"*Dance literature can—at its best—sharpen our perceptions and allow us to* see, *not merely to* watch *dance. The American dance critic Edwin Denby has claimed that writing about dance has two different aspects: one aspect is being made drunk for a second by seeing something happen; the other is expressing lucidly what you saw when you were drunk. Perhaps this is the true function of dance literature: to illuminate intoxication. And this has been my hope for this project: to compile a book of writings that would illuminate the dance, while remaining true to its exhilarating flux.*"

—from the Preface by Cobbett Steinberg

COBBETT STEINBERG is currently Dance Critic for *New West Magazine*. He is the author of *Reel Facts*, as well as numerous articles on the dance and other arts.

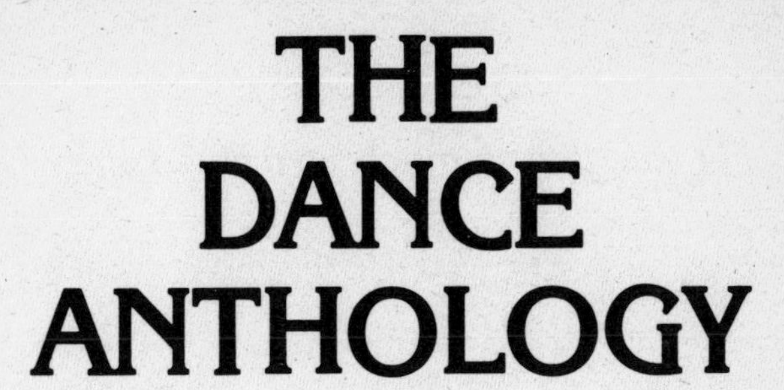

THE DANCE ANTHOLOGY

Edited by

Cobbett Steinberg

A PLUME BOOK
NEW AMERICAN LIBRARY
TIMES MIRROR
NEW YORK, LONDON AND SCARBOROUGH, ONTARIO

To Edwin Denby

For teaching so much, so well, so often

NAL BOOKS ARE AVAILABLE AT QUANTITY DISCOUNTS WHEN USED TO PROMOTE PRODUCTS OR SERVICES. FOR INFORMATION PLEASE WRITE TO PREMIUM MARKETING DIVISION, THE NEW AMERICAN LIBRARY, INC., 1633 BROADWAY, NEW YORK, NEW YORK 10019

Cover photo of Melissa Hayden of the New York City Ballet by Martha Swope.

The following pages constitute an extension of this copyright page

Translations by Cyril Beaumont of Letters I and IV from Jean-George Noverre's *Letters on Dancing and Ballet*, excerpts from Théophile Gautier's *The Romantic Ballet*, and "The New Ballet" from *Michel Fokine and His Ballet*, and selection from Cyril Beaumont's *A Short History of Ballet* reprinted by permission of P. J. Pearson of the Imperial Society of Teachers of Dance.

"Notes on Choreography" and "The Dance Element in Stravinsky's Music" by George Balanchine reprinted by permission of author.

Selections from *The Art of the Dance* by Isadora Duncan reprinted by permission of Theatre Arts Books, N.Y. Copyright 1928 by Helen Hackett, Inc., renewed 1956. Copyright 1969 by Theatre Arts Books.

"A Modern Dancer's Primer for Action" by Martha Graham from *Dance: A Basic Educational Technique*, Frederick R. Rogers, ed., copyright 1941 by Macmillan Publishing Co., Inc., renewed 1969 by Frederick R. Rogers. Reprinted by permission of publisher.

Interview with Merce Cunningham from *The Creative Experience*, Stanley Rosner and Lawrence Abt, eds. Copyright 1970 by Stanley Rosner and Lawrence Abt. Reprinted by permissions of authors.

Selection from *Marie Taglioni* by André Levinson, copyright © 1977 Dance Books Ltd., London. Reprinted by permission of publisher.

Selection from *The Birth of Ballet Russes* by Prince Peter Lieven reprinted by permission of Catherine Ritter de Lieven.

Selection from *Dance to the Piper* by Agnes de Mille copyright 1951, 1952 by Agnes de Mille. Reprinted by permission of Harold Ober Associates.

Selections from *Dancers, Buildings and People in the Streets* copyright 1965, and *Looking at the Dance*, copyright 1949, by Edwin Denby. Reprinted by permission of Horizon Press, N.Y.

Selections from *Afterimages* by Arlene Croce copyright © 1974, 1975 by Arlene Croce. Reprinted by permission of Alfred A. Knopf, Inc. All selections originally appeared in *The New Yorker*.

Selections from *Footnotes to the Ballet*, Caryl Brahms, ed., reprinted by permission of editor and The Lantz Office Inc.

"Composer/Choreographer: A Symposium" and "In Search of Design" by Rouben Ter-Artunian copyright 1963, 1966 by Dance Perspectives Foundation. Reprinted by permission.

Selection from *A Sculptor's World* by Isamu Noguchi, copyright 1968 by Isamu Noguchi. Reprinted by permission of Harper & Row Publishers, Inc.

Selection from *American Ballet Theatre* by Charles Payne copyright © 1978 by Charles Payne. Reprinted by permission of Alfred A. Knopf, Inc.

"The School of American Ballet" by Nancy Goldner excerpted from *Repertory in Review: 40 Years of the New York City Ballet* by Nancy Reynolds, with an introduction by Lincoln Kirstein. Copyright © 1977 by Nancy Reynolds. Interviews by Charles France and essays by Lincoln Kirstein, Walter Sorrell, and Nancy Goldner copyright © 1977 by The Dial Press. Reprinted by permission of The Dial Press.

Selections from *Mornings in Mexico* by D. H. Lawrence copyright © 1927 by Alfred A. Knopf Inc. Reprinted by permission of publisher.

"The Egalitarian Waltz" by Ruth Katz reprinted from *Comparative Studies in Society and History*, June 1973, copyright 1973 by Ruth Katz. Reprinted by permission of Cambridge University Press.

"The Spirit of the Classic Dance" by André Levinson reprinted from *Theatre Arts Anthology* by permission of Theatre Arts Books, N.Y. Copyright © 1950 Theatre Arts Books.

Selection from *Aesthetics* by Paul Valéry, Ralph Manheim, trans., copyright 1964 by Princeton University Press. Reprinted by permission of publisher.

Selection from *Problems of Art* by Susanne K. Langer copyright © 1951 by Susanne K. Langer. Reprinted by permission of Charles Scribner's Sons.

Selection from *Studies in Seven Arts* by Arthur Symons copyright 1925 by E. P. Dutton & Co., Inc., renewal 1953 by Miss Nona Hill. Reprinted by permission of publisher.

Selection from *The Dancer's Heritage* by Ivor Guest copyright © 1978 by Ivor Guest. Reprinted by permission of author.

Selection from *Ballet: An Illustrated History* by Mary Clarke and Clement Crisp copyright © 1973 by Universe Books. Reprinted by permission of publisher.

Selection from *The Dance Through the Ages* by Walter Sorell copyright © 1967 by Walter Sorell. Reprinted by permission of Grosset & Dunlap, Inc.

Selection from *The Colourful World of Ballet* by Clement Crisp & Edward Thorpe copyright 1977 by Clement Crisp and Edward Thorpe. Reprinted by permission of David Higham Associates, London.

Selection from *Dance* by Jack Anderson copyright 1974 by Jack Anderson. Reprinted by permission of Newsweek Books.

PLUME TRADEMARK REG. U.S. PAT. OFF. AND FOREIGN COUNTRIES
REGISTERED TRADEMARK—MARCA REGISTRADA
HECHO EN FORGE VILLAGE, MASS., U.S.A.

SIGNET, SIGNET CLASSICS, MENTOR, PLUME, MERIDIAN and NAL BOOKS are published *in the United States* by The New American Library, Inc., 1633 Broadway, New York, New York 10019, *in Canada* by The New American Library of Canada Limited, 81 Mack Avenue, Scarborough, Ontario MIL IM8, *in the United Kingdom* by The New English Library Limited, Barnard's Inn, Holborn, London ECIM 2JR, England

Library of Congress Cataloging in Publication Data

Main entry under title:

The Dance anthology.

Bibliography: p.
1. Dancing—Addresses, essays, lectures.
I. Steinberg, Cobbett.
GV1599.D26 793.3 79-27476
ISBN 0-452-25233-4

First Printing, March, 1980

1 2 3 4 5 6 7 8 9

PRINTED IN THE UNITED STATES OF AMERICA

Contents

PREFACE xi

I. Dance: The Collaborative Art 1

The Choreographers 3

Letters on Dancing and Ballet *by Jean-Georges Noverre* 8
Theories on the Art of Ballet *by Michel Fokine* 17
Notes on Choreography *by George Balanchine* 28
The Art of the Dance *by Isadora Duncan* 35
Primer for Action *by Martha Graham* 44
Choreography and the Dance *by Merce Cunningham* 52

The Dancers 63

Marie Taglioni *by André Levinson* 68
Fanny Elssler *by Théophile Gautier* 77
Vaslav Nijinsky *by Prince Peter Lieven* 84
Martha Graham *by Agnes De Mille* 91
Alicia Markova *by Edwin Denby* 105
Suzanne Farrell *by Arlene Croce* 112
Mikhail Baryshnikov *by Arlene Croce* 120

The Composers, Designers, and Librettists 126

Music and Action *by Constant Lambert* 131
Composer/Choreographer: A Symposium *by Louis Horst, Norman Dello Joio, Gunther Schuller, and Norman Lloyd* 138
The Dance Element in Stravinsky's Music *by George Balanchine* 149
Decor and Costume *by Alexandre Benois* 153

In Search of Design *by Rouben Ter-Arutunian* 171
Designs for Dance *by Isamu Noguchi* 183
Writing *Giselle by Théophile Gautier* 192

The Teachers and Schools, Companies and Directors 200

The School of American Ballet *by Nancy Goldner* 202
Directing a Ballet Company *by Lucia Chase* 219

II. Speculations: Dance Aesthetics, Theory, and Philosophy 235

Dance and Society 237

The Dance of Life *by Havelock Ellis* 238
The Hopi Snake Dance *by D. H. Lawrence* 255
The Egalitarian Waltz *by Ruth Katz* 270

Dance Aesthetics 282

Meaning in Ballet *by Edwin Denby* 283
The Spirit of the Classic Dance *by André Levinson* 294
The Ideal of Ballet Aesthetics *by John Martin* 300
Forms in Motion and in Thought *by Edwin Denby* 311

Dance Theory 329

The Philosophy of the Dance *by Paul Valéry* 330
The Dynamic Image *by Susanne Langer* 339
The World as Ballet *by Arthur Symons* 346

III. In Search of Lost Time: A Short History of Theatrical Dance 349

From the Courts to the Theater *by Cyril W. Beaumont* 351
The Romantic Movement *by Mary Clarke and Clement Crisp* 361
The Age of Petipa *by Ivor Guest* 374

The Diaghilev Era *by Walter Sorell* *382*
Contempory Ballet *by Clement Crisp and Edward Thorpe* *397*
The Modern Dance *by Jack Anderson* *418*

APPENDIX I: A CHRONOLOGY OF DANCE *431*

APPENDIX II: THE FAMILY TREES OF DANCE *441*

APPENDIX III: A GUIDE TO DANCE LITERATURE, LIBRARIES, AND BOOKSHOPS *447*

NOTES ON CONTRIBUTORS *463*

"Ballet is important and significant,
but first of all it is a pleasure."

—George Balanchine

Preface

In *Dance to the Piper* Agnes De Mille recounts how in her youth she would often talk to her father of her wish to become a professional dancer. Mr. De Mille—a man of letters— was not at all pleased by the prospect: dancing simply was not respectable enough, intellectually or morally.

"Do you honestly think," he asked his daughter one evening, "that dancing has progressed since the time of the Greeks?"

"No," Agnes replied snappily. "Do you think you write any better than Euripides?" (That ought to hold him, she figured.)

He looked at her long and slow. "No, my dear," he said, "but we have Euripides's plays. They have lasted. A dancer ceases to exist the minute she sits down."

For the first time, De Mille writes, she understood death. No matter how fine her work, oblivion would be her true collaborator.

Dance is, of course, the most ephemeral of all the arts, the most difficult to capture. As Jerome Robbins once said, dance is like life, and watching a performance "reminds people much too poignantly of their own mortality." The dance—unique in its fragility—has remained immune to the staying powers of pen and camera. Always destroying what it has just created, dance is the most elusive art: it will not be caught, it will not hold still so we can survey it at leisure. As George Balanchine once noted, dance dares to go where there are no names for anything—it defies verbal analysis. But if this defiance is often frustrating, it is also one of dance's main attractions.

So why an anthology of dance *writings?* Why collect essays that approach but never capture their subjects?

Of course dance literature is no substitute for dance, but it can—at its best—sharpen our perceptions and allow us to *see*, not merely to *watch*, dance. The American dance critic Edwin Denby has claimed that writing about dance has two different aspects: one aspect is being made drunk for a second by seeing something happen; the other is expressing lucidly what you saw when you were drunk. Perhaps this is the true function of dance literature: to illuminate intoxication. And this has been my hope for this project: to compile a book of writings that illuminate the dance, while remaining true to its intoxicating flux.

PART I

Dance: The Collaborative Art

"For me, the dance is theatre and everything proceeds from that fact. When you work in the theatre, work toward the act of theatre which is the performance, you collaborate at almost every step. The task is to fuse many individual artistic acts into one single act: dance, music, setting, lighting, costumes . . . all must come together as the whole audience experiences. This may seem obvious to say unless you remember that it is not really natural for artists to work together. True artists, I mean. Painters, sculptors, poets do not have to work in this public way: they are on their own, in their privacy, and between the time they finish their work and the time that it is experienced by others, little more than mechanics intervenes. To anyone working in the theatre, no such privacy is conceivable, and none of us can ever know the unique pleasure . . . and pain, perhaps . . . of such independence. We know other pleasures and other pains. We are at the mercy of time and of each other, and this makes it all very complex and risky. There are no laws, no rules, no fixed methods to go by when one artist sets out to work with another. And there is only one certainty: before the collaboration is through, you will have revealed yourselves to each other; you will be absolutely exposed. A certain blind courage is necessary in the face of this."

—MARTHA GRAHAM
Source: From *Dance Perspectives*,
Number 16, 1963.

The Choreographers

In *Balletomania* the noted British dance critic and historian Arnold Haskell tells an amusing anecdote about a woman who, having attended two performances of a particular ballet, was both amazed and disappointed by the fact that the two performances were identical. "I thought that those clever dancers made them up as they went along," she admitted. The woman's view, Haskell noted, though extreme, is really not so completely uncommon: uninformed of a choreographer's complex functions, the general public tends to take choreography for granted. Dancers, not choreographers, initially attract most people to the ballet, and even sophisticated viewers like Haskell remain more balletomane than choreographile: "My interest in dancers had always been so strong," Haskell confesses, "that I had given little thought to balletic structure."

Before the twentieth century, choreography was, in fact, considered a minor art—a craft really, a "useful kind of carpentry" as Lincoln Kirstein has described it, "by which a regimented corps could be moved tidily and ingeniously through charming parades that would set off the performances of the stars." Choreography was too "inconsequential" to copyright: when Perrot refused Marius Petipa permission to perform one of his (Perrot's) pieces, Petipa—by his own admission—merely made a few alterations in the choreography and, changing Perrot's title, performed it anyway. Critics similarly slighted the art, rarely mentioning the choreographer's part in a ballet. Even Théophile Gautier, the most astute of nineteenth-century reviewers, gave only a few brief words to Coralli's choreography when reviewing *Giselle* and did not even mention Perrot, who composed the choreography for the ballet's leading character.

And yet choreography is the *sine qua non* of theatrical dance. Dance design—to quote Kirstein again—"is not simply one element; it is that without which ballet cannot exist. As aria is to opera, words to poetry, color to painting, so sequences in steps—their syntax, idiom, vocabulary—are the stuff of stage dancing." Choreography of course is not *all* there is to dance; we all know what it's like to be captivated—stunned almost—by the sensual specificity of a dancer's body. But choreography is the primary organizing force behind dance, and it is the choreographer, even more than the dancer, who can and has changed the direction of ballet history, extending, transcending, and subverting the accepted idiom and providing us with new visions of the human body in motion.

The essays included in this section detail many of those historic changes. These essays—all written by choreographers themselves—are largely theoretical, occasionally even visionary: this is how the most influential choreographers conceive dance, what they want dance to be.

It has been said that the entire history of ballet has see-sawed between two approaches to dance. There have been choreographers like Noverre, Fokine, and Graham who advocate that dance should be a tightly woven tapestry of movement, drama, character, and design, a *ballet d'action*. And then there are choreographers like Petipa, Balanchine, and Cunningham who, believing that movement in and of itself is the basis of dance, argue that a ballet can indeed be constructed around a suite of display dances (*divertissement*) or can in fact do away with plot entirely (an "abstract" ballet). So although each of the choreographers included here has his or her approach to dance, their approaches can be roughly divided into two groups: Noverre, Fokine, and Graham stress the theatrics of dance—dramatic expression, gestural significance, thematic resonance; Petipa, Balanchine, and Cunningham are interested in dance in and of itself.

The French-born Jean-Georges Noverre (1727–1810), one of the most important reformers in the history of dance (Garrick called him "the Shakespeare of the dance"), wanted to raise dance above the level of mere diversion. Like Isadora Duncan and Graham after him, Noverre believed the powers of dance had seriously declined since ancient times. Disavowing the acrobatics popular in his day ("to hasten the progress of our art and bring it nearer the truth, we must sacrifice all our over-complicated steps"), he wished to reunite dance with expression and purpose. His aesthetics were basically those of psychological realism: "Nature"—that great eighteenth-century buzzword—was his model. Under his guidelines, ballets—neither transgressing truth nor shocking probability—would study man's passions, would "speak to the soul through the eyes." There was hardly an aspect of dance production he did not examine: costumes, plot, technique, and choreography all came under his scrutiny. His famous *Letters on Dancing and Ballets*, as British dance scholar Cyril W. Beaumont has written, "have no equal in the whole of the literature devoted to the art, and no book has exerted so incalculable an influence for good on the manner of production of ballets and dances."

Many of Noverre's reforms were, however, ignored by the greatest of nineteenth-century choreographers, Marius Petipa (1818–1910). As the principal ballet master of St. Petersburg's Imperial Ballet for more than forty years, Petipa catered to the Russians' near-insatiable appetite for spectacle and virtuosity, choreographing during his tenure more than sixty (!) full-length ballets, among which are two of the best-known works in the international repertory: *Swan Lake* and *Sleeping Beauty*. Unlike Noverre, Petipa was meticulously concerned with dance form: whereas Noverre abhorred symmetry for its artificiality ("symmetry should always be banished from dances with action"), Petipa created some of the most dazzling symmetrical designs ever devised in dance. Petipa was fascinated by technique, by the sequence and structure of steps, and he did not hesitate to capitalize upon a dancer's particular strengths—putting, for example, the famous series of thirty-two *fouettés* in the third act of *Swan Lake* because his ballerina, Pierina Legnani, was so good at them. His talent for grandeur was undeniable: the fourth act of his *La Bayadère*, with its famous single-file entrance down a ramp, is dynamic in design and audacious in scale. Although he followed the standard formulas of his time—slight story, five schematic acts—he managed to produce some of the most original achievements in ballet history. By the turn of the century, however, many younger choreographers found his work old-fashioned and his memoirs, written in his later years, reveal the bitterness of neglect. (Petipa's notes and diaries are only now being translated into English, and hence could not be included in this section. See "The Age of Petipa" in Section III for a further consideration of Petipa.)

The best-known of these younger choreographers was Michel Fokine (1880–1942), the principal choreographer of the Ballets Russes during its early years and creator of its first masterpieces: *Les Sylphides*, *Firebird*, and *Spectre de la rose*. Weary of mechanical plots and incongruous costumes, Fokine wanted to provide dance with the dramatic and stylistic unity advocated by Noverre. In a letter published in the London *Times* on July 6, 1914, he outlined his five artistic principles (Haskell has dubbed them the "Magna Carta" of modern choreography) that challenged prevailing practices, including the dependence on mime so beloved by Noverre. Movement and expression should be one, Fokine urged: the dances should not "interrupt" the story, and the story should not merely be a convenient peg on which to hang a succession of display pieces. Like Noverre, Fokine tried to give meaning to movement, to differentiate dance from gymnastics. Expressiveness was his goal, dramatic unity his means. And although he could be too literal-minded—his desire for historically accurate costumes at times degenerated into mere archeological authenticity, making ballet an adjunct to the museum—he was undeniably one of the great men responsible for the genius of the Ballets Russes.

The early ballets of George Balanchine (1904–) were also choreographed for the Ballets Russes, but it is Petipa rather than Fokine who is Balanchine's true mentor. Like Petipa, Balanchine has been concerned with the basic materials of choreography—the linkage of steps, the design of movement. But unlike Petipa, he has managed to free dance from the demands of story: he is, of course, the choreographer most closely associated with the plotless ballet, sometimes called—inaccurately, Balanchine says—the "abstract" ballet. Unlike Noverre or Fokine, Balanchine is not especially interested in the pictorial or literary aspects of dance, and excessive emotions—what Noverre called "the passions"—don't concern him. Although he has been a great innovator, combining steps in new and interesting ways, Balanchine remains committed to academic dance. Much of his essay here pays tribute to the necessity of classical training, and in these notes—as in his ballets—Balanchine seeks out the roots of classicism, the unchanging principles on which classicism rests. His attention is on movement, not "meaning." Although some critics have found his ballets "cold and mechanical," Balanchine's choreography is in fact not a denial of emotion but a refinement of it, and it definitely does not exclude sensuality. The immaculate, scrupulously clean style for which Balanchine is so rightly celebrated may not have dramatic content, but it certainly has dramatic effects. The plots of nineteenth-century ballets may have been about transcendence, but Balanchine's style itself suggests transcendence: there is something magical, mysterious, and stirring about the drawing of those invisible lines in space. Nietzsche once said there were two kinds of classicism—the static and the dynamic. Balanchine is obviously the second kind of classicist: his formalism is a testimony to the exciting expressivity inherent in human movement.

Isadora Duncan (1878–1927)—often considered the founder of modern dance, or at least its foremost forerunner—wished to free dance from the codified restraints of ballet. Trying to regain the purity and simplicity of ancient—especially Greek—dance, she abandoned tights and tutus in favor of loose-fitting tunics in the manner of Hellenic sculpture. She was a great champion of the "natural" and sought to discover in dance, not the principles of its own formalism (as has Balanchine), but the principles dance shares with all the universe. "All of the movements of the earth," she said, "follow the lines of wave motion," and it was this wave motion, natural to all she felt, that was the beginning of body movement as well.

Like Fokine (whom she is often said to have influenced) and Noverre, Duncan was interested in the emotional and expressive capacities of dance. "Art," Fokine said, "stems from feelings," and Duncan agreed. But unlike Fokine and Noverre, Duncan did not attempt to reveal emotions through carefully constructed, coherent stories; rather, her dances were more like poems in which she embodied some abstract feeling: Joy, Immortality, Oppression. Dance for Duncan should express not a contrived character but the Self—unadorned and glorified. She fought against the alleged silliness of ballet, seeking to recapture the religious qualities of dance. The body to her was spiritual, communicative in and of itself. Whereas Noverre believed that "intelligence and taste do not reside in the feet," Duncan claimed that the expression and intelligence of the human foot was "one of the greatest triumphs of the evolution of man." The body needed not training but freedom. Although Duncan founded no lasting school or discovered no new technique, her influence is still incalculable: much of what has happened in twentieth-century dance would not have been possible without her example.

Martha Graham (1894–), the most famous member of the second generation of modern dance, has also aimed to restore spirituality to dance, "to make it significant," as she says here. Duncan had argued that the dance of the future was the dance of the past, and Graham agreed: "to understand dance for what it is," she once said, "it is necessary we know from whence it comes." Like Duncan, Graham sees the body as an instrument of revelation: the body is its own form of truth, it does not lie. But whereas Duncan believed the body could best reveal itself unencumbered by any codified technique, Graham is committed to discipline. "There must be a disciplined way of dancing," she writes. "This means learning a craft, not by intellection, but by hard physical work." Much of her essay here—like much of Balanchine's—details the necessity of technique. But of course unlike Balanchine, Graham has used technique not as an end in itself but as the means to free the body to become "its ultimate self." No other choreographer has so consistently and so ingeniously examined the human psyche. The function of dance for Graham is to make visible the "interior landscape," much as Noverre wished to make dance "speak to the soul through the eye." (In fact, many of Noverre's beliefs—that the inner passions give force to exterior movements, for example—sound like Graham pronouncements.) Although she has on occasion been a bit too solemn, almost pretentious at times (some of her later works look like parodies of earlier ones), her oeuvre is an incredible testament to the dramatic and expressive powers of dance, reminding us that dance can embody the vision not only of the individual but of an entire nation.

Merce Cunningham (1919–), the most influential choreographer of the third generation of modern dance, has left behind Graham's literary and dramatic ways. As he says here, his dances start with steps, not with characters, emotions, or plots. Although he has been one of America's most consistent and inventive experimentalists, his choreography is informed by a classicist's urge to treat movement as sufficiently interesting to be its own subject. Cunningham is committed to dancing exclusive of decor and (unlike Balanchine) independent of music. To the tradition of modern dance solemnity, he has added rarefied whimsy. And he has drastically changed our notions of both dance space (every part of the stage is equally interesting in Cunningham's decentralized and democratized universe) and time (his dances don't always have obvious beginnings, middles, and ends). Vehemently attacked and ardently praised, he has remained our most durable avant-gardist, our best radical classicist.

Letters on Dancing and Ballets

by Jean-Georges Noverre

Letter I

Poetry, painting and dancing, Sir, are, or should be, no other than a faithful likeness of beautiful nature. It is owing to their accuracy of representation that the works of men like Corneille and Racine, Raphael and Michelangelo, have been handed down to posterity, after having obtained (what is rare enough) the commendation of their own age. Why can we not add to the names of these great men those of the

Source: From *Letters on Dancing and Ballets*, trans. Cyril W. Beaumont (New York: Dance Horizons, 1966), from the revised and enlarged edition published in St. Petersburg, 1803.

maîtres de ballet[1] who made themselves so celebrated in their day? But they are scarcely known; is it the fault of their art, or of themselves?

A ballet is a picture, or rather a series of pictures connected one with the other by the plot which provides the theme of the ballet; the stage is, as it were, the canvas on which the composer expresses his ideas; the choice of the music, scenery and costumes are his colours; the composer is the painter. If nature have endowed him with that passionate enthusiasm which is the soul of all imitative arts, will not immortality be assured him? Why are the names of *maîtres de ballet* unknown to us? It is because works of this kind endure only for a moment and are forgotten almost as soon as the impressions they had produced; hence there remains not a vestige of the most sublime productions of a Bathyllus and a Pylades.[2] Hardly a notion has been preserved of those pantomimes so celebrated in the age of Augustus.[3]

If these great composers, unable to transmit to posterity their fugitive pictures, had at least bequeathed us their ideas and the principles of their art; if they had set forth the laws of the style of which they were the creators; their names and writings would have traversed the immensity of the ages and they would not have sacrificed their labours and repose for a moment's glory. Those who have succeeded them would have had some principles to guide them, and the art of pantomime and gesture, formerly carried to a point which still astonishes the imagination, would not have perished.

Since the loss of that art, no one has sought to re-discover it, or, so to speak, to create it a second time. Appalled by the difficulties of that

[1] As a general rule, whenever Noverre uses the term *maître de ballet*, he employs it in its old sense of meaning the person who composes the dances in a *divertissement* or ballet. Nowadays, such a person is termed the *chorégraphe*, while the designation *maître de ballet* is applied to the individual responsible for the training of the dancers and the maintenance of their technique at the requisite standard of efficiency. [These notes are the translator's.]

[2] Bathyllus and Pylades were two celebrated mimes famous about 22 B.C. Bathyllus of Alexandria, the freedman and favourite of Mæcenas, together with Pylades of Cicilia and his pupil Hylas, brought to a fine degree of perfection, during the reign of Augustus, the imitative dance termed *Pantomimus*, which was one of the most popular public amusements at Rome until the fall of the Empire. Bathyllus excelled in the interpretation of comic scenes, while Pylades was unsurpassed in the representation of tragic themes. At first, the two actors gave performances in common, then, becoming jealous of each other's fame, they quarrelled and established rival theatres. Each founded a school and each had a numerous band of followers whose fierce partisanship led to many brawls and sometimes bloodshed.

Some account of these actors will be found in Castil-Blaze. *La Danse et les Ballets*, 1832, Chapter I. For a description of their performances, consult Smith (W.). *A Dictionary of Greek and Roman Antiquities.* 2 Vols. 1891. Vol. 2, p. 334, *Pantomimus.*

[3] The first Emperor of the Roman Empire. Born Sept. 23rd, B.C. 63. Died Aug. 29th, A.D. 14.

enterprise, my predecessors have abandoned it, without making a single attempt, and have allowed a divorce, which it would appear must be eternal, to exist between pure dancing and pantomime.

More venturesome than they, perhaps less gifted, I have dared to fathom the art of devising ballets with action; to re-unite action with dancing; to accord it some expression and purpose. I have dared to tread new paths, encouraged by the indulgence of the public which has supported me in crises capable of rebuffing one's self-esteem; and my successes appear to authorise me to satisfy your curiosity regarding an art which you cherish, and to which I have devoted my every moment.

From the reign of Augustus to our days, ballets have been only feeble sketches of what they may one day become. This art, born of genius and good taste, can become beautiful and varied to an infinite degree. History, legend, painting, all the arts may unite to withdraw their sister art from the obscurity in which she is shrouded; and it astonishes one that *maîtres de ballet* have disdained such powerful assistance.

The programmes of the ballets which have been given, during the past century or so, in the different courts of Europe, incline one to believe that this art (which was still of no account), far from having progressed, is more and more declining. These kinds of traditions, it is true, are always strongly suspect. It is with ballets as with entertainments in general; nothing so grandiose and so alluring on paper, and often nothing so dull and ill-arranged in performance.

I think, Sir, that this art has remained in its infancy only because its effects have been limited, like those of fireworks designed simply to gratify the eyes; although this art shares with the best plays the advantage of inspiring, moving and captivating the spectator by the charm of its interest and illusion. No one has suspected its power of speaking to the heart.

If our ballets be feeble, monotonous and dull, if they be devoid of ideas, meaning, expression and character, it is less, I repeat, the fault of the art than that of the artist: does he ignore that dancing united to pantomime is an imitative art? I shall be tempted to believe it, because the majority of composers restrict themselves to making a servile copy of a certain number of steps and figures to which the public has been treated for centuries past; in such wise that the ballets from *Phaéton*,[4]

[4] A lyrical tragedy in five acts and a prologue, with libretto by Quinault and music by Lully. It was first played before the Court on Jan. 6th, 1663. The first public performance was given at the Académie Royale de Musique, on April 27th, of the same year. It had an immense success due to its many charming airs and the wealth of the mechanical effects introduced. Its theme was the return of the Golden Age, and it was intended as a panegyric in honour of Louis XIV.

or from another opera, revived by a modern composer, differ so little from those of the past that one would imagine they were always the same.

In fact, it is rare, not to say impossible, to find genius in the plans, elegance in the forms, lightness in the groups, precision and neatness in the tracks which lead to the different figures; the art of disguising old things and giving them an air of novelty is scarcely known.

Maîtres de ballet should consult the pictures of great painters. This examination would undoubtedly bring them in touch with nature; then they should avoid, as often as possible, that symmetry in the figures which, repeating the same thing, offers two similar pictures on the same canvas. That is not to say that I condemn in general all symmetrical figures or to think that I claim to abolish the practice entirely, for that would be to misinterpret my views.

The abuse of the best things is always detrimental; I only disapprove of the too frequent and too repeated use of these kinds of figures, a practice which my colleagues will feel to be vicious when they essay to copy nature faithfully and to depict on the stage different passions with the shades and colours which appertain to each in particular.

Symmetrical figures from right to left are, in my opinion, only supportable in the *corps d'entrées*,[5] which have no means of expression, and which, conveying nothing, are employed simply to give the *premiers danseurs* time to take breath; they can have a place in a *ballet général* which concludes a festival; further, they can be tolerated in *pas d'execution*, *pas de quatre*, *pas de six*, etc., although, to my mind, it would be ridiculous, in these fragments, to sacrifice expression and feeling to bodily skill and agility of the legs; but symmetry should give place to nature in *scènes d'action*. One example, however slight it may be, will make my meaning clear and suffice to support my contention.

A band of nymphs, at the unexpected sight of a troupe of young fauns, takes flight hurriedly in fear; the fauns, on their side, pursue the nymphs with eagerness, which generally suggests delight: presently, they stop to examine the impression they have made on the nymphs; at the same time the latter suspend their course; they regard the fauns with fear, seek to discover their designs, and to attain by flight a refuge which would secure them against the danger which threatens; the two

[5] An *entrée* is a *divertissement* executed by a number of dancers.

Compan, in his *Dictionnaire de Danse* (1787) gives the following definition: "The usual division for all kinds of ballets is five acts. Each act consists of three, six, nine, and sometimes twelve *entrées*. The term *entrée* is given to one or more bands of dancers who, by means of their steps, gestures and attitudes, express that portion of the whole theme which has been assigned to them."

troupes approach; the nymphs resist, defend themselves and escape with a skill equal to their agility, etc.

That is what I term a *scène d'action*, where the dance should speak with fire and energy; where symmetrical and formal figures cannot be employed without transgressing truth and shocking probability, without enfeebling the action and chilling the interest. There, I say, is a scene which should offer a ravishing disorder, and where the composer's art should not appear except to embellish nature.

A *maître de ballet*, devoid of intelligence and good taste, will treat this portion of the dance mechanically, and deprive it of its effect, because he will not feel the spirit of it. He will place the nymphs and the fauns on several parallel lines, he will scrupulously exact that all the nymphs be posed in uniform attitudes, and that the fauns have their arms raised at the same height; he will take great care in his arrangement not to place five nymphs to the right and seven to the left, for this would transgress the traditions of the *Opéra*, but he will make a cold and formal performance of a *scène d'action* which should be full of fire.

Some ill-disposed critics, who do not understand enough of the art to judge of its different effects, will say that this scene should offer two pictures only; that the desire of the fauns should express one, and the fear of the nymphs depict the other. But how many different gradations are there to contrive in that fear and that desire; what oppositions, what variations of light and shade to observe; so that from these two sentiments there result a multitude of pictures, each more animated than the other!

All men having the same passions, differ only in proportion to their sensibilities; they affect with more or less force all men, and manifest themselves outwardly with more or less vehemence and impetuosity. This principle stated, which nature demonstrates every day, one should vary the attitudes, diffuse the shades of expression, and thenceforth the pantomimic action of each person would cease to be monotonous.

It would result in being both a faithful imitator and an excellent painter, to put variety in the expression of the heads, to give an air of ferocity to some of the fauns, to others less passion; to these a more tender air, and, lastly, to the others a voluptuous character which would calm or share the fear of the nymphs. The sketch of this picture determines naturally the composition of the other: I see then the nymphs who hesitate between pleasure and fear, I perceive others who, by their contrasting attitudes, depict to me the different emotions with which their being is agitated; the latter are prouder than their companions, the former mingle fear with a sense of curiosity which renders the picture more seductive; this variety is the more attractive in its likeness to nature. You must agree with me, Sir, that symmetry should always be banished from dances with action.

I will ask those who usually are prejudiced, if they will find symmetry in a flock of stray sheep which wish to escape from the murdering fangs of wolves, or in a band of peasants who abandon their fields and hamlets to avoid the fury of the enemy who pursues them? No, without a doubt; but true art consists in concealing art. I do not counsel disorder and confusion at all, on the contrary I desire that regularity be found even in irregularity; I ask for ingenious groups, strong but always natural situations, a manner of composition which conceals the composer's labours from the eyes of the spectator.

As to figures, they only deserve to please when they are presented in quick succession and designed with both taste and elegance.

Letter IV

Dancing and ballets, Sir, have become the vogue of the day; they are received with a kind of passion and never was an art more encouraged by applause than our own. The French stage, the richest in Europe in dramas of all kinds and the most prolific in eminent performers, has been forced in some degree, in order to gratify the public taste and to be in the fashion, to include dancing in its programmes.

The lively and pronounced taste for ballets is general; every sovereign employs them to adorn his stage spectacles, not so much to copy our customs, as to minister to the eager interest which this art excites. The most insignificant touring company trails after it a swarm of dancers of both sexes, indeed, charlatans and vendors of quack medicines have more confidence in the merit of their ballets than in their nostrums; it is with *entrechats* that they attract the staring eyes of the crowd, and the sales of their remedies rise and fall accordingly as their entertainments are more or less numerous.

The indulgence with which the public applauds such trifles should, in my opinion, urge the artist to seek perfection. Praise should encourage and not dazzle us with the idea that the highest achievement has been attained and that there remains nothing more to accomplish. The false confidence resident in the majority of *maîtres de ballet*, and the little trouble they take to attain further improvement, inclines me to suspect that they imagine they have nothing more to learn.

The public, for its part, takes delight in deluding itself that the taste and talents of its time are far superior to those of preceding epochs; hence the florid steps and grimaces of our dancers are received with the most enthusiastic applause. I am not speaking of that section of the public which is its life and soul, of those intelligent men who, incapable of being swayed by popular prejudice, deplore the bad taste of their contemporaries, who listen without talking, who regard everything with attention, who consider carefully before they judge, and only applaud those passages which move, affect and transport them. That applause lavished at a whim and without discernment, often proves the ruin of young men training for a stage career. I know that applause is the food of the arts, but it ceases to be wholesome if administered indiscriminately; and the nutrition is so rich that, far from strengthening the constitution, it disturbs and enfeebles it. Stage beginners are similar to those children totally spoiled by the blind affection of their parents. Faults and imperfections are perceived as the illusion wears off and the attraction of novelty diminishes.

Painting and dancing have this advantage over the other arts, that they are of every country, of all nations; that their language is universally understood, and that they achieve the same impression everywhere.

If our art, imperfect as it is, seduce and captivate the spectator: if dancing stripped of the charm of expression sometimes occasion us trouble and emotion, and throw our thoughts into a pleasing disorder; what power and domination might it not achieve over us if its movements were directed by brains and its pictures painted with feeling? There is no doubt that ballets will rival painting in attraction when the executants display less of the automaton and the composers are better trained.

A fine picture is but the image of nature; a finished ballet is nature herself, embellished with every ornament of the art. If a painted canvas convey to me a sense of illusion, if I am carried away by the skill of the delineator, if I am moved by the sight of a picture, if my captivated thoughts are affected in a lively manner by this enchantment, if the colours and brush of the skilful artist react on my senses so as to reveal to me nature, to endow her with speech so that I fancy I hear and answer her, how shall my feelings be wrought upon, what shall I become, and what will be my sensations, at the sight of a representation still more veracious and rendered by the histrionic abilities of my fellow-creatures? What dominion will not living and varied pictures possess over my imagination? Nothing interests man so much as humanity itself. Yes, Sir, it is shameful that dancing should renounce the empire it might assert over the mind and only endeavor to please the sight. A beautiful ballet is, up to the present, a thing seen only in the imagination; like the Phœnix it is never found.

It is a vain hope to re-model the dance, so long as we continue to be slaves to the old methods and ancient traditions of the *Opéra*. At our theatres we see only feeble copies of the copies that have preceded them; let us not practise steps only, let us study the passions. In training ourselves to feel them, the difficulty of expressing them will vanish, then the features will receive their impressions from the sentiments within, they will give force to exterior movements and paint in lines of fire the disorder of the senses and the tumult which reigns in the breast.

Dancing needs only a fine model, a man of genius, and ballets will change their character. Let this restorer of the true dance appear, this reformer of bad taste and of the vicious customs that have impoverished the art; but he must appear in the capital. If he would persuade, let him open the eyes of our young dancers and say to them:—"Children of Terpsichore, renounce *cabrioles*, *entrechats* and over-complicated steps; abandon grimaces to study sentiments, artless graces and expression; study how to make your gestures noble, never forget that it is the life-blood of dancing; put judgment and sense into your *pas de deux;* let will-power order their course and good taste preside over all situations; away with those lifeless masks but feeble copies of nature; they hide your features, they stifle, so to speak, your emotions and thus deprive you of your most important means of expression; take off those enormous wigs and those gigantic head-dresses which destroy the true proportions of the head with the body; discard the use of those stiff and cumbersome hoops which detract from the beauties of execution, which disfigure the elegance of your attitudes and mar the beauties of contour which the bust should exhibit in its different positions.

"Renounce that slavish routine which keeps your art in its infancy; examine everything relative to the development of your talents; be original; form a style for yourselves based on your private studies; if you must copy, imitate nature, it is a noble model and never misleads those who follow it.

"As for you young men who aspire to be *maîtres de ballet* and think that to achieve success it is sufficient to have danced a couple of years under a man of talent, you must begin by acquiring some of this quality yourselves. Devoid of enthusiasm, wit, imagination, taste and knowledge, would you dare set up as painters? You wish for an historical theme and know nothing of history! You fly to poets and are unacquainted with their works! Apply yourselves to the study of them so that your ballets will be complete poems. Learn the difficult art of selection. Never undertake great enterprises without first making a careful plan; commit your thoughts to paper; read them a hundred times over; divide your drama into scenes; let each one be interesting and lead in proper sequence, without hindrance or superfluities, to a well-planned climax; carefully eschew all tedious incidents, they hold up the action and spoil its effect. Remember that *tableaux* and groups provide the most delightful moments in a ballet.

"Make your *corps de ballet* dance, but, when it does so, let each member of it express an emotion or contribute to form a picture; let them mime while dancing so that the sentiments with which they are imbued may cause their appearance to be changed at every moment. If their gestures and features be constantly in harmony with their feelings, they will be expressive accordingly and give life to the representation. Never go to a rehearsal with a head stuffed with new figures and devoid of sense. Acquire all the knowledge you can of the matter you have in hand. Your imagination, filled with the picture you wish to represent, will provide you with the proper figures, steps and gestures. Then your compositions will glow with fire and strength, they cannot but be true to nature if you are full of your subject. Bring love as well as enthusiasm to your art. To be successful in theatrical representations, the heart must be touched, the soul moved and the imagination inflamed.

"Are you, on the contrary, lukewarm? Does your blood circulate slowly through your veins? Have you a heart of ice? Have you a soul incapable of sensation? Then renounce the stage, abandon an art for which you are unfitted. Adopt a profession or trade where imagination is of no account, with which genius has nothing to do and wherein you have need of arms and hands only."

If, Sir, the principles pronounced were followed, the stage would be disencumbered of an inestimable quantity of indifferent dancers and of bad *maîtres de ballet*, while the blacksmith's trade and others would be supplied with a number of workers much more usefully employed in administering to the wants of society, than they can ever be of service in contributing to its amusements and entertainments.

Theories on the Art of Ballet

by Michel Fokine

"The New Ballet"

I. On Ballet Routine

Before I discuss the traditions which hinder the natural development of the art of ballet, I wish to state that I shall consider what in my opinion is wrong. But I shall deal with laws and traditions, and not with the talents of the artistes. It must be admitted that the creators of the old ballet possessed genius which, however, was restricted by unnecessary rules. The traditional ballet forgot man's natural beauty. It essayed to express a psychological feeling by a fixed movement, or series of movements, which could neither describe nor symbolise anything.

Not only did the spectators fail to understand the expressions of the artistes, but one artiste did not know what another was supposed to convey to him. The audience witness a number of movements but never trouble to question whether they are expressive. Some of these are familiar to them from long acquaintance. For example, it is understood that when a dancer points one finger upwards and then touches his lips with it, he is entreating a kiss; it is curious that in all ballets only one kiss is requested. If the girl to whom he makes this sign runs away from him, proudly raises her arms, points to herself, lowers her arms in front of her and then sweeps them to one side, it is intended to intimate that her would-be lover is rich while she is poor, and consequently he would soon cast her away. This incident is repeated in *Paquita*, *Esmeralda*, and *La Bayadère*. But this series of gestures cannot even pretend to be expressive. It is hardly likely that a man desirous of obtaining a kiss would point with his finger; but that is the traditional method of making love in a ballet. The expressiveness of the action is relatively unimportant, it is the beauty of the poses and movements,

Source: "The New Ballet" from the article contributed by Fokine to the Russian periodical, *Argus*, No. 1, 1916. "Letter to 'The Times' " from the letter written by Fokine to the London *Times*, July 6, 1914. Both of these pieces can be found in Cyril W. Beaumont's *Michel Fokine and His Ballets* (London: Beaumont, 1935).

the graceful action of pointing one finger to Heaven that is all important.

Then there is the famous gesture where a man raises the right hand and sweeps it in a circular movement about his face. This is supposed to convey to the audience that his sweetheart is beautiful. But does it really mean anything? If you follow such a scene in a ballet it is easy to observe that both artistes and audience are indifferent to these signs which, in fact, are only employed as a means of filling up so many bars of the music. Consider *Le Lac des Cygnes.* Siegfried's tutor comes on the stage and says: "Benno is coming here." The latter enters and remarks: "Siegfried is coming here." Then Siegfried enters, greets the peasants and his friends, drinks some wine and begins to talk. What does he say? "My mother is coming here." In this way several pages of music are disposed of. In many ballets the newcomer says: "I have come here." Surely his presence is sufficiently obvious. But follow the appearance of Siegfried's mother, a character who seems inseparable from so many ballets. When she appears on the scene, she circles round the stage; but can any mother explain why she does this? Then she begs her son to renounce drinking and marry. She clasps her hands and entreats: "Please marry." He replies: "No!" She repeats: "Please marry." He replies again: "No!" She beseeches him for the third time and he consents. Is it not clear that such a dialogue is possible only as a result of the complete absence of expressive signs in ballet, for if these signs were comprehensible, so that the audience was interested in the logic of the scene, it could not take place? But expressive signs are replaced by fixed movements which none can understand.

II. The Development of Signs

I have mentioned the above details because, in my opinion, a dance is the development and ideal of the sign. The ballet renounced expression and consequently dancing became acrobatic, mechanical, and empty. In order to restore dancing its soul we must abandon fixed signs and devise others based on the laws of natural expression. "But," it may be asked, "how can a dance be built on a sign?" Consider the *arabesque* of the good old times. "But," it may be argued, "you employed *arabesques* in *Les Sylphides.*" Certainly, an *arabesque* is sensible when it idealises the sign, because it suggests the body's straining to soar upward, the whole body is expressive. If there be no expression, no sign, but merely a foot raised in the position termed *en arabesque*, it looks foolish. That is the difference between the good old, and the merely old.

Examine the prints of Cerrito, Grisi, Elssler, and Taglioni, it will be found that their poses have a certain expressiveness. Now look through a history of dancing, on the concluding pages of which will be found the dancers of the end of the last century. Their poses are quite different. There is no sign. What does their pose express? Simply a leg extended backwards. It is neither the beginning nor end of the sign, nor its development. Instead of expressing something, the body seeks balance to avoid falling on account of the raised leg.

There is a vast difference between the dancers of the beginning of the nineteenth century, when the ballet reached its height in beauty, and those at the end of the century, when beauty was forced to give place to acrobatics. There is a complete difference in principle. Taglioni raises herself *sur les pointes* in order to be so light as to seem hardly to touch the ground. The dancer of the period when ballet was in decline uses her *pointes* in order to astonish the audience with their strength and endurance. She fills up the toe of her satin shoe and jumps on it so that the shoe hits the ground with all the strength of her muscular feet. The "steel" toe is a horrible invention of the ballet in decline. In its days of greatness, supernatural lightness was the ideal. Now, the steel toe, hard legs, and precision in execution, are the ideals.

III. The Old and the New in Ballet. The Creative Power in Ballet

I ask for the careful preservation of the beauty of the dance as Taglioni knew it. That world of fragile dreams could not support the rude acrobatic ballet and has fled from us. It will never return if we do not exert all our strength to save this highest form of the dance. But, having preserved it, this style must be employed only when it is applicable. No single form of dancing should be adopted once and for all. The best form is that which most fully expresses the meaning desired, and the most natural one that which most closely corresponds with the idea to be conveyed. For example, ballet steps executed *sur la pointe* cannot be used in a Greek Bacchic dance, on the other hand it would be unnatural to dance a Spanish dance in a Greek *chiton*.

If the music be in character with Spanish folk melodies and rhythms, the dance must also express the same national character. Climate and history have created the temperament which naturally gave birth to those particular forms. The rhythmic tapping of the heel, the sensuous swaying of the whole body, the snake-like movement of the arms, are more natural in this case than the most natural dance of the barefoot school. Whatever the period required by the theme, the ballet must always create a dance which correspondingly expresses that period. I do not wish to imply by this an ethnological accuracy or archæological exactitude; but there must be co-ordination of style and movement with the style of the period.

Man has always changed his plastic language. He had expressed in the most varied forms his sorrows, his joys, and all the emotions he experienced, hence his mode of expression cannot be fixed according to any one rule. The old method of production consisted in creating dances from fixed movements and poses, the mimed scenes were always expressed by a fixed manner of gesticulation, and thus the audience had to understand the theme. The most prominent creators of ballet were bound hand and foot by those laws and traditions. We must denounce this. Work of this kind is very easy for the producer and the artistes, and lightens the work of the critic. It is easy to judge whether a dancer has executed correctly the steps which he or she has performed a hundred times in other ballets. But there is one drawback to this method, a ready-made pattern does not always fit.

IV. Confusion

Creators of ballets should always endeavour to seek out that form of dancing which best expresses the particular theme, for this principle leads to great beauty. However varied the rule of ballet might become, life would always be more varied still; while ballet having no relation to reality and circumscribed by tradition naturally becomes ludicrous. The old ballet has confused periods and styles. It uses Russian top-boots and the French school of dancing in one ballet, the short ballet-skirt and historically correct Egyptian costume in another, and so forth. Is not that confusion? The style of the dance is always inharmonious with that of the costumes, theme, and period. Moreover, there is one style for classical dances, another for character dances; and all these appear in one ballet and at the same time. Such is tradition. And to give one homogeneous, harmonious thing is to sin against it, because in order to comply with ballet æsthetics it is imperative to reproduce dual styles.

V. Ballet Rules

The classical ballet came into being as a pleasure of the aristocracy and part of court ceremony. The bowing before the public, the addressing of hand movements to them, and so on, are the foundations on which the rules of ballet were built. Examine the photographs of academic dancers in, for instance, a *pas de deux;* the *danseur* always stands behind the *danseuse*. He holds her waist and looks at her back, while she faces the audience. He displays her. If I do not agree with this style of dancing, it does not mean that I ignore the school. On the contrary, I think that in order to create anything of value one must study and pass through a proper school which, however, should not be confined to the study of fixed poses and steps.

First, one must study oneself, conquer one's own body, and try to learn to feel and develop an ability to perform various movements. Ballet gymnastics are limited, they do not develop the whole body nor instil a feeling for pose and movement in all their variety. The ballet at the end of the last century was limited to several rules handed down without explanation as dogmas. It was of no avail to inquire the why and the wherefore because no one could answer such questions, they were too old. One had to accept the creed that the feet should keep to the five positions and that all movements consisted in combinations of these positions; that the arms should be rounded, the elbows held sideways facing the audience, the back straight, and the feet turned outwards with the heels well to the front. It is difficult to lose faith in these five positions in order to realise that beauty of movement cannot be limited by them.

The practice of turning the legs outward certainly develops the flexibility of the lower limbs, but exercises *en dehors* develop the feet to one side only. In order to make sure it is sufficient to look at a dancer with turned out feet in a dance requiring the feet to be in a natural position. It is obvious that she is ill at ease. Her feet are not under control. I appreciate the "turning out" of the feet in preliminary exercises, but as soon as the exercises are finished the "turning out" should cease, except in Siamese, Hindu, and exotic dances, when the feet should harmonise with the angular positions of the arms. But a barefoot dance with the feet turned out is absurd.

Another failing of ballet technique is that it is concentrated in the dancing of the lower limbs, whereas the whole body should dance. The whole body to the smallest muscle should be expresssive, but ballet schools concentrate on exercises for the feet. The arms are limited to a few movements and the hands to one fixed position. What variety would not be possible if the dancer renounced the mannerism of rounded arms. And the movement of the upper part of the body, to what does that lead? A straight back, that is the ideal. One must be deaf not to become furious when the teacher continually repeats for eight or nine years one and the same rule—hold up your back. What store of beauty have painters not taken from the different positions of the body? The academic dancer, however, always faces the audience in a straight line.

The conservative critics were furious because the dancers in certain of my ballets wore sandals and Eastern shoes, and only used the traditional ballet-shoe in some ballets. The admirers of academic dancing could not understand the view that *pointes* should be used as a means and not as the sole aim of ballet. *Pointes* should be employed where they are suitable and renounced without regret where they would not serve any artistic purpose. For instance, in Eastern ballets, the bare foot or a soft shoe is more pleasing than a ballet-shoe, but the dancer in *Le Cygne* does not offend when she uses her *pointes* to suggest a soaring movement. It is right if all her body express the same feeling, but wrong if she use her *pointes* to display her "steel" toe. She degrades herself before the audience which is watching for the strength of her toes. It is a complete misunderstanding of this beautiful mode of progression.

Forgetful of its artistic aims, ballet began to use *pointes* for quite opposite means, in fact merely to display the endurance and strength of the toes. The shoe was filled up with leather, cotton wool, and cork. But this did not make any difference to anyone, because a competition began as to who could make the most turns *sur la pointe*. The dancer's toes became ugly and it became impossible for her to show her foot without the shoe. That also did not matter. If we admit that ballet should develop mime for most styles of dancing, the basis of the school should be the teaching of natural movement. One should be able to move naturally and control the body to this end. The natural dance should follow and then one could advance to the dance of artificial movement. Ballet however begins at the end. It renounces natural movement, but surely the ballet has no right to discard what it did not possess. Vrubel had the right to paint a mutilated demon because he could draw a beautiful human body.

VI. Basic Movements

There are very few dancers who can walk and run about naturally. At first, when I asked a dancer not to execute *pas de bourrée* but simply run, she would become shy and say: "No, I cannot." But dancing is developed from these basic movements. The natural dance is built on raising the foot backwards and forwards just as in the action of walking.

The ballet, however, abounds in sideway movements. The so-called second position, so inæsthetic, is the one most used in academic dancing. What could be more ugly and vulgar than the feet wide apart. But many steps are built on it, such as *glissade*, *échappé*, and so forth. The chief reason for it is because ballet is danced mostly facing the public, whom the dancer respects and from whom he or she awaits approval. If it be agreed that every pose should express the inner self, that every movement should be logical, then it is obvious that sideway movements are senseless, expressionless, and ugly.

Gautier, who lived in the period of the highest development of the classic ballet, was very much opposed to the "turned out" dance. Is it no strange that this turned out dance is championed by so many admirers of the classical ballet?

VII. Delightful Nonsense

The step from the senseless to the expressive dance does not lead to cheap drama, to the narrow dramatisation of the dance; it expresses everything that is in the human soul. "Why," it is argued, "should ballet contain expression and drama when it should be unreal and irrational?" Someone has styled ballet "delightful nonsense." I am glad that ballet is considered "delightful," but if it were not nonsense it would have gained. Expression is as necessary to ballet as any other art, even more so. If colours and sounds do not speak they are tolerable, but an expressionless human body resembles a doll or a corpse. In pictures we look for the painter's soul. We do not accept a picture which expresses nothing; how then can we tolerate a man without expression?

If ballet forsake its direct aim for expression, the result is that one part expresses one thing, and the other the opposite. The most typical example is the *fouetté*. For me this is the most hateful invention of the ballet. The dancer expresses ecstasy and joy, but her face—what does that express? Quite the opposite. She seeks for balance and the whole face proclaims it. The body is straight, the head also, the hands are symmetrical, the eyes fixed on one point. The face betrays her fear of losing her balance. There are few who can watch the expression of her features while she moves; what a contradiction! Unity of pose and movement is a law which, to my regret, is not felt by everybody. This can only be explained by the undeveloped ability to seize quickly poses and movements.

VIII. Acrobatism

What is the difference between a dancer who executes thirty-two pirouettes and an acrobat who performs twice as many? I think that an acrobat does his with more certainty, but there should be another difference. Everything that an acrobat does is for the purpose of effect, to astonish, to amuse, and establish a record. This is in the nature of sport which element should be quite foreign to the ballet. The aim of every movement in ballet should be expression. A dancer representing a satyr can do somersaults, roll on the ground, and, if he conveys the impression that he is half-man, half-animal, he has fulfilled his mission as an artist. But if a dancer representing a princess turns like a top, she must renounce all pretence of being an artist. The impression given would be strong but of a quite different character.

Just as acrobats have broken bones, so ballet dancers have "turned out" feet. If this were æsthetic, this form of beauty would long ago have been revealed to us by painters. Let us examine the best works of sculpture and painting from the point of view of a *maître de ballet* of the old school. All the marble gods of Greece would appear in faulty poses, since none of them have "turned out" feet or hold their arms in ballet positions. All the figures of Rodin, Michaelangelo, Raphael, and the Renaissance period would be incorrect. And to be a true follower of classical ballet we should denounce all the treasures of beauty stored for thousands of years by man's genius and declare them to be wrong.

I am far from desirous of laying down any rules prohibiting certain forms of dance and mime. I even admit that a figure with "turned out" feet can be interesting and beautiful, if it be the product of a national or exotic character so that the whole figure harmonise with "turned out" feet and arms, such as may be observed in the statues adorning Indian temples. The natural position of the body is the point of departure for all styles and it would be a mistake to renounce the possibilities of the artificial dance. Observe Indian sculpture, the figures of ancient Assyria, Babylon, Egypt, and Greece, poetical Persian miniatures, Japanese and Chinese water-colours. All these depict unnatural movements and are opposed to the theory of the free and natural dance, but they possess so much beauty, such variety of style, and express the ideals of the various nationalities. How then can we sacrifice this variety for a fixed formula? The artist of the dance should admit the life and art of all humanity and not confine himself to a few poor rules and old-fashioned traditions of the ballet school.

Letter to "The Times"

To the Editor of "The Times."

Sir—I am extremely grateful to the English Press for the attention which it has given to the "Russian Ballet," now appearing at Drury Lane Theatre, but at the same time I should like to point out certain misconceptions which exist as to the history of that ballet and the principles on which it is founded.

The misconceptions are these, that some mistake this new school of art, which has arisen only during the last seven years, for the traditional ballet which continues to exist in the Imperial theatres of St. Petersburg and Moscow, and others mistake it for a development of the principles of Isadora Duncan, while as a matter of fact the new Russian ballet is sharply differentiated by its principles both from the old ballet and from the art of that great dancer.

The Old Conventions

The older ballet developed the form of so-called "classical dancing," consciously preferring to every other form the artificial form of dancing on the point of the toe, with the feet turned out, in short bodices, with the figure tightly laced in stays, and with a strictly-established system of steps, gestures, and attitudes. Miss Duncan rejected the ballet and established an entirely opposite form of her own. She introduced natural dancing, in which the body of the dancer was liberated not only from stays and satin slippers, but also from the dance-steps of the ballet. She founded her dancing on natural movements and on the most natural of all dance-forms—namely, the dancing of the ancient Greeks.

The new ballet, which also rejects the conventions of the older ballet, cannot nevertheless be regarded as a follower of Miss Duncan. Every form of dancing is good in so far as it expresses the content or subject with which the dance deals; and that form is the most natural which is most suited to the purpose of the dancer. It would be equally unnatural to represent a Greek Bacchic dance with ballet-steps on the point of the toes, or to represent a characteristic Spanish national dance by running and jumping in a Greek tunic and falling into attitudes copied from paintings on ancient Greek vases. No one form of dancing should be accepted once and for all. Borrowing its subjects from the most various historical periods, the ballet must create forms corresponding to the various periods represented. I am not speaking of ethnographical or archæological exactitude, but of the correspondence of the style of the dancing and gestures with the style of the periods represented. In the course of the ages man has repeatedly changed his plastic language and expressed his joys and sorrows and all his emotions under a great variety of forms, often of extreme beauty. For man is infinitely various, and the manifold expressiveness of his gestures cannot be reduced to a single formula.

The art of the older ballet turned its back on life and on all the other arts and shut itself up in a narrow circle of traditions. According to the old method of producing a ballet, the ballet-master composed his dances by combining certain well-established movements and poses, and for his mimetic scenes he used a conventional system of gesticulation, and endeavoured by gestures of the dancers' hands according to established rules to convey the plot of the ballet to the spectator.

The New Ideas

In the new ballet, on the other hand, the dramatic action is expressed by dances and mimetic in which the whole body plays a part. In order to create a stylistic picture the ballet-master of the new school has to study, in the first place, the national dances of the nations represented, dances differing immensely from nation to nation, and often expressing the spirit of a whole race; and, in the second, the art and literature of the period in which the scene is laid. The new ballet, while recognizing the excellence both of the older ballet, and of the dancing of Isadora Duncan in every case where they are suitable to the subject to be treated, refuses to accept any one form as final and exclusive.

If we look at the best productions of sculptural and pictorial art from the point of view of a choreographer of the old school thoroughly versed in the rules of traditional gesticulation and of dancing with the toes turned out we shall find that the marble gods of Greece stood in entirely wrong attitudes; not one of them turned his toes out or held his hands in the positions required by the rules of ballet dancing. Equally faulty from the old-fashioned ballet-master's point of view are the majestic statues of Michael Angelo and the expressive figures in the paintings of the Renaissance, to say nothing of the creations of Raphael and of all modern art from Rodin down. If we are to be true to the rules of the older ballet we must turn our backs on the treasures of beauty accumulated by the genius of mankind during thousands of years, and declare them all to be wrong.

If we look from the point of view of the natural dancing of Miss Duncan, the fantastic attitudes of statues which adorn the temples of India, the severely beautiful figures of ancient Egypt, Assyria, and Babylon, the poetic miniatures of Persia, the water-colours of Japan and China, the art of prehistoric Greece, of the popular chap-books and broadsides of Russia—all alike are far removed from the natural movements of man, and cannot be reconciled with any theory of free and natural dancing. And yet they contain an immense store of beauty, an immense variety of taste, and are clear expressions of the character and ideals of the various nations which produced them. Have we any right to reject all this variety for the sake of adherence to a single formula? No.

The Five Principles

Not to form combinations of ready-made and established dance-steps, but to create in each case a new form corresponding to the subject, the most expressive form possible for the representation of the period and the character of the nation represented—that is the first rule of the new ballet.

The second rule is that dancing and mimetic gesture have no meaning in a ballet unless they serve as an expression of its dramatic action, and they must not be used as a mere divertissement or entertainment, having no connection with the scheme of the whole ballet.

The third rule is that the new ballet admits the use of conventional gesture only where it is required by the style of the ballet, and in all other cases endeavours to replace gestures of the hands by mimetic of the whole body. Man can be and should be expressive from head to foot.

The fourth rule is the expressiveness of groups and of ensemble dancing. In the older ballet the dancers were ranged in groups only for the purpose of ornament, and the ballet-master was not concerned with the expression of any sentiment in groups of characters or in ensemble dances. The new ballet, on the other hand, in developing the principle of expressiveness, advances from the expressiveness of the face to the expressiveness of the whole body, and from the expressiveness of the individual body to the expressiveness of a group of bodies and the expressiveness of the combined dancing of a crowd.

The fifth rule is the alliance of dancing with other arts. The new ballet, refusing to be the slave either of music or of scenic decoration, and recognizing the alliance of the arts only on the condition of complete equality, allows perfect freedom both to the scenic artist and to the musician. In contradistinction to the older ballet it does not demand "ballet music" of the composer as an accompaniment to dancing; it accepts music of every kind, provided only that it is good and expressive. It does not demand of the scenic artist that he should array the ballerinas in short skirts and pink slippers. It does not impose any specific "ballet" conditions on the composer or the decorative artist, but gives complete liberty to their creative powers.

These are the chief rules of the new ballet. If its ideals have not yet been fully realized, its purpose has at any rate been declared plainly enough to split not only the public and the Press but also the members of the St. Petersburg ballet, into two opposing groups, and has led to the establishment of that "Russian Ballet" which visits all foreign countries and is often mistaken for the traditional Russian Ballet which still continues its existence in Moscow and St. Petersburg.

No artist can tell to what extent his work is the result of the influence of others and to what extent it is his own. I cannot, therefore, judge to what extent the influence of the old traditions is preserved in the new ballet and how much the new ideals of Miss Duncan are reflected in it. In accordance with the principles of the new ballet which I have set out above, in composing the ballets which (together with the old ballet, *Le Lac des Cygnes*) constitute the repertory of the "Russian Ballet" at Drury Lane I was not only under the influence of the artists of the historical periods represented, but deliberately sought that influence. When I composed an ancient Greek ballet I studied the artists of ancient Greece; when I produced *Le Coq d'Or* I studied the old Russian chap-books and broadsides; and when I produced *Schéhérazade*, *Cleopatra*, *Le Spectre de la rose*, and the Polovtsian dances in *Prince Igor*, in each case I made use of different materials appropriate to the ballet in hand.

Yours faithfully,

MICHEL FOKINE.

Notes on Choreography

by George Balanchine

We must first realize that dancing is an important independent art, not merely a secondary accompanying one. I believe that it is one of

Source: From *Dance Index*, Volume IV, Numbers 2–3, February–March 1945.

the great arts. Like the music of great musicians, it can be enjoyed and understood without any verbal introduction or explanation. Nowadays at concerts of the greatest philharmonic orchestras in the world, the receptivity of the audience is so low that they have to be provided with little stories explaining the action. I have seen row upon row of listeners at a concert following the "plot" in their programs while a symphony is being played—a note on the bassoon, the entrance of the villain; drums, a thunderstorm is coming. And at the ballets, some of which, unlike the symphonies, actually cannot be understood without program notes, the audience is constantly referring to the libretto to learn that the two women on the stage are mother and daughter and that the gentleman who enters is the brother-in-law of one of them. In the times of St. Leon and Petipa the things in a ballet which could not be conveyed in simple dance movements were told in pantomime. However, this elaborate art is almost completely neglected now, and has been increasingly replaced by written "plots."

The important thing in ballet is the movement itself, as it is sound which is important in a symphony. A ballet may contain a story, but the visual spectacle, not the story, is the essential element. The choreographer and the dancer must remember that they reach the audience through the *eye*—and the audience, in its turn, must train itself actually to *see* what is performed upon the stage. It is the illusion created which convinces the audience, much as it is with the work of a magician. If the illusion fails the ballet fails, no matter how well a program note tells the audience that it has succeeded.

Everything cannot be conveyed by ballet, only those things which can be shown on the stage. Dance is not as inclusive an art as literature. Many things, however, can be shown or implied by the simple means of entrances, exits, solo dances, *pas de deux* or group movements. Moreover, as in music, the audience should be able to enjoy the movement, regardless of the story.

The dance proves that movement is important in itself, for though the other visual arts, such as painting and architecture, are stationary, dance is continually in motion and any single position of a ballet is before the audience's eye for only a fleeting moment. Perhaps the eye does not see motion, but only these stationary positions, like single frames in a cinema film, but memory combines each new image with the preceding image, and the ballet is created by the relation of each of the positions, or movements, to those which precede and follow it.

This accounts for the fact that action photographs of performances of my ballets do not show anything, because they catch only attitudes, the flavor and meaning of which depend on their place in a steady progression. When every emphasis in a ballet is placed on movement it is obvious that a still photograph cannot catch the feeling of it. (It is possible sometimes, however, to succeed by arranging dancers for posed studio photographs.)

The majority of the public may want to relax and make no effort when they go to the theatre, but all art requires a certain amount of effort and ability on the part of the audience. To enjoy a ballet of any value necessitates concentration comparable to that necessary to read a book of value. Each normal person possesses a certain ability to see, but he often does not make any effort to do so. Some people see more than others, not because they have sharper vision, but because they want to see as much as possible and make the effort. When someone stares fixedly at a point, his mind is usually wandering and his visual intensity is weakened. The spectator must be willing to assimilate what is shown on the stage, and possibly to be disturbed by it (for the ballet has spiritual and metaphysical elements, not merely physical ones) and to retain in his memory the preceding movements which will give significance to the ones that are being performed and the ones which are to follow.

Choreographic movement, used to produce visual sensations, is quite different from the practical movement of everyday life used to execute a task, to walk, to lift an object, to sit down. Choreographic movement is an end in itself, and its only purpose is to create the impression of intensity and beauty. No one intends to produce beautiful movements when rolling barrels or handling trains or elevators. In all these movements, however, there are important visual dynamics if one will seek them. Choreographic movements are the basic movements which underlie all gesture and action, and the choreographer must train himself to discover them. It is necessary for the choreographer to see things which other people do not notice, even though they are before their eyes, and to cultivate his visual sense. (It amazes me, for instance, that some people never notice the tops of buildings.)

It is natural that these basic movements will be at first seen affected and artificial to the body which is accustomed only to the practical movements of everyday life. The object of the dancer's technical training is to enable him to perform with perfect ease choreographic movements, movements not limited by considerations of practical, daily life.

Children should begin to study ballet at the age of eight or nine. Before that age ballet exercises could be actually detrimental if performed with the required effort and intensity. In addition, few children under eight years have the faculty to concentrate and to submit to the discipline of a serious ballet class.

Even with eight or nine year-old children, we must always keep in mind the fact that their bones are still soft and their muscles (particularly the ones around the knee) are still unformed. For this reason one should never force the feet of children to attain perfect ballet positions, nor insist on their making an effort to turn out their legs.

At the start each of the five ballet positions must be demonstrated to the children and explained very simply and plainly. Then the children are stood facing the wall with both hands on the bar, so that their weight is evenly supported by both hands. Standing this way, they must first learn to stand in each of the five positions until they become completely familiar with them and can adopt one or another at random, but as yet without any connecting exercises. The children's attention should be drawn to correct posture from the beginning; they should be taught to keep their back straight, their shoulders down, etc. Next they should learn to *demi-plier* very slowly in each of the five positions, always paying strict attention to posture.

Children must be watched to see when they have enough of each exercise. Never strain them in order to speed their progress. The training of children requires a long time and trying to shorten it by hurrying the child does no good whatsoever.

When the children are familiar with the five positions, they must learn how to change from one position to another by means of connecting movement. Next, they learn *battements tendus*, beginning with the simplest: from 1st position to 2nd position and back. They should be taught *battements* only in front, then only sideways, then in back, separately. All the foregoing should be taught first with both hands on the bar. Next the same exercises can be performed with only one hand on the bar. The free arm should be held down at first (in the first position of the arm) and later it should be held horizontally. At this point the children learn how the hand and fingers should be held. (Like the foot, the hand does not change its position but follows the movements of the arm.) Then, away from the bar, the children are taught the positions of the arms.

After this, very simple exercises such as *ronds de jambe par terre* can be gradually added to the lesson. Needless to say, these are performed at the bar.

The children should respect the teacher. Good manners are a very important thing and a definite part of the tradition of ballet which is an aristocratic, that is, an exclusive art, completely understood only by those who are willing to expend a great deal of effort and time on it. In this sense, it is also a democratic art, open to *all* who are willing to do so. To be respected the teacher must carry himself well and be polite to his pupils. Discipline becomes easy if people respect each other. The teacher thanks the pupils at the end of the lesson and has them acknowledge this by a *reverence* which will be so important to them later for bowing gracefully on the stage.

Without technical background dancing can only be improvisation. You want to please yourself and others by expressing something, but you don't know how. I often think how wonderfully I could play a certain violin concerto, with what feeling and expression—only, unfortunately, I do not play the violin!

All ballet positions and movements are based on two principles: the horizontal alignment of each movement in space, and the vertical balance of the human figure.

The alignment is an invisible horizontal line on which the dance is built; it extends unbroken from the point where the dance begins to where it ends. Upon it the movements of the dancers exist, as upon a thread a string of pearls is held.

The vertical balance of the human figure is at the basis of the positions from which every ballet movement originates and in which every ballet movement ends. In the five initial positions the body is balanced on both feet. When a movement is started with one foot from one of these positions, the body remains balanced on the second, supporting foot, erect, as though an invisible vertical line were drawn from the dancer's head to the floor.

After learning the basic positions, dancers are taught a series of exercises which begin and end in these positions. They repeat these exercises, such as *battements tendus*, for example, a great many times, not so much for the purpose of building up certain muscles, as in order to familiarize themselves so completely with each ballet movement that its correct execution will become second nature to them. Only by repeating each movement until it becomes their own can they be sure that their feet and arms will always be in the right position, for they cannot be expected to check every detail consciously while performing.

In order to execute a movement the dancer must make some preparation. The classical positions are stances in which he can both begin and end a motion so that no preparation is necessary between movements and he performs smoothly. The basic positions through which he passes at the end of each movement recover his balance without any extra motion. The fact that after each movement the dancer must revert to an initial ballet position in order to recover his balance, naturally limits the vocabulary of dance movements. However, the combinations of these movements are unlimited in number.

After the first two years of training these elementary movements should be as familiar to the dancer as the alphabet, and he should no more need correction in them than a high school student needs correction in the alphabet. When he has achieved knowledge of these movements, he can perform them without thinking about them. He can *not* do them incorrectly. And when he really knows these basic principles well, he also knows his personal limitations and how to compensate for them, and he can become a good dancer even though he does not have the ideal physical qualifications for it.

Ballet is greatly simplified by the fact that it has not only exact separate movements, but set combinations of positions and movements in which balance is always present.

Jumps, like all other ballet movements, start from and return to one of the set ballet positions. The foot remains immobile through the jump also. As the dancer has only two feet he is limited to five kinds of jumps: from two feet to two feet; from one foot to two feet, from one foot to the same foot, from two feet to one foot, and from one foot to the other. But here again, we have an endless number of combinations. In general, the number of combinations of ballet positions and movements are not restricting but so large that we are unable to use them all.

The positions of the arms are also determined by consideration of balance as well as line. For instance in the second position, the arms are held slightly above and in front of the head, just so the dancer can see her hands if she raises her eyes. If the hands were held directly above her head they would pull the shoulders too far back, and if they were held further in front of the head they would tip the balance of the body forward.

The choreographer frees his mind from the limitations of practical time in much the same way that the dancer has freed his body. He turns not away from life, but to its source. He uses his technical proficiency to express in movement his essential knowledge. Talent, inspiration and personality are not sources which come to an artist in a flash and go away, but are the accumulated results of all he has felt, thought, seen and done—the stories he heard as a child, the art he has enjoyed, his education and his everyday life—and are always with him, capable of being reached by his technical ability and transformed into dynamic designs of the utmost intensity.

If movement is the main, possibly the only means of presenting the art of dancing in its fullest significance, it is easy to understand the importance of connecting movements to each other with subtle care, yet at the same time emphasizing, by contrast, their continuity. For example, very brief and small movements to a fast or slow tempo, in every angle or degree of angle, are developed in relation to following broad, large movements in the identical tempo, and increased from their use by one dancer to their use by many dancers. A kaleidoscope of such movements lives within the choreographer's brain, not yet, of course, set to any tempo. They are as yet only abstract memories of form. Of these, silence, placidity and immobility are perhaps the most powerful forces. They are as impressive, even more so, than rage, delirium or ecstacy. When the body remains transfixed and immobile, every part of it should be invisibly tense, and even in relaxation there should be an inner muscular control.

The steps which a dancer has learned (and after he has studied about ten years with good teachers he should have an impressive vocabulary of movements) are, when separate, devoid of meaning, but they acquire value when they are coordinated in time and space, as parts of the continual, rhythmic flow of the whole.

The student choreographer should at first work out simple technical exercises; for example, fitting eight bars of movement to eight bars of music. Many different interpretations may be given to music; there is no single meaning behind it which the listener must discover, and the choreographic student can fit any number of combinations of movements to the same eight bars of music. On the other hand, he can fit the same combination of movements to several different pieces of music. Or he can fit bars of movement to silence, which has a tempo of its own. But if he uses music he must be sure to fit the movements to it completely.

There is a lot of talk about counterpoint in dancing. It is generally believed that counterpoint is based on contrasts. Actually, counterpoint is an accompaniment to a main theme which it serves to enhance, but from whose unity it must not detract. The only kind of counterpoint that I can see in dancing are the movements of arms, head, and feet which are contrapuntal to the static or vertical position of the body. For instance, in the *croisé* position the body is vertical, but one arm is raised, the other horizontal, one foot points forward while the other supports the body, and the head is inclined towards one of the shoulders. All this is an accompaniment to the main theme, which is the vertical position of the body. In dancing one should not strive to achieve counterpoint by contrasting the movements of two dancers or two groups of dancers on the stage. This results not in counterpoint, but in disunity. (There is no need to apply musical terms to the dance, but if it is done their meaning must be clearly understood.)

The eye can focus perfectly only on objects which are in the center of its field of vision. Those objects which are not head-on are seen clearly only because the observer knows and imagines what they are, while he focuses on the center object. If some new or different form is placed in the secondary part of a composition, the eye instinctively changes its focus and convinces itself of the identity of each individual form. And as vision is the channel through which the art of choreography reaches its audience, this inevitably results in confusion, and a loss of attention to the main theme. But the eye can follow the movements of a large group of dancers if these form a harmonious pattern within its central field or vision.

The Art of the Dance
by Isadora Duncan

The Dance of the Future

A woman once asked me why I dance with bare feet and I replied, "Madam, I believe in the religion of the beauty of the human foot." The lady replied, "But I do not," and I said, "Yet you must, Madam, for the expression and intelligence of the human foot is one of the greatest triumphs of the evolution of man." "But," said the lady, "I do not believe in the evolution of man"; at this said I, "My task is at an end. I refer you to my most revered teachers, Mr. Charles Darwin and Mr. Ernst Haeckel." "But," said the lady, "I do not believe in Darwin and Haeckel." At this point I could think of nothing more to say. So you see that to convince people, I am of little value and ought not to speak. But I am brought from the seclusion of my study, trembling and stammering before a public and told to lecture on the dance of the future.

If we seek the real source of the dance, if we go to nature, we find that the dance of the future is the dance of the past, the dance of eternity, and has been and will always be the same.

The movement of waves, of winds, of the earth is ever in the same lasting harmony. We do not stand on the beach and inquire of the ocean what was its movement in the past and what will be its move-

Source: From *The Art of the Dance*, edited by Sheldon Cheney (New York: Theatre Arts Books, 1969).

ment in the future. We realize that the movement peculiar to its nature is eternal to its nature. The movement of the free animals and birds remains always in correspondence to their nature, the necessities and wants of that nature, and its correspondence to the earth nature. It is only when you put free animals under false restrictions that they lose the power of moving in harmony with nature, and adopt a movement expression of the restrictions placed about them.

So it has been with civilized man. The movements of the savage, who lived in freedom in constant touch with Nature, were unrestricted, natural and beautiful. Only the movements of the naked body can be perfectly natural. Man, arrived at the end of civilization, will have to return to nakedness, not to the unconscious nakedness of the savage, but to the conscious and acknowledged nakedness of the mature Man, whose body will be the harmonious expression of his spiritual being.

And the movements of this Man will be natural and beautiful like those of the free animals.

The movement of the universe concentrating in an individual becomes what is termed the will; for example, the movement of the earth, being the concentration of surrounding forces, gives to the earth its individuality, its will of movement. So creatures of the earth, receiving in turn these concentrating forces in their different relations, as transmitted to them through their ancestors and to those by the earth, in themselves evolve the movement of individuals which is termed the will.

The dance should simply be, then, the natural gravitation of this will of the individual, which in the end is no more nor less than a human translation of the gravitation of the universe.

The school of the ballet of today, vainly striving against the natural laws of gravitation or the natural will of the individual, and working in discord in its form and movement with the form and movement of nature, produces a sterile movement which gives no birth to future movements, but dies as it is made.

The expression of the modern school of ballet, wherein each action is an end, and no movement, pose or rhythm is successive or can be made to evolve succeeding action, is an expression of degeneration, of living death. All the movements of our modern ballet school are sterile movements because they are unnatural: their purpose is to create the delusion that the law of gravitation does not exist for them.

The primary or fundamental movements of the new school of the dance must have within them the seeds from which will evolve all other movements, each in turn to give birth to others in unending sequence of still higher and greater expression, thoughts and ideas.

To those who nevertheless still enjoy the movements, for historical or choreographic or whatever other reasons, to those I answer: They see no farther than the skirts and tricots. But look—under the skirts, under the tricots are dancing deformed muscles. Look still farther—underneath the muscles are deformed bones. A deformed skeleton is dancing before you. This deformation through incorrect dress and incorrect movement is the result of the training necessary to the ballet.

The ballet condemns itself by enforcing the deformation of the beautiful woman's body! No historical, no choreographic reasons can prevail against that!

It is the mission of all art to express the highest and most beautiful ideals of man. What ideal does the ballet express?

No, the dance was once the most noble of all arts; and it shall be again. From the great depth to which it has fallen, it shall be raised. The dancer of the future shall attain so great a height that all other arts shall be helped thereby.

To express what is the most moral, healthful and beautiful in art—this is the mission of the dancer, and to this I dedicate my life.

These flowers before me contain the dream of a dance; it could be named "The light falling on white flowers." A dance that would be a subtle translation of the light and the whiteness. So pure, so strong, that people would say: it is a soul we see moving, a soul that has reached the light and found the whiteness. We are glad it should move so. Through its human medium we have a satisfying sense of movement, of light and glad things. Through this human medium, the movement of all nature runs also through us, is transmitted to us from the dancer. We feel the movement of light intermingled with the thought of whiteness. It is a prayer, this dance; each movement reaches in long undulations to the heavens and becomes a part of the eternal rhythm of the spheres.

To find those primary movements for the human body from which shall evolve the movements of the future dance in ever-varying, natural, unending sequences, that is the duty of the new dancer of today.

As an example of this, we might take the pose of the Hermes of the Greeks. He is represented as flying on the wind. If the artist had pleased to pose his foot in a vertical position, he might have done so, as the God, flying on the wind, is not touching the earth; but realizing that no movement is true unless suggesting sequence of movements, the sculptor placed the Hermes with the ball of his foot resting on the wind, giving the movement an eternal quality.

In the same way I might make an example of each pose and gesture in the thousands of figures we have left to us on the Greek vases and bas-reliefs; there is not one which in its movement does not presuppose another movement.

This is because the Greeks were the greatest students of the laws of nature, wherein all is the expression of unending, ever-increasing evolution, wherein are no ends and no stops.

Such movements will always have to depend on and correspond to the form that is moving. The movements of a beetle correspond to its form. So do those of the horse. Even so the movements of the human body must correspond to its form. The dances of no two persons should be alike.

People have thought that so long as one danced in rhythm, the form and design did not matter; but no, one must perfectly correspond to the other. The Greeks understood this very well. There is a statuette that shows a dancing cupid. It is a child's dance. The movements of the plump little feet and arms are perfectly suited to its form. The sole of the foot rests flat on the ground, a position which might be ugly in a more developed person, but is natural in a child trying to keep its balance. One of the legs is half raised; if it were outstretched it would irritate us, because the movement would be unnatural. There is also a statue of a satyr in a dance that is quite different from that of the cupid. His movements are those of a ripe and muscular man. They are in perfect harmony with the structure of his body.

The Greeks in all their painting, sculpture, architecture, literature, dance and tragedy evolved their movements from the movement of nature, as we plainly see expressed in all representations of the Greek gods, who, being no other than the representatives of natural forces, are always designed in a pose expressing the concentration and evolution of these forces. This is why the art of the Greeks is not a national or characteristic art but has been and will be the art of all humanity for all time.

Therefore dancing naked upon the earth I naturally fall into Greek positions, for Greek positions are only earth positions.

The noblest in art is the nude. This truth is recognized by all, and followed by painters, sculptors and poets; only the dancer has forgotten it, who should most remember it, as the instrument of her art is the human body itself.

Man's first conception of beauty is gained from the form and symmetry of the human body. The new school of the dance should begin with that movement which is in harmony with and will develop the highest form of the human body.

I intend to work for this dance of the future. I do not know whether I have the necessary qualities: I may have neither genius nor talent nor temperament. But I know that I have a Will; and will and energy sometimes prove greater than either genius or talent or temperament.

Let me anticipate all that can be said against my qualification for my work, in the following little fable:

The Gods looked down through the glass roof of my studio and Athene said, "She is not wise, she is not wise, in fact, she is remarkably stupid."

And Demeter looked and said, "She is a weakling; a little thing—not like my deep-breasted daughters who play in the fields of Eleusis; one can see each rib; she is not worthy to dance on my broad-wayed Earth." And Iris looked down and said, "See how heavily she moves—does she guess nothing of the swift and gracious movement of a winged being?" And Pan looked and said, "What? Does she think she knows aught of the movements of my satyrs, splendid ivy-horned fellows who have within them all the fragrant life of the woods and waters?" And then Terpsichore gave one scornful glance; "And she calls that dancing! Why, her feet move more like the lazy steps of a deranged turtle."

And all the Gods laughed; but I looked bravely up through the glass roof and said: "O ye immortal Gods, who dwell in high Olympus and live on Ambrosia and Honey-cakes, and pay no studio rent nor bakers' bills thereof, do not judge me so scornfully. It is true, O Athene, that I am not wise, and my head is a rattled institution; but I do occasionally read the word of those who have gazed into the infinite blue of thine eyes, and I bow my empty gourd head very humbly before thine altars. And, O Demeter of the Holy Garland," I continued, "it is true that the beautiful maidens of your broad-wayed earth would not admit me of their company; still I have thrown aside my sandals that my feet may touch your life-giving earth more reverently, and I have had your sacred Hymn sung before the present day Barbarians, and I have made them to listen and to find it good.

"And, O Iris of the golden wings, it is true that mine is but a sluggish movement; others of my profession have luted more violently against the laws of gravitation, from which laws, O glorious one, you are alone exempt. Yet the wind from your wings has swept through my poor earthy spirit, and I have often brought prayers to your courage-inspiring image.

"And, O Pan, you who were pitiful and gentle to simple Psyche in her wanderings, think more kindly of my little attempts to dance in your woody places.

"And you most exquisite one, Terpsichore, send to me a little comfort and strength that I may proclaim your power on Earth during my life; and afterwards, in the shadowy Hades, my wistful spirit shall dance dances better yet in thine honour."

Then came the voice of Zeus, the Thunderer:

"Continue your way and rely upon the eternal justice of the immortal Gods; if you work well they shall know of it and be pleased thereof."

In this sense, then, I intend to work, and if I could find in my dance a few or even one single position that the sculptor could transfer into marble so that it might be preserved, my work would not have been in vain; this one form would be a gain; it would be a first step for the future. My intention is, in due time, to found a school, to build a theatre where a hundred little girls shall be trained in my art, which they, in their turn, will better. In this school I shall not teach the children to imitate my movements, but to make their own. I shall not force them to study certain definite movements; I shall help them to develop those movements which are natural to them. Whosoever sees the movements of an untaught little child cannot deny that its movements are beautiful. They are beautiful because they are natural to the child. Even so the movements of the human body may be beautiful in every stage of development so long as they are in harmony with that stage and degree of maturity which the body has attained. There will always be movements which are the perfect expression of that individual body and that individual soul; so we must not force it to make movements which are not natural to it but which belong to a school. An intelligent child must be astonished to find that in the ballet school it is taught movements contrary to all those movements which it would make of its own accord.

This may seem a question of little importance, a question of differing opinions on the ballet and the new dance. But it is a great question. It is not only a question of true art, it is a question of race, of the development of the female sex to beauty and health, of the return to the original strength and to natural movements of woman's body. It is a question of the development of perfect mothers and the birth of healthy and beautiful children. The dancing school of the future is to develop and to show the ideal form of woman. It will be, as it were, a museum of the living beauty of the period.

Travellers coming into a country and seeing the dancers should find in them that country's ideal of the beauty of form and movement. But strangers who today come to any country, and there see the dancers of the ballet school, would get a strange notion indeed of the ideal of beauty in that country. More than this, dancing like any art of any time should reflect the highest point the spirit of mankind has reached in that special period. Does anybody think that the present day ballet school expresses this?

Why are its positions in such contrast to the beautiful positions of the antique sculptures which we preserve in our museums and which are constantly presented to us as perfect models of ideal beauty? Or have our museums been founded only out of historical and archaeological interest, and not for the sake of the beauty of the objects which they contain?

The ideal of beauty of the human body cannot change with fashion but only with evolution. Remember the story of the beautiful sculpture of a Roman girl which was discovered under the reign of Pope Innocent VIII, and which by its beauty created such a sensation that the men thronged to see it and made pilgrimages to it as to a holy shrine, so that the Pope, troubled by the movement which it originated, finally had it buried again.

And here I want to avoid a misunderstanding that might easily arise. From what I have said you might conclude that my intention is to return to the dances of the old Greeks, or that I think that the dance of the future will be a revival of the antique dances or even of those of the primitive tribes. No, the dance of the future will be a new movement, a consequence of the entire evolution which mankind has passed through. To return to the dances of the Greeks would be as impossible as it is unnecessary. We are not Greeks and therefore cannot dance Greek dances.

But the dance of the future will have to become again a high religious art as it was with the Greeks. For art which is not religious is not art, is mere merchandise.

The dancer of the future will be one whose body and soul have grown so harmoniously together that the natural language of that soul will have become the movement of the body. The dancer will not belong to a nation but to all humanity. She will dance not in the form of nymph, nor fairy, nor coquette, but in the form of woman in her greatest and purest expression. She will realize the mission of woman's body and the holiness of all its parts. She will dance the changing life of nature, showing how each part is transformed into the other. From all parts of her body shall shine radiant intelligence, bringing to the world the message of the thoughts and aspirations of thousands of women. She shall dance the freedom of woman.

Oh, what a field is here awaiting her! Do you not feel that she is near, that she is coming, this dancer of the future! She will help womankind to a new knowledge of the possible strength and beauty of their bodies, and the relation of their bodies to the earth nature and to the children of the future. She will dance the body emerging again from centuries of civilized forgetfulness, emerging not in the nudity of primitive man, but in a new nakedness, no longer at war with spirituality and intelligence, but joining with them in a glorious harmony.

This is the mission of the dancer of the future. Oh, do you not feel that she is near, do you not long for her coming as I do? Let us prepare the place for her. I would build for her a temple to await her. Perhaps she is yet unborn, perhaps she is now a little child. Perhaps, oh blissful! it may be my holy mission to guide her first steps, to watch the progress of her movements day by day until, far outgrowing my poor teaching, her movements will become godlike, mirroring in themselves the waves, the winds, the movements of growing things, the flight of birds, the passing of clouds, and finally the thought of man in his relation to the universe.

Oh, she is coming, the dancer of the future: the free spirit, who will inhabit the body of new woman; more glorious than any woman that has yet been; more beautiful than the Egyptian, than the Greek, the early Italian, than all women of past centuries—the highest intelligence in the freest body!

Movement Is Life

Study the movement of the earth, the movement of plants and trees, of animals, the movement of winds and waves—and then study the movements of a child. You will find that the movement of all natural things works within harmonious expression. And this is true in the first years of a child's life; but very soon the movement is imposed from without by wrong theories of education, and the child soon loses its natural spontaneous life, and its power of expressing that in movement.

I notice that a baby of three or four coming to my school is responsive to the exaltation of beautiful music, whereas a child of eight or nine is already under the influence of a conventional and mechanical conception of life imposed upon it by the pedagogues. The child of nine has already entered into the prison of conventional and mechanical movement, in which it will remain and suffer its entire life, until advancing age brings on paralysis of bodily expression.

When asked for the pedagogic program of my school, I reply: "Let us first teach little children to breathe, to vibrate, to feel, and to become one with the general harmony and movement of nature. Let us first produce a beautiful human being, a dancing child." Nietzsche has said that he cannot believe in a god that cannot dance. He has also said, "Let that day be considered lost on which we have not danced."

But he did not mean the execution of pirouettes. He meant the exaltation of life in movement.

The harmony of music exists equally with the harmony of movement in nature.

Man has not invented the harmony of music. It is one of the underlying principles of life. Neither could the harmony of movement be invented: it is essential to draw one's conception of it from Nature herself, and to seek the rhythm of human movement from the rhythm of water in motion, from the blowing of the winds on the world, in all the earth's movements, in the motions of animals, fish, birds, reptiles, and even in primitive man, whose body still moved in harmony with nature.

With the first conception of a conscience, man became self-conscious, lost the natural movements of the body; today in the light of intelligence gained through years of civilization, it is essential that he consciously seek what he has unconsciously lost.

All the movements of the earth follow the lines of wave motion. Both sound and light travel in waves. The motion of water, winds, trees and plants progresses in waves. The flight of a bird and the movements of all animals follow lines like undulating waves. If then one seeks a point of physical beginning for the movement of the human body, there is a clue in the undulating motion of the wave. It is one of the elemental facts of nature, and out of such elementals the child, the dancer, absorbs something basic to dancing.

The human being too is a source. Dancing expresses in a different language, different from nature, the beauty of the body; and the body grows more beautiful with dancing. All the conscious art of mankind has grown out of the discovery of the natural beauty of the human body. Men tried to reproduce it in sand or on a wall, and painting thus was born. From our understanding of the harmonies and proportions of the members of the body sprang architecture. From the wish to glorify the body sculpture was created.

The beauty of the human form is not chance. One cannot change it by dress. The Chinese women deformed their feet with tiny shoes; women of the time of Louis XIV deformed their bodies with corsets; but the ideal of the human body must forever remain the same. The Venus of Milo stands on her pedestal in the Louvre for an ideal; women pass before her, hurt and deformed by the dress of ridiculous fashions; she remains forever the same, for she is beauty, life, truth.

It is because the human form is not and cannot be at the mercy of fashion or the taste of an epoch that the beauty of woman is eternal. It is the guide of human evolution toward the goal of the human race, toward the ideal of the future which dreams of becoming God.

The architect, the sculptor, the painter, the musician, the poet, all understand how the idealization of the human form and the consciousness of its divinity are at the root of all art created by man. A single artist has lost this divinity, an artist who above all should be the first to desire it—the dancer.

Dancing, indeed, through a long era lacked all sense of elemental natural movement. It tried to afford the sense of gravity overcome—a denial of nature. Its movements were not living, flowing, undulating, giving rise inevitably to other movements. All freedom and spontaneity were lost in a maze of intricate artifice. The dancer had to be dressed up artificially to be in keeping with its unnatural character.

Then when I opened the door to nature again, revealing a different kind of dance, some people explained it all by saying, "See, it is *natural* dancing." But with its freedom, its accordance with natural movement, there was always design too—even in nature you find sure, even rigid design. "Natural" dancing should mean only that the dance never goes against nature, not that anything is left to chance.

Nature must be the source of all art, and dance must make use of nature's forces in harmony and rhythm, but the dancer's movement will always be separate from any movement in nature.

A Modern Dancer's Primer for Action

by Martha Graham

1. Certain Basic Principles

I am a dancer. My experience has been with dance as an art.

Each art has an instrument and a medium. The instrument of the dance is the human body; the medium is movement. The body has always been to me a thrilling wonder, a dynamo of energy, exciting,

Source: From *Dance: A Basic Educational Technique*, edited by Frederick R. Rogers (New York: Macmillan, 1941).

courageous, powerful; a delicately balanced logic and proportion. It has not been my aim to evolve or discover a new method of dance training, but rather to dance significantly. To dance significantly means "through the medium of discipline and by means of a sensitive, strong instrument, to bring into focus unhackneyed movement: a human being."

I did not want to be a tree, a flower, or a wave. In a dancer's body, we as audience must see *ourselves*, not the imitated behavior of everyday actions, not the phenomena of nature, not exotic creatures from another planet, but something of the miracle that is a human being, motivated, disciplined, concentrated.

The part a modern art plays in the world, each time such a movement manifests itself, is to make apparent once again the inner hidden realities behind the accepted symbols. Out of this need a new plasticity, emotional and physical, was demanded of the dance. This meant experiment in movement. The body must not only be strong, be facile, be brilliant, but must also be significant and simple. To be simple takes the greatest measure of experience and discipline known to the artist.

It may be possible for an individual dancer to proceed instinctively along these lines, but when dance involves more than the solo figure, some uniform training is necessary. Several of us, working separately, found methods of training, evolving as we worked.

The method, however, was secondary. Training, technique, is important; but it is always in the artist's mind only the means to an end. Its importance is that it frees the body to become its ultimate self.

Technique and training have never been a substitute for that condition of awareness which is talent, for that complete miracle of balance which is genius, but it can give plasticity and tension, freedom and discipline, balancing one against the other. It can awaken memory of the race through muscular memory of the body. Training and technique are means to strength, to freedom, to spontaneity.

Contrary to popular belief, spontaneity as one sees it in dance or in theatre, is not wholly dependent on emotion at that instant. It is the condition of emotion objectified. It plays the part in theater that light plays in life. It illumines. It excites. Spontaneity is essentially dependent on energy, upon the strength necessary to perfect timing. It is the result of perfect timing to the Now. It is not essentially intellectual or emotional, but is nerve reaction. That is why art is not to be *understood*, as we use the term, but is to be *experienced*.

To experience means that our minds and emotions are involved. For primarily it is the nervous system that is the instrument of experience. This is the reason music, with its sound and rhythm, is universally the great moving force of the world. It affects animals as well as human beings.

A program of physical activity which involves only, first, exercises for strength, and second, a means of emotional catharsis through so-called "self-expression dancing," will never produce a complete human being. It is a dangerous program, for it does not fit a child or an adolescent for the virtue of living.

Living is an adventure, a form of evolvement which demands the greatest sensitivity to accomplish it with grace, dignity, efficiency. The puritanical concept of life has always ignored the fact that the nervous system and the body as well as the mind are involved in experience, and art cannot be experienced except by one's entire being.

In life, heightened nerve sensitivity produces that concentration on the instant which is true living. In dance, this sensitivity produces action timed to the present moment. It is the result of a technique for revelation of experience.

To me, this acquirement of nervous, physical, and emotional concentration is the one element possessed to the highest degree by the truly great dancers of the world. Its acquirement is the result of discipline, of energy in the deep sense. That is why there are so few great dancers.

A great dancer is not made by technique alone any more than a great statesman is made by knowledge alone. Both possess true spontaneity. Spontaneity in behavior, in life, is due largely to complete health; on the stage to a technical use—often so ingrained by proper training as to seem instinctive—of nervous energy. Perhaps what we have always called intuition is merely a nervous system organized by training to perceive.

Dance had its origin in ritual, the eternal urge toward immortality. Basically, ritual was the formalized desire to achieve union with those beings who could bestow immortality upon man. Today we practice a different ritual, and this despite the shadow over the world, for we seek immortality of another order—the potential greatness of man.

In its essentials, dance is the same over the entire world. These essentials are its function, which is communication; its instrument, which is the body; and its medium, which is movement. The style or manner of dance is different in each country in which it manifests itself. The reason for this is threefold—climate, religion, and social system. These things affect our thinking and hence our movement expression.

Although its concept was the product of Isadora Duncan and Ruth St. Denis, modern dance in its present manifestation has evolved since the World War. At that time a different attitude towards life emerged.

As a result of twentieth-century thinking, a new or more related movement language was inevitable. If that made necessary a complete departure from the dance form known as ballet, the classical dance, it did not mean that ballet training itself was wrong. It was simply found not to be complete enough, not adequate to the time, with its change of thinking and physical attitude.

A break from a certain rigidity, a certain glibness, a certain accent on overprivilege was needed. There was need of an intensification, a simplification. For a time, this need manifested itself in an extreme of movement asceticism; there has now come a swing back from that extreme. All facilities of body are again being used fearlessly, but during that time of asceticism, so-called, much glibness was dropped, much of the purely decorative cast aside.

No art ignores human values, for therein lie its roots. Directed by the authentic or perverted magnificence, which is man's spirit, movement is the most powerful and dangerous art medium known. This is because it is the speech of the basic instrument, the body, which is an instinctive, intuitive, inevitable mirror revealing man as he is.

Art does not create change; it registers change. The change takes place in the man himself. The change from nineteenth- to twentieth-century thinking and attitude toward life has produced a difference in inspiration for action. As a result, there is a difference in form and technical expression in the arts.

2. *Posture, Movement, Balance*

One of the first indications of change, because it is the total being—physical, emotional, mental, and nervous—is posture.

Posture is dynamic, not static. It is a self-portrait of being. It is psychological as well as physiological.

I use the word "posture" to mean *that instant of seeming stillness when the body is poised for most intense, most subtle action, the body at its moment of greatest potential efficiency*.

People often say that the posture of this dancer or that dancer or of all dancers is not natural. I ask, "Not natural to what?—natural to joy, sorrow, pain, relaxation, exaltation, elevation, fall?"

Each condition of sensitivity has a corresponding condition of posture. Posture is correct when it is relative to the need of the instant.

There is only one law of posture I have been able to discover—the perpendicular line connecting heaven and earth. But the problem is how to relate the various parts of the body. The nearest to the norm, as it has been observed and practiced over centuries, has been the ear in line perpendicularly with the shoulder, the shoulder with the pelvic bone, the pelvic bone in line with the arch of the foot.

The criticism that the posture of some dancers is bad because they appear to have a "sway back" is usually not justified, for a "sway back" is a weak back. Often the development of the muscles for jumping, leaping, and elevation, all of which concentrate in the hips and buttocks, is so pronounced as to give the appearance, to the uninformed critic, of "sway back."

Through all times the acquiring of technique in dance has been for one purpose—so to train the body as to make possible any demand made upon it by that inner self which has the vision of what needs to be said.

No one invents movement; movement is discovered. What is possible and necessary to the body under the impulse of the emotional self is the result of this discovery; and the formalization of it into a progressive series of exercises is technique.

It is possible and wise to teach these exercises even to the person who has no desire to dance professionally. It must, however, be emphasized that performance of these exercises is not a mere matter of "having a good time," but of achieving a center of body and mind which will eventually, but not immediately, result in a singing freedom. Throughout the performance of these technical exercises, a woman remains a woman, and a man a man, because power means to become what one *is*, to the highest degree of realization.

As in any other architectural edifice, the body is kept erect by balance. Balance is a nicety of relationship preserved throughout the various sections of the body. There are points of tension which preserve us in the air, hold us erect when standing, and hold us safely when we seem to drop to the floor at incredible speed. We would possess these naturally if they had not been destroyed in us by wrong training, either physical, intellectual, or emotional.

Contrary to opinion, the dancer's body is nearer to the norm of what the body should be than any other. It has been brought to this possible norm by discipline, for the dancer is, of necessity, a realist. Pavlova, Argentina, and Ruth St. Denis all practiced their art past the age of fifty.

3. The Aim of Method

There is no common terminology for describing the technique of modern dance. Furthermore, to describe two or three exercises would give an accent to these few beyond their importance. Therefore, rather than being a description here of actual specific practice of exercises, this is intended as an exposition of the theory behind the practice of the technical training I employ.

The aim of the method is coordination. In dance, that means unity of body produced by emotional physical balance. In technique, it means so to train all elements of body—legs, arms, torso, etc.—as to make them all equally important and equally efficient. It means a state of relativity of members in use that results in flow of movement. I have discovered whatever it is that I have discovered through practice and out of need. My theory, if it can be called such, had its origin and has its justificiation in practical experience.

What I say is based on one premise—dance is an art, one of the arts of the theatre. True theatricality is not a vain or egotistic or unpleasant attribute. Neither does it depend on cheap tricks either of movement, costume, or audience appeal. Primarily, it is a means employed to bring the idea of one person into focus for the many. First there is the concept; then there is a dramatization of that concept which makes it apparent to others. This process is what is known as theatricality.

I believe dancing can bring liberation to many because it brings organized activity. I believe that the exercises I use are as right for a lay person as for a professional dancer, because they do no violence anatomically or emotionally. The difference in their use for the lay person and for the professional dancer is not in their basic approach but in the degree and intensity of their application. I have always thought first of the dancer as a human being. These exercises, though their original intention was the training of professionals, have been taught to children and adolescents as well.

What follows might be termed a "Primer for Action."

4. *Primer for Action*

A. An Attitude Toward Dance.

1. There must be something that needs to be danced. Dance demands a dedication, but it is not a substitute for living. It is the expression of a fully aware person dancing that which can be expressed only by means of dance. It is not an emotional catharsis for the hysterical, frustrated, fearful, or morbid. It is an act of affirmation, not of escape. The affirmation may take many forms—tragedy, comedy, satire, lyric or dramatic.

2. There must be a disciplined way of dancing. This means learning a craft, not by intellection, but by hard physical work.

B. A Dancer's Attitude Toward the Body.

The body must be sustained, honored, understood, disciplined. There should be no violation of the body. All exercises are but the extensions of physical capabilities. This is the reason it takes years of daily work to develop a dancer's body. It can only be done just so fast. It is subject to the natural timing of physical growth.

C. An Attitude Toward Technique.

Technique is a means to an end. It is the means to becoming a dancer.

1. All exercises should be based on bodily structure. They should be written for the instrument, a body, male *or* female.
2. As the province of dance is motion, all exercises should be based upon the body in motion as its natural state. This is true even of exercises on the floor.

D. Technique Has a Three-Fold Purpose.

1. Strength of body.
2. Freedom of body and spirit.
3. Spontaneity of action.

E. Specific Procedure in Technique.

All exercises are in the form of theme and variations. There is a basic principle of movement employed which deals specifically with a certain region of body—torso, back, pelvis, legs, feet, etc. The theme of the exercise deals directly with its function for body control. It is stripped of all extraneous movement or embellishments. The variations become increasingly wider in scope, moving from the specific to the general movement which embraces the use of the entire body. Variation still keeps, however, no matter how involved it becomes, its relationship to the theme.

F. Four Main Classes into Which Technique Is Divided.

1. Exercises on the floor.

All exercises on the floor are direct preparations for standing and elevation later. The first principle taught is body center. The first movement is based upon the body in two acts of breathing—inhaling and exhaling—developing it from actual breathing experience to the muscular activity independent of the actual act of breathing. These two acts, when performed muscularly only, are called "release," which corresponds to the body in inhalation, and "contraction" which corresponds to exhalation. The word "relaxation" is not used because it has come to mean a devitalized body.

In the professional class, the floor exercises take approximately twenty minutes. They comprise: a. stretching; b. back exercise; c. leg extensions.

N.B. No stretch is made by pushing the back of the student to the floor. The down movement is never helped. The spine is never touched. The leg is never stretched suddenly or forcibly by pressure. The hand never tries to straighten the knee by pressure. The leg is straightened only by slow and gradual extension.

2. Exercises standing in one place.
   a. All exercises for the legs—bends, lifts, extensions, front, side, and back.
   b. Hip swings.
   c. Feet exercises.
   d. Turns in place.

   N.B. In all lifts and *pliés*, the relationship of knee to foot is closely observed. There must be no strain on knees or arches at any time. In all exercises on contraction, the shoulders and pelvic bone have a definite relationship in order to avoid all abdominal strain.

3. Exercises for elevation.
   a. Jumps in place.
   b. Open space work.
   Walks in rhythms.
   Runs.
   Turns across the floor.
   Turns in the air.
   Leaps.
   Skips.

   N.B. No elevation is attempted until at least one half hour of preliminary work is done to permit the body to become fluid. All elevation is without strain. The legs and back are strong and the body centered from the exercises which have gone before.

4. Exercise for falls.

This exercise is a series of falls forward, side, and back in various rhythms and at various speeds. The body never strikes the floor by landing on the knees, on the spine, on a shoulder, or on an elbow or head. The joints must not be jarred or any vital part struck. Falls are used primarily as preliminary to and therefore as a means of "affirmation." In no fall does the body remain on the floor, but assumes an upright position as part of the exercise. My dancers fall *so they may rise*.

Choreography and the Dance
by Merce Cunningham

Mr. Cunningham, could you describe your approach to dance?

In my choreographic work, the basis for the dances is movement, that is, the human body moving in time-space. The scale for this movement ranges from being quiescent to the maximum amount of movement (physical activity) a person can produce at any given moment. The ideas of the dance come both from the movement, and are in the movement. It has no reference outside of that. A given dance does not have its origin in some thought I might have about a story, a mood, or an expression; rather, the proportions of the dance come from the activity itself. Any idea as to mood, story, or expression entertained by the spectator is a product of his mind, of his feelings; and he is free to act with it. So in starting to choreograph, I begin with movements, steps, if you like, in working by myself or with the members of my company, and from that, the dance continues.

This is a simplified statement, describing something that can take many work-hours daily for weeks and months, but it is essentially a process of watching and working with people who use movement as a force of life, not as something to be explained by reference, or used as illustration, but as something, if not necessarily grave, certainly constant in life. What is fascinating and interesting in movement, is, though we are all two-legged creatures, we all move differently, in accordance with our physical proportions as well as our temperaments. It is this that interests me. Not the sameness of one person to another, but the difference, not a corps de ballet, but a group of individuals acting together.

This non-reference of the movement is extended into a relationship with music. It is essentially a non-relationship. The dance is not performed to the music. For the dances that we present, the music is composed and performed as a separate identity in itself. It happens to take place at the same time as the dance. The two co-exist, as sight and

Source: *The Creative Experience*, edited by Stanley Rosner and Lawrence E. Abt (New York: Grossman Publications, 1970).

sound do in our daily lives. And with that, the dance is not dependent upon the music. This does not mean I would prefer to dance in silence (although we have done that, on one notable occasion an entire program owing to a union dispute), because it would strike me as daily life without sound. I accept sound as one of the sensory areas along with sight, the visual sense.

How is the music chosen for the dances in view of the separation between dance and music?

At some point earlier or later in the work on a new piece, I will discuss with John Cage, David Tudor, and Gordon Mumma, the musicians connected with my company, the composers they might suggest as possibilities. Ordinarily the music I have is contemporary, more often than not a commission. The musicians ask me something about the piece, but I can tell them little, since it is about no specific thing. They may look at it naturally, but that isn't always helpful, as it isn't finished, and we, the dancers, are unable to show it clearly. There are details of course, the possible length, the number of dancers, its speeds, and so forth. The musicians make some decision from this as to who might be involved as the composer, or I myself may have someone in mind. Then we ask the composer if he would be interested in working with this. If he is, he may have a few questions. The two questions that Christian Wolff asked me about *Rune* were how long it should be and how many dancers would be involved. But the music is made to be separate from the dance. To push this a little further, the dancers on several occasions have not actually heard the music until the first performance; that is, until the audience hears it. There is no necessity for us to rehearse with it. It is okay if we do, if it is available, which with recent works hasn't been the case since it is usually not completed before curtain time, if then. As David Tudor once said, it's not music with dancing, it's music *and* dancing.

Most of the scores I now have, the works in the past six or seven years, are open-ended. The time structures of the scores are such that they can be any length, as are some of the dances. Therefore, in a work such as *Canfield* or *Field Dances,* I make a decision prior to the performance as to how long a given piece will be for that playing. Then we begin as the curtain goes up and end when it comes down.

Is there a great deal of structure involved in your choreography?

Our repertoire ranges from dances which are strictly choreographed, and repeated at each performance, to dances in which, though the movements have been choreographed for the dancer, he is free in the course of the performance to do them faster or slower, in part or in toto, to exit from or return to the area freely. The length of the dance varies from performance to performance. But the movements have been given. This is not, of course, improvisation, although the dancers do have various freedoms with the materials given.

What about the relationship between the structure of the dances, and the choice of dancer?

I attempt to find in a dancer something that makes him dance in his particular way. I don't mean anything psychological about this. I mean simply that one person's body is different from another's. And each therefore takes forms and shapes differently. It doesn't mean that the shapes are deformed. He does them the way he does them. Just as you see people moving in the streets and recognize their differences. So, in training dancers in class, I attempt to see the unique way in which a given person moves. For instance, here is a photograph with two dancers in it. You can see the particular way each is in the movement-shape he shows. Now, if the two were different people, they could make the same shapes. But if the girl is shorter, it doesn't happen to look the same. But a little searching in momentum with the shorter girl might bring out the way she hits the shape. Not an imitation, but a reality.

There is a further involvement here. Being a performing company, we are often touring. This means, at times, that some dancers can't go, and other dancers have to take over parts. This makes for difficulties which all dance companies have. One has to find a way to let the new dancer do the same thing, and at the same time not make demands upon that dancer which aren't suitable to his structure and timing. So, it is a constant process of dealing with the person, not with an idea, but with the person in a given physical situation.

In my choreography I am more likely to think in terms of structure, structure in time. I will have some awareness as to the length of a dance, and within that limit, the dance gets structured time-wise. So, if the dance is twenty minutes long, one section may be four and a half minutes, another five, the next two, and so on, although these lengths will change in the course of working the dance out. It's like going down a path: you follow it. If there's a tree in the way, you're not likely to go through it. You have to go around it. You might go over it. But that's more complicated. So you allow for these occurrences as the working procedure goes along.

What are the origins of the shapes and movements you find for your dancers?

There are many things dancers can do. For example, a girl can balance against a man who is holding her. The two people can balance with each other, and because he is stronger than she is normally, she can move much further away, and he can still allow for that. This kind of action is possible in different directions—into the air and on or across the floor. I think in movement terms. Human beings move on two legs across the floor, across the earth. We don't do very much on the ground. We don't have that kind of power in us. And we can't go as fast as most four-footed animals do. Our action is here on our two legs. That's what our life is about. When one thinks of falling, dying, or a loss of consciousness, this is a condition that is out of the normal range of human momentum. With jumping, although we all try to do it, we are again caught, because we can't stay up there very long. So it becomes virtuoso. You know, when someone jumps high and stays long enough for it to register, it becomes a virtuoso feat. This is the way I've thought of human movement, in terms of the fact that we stand and move on two legs, and every person moves differently. There is an enormous variety of movement to deal with.

My choreography is part of a working process. It is not necessarily always with the company. It may be with myself. But it is a working process. I begin, in the studio, to try something out. If it doesn't work for some reason or if it's physically not possible for me, I try out something else. And then I do it with myself, or with the company, or with all of us together. Just yesterday we had a little problem about one person's running into another, because I wanted to find out about certain momentums in space, and the only way to do it is to do it.

As you see, I am interested in experimenting with movements. Oh, I may see something out of the corner of my eye—the slight way a person climbs a curb, the special attack of a dancer to a familiar step in class, an unfamiliar stride in a sportsman, something I don't know about, and then I try it. Children do amazing kinds of motions, and one wonders how they got into that particular shape.

I have made dances that employ different compositional continuities. For instance, now I rarely make a dance in which I start at the beginning and go on through to the end. More likely I make a series of things, short sequences, long passages, involving myself alone, and maybe one or more of the other dancers, sometimes the entire company. Then by chance or other methods I make a decision about the order. So I cannot have a specific idea which starts here and goes through, that someone could pin down that way. After one performs a piece for a period though, however strange it may have seemed at the beginning, it takes its own continuity. It's as if one enters a strange house and has to follow unfamiliar paths. After a time, the paths are no longer strange.

I often use a random method to find out the order of the various sequences in a dance. This can act to jump the continuity of the dance out of my personal feelings about order or out of my memory of physical coordinations. This has been done by breaking the movement into small fragments or dividing it into big sections. I have on occasion changed the order of dances after we have performed them. This is a process of taking the given material and changing the order, which we did most recently with a piece called *Scramble*. Another work, *Canfield*, not only changes the order from performance to performance, but the various sections done at one performance can be replaced by others at the next, so though the temper of the piece is the same, the details (material, time, space) are different.

Do you attempt to express moods or feelings in your dances?

There is no specific expressive intent in the dances, although an individual spectator looking at one may decide there is something particular in it. I can give you a description of a piece we have in the repertoire called *Winterbranch*, made in 1964, which has been received by spectators in many different ways. The material of the dance is made up of a person's falling in one way or another. The structure of the piece is that one or more dancers enter an area, walking, and at a point in the area, originally figured out by random means, perform a certain kind of falling configuration. The number of dancers in any sequence ranges from one to six. Ordinarily the dancers will finish the sequence and walk out of the area. But to allow for variety in this, I saw there were several possibilities of a girl's being dragged off the stage. Then there's this terrible problem about splinters. We have to play on many different kinds of stages. So rather than make that a problem, I thought, perhaps she could fall on something, and be dragged off. I practiced with towels, tried it with the dancers, and decided some kind of material could be used.

Robert Rauschenberg did the designing for the dance, and I told him that the clothes we wore should be practical for falling. I also said we had to have something on our feet. It has something to do with the nature of the motion. I also thought of the piece as taking place at night rather than during the day, not with moonlight, but with artificial illumination which can go on and off. The lighting could change from performance to performance (as did the dance originally).

So Mr. Rauschenberg went away and came back some time later with the idea that we wear sweat clothes and dance in the dark. He put black paint under our eyes, such as skiers and football players wear. We had white sneakers. The materials on which we fall are old pieces of canvas. The light changes everytime at each performance. Sometimes the light is turned directly into the eyes of the audience. It may be strong or weak, depending upon what is available in the lighting situation. The lighting changes each time. The order of the dance could change too, except when we have to perform it often, since it is hard for us to rehearse a change quickly. I found that it's physically tiring, and there can be accidents. I try to avoid them.

As to the music part, I brought this to Mr. Cage, and he thought the composer La Monte Young might work in this particular situation. We spoke to Mr. Young. He suggested that we could use his piece which is called *Two Sounds*, which has one low decibel and one high decibel sound in it. These sounds go on continuously at the same level for about half the dance, ten to twelve minutes.

These are three separate things put together. The lighting does not relate to the movement at all. That is, it does not reveal or disguise any particular movement. There are times when the stage is in total darkness, which is difficult for us too, since we feel we might fall off the stage.

How did this treatment of lighting come about?

I thought that perhaps something about night rather than day could be tried. That's what brought that on. But then the lighting man was free to do what he liked with it, to show or not show any particular part of the piece. It's evident, of course, that it has a striking dramatic punch to it, simply because of turning on and off lights. We have equipment available now which was not available fifty years ago. We couldn't do it quite that way then. But now these things are possible in the theatre. And I hope in the future that there are going to be a few more.

Did you have any thoughts as to the origins of writing a dance about falling when you wrote Winterbranch?

First of all I don't write a dance. I choreograph a dance. Falling is one of the ways of moving. Sometimes the dances involve many kinds of movement, sometimes few. *Winterbranch* got into different kinds of falling. As to why that came up instead of jumping, I don't know. Why an apple instead of an orange?

As I have tried to indicate earlier, I am more interested in the *facts* of moving rather than my feelings about them. Naturally, movement possibilities are limited for me, since I am limited by what I can do physically or can think up for someone else to do. But I always hope to find something I don't know about. I would prefer to come upon something, whether by random means or other, that I don't know how to do, and try to find out about it. Perhaps that was the situation with falling. I didn't know much about it, and this was one way to find out.

Is your more formal kind of choreography related to the work of Ann Halprin?

One of the major differences between Ann Halprin and myself is that I work with a formally trained dance company. I accept this situation as more or less the base on which I work. From what I know of her work, she has dealt with both trained and untrained dancers in different kinds of environmental situations. But I would think that one thing we have in common is that we are not interested in the old ways or forms of making things. She is often concerned with a particular environment and the individual's reaction to it. Well, I do that in a certain way too, but it is different because we are a troupe of dancers. We are a repertory company, and we tour and do pieces over and over in changing theatre situations, so that we have to keep adjusting ourselves in a given dance anew.

How did you become interested in choreography?

When I came to New York, I was in the company of Martha Graham. I became disinterested in that work and decided to work for myself, and I began to make solos and give programs. Then I did not want to work just with myself. I wanted to work with other dancers, to have a company. I was interested in making pieces with other people involved along with myself. I began to look around and discovered that I didn't like the way they danced. It was not a kind of dancing that interested me. I went a little further in thinking of ways to train them. If one doesn't like what someone else does, then the only thing to do is to make something oneself, rather than complaining. In time, I began to teach in order to have dancers trained in the way I thought interesting. Basically it was that with just a few years in between.

In training, my concern has been to make the body as flexible, strong, and resilient as possible, and in as many directions as I could find. The human body is the instrument that dancing deals with. The human body moves in limited ways, very few actually. There are certain physical things it can't do that another animal might be able to do. But within the body's limitations, I wanted to be able to accept all the possibilities. I also felt that dancing concerned with states of mind involved one with one's own personal problems and feelings, which often had little or nothing to do with the possibilities in dancing; and I became more interested in opening that out to society and relating it to the contemporary scene, rather than hedging it in.

That was surely one of the reasons I began to use random methods in choreography, to break the patterns of personal remembered physical coordinations. Other ways were then seen as possible. When I talk about these ideas of chance to students, they ask if something comes up you don't like, do you discard it? No, rather than using a principle of likes and dislikes, I prefer to try whatever comes up, to be flexible about it rather than fixed. If I can't handle it, perhaps another dancer can, and further there's always the possibility of extending things by the use of movies or visual electronics. I did not want the work turned in, preferably turned out, like dancers.

Is your interest in movement and body strength related to anything in your particular personal life history?

Anyone's work is involved with his life. But I don't want to stop there. My hope is that in working the way I do, I can place the dancer (and this is involved in my student work too), in a situation where he is dependent upon himself. He has to be what he is. He has as few guides or rules as need be given. He finds his way. It's concerned with his discovery. I think a good teacher keeps out of the way. That's why, in the classwork, although there are certain exercises which are repeated every day, they are not exact repetitions. They are varied slightly or radically. Each time the dancer has to look again. The resourcefulness and resiliency of a person are brought into play. Not just of a body, but a whole person. It doesn't make a difference as to simplicity or complexity. When an exercise is presented to a group of students, each has to deal with himself, but also with everyone else in the room, to avoid, among other things, running smack into another. It's like yoga. The mind has to be there.

Who influenced your work in choreography?

John Cage has been a strong influence because of his ideas about the possibilities of sound and time. Then I had a marvelous tap-dancing teacher when I was in high school. She had an extraordinary sense of rhythm and a brilliant performing energy. I think influences are difficult to pinpoint since there are probably many of them. There are many things in one's life that serve to influence one's ideas and one's actions on them. But certainly Mr. Cage's ideas concerning the separate identities of music and dance were influential from the beginning. When we began to work together (these were during the solo program days), he would compose the music quite separately from the dance, although in those early dances, there were structure points in the music that related to the dance. Now even that has vanished. We start as though to take off from the earth and then go to the moon!

It would be erroneous to think that my work is not structured. It's clearly structured, but in a different way. The structure is in time, rather than themes or through an idea. It's not dissimilar to the way continuity in television acts. Television shows fit the time between the commercials, which are spaced so many within the allotted half or hour period. TV has trouble with movies and commercials, as the movies were made another way. Composers now write for the length of recordings. They gear the composition to be within the time of a record. The expression fits the time.

In my work a dance may be forty-nine minutes long, and the structure twenty-one, ten, and eighteen. This is the case in *Walk Around Time*. The first part is twenty-one minutes, the entre'acte ten, and the second half is eighteen. The total, forty-nine, is a seven by seven structure. In the past when Mr. Cage and I worked together, he would have written music that would be as long as the dance. At present, he would more likely make a sound situation which could be of any length, and then for the purpose of the dance, it would end when the dance ended.

Would it be correct to say that every time your company performs a dance, that at a certain time when a certain note is played in the music, that the dancers would be performing a certain movement?

In answer to your question, no. The dance movement and the musical sound would not coincide the same from performance to performance. I can illustrate this again by one of the dances. The piece is called *How To Pass, Kick, Fall, and Run*. It is twenty-four minutes long. For this I asked Mr. Cage if he would do something. He asked me how it was made. I explained the length and the structure points. After seeing the dance, Mr. Cage decided to make a sound accompaniment of stories. Each story in its telling would take a minute. He tells on an average of fifteen stories in the course of the twenty-four minutes, so there are lengths of silence as the dance continues. Using a stopwatch, he governs the speed of each telling, a story with few words being spaced out over the minute, a story with many having a faster rhythm. Since from one playing to another playing of the dance he never tells the same story at the same point in time, we cannot count on it to relate to us. Often audiences, having made a relationship for themselves, will say, it is funny when he told the story about my mother and a policeman, and I was doing a solo. But the next time, if he told the story again I might not be on stage at all.

One of the better things to do on plane trips across the country is to watch Joe Namath on the professional football reruns, and plug the sound into the music channel. It makes an absorbing dance. Probably that's something new for the spectator. He has choices to make now. Of course, he always did. He could get up and leave, and often did.

This must give dance critics a hard time in view of the departure from traditional dance.

Well, they are getting used to it now, though they do not write a great deal about the dance, and they rarely like the music. They sometimes write of the dancers, but they have trouble with the dancing so they pick out other things. For instance, one of the dances, *Variations V*, is a work involved with dance, movies, slides, electronic sound, and was given first at Lincoln Center in 1965. Now it would be called mixed-media. The dancers had to dance over wires taped to the floor because these were attached to a dozen microphone-type poles on the stage which were antennae for sound when we came within a six-foot radius of any one of them. We triggered the sound, then the musicians and electricians on the platform behind us could change, distort, extend, and delay that sound. Behind this on screens were movies and slides. There were a few special sound-producing actions the dancers did; for example, two of us potted a plant, which was wired and, when touched, produced sound. The piece is forty-five minutes long, and for about thirty-five of that there is dancing by one or more. Probably in the middle of all the rest, the reviewers could not see the dancing, but they all saw me riding a bicycle for about a minute and a half at the end of the work. Perhaps spectators cannot see a difficult dance if it doesn't relate to the music. But we now have to relate daily to things in a variety of ways in this society, and not in just one way. Of course, the sound in our piece is difficult for audiences, too. First because it is unfamiliar, and sometimes, because it is loud. It is primarily electronic and a kind they may not be accustomed to. Yet my feeling is that the work we have done goes along with the society around us.

Could you tell us something about the influence of your family background on your career in the dance?

My family was never against my wanting to be in the theatre. My father was a lawyer, and my mother enjoyed traveling. But they had no particular awareness of the arts. They didn't stop me from tap-dancing when I was an adolescent. My father said, "If you want to do it, fine. All you have to do is work at it." There was no personal objection. It is curious perhaps, since my two brothers followed him, one being a lawyer, the other, a judge.

I think it is difficult to talk about dancing even conventionally, because it so easily becomes a kind of gossip about a particular dancer in a given work and her good and bad points. Even more so now because of the enormous changes in the way we act in space and time. We can't equate minutes with footsteps now, so much as continents. Rather than one point being the most interesting, and others relating to it, say like colonialism, any point is interesting now. Any place that something is put, is as interesting as any other place. So with time, you don't lead up to something: whatever place you are in, is fine.

I think dancing is a fascinating art, and I also feel that it lies at this moment at a great point of change. So many different areas are being explored by the dancers now, and our visual shifts have been so sharp in recent years, it gives dancing a chance to be more than just an expression of a private concern, and moves more into the everyday world of activity of people in the streets or on the stage.

The Dancers

According to legend, a group of Russian balletomanes was so obsessed with Marie Taglioni's dancing that they bought a pair of the famous ballerina's slippers, had them cooked with a special sauce, and ate them at a banquet. Although few dancers may know such extreme adulation, it is indeed the dancer—not the choreographer, composer, librettist, or designer—who has had the strongest and most persistent hold on the public's imagination.

It's easy to understand why: because dance lives only in actual performance, leaving behind no record, no text, no score. Dance is identified with its performers to a degree untrue of any other art: it does not really exist apart from dancers. As Yeats once wrote, it is indeed difficult to know the dancer from the dance. Embodying his art, the dancer is at once artist and art form—he combines the purity of abstract design with the seductive specificity of the human body, a combination that is indeed hard to resist.

Despite the attention understandably lavished upon dancers, very little has actually been written about the particularities of various dancers' styles. Dancers have so frequently been praised for their "grace," "elegance," and "brilliant technique" that descriptions of one dancer become indistinguishable from those of others: Baryshnikov begins to sound like Nureyev who begins to sound like Nijinsky. Arlene Croce, America's finest contemporary dance critic, once complained that dancers have not been so much described as placed into simple good-better-best categories. But the important question to ask, Croce reminds us, is not How good is a dancer? but What is he doing?

The essays included in this section were chosen because they do indeed describe and not merely judge some of the most famous dancers of the nineteenth and twentieth centuries. These essays—which, with the exception of André Levinson's, are eyewitness accounts—capture the specific dance styles of their subjects; they allow us to distinguish, let's say, the particularities of Nijinsky's genius from those of Baryshnikov's. For one of the great joys of balletomania is perceiving how a dancer—within the rigid standards dictated by classical technique—can still illuminate a ballet with his own style, how his line, phrasing, musicality, and dramatic powers give meaning to movement and turn "steps" into choreography.

In ballet, an arabesque is not an arabesque is not an arabesque. Rather a dancer will inform steps with his own special style. For example, today Nureyev, unlike most classical dancers, makes his exertion visible. He accentuates the ardor of action and gives his dance a strained but heroic quality. Nureyev lets us see the price of movement, just how much those steps cost him. Where a dancer like Baryshnikov, with his all-but-invisible preparations, suggests utopia—a paradise where energy is plentiful but not excessive—Nureyev evokes a more complicated, less perfect world, a fallen world where energy must be nothing less than extravagant, and where movement is not a natural birthright but a challenge to one's body. Where Baryshnikov usually seems to occupy just the right amount of space, Nureyev never seems to have enough; you always get the impression that he needs and wants more. Baryshnikov is, as one critic described him, an "innocent prodigy"—he can play Apollo to Nureyev's Prometheus—but Nureyev is a hungry dancer who treats dance not as a fulfillment of his instincts, but as a series of tests, a quest without interval or pause or satiety. Even executing the same steps, Baryshnikov and Nureyev will thus evoke different worlds. The essays included in this section describe the worlds evoked by seven of the most interesting dancers the world has known.

Although a dancer is at the mercy of a choreographer and must remain the choreographer's creature, dancers are not simply passive collaborators. A dancer can make innumerable contributions during the creation of a particular ballet; when Suzanne Farrell realizes Balanchine doesn't have a step in mind or the step he thought of doesn't exactly fit or look right, she will "fall" into a step or a pose that Balanchine will then often use. A dancer can even influence the course of a choreographer's career or that of an entire era: Taglioni's delicate, spiritual style revolutionized ballet in the mid-1800s.

Agnes De Mille, herself both dancer and choreographer, paid tribute to just how much a choreographer depends upon his dancers. "Well, there they stand," De Mille said, "the material of your craft, patient, disciplined, neat and hopeful in their woolens. They will offer you their bodies for the next several weeks to milk the stuff of your ideas out of their muscles. They will submit to endless experimentation. They will find technique that has never been tried before; they will submerge their personalities and minds to the blindest, feeblest flutterings of yours. They will remember what you forget."

Because the essays included below are lively accounts rather than historical overviews, the following brief biographies are included:

MARIE TAGLIONI (1804–1884), the most famous ballerina of the Romantic era, was celebrated for her ethereality. Trained by her father who choreographed many of her best-known roles, Taglioni achieved overwhelming success in the title role of *La Sylphide* (1832), a role that is often said to have inaugurated Romanticism in ballet. Taglioni's spirituality—her ability to turn pointe work into poetry—revolutionized ballet. She traveled throughout Europe where she enjoyed enormous popularity: forty aristocrats in Vienna unhitched her horses and drew her carriage themselves through the streets. In Paris, however, Taglioni had to contend with the success of her rival, Fanny Elssler. Taglioni gave her farewell performance in 1847, after which she maintained her interest in dance, choreographing *Le Papillon* in 1860, teaching at the Paris Opera, and guiding the careers of younger dancers.

FANNY ELSSLER (1810–1884), the daughter of Joseph Haydn's valet and copyist, embodied the sensual, earthy side of Romanticism. Gautier, one of her early champions, called her a "pagan" dancer, as opposed to Taglioni, whom he termed a "Christian" ballerina. The rivalry between the two dancers was, as mentioned, notorious. Excelling in fiery, voluptuous roles—her Cachucha solo in Coralli's *Le Diable boiteux* (1836) was reportedly explosive—Elssler introduced to ballet what we now think of as character dancing. Her tours throughout Europe and America were so successful she accumulated a fortune in excess of one million dollars, retiring in comfort at the age of forty-one at the height of her career.

VASLAV NIJINSKY (1888–1950) was born in Kiev and received his training at the Imperial School of Ballet at St. Petersburg, where his extraordinary elevation and ballon (the ability to appear to pause in mid-air) brought him to the attention of his teachers. Upon graduation, he joined the famous Maryinsky company and was among the Russian dancers Diaghilev took to Paris for that famous first season of the Ballets Russes in 1909. Nijinsky astounded French audiences with his dramatic and technical powers and soon became, under Diaghilev's watchful eyes, the company's star dancer. Nijinsky was featured in most of Fokine's early works—*Scheherazade* (1910), *Spectre de la rose*

(1911), *Petrushka* (1911)—and brought male dancing to a prominence it had not known in generations. Although his leaps were spectacular and his beats wickedly fast and precise, Nijinsky was celebrated not only for his technique but for his interpretive genius: contemporary reports claim he looked completely different in each role. Encouraged by Diaghilev, he tried his hand at choreography, creating three works—*Afternoon of a Faun* (1912), *Jeux* (1913), and *Rite of Spring* (1913)—which, though not popular at the time, have since been hailed as precursors of modern ballets. When Nijinsky unexpectedly married in 1913, Diaghilev was so enraged (Nijinsky had been his constant companion), he dismissed Nijinsky from the Ballets Russes. Although Nijinsky did dance with the company again during its American tours (during which he created *Till Eulenspiegel* in 1916), his career declined rapidly. He gave his last solo performance in 1919 and began suffering from severe mental disorders. He lived in and out of institutions for the remainder of his life.

MARTHA GRAHAM (1894–), born of Presbyterian parents in Allegheny, Pennsylvania, was raised in California. Forbidden by her father to pursue a career in dance, she did not begin her professional training until after his death, taking classes in 1916 at Denishawn (the school of Ruth St. Denis and Ted Shawn, the two founding parents of American modern dance) in Los Angeles. Graham performed with Denishawn until 1923, when she began pursuing her own style of dance, giving her first solo recital in 1926. Founding the Martha Graham School of Contemporary Dance in 1927, she began giving company performances in 1929; all of the company's works were choreographed by Graham herself. She became one of the most influential personalities in modern dance, creating new styles (angular, earthbound, emphatic) and finding narrative techniques (flashbacks, fragmented plot lines, multiple perspectives) new to dance. She gave to her works—even her Greek-myth ballets—a particularly American slant. She was, moreover, one of the most powerful and long-lived performers the American stage has ever known; she continued dancing, in fact, until the early 1970s. She still choreographs new works, revives some of her earlier classics, and often appears with her company as an elegant and learned lecturer.

ALICIA MARKOVA (1910–) was born in London, studied with such great teachers as Legat and Cecchetti, became a member of Diaghilev's Ballets Russes when she was only fourteen, and danced the title role in Balanchine's *Le Rossignol* in 1926. After Diaghilev's death in 1929, Markova danced with several companies in England, creating many of the roles in the early British ballets such as Ashton's *Facade* (1931) and *Mephisto Valse* (1934), Tudor's *Lysistrata* (1932), and de Valois' *The Rake's Progress* (1935). With Anton Dolin, she formed the Markova–Dolin Company in 1935, but she then joined the Ballet Russe de Monte Carlo in 1938. From 1941 to 1945 she danced in America with Ballet Theatre. She was at the height of her powers: her Giselle is considered one of the finest in dance history and she was celebrated for her purity, delicacy, and astute musicality. Markova stopped dancing in 1962, served as director of the New York Metropolitan Opera from 1963 to 1969, and taught at the University of Cincinnati in the early 1970s. Since 1973 she has been a Governor of the Royal Ballet.

SUZANNE FARRELL (1945–) was born in Cincinnati, where she received her first training before studying with the School of American Ballet, the official school of the New York City Ballet. Farrell became a member of the company in 1961 and a soloist in 1965. Noted for her leggy sensuality and her plush extensions, she became the quintessential Balanchine dancer of the late 1960s, creating roles in his *Movements for Piano and Orchestra* (1963), *Don Quixote* (1965), *Jewels* (1967), and many other ballets. It has been said that no other ballerina has been so influential in Balachine's career or so favored by him: in 1968 Farrell was featured in twenty-two of the company's forty-one ballets. In 1969 she left the New York City Ballet in a much publicized departure. She danced with Bejart's Ballet of the Twentieth Century from 1970 to 1974 and rejoined the New York City Ballet in 1975. Audiences noticed a new maturity and a heightened authority in Farrell after her Bejart years, and she has in recent years became one of America's finest ballerinas.

MIKHAIL BARYSHNIKOV (1948–) first studied at the Riga Choreographic School in Russia and then at the Leningrad Choreographic School where Nijinsky, Pavlova, Balanchine, and Nureyev had also studied. (Baryshnikov and Nureyev were both taught by Alexander Pushkin.) Winning the Gold Medal in Varna in 1966, Baryshnikov joined the Kirov Ballet upon graduation and soon became one of the company's most brilliant soloists. When touring Canada with a group of Soviet dancers in 1974, Baryshnikov chose to defect from the company and began dancing with Western companies, most notably the American Ballet Theatre. He staged *Nutcracker* (1976) and *Don Quixote* (1978) for American Ballet Theatre, before shocking the dance world with his move to Balanchine's New York City Ballet in 1978. (As of September 1980, Baryshnikov will be the artistic director of A.B.T., having left N.Y.C.B. in October 1979.) He has always astounded audiences with his indescribable virtuosity in both classic and modern roles; by even the most conservative estimates, he is one of the greatest technicians in the history of dance.

Marie Taglioni (1804–1884)

by André Levinson

"Regardez-la courir. Rien de mortel en elle."

—Méry.

"The famous *ballerina* Taglioni came to St. Petersburg with her father, a little old man," relates a former pupil of the Imperial Theatre School, in her *Memoirs*. "She came to the school to do her exercises. The director and his assistants paid the foreigner every attention. Taglioni was very plain and excessively thin; her little sallow face was covered with tiny wrinkles. I blushed for the pupils who, after class, surrounded Taglioni and said to her in compassionate tones: 'What an ugly mug you've got; how wrinkled you are!' Taglioni, who imagined she was listening to compliments, tossed her head, smiling, and murmured in French: 'Thank you, children.' "

Another of these frolicsome pupils sounds a different note in her *Recollections*: "We looked upon her," she declares, "as a goddess. She was not what one would call a beauty, but she had supremely elegant manners. She was quite ethereal."

Despite their difference in tone, the two extracts quoted both indicate a prematurely faded young woman (at the time of her visit to Russia, Taglioni was barely thirty-three), whose charm lay more in her manner than in her physical attractions. She had nothing of the statuesque beauty of Fanny Elssler. Of the attributes of a pretty woman, she had nothing beyond what was required to make a great dancer.

"That a dancer, thirty years ago, should have been able to bring about a revolution in the art of dancing which is still effective, is in itself astonishing," declares the author of *Petits Mémoires de l'Opéra;* "but that this dancer, this great revolutionary, should have been an ill-made woman, almost hump-backed, without beauty and without any of those striking exterior advantages that command success, amounts to a miracle." . . .

Source: From *Marie Taglioni*, translated by Cyril W. Beamont (London: Dance Books, 1977). First published in Paris, 1929.

Another anecdote, related by M. Ehrhard, the excellent biographer of Taglioni's rival, Elssler, has it that when Taglioni's father took her to Coulon's class, her fellow-pupils made fun of her, saying: "How can that little hunchback ever learn to dance?" This is another version of Hans Christian Andersen's story of the "Ugly Duckling," who, despised by her kind, one day turns out to be a swan, and spreads her white wings.

The celebrated ugliness of the actor Lekain played a considerable part in his posthumous fame. The memory of his ravaged mask survives where innumerable cameo-like profiles have been forgotten in the limbo of time. Were not the Sylphide's supposed infirmities the very marks of her genius? What difference did it make if, when she flew to the ground, the spread of her wings, like those of the albatross in *Les Fleurs du Mal*, prevented her from walking?

In this wasted body of paradoxical proportions everything functioned, everything was in accordance with some secret design, favourable to soaring flight. There are musical instruments, violins fashioned by an Amati or a Stradivarius, dwellings for souls, which have the contour and reactions of a living being. By a miracle of contrariness, the divine craftsman fashioned of Marie Taglioni, a woman without any sensual appeal, owing to her emaciated and bruised frame, an incomparable instrument, which, setting metaphors aside, we shall endeavour to take to pieces and describe.

But at this juncture our literary sources cease to be reliable. The opinions of her contemporaries are eloquent, but never concrete and explicit. "Light, ethereal, seraphic," are all very well; but such epithets merely enumerate the attributes of an object; they do not describe it. Circumlocutions abound. In praising Taglioni, poets and critics alike perceive nothing of the being of flesh-and-blood; they conduct us through "a forest of symbols." Each gesture and each bound are recorded figuratively.

Is it surprising that a Jules Janin should fail to find the right word to give life to his portrait? But even Gautier, the vigorous craftsman of *Fusains et Eaux-fortes*, did not succeed in condensing the vaporous vision. When he is dealing with Carlotta Grisi, "*la belle dame sans merci*," he gives an impression of her which, despite his emotion, has all the precision of an official document:

"Carlotta . . . is fair, or at least auburn. She has blue eyes, of an extraordinary limpidity and softness. Her mouth is small, dainty and childlike. . . ."

And so on. When he undertakes to depict Mlle. Fanny Elssler for the subscribers to the *Figaro*, we not only learn that the Florindo of the

Diable Boiteux is tall, supple and well set-up, but also that she has "slender wrists and dainty ankles," that "her knee-caps are well defined, stand out in relief, and make the whole knee beyond reproach," and that "her hands are slim and delicate."

But, when he turns to Taglioni, our poet no longer says: "She is this or that," but: "She makes us think of . . ." And he proceeds to draw comparisons. Amid that cloud of white muslin, he no longer regards her as a beautiful and desirable feminine body, but as an allusion to something inexpressible in words. Faced with such a bankruptcy of description, we are obliged to have recourse to pictures.

There is an innumerable quantity of portraits of Taglioni, both drawn and engraved. The iconography of her in Russian, prepared by N. V. Soloviev, gives seventy-one items; and this list is far from complete. So we must again search through this bulging portfolio in order to obtain a reasonable likeness of the Sylphide.

The print of the romantic era is as conventional as the designs used by Ionian potters. Allowance must be made for the stylisation which reduced the lithographs of dancers to a type conforming to the fashion of the day and stamped with a commonplace banality.

There is nothing of value to be gleaned from the official portrait by Grevedon. It is a full-face portrait in which he strives to treat Taglioni in the manner of a vignette from a *Keepsake;* this document is of interest merely on account of the pains taken to render the details of this wax doll's head-dress. The print by Jean Gigoux, the fertile illustrator of *Gil Blas,* is little better, being executed in the same conventional manner and "one of a series." There are some more authentic engravings that afford us a few details. But the truth is to be found in the work of one painter only, that of A. E. Chalon, of the Royal Academy, London (who also had the honour of being hung in the National Gallery). His *Six Sketches*, as well as his coloured lithograph, dated 1845, of the famous *Pas de Quatre*, which marked the fullest development of the romantic ballet just before it began to decline, do suggest the idea of Taglioni as we had imagined her. Chalon, a man of perception, did not attempt to correct the natural features of his model to make them conform to some abstract ideal. Hence we can always turn to him when in doubt. Thanks to such testimony, it is possible to reconstruct a hypothetical portrait of Taglioni.

The very first thing that strikes us about the Sylphide's physiognomy is the very high and slightly domed forehead, which, rather than the eyes, illumines the face and extends the irregular, oval form suggested by the wide jaws and short, sharp chin. The smooth bands of chestnut hair leave the temples free. The nose is thin and long; the narrow lips are raised at the corners in a smile. The curve of the eyebrows is very flat; the eyelids, weary and pallid, droop over hazel eyes that are fairly small.

Her complexion has no bloom; the skin, which is exceedingly delicate, is jaded from the use of cosmetics. The expression of her face is serene, though tinged with melancholy, and she has the appearance of great intelligence. To be frank, Marie Taglioni looks like a sickly old maid who has suffered many woes and made up her mind to take the veil.

Her head is small, set upon a long, undulating neck, the swan neck beloved of poets, which painters such as a Domenico Veneziano or a Pisanello, in their portraits, bestowed on high-born Tuscan ladies of the fifteenth century. This sinuous neck joins the sloping shoulders in a lovely curve; the falling-away of the bust makes the back of the "little humpback" seem round-shouldered. The collarbones are prominent; the bosom is small and low; the waist short and delicate, a wasp waist. The slender, tapering arms are abnormally long and end in very small wrists and slim fingers. In a foot-note to his *Manual of Classical Theatrical Dancing*, the well-known teacher Enrico Cecchetti tells us that Taglioni's father taught her to cross her arms in order to conceal this defect; in this way an unsightly blemish yielded a charm the more. On the other hand, the choregrapher Saint-Léon, who partnered Taglioni, declares that: "there were *balletomanes* who took exception to the way she generally held her arms in a low position, quite contrary to the custom of the other dancers; they also criticised her deportment, for she held her body much further forward that was customary in the dancing schools of that day."

At the same time, her legs are too long in proportion to the rest of her body. The "portrait" which we have of one of these legs shows it to be extremely well-shaped, with the exception of a slight thickening of the calf, the characteristic blemish found in the professional dancer, the result of muscular strain. The instep, delicately fashioned, smooth and slender, seems to move under the silken tights. The foot is long and pointed, the instep arched, the toe-joints elongated, the sole of the foot so curved that it seems to be breaking the ballet shoe. Achille Devéria's celebrated lithograph, after Barre's statuette, represents, with a happy stretch of imagination, the Sylphide dancing in bare feet over the flowers of her celestial garden. The big toe seems to be short, the other toes long. Is this conformation based on fact? Or is it a concession to some "ideal of beauty" applied to the foot of a goddess?

But the most important question of all concerns that indescribable foot which Victor Hugo likened to a wing. Was it small? In his exquisite *Souvenir de Marie Taglioni, Danseuse*, M. Gilbert de Voisins, her respectful grandson, recalls, among many memories, a scene where a young friend who was calling on the lady who had been the Sylphide, wondered at the "slender elegance, the incredible narrowness" of the shoes preserved by the dancer in a little amaranthine casket, and declared that it seemed impossible that they could ever have fitted any woman's foot.

Thanks to the munificence of Mme. Robert Brussel, the Musée de l'Opéra has a duplicate of this family treasure. An examination of this winged sandal does not entirely confirm the legend of Cinderella's slipper. In fact, the shoe of Fanny Elssler, Taglioni's rival, is not only smaller, but noticeably shorter. Taglioni's foot, besides being extremely narrow, is very long in proportion. If it be compared with one of the shoes that belonged to some famous beauty, such shoes as those preserved in the Musée de Cluny, it does not remind us of the pattens of a Chinese beauty, or of the silken mules of the Princesse de Lamballe, but rather the black satin slippers once worn by the Empress Josephine.

It is certainly not the foot of a pretty woman, a coquettish *bibelot* of flesh and blood, mincing along with tiny steps; it is not the kind of foot one would choose to cross a ball-room with, or trip to a lover's tryst.

The conclusions to be drawn from this comparative study of the documentary evidence and exhibits are almost self-evident. In general, our inquiry narrows down to an individual singularly lacking in physical attractions, whose anatomy violates all our preconceived ideas of feminine beauty. With very little exaggeration, Taglioni could be called deformed!

This being so, how can this dancer's fascination be explained? It is a fact that, although small of stature, she appeared tall to those critics who sought to express "the characteristic qualities of her beauty." Stage lighting, coupled with the glamour of the theatre, can of course do much; but all this did not prevent the "spirit-like arms" of the emaciated Fitz-James from arousing laughter. The mystery remains, only to be explained by the fact that plastic perfection and choregraphic beauty are two separate things.

In a statue, we admire a body in stable equilibrium, resting on its base, invoking the immutable harmony of masses and planes. Dancing is a kinetic art which, instead of avoiding the movement that displaces the lines of the composition, traces figures in space only to erase them at once. In dancing of the classic school, these ideal figures attain a geometric purity of outline where there is a play of sweeping curves around intersections of straight lines. A vertical line intersected at a determined angle by two parallels—such, for instance, is the outline of an *arabesque sur la pointe*, in which exhibition of shifting equilibrium Taglioni excelled. The *pointe tendue* extends the vertical line of equilibrium. Her abnormally long arm stretched out in front, indicates a line that continues to infinity. This characteristically romantic pose expresses the final moment of hesitation before taking flight in the empyrean.

But this is mere technique. My intention was to bring about a "clearer understanding" of the "structural defects" of the Sylphide—defects which prove to be essential to the beauty of dancing.

This inquiry reminds me of a witticism attributed to M. Max Liebermann, the great impressionist painter of Berlin. When an official drew his attention to Cezanne's *Garconnet au Gilet Rouge*, declaring that the arm was far too long, he retorted: "When an arm is painted in that manner it cannot be long enough." This reply bears on Taglioni's arm. The shortened trunk and the abnormal development of the legs predestined this dancer for travelling movements and *pas d'élévation*. Her covering power is enormous, the length of the spring enables her to leap into the air in a tremendous parabola. This is the way the grass-hopper is made and, if you will, the kangaroo. Nature, who thus equipped the insect and the ruminant, also made Taglioni, the dancer.

As soon as she touches the ground, she is vulnerable. In Nourrit's little plot, the Sylphide dies as her wings fall off. There is a lithograph of Chalon's that has caught, with an effect of foreshortening that anticipates Degas, a choregraphic curtsy of Taglioni. In this, where she bends her knees in the fourth position, the peculiarities of her physical structure are emphasised to the point of unintentional caricature.

Was this chosen of the gods, then, really a freak of nature? Yes—just as all pure spirit changes when it becomes incarnate, like the four-handed Siva of the Hindus, the Ariel of Shakespeare, or the winged Eros of the ancients.

To write a poem, words are necessary. Whence did Taglioni derive her vocabulary? She adapted to her use the traditional language of the classic school. If she enriched it with a new play of fancy, she restricted or forbade the use of certain other choregraphic terms. Hence, if we may credit Charles Maurice, she created "not a manner, but a style."

Our authorities enable us to define this style. It favoured *form denuded of ornament*, big simple lines, sweeping trajectories. This saltatory plain-song renounced such grace notes as *batterie*, the swift impact of double *cabrioles*, the zigzag of the *entrechat* making a fantastic broken line while the dancer rises. Gyration is limited to some rare enveloping movement; never would the Sylphide be engulfed in the dionysiac fury of a series of *pirouettes*. The low and barbed *pointe* seems to perfect the vertical line of equilibrium, not to support the body in bold and varied *équilibres*. Moving with great bounds, she appeared to be suspended in the air, then sank to earth, hovering, when, like a spring-board, the resilient spring of her muscles impelled her into the air once more. This elasticity of knee and, above all, of instep, overcame weight, lessened the effect of gravitation, and enabled her to alight without the slightest noise. There is a story about her father's threatening to curse his daughter if he ever *heard* her dance.

These sustained and soaring flights corresponded to the slow progress of *développés* on the ground. The cautious raising of the *pointe* in a line with the shin, the *dégagé* of the leg, its passing to *grande seconde*, the twisting of the torso, gave birth to an *arabesque*, the supreme formula of a spiritualistic choregraphy which conveys the soul of dancing. A print, a miniature by the Russian artist Timm, shows us one of Taglioni's *arabesques penchées*, or rather an *attitude allongée*, to make use of the language of pedantry, because the dancer's hands are joined in an attitude of supplication.

However it may be, it was not what she did in conformance with tradition that impressed her contemporaries, but that in which she diverged from or surpassed them. "This manner of execution, at once brilliant and continuous, which had nothing in common with the *tours de force* of the classic school (so says Alphonse Royer, the historian and director of the Opéra), produced by its novelty a profound surprise." "The old school of *entrechats* and *ronds de jambe*," declares for its part the *Nouvelle Biographie Didot* (1865), which goes back to the seventeenth century, "was stricken to death by the novelty of her dancing." Nothing could be more erroneous than this judgment, but nothing is more indicative of the general blindness. If the "purist" happens to introduce some superfluity, some brilliant flourish into her dancing, astonishment is unanimous.

"I tell you, gentlemen, she did an *entrechat!*"

"Impossible! Are you sure?"

"Two *entrechats*, three *entrechats*."

This dialogue, recorded by Jules Janin in his account of September 30th, 1833, proves the disconcern caused by Taglioni's beating a *pas*. "She dances like all dancers before her, and as others no longer dance after her!" The "lions" were moved by such a heresy as the heads of the romantic school would have been at listening to Théramène's recital. "Mlle. Taglioni is the George Monk of the Opéra," concludes the journalist, "the classic dance is indebted to her for its restoration."

In Taglioni's customary simplicity, in her renunciation of the pomps and vanities of an elaborate and sophisticated method of execution, eyes blinded by hate discovered many weaknesses.

Charles Maurice, that traitorous panegyrist, went so far as to refuse her all originality: "Mlle. Taglioni's success," insinuates the viperish critic, "originally founded on incontestable merit and methods of execution which were novel to those who did not know where this dancer had slavishly copied them. . . . The continual recurrence of five *temps*, of which the whole of this dance is composed, soon exhausts attention." And resuming the supposed statements of an important paper, he reproaches his victim for her "academic poses, soft and languorous gestures, affected balance, fanciful *entrechats* and *pirouettes.*" Lastly, on the very eve of her inexpressible triumph in *La Sylphide*, the *Courrier des Théâtres* delivers a funeral oration over this reign that has ended: "No balance, toes in the air, beats of the knees, plenty of grimaces, *ungainliness* and a great deal of charlatanism, that is what she shows us."

Thus is presented, translated into the slang of the "wings" and the language of envy, the inventory of the Taglionesque style. But, truth to tell, the analysis of this style can only be falsified by a purely technical and professional examination. That the existence of such astonishing harmony between the amplitude of movement and the dancer's height had modified the aspect of certain conventional poses and *pas* is no more than an exterior sign of that *novelty* whose spirit we seek. Because it is not only a question of *craft*, but a manifestation of *style*. In the course of this study we have, on more than one occasion, attempted to define this style by setting the testimonies of eye-witnesses side by side. Let the "bourgeois of Paris," His Majesty Véron I (if it be not the "ghost" who wrote his *Memoirs*), recapitulate Taglioni's assets and her father's teaching:

"Like the artists of great periods of painting, Taglioni *père* founded a new school of dancing, very different from the style and philosophy governing that of Gardel and Vestris. Vestris taught grace and seduction; he was a sensualist. . . . [Taglioni] demanded a graceful facility of movement, lightness, elevation above all, and *ballon;* but he would not allow his daughter to make a single gesture or attitude lacking in decorum or modesty. He told her: 'Mothers and daughters should be able to see you dance without blushing.' . . . Vestris required pupils to dance as they did at Athens, like bacchantes and courtesans. Taglioni required of the dance an almost mystic and religious artlessness, while the other preferred a more catholic conception. But these transcendental *pas* and esoteric *cabrioles* had to be wrested from unwilling nature. Some idea of the daily labour imposed on the Sylphide by the well-meaning and implacable paternal tyranny may be gleaned from another passage in the same *Memoirs:* 'Abundant sweats, overwhelming hardships, tears—nothing softened the heart of that father, dreaming of glory for the talent that bore his name.' And Albéric Second, in his amusing *Petits Mystères de l'Opéra* says: 'I have seen Mlle. Taglioni, after her father had given her a two hours' lesson, almost drop dead on the carpet of her room, where she let herself be undressed, sponged and re-dressed, without seeming to know what was taking place."

When one is thus made aware of the price paid for that unfettered and ethereal mastery, one can no longer be astonished at the penury of the sentimental life of such a dancer, a willing martyr to her profession.

Did Taglioni's influence give an impetus to theatrical dancing? It is a difficult question to answer. The Sylphide had enlarged the sphere of ballet by her conquest of the land of dreams. But genius not being transmissible, the whole burden of this spiritual royalty devolved on her frail shoulders. The spectacle as a whole was sacrificed to her creative personality; the *corps de ballet* being reduced to a discreet accompaniment, the *ensemble* withered away. Taglioni was an *artist*, but she inevitably inaugurated the age of *virtuosi*.

A graver thing still, in causing the *eternal feminine* to triumph she evicted male dancing. The eclipse was complete. Not a single great male dancer arose between Perrot the Aerial and Nijinsky. "The male dancer has fallen into decline," says Saint-Léon. And he had been pre-eminent in the days of the Vestris! "It may be said that to-day the male dancer exists no longer," observes Charles de Boigne in 1856. "A few years have sufficed to turn them into fossils . . . male dancers fill the posts of teachers, mimes or *maîtres de ballet*." Henceforth, what was expected of a Lucien Petipa, or a Mérante? To serve as a living pivot for the *tours* of a *danseuse* and to "juggle not too clumsily with a hundred-pound weight." "We have suppressed male dancers," confirms Jules Janin.[1] When Guerra, a native of Milan and the best of the pupils of the great Carlo Blasis, who codified the classical ballet, took it into his head to come and dance at the Opéra, he was received with a storm of hisses, so unusual a spectacle had the male dancer become. In the Spanish ballet, *Paquita*, arranged by Mazilier, women dressed as men took part in the *Grand Pas des Gitanes*. This happened in 1846. We find it curious that female characters should have been taken by men in

[1] The season of 1832, the year in which *La Sylphide* was produced, was fatal to male dancers, the disfavour in which they were held was such that their number was reduced, while that of the *danseuses* was increased, a measure which perpetuated the decline of the male dancer. [Levinson's note.]

the theatre of Shakespeare's day, or in the Nōh plays of Japan. But, even in our time, male characters in *Coppélia* or the *Deux Pigeons* continue, at the Opéra, to be taken by women, so that fantastic customs in matters of dancing die hard.

Thus did feminine romanticism lay waste the domain of ballet. The Taglionesque exaltation, hypertrophy of the soul, paved the way for a period of sterile virtuosity. A whole century had to pass ere another dancer of her rare quality came to add to the elegy of the *Sylphide* the nocturne of the *Mort du Cygne*.

Fanny Elssler (1810–1884)
by Théophile Gautier

Reviews are but little concerned with the talent and acting of actresses. Their beauty is not analysed, they are never considered from the purely plastic viewpoint. Only rarely is mention made of their grace, or their prettiness, and nothing of anything else.

However, an actress is a statue or a picture which is exhibited to you, and can be freely criticised; she can be reproached for her uncomeliness just as a painter is criticised for a fault in drawing (the question of compassion for human imperfections does not arise here), and can be praised for her charms, with the same composure that a sculptor, on viewing a statue, says: "Here is a beautiful shoulder or a well-modelled arm."

No journalist makes a virtue of this important point; so that the reputations of pretty actresses depend on chance, and in many cases are far from being deserved; besides, so many of these reputations for beauty have endured for nearly half a century; surely that is too long.

A host of heroic generals, of delightful officials of the Empire, and of no less delightful countrified people, nay, even Parisians by birth, still admire the traditional and mythological bloom, going back for fabulous ages, of Mlle. Mars, the inimitable Celimène.

In general, beautiful actresses are plain enough, it is only fair to say

Source: From *The Romantic Ballet As Seen By Théophile Gautier*, translated by Cyril W. Beaumont (New York: Dance Horizons, 1972). Originally published in London 1932, and revised edition 1947.

that, had they not the stage for pedestal, no one would give them a glance; they would be classed among ordinary women or honest women, who themselves have no other merit than that of not being men, of which we are convinced when they doff the clothes of their own sex in order to don ours.

This does not apply to Mlle. Fanny Elssler, who is in the full flower of her youth and her beauty, and who has the advantage of not having been admired by our grandfathers.

Mlle. Fanny Elssler is tall, supple, and well-formed; she has delicate wrists and slim ankles; her legs, elegant and well-turned, recall the slender but muscular legs of Diana, the virgin huntress; the knee-caps are well-defined, stand out in relief, and make the whole knee beyond reproach; her legs differ considerably from the usual dancers' legs, whose bodies seem to have run into their stockings and settled there; they are not the calves of a parish beadle or of a jack of clubs, which arouse the enthusiasm of the old *roués* in the stalls and make them continuously polish the lenses of their opera-glasses, but two beautiful legs like those of antique statue, worthy of being cast and studied with care.

We shall be pardoned, we hope, for having discoursed at such length on legs, but we are speaking of a dancer.

Another praiseworthy feature is that Mlle. Elssler has rounded and well-shaped arms, which do not reveal the bone of the elbow, and have nothing of the angular shape of the arms of her companions, whose awful thinness makes them resemble lobster-claws dabbed with wet-white. Her bosom is full, a rarity among dancers, where the twin hills and mountains of snow so praised by students and minor poets appear totally unknown. Neither can one see moving on her back those two bony triangles which resemble the roots of a torn-off wing.

As to the shape of her head, we must admit that it does not seem to us to be as graceful as it is said to be. Mlle. Elssler is endowed with superb hair which falls on each side of her temples, lustrous and glossy as the two wings of a bird; the dark shade of her hair clashes in too southern a manner with her typically German features; it is not the right hair for such a head and body. This peculiarity is disturbing and upsets the harmony of the whole; her eyes, very black, the pupils of which are like two little stars of jet set in a crystal sky, are inconsistent with the nose, which, like the forehead, is quite German.

Mlle. Elssler has been styled a *Spaniard from the North*, which phrase has been intended as a compliment; but that is her defect. She is German in her smile, the whiteness of her skin, the shape of her body, the placidity of her forehead; she is Spanish in her hair, her little feet, her tapering and dainty hands, the somewhat bold curve of her back. In her, two nations and two temperaments are opposed: her beauty would gain were she to decide to be one or the other of these two types. She is pretty, but cross-bred; she wavers between Spain and Germany. And that same indecision is to be observed in the character of her sex; her hips are but little developed, her breast does not exceed the fulness of an hermaphrodite of antiquity; just as she is a very charming woman, so she might be the handsomest young man in the world.

We shall conclude this portrait with a few words of advice. Mlle. Elssler's smile is not open often enough; it is sometimes restrained; it allows too much of the gums to be seen. In certain leaning poses, the lines of the body show to disadvantage, the eyebrows become blurred, the corners of the mouth turn up, the nose becomes pointed; all this accords the features a displeasing expression of malicious cunning. Mlle. Elssler should arrange her hair more at the back; her hair, placed lower, would break the rigid line between her shoulders and the nape of her neck. We also counsel her to tint the tips of her pretty, tapering fingers with a paler shade of pink; it is a needless embellishment. — *October 19, 1837*

Fanny Elssler in "Le Diable Boiteux"

She comes forward in her pink satin *basquine* trimmed with wide flounces of black lace; her skirt, weighted at the hem, fits tightly over the hips; her slender waist boldly arches and causes the diamond ornament on her bodice to glitter; her leg, smooth as marble, gleams through the frail mesh of her silk stocking; and her little foot at rest seems but to await the signal of the music. How charming she is with her big comb, the rose behind her ear, her lustrous eyes and her sparkling smile! At the tips of her rosy fingers quiver ebony castanets. Now she darts forward; the castanets begin their sonorous chatter. With her hand she seems to shake down great clusters of rhythm. How she twists, how she bends! What fire! What voluptuousness! What precision! Her swooning arms toss about her drooping head, her body curves backwards, her white shoulders almost graze the ground. What a charming gesture! Would you not say that in that hand which seems to skim the dazzling barrier of the footlights, she gathers up all the desires and all the enthusiasm of the spectators?

We have seen Rosita Diez, Lola, and the best dancers of Madrid, Seville, Cadiz, and Granada; we have seen the gitanas of Albaicin; but nothing approaches that Cachuca danced by Elssler.

Fanny Elssler in "La Tempête"

Mlle. Fanny Elssler has made her reappearance in the part of Alcine in *La Tempête*. The ballet *La Tempête* is a ballet, that is the most favourable remark that can be made about it. Furthermore, it has the advantage of spoiling one of the finest themes for an opera that could ever be imagined. It is not quite clear in this piece why Prospero should be replaced by Oberon; Oberon is inseparable from *A Midsummer Night's Dream*, he cannot move without his wife, Titania; Alcine, that bewitching creation of Ariosto, appears quite out of her element in the isle of *The Tempest*, beside Caliban, and I doubt very much whether Fernando can make him forget that brilliant knight, Roger. But we shall not prosecute too far our observations regarding the intrinsic merit of the theme; the literature of legs is hardly a subject for discussion; let us come at once to Fanny Elssler. Much applause bursts forth and the gauze curtain parts to reveal the captivating enchantress, and no one has any doubt but what the virtuous Fernando will soon be unfaithful to the memory of Lea, Oberon's ward.

Fanny Elssler's dancing is quite different from the academic idea, it has a particular character which sets her apart from all other dancers; it is not the aerial and virginal grace of Taglioni, it is something more human, more appealing to the senses. Mlle. Taglioni is a Christian dancer, if one may make use of such an expression in regard to an art proscribed by the Catholic faith: she flies like a spirit in the midst of the transparent clouds of white muslin with which she loves to surround herself, she resembles a happy angel who scarcely bends the petals of celestial flowers with the tips of her pink toes. Fanny is a quite pagan dancer; she reminds one of the muse Terpsichore, tambourine in hand, her tunic, exposing her thigh, caught up with a golden clasp; when she bends freely from her hips, throwing back her swooning, voluptuous arms, we seem to see one of those beautiful figures from Herculaneum or Pompeii which stand out in white relief against a black background, marking their steps with resounding cymbals; Virgil's line:

Crispum sub crotalo docta movere latus,

involuntarily springs to the mind. The Syrian slave whom he loved so much to see dancing beneath the pale arbour of the little inn would have had much in common with Fanny Elssler.

Undoubtedly, spiritualism is a thing to be respected; but, as regards dancing, we can quite well make some concessions to materialism. After all, dancing consists of nothing more than the art of displaying beautiful shapes in graceful positions and the development from them of lines agreeable to the eye; it is mute rhythm, music that is seen. Dancing is little adapted to render metaphysical themes; it only expresses the passions; love, desire with all its attendant coquetry; the male who attacks and the female who feebly defends herself is the basis of all primitive dances.

Mlle. Fanny Elssler has fully realised this truth. She has dared more than any other dancer of the Opera; she was the first to transport to these modest boards the audacious Cachuca, without its losing any of its native zest. She dances with the whole of her body, from the crown of her head to the tips of her toes. Thus she is a true and beautiful dancer, while the others are nothing but a pair of legs struggling beneath a motionless body! —*September 11, 1837*

Revival of "La Sylphide"

It must be stated that the Opera lacks ballets and does not know how to find employment for its army of dancers and pretty supers; it appears that the literature of legs is the most difficult of all styles, for no one can succeed at it.

The revivals of *La Fille Mal Gardée*, *La Somnambule*, and *Le Carnaval de Venise* have only attained a comparative success, without any effect on the box-office receipts.

To see these old-fashioned pieces which delighted our fathers, and whose melodies, ground out by barrel-organs at every street-corner, lulled us to sleep in our earliest years, one became conscious of a kind of bitter-sweet emotion, as though, in rummaging in a corner of some dusty drawer, one came across some iridescent skirts, a few pieces of discoloured lace, a broken fan, with an episode from Rousseau's *Confessions* painted on one side and a pastoral on the other, forgotten relics of a grandmother or a great-aunt, long since departed.

But this altogether poetic sentiment, although not without its fragrance, does not suffice to fill the auditorium at the Opera; besides, the shabbiness of the scenery, completely faded and torn in every fold, forbade the exhumation of these mummies of ballets which, twenty years ago, perhaps, had fresh and youthful bodies and charming features with happy smiles, but which will always seem to us somewhat ridiculous, out-of-date, and old-fashioned.

For some time past there has been talk of Mlle. Fanny Elssler's reviving Mlle. Taglioni's parts in *La Sylphide* and *La Fille du Danube;* the Taglionists gave vent to cries of sacrilege and the abomination of desolation—one would have thought that it was a question of laying hands on the Ark of the Covenant. Mlle. Elssler herself, with that modesty which so well becomes her talent, shrank from encroaching on parts in which her illustrious rival had shown herself to be perfect, but it was not right that so charming a ballet as *La Sylphide* should be struck out of the repertory because of exaggerated scruples; there are a thousand ways of playing, and, above all, of dancing the same character, and the pre-eminence of Mlle. Taglioni in comparison with Mlle. Elssler is a matter that can quite well be contested.

Mlle. Taglioni, tired out from her interminable travels, is no longer what she was; she has lost much of her lightness and her elevation. When she appears on the stage, you always see the white mist bathed in transparent muslin, the ethereal and chaste vision, the divine delight which we know so well; but, after some bars, signs of fatigue appear, she becomes short of breath, perspiration bedews her brow, her muscles seem to be under a strain, her arms and chest redden; formerly, she was a real sylphide, but now she is merely a dancer, the first dancer in the world, if you will, but nothing more. The princes and kings of the North have so applauded her, so wearied her with compliments, caused so many showers of flowers and diamonds to fall upon her, that they have weighed down her tireless feet, which, like those of the amazon Camilla, could run over blades of grass without bending them; they have loaded her with so much gold and so many precious stones that Marie full of grace has not been able to take to flight again, and only timidly skims the ground like a bird with wet wings.

Mlle. Fanny Elssler to-day is in the full flower of her talent, she can only vary her perfection and not transcend it, because above very good is too good, which is nearer to bad than may be thought; she is the dancer for men, as Mlle. Taglioni was the dancer for women; she has elegance, beauty, a bold and petulant vigour, a sparkling smile, an air of Spanish vivacity tempered by her German artlessness, which makes her a very charming and very adorable creature. When Fanny dances, one thinks of a thousand pleasant things, in imagination one wanders into marble palaces flooded with sunlight and silhouetted against a deep-blue sky, like the friezes of the Parthenon; you feel yourself leaning on your elbow on the balustrade of a terrace, with roses round your head, a cup full of Syracusan wine in your hand, a white greyhound at your feet, and beside you a beautiful woman with a plumed head-dress and robe of crimson velvet; you hear the thrum of tambourines and the silvery tinkle of small bells.

Mlle. Taglioni reminded you of cool and shaded valleys, where a white vision suddenly emerges from the bark of an oak to greet the eyes of a young, surprised, and blushing shepherd; she resembled unmistakably those fairies of Scotland of whom Walter Scott speaks, who roam in the moonlight near the mysterious fountain, with a necklace of dewdrops and a golden thread for girdle.

If one may make use of the expression, Mlle. Taglioni is a Christian dancer, Mlle. Fanny Elssler is a pagan dancer—the daughters of Miletus, beautiful Ionians, so celebrated in antiquity, must have danced in the same manner.

Hence Mlle. Elssler, although not fitted by temperament for Mlle. Taglioni's parts, can replace her in every way without any risk or danger; because she has sufficient versatility and skill to adapt herself to suit the particular style of the part.

The theme of *La Sylphide* is one of the most delightful themes for a ballet that could possibly be encountered; it includes an idea at once moving and poetic, a rare thing in a ballet, and we are delighted that it is to be staged again; the action is self-explanatory and can be understood without any difficulty, and lends itself to the most graceful pictures—in addition, there are hardly any dances for men, which is a great comfort.

Mlle. Elssler's costume was of a delicious freshness; her dress might have been fashioned of dragon-flies' wings and her feet shod with satin made from lilies. A garland of convolvulus of an ideal shade of pink encircled her beautiful brown hair, and behind her white shoulders quivered and trembled two little wings made of peacocks' feathers, superfluous with such feet!

The new Sylphide was frantically applauded; she invested the *rôle* with an infinity of delicacy, grace, and lightness—she appeared and vanished like an intangible vision; when you believed her to be in one place she was in another. She surpassed herself in the *pas* with her sister; it is impossible to see anything more perfect or more graceful; her miming, when she is caught by her lover in the folds of the enchanted scarf, expresses with a very poetic regret and pardon the feeling of disaster and of error beyond repair, while her last long look at her wings which have fallen to the ground is full of a great tragic beauty.

At the beginning of the ballet, there took place a little accident which, unfortunately, had no serious consequences, but which at first alarmed us: at the moment when the Sylphide disappears through the fireplace (a strange exit for a sylphide) Mlle. Fanny Elssler, being carried too quickly by the counter-weight, knocked her foot violently against the frame of the chimney-piece.

Fortunately, she did not hurt herself; but we take this opportunity of inveighing against these "flyings" which are a tradition of old opera. We see nothing graceful in the spectacle of five or six unfortunate girls almost dying of fright from being suspended in mid-air by iron wire which may quite well give way; these poor wretches who distractedly move their arms and legs like toads out of their element involuntarily remind one of stuffed crocodiles hung from a ceiling. At the performance given for Mlle. Taglioni's benefit, two sylphides remained suspended in mid-air, it was impossible to pull them up or lower them down; people in the audience cried out in terror; at last a machinist risked his life and descended from the roof at the end of a rope to set them free. Some minutes later, Mlle. Taglioni, who only spoke this once in all her life (at the theatre, of course), went towards the footlights and said: "Gentlemen, no one has been hurt." The following day two sylphides of the second class received a present from the real Sylphide. It is not unlikely that another difficulty of this sort will soon recur. —*September 17, 1838*

Vaslav Nijinsky (1888–1950)

by Prince Peter Lieven

To understand and appreciate Nijinsky to the full it must be known that he came of a family connected with the circus. I foresee much indignation and protests at such a statement: "What! Nijinsky! The God of the Dance! The highest, the greatest genius that the ballet art has produced . . . and you dare to mention circuses!"

But it is the truth, and, to my mind a necessary truth. Both his father and his mother were connected with the circus and to this day his uncle works as a clown in some show or other.

Without this circus lineage, these generations of acrobats behind him, it would be difficult to explain his extraordinary physical gifts. His lightness which was beyond all technique, his renowned *élévation* would be quite inexplicable. It would, of course, be absurd to credit the circus with all that this man accomplished, his genius was developed in quite another sphere—that of the ballet. Yet his natural and inherent physical gifts were due to and sprang from the circus.

Source: From *The Birth of the Ballets-Russes*, translated by L. Zarine (New York: Dover, 1973). First published in London, 1936.

There is, moreover, nothing degrading in the art of the circus; it attains the same heights as any other art. Did it not produce that wonder of wonders, Little Tich? Is not clowning the art of one of our most gifted contemporaries—Charlie Chaplin? The circus, nowadays, has become a forgotten art, it has been submerged and its possibilities are underrated by us. It is in approximately the same plight as the ballet art was in Western Europe prior to the advent of Diaghilev. Yet in the circus we find that which is most essential to art, namely, art-tradition. True classical clowning has not yet died out, its root must be sought as far back as the Italian Harlequinade and the Commedia dell'Arte. A good circus has traditions and therefore, style, in the true sense of the word. It is the branch of art which is on the brink of a renaissance, all it needs is a leader, and creators, who will raise it back to its true level as a great and noble art.

I think that Romola Nijinska was ill-advised when she carefully withheld in her book any precise information as to the "theatres" in which her husband's people worked. There is nothing shameful in the fact that these were, for the most part, circuses. Nijinsky's art ranks so high in the history of human achievement that the slightest detail is both important and essential, provided it throws some light on his unusual gifts.

Of all the people I have met in the course of more years than I like to remember, I can apply the term "genius" only to Chaliapine in his youth, and Nijinsky. In the latter there was something rare which was not to be found in other people. He danced as birds sing, with that joy and simplicity natural only to one who found dancing the one way in which to pour out his soul. He seemed to have been born for dancing and for nothing else. His every movement was natural, light, and unique. No other dancer used his hands, inclined his head or moved his body as he did. His movements were so plastic and yet so surprisingly simple and convincing: there was nothing artificial, strained, or faked about him. He seemed to speak to you from the stage in his own particular and natural language of movement, and you seemed to grasp the meaning of his message although you could never translate it into words.

His *élévation*, by which I mean the way he had of rising in the air, remaining motionless and slowly descending, has always remained a mystery to me; it seemed obvious that the law of gravity did not exist for him. He remained in the air as long as he pleased and returned to earth just when he felt like it, not when he was compelled. I have often pondered over this strange "illusion," longing to get to the bottom of it and to discover the "trick." I timed his leaps and tried them myself at home. My time was the same—I was young then and could jump. But whereas Nijinsky floated in the air, I saw myself through the looking glass falling heavily like a sandbag. The secret of this illusion might have been in the extraordinary plastic quality of his jump: it was so free and beautiful. Whether he rose or whether he fell, he swept into the air without the slightest effort and the lightness and beauty of this dive into space was beyond words. It might have been that the secret was in the impression he conveyed of all that he still had in reserve to give. In just the same way, certain Italian tenors, reaching the topmost and most dramatic note of their arias give the impression that they could go much higher. Having reached the top "C" they could, it seems, go up through the whole scale. Nijinsky gave the same impression of unexploited and infinite possibilities. When he did his famous *entrechat* ten you were firmly convinced that he could do a twenty.

Nijinsky accomplished every variety of movement with marvellous ease. In *Le Spectre de la rose* there is a scene where, jumping from foot to foot, like children do, he would make the whole round of the stage. I can remember the audience of the Metropolitan Opera in New York —one of the most stolid and immovable audiences in the world—letting out, at the sight of him, something which was between a sigh and a groan. There was no applause—just that strangled cry. Nijinsky travelled through the air, just above, but never seeming to touch the ground. Like an autumn leaf he came lightly down.

Carnaval was another of his ballets. Nijinsky as Harlequin was something quite different. Like a bouncing rubber ball he rose and fell from the floor as if there was something there that refused to keep him but sent him on again into the next jump.

In another ballet, the classical *Les Sylphides*, he seemed to be caught up like a feather, his hands and feet just flashed in the happiness of an airy dance and his soul lived in it.

In *Petrushka* his movements were again quite different. His first dance on emerging from the fair booth, a Russian dance, was very *terre à terre*, rhythmical, and full of energy. It was the weird, mechanical dance of a clockwork doll, angular and full of kinetic temperament.

I pity from the depths of my heart all those who did not see him. No words can describe the lasting impression that he produced. It was a peculiar impression, he was so unlike anyone else, his manner was so clearly individual and personal. You could not say: "Woizikovski and Massine are different from Nijinsky because . . ." It would not have explained anything. In technique it is easier to explain—one can say, for instance, that his technique was so perfect that it was no longer noticeable, looking at his dance you found it so simple that you felt that you yourself could have done it. But artistically, Nijinsky cannot be described or explained. When his career came to an end his art died, like the art of many histrionic geniuses. It has not been preserved by any mechanical means and those who did not see it will never feel it or understand.

In addition to this unique gift of the dance, Nijinsky had a great dramatic gift. He could be expressive—amazingly so. Petrushka's last gesture, when he appears above the fair booth and looks down on the terrified magician, doll in hand, was shattering. The outstretched hands and crooked fingers, the broken, puppet-like bend of the body, and the face grimacing tragically as in the throes of some macabre passion he seemed to be reproaching the magician: "What have you done to me? Why have you ruined my poor immortal soul?" The curtain fell on this arresting movement whilst the orchestra shrieked this tragic, unfinished and questioning phrase.

Nijinsky's influence on the art of the ballet was great. There had always been male dancers on the Russian Imperial stages. So long ago as the seventies, Gert the magnificent, was already renowned. The brothers Legat were brilliant dancers in a later period, and they were followed by others. Every year the Imperial schools sent out batches of highly accomplished pupils. Without this tradition of the St. Petersburg schools there would have been no Nijinsky. But the significance of male choreography changed with Nijinsky. Previously the rôle of the male dancer had been auxiliary, he had merely been the supporter of the prima ballerina. There had been male *pas seuls*, but they were short ones to which no one attached great importance. They merely gave the ballerina a rest. Dramatic talent, mimicry, and character dancing were more important in male dancing. It was only after Nijinsky that a man could take the principal part in a classical ballet. He made the male dancer the equal of the ballerina and established equality between the male and female elements of the ballet. In this way he influenced the moulding of the ballet art and of the librettos. Such productions as *Le Spectre de la rose*, *Narcisse*, and *Petrushka*, where the male dancer takes the center of the stage, did not make their appearance in the repertoire of the *Ballets-Russes* until its third season, late in 1911. This was the immediate result of Nijinsky's genius and his two years of overwhelming success.

Was the man a creator as well as a gifted dancer? It is a hard question to answer and any answer could only be surmise. According to the reminiscences of his wife Nijinsky was a great choreographic innovator. Unfortunately one cannot rely on her book as one which provides solid material on which to build. It is, actually, difficult to define Nijinsky's part in productions, hard to tell where he begins and where

Diaghilev leaves off. It would have been easier if Nijinsky, after the break with Diaghilev, had proved his creative powers in some way. Unfortunately he did not do so. His attempt in 1914 to run his own ballet company in London was a sudden and complete failure. Whether Nijinsky had in him the makings of a gifted choreographer may be questionable, but there is no doubt that he was quite unsuited to the job of theatrical manager. Moveover, his enterprise in London was tacitly taboo—to go to the *Ballets-Russes* and to applaud and get enthusiastic about its productions was not only permissible, but was "the thing" in the snobbish social sense, but to patronize the Nijinsky productions was decidedly a social *faux pas*.

According to the account that Benois gives, Nijinsky's plans and ballet theories at that time (he was then seeking a reconciliation with Diaghilev) were hazy, naïve, and even childish. Benois was frankly sceptical about his ability for independent artistic creation. I believe the only attempt of Nijinsky in that direction apart from the 1914 London production was the ballet *Till Eulenspiegel* to Richard Strauss's music, which he did in America in 1916. It was only given three times and left no impression on the ballet art.

Nijinsky, during his friendship with Diaghilev, is supposed to have produced three ballets—*L'Après-midi d'un Faune*, *Les Jeux*, and *Sacre du Printemps*. It is hard to say who was the real author of these ballets. *L'Après-midi d'un Faune* certainly bears traces of Bakst's passion for archaic Greece. Bakst and Serov had just returned, delirious with rapture, from a tour of Crete and Greece. They did more than give verbal expression to their enthusiasm, the tour inspired from Serov the painting *The Rape of Europa*, and from Bakst *Terror Antiquus*. The ballet *Narcisse* must also be put down to Bakst's enthusiasm. We find the same idea in *L'Après-midi d'un Faune*.

Diaghilev always liked to push his fellow workers into the limelight; like the good owner of a large stable he loved his racehorses, he showed them off and was proud of them. This sentiment, naturally, was very strongly expressed in Nijinsky's career—the urge to make a choreographer of him was one of the few mistakes in Diaghilev's life. Nijinsky was his *grande passion* and Diaghilev found it difficult to view him impartially. His unmistakable genius and his overwhelming success as a dancer were not enough for Diaghilev, who did not love lightly. He believed that with his help and with the artistic milieu that he had built around him, Nijinsky would become an independent constructor. He was mistaken.

Just as the impression left by Nijinsky the artiste was so great and unforgettable, so the impression created by the man was slight and disappointing. I have never come across such a striking contrast. As a rule the talented artiste can be distinguished in private life. Sir Beerbohm Tree was a cultured and delightful conversationalist; Gordon Craig, when he chose, could be brilliant.[1] Diaghilev was one of the most brilliant conversationalists I have ever met. But Nijinsky was a nonentity, an absolute and thorough nonentity. After five minutes in any society his existence was completely forgotten.

I made Nijinsky's acquaintance as late as 1916 behind the scenes of the Metropolitan Opera House, New York. He produced a strange impression, he was silent, but not as people are wont to be silent. It was not the ordinary silence of an untalkative man, not that the dancer was averse to speech, but rather that he was not there at all. His manner of greeting you was characteristic—it was exaggeratedly and unexpectedly cordial. I have noticed the same thing in blind people. Whether he was intelligent or whether he was stupid I cannot say. I think he belongs to a class of people who cannot be described by either term. At any rate, if I called him stupid it would convey nothing. I think the neatest and at the same time the truest estimate of Nijinsky's intellect was given me by Misia Sert, one of Diaghilev's best friends. She called him an "idiot of genius." This is no paradox. In our enthusiasm over the "entity of an image" our admiration goes to the dancer's creative instincts and not to the conception of his brain, as for example, his rôle in *Petrushka*.

I am bound to say that he did not strike one as an ordinary man. Was he always pre-occupied with his art? I do not think so. I think rather that outside his work and off the stage he simply did not exist. There was something vague, childish, and even absurd about him; it seemed that if you took him by the hand and led him somewhere he would follow without asking where and why he was being taken. The story of his marriage proves this.

As a worker Nijinsky was untiring. Every day, for hours at a stretch, no matter where he was, even in the theatre, he could be found practising.

His physical build was most unusual. The top half of his body seemed to belong to one person and the lower half to another. You had to see him training to appreciate this to the full. From the waist up his body was that of a normally developed, strong, and healthy youth. Below that were thighs and calves with extraordinarily developed muscles. All that part of his body struck one as being abnormally developed and massive compared with the top half. On the stage, thanks to the

[1] I remember Tree's answer when I asked him what he thought of Craig. "Oh, he is very good to steal from." It would be difficult to describe Craig's quality more aptly. [Lieven's note.]

costume and lighting this was not noticeable. There Nijinsky seemed to possess the figure of an Apollo. Off the stage his appearance, of course, was disappointing. With his pale face, his small and slightly Mongol eyes, and his thin hair, nondescript blonde in colour, he was not beautiful. Seeing him you could hardly believe your eyes. "What! This is the same Nijinsky who was just now so perfect in *Le Spectre de la rose?*" It was simply unbelievable. That same colourless figure seemed queer and unhuman in his ballet working garb; he repeated the same steps, leaps, and *entrechats* a hundred times.

Let us hear what Alexandre Benois has to say about him.

"He was a modest, quiet, and silent youth. I cannot remember any of his conversation—he had none. If he had not been the famous Nijinsky he would have passed quite unnoticed. I remember when they came to see me in Montagnola—Diaghilev, Stravinsky, and Nijinsky—it was a week of reconciliation. I can remember all the details and all the conversation. There was Diaghilev and Stravinsky, but no Nijinsky. I know he was there but I cannot remember anything about him.

"He himself found his meteoric triumphs most unexpected. He was the first spectator to witness his own performances. When visiting he always sat with a broad smile on his face and seemed quite delighted. He was always unruffled and even-tempered, although when things did not run smoothly, if, for instance a costume did not fit or some other trifling matter upset him, he would suddenly become excited. But his attitude was never that of the spoilt darling of the public; he was always like the small child who complains but never demands.

"We hardly ever saw him without Diaghilev. Serge isolated him from the outside world, he even attached bodyguards, who protected him night and day. It was usually Vasili Zouikoff, Diaghilev's devoted servant, sometimes Pavel Koribout-Kubitovitch, Diaghilev's equally devoted cousin.

"Years later, after the break with Diaghilev, Nijinsky turned up at my place in Paris unexpectedly and proved suddenly talkative. He wanted at all costs to make it up with Diaghilev and was full of plans and projects. He kept repeating that they were not doing what they ought to do in ballet, that everything ought to be quite different and that he would try to explain what he had in mind. I must confess that what he had to say was all very hazy and childish."

Four years spent in the constant companionship of Diaghilev had a disastrous effect on Nijinsky. Having cut him off from the outside world Serge, during that time, educated him despotically. He instilled, as it were, his own brains into Nijinsky. The thoughts forced up by this premature and hot-house system of education were hazy and faltering. This artificial spiritual growth, together with Nijinsky's readiness to be influenced by others, was fatal to him.

As a dancer he is unforgettable. Practically all his appearances, beginning with *Le Pavillon d'Armide* at the Maryinsky Theatre to the last Diaghilev production, were masterpieces. He was a born, God-sent dancer and a first-class dramatic artiste. His gracefulness, his lightness, and his *élévation* were quite unique. He *took time* to come down, it was a real illusion. I put this down to his will power. As he sprang he must have believed that he was floating through the air and this belief communicated itself to the audience. It was a phenomenon which might be described as mass hypnotism.

My last meeting with Nijinsky was in painful and tragic circumstances. Diaghilev had a sudden idea that Nijinsky's mental sickness could be lightened if he could be transplanted to the surroundings of the ballet. In January 1929 Nijinsky was one of the audience at the Grand Opera, Paris, to witness his old ballet *Petrushka*. He sat in dead silence, a frozen smile on his face, staring fixedly and uncomprehendingly at the stage. Pointing at Leon Woizikovski, who was dancing Petrushka, Diaghilev asked him what he thought of him. "Il saute bien," answered Nijinsky, and again he was silent. They could get nothing more out of him.

After the performance Diaghilev took him on the stage. There his former partner Karsavina and many other friends and collaborators crowded round him. We were photographed. How happy and gay we all looked, yet I can never remember a more gloomy and melancholy occasion.

Martha Graham (1894–)

by Agnes De Mille

I went, as Louis Horst urged, one Sunday night, to see Martha Graham.[1] She performed with the assistance of three of her pupils

Source: From *Dance to the Piper* (Boston: Little, Brown, 1952).

[1] All dance concerts except those given at Town or Carnegie Hall took place on Sunday nights. It was strictly against the law to dance in New York State on Sunday, but this was the only day theaters were available for rental. We broke the law until we were threatened, at the instigation of the Sabbath League, with arrest. Then the dancers organized and, headed by Helen Tamiris and me, we went to Albany and changed the law. [De Mille's note.]

from the Eastman School. She was impressive, certainly, but I found myself neither charmed nor moved. All of the dance public was arrested, but, at first, very few became enthusiasts. Martha, however, continued giving concerts, and no one of us ever stayed away. Each time I saw her, I saw more.

This was a stirring period in American dance history—a period of revolution and adventure. There were at least ten soloists working in New York, each making epxeriments. There were a score or more imitators expanding and developing our discoveries. Every Sunday, throughout the winter season, at least two dance concerts were given, frequently more, and the two dance critics, *Times* and *Tribune*, spent the afternoon and evening zigzagging through the forties in an effort to keep up. We all turned out en bloc for every occasion, wrangling and fighting in the lobbies as though at a political meeting.

Louis Horst played for a great portion of the concerts, sometimes accompanying Tamiris in the afternoon, dashing off to Doris Humphrey in the evening and working all night on the score of Martha's new *première*.

The dance seasons these days are quite different. They are more professional and vastly more expensive, and the elegants show up in full dress, something they never did before, but the atmosphere then was crisp with daring. We risked everything. Every one of us had thrown overboard all our traditions, ballet, Duncan, Denishawn, or what not, and were out to remodel our entire craft. No one helped us, and there were no rules. We worked alone. We struck sparks from one another. It was a kind of gigantic jam session and it lasted nine years, until the end of WPA. There are brilliant young dancer-choreographers today, but no one with the power of Graham or Humphrey, and all of them are derived from and imitative of the styles launched in the 'thirties or earlier.

I am glad I participated in the period of the originators. There is a force and wonder in first revelation that has no duplicate. Greater dancers may be coming, greater and more subtle choreography, but we worked when there was no interest, no pattern, no precedent, no chance. We made it all as we went along, and every concert was a perilous test for all of us, a perilous, portentous challenge. The whole subsequent flowering of concert dance had its seed in this period. But from the first Martha was the most startling inventor, and by all odds the greatest performer that trod our native stage.

In the early days when I first got to know her, there was a good deal of talk about Graham, a lot of it unfriendly. People wondered what she was about. They always rushed like crazy to see at the next concert.

Folks resented her unorthodoxy—the cult of her students, her temper, her tyranny, the expression of her face, the cut of her hair and, not least, her success.

The first time I saw her off stage, she was sitting in a New York theater in a melancholy which I had been told was her characteristic public pose. I had not met her, but I could not take my eyes off her. Heads were turning all around. Martha's presence, no matter how passive, cuts through attention, arrests speech, interrupts ideas. At the moment, she was sitting unmoving and silent. Her dark head with its cavernous cheeks and sunken eyes drooped on one shoulder. She held a single rose in her right hand which she sniffed from time to time. Louis Horst, to whom she did not address a word, sat stolidly beside her. She looked half starved, tragic and self-conscious. Two of these things she certainly was not. She ate enough for three. And while she was, from time to time, quite thoroughly unhappy, she was not ever, I learned, self-pitying. But she was unquestionably aloof. The first theatrical tradition she broke was that of being a good egg—one of the gang. She foresaw she had a lot to think out, and she arranged to have the privacy to do it in. This people resented. They said she was queer and arty. She wasn't queer; she just wasn't around.

I got to know her in a quite plain, folksy way because Louis Horst took us to dinner occasionally at Hugo Bergamasco's restaurant. Hugo was our flutist and served Italian dinners cooked in the back room by his mother and wife. Hugo made fine prohibition red wine and discoursed on modern music as he served the spaghetti. On the dining room walls hung signed photographs of Martha and me, the sexiest ones we could find. I almost always thought of her as a girl friend—almost, but not quite always; one does not domesticate a prophetess.

From the beginning, Graham knew what she wanted to do and did it. She was born in Pittsburgh of Scotch Presbyterian parents, and raised in Santa Barbara, California. Her father was a physician who specialized in mental ailments. So from an early age she grew accustomed to the idea that people move as they do for reasons. Her father, for instance, used to detect lying by the manner in which people held their hands. He did not wish her to dance. She had to wait until he died before she started training.

She entered the Denishawn School in Los Angeles while attending the Cumnock School and came under the spell of Ruth St. Denis. Thereafter she never took any aspect of dancing flippantly. When she was graduated from high school, she joined the troupe as a student and performed tangos with Ted, Japanese flower arrangements with Miss Ruth, and music visualizations to Doris Humphrey's choreography. I saw her during this period. I remember her hurtling through the room to Schubert, or sitting bare-legged on the polished floor with smoldering watchfulness. The mask of her face was like porcelain over red-hot iron. One felt that the gathering force within might suddenly burst the gesture, the chiffon, the studio walls, the pretty groupings of graceful girls. The intensity she brought to bear on each composition was not comfortable to watch. She went with the troupe on a European tour. Ted Shawn built an Aztec ballet around her which gave her the opportunity to vent some of her ebullience. In this she had the chance, for instance, to gnaw on his leg. No one subsequently, they told me, ever did this so well.

It was during this tour that she came under the influence of Louis Horst, then Denishawn musical director. He urged her to try her own wings. So she up and left, and with great courage came to New York and started out on her own. Horst left the home fold shortly thereafter.

Denishawn viewed this double departure poorly. Girls did not rebel this way. Not since Miss Ruth herself dressed up as an Egyptian cigarette ad in 1906 and gave Oriental mysticism a new lease on life by undulating in a roof-garden restaurant had a young woman broken with tradition so flagrantly. For the last two decades dancing had been Russian, which was art; American, which was commercial (tap, acrobatic, ballroom, or musical comedy, the last a vague term applicable to anything successfully cute); Duncan, which while emotionally good for young girls was fast losing favor; or Denishawn, which combined the best features of all. Graham had the audacity to think that there might be still another way, stronger and more indigenous.

Martha put in a couple of seasons in the *Greenwich Village Follies.* Then, with a little money saved, she started serious experimenting. She taught at the Eastman School of Music, entering the project with great diffidence. But Horst believed she had genius. He accepted, however, no easy revelations. He scolded and forced and chivied; the relationship was full of storm and protest.

"You're breaking me," she used to say. "You're destroying me."

"Something greater is coming," he promised, and drove her harder. "Every young artist," he explained once, "needs a wall to grow against like a vine. I am that wall."

Louis chivied me also about many things. He never stopped urging me to leave Mother, to take lovers, to give up comedy pantomime, open my own school, to read Nietzsche, to stop practicing ballet exercises, to get away from my family, to give up all thought of marriage.

Louis had paid the rent and bills of I don't know how many pupils, had paid for their pianos, given his services, held their heads, buried their dead and taught their young. But my indication of normal well-being revolted him—or so he said, particularly in relation to Martha. She, he believed, had been set aside for a special vocation. There was neither time nor opportunity for private life. She had elected the hardest of all professions for women, and she was a pioneer in that profession. She was, I am sure, although she has never said so except indirectly through her work, also convinced in heart that it must be for her either art or life. . . . She could not have a home in the ordinary sense if she wished to serve her talent. Through her a new art form was to be revealed.

Ballet has striven always to conceal effort; she on the contrary thought that effort was important since, in fact, effort was life. And because effort starts with the nerve centers, it follows that a technique developed from percussive impulses that flowed through the body and the length of the arms and legs, as motion is sent through a whip, would have enormous nervous vitality. These impulses she called "contractions." She also evolved suspensions and falls utilizing the thigh and knees as a hinge on which to raise and lower the body to the floor, thus incorporating, for the first time, the ground into the gesture proper. All this differs radically from ballet movement. It is different from Wigman's technique, and it is probably the greatest addition to dance vocabulary made this century, comparable to the rules of perspective in painting or the use of the thumb in keyboard playing. No dancer that I can name has expanded technique to a comparable degree. She has herself alone given us a new system of leverage, balance and dynamics. It has gone into the idiom.

This may not seem much to a non-dancer. But compare her findings with the achievements of other single historical figures. Camargo in her lifetime is supposed to have invented the *entrechat quatre*, or jumps with two crossed beatings of the legs, and to have shortened the classic skirt to ankle length. Heinel created the double pirouette. Vestris, the greatest male dancer of the eighteenth century, expanded the leg beatings (batterie) from four to eight and evolved pirouettes of five or six revolutions. The father of Maria Taglioni put her up on full point although others had been making tentative efforts in this line. Legnani exploited the *fouetté* pirouette—not her own invention. None of these altered the basic principles or positions of ballet technique. Anna Pavlova is credited by Svetlov, her biographer, with adding the trill on points. These are each minute advancements for a lifetime of experimenting.

It may be argued that Duncan created a new way of moving. But this is not strictly true. She refused, rather, to accept the old way and evolved a personal expression that was based on simple running, walking and leaping. She worked almost without dance technique. Her influence has been incalculable, but her method was too personal for transference.

In the twenty years prior to the last war in Germany, Rudolf von Laban and, after him, Mary Wigman developed a fresh approach with an enormous code of technique and, being German, correlated a philosophy and psychology to go with it. But they and their schools represent the achievement of an aggregate of workers and their style stems strongly from the Oriental. Strangely enough, Graham's style, for all its Denishawn background, does not. And in evaluating her work it must be remembered that Graham's technique was clarified before ever she saw a dancer from Central Europe. The two great modern schools, German and American, evolved without interaction of any kind. It is bootless to discuss which, if either, is more influential. I am inclined to think Graham's contains more original invention.

It is noteworthy of Graham that in twenty years of composing she is still what she was at the beginning: the most unpredictable, the most searching, the most radical of all choreographers. She is one of the great costume designers of our time, as revolutionary in the use of material as Vionnet. In point of view and subject matter, in choice of music and scenery, she cuts across all tradition. And for each new phase, there was needed a whole new style. Her idiom has shown as great a variety as Picasso's.

In ideas she has always led the field. She was doing dances of revolt and protest to the posh days of 1929. She was searching religious ritual and American folkways when revolution became the young radicals' artistic line in 1931–1933. The Communists then suddenly discovered that they were Americans with grass roots down to the center of Moscow and put every pressure on Graham to make her their American standard-bearer. But she was nobody's tool. She was already through with folkways and making experiments in psychology, and while other concerts were padded with *American Suites* and *Dust Bowl Ballads*, Graham began to turn out her superb satires, *Every Soul Is a Circus* and *Punch and the Judy*, which foreshadowed some of Tudor's work and a very great deal of Robbins and de Mille. The dance world seethed with satire and Martha concerned herself with woman as artist and then woman as woman, inaugurating her poetic tragedies *Letter to the World*, *Deaths and Entrances* and *Salem Shore*, and developing the first use of the spoken word in relation to dance pattern. Everyone else began to do biographies; Graham delved deeper and deeper into anthropology—*Dark Meadow*. She began to search Greek mythology for the key to woman's present discomforts—*Labyrinth*, *Cave of the Heart*, *Night Jour-*

ney. Nowadays the doctors sit out front biting their nails and taking sharp note.

Her students plainly worshiped. She was followed by a coterie of idolaters. To the Philistines, and they included all the press except Martin of the *Times* and Watkins of the *Tribune*, she was a figure of mockery, "a dark soul," a freak. The public and critics were in turn outraged, exasperated, stimulated or adoring. No one was ever indifferent. This is the exact *status quo* today—twenty years later.

The center of all this turmoil one might have supposed was a virago, a wild-eyed harridan. Well, she could be. If she thought her prerogatives were questioned, she was a very bold woman to cross. I was told by her girls that Martha in a rage was like something on a Greek tripod.

Furthermore, she could be formidable when it takes great courage to be. In 1936 the Nazi government invited her to the Olympic Games —the only American artist so honored. This would have meant world-wide publicity and a whacking great sum she badly needed. Let anyone who so much as bought a German boat passage between 1931 and 1939 dare to look down his nose at the offer. Martha received the representatives courteously and replied, "But you see half my group is Jewish."

The Germans rose screaming in protest. Not one of them would be treated with incivility. Their status as American citizens and as her pupils would ensure their protection.

"But," said Martha, "I also am an American citizen and their friend and sponsor. And do you think I would enter a country where you treat your citizens and their people in such a manner?"

"It would be too bad," said the Germans, "if America were represented by any but the best."

"It would be too bad for you," said Martha, "because everybody would know exactly why."

Martha told me this herself and added cheerfully that she knew she was listed at the German consulate in New York for immediate attention when opportunity offered. No dancer from the United States went to Germany that year.

I saw her only once in one of her alerted moods. It was during the time she was working under the direction of Massine in his *Sacre du Printemps*. They achieved a really splendid clashing of wills. He accused her of stubbornly refusing to do anything he asked; she claimed he asked her to do what was outside her technical abilities. She had never in her life done anything she didn't believe in. He, on the other hand, was a king in the theater and used to instantaneous and terrified obedience. Stokowski rode herd. She had resigned twice before they got the curtain up: I saw her sitting on her bed in Philadelphia with a cup of cocoa in her hands.

"I wouldn't have got out for anything in the world," she said pleasantly, her eyes bright as a vixen's in the brush. "There is no power that could have made me give up. I think he hoped I would. But I won't. But of course I've had to resign repeatedly. Oh, but I was angry today. I strode up and down and lashed my tail."

Strangely enough, the impression she has always made is essentially feminine. She is small—five feet three inches. On the stage, she seems tall, gaunt and powerful. She looks starved, but her body is deceptively sturdy. She has probably the strongest back and thighs in the world. She has an instep under which you could run water, a clublike square-toed foot with a heel and arch of such flexibility and strength that she seems to use it like a pogo stick. Her feet have an animal-like strength and suppleness that makes you feel she could, if she chose, bend her knees and clear the traffic. She is able actually to do things with her feet in an inching snakelike undulation that no one else has even approximated. She has a split kick, straight up, 180 degrees.

She is well-turned-out, almost to the degree of being crotch-sprung. (I am not now speaking sartorially. She is that as well.) It was on her own body that she built her technique.

Her arms are long and inclined to be both brawny and scrawny; the hands are heartbreaking, contorted, work-worn, the hands of a washer-woman. All the drudgery and bitterness of her life have gone into her hands. These are the extremities, roped with veins and knotted in the joints, that seem to stream light when she lifts them in dance.

But all of this is statistical chatter. It is the face one sees first and last, the eyes and voice that hold one. I mentioned the other characteristics because once she starts talking, there is no time for remarking them. The shape of the face is Mongoloid with skin drawn taut over the bones. The cheeks are hollows. In the eye sockets, the great doelike orbs glow and blaze and darken as she speaks. Her eyes are golden yellow flecked with brown and on occasion of high emotional tension seem slightly to project from the lids while the iris glows like a cat's. The little nose is straight and delicate. The mouth is mobile, large, and generally half-opened in a kind of dreamy receptivity. The skin of her glistening teeth, the skin of her lips, the skin of her cheeks and nose is all exposed and waiting with sensitive delight like the skin of an animal's face, or the surface of a plant as it bends toward light; every bit of surface breathing, listening, experiencing. The posture is just this, a delighted forward thrust that exposes the mouth. In more than one way she resembles Nefertiti, the long passionate neck, the queenly head, the bending, accepting, listening posture.

Her laughter is girlish and light—quite frequently a giggle. She has a sly wit that reminds one in its incisive perception of Jane Austen, or of Emily Dickinson whom she so greatly reveres. She loves pretty female things although she lives stripped to the wheels, and she manages to dress with great chic on an imperceptible budget, having the happy faculty of always appearing right for any occasion. Her hair is black and straight as a horse's tail. Her voice is low, dark and rusky, clear and bodyless like most dancers'. Her speech—who shall describe Martha's speech? The breathless, halting search for the releasing word as she instructs a student, the miracle word she has always found. The gentle "you see it should be like this," as her body contracts with lightning, plummets to the earth and strikes stars out of the floor. "Now you try it. *You* can do it." Thus Diana to the rat catchers.

No one can remember exactly what she says, the words escape because they are elliptical. She talks beyond logic. She leaps from one flame point to another. People leave her dazed, bewitched. Young men fall in love with her after every lunch date. Young women become votive vestals, and this can get tedious. They tend to clutter up the hallways clamoring for Martha's wisdom like sparrows for crumbs.

Everyone who could has always gone to her for advice. God knows how many she has heartened through the years. She has talked vocation problems with anyone—even nondancers. She has laid a steadying hand on the back of all young men starting on the black and uncharted path of the male dancer. Having something of the quality of a nun or a nurse, she has always given one the sense of boundless strength, the reassurance that although circumstances might be tragic or dismaying, they were not outside nature. No one could say she was the healthy out-of-doors type. On the contrary, she was a thoroughly neurotic woman leading a most unusual life, but she had faith, faith in the integrity of work and in the rightness of spirit. This she has always been able to communicate. To every boy and girl who entered her studio she has said something that has illumined the theater, so that it could never grow shabby or lusterless again.

I very soon took to going to her for advice, for reaffirmation and for critical help. Although she never admitted to the role, although we worked in alien styles, she became a kind of mentor. After every concert I rushed to her for analyses. Three times she said the word that has picked me up, dusted me off and sent me marching, the word that has kept me from quitting.

Why could one believe her? Was it the sense of obsession in the face, or the sheer integrity of her life? One faced a woman who for better or worse never compromised, who, although she had known prolonged and bitter poverty, could not be bought or pushed or cajoled into toying with her principles. She was a brave and gallant creature. There are few such in the world, almost none in the theater. One stood abashed and listened. If her words sounded arbitrary, there was the seal of her life upon them and the weight of her enormous achievement. One could not turn aside lightly. In the most evanescent of all professions she is now regarded, and I believe rightly, as an immortal. Dancers for untold generations will dance differently because of her labors. The individual creations may be lost but the body of her discoveries is impressed into the vocabulary of inherited movement. Boys and girls who have never seen her will use and borrow, decades hence, her scale of movement. Technically speaking, hers is the single largest contribution in the history of Western dancing.

In 1931 she produced *Primitive Mysteries* based on the Catholic Amerindian concept of the Virgin, and with this composition our native dance theater reached a new level. Thenceforth Martha was recognized as a notable in the field of American creative art. For a new work she was granted half a Guggenheim Fellowship. (Being a dancer, although the greatest, she was naturally not entitled to the usual grant awarded a painter, or writer, or scientist.) She went to Mexico.

The following winter I had occasion to visit her in her studio on 9th Street. She said to come late, see the end of rehearsal—about eleven o'clock. (She had to work at night. Most of her girls had jobs during the day.) I came late. This was the first time I had actually seen her in the throes. At the conclusion of rehearsal, the girls were dismissed and Martha went into her little sleeping cell and didn't come out. Louis Horst said I was to wait, that Martha was out of sorts. I waited the better part of an hour. Then Louis suggested, in a dispirited way, that I might as well go in as not.

Martha's room was about five feet broad as I recall it, and it contained a bed, a chest of drawers and an armchair. Louis more than filled the armchair. I took a box. In the center of the bed was a tiny huddle buried in a dressing gown. The only visible piece of Martha was a snake of black hair. Every so often the bundle shivered. Otherwise there was no sound from that quarter.

Louis droned on through his nose, "Now, Martha, you've got to pull yourself together."

There was a great deal of wheezing and huffing as he spoke. That was because he had four chests and all his mechanics seemed to get muffled down. "You can't do this. I've seen you do this before every concert. You're a big enough artist to indulge yourself this way, to fall apart the week before and still deliver on the night. But the girls are not experienced enough. You destroy their morale. You tear them down. They're not fit to perform."

He was right. She not only rehearsed the girls and herself to the point of utter exhaustion, changing and re-creating whole sections until the very eve of performance, she always ripped up her costumes and spent the entire night before and all day when she was not lighting in the theater in a fever of sewing. Incidentally, she cut and stitched her costumes herself with the aid of a sewing woman. Apparently she had to do this as a nervous catharsis. Contrary to all rules governing athletes she never slept for two nights before an appearance.

The girls worked for nothing, of course. The box office barely paid the advertising and rental, never any of the rehearsal costs. Martha taught the year around to pay these and her living. To meet their expenses, some of her pupils waited on table. None of them were adequately fed or housed.

These girls are not to be thought of as the usual illiterate dance student who fills the ballet schools. They were all adults; many held degrees of one sort or another and had deliberately chosen this form of dancing as opposed to the traditional for serious and lasting reasons. Among their ranks they have numbered great soloists, Jane Dudley, Sophie Maslow, May O'Donnell, Dorothy Bird, Anita Alvarez, Anna Sokolow, Yuriko, Pearl Lang. No other choreographer has had a concert group of superior caliber.

These girls had a style of appearance which became widely known long before their work was understood. We always said then they looked Villagy—but the term is misleading. They may have been unorthodox in many ways, but they embraced every possible sacrifice in order to serve their work, and lived like ascetics. They took the stage with the ardor of novitiates, and the group performance was incandescent.

Their leader worked them without mercy and I am told used to grow almost desperate. She worked them until midnight every night except Sundays and holidays, when she worked them all day as well. The abandoned husbands formed a club, "The Husbands of Martha Graham's Group," to amuse one another while they waited. One New Year's Eve the men turned ugly and things eased up a bit after that.

"You cannot work your girls this hard and then depress them. They will not be able to perform," said Louis to Martha on the sad night.

Without showing her face or moving, Martha whimpered. "The winter is lost. The whole winter's work is lost. I've destroyed my year. This work is no good."

"It is good, Martha," said Louis persuasively.

"It is not good. I know whether it's good or not. It is not good."

"It may not be so successful as *Mysteries*"—whimpers and thrashings —"but it has its own merits."

"I've lost the year. I've thrown away my Guggenheim Fellowship."

"One cannot always create on the same level. The Sixth Symphony followed the Fifth, but without the Sixth we could not have had the Seventh." (This was sound thinking and I stored it away in my own breast for future comfort.) "One cannot know what one is leading into. Transitions are as important as achievements."

"Oh, please, please, leave me alone," begged the little voice. I ventured a very timid ministration. I felt like Elizabeth Arden approaching the Cross.

"Martha, dear. Dearest Martha, I thought it was beautiful." There was the sound of a ladylike gorge rising.

Louis got stern. He rose; he loomed, not over—that was impossible because of bulk—but near her. "Martha, now you listen to me. You haven't eaten all day. Get your clothes on and come out for some food."

Martha tossed the blanket a bit. The snake whisked from one side to the other.

Louis got his ulster. Louis got his cap, a flat one with a visor which sat on the top of his white hair. Louis put the coat on Max, his Dackel, and leaned to pat Martha's Maedel. Louis progressed down the street displacing the winter before him. Low in the Horst umbrage cast by street lamps the dachshund wagged on the end of a string. Louis wheezed out his disapproval in a cloud of warm breath. "It's not worth it. Every concert the same. It's not worth it. She's put us all through the wringer. She destroys us."

"But, Louis," I said, pattering after and peering up and around his coat, "she is a genius." He snorted. "Would you consider working with anyone else?"

At this he stopped. He slumped down layers of himself to a thickened halt. "That's the trouble. When you get down to it, there is no other dancer."

The date of this conversation was 1932. Up till 1949 he still played for her classes, conducted her orchestra, comforted her girls. He still stood beside her, hand in hand, to take the bows at those times more frequent in her life than in most when the power and the glory are present and spectators and performers are wrapped in mantles of bright communication.

I begged Martha to let me study with her but this she refused. I had genuine need of her help. I had need of her encouragement. Doubt, like a mold, had began to film over my hopes. It wasn't just that I was afraid I wouldn't succeed. There was also the growing belief that whatever I did, however expert I became, I would never be more than a glorified parlor entertainer, could not be for the very nature of the medium I had chosen. Martha moved; I grimaced. One gesture of true dance opened doors that were to be for me forever closed. I had therefore obviously to learn to move. I was not a good dancer and no choreographer whatever, but following the promptings of a persistent instinct, I turned my back on all I had done and faced the dark.

During the next five years I taught myself to choreograph, and I took a hostile press right in the teeth for that period of time. Five years is a long period in any girl's life; in a dancer's, it is usually one third of her career.

I was trying to learn to compose dances, not pantomimes, nor dramatic stories, nor character studies, but planned sequences of sustained movement which would be original and compelling. I did not know how to begin. Everything I attempted seemed to develop either into trite balletic derivations or misconceptions of Graham. I tried to learn form and style through studies of English and American folk dances and through reconstructions (necessarily largely guessed) of preclassic (1450–1700) European court patterns. It was slow work and it was bloodless. One does not think out movement. One moves. One thinks out pattern. One moves well if one is used to moving and originally if one has developed through exercise a spontaneous idiom of expression. But I had nowhere to dance, and no company to work with.

Out of the top of my head, from fined-down nerve points, I tried by friction of will to generate ideas. Creation is not teased this way. Creation is an opening up, a submission to the dear, unwilled forces of human life. But how was I to know this, or knowing it to respond, I who was shut away from all the good, natural happiness of the world.

I used to try not to wake in the morning, and when awake, wonder what I could do all day. When I left a rumpled room for class, I was late. My exhaustion in class prevented any progress. I ate alone. I struggled with undancing all afternoon. I resisted the temptation to run to Mother for dinner. I ate dinner alone at a restaurant. The evenings were dreadful. I couldn't work. I couldn't play. I withered, unwillingly, inch by inch, with mounting terror, and the lifeblood grew black in my heart, and I could think of no good dances.

Every creative worker goes through bad periods, but today he usually manages to keep performing. If one can but just keep moving, the creative log jam breaks. Through muscles, through the racing of the blood, the running of feet, rhythms are set up that generate below fear and one is away on a new pace before one has given it a thought. But if one does not keep dancing or if there is no reason for dancing . . . I would stand in my studio two or three hours and not know whether to start north or south, whether to lift an arm or let it alone.

Mother didn't understand what I was doing, and she didn't like it. But she never withheld her savings or refused any possible effort to help. She followed in blind loyalty, although her heart was oppressed.

Why all this fancy experimentation when I could be funny, genuinely funny? Friends expostulated. My family wailed. And I fought the mists.

These were the days when Martha Graham moved like an angel in the night. Just to know she was there finding paths where my feet trod vapor, with the strength in her spirit to leap out where I stood dumb, was companionship. "We all go through this," said Martha. "You are being tempered. You are a sword in the fire. Be glad. There is achievement ahead."

"But, practically, Martha, what do I do tomorrow between waking and sleeping?"

"You make yourself a program of activity, and you do not stop once for five minutes to consider what you are doing. You do not permit yourself to reflect or to sit down. You keep going. That is your only responsibility."

"But if someone would only give me a job."

"That is beside the point. Whether they do or they don't, we keep going."

"Martha, let me work with you."

"Certainly not. Find your own way. I won't let you lean on me."

"Martha, you have genius. You know where you're going."

"I don't know where I'm going. None of us knows that. And someday I'm going to give you a good smack."

"Martha," I said one day, beating my breast over a sundae, "I have no technique and I have no time or energy to acquire any—that is, not sufficient."

"Technique!" Her voice rang with scorn. "Technique! I can see technique at Radio City. From you I ask something greater than that. From you I ask what cannot be learned in any class. Reaffirmation. Your *'49*, your American studies, have given me courage."

Martha Graham said this to me.

Alicia Markova (1910–)
by Edwin Denby

Alicia Markova and Romeo and Juliet

The great event of any Ballet Theater season is the dancing of Markova. And this season she danced even more wonderfully than before. She appeared night after night, and even in two ballets on the same program. Once the papers said she had fainted after the performance. There is only one of her. I very much hope she is gratefully taken care of and prevented from injurious overwork.

When she dances everybody seems to understand as if by sympathy everything she does. And yet her modesty is the very opposite of the Broadway and Hollywood emphasis we are used to. A Russian girl I know who works in a defense plant brought along her whole swingshift one Sunday into standing room. They had never seen ballet, and they all unanimously fell in love with Markova. Markova has the authority of a star, but her glamor comes from what the English so well call a genuine spiritual refinement.

Watching her critically in Petipa's *Swan Lake*, in Fokine's *Sylphides*, in Massine's *Aleko*, or in Tudor's novelty, the *Romeo and Juliet*, I am constantly astonished how she makes each of these very different styles completely intelligible in its own terms. None looks old-fashioned or new-fangled. Each makes straight sense. Her new Juliet for instance is extraordinary. One doesn't think of it as Markova in a Tudor part, you see only Juliet. She is like no girl one has ever seen before, and she is completely real. One doesn't take one's eyes off her, and one doesn't forget a single move. It doesn't occur to you that she is dancing for an audience; she is so quiet. Juliet doesn't try to move you. She appears, she lives her life, and dies.

One of the qualities that strikes me more and more in Markova's dancing is her dance rhythm. Anybody who has been to the Savoy

Source: "Impressions of Markova at the Met" is from *Dancers, Building, and People in the Streets* (New York: Horizon, 1965). All other selections are from *Looking at the Dance* (New York: Horizon, 1968), which was originally published in New York, 1949.

Ballroom knows what rhythm in dancing is. But once you get away from there and start watching the art of stage dancing, you find rhythm very rarely. You find many beautiful things—exact control, intelligence, energy, variety, expression; but they aren't quite the same thing as rhythm. Of course rhythm in art dancing is not so simple as in the Savoy "folk" form. But you recognize it wherever you find it. And as anybody can hear that Landowska has rhythm, so anybody can see that Markova has it.

Markova's rhythm is not only due to her remarkable freedom in attacking her steps a hair's breadth before or after the beat, a freedom in which she shows a perfect musical instinct. I think one gets closer to it by noticing her phrasing. And what we speak of as Negro rhythm is perfection of phrasing in a very short dance phrase. What strikes me equally about their two-beat phrases and her very long ones is how clearly each separate phrase is completed. It is perfectly clear when the phrase rises, and when it has spent itself. I feel the impulse has been completed, because I have seen the movement change in speed, and in weight. (In the Lindy the thrust is hard and quick, but the finish—or recovery—of the step is light and seems even retarded; in Markova's incomparable *Sylphides* phrases she prepares during five or six steps with a gentle, uniform downwarm martellato for one slow expressive and protracted upward movement in her arms.) In musical terms there is a rubato within the phrase, corresponding to the way the balance of the body is first strained, then is restored.

Markova's way of dancing adds a peculiar quality to a ballet by Tudor. Other dancers can make his dramatic intentions clear. They show that each of his gestures carries a meaning: a nuance of emotion, of character, of social standing. They show his precision of timing and placing, so that one appreciates his extraordinary genius for visual rhythms on the stage. They are personally self-effacing, and give a thrilling intensity to the drama he intended. But Tudor's style includes many hampered movements, slow-motion effects, sudden spurts of allegro arrested incomplete, arm tensions straining into space, pelvic displacements and shifts of carriage. They are fascinating effects. On the other hand I notice that in execution the movement looks forced. The dancers have trouble with their balance, they are apt to look laborious and lose their spring. Perhaps Tudor meant the dance to look off balance, but it also looks airless. Now I see that Markova can sense and can show the dance rhythm that underlies his visual phrases. She finds their point of rest. She is easily equal to his dramatic meaning and passion, but she also gives his drama the buoyancy of dancing. As I watch her, Markova—like Duse in Ibsen—seems to be speaking poetry to the company's earnest prose.

Boisterous, Then Beautiful

Saturday night's performance of Ballet Theater at the Lewisohn Stadium was a full success. The first two ballets (*Capriccio Espagnol* and *Three Virgins and a Devil*) have the boisterous qualities that register most easily in the open air. *Giselle*, the third ballet, is anything but boisterous. But the passionate precision of Miss Markova in the lead made its subtle values intelligible a block away. It was a startling experience to see so delicate, so intimate a piece appeal without effort to an audience of ten thousand. It was a triumph for Miss Markova as a theater artist. [. . .]

Miss Markova succeeded in the role on Saturday as completely as she already had at the Metropolitan. She captivated, dazzled, and touched. In the mimed passages—for instance, the conventional gesture of madness, staring at the audience with hands pressed to frame the face—she is somehow thrillingly sincere. In the dance passages of the first act, she is gay and light with a sort of chaste abandon; in those of the second, she is partly unearthly like a specter, partly gracious as a tender memory. It is as hard to color correct academic dancing with emotion as it is to give emotional color to correct bel canto. Miss Markova makes it seem the most natural thing in the world.

One reason she succeeds is that one sees every detail of the movement so distinctly. The movement of other dancers is apt to look fuzzy or two-dimensional in comparison to hers, which looks three-dimensional. Only the greatest dancers have this, so to speak, stereoscopic distinctness. Markova also has a complete command of the impetus of dance movement. She hits the climax of a phrase—say, a pose on one toe, or a leap—without a trace of effort or excess drive. The leap, the pose, seems to sustain itself in the air of its own accord.

She does not strain either in movement or in theater projection. She is so straight upright, so secure, that she does not have to thrust her personality on the audience for an effect; the audience is happy to come to her. This makes her dance seem personal, intimate, even in the open air.

—June 28, 1943

Ballet Theater's Glory

Alicia Markova in *Giselle* is Ballet Theater's greatest glory. Last night was the second of three performances of *Giselle* on this season's programs; and it was a gala evening at the Metropolitan. Miss Markova danced once again with incomparable beauty of style—dazzlingly limpid, mysteriously tender.

There is no other dancer whose movement is so perfectly centered, and who controls so exactly the full continuity of a motion from the center to the extremities. There is no other dancer whose waist and thighs are so quick to execute the first actions that lead to an arm gesture and to a step; or who diminishes the stress so precisely as it travels outward along the arms and legs. It is this that gives her dancing figure its incomparable clarity, its delicacy and its repose. It is this, too, that makes her dance rhythm so clear to the eye and so full of variety.

This superlative dance intelligence makes her dance fascinating, both as pure motion and as motion to music. The fragility of her figure, the dramatic conviction of her characterization give her dance another and equally strong expressivity. Her physical and intellectual concentration confer on her a mysterious remoteness and isolation, and this tragic dignity makes her expressions of tenderness extraordinarily touching.

All her qualities, of dancing, of mime, of presence, find a perfect use in the part of Giselle; the extraordinary effect Miss Markova creates in this part is obvious to the thousands who watch her, whether they are familiar with ballet or not. Last night again she received a unanimous ovation.

—May 6, 1944

Glimpse of Markova

There are only two real ballerinas in the country; the senior one is the great Alexandra Danilova and the junior one is the great Alicia Markova. Miss Markova, appearing last night with Ballet Theater at the Metropolitan in two of her former ballets, *Romeo and Juliet* and *Pas de Quatre*, transformed this sadly disoriented company at a stroke into the splendid one it was during her marvelous final week with them last spring. She did it by showing them the quiet simplicity of a great style, by believing completely in the piece she was performing. They glowed, they danced, they were all wonderful.

Miss Markova's delicacy in lightness, in rapidity; the quickness in the thighs, the arrowy flexibility of the instep; her responsiveness in the torso, the poise of the arms, the sweetness of the wrists, the grace of neck and head; all this is extraordinary. But her dancing is based on a rarer virtue. It is the quiet which she moves in, an instinct for the melody of movement as it deploys and subsides in the silence of time that is the most refined of rhythmic delights. The sense of serenity in animation she creates is as touching as that of a Mozart melody.

She is a completely objective artist. Who Markova is, nobody knows. What you see on the stage is the piece she performs, the character she acts. She shows you, as only the greatest of actresses do, a completely fascinating impersonation, completely fascinating because you recognize a heroine of the imagination who finds out all about vanity and love and authority and death. You watch her discover them.

Markova's Juliet is a miracle of acting. Every nuance of pantomime is poignantly clear and every moment is a different aspect of the cumulative tragedy. Her shy loveliness in the balcony scene, her moment watching Romeo die—but one would like to enumerate them all minute by minute. And the restraint of them all, the slow-motion continuum from which they each arise as dance gestures and which flows so steadily through the whole hour-long ballet are wonders to have seen.

—*April 9, 1945*

Impressions of Markova at the Met

Alicia Markova has become that legendary figure, the last of the old-style ballerinas. Her second *Giselle* with Ballet Theatre this fall season broke a box office record at the Metropolitan Opera House. Five people fainted in standing room. She did the contrary of everything the new generation of ballerinas has accustomed us to. With almost no dazzle left, Markova held the house spellbound with a pianissimo, with a rest. A musician next to me was in tears, a critic smiled, a lady behind me exclaimed "Beautiful!" in an ecstatic, booming voice. Her dancing was queerer than anyone had remembered it. A few days later, meeting a balletomane usually far stricter than I, on the street, I asked him what he thought of her this season. "More wonderful than ever," he cried aggressively. When I asked if he thought she had shown this defect or that, he admitted each in turn, but his admiration was as pure as before. This is the sort of wonder a real ballerina awakens, one our young dancers are too modest to conceive of, and that Markova's dancing used to do for me, too. Though I wasn't carried away this time, I found watching her so-different method intensely interesting.

Details were extraordinary—the beautiful slender feet in flight in the soubresauts of *Giselle*, Act Two, how she softly and slowly stretches the long instep like the softest of talons as she sails through the air; or in the échappés just after, how they flash quick as knives; or in the "broken steps" of the mad scene of Act One, when, missing a beat, she extends one foot high up, rigidly forced, and seems to leave it there as if it were not hers. I was happy seeing again those wonderful light endings she makes, with the low drooping "keepsake" shoulders, a complete quiet, sometimes long only as an eighth note, but perfectly still. I recognized too, the lovely free phrasing of the *Sylphides* Prelude, so large, though not so easy as once. Best of all, better than before, I thought her acting in Giselle Act One. Surer than I remembered is the dance-like continuity she gives her gestures and mime scenes—all the actions of the stage business imbedded in phrases of movement, but each action so lightly started it seemed when it happened a perfectly spontaneous one. In this continuity, the slow rise of dramatic tension never broke or grew confused. It was the technique of mime in the large classic style.

In classic miming, a sense of grandeur is given by stillness that is "inside" a phrase of movement the way a musical rest is "inside" a musical phrase. Markova's strong continuity of phrasing; the clarity of shape that mime gestures have when they are made not like daily life gestures but like dance movements from deep down the back; and her special virtuosity in "rests"; these give her miming grandeur. But for dancing, her strength is too small for the grand work of climaxes. She cannot keep a brilliant speed, sustain extensions, or lift them slow and high; leaps from one foot begin to blur in the air; her balance is unreliable. In ballet it is the grand power of the thighs that give magnanimity to the action; there is no substitute and a ballet heroine cannot do without it. Once one accepts this disappointment, one can watch with interest how skillfully she disguises the absence: by cuts, by elisions, by brilliant accents, by brio, by long skirts, by scaling down a whole passage so that it will still rise to a relative climax.

A second disappointment for me was that her powerful stage presence (or projection) no longer calmly draws the audience to herself and into her story on the stage. Markova used particularly to practice that art of great legitimate theatre personalities of drawing the public to her into her own imaginary world; she used to be fascinatingly absorbed in that world. But now she often seems like a nervous hostess performing to amuse, eager to be liked; she pushes herself out on the public. It is a musical comedy winsomeness and looks poor in classic ballet. It was, I thought, a serious mistake for a ballerina of such wide experience to make. Another error, a more trivial one, was the absurd way she danced the *Nutcracker* pas de deux—more like a provincial Merry Widow number than the *Nutcracker*—with a shrunken, slovenly action, bad knees, affectations of wrists and face—and for a Sugar Plum Fairy to be carelessly dressed was unfortunate.

But despite even bad mistakes, there remains her phenomenal old-fashioned style of delicate nuances in dancing. The methods she uses showed here and there and it was fun to look. For instance the divine lightness of attack: Merce Cunningham, with whom I was discussing her technique, spoke of the illusion she gives of moving without a preparation so you see her only already full launched, as if she had no weight to get off the ground (the stretch from plié is so quick). He remarked very vividly that in a leap she seemed at once "on top of her jump, like an animal." He also pointed out how she uses this illusion to disguise the weakness of a développé—she throws the leg up in a flash with knee half extended, but all you become aware of is the adagio motion immediately after that—a slow dreamy extension of the beautiful instep.

Markova achieves her illusion of lightness not by strength—for strength she has only the instep, shoulder and elbow left. But she draws on other virtuoso resources—the art of sharply changing the speed without breaking the flow of a movement; the art, too, of timing the lightning-like preparation so that the stress of the music will underline only the *following* motion, done at the speed of the music, which is meant to be displayed. As in her phrase beginnings and leaps up, so the same transformation of speed from presto to adagio is used for her weightless descents and her phrase endings—though for the latter, it takes her a beat or two more to subside into stillness than it used to. For the full effect of being stilled and immobile, she often brings forward her low shoulders into a droop, a gesture like a folding-in of petals, like a return into herself. This motion softens the precise stop of the feet, because it carries over for an unaccented count like a feminine ending; like the diminuendo effect of a port de bras which is finished a count later than the feet finish the step. Her softening forward droop in the shoulders also alters the look of the next new start since the dancer takes an up-beat of straightening her shoulders, and so seems to lift and unfold into the new phrase. Such nuances of color or breathing or dynamics give to the old-fashioned style its fullness; but they easily become fullsome. One can watch Markova, however, use them to carve more clearly the contour of a phrase, to make it more visible and more poignant. Our current fashion in classicism is to avoid these nuances to make sure that they will not be used to conceal a cardinal weakness.

In contrast to the solid, sharp, professional, rather impatient brilliance of our grand and powerful young ballerinas, the kind of effect Markova makes seems more than ever airy and mild, transparent and still. The dancer seems to begin on a sudden impulse, and to end in an inner stillness. She seems less to execute a dance than to be spontaneously inventing. She seems to respond to the music not like a professional, but more surprisingly, more communicatively. It is an "expressive" style, as peculiar looking in New York as any Parisian one. It is one our dancers look quite clumsy at, and not only our own, who hardly ever try for it, but many Europeans too, who constantly do.

I have wanted to focus attention on the difference, but I don't mean to judge between these two styles. For my part, I enjoy our own new one because the neutral look of it, a sort of pleasant guardedness, seems to suit our dancers better. Some day they will find out how to open up, but in terms of a technique that suits them. Markova happened to learn a style that suited her physique, her temperament, her environment; and a born ballerina, she made the most of it. The public responds to her now, not because of her style, not because it is the right one, but because she is a wonderfully compelling theatre artist. For me she was, this fall, exhibiting her highly elaborated style rather than dancing a dance or a role, and that limited my enjoyment. But for fans who love classic dancing, and because they love it are happy to see as much as they can of its possibilities, of its richness and scope, it is well worth seeing her perform effects no one in our generation is likely to make so lightly and so lucidly. *(1952)*

Suzanne Farrell (1945–)
by Arlene Croce

Farrell and Farrellism

Suzanne Farrell, one of the great dancers of the age, has rejoined the New York City Ballet. She returned without publicity or ceremony of any sort, entering the stage on Peter Martins's arm in the adagio movement of the Balanchine-Bizet *Symphony in C.* The theatre was full but not packed. (Ballet Theatre was playing a one-time-only performance of *Theme and Variations* with Kirkland and Baryshnikov, at the City Center.) The lower rings were thronged with standees who did not have to push their way in. Sanity was in the air. As the long bourrée to the oboe solo began, the audience withheld its applause, as if wanting to be sure that this was indeed Suzanne Farrell. Then a thunderclap lasting perhaps fifteen seconds rolled around the theatre, ending as

Source: From *Afterimages* (New York: Knopf, 1977).

decisively as it had begun, and there fell the deeper and prolonged silence of total absorption. For the next eight minutes, nobody except the dancers moved a muscle. At the end of the adagio, Farrell took four calls, and at the end of the ballet an unprecedented solo bow to cheers and bravas. There was no distraction, no intemperateness, in either the performance or its reception. The Bizet was never one of Farrell's best roles, but it is probably the most privileged role in the Balanchine repertory. Returning in it, she returns to the heart of the company, and she could become great in it yet.

In that first moment of delighted recognition and then in the intense quiet that followed, the audience, I think, saw what I saw—that although this tall, incomparably regal creature could be nobody but Farrell, it was not the same Farrell. She has lost a great deal of weight all over, and with it a certain plump quality in the texture of her movement. The plush is gone, and it was one of her glories. The impact of the long, full legs was different, too. If anything, they're more beautiful than ever, but no longer so impressively solid in extension, so exaggerated in their sweep, or so effortlessly controlled in their slow push outward from the lower back. The largesse of the thighs is still there, but in legato their pulse seemed to emerge and diminish sooner than it used to, and diminish still further below the knee in the newly slim, tapering calf. Yet the slenderness in the lower leg gives the ankle and the long arch of the foot a delicacy they didn't have before. And it shaves to a virtual pinpoint the already minute base from which the swelling grandeur of her form takes its impetus. Farrell is still broad across the hips (though not so broad as before); in pirouettes she is a spiraling cone. But it isn't that Farrell is so terribly big; it's that she *dances* big in relation to her base of support. The lightness of her instep, the speed of her dégagé are still thrilling. You'd think a dancer moving that fast couldn't possibly consume so much space—that she'd have to be more squarely planted. Farrell defies the logic of mechanics, and in that defiance is the essence of the new heroism she brought to Balanchine's stage a little over a decade ago.

Farrell's speed and amplitude were demonstrated more compellingly in *Concerto Barocco*, two nights after the Bizet. They are old virtues, and I am happy to see them back. Farrell doesn't look muscular or drained, as I feared she might, after five years in an alien and diseased repertory. In the upper body, she is almost totally different, and vastly improved. I miss the lift in the breastbone, and I think her sight line has dropped, but the shoulders, neck, and head have a wonderful new clarity and composure. The refinement of the arms and the simple dignity of the hands are miracles I didn't expect. And here is perhaps the best news of all: a Farrell who dances with a new grace of deportment and sensitivity of phrasing. Of all the changes that have come over her, this is the most significant, the most moving. Farrell sensitive? Back in the old days, in the seasons just before her departure from the New York City Ballet, she was the exact opposite—a superdiva who distorted every one of the roles she danced except those with distortions already written in. The absurd sky-high penchées, the flailing spine and thrust hips, the hiked elbows and flapping hands were as much a part of the Farrell of that period as the prodigies of speed and scale and balance that she accomplished. She wasn't joyously vulgar, like an old-style Bolshoi ballerina; she was carelessly vulgar, with no idea of the difference between one ballet and another. But the concept of differences in ballets was in general collapse, and one couldn't blame Farrell for what the company failed to teach her. Strangely, she returns at a time when those distinctions are beginning to be felt again—when the company can be seen at its best one night in *Tchaikovsky Concerto No. 2* and again another night in the utterly different *Stravinsky Violin Concerto*. But there's a collision in the making between Farrell's new, unaffected, clean style and the style of the dancers who've been replacing her all these years.

Farrell's great promise, in which Balanchine was immersed for so long in the sixties, marks the company to this day. It is saturated with her image. What Balanchine saw in her he has projected onto other dancers, but when she left, nearly six years ago, she was still evolving and obviously under fearful pressure. For many of the dancers who got chances after she left, the Farrell image in all its negative aspects has become rigidified as a norm—even intensified as a norm. Karin von Aroldingen and Sara Leland and Kay Mazzo are much worse than Farrell ever was; they're caricatures of the caricature she had become. Beside their wild, strained excesses, the Farrell of today looks almost conventional. Of course, compared to the ballets Balanchine made for her, *Symphony in C* and *Concerto Barocco* are conventional, and these are the only pieces we've seen her in so far. The rest of the Farrell story, which may well contain contradictions of what I've been saying about her, will unfold this season in *Jewels* and *Don Quixote*. But even without having the mature Farrell around to point up the difference, one can see that the Farrell image has been grievously misconceived. Swinging pelvises, baling-hook arms, and clawing hands have become the new, cruel orthodoxy, and there's a whole cluster of young girls in the corps —thin, long-limbed girls who look hysterically overbred: the ultimate degeneration of what might be called the Farrell strain. Penelope Dudleston is one of these girls. All hinges and splays, she dances the Siren in *The Prodigal Son* with a peculiar, dehumanized force. That is to say, she has no force at all—just a limp, terrifying presence. Dudleston is the first Siren to suggest that she stems from the men's chorus of reveling creeps; she might even be taken for one of them in disguise. (And there, opposite this apparition, was Edward Villella, looking sweeter, more innocent—and more baffled—than ever.) Heather Watts, whose hyperextended joints I rather enjoy, does Allegra Kent's old role in the Webern ballet *Episodes,* while Dudleston does Diana Adams's. The great breeding cycle of which Farrell's early NYCB phase was a part has long since run its course and is now exhausting itself in mutations. Bodies like Dudleston's and Watts's are redundant in ballets like *Episodes;* they're the bodies that mad, hyperbolic choreography is about, and they get no antipathetical play—no drama—out of the deliberate awkwardnesses and non sequiturs and extreme dislocations that Balanchine invented for the more resistant bodies of Adams and Kent.

Who Cares? is, like *Episodes*, a landmark ballet, and it, too, is showing signs of erosion. When it finally gets going (with the ten demisoloists doing their relay of Gershwin hits), *Who Cares?* is a ballet I adore, but the moment it marks in the history of the company is a poignant one that I can't get out of my mind. It was Balanchine's first ballet after the break with Farrell, and in it you could feel the whole company breathing easier. Patricia McBride, who is still marvelous in it, was unexpectedly marvelous in it then; it was one of the ballets that consolidated her stardom. One of the reasons it's no longer fresh is that Von Aroldingen has trashed the beautiful part Balanchine gave her—the part that for the first time made her look like an American ballerina and that might well have gone to Farrell if she'd stayed. It was as easy in 1970 to imagine Farrell in *Who Cares?* as it was in 1957 to imagine Tanaquil LeClercq in *Agon*, and that, perhaps, is part of Von Aroldingen's problem. She's a hard-working, thoughtful, not overly endowed dancer who doesn't deserve the unseemly prominence into which Balanchine has forced her, and she hasn't borne up well as the prime custodian of Farrell's image. In her roles, one feels, Balanchine has been creating for Farrell by proxy and not really succeeding. Although on occasion (the *Violin Concerto*) he's used her and Mazzo very well, it's pretty obvious that what has been thrown up in Farrell's wake isn't a new wealth of opportunities for other dancers but a whole flock of surrogate ballerinas. Gelsey Kirkland was the one dancer to have arisen and progressed during this difficult period; when she resigned from the company last summer, only McBride was left to carry on as major star and full-time ballerina. As one of the witty dancers remarked, "Suzanne coming back is the best thing that's happened to us since she left." There are young dancers, as yet below ballerina level, who have escaped the influence of Farrell and Farrellism. Merrill Ashley and Colleen Neary (who is one of the thin, long-limbed girls, but with a soft, human core) are two of the most rewarding. It isn't amusing to speculate, even in private, on what may happen to these talented girls now that Farrell has returned, or to the less talented ones, or, indeed, to Farrell herself. The crisis is a serious one, and these are family matters. Farrell once precipitated a revolution in the company. She made audiences sweat, and, indirectly, blamelessly, she's been making us sweat ever since. Remembering those revolutionary days, one can only look with helpless fascination to the days ahead. This is 1975, a new year in the life of the most adventurous, erratic, and valuable ballet company in the world.

—February 3, 1975

Free and More Than Equal

If George Balanchine were a novelist or a playwright or a movie director instead of a choreographer, his studies of women would be among the most discussed and most influential artistic achievements of our time. But because Balanchine works without words, and customarily without a libretto, and because the position of women in ballet has long been a dominant one, we take his extraordinary creations for granted, much as if they were natural happenings. It is part of Balanchine's genius to make the extraordinary seem natural; how many contemporary male artists, in ballet or out of it, can compete with him in depicting contemporary women? Balanchine's world is pervaded by a modern consciousness; his women do not always live for love, and their destinies are seldom defined by the men they lean on. Sexual complicity in conflict with individual freedom is a central theme of the Balanchine pas de deux, and more often than not it is dramatized from the woman's point of view. The man's role is usually that of fascinated observer and would-be manipulator—the artist who seeks to possess his subject and finds that he may only explore it. For Balanchine it is the man who sees and follows and it is the woman who acts and guides. The roles may not be reversed. When the man sometimes does not "see" (one thinks of Orpheus, or the lone male figure in the Elegy of *Serenade*, or Don Quixote, who hallucinates), he continues blindly on his mission, passive in the grip of fate. But when the woman is passive and sightless it is because she is without a destiny of her own. She can belong to a man. This is what the Sleepwalker suggests to the Poet in

La Sonnambula; it is what Kay Mazzo suggests to Peter Martins in *Duo Concertant* and *Stravinsky Violin Concerto.* In both these ballets, Mazzo is blinded by Martins in a gesture both benevolent and authoritarian. They are the only pas de deux of Balanchine's I know in which the man has a fully controlling role. Even the Sleepwalker does not surrender to the Poet she tantalizes. And even Allegra Kent, who in the roles Balanchine made for her was so supple she practically invited a man to turn her into a docile toy, was uncapturable. Think of *Episodes,* in which every trap her partner sets seems to contain a hidden spring by which she can release herself—or ensnare *him;* or her role in *Ivesiana* ("The Unanswered Question"), in which she is borne like an infanta on the shoulders of four men, lifted, turned in this direction and that, dropped headlong to within inches of the ground, delivered for one burning instant into the arms of a fifth man, who is crawling wretchedly after her, and taken away into the dark whence she came. Like the Sleepwalker, she does not seem to belong to herself, yet she doesn't belong to her manipulators, either—they're a part of her mystery. (In the same ballet, another woman enters blind, groping her way forward; what seems to happen between her and the man she meets is rape.)

The image of the unattainable woman is one that comes from nineteenth-century Romantic ballet, but in Balanchine the ballerina is unattainable simply because she is a woman, not because she's a supernatural or enchanted being. He can make comedy or tragedy, and sometimes a blend of both, out of the conflict between a woman's free will and her need for a man; he can carry you step by step into dramas in which sexual relationships are not defined by sex or erotic tension alone, and in this he is unique among choreographers. He is unique, too, in going beyond the limits of what women have conventionally expressed on the stage. In *Diamonds,* the ballet that follows *Emeralds* and *Rubies* in the three-part program called *Jewels,* Suzanne Farrell dances a long, supported adagio the point of which is to let us see how little support she actually needs. There is no suggestion here of a partnership between equals, of matched wits in a power play such as there is in *Rubies,* with Patricia McBride and Edward Villella. In *Diamonds* there is no contest, and in a sense the conception is reactionary —the woman is back on her pedestal and the man is worshipful. But that is not the meaning of the dance as we see it today. There's much more substance to *Diamonds* than there was in the days when Farrell first danced it; then it seemed the iciest and emptiest of abstractions with, in the woman's part, an edge of brazen contempt. Farrell, a changed and immeasurably enriched dancer, in stepping back into the ballet has discovered it. She is every bit as powerful as she was before, but now she takes responsibility for the discharge of power; she doesn't just fire away. And whereas she used to look to me like an omnicompetent blank, she's now dynamic, colorful, tender. Her impetuosity and her serenity are forces in constant play, and one may see the action of the piece as a drama of temperament. It is a drama very different from the one I remember. Farrell's independent drive no longer seems unacceptably burdensome to her, and her mastery implies no rebuke.

And what mastery it is—of continual off-center balances maintained with light support or no support at all, of divergently shaped steps unthinkably combined in the same phrase, of invisible transitions between steps and delicate shifts of weight in poses that reveal new and sweeter harmonies of proportion no matter how wide or how subtle the contrast. Your eye gorges on her variety, your heart stops at the brink of every precipice. She, however, sails calmly out into space and returns as if the danger did not exist. Farrell's style in *Diamonds* (and the third act of *Don Quixote*) is based on risk; she is almost always off balance and always secure. Her confidence in moments of great risk gives her the leeway to suggest what no ballerina has suggested before her—that she can sustain herself, that she can go it alone. Unlike Cynthia Gregory, and many ballerinas less distinguished than Gregory, who perfect held balances, Farrell perfects the *act* of balance/imbalance as a constant feature of dancing. It is not equilibrium as stasis, it is equilibrium as continuity that she excels in. Although, as in her *Diamonds* performance, she can take a piqué arabesque and stand unaided, she's capable of much more; her conquests are really up there where the richer hazards are. In the Scherzo, going at high speed, she several times takes piqué arabesque, swings into second position and back into arabesque, uncoiling a half-turn that, because of the sudden force of the swing, seems like a complete one. In the finale, her partner (Jacques d'Amboise) is only there to stop her. She slips like a fish through his hands. She doesn't stop, doesn't wait, doesn't depend, and she can't fall. She's like someone who has learned to breathe thin air.

Of course, the autonomy of the ballerina is an illusion, but Farrell's is the extremest form of this illusion we have yet seen, and it makes *Diamonds* a riveting spectacle about the freest woman alive. The title is a misnomer. *Diamonds* finds its entire justification in a single dancer; apart from its presentation of the multifaceted Farrell, the ballet is paste. None of the ballets Balanchine created for Farrell were top-flight, and there is very little besides Farrell to justify the maintenance in repertory of his full-evening work *Don Quixote*. Farrell has little to do until the third act, where she fully recaptures her old brilliance and adds to it a new gift for dramatization. Up to that point she has outgrown the role, and the ballet is stale and boring. It was an interesting failure ten years ago, when it was new, but Balanchine's attempts to straighten out the strands that connect the Don's fantasies to the reality of persons and events around him have led to a succession of ever more futile revisions in the first act, and with the addition two years ago of a classical-Spanish divertissement he abandoned all efforts at mise-en-scène. The story of Don Quixote doesn't really get going until well into the second act, most of which is taken up with another divertissement. The ballet has always suffered from a lack of conviction; maybe it was on account of Nicolas Nabokov's music, maybe it was because giving overt dramatic expression to his theme of the elusive Ideal Woman betrayed Balanchine into unflattering revelations of self-pity. Although Jacques d'Amboise, taking over the role this season, gives the Don modesty and dignity, Balanchine seems to feel very sorry for him indeed.

Farrell's Dulcinea and her role in *Diamonds* suggest that, as a Balanchine conception, she's free and more than equal to any man. In *Bugaku*, she appeared in a contrasting role, one originally done by Kent. Here the woman is seen ribaldly as an object, and though there are moments of satire in the geisha-girl pantomime (as well as some nasty pseudo-Oriental mannerisms), *Bugaku* is the nearest thing in the New York City Ballet repertory to a Béjart ballet. Balanchine seems to have derived his inspiration for the pas de deux from Japanese pornographic prints. Farrell brought out some of the acid below the surface, but not enough. Kent can bring it all out—complicity carried to the point of mockery—so the piece becomes nearly a feminist statement; she can make the movements look insinuating and delicious at the same time. There is a close link between Kent and Farrell that Farrell's absence had obscured, but Farrell in Kent's roles rather emphasizes their dissimilarities.

—February 24, 1975

Mikhail Baryshnikov
by Arlene Croce

Glimpses of Genius

Mikhail Baryshnikov, the legendary young star of Leningrad's Kirov Ballet, is making his first appearances on this continent this summer, touring in Canada with a contingent of Bolshoi dancers. Baryshnikov became a legend even before he was admitted to the Kirov, in 1967; he was the pupil—the best, many said, and one of the last, as it turned out—of Alexander Pushkin, the great Leningrad teacher who had trained Yuri Soloviev and Rudolf Nureyev. In 1970, the year Pushkin died, Baryshnikov appeared in London, and from the way the London critics threw around the word "genius" I began to get an uncomfortable feeling about him: either he wouldn't live up to his notices or he would so fully justify them that he'd be, as a phenomenon, unrecognizable. True genius doesn't fulfill expectations, it shatters them, and the initial experience of it can be disturbing. Now that I've seen Baryshnikov perform in Montreal, I can't remember what I expected him to be like. Something on the order of Soloviev, I suppose, only smaller, higher, and faster. (That would have been genius enough.) Well, Baryshnikov is all three, but he's unlike anyone else, and he does things I've never seen any other dancer do. I was confounded, and the audiences at the Salle Wilfrid-Pelletier were, too. Although they gave him ovations, I think they really didn't get him. Probably they, like me, were bemused by the purity of Baryshnikov's style. He carries the impeccable to the point where it vanishes into the ineffable. One can't see where the dazzle comes from. When he walks out onto the stage, he doesn't radiate—doesn't put the audience on notice that he's a star. His body, with its short, rounded muscles, isn't handsome; he's no Anthony Dowell. His head and hands are large, and his face—pale, with peaked features and distant eyes—is the face of Petrouchka. He attends carefully to his ballerina and appears utterly unprepossessing. When he dances, the illusion—its size and glow—comes so suddenly that it takes you by surprise. You think from the looks of him that he might be a maverick, which would make him easy to accept, but he doesn't

Source: From *Afterimages* (New York; Knopf, 1977).

dance like one. Any hope of idiosyncrasy or impertinence is dashed the instant he leaves the floor. And yet there's no mistaking his phenomenal gift. It's obvious that Pushkin has turned out not the last of a line but a new and unique classical virtuoso.

Baryshnikov is able to perform unparalleled spectacular feats as an extension of classical rather than character or acrobatic dancing. Lovers of flashy entertainment, of sport, of raw prowess, may not take to him at once, but lovers of classical style will go mad. He gets into a step sequence more quickly, complicates it more variously, and prolongs it more extravagantly than any dancer I've ever seen. And he finishes when he wants to, not when he has to. Perhaps his greatest gift is his sense of fantasy in classical gesture. He pursues the extremes of its logic so that every step takes on an unforeseen dimension. His grande pirouette is a rhapsody of swelling volume and displaced weight. He does not turn; he is turned—spun around and around by the tip of his toe. Like the young prodigy Nadezhda Pavlova, whom the Bolshoi introduced to American audiences last year, Baryshnikov both summarizes and extends the resources of classical expression. The three performances I saw him give in Montreal were of standard pas de deux (two *Nutcrackers* and one *Don Quixote*), and while it would be absurd to judge his range on so short an acquaintance, one can certainly assume that he possesses many qualities he had no chance to display in Montreal. I can believe, for example, that he is the fine actor he's reputed to be, because of the way he altered his style to suit each of the pas de deux. In the *Nutcracker*, he was an image of elfin Mozartean grace; in the *Don Quixote*, he was diabolical, dancing with a livid force. And the dance pictures he produced in these different styles—particularly one of a high, slow jeté passé in which he arched his back at the peak of the jump—will linger long in memory. *July 8, 1974*

Baryshnikov's Day

Because his performances are as exciting for what they portend as for what they contain, it's impossible to see all there is of Mikhail Baryshnikov at the moment and to see him complete. The feeling he leaves you with is one of intense pleasure mingled with the ache of frustration, and you can't capture him whole by seeing him again. To watch Baryshnikov dance for the first time is to see a door open on the future—on the possibilities, as yet untold, of male classical style in this century. The second time, and the third and the fourth, it's the same —that same dazzling vista, crowded with prophetic shapes and rhythms; we see it clearly in a flash, and then it's like trying to recall the content of a dream we only feel the emotion of: we get the same ache. Although Baryshnikov is in no sense an unfinished artist—at twenty-six he is in his prime—every performance confirms his potential, and part of the anguish we feel comes from the fear that his potential may be wasted. He harbors the future, but his roles keep him from exploring it. If ever a dancer needed new roles, it is he, and I don't mean roles from the modern Western repertory which would be new just to him; I mean his own new roles, with advanced choreography, that would be new to us as well. Baryshnikov begins where other dancers leave off, and to confine him to an existing repertory—no matter how amply he might ornament it—would be to suppress his essential genius.

Baryshnikov crams traditional roles with new vitality, and in them he seems literally to be flying out of the nineteenth into the twentieth century. In his début performances this season with the American Ballet Theatre, he danced "on top of" the solos in *Giselle* and *La Bayadère*, giving us two and three times as much to look at as anyone had ever given us in the same unit of musical time. High-concentrate dancing is what the most progressive twentieth-century choreography is all about, but the idea has never been expressed before by a performer on so high a level of virtuosity. For Baryshnikov, a double pirouette or air turn is a linking step, and preparations scarcely exist. In the *Bayadère* variation, he turned a grande pirouette in second, in passé, in attitude—nine or ten revolutions in all, and all from one preparation. In a traveling version of the same thing, he swept from low grand jeté into an air turn à la seconde and, on landing, continued to turn in a series of perfectly placed pirouettes en dedans. His finishes are achieved in a faultless diminuendo or a sudden clean stop. He gives a new urgency to commonplace allegro steps like brisés (in the two speeding diagonals of *Giselle*), and an ordinary jump appears in all its compound splendor as grand jeté dessus en tournant battu—redefined almost past recognition, and about a mile off the ground, too. Occasionally, because the traditional dance rhetoric comes so easily to him, the pressure gets a little thin. In the coda to *La Bayadère* and in his *Don Quixote* solo, he does a circuit of barrel turns (tour de reins) that must be unmatched for height, evenness, and cleanness of execution, but the ease of his style deprives the step of the raw impact it can have when it is done by lesser dancers. He also performs invented steps. One is a turning jeté in which, at the last second, he changes the foot he's going to land on and his legs flash past each other in the air. Or, on the way to one of his pinpoint landings in assemblé, he will suddenly flex his knees. It looks like provincial hot stuff. Baryshnikov's promise lies not in novel steps but in his power to push classical steps to a new extreme in logic, a new density of interest. He is a modern classical dancer. Unfortunately, at Ballet Theatre he plays to an audience that identifies classicism with the nineteenth century or with empty displays of technique. On the evening of his first *La Bayadère*, Baryshnikov was cheered, but Cynthia Gregory was cheered twice as loudly for perverting her own beautiful style in a simpering, stunt-filled exercise called *Grand Pas Classique*.

Baryshnikov's ballerina in all four of his performances was Natalia Makarova—a partnership that is not heaven-sent. Makarova is hard to partner, especially in *La Bayadère*. She needs Ivan Nagy, who can commit himself to her completely. But in *Giselle* and in the *Don Quixote* pas de deux Makarova and Baryshnikov were wonderful to have together on the same stage. Stylistically, these two former stars of the Kirov Ballet are beautifully matched, and their Giselle and Albrecht were as psychically fused as Cathy and Heathcliff. (In the second *Bayadère*, this psychic fusion turned a bit anxious and a gray something descended which I can only describe as Kirov funk.) In the second act, Makarova's slightly rigid head positions and the line from the nape to the extended instep in fourth position had an entrancing pathos. It was her only *Giselle* of the season; she gave it up to Baryshnikov for his first appearance in America. He, in turn, played to her all evening with fervent devotion. At the end, he scattered lilies in a trail from the grave, then lay facing it as the curtain fell. —*August 19, 1974*

Old Acquaintance and New

Nothing galvanizes the general public like the advent of a new male star in ballet. Baryshnikov evenings at the American Ballet Theatre are sellouts and surpass in the feverish excitement they arouse even Nureyev's first American season with the Royal Ballet, in 1963. In those days, the hard ticket was Nureyev-Fonteyn. Nureyev by himself didn't sell out the Met until the Hurok office released its publicity barrage in 1965, and it must be remembered, too, that Nureyev's star had already ascended partly via network television. If Ed Sullivan and the *Bell Telephone Hour* were still in business, Mikhail Baryshnikov would be known to millions more Americans than know him today. As it is, he's on the verge of becoming a national household name, and only New York, Washington, Houston, Denver, and Atlanta have seen him. In the current City Center season, the clamor is as much for Baryshnikov solo in *Les Patineurs* as it is for Baryshnikov-Makarova or Baryshnikov-

Kirkland in the ballets he performs with either or both ballerinas—*Coppélia* and *La Fille Mal Gardée* and *La Sylphide* and *Giselle*.

So far, if I'd had to give my scalp for one ticket, I'd have given it for *Les Patineurs*. In this transcendent Baryshnikov performance (which, alas for the scalpers, he gave exactly twice), one didn't have to wait around for him to dance. Each appearance was an instantaneous string of firecrackers, a flaring up of incalculable human energy in its most elegant form. The Ashton ballet, thirty-eight years old, is still a model of construction. The central role is so well designed that a dancer can get by on neat execution alone. Baryshnikov embellished it like a bel-canto tenor, and, as often happens, he made the choreography look as if he had invented or at the least inspired it. A now famous Baryshnikovism, the split tour-jeté, looked right for the first time in the context of this ballet about ice skaters, and Baryshnikov produced the step as none of his imitators so far have done—coming out of a double air turn. Curiously, in the performance I saw (the second of the two), the role had none of the brash extrovert character that is associated with it. It had instead a sense of spiritual dissociation, as if the Green Skater's isolation were to be attributed to his genius. He—the "character" as Baryshnikov assumed it—suggested a boy who builds dynamos in his attic; he had that kind of tragic happiness.

Up to now, *Patineurs* is the only role in which Baryshnikov's dazzling dance power and the diffidence of his personality seem to fit together, but it isn't the role Ashton created. (Not that it matters.) As it happens, Ballet Theatre already has a superlative show-off Green Skater in Fernando Bujones, and Bujones is dazzling in an altogether different way—sharp and arrowy, while Baryshnikov is soft and sinuous. With Bujones leading what is now the strongest male corps in American ballet, and with Natalia Makarova and Cynthia Gregory and Martine van Hamel leading a female corps that includes such exceptionally talented soloists as Kim Highton and Marianna Tcherkassky, the company didn't need Baryshnikov to put over its winter season. But it has got him, and it has Gelsey Kirland, too, who left the dwindling Sugar Plums at the New York City Ballet to be the icing on Ballet Theatre's top-heavy cake. How Ballet Theatre was to handle its load of talent was a problem *before* Baryshnikov and Kirkland joined; the company's ability to attract stars isn't matched by an ability to attract choreographers, and the disproportionately small shareable repertory means that dancers are either waiting to get into a part or waiting to get out of one. A Makarova-Baryshnikov *Coppélia* this season wrung the material for all it could give, shook out a few extra gags (Makarova popping an elastic band under her chin), and wrung some more. Makarova's showmanship doesn't fail her even when her dancing does. Baryshnikov's dancing *is* his showmanship. His acting tends to be a cover for his personality, not a revelation of it. In comic roles, he's less guarded than he is in roles like James and Albrecht, in which he contorts his face and his playing is heavy and confused. He hasn't Ivan Nagy's gift, in *La Sylphide*, of putting the audience in his place. Nagy, the company's best actor in classical roles, is also Makarova's best partner. Makarova's solos were finer in the *Giselle* with Baryshnikov, but in the duets she didn't have the unearthly halation she had when Nagy lifted her.

And Baryshnikov is better with Kirkland. They did one *La Sylphide*, he in his kilt and Frankenstein makeup, she looking like a French chambermaid, yet it was wonderful—the evident climax of this first phase of their partnership. In the first act, Baryshnikov seemed to be trying out different interpretations of the role in a kind of Stanislavskian attempt to make sense of it. James is a character of stormy temperament, but his dances are light and airy. Ironies of that sort, which abound in Romantic ballet, make contemporary Russians impatient. They gave us a Stanislavski *Giselle*, and they probably can't understand how we can live with that and the light insincerities of *La Sylphide* at the same time. In the second act, Baryshnikov actually forced a new element into James's solos. That element was passion. James's buoyancy and speed were overtaken by the fury of frustrated desire. This was dark "Russian" Bournonville, but it was very different from the undirected violence that marks Nureyev in the same part. No other dancer alive could have done it. *—January 20, 1975*

The Composers, Designers, and Librettists

Composers

Early in 1878 the Russian composer Peter Tchaikovsky completed his Fourth Symphony. In Italy at the time, he mailed the recently finished score to his close friend Serge Taneiev in Russia and invited his opinion on the new work. Taneiev replied that although he enjoyed the symphony's middle movements—the Andante was "charming" and the Scherzo "exquisite"—the composition had one defect to which he could never be reconciled: "in every movement there are phrases which sound like ballet music."

"Ballet music" was often used as a term of contempt by nineteenth-century musicians, much as the phrase "movie music" has been used in this century. With its rum-ti-tum rhythms and allegedly banal tunes, dance music was held in low esteem: it was considered hack work pure and simple, composed by the yard and aimed to arouse only the most facile and obvious of emotions. Dance music was thought so inconsequential that little attention was paid to its potential. When writing for the ballet, many composers did not hesitate to "borrow" whatever they "needed" from other composers: when composing *La Fille Mal Gardée*, Ferdinand Herold, for example, took tunes from Rossini's *Cenerentola* and Donizetti's *L'Elisir d'Amore* and merely inserted them into his own work. And when reviewing a new ballet, most reviewers did not feel obliged to discuss its score: even Gautier could summarily dismiss a score as "equal to the average music of its kind." One score was thought as good—or as bad—as any other, and even today the names of two of the most prolific nineteenth-century ballet composers—Minkus and Drigo—are often comically consolidate into "Drinkus" to convey the unoriginality and interchangeability of certain ballet composers.

Although such inventive composers as Delibes and Tchaikovsky began working for the ballet in the 1870s, the status of ballet music still remained surprisingly low. When Tchaikovsky's *Swan Lake* was premiered in Moscow in 1877, it was thought too complicated and symphonic—too "good" for the ballet stage. (In fact, almost a third of the score was deleted for the first production as being too difficult to dance to.) And when Isadora Duncan in the early years of this century began dancing to the music of such traditional concert hall composers as Bach and Schubert, musical purists were enraged: such music was far too important to be compromised by dance.

The alliance between dance and music was, however, considerably strengthened when composers like Igor Stravinsky began creating undeniably innovative scores for the ballet, and when choreographers like Balanchine began treating those scores with such sensitivity, style, and wit that audiences could, as Balanchine said, "see the music and hear the dance." Stravinsky, of course, proved to be a seminal figure in the aesthetics of modern music, and his obvious love of ballet ("If I appreciate so highly the value of classical ballet, it is not simply a matter of taste on my part, but because I see exactly in it the perfect expression of the Apollonian principle.") was bound to improve composers' attitudes towards ballet music, much as Balanchine's obvious debt to music ("The music is first. I couldn't move without a reason and the reason is music.") was bound to stimulate other choreographers to treat music with greater sensitivity. It has been said, in fact, that innovations in dance during the past several decades have been inspired not by painting (as in the early part of this century) nor by literature (as in the nineteenth century), but by music.

Questions, of course, remain about the association of music and dance. *Are* some scores better suited for dance? Even Balanchine, who has used a startlingly wide range of music for his ballets—everything from John Phillip Sousa and TV commercial jingles to Webern and Xenakis—admits that it is better not to use certain types of music. "I wouldn't use Beethoven overtures because they are made for listening. I wouldn't know what to do with them."

In his essay "Music and Action," Constant Lambert—for years the musical director of the Sadler's Wells Ballet (now called the Royal Ballet) and himself a ballet composer—examines what type of music is best suited for dance. Lambert claims that music with the two-dimensional quality of present action (as opposed to music with the more subtle quality of imagined or recollected action) works best for dance. In "Composer/Choreographer," several composers prominently associated with American modern dance discuss the several ways choreographer and composer can collaborate, as well as ask what is the best relation of dance to music: Should the dance merely illustrate the music or actually illuminate it? Is the music the partner of dance or its master? And in the third of these essays about dance music, Balanchine himself discusses the dance elements in Stravinsky's music: its inventive rhythms, structural integrity, and eloquent sparseness.

Taneiev may have criticized the balletic qualities of Tchaikovsky's Fourth Symphony, but it is Tchaikovsky who has had the last word: "What difference does it make if the ballet dances to it? Is it good? That is the only question that matters."

Designers

Dance designers work within limitations not imposed on other designers: dance decor and costumes must neither impede nor obscure movement, two requirements that can put quite a damper on many designers' imaginations. A dance costume, for example, must not only convey the appropriate atmosphere of period or character (the function of any theatrical dress), it must first provide enough freedom and comfort for the dancer to move with considerable ease (requirements peculiar to dance alone). Dance costumes must reveal the body—its line, its plasticity. The art of dressing dance is, in many ways, the art of undressing dance.

Even as early as 1681, Père Ménestrier in his *Des Ballets Anciens et Modernes* advised costumers to design clothes that would "leave the legs and body quite free to dance." And in his *Letters on Dancing and Ballets*, first published in 1760, Noverre, wishing to abolish costumes that conceal all the contours of the body, called for light and simple draperies that would reveal the dancer's figure. "I would reduce by three-quarters," he angrily wrote, "the ridiculous paniers of our *danseuses*, they are equally opposed to the liberty, speed, prompt and lively action of the dance."

Because of the special requirements of dress for dance, the history of ballet has been closely bound to the history of its costumes: new styles of movement have often resulted in new costumes, and new costumes have often inspired new steps. When Marie Camargo shortened her dress by several inches in 1730—shocking her contemporaries—she was able to perform the *entrechat* (a criss-crossing of the legs in midair), the first time a woman had ever done so. And as technique developed and ballerinas strove to achieve greater virtuosity, the skirt became shorter and shorter and shorter until it became the "powderpuff" tutu; classical technique, in love with the length of the human leg, needed a costume to reveal and accentuate that love. Cyril W. Beaumont, the late British dance historian and bookseller, has even claimed that the evolution of the tutu and tights permitted "as great a change in the art of dancing as did the invention of gunpowder on warfare."

Edwin Denby once noted that because ballet dancers keep moving all over the stage and because in looking at them you keep looking at all the scenery all the time, ballet decoration is observed in a livelier manner than play or opera decoration. Just as an effective dance costume will provide enough freedom to reveal the body's contours, a successful set—even the most elaborate and detailed—will create enough space so that the dancers seem to have ample air all around to dance easily. Classical dance, which makes the body look large, unencumbered, and extravagantly free, requires space, and every designer working for ballet must create this illusion of space.

The essays about design included in this anthology detail two different approaches to the very special problems of dance design. Alexandre Benois, one of the founding forces of Diaghilev's Ballets Russes and the designer of several of its early ballets, advocates spectacle in dance decor: the set as the opulent background in front of which sumptuously attired dancers perform. In contrast, Rouben Ter-Arutunian and Isamu Noguchi, two of the leading contemporary designers (Ter-Arutunian has been closely associated with Balanchine; Noguchi with Graham) want decor to be structural rather than merely pictorial: to them, decor is integral, not incidental; it reveals, not simply adorns. Benois' approach is painterly and illustrative; Ter-Arutunian and Noguchi's is sculptural and symbolic. Props are magical accessories for Benois; extensions of the dancer's anatomy for Noguchi. Decor preserves mood for Benois; it generates meaning for Noguchi and Arutunian. But all three designers disavow realism: dance is poetry, and its landscape is that of the imagination.

Librettists

"It is not easy to write for legs," claimed Gautier, who having written the librettos for *Giselle* and *La Péri* knew exactly how difficult it was to find suitable stories for dance. Although many people imagine any plot will do for ballet—"the story's just an excuse for the dancing"—perhaps no dramatic form presents as many difficulties as the ballet. "To invent a plot whose action shall be ever visible," Gautier observed, "to find events and passions capable of being expressed in easily understood poses and gesture, to make use of considerable numbers of people, to set them in motion without creating confusion, to choose a period and a country whose costumes are brilliant and picturesque, a locality which lends itself to a beautiful setting—these are some of the cares and troubles entailed in connection with that futile amusement called ballet, which is not even literature. Many other things classed as serious pursuits can be achieved with far less effort."

Ballet does indeed face problems unknown to other narrative arts. "There are no mothers-in-law in ballet," Balanchine once wryly noted, reminding us that exposition in dance is tricky at best, impossible at worst and that dance can express only the most basic human relationships. Nor are there past and present in dance (ballet "must always conjugate its action in the present" according to Gautier), so that plot —even in the hands of an innovative storyteller like Graham—must follow rules of simple dramaturgy. (Balanchine once said that the perfect type of story for ballet was that of the Prodigal Son: once there was a man who had everything, then he had nothing, finally he had everything again.) Debarred from the nuances of language and deprived of narrative complexities, the dance librettist must find stories whose subjects can be expressed in dance terms, subjects where, as Gautier said, "dancing occurs necessarily and unavoidably and is used for the very expression of the story."

Relying on dance-related subjects, even narrative ballets are thus self-referential: like their plotless counterparts, story ballets are dances about dancing. *Giselle*, for example, may depict the love story of a peasant girl (Giselle) and a nobleman (Albrecht), but it also portrays the awesome powers of dance. It is dance—not only Albrecht's betrayal—that kills Giselle in the first act of the ballet, and it is also dance that almost kills Albrecht in the second. When a character breaks out into dance in a successful story ballet, the dance doesn't interrupt the story—it *is* the story. The dances extend and deepen the plot. They reveal the diversity of dance functions: dance as exhaustion and exaltation (*Giselle*), dance as sexual come-on (*Fancy Free*), dance as aristocratic order (*Sleeping Beauty*), dance as social integration (*Rodeo*), dance as erotic deception (*Swan Lake*, Act III).

Dance librettos have undergone several changes in fashion: the plots of eighteenth-century ballets were based on classical mythology; those of the nineteenth century on romantic legends. During the early Diaghilev years, ballets were inspired by exotic, often Oriental tales; during its later phases, by contemporary life. And in the post-Diaghilev era, ballets have often done away with story entirely: this is the "plotless" era. (It should be remembered, however, that even a plotless ballet has a subject. As Arlene Croce once said of Balanchine: "only a man who knows how to tell a story can do without a plot.")

Vernoy de Saint-Georges and Gautier's libretto for *Giselle* is often considered one of the best. Its clear-cut structure (Act I is earthly and joyous, Act II ethereal and spiritual) and dance-related story ("Giselle wants nothing more in the world but to dance to be loved by Loys") are exemplary. In the letter included in this anthology, Gautier describes the plot in detail and suggests what goes into making what he elsewhere called "the rarest thing in the world": a good ballet libretto.

Music and Action
by Constant Lambert

Music, though the most subtle of all arts in its powers of suggestion, is the most clumsy in its powers of definition. It can suggest some nostalgic half-shade of emotion with an almost mathematical precision denied to literature, yet it is incapable of the simple distinction between "He said" and "He thought" without which the art of the novel would be impossible. (Even in the works of writers like Joyce and Faulkner, who exalt the interior monologue at the expense of the action, the distinction between the two is as firmly established as in the case of Dickens.) But although music is incapable of making this distinction in so many words, or rather so many notes, it would be a great mistake to imagine that this distinction does not exist.

We use the word "music" to cover the world of ordered sound in general, often without realising that music can be divided into as many distinct branches as literature—poetic drama, prose drama, novels, belles-lettres, travel books and the like. No one would dream of making a play out of Sir Thomas Browne's *Urn Burial* or Kant's *Critique of Pure Reason*, yet some of the recent choreographic assaults on famous pieces of music have not been less absurd in their misunderstanding of medium. The crude distinction between music actually written for the stage and music written for the concert-hall is naturally appreciated; but it is not so often realised that a similar distinction can exist as regards two pieces of concert-hall music—I mean the difference between what may be called direct or present action, and what may be called recollected or imaginary action.

The difference can most clearly be seen if we compare two pieces apparently in the same genre and sharing certain similarities of style: Rimsky-Korsakoff's *Scheherazade* and Balakireff's *Thamar*, two evocative

Source: From *Footnotes to the Ballet: A Book for Balletomanes*, edited by Caryl Brahms (London: Peter Davies, 1936).

orchestral works both of which were eventually turned into ballets. I am not alone in considering Balakireff's work greatly superior from the purely musical point of view, and I expect many will agree with me in preferring Fokine's choreography and Bakst's décor in *Thamar* to their work in *Scheherazade*, considered again as separate artistic elements. Yet *Scheherazade* is to me the more successful and satisfying ballet of the two, for the simple reason that the music has the direct two-dimensional quality of present action, while Balakireff's work has the more subtle quality of imagined or recollected action. The success is all the more remarkable when we remember that the scenario of *Thamar* follows closely the Lermontoff poem round which Balakireff wrote his symphonic poem, while the scenario of *Scheherazade* has nothing in common with the stories round which Rimsky-Korsakoff wrote his symphonic suite. The point, I think, is this: Rimsky-Korsakoff's formal outlook being as simple and direct as the narrative methods of the *Arabian Nights* themselves, his music lends itself to any tale of a type similar to those he actually chose to illustrate. Balakireff, on the other hand, approaches his subject with something of the formal subtlety of a Conrad, and hence even the most painstaking realisation of his tale does a certain violence to the musical content. There is in *Thamar* none of the obvious physical climax which lends itself so successfully to action in the closing scene of *Scheherazade*. Instead we are given an emotional summing-up after the action is over. As a result the actual murder of the Prince on the stage is too strong an action for the music, while on the other hand the epilogue is choreographically speaking too weak.

Conrad, to whom I have compared Balakireff, provides us with a particularly good example of the difference between direct and recollected action which it is so important for the choreographer to realise when dealing with music. It is a platitude to point out that although Conrad's plots, considered as a dramatic framework, are melodramatic, his books are never melodramatic because of his oblique approach to the more theatrical incidents. When, however, he tried to turn his novels and tales into plays they became just melodramas and rather bad ones at that. It is as though some one had re-written a Greek tragedy and shown us the messenger's speech in terms of action; made us see Jocasta committing suicide, Oedipus gouging his eyes out. Such a play would be an outrage on taste, but is it less of an outrage when Massine represents the personal tragedy which lies behind the slow movement of Tchaikovsky No. 5 by a bogy-man with pantomime wings breaking in on a pair of lovers? Choreography by its very nature is denied the oblique approach to narrative or action open to the writer or composer. Hence the necessity for the choreographer and scenario-writer to exercise the utmost discrimination and reticence in the choice of a ballet theme.

To return to *Thamar*, which provides a peculiarly apt test-case for our argument. Though less suited to action than *Scheherazade* because of its emotional-cum-formal subtlety, it is, on the other hand, well suited to action because of its narrative time-sense. It cannot be emphasised too strongly that although the composer is forced to adopt time as his medium he does not always approach time in the same way. Sometimes his themes succeed each other in dramatic sequence like the acts of a play, sometimes their sequence and their position in time is dictated by purely formal reasons. In a symphonic poem by Liszt or Strauss the former is the case. The triumphant apotheoses or pathetic death-scenes which end their works are definitely the last act of the play and represent the final word on the subject in hand. But this is not so in the case of a Mozart symphony. We have it on his own authority that Mozart conceived a symphony in its full form in one moment of time. It stands to reason, then, that the return of a theme in his works can have no narrative or dramatic significance. The recapitulation balances the exposition, much as a tree on one side of a picture might balance one on the other. We do not look at a picture "reading from left to right" as in a society photograph, but take in its design as a whole; and though we inevitably have to listen to a Mozart symphony from left to right, as it were, we should try as far as possible to banish this aspect of the work from our minds and try to see it as the composer conceived it, in one moment of time.

The trouble with any choreographic interpretation of a classical symphony (as opposed to a romantic symphonic poem) is that the dancing is bound to emphasise the least important aspect of the music—its time-sequence. Let us suppose that a choreographer wished to set Mozart's G minor quintet as a ballet. (A hideous thought, but not more hideous than many recent choreographic conceptions.) Any one who appreciates this masterpiece must also appreciate the fact that the final movement, though more light-hearted in tone than the rest of the work, represents not a final "winning through" or "triumph over adversity" but a facet of experience only, no more important than the others through its being placed at the end. But if it were presented on the stage we would be bound to feel during the finale that after a *mauvais quart d'heure* the dancers were cheering up considerably. Perverse though the idea may seem, a complicated *tableau-vivant* would actually be a closer interpretation of Mozart's thought than any ballet.

It is true that there are many symphonies of a later date into which narrative element and dramatic time-sequence enter and which therefore are more suited than Mozart's symphonies to choreographic interpretation. In fact it may safely be said that the worse the symphony the more likely it is to make a good ballet. But that does not alter the fact that the symphony, of all musical forms the most concentrated, intellectual, and withdrawn from present action (as opposed to emotional retrospect), is of all musical forms the least suited to physical or dramatic expression.

That certain symphonic movements are "danceable" is really beside the point. A poem may be musical in the extreme and yet be totally unsuited to musical setting (the greater part of Keats for example). The choice of music for dancing may well be compared to the choice of words for music. The most suitable poems for music are either short lyrics definitely written for the purpose, such as the songs in the Elizabethan dramas which impose their own treatment, or rather loosely written poems with more poetic suggestion than form, such as the poems of Walt Whitman. Fletcher's "Sleep" from *The Woman Hater* is a moving poem when read in the study, but it is doubly moving when heard in Warlock's setting. Whitman's poems, or rather rough drafts for poems, become complete works of art only when supported by the music of Delius or Vaughan Williams. In each case the poem gains. But it is obvious that a speech from *Hamlet* or *The Duchess of Malfi*, an intellectual non-lyrical poem by Donne, or one of Keats's odes can only lose by any association with music because they are already complete works of art in themselves. If the music parallels their concentration and richness it will only distract our attention from the words; if it remains in the background allowing the words to speak for themselves then it is superfluous.

Exactly the same situation can be observed in the world of ballet. Tchaikovsky's short dance tunes or *variations* may be compared to madrigal verse. They "dance themselves" in the way an Elizabethan lyric "sings itself." For all their charm they are only heard to full advantage when in collaboration with the dance. (Imagine the flat effect of a concert performance of the brilliantly conceived *Blue Bird* numbers.) The music of the impressionist composers (in which I would include, of course, early Stravinsky) provides the equivalent of the loosely written *vers libre* of the Whitman type, even when it is specifically written for stage action. That is to say it has more pictorial suggestion than form and does not achieve artistic completeness until defined and pinned down by action. *Petrouchka* is meaningless in the concert-hall unless one knows the ballet; *L'Oiseau de Feu* is only possible when reduced to suite form and even then loses half its effect.

One is in no way decrying these composers by pointing this out. Tchaikovsky and Stravinsky are undoubtedly the two greatest composers the ballet has seen, the one representing the classical opera side of ballet, the other the music-drama side. They would indeed have failed as ballet composers were their work to be satisfying in the concert-hall. But a Beethoven symphony, like a speech in *Hamlet* or an ode by Keats, satisfies us completely in its present form. Any action which might accompany it would either be an irritating distraction or a superfluous echo.

That the greatest of stage composers were thoroughly conscious of the difference between real and imagined action, between statement and reflection can be seen clearly if we look at the work of two composers who divided their attention equally between the concert-hall and the theatre, Mozart and Tchaikovsky. While it would not be quite true to say that the essential style of their music changes when they write for the theatre, it is certainly true that the physique of their music changes. I can think of no tune in any Mozart opera which Mozart could have used as the first or second subject in a symphony, and the same is true of the tunes in Tchaikovsky's ballets. In such a dance as the *pas de deux* in *Lac des Cygnes*, Act II, the very shape of the fiddle solo is determined by the "lifts" in the choreography. We find no such melodic figuration in his symphonies, still less in any classicial symphonies. It is most interesting to compare the minuets Mozart actually wrote for dancing with the symphonic minuets in which the dance form merely crystallises some phase of emotion and does not call to action. It is even more interesting to compare the valses in Tchaikovsky's ballets with the valses in his Third and Fifth symphonies.

Impure symphonist though he was, Tchaikovsky only once included in his symphonies a movement more suited to the theatre than the concert-hall. I refer to the finale of the Second Symphony, a straightforward peasant dance which, apart from some sequential passages of development, is no more symphonic in style than the *Kazatchok* of Dargomizhky which it emulates. This movement, by the way, was the only piece of symphonic music (technically speaking) ever used by Diaghilev. The phrase "symphonic suite" as applied to *Scheherazade* has very little meaning, and it is worth noticing that the first movement, which most nearly approaches to symphonic style, was used as an overture only.

To say to the choreographer that he should restrict himself to ballet music written specifically as such by a master of the art like Tchaikovsky or Stravinsky is obviously a vain counsel of perfection. To start with, the supply of such music is by no means equal to the demand.

The days when the greatest composers turned naturally and easily to ballet seem to be gradually passing (it is a sign of the times that Stravinsky should have written only one true piece of ballet music since the war—*Le Baiser de la Fée*), and a large number of the ballets written by contemporary composers approach the art from far too literary and operatic a point of view. This is particularly true of the miming scenes where the average composer tries to suggest in the score each inflection of the action. He would be well advised to take a leaf out of Tchaikovsky's book. Tchaikovsky's miming scenes are always admirable because he is content to establish only the general atmosphere of the scene, and does not try to emphasise imaginary words in operatic recitative style. How tiresome by contrast is the opening of *The Three-Cornered Hat* where the music underlines every little detail in the scenario. Falla's ballet (admittedly a first-rate work when viewed as a whole) does not get really going until the dance of the neighbours, which though inessential from the dramatic point of view is good theatre for the simple reason that it is good ballet.

The supply of true ballet music, then, being so inadequate it is only natural that at least half the ballet repertoire should be founded on music written for its own sake. When this music is suited to the dance in texture and rhythm, and not too introspective or philosophical in mood, it can often be as satisfactory as ballet music written for the purpose: witness *Les Sylphides* among classical ballets, and *Cotillon* among modern ballets. But the question of arranging ballets to classical or non-dramatic music immediately raises the most important problem of all for the choreographer: How closely should the dancing follow the music?

There seems to be a growing theory that dancing which represents visually the formal devices and texture of the music must of necessity be pleasing to the musical mind. Nothing could be further from the truth. I am sure there must be innumerable musicians beside myself who experience the same feeling of exasperation when the choreographer turns the stage into a vast lecturer's blackboard and, by associating certain dancers with certain themes, proceeds to underline obvious formal devices in the music which any one of average intelligence can appreciate with half an ear. Literal translations from one language into another are always unsatisfactory and usually ridiculous. "Symphonic" ballets are no exception to this rule. Moreover, the choreographer is debasing his art if he thus makes dancing a mere visual *exposé* of the music. The dance should not be a translation of the music but an interpretation of it. It should not slavishly imitate the musical texture but should add a counter-subject of its own. Choreography which does this is truly contrapuntal, whereas choreography which interprets a fugue in the Dalcroze manner is merely a species of choreographical "vamping," far more harmonic than contrapuntal in feeling.

It is significant that Balanchine, who undoubtedly has the greatest technical knowledge of music among present-day choreographers, is also the most free in his treatment of the music. He is one of the few choreographers with the intelligence to realise that visual complexity is not the most suitable accompaniment to aural complexity. The reverse, surely, is the case. (I am not speaking now of dramatic, narrative ballets where the purple patches in the choreography must inevitably coincide with the purple patches in the story and music.) A complicated fugue occupies, or should occupy, so much of our aesthetic concentration that we cannot assimilate an equal elaboration of physical design at the same time. On the other hand a simple valse tune lends itself to the richest and most complex design on the stage.

I hope I may be pardoned a personal reference in pointing to two highly successful examples of the choreographic counterpoint I am trying to define. One was Ashton's treatment of a three-part *fugato* in *Pomona* as a lyrical dance for a *solo* dancer; the other was the astonishing choreographic fugue which Nijinska arranged to a purely homophonic passage in the finale of *Romeo and Juliet*. We can find examples of the same kind of thing even in the ballets of Massine, who for all his brilliant and indeed unsurpassed sense of purely choreographic design shows only a mechanical and superficial appreciation of musical design. The finales of *Amphytrion* and *Le Pas d'Acier*, for example, where he erects a choreographic structure of remarkable complexity on a comparatively simple musical basis, are to my mind far more successful than the finale of *Choreartium*, which rivals the music in complexity but never in intensity. These two ballets, however, were composed before he had started the vogue for "symphonic" ballet, which marks the nadir of the collaboration between music and the dance.

In a brief essay such as this it is impossible to do more than to adumbrate a few lines of approach to a highly controversial subject which as yet has received little serious attention. I have not attempted to propound anything in the nature of an aesthetic theory. The art of ballet is still too young for that. Ballet did not reach its Wagnerian stage until the pre-war Diaghilev days, and though it has made up since for lost time it is still inclined to lag behind. It will lag farther behind if choreographers, instead of finding new forms inspired by their own medium, pin themselves to forms which belong essentially to another medium, forms, moreover, which (save in a few rare instances) have already outlived their period of aesthetic significance.

Composer/Choreographer: A Symposium

by Louis Horst, Norman Dello Joio, Gunther Schuller, and Norman Lloyd

Louis Horst

In 1915 I had no particular interest in dance; I was a musician. I became musical director for Ruth St. Denis and Ted Shawn then because they thought that someone who had accompanied singers could also accompany dancers. At that time, there was no such thing as a dance accompanist.

Dance music then consisted of pieces selected from records—a bit of this and a bit of that. The dancer heard some music that made him feel like moving, and he interpreted what he heard. The idea back of it was that dance was considered the handmaiden of music. The dancer caught the mood of the music, and made a dance to it. If the score was too long—as it frequently was—I was asked to cut it. Often the cuts amounted to chasms. The method was invalid, both musically and choreographically, but this is what my first experiences of dance music were like.

Then we began to hear about what Mary Wigman was doing in Germany. She, we were told, thought of dance as an independent art, one that could come into being and exist without music. For her, the motivation was not the work of another person—the composer—but her own feelings. The dance was created from within.

When Martha Graham left the Denishawn company and created *Frontier*, she choreographed the entire dance to counts. After she showed me the dance, I wrote the music to the counts she gave me. We used the same procedure with *Primitive Mysteries*. Other composers have written for her, not from counts, but from a script. She outlined the action, or the mood, and set the duration of the section. Sometimes, with both methods, adjustments would have to be made. I would ask: "Could you continue this movement a few bars longer? I need more time to make this section musically complete."

Either way, the fact of starting with the dance is important, because the dance should be the center of interest, the point of tension. The music should be transparent, open and spacious, so the audience can

Source: From *Dance Perspectives*, Number 16, 1963.

I admire the dancer who brings out the emotional content of the music. To me, Antony Tudor is one of the most musical of choreographers. No matter what score he takes he seems to capture its essence. His choreography adds a needed dimension, while his individuality remains. And Martha Graham. Her choreography stems from the music but then goes off into areas that are hers alone. The work becomes a real duet.

Music has emotional connotations, over-all effects, that lead the listener to associate sounds with dramatic meanings. These are present for the choreographer to discover. Finally, music has an abstract life of its own, which persists even when the music is heard without the addition of the dance for which it was written.

Gunther Schuller

It is not in my nature as a person or an artist to state a categoric either-or position on a subject as general as the relationship of music to dance. As a composer I have experienced the choreographic treatment of my music in terms of several approaches, and discovered thereby that there is no single concept of translating music into physical movement that is inherently superior to any other. Ultimately it is a matter of artistic inspiration, imagination, and control of metier, and I would consider it theoretically possible that any reasonably enlightened conceptual approach would be capable of producing a work of art in the hands of a fine creative artist.

I am aware that there are two schools of thought regarding the role of the dance vis-a-vis the music to which it is choreographed. Some claim that the dance must be "autonomous." Quite apart from the semantic ambiguity of such a term, is it really possible for a dance movement to be autonomous of the music to which it is set? Somehow at the most fundamental level—and therefore precisely the most important, internal level—the choreographer receives *some* degree of stimulus from the music, and no matter to what extent he wishes to disguise this relationship, it is an inextricable part of the whole. The only truly "autonomous" dance is one which is unaccompanied.

This is not to say that the dance must therefore be of an illustrative nature. This seems to me to be the other extreme. A choreographic "illustration" of a given piece of music may serve a particular function in certain types of narrative dance, and it may be very entertaining. But aside from this exception, I think we would all agree that the dance —like music—is a language whose communicative power stands in exact ratio to its degree of abstraction. It can say so much precisely because (or when) it says nothing specific.

In this sense, it is perhaps true that all arguments regarding this aesthetic question reduce themselves to a matter of degree. Eliminating the two extremes of dance, on the one hand, as an illustrative decorative art and, on the other hand, as an allegedly autonomous abstraction of movement—it seems to me that all choreographers are *in varying degrees* after the same thing. It is ultimately a matter of the most personal subjective nature as to whether a choreographer looks upon his creation as a fusion of two media or as the superimposition of one over the other. We know of choreographers who let the music impose itself on their choreography in both its small and larger aspects.

Others have choreographic preconceptions to which the music is fitted, often to the extent of distorting or altering the music. I do not think this latter approach is ever justifiable if unilaterally carried out by the dancer, and it certainly does not create much mutual respect between dancers and musicians. The sins that have been committed by dancers in this respect are legendary, and I need not dwell on them here. Suffice it to say that it is very disturbing to a composer to contemplate a choreography which consistently ignores the metric and phrasing shapes of the music—and I am certain that such discrepancies make themselves felt in some dim way to even a lay audience. It is like reading a book in which the printer has put all the commas and periods in the middle of sentences and clauses.

Perhaps what I am trying to say is that the choreographer and dancer must choose between two conceptions: "paraphrase" or "parallel." Of the two, certainly the former is the preferable approach. If a piece of music is inspired in its content, it does not need a parallel translation into physical movement. This creates only a meaningless redundancy. A choreographic "paraphrase," on the other hand, can—through emphasis and statement at several levels—expand or concentrate the meaning of the music; it can reinterpret it in a different perspective; at its best it can add an extra dimension that the music itself cannot have. Such was the case, I believe, in Balanchine's remarkable Webern *Episodes*.

At this highest level such secondary questions as whether the music comes first, whether it should be written especially for a given dance, whether the dance movement should come first—all are irrelevant. Inspired creativity can cut through any seeming barriers between the two forms of expression.

Obviously more choreographers who can read music would be a help, although this is by no means the whole answer. At an uninspired level this can so easily lead to an academic parallelism between dance and music. Thus I come back to my original point, the truism that in the arts there are no formulas which guarantee a superior product; only artistic inspiration in conjunction with a high measure of technical skill can give us that. But if I had to make a plea for one as yet relatively untried method, it would be for having the composer—possibly in consultation with the choreographer—actually notate into the score, in very general terms, rhythm and movement patterns which could then be expanded into an actual choreography. This kind of collaborative effort would still leave the choreographer free to create the specifics of his dance. At the same time, with the basic structuring of the dance patterns built right into the music at its inception, I think one could guarantee a modicum of artistic and stylistic unity. Dance and music would both be fathered by a single germinal idea, divisible and indivisible at will depending on the needs of the work—an idea that would, at the minimum, guarantee the integration at a primary level of that element which fundamentally distinguishes dance and music (and the film) from all the other arts: the element of time. Time would be the unifying force, while the dance would deal separately with space, and music with sound—both revolving, so to speak, around the axis of time.

Norman Lloyd

In writing music for dance the composer should have but one aim: to create music that makes the total work successful. If the music, or a part of it, is good enough to stand on its own—so much the better. The composer will have scored a double bull's-eye when he writes music which suits the dance perfectly and also has enough interest in its own right to be heard as music. Copland's *Appalachian Spring* and Stravinsky's *Sacre* and *Petrouchka* achieved this. Parts—and only parts—of some of the finest dance scores can also be included in this category: Tchaikovsky's three ballets and Riegger's music for Doris Humphrey's *New Dance*. But what about the many successful dance scores that are not played as concert works? Are they less important or less valid than the self-sufficient ones? Where do the differences lie? These questions lead to a consideration of the nature of dramatic and theatrical music.

Dance, opera, a play with incidental music, and vocal music with a text are forms in which music is combined with movement, words, lighting, sets and/or costumes. These forms have ancient roots—many of them are traceable to primitive religious rituals. To relegate such music to a secondary place in a musical hierarchy, behind so-called "pure" or instrumental music is a bit naive. Such an attempt to rank different types of music shows a lack of understanding of the many natures of music, which exists for many different purposes and in many different ways. In comparisons one might say that a certain piece of instrumental music is more interesting than another piece of instrumental music, or that one dance score is more effective than another. What cannot be said is that one category, by its very nature, is better than another. Such reasoning would lead to the statement that any dull symphony is better than a fine dramatic score. Unfortunately, this approach to criticism is all too prevalent. It confuses intent with content. It attempts to narrow the experiences that a great art makes possible.

Why should dance music be singled out for such controversy? One does not ask of a song accompaniment that it sound well when played as a piano solo. Nor is it expected that the orchestral background of an opera become an independent concert piece. Of the four evenings of music in Wagner's *Ring of the Nibelungen* only a few excerpts, aside from the preludes, are ever played on orchestral programs. Similar statements could be made of such theatrical masterpieces as Mozart's *Don Giovanni* and Verdi's *Otello*. Yet a dance score which does what it sets out to do—that is, make a complete theatre piece—is criticized for not making its way on symphonic programs.

Since there are several different kinds of dance, there are different kinds of dance music. There is the dance of design where the pleasing patterns of the dancers counterpoint the flow of lyrical music. This lends itself to set forms, generous enough in length and breadth to make a receptacle into which a gifted composer pours music that can eventually stand by itself. Perfect examples are the various court dances of the seventeenth and eighteenth centuries which formed the basis of the ballets of their time.

Then there is the dance of mood, which allows the composer to write a score that is all of a piece. This is often short and a part of a long theatre work. Gluck's "Dance of the Blessed Spirits" and "Dance of the Furies" from his opera *Orpheus and Euridice* are such dances.

There is the dance that is primarily rhythmic, requiring a score that is itself highly rhythmic. The dance music of de Falla, Surinach, Bernstein and Ellington not only supports movement but has proven listenable in itself.

Opposed to such dances, and the opportunities they provide for the composer, is the dramatic dance. A composer following a purely dramatic form will find that it often refuses to be forced into a musical form. In the fugue or the sonata, phrase balances phrase, section balances section. Time is needed to accomplish the total effect of the form. The interest lies in how musical material develops, in how one harmony leads to another, in how suspense is built up so that the restatement of a theme comes as a welcome climax.

Dramatic music, on the contrary, makes its point *now*—immediately. It might use a shuddering tremolo in the strings, the throbbing of slow tympani beats, the ominous threat in the sound of a chord played by low, muted brass. Heard as isolated sounds in a concert piece such dramatic devices would leave the audience wondering what program the composer had in mind. The same audience would accept these sounds if they were used in an opera, dance, or film score to heighten the emotional impact of the whole work. The first great theatrical composer, Monteverdi, understood the necessity of making a dramatic point immediately when he used instrumental effects such as the tremolo and the pizzicato instead of relying on slower-acting harmonic sounds and melodic motion.

Musical interest versus dramatic impact is most evident at a circus. As an aerialist balances on the high wire the tension is built by a crescendo roll on the snare drum. The most beautiful score in the world cannot equal the effectiveness of that drum roll. Nor could any amount of thematic manipulation, clever as it might be, so focus the attention of the audience on the performer and make the collective pulses beat a bit faster. Comparable in effectiveness to the snare drum roll, but in a different part of the dramatic spectrum, is the muffled beat of drums accompanying a funeral procession. The hollow sound puts a damper on the heart beats of those who watch and listen. Yet neither of these drum sounds could be listened to as concert music.

Much dramatic music is gestural—that is, it imitates or suggests in sound what is happening in action. Carried to an extreme it becomes a kind of musical cartooning. In fact among film composers such a technique is called "Mickey-Mousing" (although the technique pre-dates Mr. Disney by many thousands of years). In European music the madrigal composers of the sixteenth century used running passages to accompany the word "run." Rameau, in the eighteenth century, used falling scale lines to accompany the descent of gods arriving on stage via cloud machines. The same composer wrote trills and short rushing patterns to suggest the movement of Zephyrs as they swept across the stage.

A study of Rameau's operas and ballets reveals the differences that separate excerptable dance music from motion music, which is so integrated with dramatic action that by itself it means nothing. It is the set pieces by Rameau—the minuets, bourrées and chaconnes—that have been made into orchestral suites. The dramatic gestural music is heard only in performances of the complete work.

Which aspect of Rameau's music is more important? We come back to the old question—is there special merit in dance music that is self sufficient?

There is no categorical "yes" or "no" answer. Each musical score must be thought about in terms of what it sets out to do and how well it does it. Beethoven understood this when he made vastly different treatments of the same theme for the finale of his ballet *The Creatures of Prometheus* and for the finale of his *Eroica* symphony. Beethoven was not the world's greatest theatrical composer, but he was one of the greatest composers of dramatic music. He knew that his symphonic treatment of the theme might have overwhelmed Vigano's choreography. On the other hand, the *Prometheus* variations would not have served well as the climax to one of the most gigantic of all symphonies. Does this mean that the *Prometheus* score is less good than the *Eroica?* For a symphony—yes. But the finale of the *Eroica* might not be good for a ballet.

Many music-lovers have adopted an attitude of preciousness, saying that a piece of music is too good to be used for dance. They might mean that it would present almost insurmountable problems. But they might also be giving voice to a kind of nonsensical, romantic hushed-voice reverence. Such biased criticism was used, for example, against Doris Humphrey when she made her beautiful dance to Bach's *Passacaglia in C Minor*. Such critics forget that the passacaglia was originally a dance form—from which came music. They treat certain musical works as though they were brought down by Moses along with the Ten Commandments. They forget that music is man-made, even though it is God-given.

Probably no piece of music is too good or too poor, too simple or too complex, to be used for a dance. What is needed is a choreographer with sufficient imagination to see in his mind the total effect of setting his movement to a certain piece of music. Leonide Massine, Anna Sokolow, Doris Humphrey, George Balanchine, Merce Cunningham, Martha Graham, Antony Tudor, and José Limón have shown us the dance possibilities in the dissimilar music of Offenbach, Berg, Britten, Bizet, Cage, Schuman, Mahler, and Purcell. If any of this music was "too good" or "too poor," the dances would have been unsuccessful instead of becoming *Gaité Parisienne*, *Lyric Suite*, *Ruins and Visions*, *Symphony in C*, *Antic Meet*, *Night Journey*, *Dark Elegies*, and *The Moor's Pavane*.

The Dance Element in Stravinsky's Music
by George Balanchine

In Stravinsky's music, the dance element of most force is the pulse. It is steady, insistent yet healthy, always reassuring. You feel it even in the rests. It holds together each of his works and runs through them all. The time in *Le Sacre* changes from measure to measure; in *Oedipus* the rhythms are four-square; in *Apollon* the patterns are uncomplicated, traditional; the *Symphony* of 1945 reviews almost everything he has done before. But in each work his pulse builds up a powerful motor drive so that when the end is reached you know, as with Mozart, the subject has been completely stated, is in fact exhausted.

Stravinsky's strict beat is his sign of authority over time; over his interpreters too. A choreographer should, first of all, place confidence without limit in this control. For Stravinsky's rhythmic invention, possible only above a stable base, will give the greatest stimulus to his own powers.

A choreographer can't invent rhythms, he only reflects them in movement. The body is his medium and, unaided, the body will improvise for a short breath. But the organizing of rhythm on a grand scale is a sustained process. It is a function of the musical mind. Planning rhythm is like planning a house, it needs a structural operation.

As an organizer of rhythms, Stravinsky has been more subtle and various than any single creator in history. And since his rhythms are so clear, so exact, to extemporize with them is improper. There is no place for effects. With Stravinsky, a fermata is always counted out in beats. If he intends a rubato, it will be notated precisely, in unequal measures. (Elsewhere, of course, a good instrumentalist, Milstein, for instance, or a resourceful dancer, can give the feeling of rubato in Stravinsky's music without blurring the beat.)

Stravinsky's invention is fascinating, not just because of his free shifting of bar lengths or accents. He can be very brilliant in this manipulation. But if he had merely followed the line of *Le Sacre* he would have burned out his own interest and ours too.

Source: From *Dance Index*, Volume VII, Numbers 10–12, Also published in *Stravinsky in the Theatre*, edited by Minna Lederman (New York: Da Capo, 1975), which was first published in book form in New York, 1949.

What holds me, now and always, is the vitality in the substance of each measure. Each measure has its complete, almost personal life, it is a living unit. There are no blind spots anywhere. A pause, an interruption, is never empty space between indicated sounds. It is not just nothing. It acts as a carrying agent from the last sound to the next one. Life goes on within each silence.

An interpreter should not fear (unfortunately many do) Stravinsky's calculated, dynamic use of silence. He should give it his trust and what's more, his undivided attention. In this use of time, in the extreme, never-failing consciousness of it, he will find one of the living secrets of Stravinsky's music.

Dazzling too is the contour of Stravinsky's melodic line, so carefully weighted and balanced, so jewel-sharp in the molding. It now appears to have absorbed and to reflect in wonderful transformation the whole dance idiom of Western music—the waltzes, polkas, gavottes, marches, can-cans, tangos and ragtimes; the inventions of Mozart and Gounod; of Offenbach, Lanner and Strauss; of Delibes and Tchaikovsky. . . .

People sometimes complain that Stravinsky is too deliberately complicated, that he makes himself remote. But may not the fault lie in their own carelessness and laxity? They call his music dry or dissonant. What do they mean? After all, dissonance makes us aware of consonance; we cannot have the cool shadow without light. And we know that to find a wine too dry is merely to express a personal limitation.

Speaking for myself I can only say Stravinsky's music altogether satisfies me. It makes me comfortable. When I listen to a score by him I am moved—I don't like the word inspired—to try to make visible not only the rhythm, melody and harmony, but even the timbres of the instruments. For if I could write music it seems to me this is how I would want it to sound.

And I don't understand either what is meant when Stravinsky's music is called too abstract. This is a vague use of words, as unclear to me as when my ballets are described that way. Does it mean that there is an absence of story, or literary image, or even feeling—just sound and movement in a disembodied state?

No piece of music, no dance can in itself be abstract. You hear a physical sound, humanly organized, performed by people. Or you see moving before you, dancers of flesh and blood, in a living relation to each other. What you hear and see is completely real.

But the after-image that remains with the observer may have for him the quality of an abstraction. Stravinsky's music, through the force of its invention, leaves strong after-images. I myself think of *Apollon* as white music, in places as white-on-white. . . . For me the whiteness is something positive (it has in itself an essence) and at the same time abstract. Such a quality exerts great power over me when I am creating a dance; it is the music's final communication and fixes the pitch that determines my own invention.

Whether a ballet has a story, like *Le Baiser de la Fée*, or none, like *Danses Concertantes*, the controlling image for me comes from the music. This is different of course from the method of Fokine. Take *Petrouchka*, for instance. You can see that what he has chiefly in mind are the characters of the story. He thinks of a coachman on a Russian street and therefore he recalls the stereotyped folk-movement of beating the chest with the arms, over and over, to keep warm. The music accommodates him by supplying the right beat—here Stravinsky uses folk-tunes and they serve Fokine very well. But perhaps Rimsky-Korsakov would have done even better! In the death of *Petrouchka*, however, it is doubtful whether Stravinsky's marvelous passage for wind instruments quite accurately represents what is happening on the stage.

Stravinsky's effect on my own work has been always in the direction of control, of simplification and quietness.

Rossignol, in 1925, was a first attempt, an exercise set me by Diaghilev. The problem was to dance a story with a Chinese background, already composed as an opera. But *Apollon* three years later was a collaboration.

Apollon I look back on as the turning point of my life. In its discipline and restraint, in its sustained oneness of tone and feeling the score was a revelation. It seemed to tell me that I could dare not to use everything, that I, too, could eliminate. In *Apollon*, and in all the music that follows, it is impossible to imagine substituting for any single fragment the fragment of any other Stravinsky score. Each piece is unique in itself, nothing is replaceable.

I examined my own work in the light of this lesson. I began to see how I could clarify, by limiting, by reducing what seemed to be multiple possibilities to the one that is inevitable. The ballet, *Pastorale*, which I had set previously to a score by Georges Auric, contained at least ten different types of movement, any one of which would have sustained a separate work.

It was in studying *Apollon* that I came first to understand how gestures, like tones in music and shades in painting, have certain family relations. As groups they impose their own laws. The more conscious an artist is, the more he comes to understand these laws, and to respond to them. Since this work, I have developed my choreography inside the framework such relations suggest.

Apollon is sometimes criticized for not being "of the theatre." It's true there is no violent plot. (A thread of story runs quietly through it, however.) But the technique is that of classical ballet which is in every way theatrical and it is here used to project sound directly into visible movement.

Le Baiser de la Fée, which I first arranged in 1936, took me a step further in simplifying. It has a freer, easier use of repetition, as in the grand pas classique of the scene in the mill. And again taking my cue from Stravinsky, who in *Le Baiser* makes a specific quotation from Tchaikovsky, I modeled my choreography after the Petipa style.

Jeu de Cartes and *Danses Concertantes*, in contrast to these earlier scores, are more playful. They suggest the Italian spirit of the commedia dell'arte. Though not alike in texture, both are rhythmically complex. So in them I have used the bodies of dancers to feel out this volatile quality of the rhythm. Perhaps that is why as ballets they seem to the public more theatrical than *Apollon*, which is rhythmically simple.

Stravinsky, as a collaborator, breaks down every task to essentials. He thinks first, and sometimes last, of time duration—how much is needed for the introduction, the pas de deux, the variations, the coda. To have all the time in the world means nothing to him. "When I know how long a piece must take, then it excites me."

We can't measure yet what Stravinsky has given to the dance or to music. Like Delibes and Tchaikovsky, who elaborated the dance variation and with it composed full-bodied works for the theatre, he too has organized great forms for the use of dancing. But at the same time he constantly draws elements of the dance into our broader musical speech. For dancing he has extended the range of music. To music he brings his own special eloquence of movement continuously felt and most completely expressed.

Nearly forty years ago he began to deliver his amazing works to the theatres of the world. Each of his periods has been a milestone in contemporary art. Today he shows us the humanist values that bind the past to the present. His new scores, grave and deliberate, suggest the discipline and the grandeur of the heroic human body. Stravinsky is himself an Orpheus of the twentieth century.

Décor and Costume

by Alexandre Benois

It is essential in ballet to differentiate between theory of décor and theory of costume. Admitted that the ultimate aim of any spectacle (and more especially ballet) is the preservation of mood or atmosphere, to which all the component parts should contribute, it follows that décor and costume must blend together into the common harmony. Nevertheless, the conditions governing décor differ from those governing costume. Décor plays no immediate part in the action—in the actual performance of the players—yet the main essential of ballet lies in its action, whether dance or pantomime; and outside action, ballet, as such, does not exist. This, then, is the somewhat independent attitude of décor. Décor is the "background" in front of which something is performed—that something being nearly always detached from it.[1] Costume, on the other hand, takes a part in the performance itself and aids the actor in creating the character demanded by the context.

Nevertheless, though not participating in the action, décor plays a substantial rôle in ballet, at any rate in the traditional classical ballet, which to a considerable number of followers, including the writer, is the only real ballet. I am not referring here to suites of dances, *divertissements* and such: we are talking of ballet, and by that word I mean that particular and separate form of theatrical spectacle in which all the varied elements must blend into a whole to constitute what Wagner called "Gesamtkunstwerk." It was with this "real" ballet that I fell in love, ardently and irrevocably, on the very day when I first witnessed it, when, being still a child, I was quite incapable of any theoretical appreciations. It is to this "real" ballet that I have remained faithful all my life, and it is to its service that I have dedicated the greater part of my creative power. Lastly, it was this "real" ballet that we took, with Diaghilev, to show to Europe—to that Europe where it was first born and reared but which, at the time of our arrival, had contrived to lose with it all vital relationship.

Source: From *Footnotes to the Ballet: A Book for Balletomanes*, edited by Caryl Brahms (London: Peter Davies, 1936).

[1] Décor takes a part in the action only in such instances as when a player makes his exit through a door cut in the scenery, looks out of a window, etc. [Benois' note, as are the others in the essay.]

It is for this real traditional ballet that I, with all my soul, wish further prosperity and progress. But do not imagine that my feelings are prompted by that conservative inertness so easily attributed to people who have reached a certain age—or, if you prefer it, dotards. I am not antagonistic to new form; it is inconceivable that I should desire to turn a live art like ballet into a sort of museum relic. Ballet must live and progress. But all the same ballet must remain ballet—that is, in the theatrical form that was evolved in the eighteenth and nineteenth centuries and which to its followers is immeasurably precious. To protect that form ballet must remain "Gesamtkunstwerk," that is, maintain in its entirety all its combining elements, among which, of equal importance with music and dancing, is scenery—i.e. décor.

Décor is that content which achieves the transformation of a ballet into a picture. Through décor "Gesamtkunstwerk" ballet becomes a branch of painting—a branch at once enchanting and exciting. If so many artists, painters (not merely professional decorators), have bent their forces to ballet, then the explanation of the phenomenon lies in the fact that ballet offered the painter an exceptionally wide field for his fantasy. Here he could create canvases gigantic and imposing, but besides this the artist found in ballet the most complete fulfilment of his dreams. He was present while the portrait created by his brush awoke and blossomed into music-pulsating life.

The purpose of décor is to fix the time and place of the action. As the curtain rises it informs the spectator *à quoi s'en tenir*—when and where the action passes and also the type of spectacle that he may expect. Décor is the introduction to spectacle, the creator of the desired poetic atmosphere. But of course not all scenery achieves this somewhat ambitious effect. It succeeds only in those cases where it is the product of a genuine aesthetic emotion, and further (and more particularly) of a painstaking concentration by the creating artist upon his problem. On the whole, the perfect ballet décor can be achieved only by an artist who understands ballet. He must study its specialised interests with no less attention than its actual interpreters. The problem of designing décor for a ballet is a difficult and responsible problem; however, when one does succeed in solving it, the result is sheer beauty, and the first to rejoice in that beauty is the creator himself—the artist.

What then is this décor of ballet, and in what way does it differ from the décor of drama, opera, and other theatrical spectacle? The difference is fairly obvious. The ordinary drama deals in the main with problems of psychology, and aims, in the majority of cases, at portraying real life. When, however, drama leaves this realist basis it loses its specific form and its décor may then borrow qualities that strictly speaking belong to the décor of ballet or opera. Plays such as *A Midsummer Night's Dream* or *The Tempest* call for the type of décor that is styled "operatic or ballet." On the other hand, *Henry VIII*, *Tartuffe*, *The School for Scandal*, *The Government Inspector*, or *La Puissance de Tenêbres* can only be performed amid scenery that conveys an impression of reality. In plays it is the text that dominates; ballet is built upon poetry and music, and enacted on a plane that bears but a vague relation to the material world. Opera falls half-way between ballet and drama—which explains why some operas are performed with scenery equally suitable for plays (e.g., *Carmen*), while others (*Faust*, *Aida*) are performed in décor that could also serve for ballet. In opera both words and music are significant; there are operas that approximate to Drama (and Realist Drama at that) and there are operas, built on verse and fantasy, in which Realism has no part. It is possible to add many shades to this somewhat rough-and-ready classification, and it might be interesting to draw up a list of operas, subdivided according to their tendency of approach to the kingdoms of Thalia and Melpomene, or the kingdom of Terpsichore. Entering this last kingdom, we, in any case, find ourselves in an absolutely separate domain.

The décor of ballet, as such, undeniably exists, and stands out as far more definite and clear-cut than the décor of opera, which falls halfway between the décor of drama and ballet. On the other hand, to define the particular points that distinguish the décor that is essentially ballet is not easy. Generally, in art, definitions are dangerous, dangerous even in those cases when in making use of some verbal expression we quite clearly envisage the meaning we are trying to convey. In no other art is the explanation of established technical terms quite so difficult as in ballet. Every *balletomane* is conscious of the images called up in his mind by the use of any particular technical term, but to formulate these images into words is at once cramping and undesirable, like the contact of something coarse to something delicate and fragile.

Much the same may be said regarding the problem of décor for ballet. A sort of abstract theory of décor, with an undefined ideal, indubitably exists; but any attempt to confine that ideal within the bounds of a rigid verbal formula would be restricting. Incidentally many styles of décor approach and even conform completely to this undefined ideal. Charming, for instance, as portrayals of ballet décor, were the baroque fantasies of Bibben, Gaspar and Valerian. Delightful, the ballet of the Romantic Epoch, with the settings of Cicéri, Quaglio and Roller. In quite another vein were the scenic inventions of Gonzalo, Sanquirico and Corsini in the Imperial Epoch. And in yet another vein, bold in conception, sonorous in colour, the décors of the early twentiety century. Certain décors are almost over-rich with innumerable details; in others, in accordance with the conception of the artist, everything is reduced to the simplest synthesis. The décor of ballet can also be created with the aid of the system originated by Appia, in which painted décor is replaced by plastic forms, terraces, platforms, columns, staircases, etc. But all the same the mirage of ballet undoubtedly blends better with painted scenery, which gives the artist full scope for his imagination and leaves the stage unencumbered for dancing.

The subdivision of the types of ballet décor hinges on the subdivision of the types of ballet. Some ballets demand the heroic note in their décor, others an elegiac languidness, others tenderness. There are even ballets that call for a certain amount of realism or the grotesque, foreign to the majority of ballets. But though we may feel that there is something in common uniting all these diversities, yet we cannot define that "common," even as we cannot define which type of music is essentially "ballet music." Why, even the condition that the music should lend itself to dancing—i.e. be subordinate to a distinct rhythm—can no longer be considered "irrevocable," as many ballets have been composed during the past few years where the music could not be accurately described as such. And yet these ballets can be ranked as successful and even included among those conforming to the ballet "ideal."

To me, at any rate, it seems an undeniable assertion that any ballet spectacle must include décor, and further that such décor must possess its own individual character. Possibly some people may find in this a sort of propaganda—*pro doma sua*—possibly they will imagine that the decorator is defending his own professional interests. But the point is that I am not a professional decorator—merely a man passionately in love with theatre and more passionately still in love with ballet. Even if part of my life has been devoted to the design of décor (by the way not only ballet décor, but also the décor of opera and drama), yet always in the foreground of my life I have been primarily a spectator—one of the audience. My assertion that décor must exist is based on my experience as a spectator, inasmuch as I could only extract complete satisfaction from ballet in those cases where décor played a significant part in the formation of some complete exciting impression.

I have nothing against the so-called dance-recitals, and I willingly admit of having been impressed by the dances of Loie Fuller, Isadora, Sakharoff, and other dancers or troupes of dancers performing against a neutral background—a background that depicts nothing. I do not deny that these dancing recitals come within the kingdom of aesthetics. But they are not ballet, and the pleasure I derive from them differs sharply from the specialised type of pleasure I extract from ballet. Ballet, real ballet, is that type of stage spectacle which, even though it budded among the people of the very distant past, and passed through many stages of experiment, did not flower into full form until the second half of the eighteenth century—a flowering due to the so-called "reform" of Noverre, which in reality was not so much a reformation as the uncovering of a submerged ideal. This ideal, having at last crystallised into a distinct form, has survived to this day, adapting itself to the changing tastes, but remaining true to its fundamental doctrine. Into this form of ballet, into whose component parts enter rhythmic movement (dancing), dramatic action (pantomime), and music, must enter also design (décor). Among the primary conditions of the ideal "Gesamtkunstwerk" is the equal right of all these parts to expression, though any and all of them must be subjugated to the mutual idea. When all these conditions are fulfilled, only then is the result real ballet and only then do we get that miracle which for lack of a better term I call "balletic suggestion."

I repeat that I became a *balletomane* from my very first contact with ballet; and it seems to me that my capacity for this spontaneous enthusiasm was due to my immediate instinctive understanding of ballet, which lay not in the separate evaluation of this or that element entering into its composition, but in the blend of all these elements into a harmonious conjunction. The impression made on me in 1887 by *La Bayardère*, that dear old ballet of romantic dreams and exotic fantasy, was so powerful that I actually fell ill with ecstasy, and in my delirium raved of processions with multi-handed idols, angels in muslin dresses and palm-surrounded temples. On my subsequent visits to ballet (I was taken to the theatre comparatively often, and twice a year, at Christmas and Easter without fail, to the ballet) I came to appreciate more and more that charm particular to ballet that I could find in no other spectacle, even though I derived considerable pleasure from both comedy and opera. Gradually, and without in any way becoming conscious of it, I began to understand ballet, so that with the arrival of Virginia Zucchi in 1885, though only a boy of fifteen, I merited the title of *balletomane* in the fullest sense of the word. My balletomania infected the friends of my Gymnasia and University days, which was not surprising, as my ardour for ballet was combined with the fiercest propaganda on its behalf. Deriving, as I did, such unique sensations from ballet, I endeavoured by every means in my power to persuade my friends into sharing these sensations, and it needed only my urging to stimulate their latent appreciation not only of the theatre as a whole but of ballet in particular. In that period (*Sturm und Drang*) I developed an antipathy to many quite harmless and even talented young men, whose attitude to ballet suggested to me a certain obstinacy, and even parted with those of them who persisted in regarding ballet as something not quite dignified. Remember that at that time the majority of Russians looked upon ballet as one of the manifestations of the senseless, depraved luxuries that characterised the Tsarist régime. It is interesting to note that Serge Diaghilev, arriving from the provinces in 1890, more or less shared this outlook on ballet and was only gradually infected by our enthusiasm, so that finally he caught balletomania but without suspecting the enormous part he was destined to play in its future history.

However, after Diaghilev had joined us, eighteen years had to elapse before that momentous day when our balletomania took on a creative character. Our first entry into the public arena was as critics of our journal *Mir Isskustva* (The World of Art), a journal which during the six years that it flourished exerted an enormous influence on Russian art and culture in general. It was under our keen collaboration and criticism that there emerged what gradually became known as Russian Ballet. Off we went to show Europe that towards which we all (though now grown from raw youngsters into mature adults) still retained the enthusiasm of youth. Off we went to show the world not merely the art of Russian dancing, not merely our gifted Russian artists, not merely our wonderful Russian music, but ballet—ballet in its entirety—real ballet.

However, having undertaken the job of exporting a so-called Russian ballet, we had little desire to show Europe something ready-made, something already in existence, something that had already delighted us for many years. Instead we preferred to create something quite fresh, something more nearly approximating to the ideal fixed in our minds, and it was with such ballet, complete in every detail, and as yet unperformed in its native land, that we ventured abroad in 1909. Included in our project of acquainting the world with Russian ballet, on a par with dancing and music, was painting-décor—the ensemble of a theatrical picture. The main initiative of the whole undertaking came from the artists, and these artists were not professional decorators but emancipated painters, whose outlook on art and the theatre was unhampered by any professional tradition or routine.

Incidentally one of the ballets with which we opened in Paris had already been performed on the stage of the Maryinsky Theatre. This was my ballet *Le Pavillon d'Armide.* Its ultra-romantic plot was the conception of Théophile Gautier, its expressive music composed by Tcherepnin, to whom I was allied by our cult of Terpsichore. But the fact that *Le Pavillon* had already been included in the repertoire of the Imperial theatres does not contradict what I have already written. *Le Pavillon* was first presented to the world only a year before our Paris invasion, and its décor then appeared somehow as the prelude to the adventure. While designing *Le Pavillon* I was stimulated by the desire to acquaint the public with my own conception of ballet, which differed slightly from the then existing tradition. I was what is known as "*plus royaliste que le roi,*" a more fanatical follower of ballet than the orthodox *balletomane;* the latter being wholly in accord with all that which in our glorious St. Petersburg ballets suggested to me a certain decline and decay. In my ballet everything had to be somehow essentially "balletic" and conform to that ideal that I had for so many years carried next to my heart. As a great lover of pantomime I assigned to pantomime the major part in the development of my subject. *Le Pavillon d'Armide* begins with pantomime and ends with pantomime. The middle part of the ballet, however, is devoted to the art of dancing, constituting in its essentials a large-scale *divertissement*, representing the celebrations with which Armide fêtes Rinaldo. But even this fête as a whole assumes a melancholy and, towards it close, almost a nightmarish character, as it takes place in the enchanted gardens of King Hydraot, with its surging fountains and the grandiose castle in the distant background. Towards the end of the fête the shadows of black clouds trail across the brilliant colours of the groups of courtiers, while glowing lanterns penetrate this *crépuscule*, trailing a sort of funereal note across the whole festival. The uniting link between this finale to the fête and the subsequent tragic development of the story, was a symphonic number depicting in the manner of the *pastorale* the coming of dawn dispersing the shadows of the night. . . .

Being at the same time both the author and the artist responsible for the setting of my ballet, I endeavoured by strictly picturesque means to interpret the same diversity, the same succession of moods as was imprisoned in the context. Of the three scenes, two took place in the magnificent but neglected arbour of the middle eighteenth century, in the shelter of which a traveller overtaken by the storm finds refuge. The middle scenes were entirely given over to the joyous visions dreamt by this youth, in which by the error of a goblin, he finds himself the betrothed of daemon beauty. The contrast in décor corresponded with the contrast in costume. The pantomime—the prologue and epilogue—were played in the ordinary costumes of the Restoration period: the hero was dressed in a travelling raglan with tall top-hat and jack-boots; her servants were in livery. On the other hand in the inner scenes everything shone with gold, silver, and precious stones, everything was reminiscent of the court of the Versailles Masquerade. Heads were adorned in golden-curled wigs. Innumerable Arab boys in green caftans lent an Oriental note. The satins of *robe ronde* and *pannier* worn by the ladies of the court were thickly embroidered with baroque designs. Crusaders in silver coats of mail wore high plumage in their helmets. Heralds trailed enormous trains behind them.[2]

My greatest difficulty was in judging how far I had succeeded in realising my own dreams of ballet. At that time I was inclined to consider much of it as still far removed from my idea of perfection. But nevertheless its performance on the St. Petersburg stage proved a dazzling success—and that in spite of the ill-natured intrigues of my enemies, and the shocked comments of the orthodox critics. It made a profound impression on the whole circle of my friends, among them Diaghilev. Our plan for the presentation of Russian ballet abroad dates from that success, when it was decided to show *Le Pavillon d'Armide* to Europe. It was also the production of *Le Pavillon* that saw the beginning of my acquaintance with Fokine, who I afterwards introduced into our circle, and with V. Nijinsky, who had then just concluded his training in the Ballet School. When it became clear that the antagonistically inclinced directorate of the Imperial theatres were hardly likely to lend us the scenery and costumes that we had just created for them, we decided that for Paris we would re-create the same *Le Pavillon* in its entirety, a decision that I personally welcomed, as I hoped in this second edition to avoid the mistakes that my inexperience had occasioned in the first. Actually this second Paris version of *Le Pavillon* emerged more complete, more sharply defined in every sense. In context and music the improvement was due mainly to a certain amount of "cutting" and an even more notable improvement was achieved in décor and costume.

In the first St. Petersburg version both décor and costume suffered

[2] Diaghilev ranked this scene from *Le Pavillon* as the most magnificent of his then existing repertoire, and had it produced at the gala performance at Covent Garden on the occasion of the coronation of His Majesty King George V in 1911. For this performance all the costumes were renovated and, in addition, I designed a few further effects of super-magnificence.

to some extent from overloading. This was the result of my effort to instil into my "baby" everything that seemed of interest. I could not in this, my first effort, ward off the temptation to be different—to "show them." In the Paris version of *Le Pavillon* I succeeded in achieving a better harmony, a greater calm, and at the same time more vitality, and as in form, so in colour. This version corresponded far more nearly to my ideal.

Many people may fail to understand why we, the fanatical worshippers of Russian ballet[3]—the ballet that we admired on the stage of the Maryinsky Theatre—did not, in addition to *Le Pavillon*, select one or two of the ballets which we professed to love so much, for example, *The Sleeping Beauty*, or *Raymonda*. I imagine that if we could have conceived the bold project of showing Russian ballet to Europe at the time when these ballets were first staged, then it is probable that we should have chosen these very ballets, and that without making a single change in any of them. We would have performed an act of simple piety towards that which we at the time worshipped almost unconditionally.

But by 1909, nineteen years after the production of *The Sleeping Beauty* and ten years after the production of *Raymonda*, we had had time to grow up, our sense of values had become more mature. And in any case the settings for these ballets, governed like everything else in theatre by the merciless law of perishability, had decayed to a considerable extent. The scenery was faded, the costumes falling to pieces. Further, assuming that we were prepared to renovate the settings for this ballet, assuming even that we were in accord with their music, ideas, and style, we were far from being in accord with their past

[3] The subject is a highly debatable one, inasmuch as what is to-day held to be Russian ballet is actually something that is nationally Russian. In Russia and only in Russia till the end of the nineteenth century survived inviolate the classic form of ballet, originated and evolved on the stages of Italy, Paris, Berlin, and Vienna; which, by some miracle, remained intact under the Russian Tsars, while fading out in the places where it had been born. In reality we showed Paris their own child, where its presentation towards the close of the nineteenth century had become obscured by all sorts of blind prejudices and mutilating routine—in fact all that to which people refer as "tradition." The distinguishing note of Russian ballet was that it managed to preserve all the real tradition, practically unhampered by routine, and for this preservation of authentic tradition full credit must be given to that director of the Imperial theatres, who being himself a genuine lover of ballet, brought Russian ballet to life during the whole of his twenty-year management. I am referring to Ivan Alexandrovitch Vsevolojsky. In 1880 his influence was already apparent, and as his influence grew stronger and took on a more constructive form so did my own enthusiasm develop. Ivan Vsevolojsky is really the man responsible for the awakening of Russian ballet, and the culminating point of this awakening was his production in 1889–90 of *The Sleeping Beauty* with music by Tchaikovsky.

manner of presentation, and especially with the past décor—a décor that was the product of a professional routine, dull, vain and tasteless. And as it was out of the question to transport that which was still dear to us but "unpresentable," it became a temptation to create for ourselves something quite new—not a "neo" to startle everybody by its originality but a "neo" to embody all the beloved old with a fresh and stimulating manner of presentation. This was also much more "amusing" (in the modern use of the word), and the "amusing" in general influenced us largely in all our undertakings.

It must be added that, in addition to their faded sceneries, the Moscow and Maryinsky also possessed some new ones. However, we did not care to make use of these either. All that was old and dear to our hearts could not be shown, as it had decayed and withered. The new displeased us—although we were the first to admire the purely technical merits of two Moscow artists, Korovin and Golovin, with both of whom our relations were friendly and whose work we admired, defending it from the attacks of both the public and Press. They were accused of leanings towards decadence, an accusation which by the way was also frequently levelled against us—that is myself, Bakst, Serov, Roerich and Doboujinsky. Korovin and Golovin occupy an entirely unique niche in the annals of scenic painting. With them, dating from their work, for the independent opera of *S. Mamontoff*, began the attraction to scenic design of the outside artists—and it was their work that was largely responsible for revealing the aesthetic potentialities of décor. Korovin and Golovin directed a blast of fresh air on to the stage; under their brushes colours rang out, sang with a new element of sonorousness, and even their style, which consisted of reducing décor to the greatest simplicity—to the barest essentials—contained in itself some quality of deliberate fascination.[4]

But Korovin and Golovin, though achieving triumph after triumph in designing sets for opera and drama, could not scale anything like these heights when it came to ballet. Much as they delighted us by

[4] After the retirement of the famous theatrical designer, André Roller (1805–88), a host of skilful masters joined the Imperial theatres: M. A. Shishkov, M. I. Bocharov, Ivanov, and later, C. K. Allegri and P. I. Lambin. All these were first-rate practitioners and connoisseurs of perspective. They succeeded in creating canvases in which the traditional craftsmanship blended admirably with the poetical. Intermixed with their work, there was also the work of foreigners—the Frenchman Levot and the Italian Tzykarelli. The décors of the latter proved that the art, once represented by Bibbieni and Gonzaro, was still alive in Italy. Some of the work created by the above artists for ballet approached to some extent the balletic ideal and contributed largely to the success of some of the productions, notably *The Sleeping Beauty*. But in general, décor after the Roller and before the Tsarist period, suffered from slackness and lack of style.

their picturesque settings for *Carmen*, *The House of Ice*, and *Boris Godounov*, so did they let us down when they tried their hand on *The Enchanted Mirror* and *The Sleeping Beauty*. I would even go as far as to say that it was from the moment that their conception of ballet décor appeared on the stage that our conception of the balletic ideal crystallised into sharper outline. It was here that the differences of our aesthetic training became emphasised. Both artists possessed flourish and vigour, but at the same time they disappointed us with their lack of finer taste and understanding. The Moscow school of ballet differed sharply from the St. Petersburg school in that particular, which its followers described as "the despotism of temperament" and which, to us, appeared as akin to ignoring the very essence of ballet. The Moscow-ism of Golovin and Korovin shocked and offended us in ballet, which is why we used the work of these artists only in *Boris Godounov* (by Golovin) in 1908 and *Ivan the Terrible* (by Korovin) in 1909, and did not commission their work when it came to ballet, the task nearest to our hearts, the task that we felt that we knew and understood so much better than they.

Here it is appropriate to mention the one feature—and quite a substantial feature at that—that was entirely absent from our project of exporting Russian ballet, and that is "snobbism," in the "Continental" meaning of this English word. We produced Russian ballet with the idea of sharing our rapture with the audiences of the world—and we had attained this rapture from that which was already in existence and evinced only a few symptoms of an approaching decline. It was never in our minds to create new Russian ballet music; our most gifted composers had presented ballet with several *chefs-d'œuvres*, and our selected balletmaster, Fokine, was merely a "renovator," not by any means a fanatical innovator. Fokine himself was far too deeply in love with what had helped to formulate his aesthetic consciousness to wish to destroy it and create instead something essentially his own and entirely original.

And we, even less, desired to destroy and create something "never yet seen on any stage"—we, the painters Bakst, Roerich, Anisfeld. It is understood, of course, that we were far from desiring merely to copy the old, even though we loved it. Naturally, all that we produced was new, but it was not actuated by the desire to startle—*coûte que coûte*—by its modernity. It emerged in all sincerity, even as the new must inevitably emerge in all those cases when it is born in the soil of enthusiasm, and that enthusiasm we had in abundance.

In general we had no intention of separating décor from one of its potent means of scenic seduction—from illusion—and from one of the tried methods of creating illusion—from perspective. But I personally refrained from reproduction and perspective and its consequences. It has so happened that this problem during the past few years has become very complex and obscure. Modernism (the strange blend of absolute, rigid, immutable laws that are allied under that term) has ordered the theatre to turn its back on illusion, under the plea that all this is somehow "puerile," and gradually this abstention from illusion has become a principle, almost a fashion.

However, everything else in the theatre has remained obedient to illusion, and one cannot take a step without recognising this fact. Why, even such an incorrigible experimenter as Meyerhold (who clutters up the stage with trestles, props and ladders, and uses a bare wall as a background) still demands that his actors should represent real figures and that their acting should convey the impression of something living—that is, that it should give the illusion of life! And are not the conquests achieved by the cinematograph as much conditional on the photographic reproduction of the surrounding settings as on the drama depicted? The art of the cinema attains a height of illusion undreamt of by the theatre, even in the days of its greatest craftsmanship in illusionist painting. On the other hand, precisely that which does not permit the theatre to attain the absolute illusion of the cinema imposes special boundaries and special demands on illusion in the theatre. But this does not affect the principle of illusion; it merely confirms it.

Photographic illusion would be particularly undesirable in the more established branches of theatrical art—in ballet—but it does not follow from this that ballet must be barred from all means of theatrical "conviction" and among them the verisimilitude of illusion in its setting. It is only with the "persuasiveness" of the theatrical setting that there is born the mood of the ballet, and this persuasion, this sense of rightness, can be attained even in those instances when it seems as if everything that is happening on the stage is contrary to sober reason. Music takes the predominant rôle in ballet, but this music only fulfils its basic function when it contains the power of persuasion, something spellbinding that compels us to believe in the most improbable occurrences. For this reason Delibes, Tchaikovsky, Stravinsky must all be ranked as first-rate composers of ballet music, inasmuch as their work, quite apart from any musical merits, possesses that wonderful power of "persuasion," inducing us to accept unquestionably all that we are seeing and hearing.

The magic side of this reaction to ballet is particularly surprising, as it would seem at first glance that ballet, by its very muteness, must spoil illusion. But in practice, this muteness aids illusion, while in opera the effect of the characters singing their words nearly always spoils it. The dancing on the stage only underlines the music, its rhythm ranks somehow as a "second" music. Of course, in those cases where the dances are merely numbers to display the virtuosity of the artists, there is no illusion; but then, though the spectacle may be agreeable, there is also no ballet. A dance in itself does not pretend to illusion. But dancing, when it takes part in the action and does not contradict the illusion, is the most indispensable part of ballet. And this applies not only to the *pas d'action*, a word that can cover a whole programme of ballet, but to other dances when they emerge naturally from the context, when they do not acquire an independence of their own apart from the unity of the action. The main reason for the decline of ballet in Europe was the neglect of this Principle of Persuasiveness. Everything was focused upon the dancing, with a resultant confusion of ballet with its genre; and ballet, having lost all power to persuade, began to resemble nothing but a senseless jumble or revue.

It is to this same contempt for "persuasion," for illusion, that may be attributed the gradual disappearance of the male element from the European stage. With the disappearance of the belief in ballet as a dramatic representation, the whole outlook on ballet became light-hearted—it became looked upon as almost nothing more than the evolutions of pretty and reasonably accessible "*petites femmes.*" When we Russians brought with us in 1909 not only first-rate *ballerine* but first-rate male dancers—among them one genius—Paris looked upon it as something quite out of the ordinary. And even though this same Paris had in its time applauded the Vestris and more recently the members of Petipa's dynasty. And it had so happened that it was one of the Petipas, Marius, whose long and unremitting service had succeeded in preserving on the Russian stage the real basis of ballet—those strict relations that called for, among other things, the inclusion of the male element, on a par with the female. This demand is based on the fact that it is only with the presence of both sexes that ballet develops real dramatic effect, becomes theatrical art in the full sense of the word, and acquires "persuasiveness."

Thus both in music and dancing, ballet must be convincing, must persuade, must create illusion. Why then expel illusion from the third of the arts that make up the ballet spectacle, from that very art that up to now had contributed most of all to illusion—from painting? No scenic illusion is required for those theatrical compositions of a dancing character, in which everything is co-ordinated into a sort of abstract pattern. But such compositions are not ballet in the strictest sense of the word. On the other hand, the actual forms of illusion are of a varied character. It is not always necessary for full-size palaces, halls, city streets, mountains, to appear on the stage, neither is it imperative for any of these to appear in realist guise—to resemble the real thing. Illusion does not demand a complete *trompe-l'œil*, i.e. that the separate parts that compose the scene should each produce an absolute effect of reality. In many cases one can manage without that, and sometimes it is even useful to refrain from it. For *Pulcinella*, Picasso composed a décor that creates a complete illusion of a night in Naples. We believed both in that toy house, in that childishly painted moon, and in that barque. And all of it, according to scheme, blended miraculously with the paradoxical nature of the music. Another example: In his first version of *Carnaval*, Bakst hung his scene with deep blue curtains with a narrow ornamental frieze at the top. The players entered the stage through these curtains and vanished into their folds. The illusion was created that a *bal masqué* was taking place somewhere behind these curtains and that here on the stage was a sort of hastily erected tent *promenoir* in which the various amorous couples took convenient refuge. But when later Bakst produced the same ballet on the stage of the Maryinsky Theatre, replacing the draperies by an entire garden plus some sort of bridge, the effect was not nearly so strong, and the illusion lessened even though the décor, as a whole, was much more probable.

The problem of creating illusion and the methods by which it can be solved is a question belonging to a different category. But the décor of *Pulcinella*, with its synchronisation of costume, reached an enchanting perfection in this sphere, so that everything emphasised the shades of parody in the music with which Stravinsky expressed his admiration of the fantasticism of Pergolesi. But one cannot visualise *Le Pavillon* or *The Sleeping Beauty* in décor of this genre—neither was such décor ever contemplated in their production. Bakst's version of *Carnaval* was delicious, but were one to attempt to perform *Swan Lake* or *Scheherazade* in such a setting the result would be an absurdity or, worse still, tasteless. *L'imagerie populaire* of Derain in *Concurrence* was sheer delight and quite in keeping with this admirable ballet-bouffe—but should one attempt that kind of décor for *Giselle . . . !*

A certain genre of ballet calls for a wealth of décor, demands all that is intricate and expert in painted illusion, i.e. the depicting of given situations by means of painting. One must almost smell the spice-laden atmosphere of the Eastern harem in the décor of *Scheherazade*. One must feel oneself in the charming interiors of our grandfathers' days when the curtain rises on the first scenes of *The Nutcracker*. Again, it is essential that the first and fourth scene of *Petrouchka* should admit the spectator to the Admiralsky square in St. Petersburg in 1830, should create the impression of the holiday fever abroad on a mild frosty day.

And what unlimited scope the existing ballet literature offers to the creative powers of painters! What wealth is here as yet unsaid, how much more to say, and how much more to learn in accurate and persuasive portrayal of ideas! But it must always be understood that Terpsichore must remain the Muse of Inspiration—it is quite out of order to use the scenery of a ballet as an excuse for all sorts of pointless ingenuity. Incidentally, I have noticed that it is only the people casually attracted to ballet who permit themselves this licence. Artists who understand ballet and love its specific form are quite incapable of such tactlessness. Those who have had the good fortune to feel in ballet something unique and deeply poetical simply lack the heart to lift a hand towards such distortion. To such artists each problem set by ballet will whisper its solution, tell them how best to employ their crafstmanship to honour the spectacle of ballet in its entirety—the ballet that is "Gesamtkunstwerk."

And now just two words about costume in ballet. Every one knows of the enormous influence exerted on the development of costume by the teachings of Noverre in the last quarter of the eighteenth century. Even before his day, voices (among them the voice of Glück) had been raised in protest against the standardised traditional fineries that the unfortunate artists were forced to flaunt, the overelaboration of which was fast approaching the level of caricature. At that time it was quite out of the question to perform a ballet (or opera) in rational costume. There was in existence a special ballet-operatic formula demanding that the Gods and Heroes of ancient days should strut about the stage in long curly wigs, draped in pompous gold-and-lace-embroidered cloaks, with helmets surmounted by mountains of plumage. Another formula was in vogue for comic costumes, in which the masks of Italian comedy predominated. And there was yet a third no less rigid formula for depicting costumes of different nationalities and the amorous couples of the Pastoral. Jean Berain, a veritable dictator of settings for ballet and opera towards the close of the seventeenth century, managed to infuse endless variety into these specifically theatrical costumes, but towards the middle of the eighteenth century the system founded by Berain had become quite impossible. It was then the protests in the name of respect for the old, or simply in the name of healthy common sense, began. Noverre expressed these protests in a more practical form, from which sprang the reform of costume and décor for those ballets that he produced; and shortly afterwards, in the epoch of the triumph of the classic (which coincided with the triumphs of Napoleon) the reform had become universal. The ballets of mythology were danced in Grecian tunics, and other ballets in such clothes in which the theatrical costumiers of the day endeavoured to manifest their knowledge of ethnology and history.

It seemed as though *le bons sens* established on the ballet stage must now remain the permanent ruler over the setting. But here a tiny detail, playing, one would imagine, a microscopic part in the general aspect of ballet, crept in to spoil the theme. This detail was the ballet shoe, essential for the execution of those dances called "classical," which had attained full development in the first third of the nineteenth century and had achieved the significance of an implacable dogma.

The Classical, in the form in which it emerged in 1830, with the appearance of the blocked shoe, not only influenced the manner of presentation of the dance, but the whole style of ballet setting. And such a result must not be considered surprising as, whatever our reactions to the blocked shoe, it is the ballets composed during the reign of this system that possess to such an extent the quality of mood that is so dear to us. The clamour to get rid of convention and inaugurate a more rational system in contemporary ballet arose more than once, but all these outcries terminated in defeat. To be quite fair, the "classical ballet" in the steel support does endow point-work with a special brilliance and lends vividness to the whole effect. The classic system also promoted the uniformity and discipline so vitally necessary for the management of masses. There was a time when the laws of Noverre, and other ballet masters—"to seek in ballet the natural, the immediate and the simple"—were held in respect. These laws indirectly influenced dancing, and though they preserved all the conventions nevertheless imbued them with a tinge of freedom. But in those places where the cult of the natural entirely elbowed out the classic discipline there resulted dilettantism and, what was even more intolerable, disorder. For ballet, together with music, is specifically that art which, owing to its discipline and scholasticism, can repel the attacks of anarchy—and that is precisely one of its most vital qualities.

Why then, you will ask, did the blocked shoe and unavoidable use of a sort of *chausson de danse* that it involved, influence so strongly the whole ensemble of ballet? After all, in the real strict traditional ballet there are male dancers whose need for a special shoe is not so great, who are permitted every conceivable kind of footwear. There is a mass of character dances, occurring even in the most classical of ballets, that can be danced without special footwear either for men and women. However, it is essential to possess a slight acquaintance with the process of designing theatre and ballet costume to understand the whole business.

We will begin with the obvious fact that the concession of a particular form of shoe to the ballerina, enabling her to perform the classic point-work, immediately influences the entire costume. You cannot dress up a ballerina as a historically accurate Greek or Egyptian maiden, a lady of the seventeeth century, a marquise of the eighteenth, and then add to the whole the ballet shoe. The result would be ugly and absurd. To soften this absurdity, to transform the ugly into the elegant, one must resort to further concession, to compromise, and as a result of these concessions, there arises a whole series of standards. It was out of these standards that there grew up the canons of the ballerina's costume. The frock must be lifted high enough from the ground to permit the movement of the legs to be seen; this frock must be made of very light material so that it does not impede action, or weigh down. These standards led to the creation of the special ballet frock, called a *tu-tu*, made of tarlatan and gauze. This frock grew longer or shorter, but throughout all its changes it continued to resemble the calyx of a flower and lent the ballerina her specific form. A ballerina is a girl whose feet are clad in heelless shoes, around whose legs are flesh-coloured tights, extending to the waist, around which is placed something akin to a fleecy cloud. Her hands must be bare, her neck free, her coiffure not over-sumptuous. This must be the appearance of all those in the cast of the ballet entrusted with parts of importance, and this must be the appearance of the *prima ballerina* herself—the queen of the ballet spectacle. But if this is so, if to achieve it one has to abandon any pretence at probability, history, common sense, etc., then how, without ruining the entire harmony, can one neglect the rest of the cast? A few exceptions may be made in respect of performers farthest removed from the *prima* and her suite, and such exceptions are invariably made. They are made in all cases of episodic dancing interpolations and it is these interpolations that infuse life and variety into ballet (whether the dances are national, comic or acrobatic). But even when designing the costumes for such interpolations, the designer cannot but concern himself with their blend with the principal costumes, which obey the demands of the classic standards. When this is not carefully supervised the result is apt to be wild, ugly, or even stupid.[5]

May I be permitted to conclude these remarks upon ballet décor with

[5] Sometimes such wildness enters into the programme, not as a result of carelessness, but in answer to a definite purpose. Thus, in *Petrouchka*, only the ballerina and the two organ-grinders were allowed ballet shoes, the rest of the dancing masses and the cast wore normal footgear. Thus Derain in *Concurrence* deliberately superimposed the comic costumes of 1890 on the grotesque figures, with the purely balletic costume on the figures representing something of the ideal. However, these are only the exceptions that prove the rule.

a eulogy upon those conventions without which ballet, our beloved ballet, cannot exist. If anything must be considered surprising and marvellous it is that these inexorable conventions not only do not hamper the action, but on the contrary, being based on its nature, appear as its chief delight. It really is remarkable that we should go into raptures over a spectacle in which human speech is replaced by gestures, in which everything is mute, in which for the slightest reason, or for no reason at all, the characters start leaping, in which occasionally the weirdest events take place against a fantastic background, in which nothing is rational and in which—*enfin*—there is no room for any relation to everyday life. And yet, with all this, there is no other spectacle that can create such an atmosphere of poetry, that can persuade as strongly as ballet. Actually a sort of enchantment is at work here. But this enchantment is undeniably caused by the whole ensemble, and not by a particular branch of ballet. Take away from ballet its music and it will become immediately quite mute—that is, something agonisingly ill, something crippled. Take away its painting and it loses a major part of the persuasiveness of its mood, its poetry. Attempt to destroy any of its conventions and this will not only fail to lead to any improvement in ballet, but will appear as a crude invasion of reason, an attack against its very nature.

Ballet and everything concerning ballet must be artifically conditioned, must be a beautiful lie, and only under these conditions is ballet "good." Only in such cases does it speak the truth that answers to the fundamental demands of human nature, which understands truth far more easily when it is presented in the guise of fiction—that is poetry. The late A. I. Levinson, in one of his delicately thought-out *études* on ballet, quotes the words of Gautier on this spectacle, which he defines as "the realisation of the imagined" and, speaking of romantic ballet, Levinson adds for himself that this ballet was in reality an immediate and unconscious expression of "spiritual metaphysics"—in other words its own kind of "mystery." But that with which Levinson is trying to characterise the romantic ballet alone can to my mind be applied to the whole of ballet in general, and from that there arises the question: Can ballet exist without romanticism? Can this form of spectacle, in which all that is romantic has acquired such convincing expression, exist outside these influences? On the other hand, that which we call romanticism is not merely a "fashion" inherent only to one particular moment in the history of human culture. Romance existed before romanticism; it found expression both in architecture and music and in plastic art. And ballet, from the earliest days of its infancy, satisfied almost entirely this ideal of romanticism.

Romance, outside romanticism, continues to exist in our time, for is not the present vogue for ballet caused by the fact that we find it a miraculous compensation for all the over-prosaic that we have to endure in everyday life? We, the followers of ballet, know how it satisfies us more than any other spectacle, how it heals and consoles us. But ballet only retains this "magic" while it enshrines our ideals, the wonderful illusions, the dreams of the poet, dreams that turn their backs on sordid reality. And is not this romanticism?

In Search of Design

by Rouben Ter-Arutunian

The curtain rises. A sight wave rushes forward toward the audience. A series of impulses, concentrated for immediate release, bursts upon them, like waters gushing through a suddenly opened barrage—reaching for the individual first, but quickly immersing the entire audience. The mechanism of a carefully calculated illusion is in motion.

This is the moment when the spectators instinctively accept or reject the décor, which establishes the climate for the production, sending it off to success or failure. The illusion of the stage triggers the imagination of the audience. No matter how much this illusion is couched in realism, no matter whether it uses the technique of the proscenium stage or the theatre-in-the-round, the music hall, the circus, the platform of wandering minstrels—it remains an illusion, make-believe. The artistic and technical personnel have assembled, according to prearranged appointment, and—through combined talent, discipline, and concentrated effort—seduce the audience to participate in this preconceived illusion. The performance is on.

Part of the illusion is conjured up by the visual impact of décor and costumes. Already, by itself, without performers, the décor establishes a definite atmosphere, evokes a mood. No matter whether it is made out of steel pipes, painted floppy canvas, or just two small square blocks that sit on the empty stage. The selection has been made by the designer (we hope!), and there it is. The décor, through its organization

Source: From *Dance Perspectives*, Number 28, Winter 1966.

of space, its color, its texture, its response to light, makes either a positive contribution to the total illusion—or interferes with it.

For ballet, physical interference can be fatal, and need not even be discussed. Dancers have to move, and they must have space.

Aesthetic interference is likely to happen more often and is possibly as dangerous, though it is far more difficult to determine. The set might become annoying to look at in connection with the movement. There might be a variety of shapes, lines, patterns, and colors that clash as they are suddenly brought out through motion and impose their presence to the point of distraction.

Today one is more and more inclined to less décor. One tends to like everything stripped—the stage uncluttered, sufficiently clean and well organized at its periphery, and in the right scale with the character of the work. This, one believes, is the condition most favorable for the performer. But this can be exaggerated to a degree of unimaginative dryness. Then something is missing. The performer is robbed of an important ingredient he could feed upon, another dimension that could have further challenged the involvement of both himself and his audience.

Dance, a faculty of motion, feeds on space. The basis of any décor for the dance is space. Dancers move essentially on the stage floor, but the audience is far less aware of the floor than of the comparatively large space in height, mostly in back of the stage, and to the left and right of it, against which the movement is visually inscribed. This is the area that the designer is most concerned with, and whatever he decides to place on the stage floor has to relate to this large, often permanently visible, high plane. In his final composition the designer has to take into account the movement of the dancer's body, which should become the unifying and animating factor that connects these two basic elements—the decorative object related to the stage floor and the expanse in back of and above it.

The stage space, when left without movement, is essentially perceived by the audience in two dimensions. It is the movement of the dancers that reveals to them the presence of the third dimension. Most likely it is the contemporary tendency to favor a unified aesthetic concept that makes the three-dimensional setting appear emotionally more appropriate. Yet the old-fashioned, two-dimensional one—made out of a few sticks of wood and canvas and paint—performs essentially the same function: it organizes the space. Here the designer must particularly collaborate with the choreographer to determine the position of the setting on the stage floor, its relation to the space around it, and its proportion—especially its height—in relation to the human scale. Hopefully, this has been discussed and solved (which it can be) ahead of time.

Now comes the question of the surface of this projected décor—the color, the texture, the direction of linear pattern, the response to light, and the practical function it has to serve.

It is the discretion of the designer to determine the character of a setting. Through his sensitive ingenuity, which guides his instinct in the analysis of the original intentions of the author, the designer establishes an affinity with his project that conditions him for his undertaking.

Stage design should be achieved through the fusion of the instinctive visions of the director and the designer, which are evoked through an objective searching of the author's intention. The fused vision is, in fact, an assemblage. George Balanchine always says, "I don't create; I just collect here and there. It is Tchaikovsky who gives me this, and Gluck who gives me that." Exactly something like this ought to happen, otherwise it is only a pre-fabricated skin that is being stretched over the skeleton of the author's thoughts. It always ought to be a different skin to fit that differently shaped skeleton.

But it is not only by drainage of the author's thoughts and their conscious assemblage that the creative process evolves. There is that certain unknown factor, which plays an important part—the "divine" inspiration leading to a sudden vision. Sometimes this vision is sparked by someone outside the triumvirate of author, director-choreographer, and designer—someone who acts as a catalyst between them.

Serge Diaghilev must have been this to the artists of his circle, as Lincoln Kirstein is today. There is something about such rare men who, with a word or a gesture, invoke an idea that takes root and flowers. When I was designing a work for the New York City Ballet, Kirstein would often bring me a print or some other object that might not have had any direct relation to our project. It would be something he may have liked personally, or thought I might like, or perhaps he thought it might put my imagination on the right track. Or sometimes, I suspect, he would do it even to divert my thinking. Yet whatever the motive, he could suddenly open to me a whole new way of seeing or understanding the author. . . .

Designing is a give and take between minds that respond to an idea or a situation or a musical score. Out of this develops the setting.

Sometimes the choreographer provides the initiating idea. The designer visualizes this, and so it is done. When Glen Tetley choreographed *Sargasso*, he wanted a staircase, which I developed into a narrow shaft, made out of a series of steps that seemed to come from nowhere to terminate on the stage floor. The original concept was of a woman standing at a certain height and, in a gesture of desperation, beginning the self-revelation that is the theme of the ballet.

But with *Ricercare* Tetley had originally a completely different idea for the set than the one we finally used. A chance drawing changed the first concept, and even led him to start the work with the two dancers suspended symmetrically on each side of the crescent, the way I had visualized it for the set.

Martha Graham is the theatre personality a stage designer dreams about. Her ability to extract from every designed object its fundamental purpose, aesthetic and physical, is admirable. No wonder her sets are mostly three-dimensional—sculpture, props, and platforms. Even when they are linear, as in Isamu Noguchi's *Seraphic Dialogue* (my nomination for the most beautiful contemporary setting), they take on a three-dimensional function, and participate to a great extent in her choreography.

Only once have I had the privilege to design for Martha Graham. It was a few years ago, and more than ten years after I had first seen her in Paris on her first European tour. Even then I had admired the originality of what I had seen on stage. When I came to meet her, and she explained what she wanted me to design, it sounded a bit complicated. There was, I believe, a protagonist, who was caught in his inner world and was in conflict with the outer world. There had to be an area for him, and another for the outer world that was represented by a wall, which he couldn't quite scale and conquer.

The set that I designed for *Visionary Recital* was a double row of vertically strung metallic cables, placed parallel to the footlights, way at the back of the stage. These were threaded through short, clear, plastic tubes of a slightly larger diameter, of varied lengths, and placed at different heights—similar to a graph of a heartbeat. These two rows of cables, which covered the entire visible height and width of the stage, representing the back wall of the set, were far enough apart from each other to allow dancers to pass between them. Similar cables were arranged in a cluster downstage left, with the protagonist caught in them. The highly reflective surface of the clear tubes and the metallic texture of the cables provided a sharp contrast with the somber, overall background, and set a strange mood. This effect was evoked particularly when heightened by the hallucinatory passing of figures between the double row of cables—the "corridor of memories," as Martha Graham called it. Each vertical the dancers passed seemed to bisect them.

A bit like the repetitious ticking of a clock—reminiscent of the passage of time.

Often Martha Graham's dances are based either on Greek mythology, which is more or less familiar; or on some kind of philosophical subject matter, which can be more personal. The story, when one first reads it in the program, seems very important: all the characters are terribly related to one another, and they all have serious problems. But at the performance I doubt if anyone thinks about this very much. The movements have their own logic, and a beauty of extraordinary visual appeal. Of course, the story line sets the mood, influences the musical score, the décor, the costumes, the lighting, and—the choreography. But really only slightly, and only in a very abstract way. The visual impressions during the performance are so striking, the transformations of the stage space so ingenious, and the synthesis of the stage machinery (and here I include the performers and the way they are presented) is so complete and so original, that one is entirely captivated through the perfection of it all. This particular kind of theatre—the special contribution of Martha Graham!

I personally don't miss the absence of story line in most contemporary ballets because I am perfectly well served by just the music and the movement. Even when a ballet has a story, it is the score that colors the execution and the setting of the narrative. True—movements of the body can express a story. Yet it is a bit difficult to understand, no matter how much pantomine there is, and you can't really tell whether somebody is someone's grandfather or uncle. It isn't that clear, and if you haven't read the program, you don't really know. Some say that ballet would be so much better served and so much easier to understand if it had a plot. Well, I think the contrary is true. It is far more difficult with a story that doesn't belong there, and with the body trying to symbolize or interpret something that can become so involved and would be so much better expressed through another medium. I find it more logical and more attractive to go to a ballet and see only the body in motion based on music.

Music, at least to me, is terribly important. It is the springboard of my design. In designing a play, one should read it, and base the setting upon the intentions of the playwright. In designing a ballet, one should start with the music. After all, the choreographer begins his work with it, and so should the designer. Music is what I always start with.

In *The Seven Deadly Sins* I was completely guided by the intentional cheapness of Kurt Weill's score, in the vein of the tingle-tangle music of the late 1920s, the so-called *systemzeit* of the Weimar Republic. I tried for a biting, acid look in the coloring, and vulgar proportioning in the shapes of the set pieces—with a touch of the geometrical overlay so typical of that era. I used mainly two-dimensional set pieces, fragments of scenery that were flown in and out of a black stage to symbolize the various areas traveled by Anna 1 and Anna 2. The last set, "San Francisco," had a large flat, covered with silver foil and a raised linear maze of geometrical abstractions. Balanchine had talked about a cold glitter, and an area high up, through which Anna 1 would jump. Also, he had thought of the costuming of the corps de ballet in high black boots, and black belts and masks. From the last set (or even from the episode in the Boston hotel where Anna 1 is humiliated) the ballet is a staggering, touching, and frightening series of tableaux that finds its heartbreaking fulfillment in the walk across the stage of Anna 1 and Anna 2, Lotte Lenya and Allegra Kent, wrapped into a black cape with only their two faces showing. So moving—the sharp brilliance of the preceding set, merciless in its cold brightness and robot-type movement—then the simplicity of the end.

The contemporary musical scores of Igor Stravinsky, Anton Webern, Pierre Boulez, Edgar Varèse, and some of the Italians and Germans, show a rhythmic pattern and a tonal intensity that seem to me to be similar to certain tendencies in modern architecture. Assemblages of large blocks of volume, animated by glittering reflections of continuously repeated surface patterns, are placed into a controlled environment, where they are set against stretches of open emptiness. In music, a concentrated sonority of plucked chords, enveloped in a tinkle of intricate rhythmic patterns, is contrasted with sustained silences. The musical style demands an extended attention from the audience, almost forcing it to listen double—toward sound and toward silence. It is not unlike looking at a painting or a sculpture where first the dominant, positive form is registered by the eye; and then its negative, enveloping surround is perceived.

These particular characteristics of the contemporary score affect the movement of the dancer, demanding a particularly refined sense of rhythm and hearing, forcing a precarious musical timing of body control and muscle release to alternate punctuated movement and flowing repose. Balanchine's choreography to Stravinsky's recent works is the ideal example of complementing such a score with movement, and of extending it onto a visual plane. His is a consistent series of discoveries of movements for the body. Yet the movements seem so strangely natural that we are surprised not to have seen them before. They are all so logical, yet they have a certain edge of revelation. It is a marriage of sound and movement, overpoweringly striking in its simplicity, and of such a personal character that it is almost a dialogue between the choreographer and the composer. Understandably, they don't want to take a chance, which is not absolutely necessary, by calling for a third collaborator. But what a challenge it would be for a designer!

In my work for the New York City Ballet the choice of style for décor has been mostly a traditional one. Four ballets that I designed were all to be part of the dressed-up repertory in the company's new home at Lincoln Center.

The décor for *Swan Lake* used "old-fashioned," painted canvas to create the illusion of a lake surrounded by a dark forest, German-medieval in character. The lake: silver-gray, touching the tormented sky; a series of small islands stretching into infinity. In the foreground: a large mountain, rising out of the lake, topped by mysterious, castle-like rock formations—all this painted on the backdrop! At the sides and the borders overhead: the foliage of the dark green forest, tinged with gold. It was the kind of set that could have been conceived technically a very long time ago, even years before the creation of the ballet itself.

Certainly this is not the only possible approach to designing a classical ballet today. Yet even with an entirely different and not at all literal solution, certain elements and characteristics have to be recognizable. Whether the designer uses floating, abstract shapes; diaphanous surfaces with lack of color; a great luminosity; or dispersed, dark scintillating forms receding into darkness—the result has to suggest an ethereal lake, surrounded by a forest, and a castle in the distance. There has to be an area for the entrance of the Magician and the presence of the swans. The transformation of the Swan Queen has to be solved. Over-all there must be a feeling of melancholy, of possible danger and mystery. After all, it is a fairy tale to be done with great elegance. Aristocracy—swans!

Harlequinade used the scenery previously designed for a New York City Opera production of Rossini's *La Cenerentola*, and it was only a question of inventing a Commedia dell'Arte house that would serve all kinds of slapstick action, and of placing it inside the red and gold stage, in the style of the Pollack Toy Theatre, that had been used for the opera. It was a very practical idea to rescue the settings of this production, and a very appropriate one. It does not happen very often that this kind of adaptation succeeds. Luck!

For *Ballet Imperial* it was a question of presenting the glory and elegance and the splendor of St. Petersburg. So the period was established. The traditional approach was decided upon.

The Nutcracker used the scenic devices that had been set at the time of its first presentation at the smaller house of the New York City Center. I was concerned mainly with the transfer of the choreographic production to the stage of the New York State Theater. The new design exploited the resources of the larger house. Fortunately, this *Nutcracker* turned out quite successfully, and in a way helped to determine the control of the New York State Theater by the City Center organization.

And about that Christmas tree . . . It is pure stagecraft, and essentially very simple. A trap opens, and the tree is pulled up. It grows and grows, as the orchestra swells. I tried to determine the right proportion for the effect, which owes a great deal also to this most wonderful score—Tchaikovsky at his very best.

The deliberate choice of traditional décor for these ballets was favored by Balanchine, whose thinking in his formative years had been conditioned by the Imperial Russian Ballet and later by the artistic circle assembled by Diaghilev. Even though Diaghilev's Ballets Russes were a novelty for the Western World, particularly through their visual impact, the technical principle of décor employed by his designers was a traditional one—essentially an animated painting. But it was the genius of his collaborators that kept it from being just that. In the early period it was particularly Léon Bakst whose instinct for the stage controlled an audacious use of glowing color, superb mastery in the application of period-flavored decorative pattern, and an extravagant use of perspective, which transformed traditional décor into a visual experience unknown before him. One of the outstanding stage and costume designers of all time.

Adolphe Appia, Gordon Craig, and the influence of Diaghilev set the standard for stage décor that we take for granted today. But it is a myth to believe that every décor done for Diaghilev had extraordinary artistic merit, and was the ideal visualization for the particular ballet. . . .

Designing costumes for dancers is, naturally, entirely different from designing for actors or singers. Dancers' costumes must show the body and the movement. Of all the costumes for dancers, the tutu is still one of the most beautiful and successful ever devised. It enhances the grace of the dancer, and accentuates the movement.

Martha Graham has found an almost equally ingenious way of costuming her girls for her way of moving. The kind of skirt/harem-pants idea she has devised for them is so simple, so intelligent, and so useful. The covered part of the body becomes almost more visible. It is like a veil that reveals and accentuates the legs. Of course, it would not be suitable for classical ballet, nor even for all contemporary styles. In the case of modern dance, where each choreographer works so differently, it is nearly impossible to design the right costume without a knowledge of the particular kind of movement.

But freedom and accentuation of movement are not the only important factors affecting the success of the costumes. They must also be worn well. It is a great talent to be able to manipulate a costume, and I am afraid not much attention is placed on this today. I found it fascinating to design for Carmen de Lavallade because her ability to work with costumes is unsurpassed. She has a gift to handle fabric of just about any quantity and, not only to make herself look beautiful, but to show her movement as well.

Most performers now want to have less costume, and they insist on being unencumbered by it. There is, for instance, this problem of skirts that touch the floor, and I don't mean lie on the floor, which would be so much more beautiful. So even if they only touch the floor, there are already complaints. They can't walk, they are afraid of tripping—they have to sing, and they have to act, and they have to carry a book or a purse, and that's just too much—they can't do all that at once. Well, of course, the performer must be at ease in his costume, but there are certain necessities that the costume imposes even with a certain discomfort, that can be used to advantage.

A dedicated performer—Katherine Hepburn, for instance—will rehearse for hours with a skirt that is much too long, much too big, but just right for the character. She works on the costume as she works on the role. Some performers might find this completely unnecessary. They would rather concentrate on coughing correctly and scratching the right way, without paying attention to the costume. The proper use of costume is an art that is dying here; unfortunately, this robs the performer of a great deal of additional effectiveness in his interpretation.

Costume for the stage is bound to be influenced by fashion. The contemporary trend is to reveal, to see more, to see through, and to partake. The body-consciousness, the form-fitted clothes, have conditioned us to accept basic facts about the masculine and feminine body, which seem to have escaped the previous generation. We have come to live with more awareness of our bodies. Not only is the silhouette of the body accentuated, but the body itself is revealed—the transparent look, the nude look, clear plastics used for clothing. This development will influence costume design.

Audiences are now willing to accept the modern setting, the architectural look,—however more on the dramatic than on the lyric stage (at least in this country). Yet they are still reluctant to see characters dressed the way we are. It seems that productions with characters in modern dress are less successful. The reason is often that these modern dress costumes are assembled without much discrimination in taste or imagination. It isn't as easy as going shopping at Orhbach's. Still, I am positive that the tendency in stage costumes will be toward the more contempory look. This is accepted in the English theatre. Peter Brooks' *King Lear*, in its choice of materials and in its simplicity of line, had several very successful solutions. On the operatic stage in Europe, the contemporary style has now become an accepted tradition, championed to a great degree by both brothers Wagner at Bayreuth. The only trouble there is that the performers don't look attractive, possibly because of the intentionsl uniformity of the Bayreuth look.

I feel that the authenticity of the stage has its own rules, based on its dramatic or lyric character, and these take preference over historical rules.

I guess it is the degree of our enlightenment, together with a greater visual notion about the past, which has conditioned us to regard authenticity of period in the theatre as important. I think that an authentic historical climate, a correct suggestion of the period for the historical play might be desirable. I don't like to be more authentic than that, as long as there is not an obviously jarring note about something that really couldn't be part of the period. What is even more important is that it not be contradictory to the feeling and atmosphere of the situation or scene. Whenever one wants pure historical authenticity, one ought to go into a museum and look at it in the display cases. In themselves authentic costumes are relics of the past; they have no dramatic function. On the stage, costumes ought to heighten characterization and express the atmosphere of the scene as conceived by the author.

There are times, of course, when a quite authentic costume—or at least an adaptation of an authentic costume—is essential to the point of the work. In *Souvenirs* the costumes were taken from the era of silent films and based on a set of fashion plates that Todd Bolender had found. The Vamp was wonderfully staged, particularly her entrance with the cigarette holder, and later her tango with the Gigolo. The ballet was a spoof of a certain aura of pre-World War I, and the set was more a series of prop pieces than a décor as such. There was the prop of the elevator; a few palms, suggesting the court of a European-type spa; a round banquette, found often in the vestibules of these hotels. Later there was a set of doors; a couch with a tiger, and a beaded curtain; then, at the end, a pole with banners and a virile lifeguard. There was a minimum of décor. The emphasis was on the costumes, which brought out the satire.

Sometimes there is a particular idea that one tries to explore, either in stage design or in costuming. Or it happens, and one realizes afterwards that one had been unconsciously influenced by a certain idea. This happened with Menotti's *Maria Golovin*, which had a blind protagonist who was preoccupied with the construction of bird cages—a way to find release from the net of his psychological tensions. The design for the set, a room, turned out to have walls and a ceiling made out of a series of thin metal rods, not unlike a prison—or a bird cage. But the intention was not to stress symbolism. The outcome was arrived at unconsciously, though it was dramatically appropriate.

Something similar happened with my first design for Paul Taylor, for his choreography to Schönberg's *Five Pieces for Orchestra*. The work came to be called *Fibres*, I guess because of the sketch for the setting. It had a series of lines arising from a center core, and this was interpreted as the tree of life, or given some other symbolic meaning. Actually, it was only a linear separation of the space in height and depth, and hardly anything else. I wanted to underscore the movement of the dancers, and create a focus for the choreography. The dancers seemed always to return to one special area on the stage to which they appeared to be related in many ways, so this then became the root, the vertical meeting point, of all these nervous lines. We used different types of thin telephone wires, and spent hours tying those wires together.

The idea for the costumes had a related motif. I had thought to destroy the surface of the body, but to reveal its functioning mechanism. Possibly I was influenced by the remarkably beautiful anatomical plates of Vesalius. I invented small shapes made of Celastic (a material similar to papier maché), painted in vivid colors, and held on the naked body by colored elastic tapes of various widths. The head was originally covered by a mask and bandaged with white tape. The strong colors of these shapes destroyed the surface of the body, but emphasized the form of the muscles. It looked as if the skin had been removed by surgical incision, revealing the structure of the muscles. In a peculiar way the costume complemented the shape of the body and accentuated its movements. . . .

Dance is the most progressive, the most individual, the most contemporary artistic expression of America, and American dance is leading the world. Russian ballet is magnificent in the effectiveness of its technique, the abundance of its human material, the perfection and skill of its dancers. But what is being done with it? Choreographically it is still at the turn of the century. The Russians only now are becoming aware of discoveries about the human body and about the various possibilities for its movement that have been explored in the West.

I would put dance in America way above painting and sculpture. The latter are not as individual. They don't seem to have a vocabulary, and they lack the degree of tradition that choreographers have been able to give to the American dance. In painting and sculpture there is not such an obviously typical American look or typically American substance as has already manifested itself in the body of the American dancer. One can see trends in painting and sculpture: there is a certain geometry, a certain relation of shapes and a linear interplay based on geometrical forms, particularly the circle. There is a steel-like incision of the surface, so predominant in the painting of the American Primitives. There is a not very sensitive and not very refined use of color, which is yet quite appealing in its freshness and naïveté. American paintings and sculptures have created a great interest abroad, but one can't say that their success has been as unanimous as that of touring American dance companies.

Whether classical or modern, the ideal dancer's body here—particularly the girl's—has been sculptured to a great extent by Balanchine. He has really set the norm of the ideal body, an ideal of beauty that is pursued everywhere now. Even in Russia, women are most anxious to adopt the Western beauty ideal and attempt to diet—which they really should. The film of Balanchine's *A Midsummer Night's Dream*—I have never seen so many beautiful girls on the screen. Each one is remarkable, and they are gloriously put together. They look beautiful, and they move beautifully. They are magnificent—slim figures, long legs, long necks, small heads that are unencumbered by hair that always gets in the way—absolutely perfect.

Dance in Europe can become over-sentimental. Even when it is being presented as an abstract choreographic essay in the style of Balanchine, it very often seems to carry a certain message or wants to have a literary gloss and chic. It can get to be a charming and athletic interplay, without ever coming close to the dynamic ideal of Jerome Robbins.

In America there seems to be less concern with the over-elaborate façade, and I certainly don't refer only to Balanchine. There is something skeletal and organic about the choreographic approach to the score and the movement. Accentuating the essentials—less involved with effect, less literal. A distillation of the idea . . .

A most important kind of artistic discipline: Discipline of creation, of being able to concentrate and trim away everything unnecessary, only to use what is absolute. What I admire and what I really try to learn and try to reach is a harmony and an originality in the balance of forms, shapes, color, and line; and the economy of their use. Yet there ought to be something in addition to all this —a graciousness and an elegance I can't really describe. Mozart has it, and Balanchine has it. This is what I cherish.

Designs for Dance

by Isamu Noguchi

We breathe in, we breathe out, inward turning, alone, or outgoing, working with others, for an experience that is cumulative through collaboration. Theater is the latter kind. My interest is the stage where it is possible to realize in a hypothetical way those projections of the imagination into environmental space which are denied us in actuality.

The theater of the dance in particular adds the movement of bodies, in relation to form and space, together with music. There is joy in seeing sculpture come to life on the stage in its own world of timeless time. Then the very air becomes charged with meaning and emotion, and form plays its integral part in the re-enactment of a ritual. Theater is a ceremonial; the performance is a rite. Sculpture in daily life should or could be like this. In the meantime, the theater gives me its poetic, exalted equivalent.

My first experience with theater was in 1926, when I made papier-mâché masks for the Japanese dancer, Itō Michio, to do the Noh Drama by W. B. Yeats called *At Hawks Well*.

My friendship with Martha Graham goes back to 1929, when I made two heads of her. I often watched her in classes, evolving her new and fundamental approach to the dance. Thus it was as a familiar that I did my first set for her *Frontier* in 1935.

In our work together, it is Martha who comes to me with the idea, the theme, the myth upon which the piece is to be based. There are some sections of music perhaps, but usually not. She will tell me if she has any special requirements—whether, for example, she wants a 'woman's place'. The form then is my projection of these ideas. I always work with a scale model of the stage space in my studio. Within it I feel at home and am in command. With Martha, there is the wonder

Source: From *A Sculptor's World* (New York: Harper & Row, 1968).

of her magic with props. She uses them as extensions of her own anatomy.

In 1939 I did *Chronicle* to music by Wallingford Riegger, and in 1940 *El Penitente*, with music by Louis Horst; but it was in 1943 that my major series of collaborations with Martha Graham may be said to have started when in the spring of that year I was asked by the Elizabeth Sprague Coolidge Foundation to design three dance pieces, to be presented in the Chamber Music Theater of the Library of Congress in Washington, DC. These were *Appalachian Spring*, *Herodiade* and *Imagined Wing.* Only the last with music by Darius Milhaud did not remain for numerous other performances.

In order to give this formal concert stage a feeling of theater and dedication, I transformed it into a place of the imagination, by building my own proscenium arch, with light baffles as wings and on the ceiling.

1935 Frontier
Music: Louis Horst

Frontier was my first set. It was for me the genesis of an idea—to wed the total void of theater space to form and action. A rope, running from the two top corners of the proscenium to the floor rear center of the stage, bisected the three-dimensional void of stage space. This seemed to throw the entire volume of air straight over the heads of the audience.

At the rear convergence was a small section of log fence, to start from and to return to. The white ropes created a curious ennobling—of an outburst into space and, at the same time, of the public's inrush toward infinity.

This set was the point of departure for all my subsequent theater work: space became a volume to be dealt with sculpturally.

1940 El Penitente
Music: Louis Horst

The rites of the flageolants as depicted in the art of the South West. The Santos danced by Erick Hawkins.

1944 Appalachian Spring
Music: Aaron Copland

New land, new home, new life; a testament to the American settler, a folk theater.

I attempted through the elimination of all non-essentials, to arrive at an essence of the stark pioneer spirit, that essence which flows out to permeate the stage. It is empty but full at the same time. It is like Shaker furniture.

1944 Herodiade
Music: Paul Hindemith

The most baroque and specifically sculptural of my sets.

Within a woman's private world, and intimate space, I was asked to place a mirror, a chair, and a clothes rack. Salome dances before her mirror. What does she see? Her bones, the potential skeleton of her body. The chair is like an extension of her vertebrae; the clothes rack, the circumscribed bones on which is hung her skin. This is the desecration of beauty, the consciousness of time.

1946 Dark Meadow
Music: Carlos Chavez

My homage to Mexico. I made four primordial shapes to define space and as counterpoint to action. They are not stones, but serve the same purpose of suggesting the continuity of time. They move and the world moves. 'It is the world of great symbols, the place of experience, the dark meadow of Ate, the Meadow of choice—the passage to another area of life.'—Martha Graham.

1946 Cave of the Heart
Music: Samuel Barber

A dance of transformation (as in the Noh Drama). Medea, priestess of the mother goddess, slays the offspring of her union with Jason and is transformed and finally consumed by, the flaming nimbus of the setting sun (her father).

I constructed a landscape like the islands of Greece. On the horizon (center rear) lies a volcanic shape like a black aorta of the heart; to this lead stepping stone islands. (Jason's voyage, the entry bridge of drama). Opposite (stage left) is coiled a green serpent, on whose back rests the transformation dress of gold (metal).

1947 Errand into the Maze
Music: Gian-Carlo Menotti

The theme, based on the story of the Minotaur, is the extremity we must all face: ourselves.

I tried to depict the way, or the labyrinth, as the interior spaces of the mind by means of rope, as I had done in *Frontier*. But this time the effect was altogether different: a space confined like the cave of the mind.

The 'doorway' is like suppliant hands, like pelvic bones, 'from which the child I never had comes forth, but the only child that comes forth is myself.'—Martha Graham.

1947 Night Journey
Music: William Schuman

Incest. I created a bed, raised on legs of gold, as the central sculpture, a double image of male and female.

The approach to this is like fragments of archaeology, the spirits of his ancestors, over whom Oedipus must mount. The chair is Jocasta's place as woman in the shape of an hour glass. Truth is the staff of Teresias, 'who was for seven years a woman.'

'The umbilical cord is a white gleaming thing that links man and woman who love each other.'

1948 Diversion of Angels
Music: Norman Dello Joio

When this dance was first presented at Connecticut College I devised a full burlap backdrop, stretched along all its edges by ropes through grommets. From behind, here and there, long rods were pushed to modulate the cloth into undulating clouds of breasts and valleys. Unfortunately this was considered too distracting for the dance, and so was dropped.

1950 JUDITH
Music: William Schuman

I carved the tent of Holofernes out of balsa wood in the shape of an animal (stage left); Judith's place as a lyre or a loom (stage right). Between these two the action takes place.

This was presented in Carnegie Hall before the Louisville Symphony Orchestra, for which it was commissioned. With the large orchestra in full view there was only a narrow space to dance in.

The problem was how to distract the audience's consciousness away from the orchestra. To hide it, as we attempted with a scrim, in Carnegie Hall, was unsatisfactory (I dislike the ambiguous quality of scrim). However, I was later given another chance to resolve this problem upon the occasion of the opening of 'Kongresshalle' in Berlin (September 1957), when there was no means even to hang a scrim. I there devised a way of camouflaging the orchestra by superimposing an even greater distraction between it and the dancer. White cloth shapes were sewed on stands of fishnet, so that the audience was effectively blinded from seeing the orchestra and their light stands.

'The Story of Judith is a fertility rite, that involves the releasing of the waters. When death is overcome or obviated, then she emerges with white flowing branches—after a tragedy to accept life, to shed the garments of sadness, to put on those of gladness.'—Martha Graham.

1953 VOYAGE
Music: William Schuman

Based on the poem *Anabasis* of St. John Perse which deals with migration to a new land in terms of an Arabian allegory.

Why I did a boat and sail for a desert caravan I do not know. Obviously, the set seemed made for something else. By strange inevitability and the genius of Miss Graham the same set was reused ten years later for an entirely different theme in *Circe*.

1955 SERAPHIC DIALOGUE
Music: Norman Dello Joio

I depicted the life of Joan of Arc as a cathedral that fills her consciousness entirely. To do this, I constructed a transparent edifice of brass tubing—articulated like a church steeple, as I had done for *The Bells*, a ballet in 1944 for the Ballet Russe de Monte Carlo, but with a different purpose. The construction was a precision operation, made possible by my friend, Edison Price.

'It is like all cathedrals, but also like no cathedral on earth, more like the golden lines which for us is a cathedral, whether the lines of the arches or the arches made by the light of candles and gold.'—Martha Graham.

1958 Embattled Garden
Music: Carlos Surinach

The Garden of Eden is the time of puberty. The symbol of the apple was made into a dance platform. Pierced with two large ovals, like the core, but in color patterns like the skin of the apple. From this rises a jungle of green rattan rods. These vibrate with the dance which takes place between and around them. To the side is the tree.

'The Garden of Eden has violence, it is only idyllic now in retrospect.'—Martha Graham.

1958 Clytemnestra
Music: Halim El Dabh

A dance of retribution after death. Out of the dark unconscious comes memory—the terrible devastation 'when the war spears clashed in Troy.'

The unencumbered stage. Space is isolated only by props which focus the eye of the imagination. Crossed spears, the throne of Knossos, the golden cloak of Agamemnon fills the sky. Continuous change covering forty-five minutes.

1960 Acrobats of God
Music: Carlos Surinach

A satiric idyl on the instruction of dance. The void of theater space is used three-dimensionally with a huge transfigured practice bar with which, on which and under which the action takes place. Meaningless symbols float in and out. Martha appears and disappears behind a small suspended plaque which hides only her face. The music rack of the three mandolin players on stage is also suspended.

1960 ALCESTIS
Music: Vivian Fine

Satiric but gentle commentary on death. Nothing comes from nothing; only submission to unconscious memory. The circular stone is the door opening both to life and to death. The sun that creates, then destroys. The home is the right angle. Hercules drags the bed from the fear of death to an area of life.

An example of my interweaving of interests: this was made while doing the Yale Library garden with a similarity of rudimental geometry.

1962 PHAEDRA
Music: Robert Starer

The unenviable bed of lust. The shrine of Aphrodite, like a giant butterfly or womb, opens to reveal the goddess transfixed (stage left).

Stage right, the moon goddess Artemis is on her platform. Between them, Phaedra on her golden bed.

Stage right rear, Hyppolitus is inside his blue and black horned capsule whose small doors open to reveal his anatomy. He is the cosmonaut weary of this world. The man and woman's area, right and left, *droit* versus *maladroit*, the unknown, sinister. The crossroad of decision.

1963 CIRCE
Music: Alan Hovhaness

Circe, the great enchantress, has turned all of Ulysses' companions into beasts. This is survival, stripped to essentials. The choreographic image is the curious mixing of people, set and space: submission to the image of desires.

The sail, the boat are now in splendid harmony.

1966 CORTEGE OF EAGLES
Music: Eugene Lester

Based on the Hecuba of Euripides. I wished to contrast the exquisite artistocratic rule of Troy destroyed by the rough dynamics of Greece, and likewise the dissolution and transformation of the noble queen (through the use of mask) into a mad dog. There were seven masks; and large kite-like forms moving into architectural and dynamic relationships. A sky floats in as well as, finally, the ghost of Hector. A significant invention was that of Charon the ferryman of the dead, as a master of ceremonies with a grotesque mask held between the teeth with one wild white eyeball and a lewd foot-long tongue.

I have done altogether twenty sets for Martha Graham; many, as old as twenty years, are still presented. Included in these were innumerable props, jewelry, etc., but not costumes, excepting the flame dress of Medea in *Cave of the Heart*.

I twice did sets for members of her company, Erick Hawkins and Yuriko.

The three ballet sets I have done included costumes as well. Of these, *Orpheus* is still performed.

1944 THE BELLS

Choreography: Ruth Page
Music: Darius Milhaud

The Bells depicts, within a rhythm of tingling resonance captured from the poem of Edgar Allen Poe, the various aspects of life and decay.

The church steeple was a very large prop. Situated stage center rear, it gradually rose and at the end collapsed in a tangled wreck. This was accomplished by articulating it like a puppet.

My favorite costumes were those of black bells which, hanging from over their heads, covered everything but the dancer's feet.

1947 THE SEASONS

Choreography: Merce Cunningham
Music: John Cage

I saw *The Seasons* as a celebration of the passage of time. The time could be either a day, from dawn through the heat of midday to the cold of night, or a year, as the title suggests, or a life-time.

In the beginning there is darkness or nothingness (before consciousness). It is raining as the light grows to bare visibility, to die, and then to revive again, pulsating and growing ever stronger.

Suddenly in a flash (magnesium flash), it is dawn. (All this is done with light machines). Birds (beaks for boys, tail feathers for girls) dance to the morning.

The light becomes hotter, the throbbing heat becomes intense, until with violence it bursts into flames (light projections throughout).

Autumn follows, with strange, soft moon shapes, then the cold of winter. It is snowing; lines of freezing ice transfix the sky (ropes), and the man of doom walks into the dark.

Although *The Seasons* was presented only three times, I have always felt it to be one of my best contributions. The costumes were comic and sad—like the human condition—somewhat like Mack Sennett bathing costumes, like birds with and without tail feathers. The beaks of red cellophane cones, mounted on white circular disks, were held in the dancers' teeth.

1948 Orpheus
Choreography: George Balanchine
Music: Igor Stravinsky

Never was I more personally involved in creation than with this piece which is the story of the artist. I interpreted *Orpheus* as the story of the artist blinded by his vision (the mask). Even inanimate objects move at his touch—as do the rocks, at the pluck of his lyre. To find his bride or to seek his dream or to fulfill his mission, he is drawn by the spirit of darkness to the netherworld. He descends in gloom as glowing rocks, like astral bodies, levitate: and as he enters Hades, from behind a wildly floating silk curtain the spirits of the dead emerge. Here, too, entranced by his art, all obey him; and even Pluto's rock turns to reveal Eurydice in his embrace (she has been married to Death, as in the Japanese myth of Izanagi-No-Mikoto and Izanami-No-Mikoto).

With his music Orpheus, who is blinded to all material facts by the mask of his art, leads Eurydice earthward. But, alas, he is now beset by doubts of material possession. He tears off his mask and sees Eurydice as she really is, a creature of death. Without the protection of his artistic powers, he is even weaker than ordinary mortals, and he is torn apart by the Furies. But his art is not dead; his singing head has grown heroic as his spirit returns; and as a symbol of this resurrection, a flowering branch ascends to heaven.

Writing *Giselle*
by Théophile Gautier

My dear Heinrich Heine, when reviewing, a few weeks ago, your fine book, *De L'Allemagne*, I came across a charming passage—one has only to open the book at random—the place where you speak of elves in white dresses, whose hems are always damp, of nixes who display their little satin feet on the ceiling of the nuptial chamber; of snow-coloured *Wilis* who waltz pitilessly, and of all those delicious apparitions you have encountered in the Harz mountains and on the banks of the Ilse, in a mist softened by German moonlight; and I involuntarily said to myself: "Wouldn't this make a pretty ballet?"

In a moment of enthusiasm, I even took a fine large sheet of white paper, and headed it in superb capitals: *Les Wilis*, a ballet. Then I laughed and threw the sheet aside without giving it any further thought, saying to myself that it was impossible to translate that misty and nocturnal poetry into terms of the theatre, that richly sinister phantasmagoria, all those effects of legend and ballet so little in keeping with our customs. In the evening, at the Opera, my head still full of your idea, I met, at a turning of the wings, the witty man who knew how to introduce into a ballet, by adding to it much of his own wit, all the fairy caprice of *Le Diable Amoureux* of Cazotte, that great poet who invented Hoffmann in the middle of the eighteenth century.

I told him the tradition of the *Wilis*. Three days later, the ballet *Giselle* was accepted. At the end of the week, Adolphe Adam had improvised the music, the scenery was nearly ready, and the rehearsals were in full swing. You see, my dear Heinrich, we are not yet so incredulous and so prosaic as you think we appear. You said in a moment of ill-humour: "How could a spectre exist in Paris? Between midnight and one o'clock, which has ever been the hour assigned to ghosts, the most animated life still fills the streets. At this moment the Opera resounds to a noisy finale. Joyous bands flow from the Variétés and the Gymnase; everyone laughs and jumps on the boulevards, and everyone runs to evening parties. How miserable a stray ghost would

Source: From *The Romantic Ballet As Seen By Théophile Gautier*, translated by Cyril W. Beaumont (New York: Dance Horizons, 1972). Originally published in London 1932, revised edition 1947.

feel in that lively throng! Well, I had only to take your pale and charming phantoms by their shadowy finger-tips and present them, to ensure their receiving the most polite reception in the world. The director and public have not offered the least objection *à la Voltaire*. The *Wilis* have already received the right of citizenship in the scarcely fantastic rue Lepelletier. Some lines where you speak of them, placed at the head of the *scenario*, have served them as passports.

Since the state of your health has prevented your being present at the first performance, I am going to attempt, if a French journalist is permitted to tell a fantastic story to a German poet, to explain to you how M. de Saint-Georges, while respecting the spirit of your legend, has made it acceptable and possible at the Opera. To allow more freedom, the action takes place in a vague country, in Silesia, in Thuringia, even in one of the Bohemian sea-ports that Shakespeare loved; it suffices for it to be on the other side of the Rhine, in some mysterious corner of Germany. Do not ask more of the geography of the ballet which cannot define the name of a town or country by means of gesture, which is its only tongue.

Hillocks weighed down with russet vines, yellowish, warmed and sweetened by the autumn sun; those beautiful vines from which hang the amber-coloured grapes which produce Rhine wine, form the background; at the summit of a grey and bare rock, so precipitous that the vine tendrils have been unable to climb it, stands, perched like an eagle's nest, one of those castles so common in Germany, with its battlemented walls, its pepper-box turrets, and its feudal weathercocks; it is the abode of Albrecht, the young Duke of Silesia. That thatched cottage to the left, cool, clean, coquettish, half-buried among the leaves, is Giselle's cottage. The hut facing it is occupied by Loys. Who is Giselle? Giselle is Carlotta Grisi, a charming girl with blue eyes, a refined and artless smile, and an alert bearing; an Italian who tries to be taken for a German, just as Fanny, the German, tries to be taken for an Andalusian from Seville. Her position is the simplest in the world; she loves Loys and she loves dancing. As for Loys, played by Petipa, there are a hundred reasons for suspecting him. Just now, a handsome esquire, adorned with gold lace, speaks to him in a low voice, standing cap in hand and maintaining a submissive and respectful attitude. What! A servant of a great house, as the esquire appears to be, fails to lord it over the humble rustic to whom he speaks! Then, Loys *is not what he appears to be* (ballet style), *but we shall see later*.

Giselle steps out of the cottage on the tip of her dainty foot. Her legs are awake already; her heart, too, sleeps no longer, for it is full morning. She has had a dream, an evil dream: a beautiful and noble lady in a gold dress, with a brilliant engagement ring on her finger, appeared to her while she slept and seemed about to be married to Loys, who himself was a great nobleman, a duke, a prince. Dreams are very strange sometimes! Loys does his best to reassure her, and Giselle, still somewhat uneasy, questions the marguerites. The little silver petals flee and scatter: "He loves me, he loves me not!" "Oh, dear! How unhappy I am, he loves me not!" Loys, who is well aware that a boy of twenty can make the daisies say whatever he chooses, repeats the test, which, this time, is favourable; and Giselle, charmed with the flowers' good augury, begins to leap about again, despite her mother, who scolds her and would rather see that agile foot turning the spinning-wheel that stands in the window, and those pretty fingers questioning marguerites busied in gathering the already over-ripe grapes or carrying a vine-dresser's basket. But Giselle scarcely listens to the advice of her mother, whom she soothes with a little caress. The mother insists: "Unhappy child! You will dance for ever, you will kill yourself, and, when you are dead, you will become a *Wili.*" And the good woman, in an expressive pantomime, relates the terrible legend of the nocturnal dancers. Giselle pays no heed. What young girl of fifteen believes in a story with the moral that one should not dance? Loys and dancing, that is her conception of happiness. This, like every possible happiness, wounds unseen a jealous heart; the gamekeeper, Hilarion, is in love with Giselle, and his most ardent desire is to injure his rival, Loys. He has already been a witness of the scene where the esquire Wilfrid spoke respectfully to the peasant. He suspects some plot, staves in the window of the hut and climbs through it, hoping to find some incriminating evidence. But now trumpets resound; the Prince of Courland and his daughter Bathilde, mounted on a white hackney, wearied from hunting, come to seek a little rest and coolness in Giselle's cottage. Loys prudently steals away. Giselle, with a timid and charming grace, hastens to set out on a table shining pewter goblets, milk, and some fruit, the best and most appetising of everything in her homely larder. While the beautiful Bathilde lifts the goblet to her lips, Giselle approaches with cat-like tread, and, in a rapture of artless admiration, ventures to touch the rich, soft material of which the lady's riding costume is composed. Bathilde, enchanted by Giselle's pleasant manners, places her gold chain round her neck and wishes to take the girl with her. Giselle thanks her effusively and replies that she wants nothing more in the world but to dance and to be loved by Loys.

The Prince of Courland and Bathilde withdraw into the hut to snatch a few moments' rest. The huntsmen disperse into the wood; a call on the prince's horn will warn them when it is time to return. The vinedressers return from the vineyards and arrange a festival of which Giselle is proclaimed the Queen and in which she takes the principal part. Joy is at its height when Hilarion appears carrying a ducal mantle, a sword, and a knightly order found in Loys's hut—all doubt is at an end. Loys is simply an impostor, a seducer who has been playing on Giselle's good faith; a duke cannot marry a humble peasant, not even in the choreographic world, in which one often sees kings marrying shepherdesses—such a marriage offers innumerable obstacles. Loys, or rather Duke Albrecht of Silesia, defends himself to the best of his ability, and declares that no great harm has been done, for Giselle will marry a duke instead of a peasant. She is pretty enough to become duchess and lady of the manor. "But you are not free, you are betrothed to another," asserts the game-keeper; and, seizing the horn left lying on the table, he blows it like a madman. The huntsmen run up. Bathilde and the Prince of Courland come out of the cottage and are amazed to see Duke Albrecht of Silesia in such a disguise. Giselle recognises in Bathilde the beautiful lady of her dreams, she doubts her misfortune no longer; her heart swells, her head swims, her feet shake and jump; she repeats the measure she danced with her lover; but her strength is soon exhausted, she staggers, sways, seizes the fatal sword brought by Hilarion and would have fallen on its point if Albrecht had not turned it aside with the quickness born of despair. Alas, the precaution is in vain; the blow has struck home; her heart is pierced and Giselle dies, consoled at least by her lover's profound grief and Bathilde's tender pity.

There, my dear Heine, that is the story invented by M. de Saint-Georges to bring about the pretty death we needed. I, who ignore theatrical effects and the demands of the stage, had thought of making the first act consist of a mimed version of Victor Hugo's delightful poem. One would have seen a beautiful ballroom belonging to some prince; the candles would have been lighted, flowers placed in vases, buffets loaded, but the guests would not yet have arrived; the *Wilis* would have shown themselves for a moment, attracted by the joy of dancing in a room glittering with crystal and gilding in the hope of adding to their number. The Queen of the *Wilis* would have touched the floor with her magic wand to fill the dancers' feet with an insatiable desire for contredanses, waltzes, galops, and mazurkas. The advent of the lords and ladies would have made them fly away like so many vague shadows. Giselle, having danced all the evening, excited by the magic floor and the desire to keep her lover from inviting other women to dance, would have been surprised by the cold dawn like the young Spaniard, and the pale Queen of the *Wilis*, invisible to all, would have laid her icy hand on her heart. But then we should not have had the lovely scene, so admirably played, which concludes the first act as it is; Giselle would have been less interesting, and the second act would have lost all its element of surprise.

The second act is as nearly as possible an exact translation of the page I have taken the liberty of tearing from your book, and I hope that when you return from Cauterets, fully recovered, you will not find it too misinterpreted.

The stage represents a forest on the banks of a pool; you see tall pale trees, whose roots spring from the grass and the rushes; the water-lily spreads its broad leaves on the surface of the placid water, which the moon silvers here and there with a trail of white spangles. Reeds with their brown velvet sheaths shiver and palpitate beneath the intermittent night breeze. The flowers open languorously and exhale a giddy perfume like those broad flowers of Java which madden whoever inhales their scent. I cannot say what burning and sensuous atmosphere flows about this humid and leafy obscurity. At the foot of a willow, asleep and concealed beneath the flowers, lies poor Giselle. From the marble cross which indicates her grave is suspended, still quite fresh, the garland of vine branches with which she had been crowned at the harvest festival.

Some hunters come to find a suitable place of concealment; Hilarion frightens them by saying that it is a dangerous and sinister spot, haunted by the *Wilis*, cruel nocturnal dancers, no more forgiving than living women are to a tired waltzer. Midnight chimes in the distance; from the midst of the long grass and tufted reeds, will o' the wisps dart forth in irregular and glittering flight and make the startled hunters flee.

The reeds part and first we see a tiny twinkling star, next a chaplet of flowers, then two startled blue eyes set in an alabaster oval, and, last of all, the whole of that beautiful, slender, chaste, and graceful form known as Adèle Cumilâtre; she is the Queen of the *Wilis*. With her characteristic melancholy grace she frolics in the pale star-light, which glides over the water like a white mist, poises herself on flexible branches, leaps on the tips of the grass, like Virgil's Camilla, who walked on wheat without bending it, and, arming herself with a magic wand, she evokes the other *Wilis*, her subjects, who come forth with their moonlight veils from the tufted reeds, clusters of verdure, and calixes of flowers to take part in the dance. She announces to them that they are to admit a new *Wili* that night. Indeed, Giselle's shade, stiff and pale in its transparent shroud, suddenly leaps from the ground at Myrtha's bidding (that is the Queen's name). The shroud falls and vanishes. Giselle, still benumbed from the icy damp of the dark abode she has left, makes a few tottering steps, looking fearfully at that tomb which bears her name. The *Wilis* take hold of her and lead her to the Queen, who herself crowns her with the magic garland of asphodel and verbena. At a touch of her wand, two little wings, as restless and quivering as those of Psyche, suddenly grow from the shoulders of the youthful shade who, for that matter, had no need of them. All at once, as though she wished to make up for the time wasted in that narrow bed fashioned of six long planks and two short ones, to quote the poet of *Leonore*, she bounds and rebounds in an intoxication of liberty and joy at no longer being weighed down by that thick coverlet of heavy earth, expressed in a sublime manner by Mme. Carlotta Grisi. The sound of footsteps is heard; the *Wilis* disperse and crouch behind the trees. The noise is made by some youthful peasants returning from a festival at a neighbouring village. They provide excellent quarry. The *Wilis* come forth from their hiding-place and try to entice them into the fatal circle; fortunately, the young men pay heed to the warnings of a wiser greybeard who knows the legend of the *Wilis*, and finds it most unusual to encounter a bevy of young beings in low-necked muslin dresses with stars on their foreheads and moth-like wings on their shoulders. The *Wilis*, disappointed, pursue them eagerly; this pursuit leaves the stage unoccupied.

Enter a young man, distracted, mad with sorrow, his eyes bathed in tears; it is Loys, or Albrecht, if you prefer it, who, escaping from his guardians' observation, comes to visit the tomb of his well-beloved. Giselle cannot resist the sweet evocation of so true and profound a grief; she parts the branches and leans forward towards her kneeling lover, her charming features aglow with love. To attract his attention, she picks some flowers which she first carries to her lips and throws her kisses to him on roses. The apparition flutters coquettishly, followed by Albrecht. Like Galatea, she flies towards the reeds and willows. The transverse flight, the leaning branch, the sudden disappearance when Albrecht wishes to take her in his arms, are new and original effects which achieve complete illusion. But now the *Wilis* return. Giselle tries to hide Albrecht; she knows too well the doom that awaits him if he is encountered by the terrible nocturnal dancers. They have found another quarry. Hilarion is lost in the forest; a treacherous path brings him back to the place from which he had only just fled. The *Wilis* seize hold of him, pass him from hand to hand: when one waltzer is tired, her place is taken by another, and always the infernal dance draws nearer to the lake. Hilarion, breathless, spent, falls at the Queen's knees and begs for mercy. But there is no mercy;

the pitiless phantom strikes him with a branch of rosemary and immediately his weary legs move convulsively. He rises and makes new efforts to escape; a dancing wall bars his passage, the *Wilis* make him giddy, push him on, and, as he leaves go of the cold hand of the last dancer, he stumbles and falls into the pool— Good night, Hilarion! That will teach you not to meddle in other people's love affairs! May the fish in the lake eat your eyes!

What is Hilarion but one partner for so many dancing women? Less than nothing. A *Wili*, with that wonderful woman's instinct for finding a waltzer, discovers Albrecht in his hiding-place. What good fortune, and someone who is young, handsome and light-footed! "Come, Giselle, prove your mettle, make him dance to death!" It is useless for Giselle to beg for mercy, the Queen refuses to listen; and threatens to give Albrecht to the less scrupulous *Wilis* in her band. Giselle draws her lover towards the tomb she has just left, signs to him to embrace the cross and not to leave it whatever may befall. Myrtha resorts to an infernal and feminine device. She forces Giselle, who, in her capacity of subject, must obey, to execute the most seductive and most graceful poses. At first, Giselle dances timidly and reluctantly; then she is carried away by her instinct as a woman and a *Wili;* she bounds lightly and dances with so seductive a grace, such overpowering fascination, that the imprudent Albrecht leaves the protecting cross and goes towards her with outstretched arms, his eyes burning with desire and love. The fatal madness takes hold of him, he pirouettes, bounds, follows Giselle in her most hazardous leaps; the frenzy to which he gives way reveals a secret desire to die with his mistress and to follow the beloved shade to her tomb; but four o'clock strikes, a pale streak shows on the edge of the horizon. Dawn has come and with it the sun bringing deliverance and salvation. Flee, visions of the night; vanish, pale phantoms! A celestial joy gleams in Giselle's eyes: her lover will not die, the hour has passed. The beautiful Myrtha re-enters her water-lily. The *Wilis* fade away, melt into the ground and disappear. Giselle herself is drawn towards her tomb by an invisible power. Albrecht, distracted, clasps her in his arms, carries her, and, covering her with kisses, places her upon a flowered mound; but the earth will not relinquish its prey, the ground opens, the flowers bend over. . . . The hunting-horn resounds; Wilfrid anxiously seeks for his master. He walks a little in front of the Prince of Courland and Bathilde. However, the flowers cover Giselle, nothing can be seen but her little transparent hand . . . this too disappears, all is over!—never again will Albrecht and Giselle see each other in this world. . . . The young man kneels by the mound, plucks a few flowers, and clasps them to his breast, then withdraws, his head resting on the shoulder of the beautiful Bathilde, who forgives and consoles him.

There, my dear poet, that, more or less, is how M. de Saint-Georges and I have adapted your charming legend with the help of M. Coralli, who composed the *pas*, groups, and attitudes of exquisite novelty and elegance. For interpreters we chose the three graces of the Opera: Mlles. Carlotta Grisi, Adèle Dumilâtre, and Forster. Carlotta danced with a perfection, lightness, boldness, and a chaste and refined seductiveness, which places her in the first rank, between Elssler and Taglioni; as for pantomime, she exceeded all expectations; nor a single conventional gesture, not one false movement; she was nature and artlessness personified. True, she has Perrot the Aerial for husband and teacher. Petipa was graceful, passionate, and touching; it is a long while since a dancer has given us so much pleasure or been so well received.

M. Adam's music is superior to the usual run of ballet music, it abounds in tunes and orchestral effects; it even includes a touching attention for lovers of difficult music, a very well-produced fugue. The second act solves the musical problem of graceful fantasy and is full of melody. As for the scenery, it is by Ciceri, who is unequalled for landscapes. The sunrise which marks the conclusion is wonderfully realistic. . . . La Carlotta was recalled to the sound of the applause of the whole house.

So, my dear Heine, your German *Wilis* have succeeded completely at the French Opera. *—July 5, 1841*

The Teachers and Schools, Companies and Directors

Teachers and Schools

"To enter the School of the Imperial Ballet," Pavlova wrote in her memoirs, "is to enter a convent whence frivolity is banned, and where merciless discipline reigns." Perhaps the training of no other kind of artist begins as early, lasts as long, and is as rigorous as that of the classical dancer. As long as he or she is performing, even the most famous of professional dancers begins the day as a student: by taking class.

These classes, similar the world over, can be traced back at least as far as 1661, when Louis XIV founded the Académie de Danse in a room in the Louvre, an institution which still exists today in the form of the Paris Opera. In 1671 Pierre Beauchamp was appointed the first ballet master of the Académie, transforming dance from a court pastime into a profession, and most of today's professional dancers can, in fact, trace their lineage to these very beginnings of ballet. (See Appendix II.)

The daily class—remarkably similar for the beginner and professional alike—may initially seem dreary, but as Agnes De Mille has remarked, "these were the exercises that built Taglioni's leg. These repeated stretches and pulls gave Pavlova her magic foot and Legnani hers and Kchessinska hers. . . . Here was an ancient and enduring art whose technique stood like the rules of harmony. All other kinds of performance in our Western theater had faded or changed. What were movies to this? Or Broadway plays?"

The five classic positions and the basic arm postures were named and codified by the first ballet teachers: Pierre Beauchamp (1636–1705?), Louis Pécourt (1653?–1729), and Pierre Rameau (dates unknown). Although subsequent great teachers such as Jean-Georges Noverre (1727–1810), Auguste Vestris (1760–1842), Carlo Blasis (1797–1878), August Bournonville (1805–1879), Enrico Cecchetti (1850–1928), and Agrippa Vaganova (1879–1951) revised and enlarged the codified steps and the fashion in which they are taught, the steps have remained largely unchanged. "The more one considers the five positions," Lincoln Kirstein has said, "the more absolute their logic seems. Simplicity itself, the underlying principle is based on human anatomy, reduced to its essential capacities. It permits a five-note scale from which an infinitude of visual chords in innumerable keys may be rationally arranged."

The importance of good teachers and their contribution to the art of dance should thus be obvious. Dance is, so to speak, a hand-me-down art and the teachers, to a great extent, do the handing down. Tamara Karsavina, the great Russian ballerina and Nijinsky's most frequent partner, claimed that the intangible treasure of ballet could only be transmitted through the medium of a great teacher. Pavlova herself once confessed that her success was due largely to the merits of her teachers, and premier danseur André Eglevsky thought so highly of the exercises given to him by his teacher Nicholas Legat that he always took Legat's notes with him on tour.

The labor of the classroom leads to the magic on the stage: the basis of even the most advanced choreography is the instruction learned so rigorously in the daily class. As Vera Volkova, one of the great modern Soviet teachers has succinctly put it: "It is our job as teachers to see that the rules are maintained and that the dancers understand the rules. It is the job of the choreographer then to break all the rules, to use distortions from the basic classroom technique."

During the eighteenth century most of the great dance teachers were French; during the nineteenth century, Italian; and during the twentieth century, Russian. When Lincoln Kirstein brought Balanchine to America in 1933 to start an American ballet company, the two men agreed that if America were ever going to produce a great company it would first need a great school. So in 1934 the School of American Ballet opened, the official training organization for what has now become the New York City Ballet. In her essay included here, Nancy Goldner details the school's history and current curriculum and provides us with insights into the important collaboration between teacher and choreographer.

Companies and Directors

Reading Petipa's *Memoirs* can be maddening. You race through the chapters, hungry to learn more about this great choreographer's work —how he conceived *Sleeping Beauty*, what he thought of his collaboration with Tchaikovsky, how he created the fourth act of *La Bayadère*—only to find a series of rather mundane anecdotes about contracts, directors, and company politics. We learn very little about Petipa's work and more than enough about his business matters. Petipa's *Memoirs* remind us that ballet, often thought the most refined and spiritual of the arts, has its practical side as well: its art is surrounded by the wheeling-dealing intrigues of powerful companies and their imperious directors.

Although Pavlova frequently performed without being formally affiliated with a dance company and Nureyev has hopped around from one company to another during his career in the West, traditionally most dancers and choreographers are closely associated with a particular dance company, much as most film actors and directors up until the 1950s worked within the confines of the studio system. And just as American filmmaking can not be completely understood without taking into account its studios, a good survey of dance must examine the influence of companies and their directors.

Although a director's contribution to dance is certainly not on a par with that of a choreographer or dancer, it would be foolish to deny that companies have shaped and even changed the history of dance. Arlene Croce once remarked that all dance companies are crazy, each in its own way, and it is a company's "craziness"—its prejudices, beliefs, habits, and style—that is bound to influence its dance. In her essay included here, Lucia Chase—the cofounder and codirector of American Ballet Theatre—discusses her role as director of one of the world's major dance companies and gives us a behind-the-scenes glimpse of ABT's own breed of "craziness."

The School of American Ballet

by Nancy Goldner

The School of American Ballet is an institution unique in America because its purpose is to train *professional* ballet dancers. Today, with ballet a widespread fact of cultural life, the desire to dance on the stage is relatively acceptable; in 1934, however, when the School of Ameri-

Source: From *Repertory in Review: Forty Years of the New York City Ballet* by Nancy Reynolds (New York: Dial, 1977).

can Ballet opened, ballet was something Europeans did. The purpose of Lincoln Kirstein's invitation to George Balanchine to work in America was to extend ballet life as Balanchine knew it—the structure he was born into in Imperial Russia—across the ocean. Since Balanchine had already shown himself to be an outstanding and prolific choreographer by 1934, the key concept in America could afford to be permanency, the opportunity for a continual production of ballets. Choreographers need an ever-renewing supply of dancers; hence the rationale for a school-company relationship. Had Balanchine been primarily a teacher instead of a choreographer, the establishment of a school would have insured proper training—this we may assume, given his St. Petersburg schooling—but it would have been an incomplete, even sterile, undertaking. The School was not intended to offer the niceties of a liberal-arts education; it did not claim that ballet instruction had some intrinsic worth, and it certainly had no intention of shipping its graduates back to Europe. Its function was pragmatic: to prepare students for employment and to give Balanchine the material he needed. A significant, even symbolic, fact about the School of American Ballet is that in March 1934, just two months after the doors opened, Balanchine assembled his advanced students and began making *Serenade*. Just four months after that, the school had a performing wing, when *Serenade* was danced for an invited public at an estate in White Plains, New York.

Being a vocational school gives the School of American Ballet a simplicity of purpose but also means that it must operate on exact and exacting principles. Whereas people who enter medical school, for example, are old enough to know what they want and have the maturity to modify their lives according to the demands of their studies, the eight- and nine-year-olds who begin to study ballet cannot understand what they are getting themselves into. Usually their parents do not understand either, because it is not the custom in America to associate childhood with serious and hard labor. A child (the vast majority are girls) enters the School of American Ballet in a fairly blind state, buttressed perhaps only by a vision of *Serenade* as it is now performed by the New York City Ballet, or more likely by an experience with *The Nutcracker*, where she sees children not much older than herself dancing on stage. That is, if she is lucky, she enters the school with these visions. Very often it is her parents who have the visions. In the Soviet Union and Denmark, where ballet schools are subsidized by the state and where it is more generally and deeply understood that ballet is a consuming and long course of study, the little child is sent to a boarding school where all her needs are met; she is fed, clothed, instructed in academics, ballet and related fields of dance, stagecraft, and music; then she's bedded down at night. The School of American Ballet offers only ballet lessons, the point being that, in not being a boarding school, it does not have an apparatus that can become a kind of symbol of crossing a threshold. So it is more difficult for an American child than it is for a Russian child to discover what vocational training means.

Because the School of American Ballet has always been associated with Balanchine, and because from 1934 until the present Balanchine has always drawn most of his dancers from the School—whether for his various Broadway and Hollywood projects, the several predecessors of the New York City Ballet, or now the New York City Ballet—the school's professional orientation is so ingrained and ordained that the stakes inevitably become clear to students. This happens through a subtle psychological process—the School operates as though it were perfectly normal in American society for children to organize their lives around work. Naturally, the School accommodates itself to American life, but it is an accommodation. The School's expectation of professional interest and drive makes itself felt immediately.

First of all, every applicant is given an audition to see if she has sufficient promise and to determine what class her technique qualifies her for. (Auditions are held once weekly throughout the year.) Students already in their teens must qualify at least for the intermediate level. If they are not sufficiently strong for that level by the time they are fourteen, say, it is highly unlikely that they will ever become professional ballet dancers. Exceptions are made for boys, but only out of necessity. Beginning students from ages ten to thirteen are enrolled in an accelerated beginner course. Given its purpose, however, the School prefers beginners to be eight or nine years old (the Russian academies accept students at age nine) and to be *real* beginners, since it has found that most local training can be harmful and, at best, needs to be unlearned. For this group, "promise" means a well-proportioned body and, most importantly, flexible limbs and arched feet. The teacher who auditions does not ask the beginner to do actual ballet steps, but examines her feet and moves her back and legs to determine muscular temperament. At the end of the examination, the teacher asks the child to improvise to music, and notes if the child can move rhythmically and can adjust her movement to changes in tempi.

The eight- and nine-year-olds, in Children 1, attend classes only twice a week, but their hour-long baptisms are by fire, and the level of concentration demanded by the teacher is incredibly high. There is no "free movement," and since the students have so few steps at their command, there is little chance for variation. Moreover, since the students are so preoccupied with basics—standing up correctly, keeping stomachs pulled in, pointing feet, learning the muscular mysteries of turnout in the legs—the teacher can barely burden their minds with combinations of steps. At first they do four or eight battements tendus in each direction; not until later on in the year, or perhaps in the second year, are they asked to handle a more sophisticated but still very elementary combination, such as three battements tendus to the front and one to the side, three to the back and one to the side.

Of necessity, first-year studies are mostly drudgery and certainly no fun. A sense of progress or achievement is so hard-won that one can only marvel that any of the students have spirit left to feel it at all. Some react to the discipline and the humdrumness of the lessons by tuning out, so that they walk or dream themselves through class, or be becoming class cutups. As is always the case in life, boredom becomes a self-perpetuating cycle to failure. The more the student removes herself from the moment, the more difficult it is for her to jump into it later on, and so the more difficult it becomes to reap the rewards that encourage greater participation. However, a few children do learn the rare pleasure of doing something well, and all are spared the chaos of a half-baked education.

The School has a fixed schedule of attendance that gradually increases as the student progresses through the five Children divisions or the two older Beginner divisions (A1 and A 2). Teachers do not take kindly to chronic absence, tardiness, or excuses of stomachaches while class is going on. They reprimand daydreamers and, while they realize that the child has just spent a whole day at academic school, they never openly acknowledge to the students that they know it is difficult to concentrate intensely right after a day's confinement in school.

Toward the end of the year, the teachers submit brief reports on their students. On these grounds, children are advanced, left behind, dismissed, or warned that they will have to make great progress the following year in order to continue at the School. In the beginning, teachers comment as much on attitude and brightness as they do on technical proficiency. In spring of 1974, six of the thirty-seven children in Children 1 class were asked to withdraw, mostly for reasons of discipline and laziness. The School's most thorough weeding occurs before the student enters the second Intermediate level, now called B2.

Obviously, however, the dropping-out process is two-way. Much of the enrollment drop is by attrition. Students cannot cope with competition, and lose sight, or never gain sight, of the connection between classroom exercises and dancing. For many entering their teens, sexual fantasies take precedence over everything else, leaving little energy to think about pliés. Like mathematics, ballet technique advances by geometric progression, and there comes a day when many find that they just cannot keep up.

Yet because ballet has become increasingly popular and seemingly more accessible, and because the School of American Ballet has that gigantic lollipop called *Nutcracker*, children—and their parents especially—are more likely to cling to dreams of ballerinadom than they were in the 1940s and early 1950s. Thus the faculty and administration must draw an increasingly "tough" line on enrollment. To parents, the School must seem harsh indeed. To children, who usually know better than their parents what is demanded of them as would-be professionals and how well they can live with that expectation, the School is probably more resolutely fair than harsh. For the School, whose business is to produce dancers, not well-rounded, gracious young men and women or even first-rate amateurs, anything less than a tough line would negate its raison d'être.

The time slots given to classes are perhaps the School's most tangible expression of the all-consuming nature of a dance education.

Up to the first Intermediate level (B1), classes do not begin until 4:00 P.M. But B2 classes, the level at which the School does its most thorough elimination process, start at 2:30 P.M. Thus when a student enters B2, at about age fourteen, she must decide whether to enter a school with special hours, such as Professional Children's School, so that she can take the daily 2:30 class. Such private schools entail huge expense for the family and may even require a move into Manhattan. For the student, this means entering a much less "normal" world and making a formal declaration of intent regarding a career that neither she nor her teachers can yet guarantee. At this point, of course, parents and children want a firm word of encouragement from the School of American Ballet. But in most cases it cannot say, "Yes, you will be a dancer; the New York City Ballet wants *you*," because bodies and minds still go through drastic changes during adolescence. Also, beginning with the B2 level, technical demands grow disproportionately; this is the time when a young dancer's drive for excellence is severely tested and often broken. Thus the very structure of the School forces students to reckon with psychological stresses that most adults usually spend their lives avoiding, and they're reckoning at an age American society still calls childhood.

It is at the B2 level also that the required number of classes per week can discourage the less committed. Before this, boys and girls must attend four classes weekly, although many girls in B1 attend more. At B2 the number jumps to eight (six ballet classes and two toe classes).

The boys, whose classes are separated from the girls', may still be taking four or five lessons a week, since they have probably started instruction at a later age. At the C and D levels, however, both sexes are spending most of their time at the School, squeezing in academics on the off-hours.

The boys have class every day with Richard Rapp, Stanley Williams, Antonina Tumkovsky, Peter Martins, or a guest teacher from 12:30 to 2:00 P.M.[1] From 2:30 to 4:00, they must take one or two supported adagio classes and a workshop class in preparation for the school's annual concert. There is an evening men's class from 5:30 to 7:00.

The advanced girls, split into C1, C2, and D levels, have ballet class from 10:30 A.M. to noon. From 2:30 to 4:00, the C1 girls have a toe class once a week, one variations class in which Alexandra Danilova teaches them dances from the standard Russian repertory, and one supported adagio class. At the same afternoon hour, the girls in C2 and D are attending each week one adagio class, two workshops with Danilova and Suki Schorer, and a variations class with Danilova. Advanced girls also attend three more evening ballet classes from 5:30 to 7:00. (They take nine classes weekly.)

As the spring workshop performance approaches, rehearsals are added to the schedule. Thus, advanced-level students, some as young as fifteen, may attend as many as thirteen classes a week. The School requires them to enroll for at least eight classes, but this is an arbitrary number. Ten classes per week (six morning classes and four specialized classes in the afternoon) would seem to be the minimum.

The School of American Ballet has always operated with exacting and rigorous standards. The faculty has always given classes designed to turn students into first-rate dancers, and the School has always demanded that advanced students attend at least eight classes a week. Yet, until a ten-year Ford Foundation grant was given the School in 1964, and to a certain degree after that and into the present, the administration has had to negotiate an inherent contradiction: it wants only professional-caliber enrollment, but it must support itself through tuition. In the 1930s, 40s, and 50s, the student body had more dead weight as a result. During these decades, there were also fewer gradations of classes (for example, four Children's divisions instead of five, one B class instead of B1 and B2), which meant much larger class size, sometimes as many as thirty-five or forty in an evening C class, when

[1] In 1976 boys' classes were also taught by Andrei Kramarevsky, a former principal with the Bolshoi, and Jean-Pierre Bonnefous of the New York City Ballet. [Goldner's note.]

professional dancers would join the students. Each of the School's residences (previous to the present Juilliard facilities), at Madison Avenue and Fifty-ninth Street (1934–1956) and Eighty-third Street and Broadway (1956–1969), had only two large studios and one smaller one. There simply was no space for more classes, nor could the administration afford to demand that teen-age students attend early-afternoon classes.

Larger classes with fewer highly qualified students mitigated to some extent the extreme professional air and the pressure to excel, which now flourish without restraint. Children in particular are helped immeasurably by today's smaller classes. The teacher's eye is felt more directly at a time when students' ability to motivate themselves is still developing, and individualized instruction can be truly enlightening. Today classes average around 20. Total enrollment is about 350, only 25 of them boys.

The School's success in expanding and refining curriculum and in drawing better students was in large measure due to the Ford Foundation program begun in 1964, but improvements would have occurred anyway, though not so quickly or thoroughly, because they had to happen. The entire dance field was expanding, and the "cultural boom" necessitated more and better dancers. The New York City Ballet itself was growing and its roots were deepening.

Around 1960 Balanchine started to reform the School of American Ballet by hiring more faculty, instituting a special small class for the best students, and starting a complete male division. (Previously there had been only one or two men's classes a week.) In the early 1960s, when these programs had been in effect a while, the administration concluded that if the School continued to follow Balanchine's course it would plunge nicely into the red. It was also during this time that the Ford Foundation asked the school to draw up a proposal for a national program of ballet education. Like all historical processes, the growth of ballet, the City Ballet, and the School and the coming of the Ford Foundation grant converged in a mixture of coincidence and inevitability.

The Ford Foundation program was in two parts. The first centered around the School. Money was allotted for operating expenses and for renting space in the new Juilliard School at Lincoln Center. Although the School had always given some scholarships, the grant made it possible to offer more tuition scholarships, aid for private school, and living expenses of $200 a month (raised to $220 in 1975–1976) for students around the country who were thought promising enough to be transported to New York for study, either for the summer or for the entire year. The School had never found that New York alone could supply enough talent to justify its operation, and so the Ford grant enabled it to consider the United States its talent pool.

Yet even with this national scope, it does not have the resources of the Russian, Danish, or English academies to take full responsibility for nonlocal students' living arrangements. Seven younger students (ages fourteen and fifteen) live with Madame Guillerm, the mother of Violette Verdy, a principal with the City Ballet. The School tries to place other young ones with the families of local students, but sometimes a Ford Foundation scholarship necessitates the student's family moving to New York. Older recipients, sixteen and seventeen years of age, live in residences approved by the School and often rent apartments together once they have been in New York for a while. Obviously, a move to New York is beset with complications, not the least of them the emotional one of leaving home and friends. Yet it enables those who want to become dancers *to* become dancers, not only through study but through the stimulation of competition and exposure to all of New York's professional dance companies. The New York City Ballet is a prime beneficiary, but a program that concentrates talent in one place is a boon to all.

The second part of the Ford Foundation program was designed to improve ballet education in the local community. Acting as administrator, the School was essentially an intermediary between the Foundation and the nation. School faculty and dancers from the City Ballet traveled to schools that applied for aid, watched classes, and recommended scholarships for local study, subject to yearly renewal. Matching grants were given to schools that wanted to set up beginner programs for children without the financial means for study. In many instances, the Ford representative taught at the local school for a day or so, while local teachers came to the school to observe. In the program's early years, Balanchine taught master classes at the School of American Ballet, which teachers from all over the country attended.

In the academic year 1971–1972, for example, 42 schools in 12 states were observed. The number of local scholarships awarded was 233 in 68 schools, and 8 beginner groups were operating. Scholarships to the School of American Ballet's 1972 summer course were given to 93 students from 52 schools, and out of that group, 12 won scholarships to the School for the following year. At the School itself, 79 students (34 of them boys) were on tuition scholarship, 41 of whom received additional aid for living expenses and academic tuition. Some scholarship students (as well as other students) participated in lecture-demonstrations led by Suki Schorer. For these 42 performances in metropolitan-area schools, the dancers received $30 a performance and $2 an hour for rehearsals. (No scholarship students are allowed to perform without the School's permission, and no dance engagements, such as the lecture-demonstrations, may interfere with regular classes at the School for any student.)

In 1973, this pilot program terminated. The Ford Foundation then approved a second grant of $1.5 million, covering the period 1974–1979, this time contingent on the School's raising equivalent funds. An additional $500,000 will be forthcoming if this money also is matched. The present grant is entirely for the operating expenses of the School; for the moment, the regional program has been suspended.

That the School of American Ballet is the official school of the New York City Ballet gives it distinct coloration beyond its professional orientation. Balanchine hires faculty, determines curriculum, and instigates new programs, such as those carried on just before and during the Ford Foundation period. Eugenie Ouroussow, the late executive director, and Natalie Molostwoff, who now holds the post, would not hire a teacher for a single class without Balanchine's permission, and all teachers have watched Balanchine teach. In the School's early years, Balanchine was a regular member of the faculty. Today he occasionally gives a class for the advanced students, but his place is in the theater, not the School. When openings develop in the New York City Ballet's corps de ballet, he asks advanced students to take his daily company class and to become apprentices for a season. In April 1974, during the period I was observing classes, he invited six girls into his company (which effectively wiped out level D class for the rest of the year). The faculty recommends students to his attention, but he does not necessarily follow their advice. Yet he draws all of his ensemble from the School (in 1974, sixty-two of the eighty-member company were graduates). Thus a student aiming for the New York City Ballet must study at its school.

Students are very much aware of the City Ballet's existence. Company members take class at the School, and ex-members Suki Schorer and Richard Rapp and present members Carol Sumner, David Richardson, Peter Martins, and Colleen Neary teach there. Company rehearsals are sometimes held if studios are available. Advanced students learn some of the Balanchine repertory (instead of the usual series of grands battements that end a class, Schorer gives her third-year children the grand battement combination from the end of Balanchine's *Stars and Stripes!*). And of course there are the ballets that use children from the School—*Nutcracker*, *Harlequinade*, *Pulcinella*, *A Midsummer Night's Dream*, *Don Quixote*, *Firebird*, *Coppélia*, and two ballets for the Stravinsky Festival, *Circus Polka* and *Choral Variations on Bach's "Vom Himmel Hoch."* With many students, there is much bugaboo about "getting into the company." As students mature—as they understand that they may not be material for Balanchine for reasons of physique and technique, or that Balanchine might not be the material for *them* —other companies might become "the" company. Since the School is considered to be among the best in the world, directors from dance groups all over the world use the advanced classes as their supply depots. The School's grapevine on auditions flourishes, and the administration actively tries to place those of its best students not likely to be candidates for the City Ballet, or who do not want it, with other professional companies. The School serves a global ballet community as well as Balanchine.

Students at the School of American Ballet learn standard ballet technique as it is taught in Russia and, with certain deviations, in England and Denmark. Essentially this is a technique taught by Russian-trained dancers and their students. Pierre Vladimiroff, the School's first teacher, from January 2, 1934, until 1968 (died 1970), was a graduate of the Imperial School of Ballet and was a leading dancer of the Maryinsky Theater, where Balanchine studied and performed in his youth. Anatole Oboukhoff, on the faculty from 1941 until his death in 1962, also had the same background, and so do present teachers Felia Doubrovska (Vladimiroff's wife) and Alexandra Danilova. Danilova was Balanchine's classmate, and Doubrovska was also an alumna of the Imperial School; both were with Diaghilev's Ballets Russes when Balanchine was its chief choreographer. Helene Duin and Antonina Tumkovsky are graduates of the State Choreographic School in Kiev and were soloists with the Kiev State Theater of Opera and Ballet. Muriel Stuart was taught by Anna Pavlova from age eight and toured with her company. Stanley Williams comes from the Danish-Russian tradition, having graduated from the Royal Danish Ballet School and performed with the Royal Danish Ballet. Elise Reiman is the first of the School's staff to be a graduate of it and a member of Balanchine's early companies, American Ballet and Ballet Society, as well as New York City Ballet. Now Richard Rapp, Suki Schorer, and the present Company members provide more immediate links, but the major difference between their classes and those of the Russians is that they speak English better. Among the teachers, there are variations in emphasis, and all teachers have their own accents, apparent not only in what they choose to correct but in the amount of teaching they do. Some are more verbal and analytical; others let the exercises speak for themselves, so that students learn simply by doing. The ex-Company teachers are younger and so demonstrate more, but the older teachers set marvelous examples of regal carriage and of the use of épaulement, by showing how a slight shift in the shoulders or head can make the difference between an elegant and a dead-looking dancer.

The first two divisions are taught by Tumkovsky, Dudin, and Reiman. In Children 1, Tumkovsky goes from girl to girl at the barre, adjusting feet with a stick or her hands and making sure that elbows are rounded, pinkies are held out away from the other fingers, and that knees and backs are straight. She does not allow girls to turn their feet out to a full 180-degree angle if their knees must bend to support the legs in that extreme position. She does not allow them to lift their legs so high that their backs cave in. Certain steps at the barre are broken down into parts. In grand battement, the leg first points in tendu and then kicks. In rond de jambe the leg does not make a continuous circle but stops at the front, side, and back. However, even in the first year the students learn all the barre exercises that the advanced divisions do. Combinations in the center are very simple, and before each jump exercise, the children first practice it at the barre. To compensate, in a way, for the dryness of the class and to maintain a high energy level, Tumkovsky keeps the pace as quick as possible and talks in a loud voice. She ends the class on a dancy note by having the children chassé across the room. To tell the truth, this is the only part they seem really to enjoy. The rest is strange and even painful.

The students in Children 2 look markedly more alert and show more awareness of their bodies. They look more in one piece, and some already have bearing; they understand that heads must be held high in ballet. With these young children, Dudin is perhaps more concerned with their alertness than with technique. She scolds them gently when they do not pay attention, and when someone makes a mistake, she demands that the child figure out what is wrong. She will wait patiently, even if it means holding up the class for minutes, for the child to respond—and to respond with the *right* answer. Children learn from the start that details are everything. In one exercise that was done two by two, Dudin told them to look at each other before making a preparatory plié for emboîtés forward. The girls who did not first look at each other had to repeat the exercise until they did it correctly. In all levels all teachers stress the importance of épaulement—a croisé positioning of the shoulders must be croisé, en face must be en face, effacé must be effacé, écarté must be écarté. In the young divisions Reiman,

Dudin, and Tumkovsky stop the class when students are hazy about these positions, and have everyone repeat the combination with greater clarity. In other words, students must learn that to do an assemblé en face when the teacher said to land in croisé is as big a mistake as doing a jeté instead of an assemblé. Details of this sort seem to be the hardest for children to learn, especially as the combinations become more complex and quicker. The advanced students work on the same problems, but the problems become more refined. They must find just the right amount of shoulder angle and must learn how to flow from one angle to another with just the right amount of motion.

In Children 3, the technical demands and complexity of combinations rise enormously, and one can see a noticeably greater strength in the legs and backs when compared to the two earlier divisions. At the barre the adagio exercises, with développés and dégagés, are much longer. Sumner and Schorer have the students do pirouettes at the barre in preparation for turns in the center. In the center the children do more things on one leg, which requires better balance and strong muscles for the supporting leg. Sumner reminds them that in preparations for pirouettes, the back leg should be straight (their first explicit exposure to one of Balanchine's few rules). Schorer stresses posture at the barre—straight backs, eyes straight ahead, buttocks taut, hips straight, no rolling over onto the front of the foot, and so forth. Like Tumkovsky, Dudin, and Reiman, Sumner and Schorer use the time at the barre for visiting each girl and making the necessary pushes and shoves. When the teacher grasps a girl's hips so that she finds she cannot swing her legs up so easily, a knowing smile passes between teacher and student. The student learns that there's quite a difference between throwing the leg up in any manner possible and throwing it up with the hip held in place. Yet in Children 4 and 5, when students must start striving for a high leg extension, Dudin will often raise a girl's leg much higher than the girl could achieve herself with her hips held in place. Thus the student must learn to work at a problem from both ends, to know when to let a high extension take precedence over hip placement and vice versa. Then when she starts taking Balanchine's class, she must juggle the two concerns again: she must get her leg *still* higher without bringing the hip out of alignment "too much"—but how much is too much?

Pointe work begins in Children 4, during the last fifteen minutes of each class. The girls wear especially light shoes, designed by Balanchine and a Capezio engineer. The most-stressed technical aspect, in this and the B toe classes, is the manner in which the girls rise on pointe. They must roll up, not jump. All movement must go through demi-pointe, and they must learn to use their pointe shoes as flexibly as their ballet shoes. This is one reason why Balanchine requires that girls from the intermediate levels on take ballet class in toe shoes. The students' constant striving for turnout and arched feet really comes into play with pointe work, and those who have not progressed in these areas find in toe work their Waterloo. Girls in Children 5 have a weekly one-hour class devoted specifically to pointe, and here they join girls in A2.

The convergence of the five Children divisions and two older Beginners' divisions in the elementary toe class is as good a measure as any of the older students' accelerated pace. The barre in A1 is about as quick, complicated, and strenuous as that in Children 3. Because their muscles are stronger, the older beginners are expected to use more gusto in forcing their legs up and out. In A2 they learn the same refinements taught in Children 4 and 5, and teachers tend to approach the steps more analytically and from an inner, or muscular, point of view. Richard Rapp can tell them to pull up on the standing leg, to press legs out in plié, to brush the leg in frappé with sharp attack—that is, he can use concepts a ten-year-old could not understand because she does not yet have enough muscular self-consciousness. Rapp and Reiman can expect them to work on the details of exercises; for example, sometimes in battement tendu with plié, they are asked to first bring the leg to fifth position and *then* plié. This method poses a much greater challenge to turnout and forces the student to turn her heel forward in tendu. These teachers stress the muscular spring and tautness that is at the very basis of ballet technique. They demand that rather than sit in plié, the student immediately rise with resilience. All leg movements must be sharply accented on the upbeat. In battement the leg must whoosh up and come softly down without collapsing. Frappés must be strongly accented out. Every movement must be rhythmically dynamic, fast at the outset and held for a split second at the finish. Reiman's students learn what "phlegmatic" means; Schorer speaks of limp macaroni. Stuart is perhaps the most theoretical of the teachers, and students do not take her class until they reach A2 and Children 5. Her central theme is that the buttocks must be pulled up and the back muscles down. Whereas other teachers ask students for more turn-out by asking them to turn their thighs out and push their heels forward (Tumkovsky and Dudin merely order, "more turn the leg out!!"), Stuart asks them to pull their buttocks up more. She also verbalizes more extensively the "secret" that students have been slowly discovering: muscular tension and control are hidden, and the head, neck, and arms—the parts of the body that are most likely to display tension—must not be rigidly gripped, but held softly, with alertness.

In B1 girls are taught by Danilova for the first time. She does most of the barre right along with the students, but manages to keep her eye on them through the mirrors lining one wall of the studio. At the barre she gives ample time for balances at the conclusion of exercises done on demi-pointe and tends to give practical hints for balancing, such as keeping the front arm slightly above eye level in arabesque. After the barre, the girls do their own leg stretches, just about the only free movement ever allowed at the School of American Ballet. In the second half of the class, Danilova often teaches variations; at one class I watched, these were a simplified variation from *Sleeping Beauty*, a minuet to music from the same ballet, a tarantella, and a polonaise. She insists on careful épaulement, which she demonstrates in high style, and on moving exactly—but exactly—with the music. She reprimands girls who dance like wooden sticks and mimics them to make her point. Of all the teachers, Danilova seems to be most concerned with the ballerina style and with having students move slightly in anticipation of the beat.

B2 and the C and D classes are more of the same—just longer and harder. The fast exercises are faster; the slower ones slower. Combinations are trickier, requiring fast shifts in weight, and are longer, requiring more stamina. Whereas the less advanced grades do adagio movements on the flat foot in center work, now the students must rise onto demi-pointe as much as possible. Jumps are laced with batterie. Pirouettes must be triple or quadruple, although B2 girls are encouraged to give clean execution precedence over number, even if that means only a single turn. With B2 begins work on turns in arabesque, attitude, and à la seconde, and by C they are par for the lesson.

At this level students meet two more teachers, Williams and Doubrovska. Williams's time is spent mostly with men's classes and the C and D classes, but he does teach one B2 class a week. Doubrovska normally instructs only the C and D classes, but when D was temporarily suspended in mid-April 1974, she was assigned to one B2 class and now teaches B2 regularly. Doubrovska stresses virtuoso aspects—balances, big jumps, and, especially, turns. She spends much time on the use of the arms for turns and has a hawk's eye for chests and backs that are anything less than regally held. At the barre she gives some exercises, such as grands battements and ronds de jambe, at a very quick pace, almost as fast as Balanchine. She wants square hips, a taut and highly pulled-up torso, and proper placement at the conclusion of a big jump so that the student can move from jump to jump easily and quickly. Herself a model of elegant carriage, she constantly reminds her students not to collapse after a combination, but to be en garde and gracious all the time. Épaulement is a means of presenting oneself to the audience. Presentation of self is the real significance of turnout, Doubrovska implies. With Doubrovska and Danilova, the student begins to perceive herself as performer.

Williams is perhaps the most idiosyncratic teacher. Whereas all the teachers at all levels jump back and forth between basic and refined corrections, Williams directs all comments to the refinements that interest him most. He seems to be envisaging the students as *his* ideal dancers. (I write *seems* because understanding exactly what Williams is after is almost an intuitive process, with sporadic flashes of recognition.) He seems to be primarily interested in a sustained legato quality of movement. Whereas Rapp, Reiman, and Schorer often want exercises to be separated (and hold!, and hold!, and hold!), and whereas the other teachers are not so explicit about this but imply it by exhorting students to be more energetic and forceful, Williams wants exercises to be done in one sustained and steady breath, and he wants this sustained rhythm without a loss of tension. To communicate this, he says that he wants the leg to "go through" fifth position, rather like electrically charged taffy. In one B2 class I observed, which, as Williams acknowledged to the class at the end, was one of the most intense he taught, he told them that in an exercise in which the leg développés front, goes into passé, and then into arabesque, he wanted the leg to go through passé on one count, like "pulling thread through a needle." A stop in passé, or for that matter in fifth position in battement and fondu exercises, is a rest and "you've lost it," "it" being that string of tension. In adagio combinations and in adagio class, Williams always wants a sense of movement even if the body is still. In adagio class he repeatedly tells the girls not to think about balancing in promenades but about their "position." If the girls are not in position, the movement "dies." What Williams is getting at here is the problem of occupying space vibrantly and authoritatively when the body is static. For supported turns in adagio class and in unsupported turns in regular ballet class, he always tells the students not to think of the turn but of the passé or attitude. He wants an illusion that the turner is always facing front, trying to pull a single clear, crystallized image out of a blur. Williams speaks of what to think and what not to think. In the men's classes, he says not to think of a jump as a jump but as a plié, so as to get that continuity of movement between the floor and the air. He is more interested in ballon, less in elevation, more interested in a clear position in turns, less in the number of turns. More than any other teacher, Williams makes dancing a mental exercise, a matter of concentration. Most of the boys are not advanced enough to grasp or make use of his subtleties. Because he forces dancers to rethink what they are doing, while the other teachers force them merely to think of a thousand familiar things at once, the students tend to look more amateurish in his classes than in others'. But because the girls ordinarily are stronger and more experienced than the boys, their weakness proceeds from strength; they can afford to experiment on this very high level.

Do the teachers prepare students for Balanchine? It is not difficult to pick out those technical emphases Balanchine will be happy to see in his Company class, yet most of them would please most teachers. When teachers ask for energy, a high carriage of the chest, high leg extensions, extreme turnout when the leg is in effacé or à la seconde, a taut plié, spring glissades with the accent in fifth, assemblés with the legs together in the air; a straight back leg in preparation for pirouettes, precise definition of all the shoulder and head positions; when teachers work for speed; when they design combinations that develop quickness in weight shifts; and when they ask that combinations be done in reverse so as to develop mental flexibility and to discourage a habit-forming approach to movement—they are preparing students for Balanchine. The one important exception to Balanchine-teacher accord is Williams's demand that battement, fondu, and frappé series be one steady flow. Balanchine wants them separated, with a slight accent out and a larger accent in fifth position. There is also a difference in ports de bras. The teachers want arms to move in a long line and at standard distance from the body. Balanchine likes the arms closer to the body in transitional movements, so that the elbows are more prominent, and wants a bigger-than-life silhouette once the pose is hit. Generally Balanchine wants a more voluptuous look in arm movement; Schorer calls the look "juicy." Also, Balanchine wants the thumb more prominently displayed than some teachers call for. In rond de jambe some teachers want the accent out, whereas Balanchine usually wants it without accent; here Williams is in accord with Balanchine. Perhaps Rapp in his men's classes and Schorer in her advanced classes are the most doctrinaire Balanchinians, but all the other teachers share their methods qualitatively if not quantitatively. As I have written, in most cases it is a matter of emphasis.

On the other hand, no class at the School of American Ballet really prepares a student for Balanchine. First of all, there are physical matters less superficial than one might suspect. As many as eighty may attend Company class in the State Theater's big rehearsal studio. Dancers hang off the rafters, and it takes a while to find one's comfortable rafter. Then, the dancers wear individually concocted warm-up costumes. They seem to take special delight in the contradictory effect of raggedy leotards and assorted bulky woolens wrapped around their beautiful, sleek bodies. The overall effect is as dizzying as a vista of Neapolitan clotheslines such as even Eugene Berman could not duplicate in his sets for *Pulcinella*. Classes at the School are conducted at a quick clip, but Balanchine's classes are in another time zone. There is absolutely no break between the left-foot and right-foot exercises at the barre. There is barely a break when Balanchine explains what exercise he wants next. He mumbles a word or so, or makes a gesture with his hands, and the dancers go to it with what an outsider perceives to be magical anticipatory speed. At the School the barre is from thirty to forty minutes long; the class, ninety minutes. In Balanchine's one-hour class the barre is only twenty minutes, yet every exercise is covered. Balanchine condenses barre work by cutting out the frills and by setting a fast tempo.

Condensing involves heightening. Balanchine's classes are designed to present normal academic exercises and combinations in their most heightened, or difficult, form. This is the crux of the matter; and this is what no student is prepared for. The tempo for each exercise is as fast or as slow as is necessary for it to be just beyond the reach of possibility. Balanchine seems to be especially fond of a series of battements tendus and jetés that becomes faster and faster until teasingly close to the impossible. Because this series has no rest break or pliés to stretch the muscles in the opposite direction, it is extremely hard on the thighs.

The series will often be continued in the center of the room, where the dancer has no barre for support. To make matters more difficult, the arms are held down so that the dancer cannot use them to balance herself. Since the tendus go in rapidly changing directions, they call for extremely strong backs and great agility in weight shifts. Whereas an adagio combination at the School grows progressively longer, in Balanchine's class it can be longer than long. At one class I observed, he had the dancers do twelve consecutive développés on each foot; as a fillip, each was done in a different position or with different ports de bras. In the School, arabesque penché is common; in Balanchine's class the dancers must do ports de bras while in that position. Hardly anyone can do it without falling over, but falling and stumbling are common features in the professional class. Balanchine's class is truly a place to experiment, to sport with ideals, to look ungainly. Because it is the exact opposite of the performance situation, where everything must go smoothly and effortlessly, it is a haven. Yet it takes time for newcomers to discover that a situation where the premiums are on struggle and failure *is* a haven. Newcomers must develop trust, bravery, and a sense of humor before they can experience the exhilaration of a Balanchine class. In addition, a pre-warmup at the barre is a virtual necessity.

The classes assume an extra difficulty because Balanchine wants each step to be a musical and visual statement. A single développé is an aria unto itself. The movement may perhaps be done on one count but have two climaxes—when the foot leaves the ground for the ankle, and when the moving leg leaves the supporting leg as it unfolds into an extension. Again, this is not in contradiction to what is taught at the School, but an intensification. Sometimes a combination or a series of them will be built around the use of dynamics. In one class the theme was combinations with soutenu, itself an easy step. The idea was to whoosh around in the soutenu, freeze for a fraction of a second, and then whoosh into the next step, a pas de bourrée. A further complication was that the pas de bourrée was supposed to be as fast as the soutenu, which is impossible to really achieve.

In other words, Balanchine wants the dancer to have as much flexibility with his body as the musician has with his piano or violin. When done with Balanchinian dynamics, movements are easy to see and exciting to watch. But I think the crucial factor is their imitation of musical stress. It has been said many times now that watching Balanchine ballet is like seeing the music. His "eye music" is usually attributed to choreography, but the fact is that the musicality of his ballets is built right into the technique, just as the drama of Graham's ballets is built right into her technique. One may deduce from this that technique is not an *a priori* system of rights and wrongs. At the School of American Ballet, technique *is* a historically proven system of rights and wrongs enabling a dancer to dance for anyone and endowing him with a base for forms other than ballet. For Balanchine, technique is a pragmatic and on-going search for a style of moving that will please him once it is seen on the stage. His classes are workshops for the dancers, but they are also preliminary exercises for Balanchine's work as a choreographer.

Directing a Ballet Company

by Lucia Chase

When I am asked what it is I do with Ballet Theatre, I usually reply that I am in charge of the company. I realize this can lead to confusion unless the term "the company" is clearly defined and understood.

Source: From *American Ballet Theatre* by Charles Payne (New York: Knopf, 1978).

When I speak of the company I do not mean the corporate entity that administers the business affairs. These are conducted by the officers of the Ballet Theatre Foundation in accordance with policies set by the Board of Governing Trustees. The company of which I am in charge is the performing unit known as American Ballet Theatre, whose members create, rehearse, and perform the ballets of its repertory. My principal concern is with the dancers, with whom I first come in contact during the selection process.

The procedure for selecting dancers has varied considerably over the years. There was a time when we could hold "open" auditions which any dancer could attend without a special invitation. Because of the tremendous increase in the number of ballet-school graduates, this is no longer feasible. (More than three hundred dancers appear for the annual auditions to the American Ballet Theatre School alone.) Today, a limited number of recommended dancers are invited to apply in smaller groups, or from time to time individuals are asked to take a company class where they can be seen by myself, the ballet masters, and the choreographers and be judged in comparison with the dancers of the company.[1] These applicants are recommended by sources all over the country. (They used to come to us from all over the world, but new government and dancers' union regulations now require that only American citizens be chosen for the corps de ballet and that foreigners be engaged as soloists or principal dancers only under special circumstances.) We have never seriously considered restricting the applicants to graduates of our own school because we are aware that there are many talented dancers throughout the country who cannot afford to come to New York for study. As it is our aim to employ the most promising talent available, we take it where we can find it.[2]

What is looked for in a dancer and by what criteria are selections

[1] On every rehearsal or performance day, separate women's and men's classes (or a combined class) are given. A class serves the double purpose of warming up the muscles and of enabling the dancer to practice combinations of steps. The dancer begins at the barre with exercises designed to stretch and strengthen the muscles and continues on the studio floor with the performance of dancing exercises. Classes are conducted by a ballet master, who points out any bad habits the dancer may have acquired and suggests how they may be corrected. Thus these are not classes in the usual sense of the word; they are not sessions in which one is taught to dance.

[2] It is to be hoped that the time may come when funds are sufficiently available to enable us to search out young talent throughout the country and to provide scholarships to our School for the most promising. At such time we will doubtless accept more School graduates into the company. In the meantime we audition those who are recommended to us by the School faculty, by our ballet masters and choreographers, by regional teachers and companies with whom we come in contact on tour, and by our own dancers. [This, like the other footnotes to the essay, are Chase's.]

made? Standards and the procedure for examination have altered enormously since the days when, as a dancer myself, I first observed the selection process. In the 1940s it was necessary to begin by determining the extent of the applicant's mastery of the ballet technique, which often proved to be scarcely adequate. In that first decade of Ballet Theatre, it was not unusual for a dancer to be taken into the company even though she was unable to execute a series of fouettés or he could not perform a double air-turn. Today, we can assume that dancers will not be put forward for our consideration, or will not offer themselves, unless they have mastered those and other technical feats. It is no longer a question of *can* they perform. The questions now asked are can they perform with ease, with authority, and with beauty of line? We do, of course, first check the dancer's physical qualifications—the proportions and placement of the body and limbs. Today, with the company performing *La Bayadère*, for example, in which the dancers must move uniformly, it is essential that they all be able to extend the leg in high arabesque (made possible only by the proper "turn-out" at the hips). And with the addition of so many classic ballets to the repertory the possession of "good feet" has assumed even greater importance.

Poor feet and faulty turn-out are physical defects that would be deplored by the auditioners for any classic ballet company. But there are also stylistic variants that are regarded as defects at a Ballet Theatre audition. Take, for example, the matter of the arms, wrists, and hands. Through the company's and Dimitri Romanoff's early association with Michel Fokine, we acquired a taste for the rounded arm and wrist, with the fingers held in a soft, natural position. This is a matter of preference. Other companies may prefer straight, thrusting arms, with "broken" wrists and fingers extended at sharp angles. There is, of course, no "right" or "wrong" style for the classic ballets; it is, as I say, a matter of preference. But our teachers, ballet masters, and choreographers devote endless hours to inculcating our preferred style into our dancers.

These physical and stylistic attributes, together with the proportions of the body, are apparent to the eye and can be observed objectively. Other attributes are less obvious and require a certain amount of guesswork in their detection. Is the dancer attractive, does she have charm, is she alert, does she project an interesting personality, is she friendly, amiable, and good-natured? Some of these qualities, particularly the last, appear to be irrelevant, but they assume importance in a touring repertory company where the dancer must remain in close contact with her fellow dancers over protracted periods and where she must accept the vicissitudes of a constantly changing repertory that may suddenly deprive her of one of her most treasured roles. To remain a contented dancer in such a company, one must necessarily be good-natured. It would seem impossible to detect these intangible qualities during a brief audition, and yet experience has proved that a great deal can be learned from apparently casual observation at a time when the dancer is not aware of being observed—as she walks to the barre, or puts on her toe shoe, or talks with her fellow dancers, or listens to the instructions of the ballet master conducting the audition.

Chance also sometimes plays a role in the selection of a dancer. She may by good fortune have applied at just the right moment. As we prepare for each season we review the roster of dancers and determine our requirements for replacements. Our dance dramas require performers of varying sizes. The role of Lizzie Borden as a child in *Fall River Legend* or of the Youngest Sister in *Pillar of Fire* must necessarily be performed by a short dancer, as must the boys' roles of the Grooms in *Petrouchka* or of the Satyrisci in *Undertow.* When these shorter dancers are cast in the classic ballets, from *Swan Lake* down through *Etudes*, they cannot be dispersed haphazardly among the taller dancers. To present an aesthetically pleasing line of the corps de ballet it is imperative, as with a string of pearls, that the dancers be placed in graduated order with respect to size. Since I keep this continually in mind, I find myself approaching an audition with reminders such as, "We need two more short boys," or "If so-and-so leaves to get married we'll need another tall girl to replace her." Thus it is that chance and the right moment may improve the fortunes of a girl of five feet six inches who comes to our attention just at the time when we must engage a tall dancer.

And finally, in a company that presents the ballets of so many different choreographers, the quality of adaptability must be sought for in its dancer applicants. Each particular choreographer would be very happy if we engaged *every* dancer whose qualities appealed to him and who he thought would be "just right" for a role in one of his ballets. However, the roster of a repertory company cannot be enrolled on this basis. Every dancer selected must appear to be capable of performing roles created by a dozen other choreographers and, even more important, be equipped with the technique demanded in the performance of the company's increasingly dominant classic repertory.

A review of our selection actions over the years reveals that more often than not dancers, particularly those with previous ballet experience, have chosen to join Ballet Theatre rather than have been selected by us. A case in point is that of John Kriza, who came back from a tour of South America with one of Ruth Page's companies during Ballet

Theatre's first year. Unless he could find dance employment in New York he was faced with the prospect of returning to Chicago to assist in running his father's meat market. With only enough money in his pocket to pay for a last meal, he attended three auditions in the same day: for the Ballet Russe de Monte Carlo, a Broadway musical, and Ballet Theatre. He was offered employment by all three companies and chose us, where he remained to become known as "Mr. Ballet Theatre" until his retirement a quarter of a century later. For me, Johnny occupied a very special and unique position in the company—one similar to that occupied today by Mikhail Baryshnikov. Although the technical skills of these two dancers are not to be compared, as warm human beings they are twin spirits—understanding, cooperative, generous of their time and talent, blessed with a humor sometimes sly but always good, and, above all, totally dedicated to the integrity of their art. Thus, at the other end of Ballet Theatre's thirty-five years, it was not significant that *we* chose to engage Mikhail Baryshnikov. Who in his right mind would not have? The significant decision was the one Mischa made when *he* chose American Ballet Theatre as his home company.

Along with the selection of the dancing company, accomplished in consultation with the ballet masters and the resident choreographers, I also collaborate with Oliver Smith in the selection of the repertory. Here again, the elements of chance and of the "right moment" inevitably play an important role both for the choreographer and the direction. When reviewing the repertory to determine what ballets will be presented during the forthcoming season, the directors may decide, for example, that the opening ballets in the active repertory have been seen too often by the public—that a new opening ballet is required. If by chance a choreographer comes forward at that right moment with an idea for a new work suitable for use as an opening ballet, he and his idea may be accepted, whereas at another time they might have been rejected. Or the directors may conclude that a new ballet must be created for one of our principal dancers. In 1975, for instance, it was agreed that we must acquire a modern ballet that would afford Mikhail Baryshnikov an opportunity to display his unique comic talent. Previously we had been discussing the commissioning of a new work with Twyla Tharp, and when coincidentally she and Baryshnikov came together, *Push Comes to Shove* was created. If they had not met at that particular time, Ballet Theatre would still have added a Tharp ballet to its repertory and would eventually have produced a comic ballet for Baryshnikov by another choreographer, but in neither case would the result have resembled *Push Comes to Shove*.

More than in any other branch of the performing arts, the directors of a ballet company are, for the most part, forced to embark on a new production in blind faith. Opera and symphony scores or scripts of dramatic works can be played or read before rehearsals are undertaken. The producers cannot know whether the production will be a success but at least they know *what* they are producing. Ballet producers can know in advance only what is in the choreographer's head, and that is often vague or incommunicable. Much must be taken on faith. Fortunately, Richard Pleasant performed such an act of faith in 1940 when a choreographer approached him with an idea he had been mulling over for some time. The choreographer had in mind a ballet, to be called *I Dedicate*, that would trace the traumatic psychological experiences of a frustrated female who lived in terror of remaining a spinster like her older sister and yet was not willing to adopt the predatory flirtation tactics employed by her younger sister in getting her man. On the basis of this brief synopsis—and the choreographer offered little more—Dick accepted the ballet, but the sketch for the scenery he commissioned from Peter Piening indicates that the choreographer's conception had not been made clear to him. When Gerry Sevastianov took over the direction of the company, he hesitated to proceed with rehearsals of the ballet and was particularly dubious that a classical ballet could be danced on pointe to Schönberg's "Verklärte Nacht." However, he crossed his fingers and went through with the production, which by that time the choreographer, Antony Tudor, had renamed *Pillar of Fire*.

The "crossing of fingers" has become the customary course of action when the direction embarks on the production of a new ballet by an established choreographer, and the risk it runs is even greater when it commissions a work from a novice. These risks must be taken into consideration when Oliver Smith and I are deciding whether to entrust the creation of a ballet to an untried choreographer. We are aware that it will not be until the rehearsals are virtually completed, and perhaps not until after the scenery and costumes have been executed, that we will be able to tell whether we have in fact discovered a choreographer with talent or have merely found one capable of flashes of choreographic brilliance but not of creating a complete, well-constructed work. During these final rehearsals we must also determine whether further investments should be made in the new choreographer regardless of the success or failure of his first ballet. For it is then that we learn the answers to such questions as, can he communicate his thoughts and wishes to the dancers, does he understand how to use their bodies (their potentialities and limitations), and, perhaps most important, can he organize his own thinking and his use of rehearsal time? If he can do these things, he is a good risk for a second ballet even if his first has been a failure. If he cannot, his chances of being given another opportunity are diminished even if his first work is an unquestioned success. In these days when rehearsal time is severely restricted by union regulations and overtime rates are so high, a company can no longer permit a dancer to be called for rehearsal only to sit by idly, unused by the choreographer. With established choreographers, the directors must tolerate "slow periods" and those sessions in which inspiration fails, but they cannot permit the same luxury to a novice. Impatience is forced on the directors by the economics of present-day production of ballets.

Having performed the function of selecting choreographers, ballets, and dancers, I am then called upon to operate what I have come to refer to as the "complaint department." Complaints of every nature, most of them understandable and many of them justified, are directed to me not only by the choreographers and dancers but also by our subscriber-patrons, the general public, and the press. The complaints from choreographers begin with the early rehearsals, when they feel not enough rehearsal time is allotted them, and continue through the performing season, when their ballets are not scheduled often enough or in the right order. (They will protest, "My ballet should never be on the same program as such-and-such ballet," or "My ballet should always be placed in the middle of the program and should be immediately preceded only by the undramatic, neutral *Les Sylphides*.") The dancers' complaints begin at the same time as the choreographers', when during rehearsals they have not been cast in the roles of their choice, and they continue throughout the season, when they are not scheduled to perform as often as they wish the roles for which they *have* been chosen.

It will be asked how one could find fault with a choreographer's eagerness to rehearse an infinite number of hours to attain perfection. No one does find fault, but eventually facts must be faced: the number of rehearsal hours and of studios is limited, and a dancer can be made available to only one choreographer in one studio at one time. To arrange for the right dancer to be in the right studio for the right choreographer at the right time presents a formidable problem of logistics that could never be easily solved even by a computer. It is solved daily in a time-consuming juggling act performed by Enrique Martinez.

The compiling of the season's performing schedules is equally complex, as ballets are constantly shifted until they are formed into a series of programs for the season that will satisfy the demands of the dancers, the choreographers, and the public. The manipulation is generally performed by Enrique Martinez and me with suggestions and advice from Antony Tudor and from Daryl Dodson, who contributes the stage expertise he acquired while serving as production stage manager. When the final arrangement of ballets has been arrived at, we separate, usually in a state of mental fatigue, and await the receipt of typed copies. It is then, the following day, that our refreshed minds begin to make unwelcome discoveries. The phones begin to ring. Daryl, as former stage manager, calls to point out that Ballet X cannot possibly follow Ballet Y on the second Friday because the scene-shifting involved would require an intermission of not less than thirty-five minutes even if there were no hitches. Enrique is on the phone to report that the second week's schedule contains only one ballet in which Martine van Hamel performs. This means she will have only one performance that week unless we insert an additional ballet or she learns an additional role. My secretary, Florence Pettan, calls to remind me that I had agreed to let Ivan Nagy dance with Margot Fonteyn on the 17th in Montreal, the day on which I have scheduled Ballet X for the Met. "Is this a mistake or is someone else learning Ivan's role?" Daryl rings again, this time in his capacity as general manager, to report that the subscription department has discovered an error. *Petrouchka* cannot be scheduled for the third Thursday because it was seen only last season by the Thursday-night subscribers. At about that time, I notice that we have programmed Ballet Y to precede *Les Noces*, which I had promised Jerry Robbins never to do. While I am still puzzling over the solution to this problem, Nancy Zeckendorf, of the American Ballet Theatre Friends, phones to tactfully protest that the new pas de deux for dancers A and B has been scheduled for the 18th, two days before the Gala. It should be reserved for the Gala alone, but if there must be additional performances they should follow the Gala and not be announced until she has sold more of the $100 tickets.

After countless adjustments have been made and, it is hoped, all the problems have been solved, I am almost immediately pressured by the publicity department to furnish it with a list of the casting of the principal roles in all of the scheduled performances. This I cannot do until I have gone through a routine I customarily follow after the programs have been set. I review with each of the principal dancers in turn the proposed casting. I frequently find that their thought processes have differed from mine and that they are able to offer valid reasons for changes. Dancer A, for example, is scheduled to dance Giselle for the first time with Dancer B. So that she can devote more time to preparation, she would prefer that the performance of *Giselle* be scheduled *after* the premiere of the new ballet on which she is now concentrating her complete attention. Even when all adjustments have been made, the casting list as published must sometimes require change due to illness or injury. And then there are always special circumstances and unknown factors that make it impossible to state with certainty who will dance which roles weeks or months hence.

These "unknowns" differ from season to season, but those which preceded the 1976 Met season are illustrative of their general nature. Erik Bruhn had been injured during the previous season and was still recuperating in Denmark when the casting lists, announcing that he would dance Petrouchka, were issued. He had never danced the role, and not until he had returned to New York would he be able to find out whether he had recovered sufficiently to dance or whether the movements devised by Fokine could be executed without causing a recurrence of his injury. Also during the previous season, Gelsey Kirkland had fallen victim to a dietary deficiency, and she was still under a doctor's care when her performances were announced. Her recovery depended to a large extent on her own determination to get well, and there appeared to be no better way of bolstering her will power than by including her name in the published casting lists as an expression of our confidence in her rapid recovery. The third unknown was perhaps unique in the annals of ballet. Arrangements had been made for Alicia Alonso to appear in the Cuban Ballet version of *Carmen*, but at the time the programs and castings were to be released it could not be ascertained whether the Cuban and American governments would issue the necessary visas. A spate of hard words directed at each other by Fidel Castro and Gerald Ford might upset all plans. And even should Alicia arrive on schedule in this country, it was deemed inadvisable for security reasons to announce her appearances in advance. Consequently, four performances of Tudor's *Shadowplay* were scheduled. If all went well, *Carmen* would be substituted for them. If not, *Shadowplay* would be performed as announced. The castings of Bruhn and Kirkland and the scheduling of *Shadowplay* were made with honest intentions but also with the knowledge that they might not materialize. However, I did not feel they justified a protest that was registered at my complaint department by a balletomane who should have been better acquainted with the exigencies of casting predictions. "Your list," he said accusingly, "is nothing but a tissue of unmitigated lies!" Was he one of those who had, in the first place, demanded casting information so far in advance?

The complaints that come to my department from the dancers fall on more sympathetic ears because they echo my own experiences as a dancer. When they ask for roles that cannot be assigned to them, I recall that I, too, coveted roles for which I had to wait. In 1941 Anton Dolin staged *Pas de Quatre*, and although I rehearsed the role of Cerrito perhaps even from the start, it was not until 1943, when the role fell vacant because its originators, Katharine Sergava and Annabelle Lyon, were no longer with the company, that it was assigned to me. When a dancer complains about having to share a role with another dancer, I remember how I felt about *Les Sylphides.* During the first season, I happily shared the Prelude with Annabelle, but when in the following year Dick Pleasant required us to share the role with a third dancer, I resented it. It meant that Annabelle and I would be given fewer performances, being replaced, if even only occasionally, by a dancer whom neither of us recognized as her equal. Like every dancer, I had my moments of greed. Later, when Alicia Markova joined the company and replaced me in most of the important performances of *Les Sylphides*, I accepted it because she was a dancer of international reputation. I don't mean to suggest that I felt *no* resentment, I can only repeat that I *accepted* it. In still another instance, in 1965 Antony Tudor was reviving *Pillar of Fire* after it had been out of the active repertory for six years. In Lisbon, Portugal, Nora Kaye had given her last performance as Hagar, a role she had danced for eighteen years, and at the same time I had decided to hang up my toe slippers and restrict future appearances to acting roles. Consequently, Tudor had to find not only a new Hagar but a new Eldest Sister. Watching another perform the role which had been mine for so many years was not without emotional complications. Most dancers retain proprietary feelings about a role that was created on them, one they rehearsed while the choreographer was originally devising it, and one that they danced at the premiere performance—they are reluctant to share it or give it up entirely. This claim to ownership continues in varying degrees of intensity as long as the dancer performs the role and even for some time afterward.

My personal experiences as a dancer will not allow me as a director to take casually the emotional factors—or even quirks—which motivate the dancers and drive them to register complaints and demands. But an understanding of their problems does not simplify my solutions. When a dancer covets a new role, I cannot always grant her request. Aside from the obvious reason that she might not be suited to the role, there is the possibility that she might not be ready for it—that the demands of the role exceed her technical and emotional maturity. Many a career has been adversely affected because the dancer was pushed prematurely into a role requiring advanced technical and dramatic skills. The first reaction of the critics and public may be one of surprised delight, but thereafter they begin to apply more stringent criteria to the dancer, judging her by too-high standards, and causing her to lose confidence in herself. For this reason a dancer must be brought along slowly and carefully nurtured, even if it means temporarily curbing her eagerness and enthusiasm.

When a dancer (or more often an ardent fan in her behalf) complains that she is being forced too often to share a role in which she has been acclaimed by the public (especially by her own sector of the public), I can only reply that Ballet Theatre policy dictates that for every role there must be alternates and understudies. This policy is required principally because the occupational hazards of ballet dancing make it imperative that substitutes be prepared at all times to take the place of the injured. But there is an additional justification of the policy. In a repertory company it is important to provide each dancer with as many roles in as many ballets as possible. Otherwise a dancer may find herself with no role to perform in a series of performances, and for a dancer to remain idle is debilitating both to her morale and her physical well-being.

There are, of course, exceptions, dictated by the choreographer and the demands of the public. For instance, a choreographer may ask that a certain role be reserved exclusively to one dancer over an extended period. Thus for eighteen years no one but Nora Kaye danced the role of Hagar. This was Tudor's wish. But during that time it was also clear that anyone who bought tickets to see *Pillar of Fire* expected to see Nora as Hagar and would accept no substitute. The same situation sometimes occurs on Broadway when a particular star is as important as the play in which she is appearing. When such a star becomes ill, performances are suspended. In the ballet, rather than substitute another dancer in the role so closely associated with the indisposed star, the program is changed and the ballet replaced with another. More recently this has been true of the ballet *Push Comes to Shove* and the dancer Mikhail Baryshnikov. Those who bought tickets to the ballet demanded to see Mischa in the leading role. We prepared an understudy, and he danced admirably, but it became apparent that in the foreseeable future the role should be performed exclusively by Baryshnikov.

In allowing ourselves to make an exception in the case of a role particularly identified with one dancer, we have sometimes run into trouble. There have been occasions when another ballet could not be substituted at the last moment, and because we had not expected the lead to be danced by anyone but the original star, the choreographer had been indifferent to preparing an understudy and I had been negligent in not insisting that he do so. This was the case with *Theme and Variations*. Everyone who bought tickets during its early years demanded that Igor Youskevitch dance the lead role created for him by George Balanchine. When he was unavailable, performances were canceled. For the Paris season of 1950, *Theme* was on the program for the first three performances. Igor danced on the opening night with Mary Ellen Moylan and woke up the next morning too ill to perform; he was unable to dance for the next ten days. We had no choice but to substitute another ballet for the remaining two scheduled performances, and so advised the French impresario, who sternly informed us that this could not be done. Programs were not capriciously changed in France; there was, in fact, a law against it, and the impresario spoke with a touch of hysteria about the possibility of police intervention. Surely, he protested, a company calling itself the American National Ballet Theatre (as we did on that tour) must be of such magnitude that it could provide at least one other premier danseur capable of replacing Youskevitch! We did have Johnny Kriza (Erik Bruhn was on leave), but his enormous talents did not include a facility for performing double air-turns—and *Theme* called for eight of them to be executed in rapid succession. With reluctance I telephoned him. It was unfair to ask him to make his debut in the ballet at such short notice and doubly unfair to require him to do so before a hypercritical Paris audience. However, he arrived before noon at the Palais du Chaillot, where he rehearsed with Alicia Alonso and danced the next two performances. Alicia was not surprised. She had often danced the *Don Quixote Pas de Deux* with him and was aware that he worried little about technical limitations. In the wings he would say, "Let's get out there and enjoy ourselves." I'm afraid this daring and "joy of dancing" is sometimes missing from much of today's performing as dancers concentrate overmuch on their techniques.

Not infrequently dancers approach my complaint department with certain illusions concerning my powers in regard to casting. They will assert confidently, "Lucia, if you really wanted to, you could give me a performance of such-and-such a role." And then they refuse to believe or prefer to ignore the fact that I am not omnipotent, that I am subject, if not to the dictates, at least to the pressures applied to me by the choreographers, my business associates, and the public. The degree of control exercised by choreographers varies according to the provisions in their contracts. The standard choreographer's agreement provides that he will have the right to choose the first cast from among the members of the company. On his part, he agrees to rehearse a second, understudy cast, to be chosen jointly by himself and the directors. He retains no control over castings in future years. This does not, however, represent the complete picture. Not all contracts are in the standard form and not all casting decisions are made in strict accordance with the contract provisions. In the interest of maintaining cordial relationships, concessions to which the choreographer is not entitled contractually are often made. And each choreographer must be dealt with as an individual. With Antony Tudor, who in his capacity as associate director is almost continually at hand to make casting decisions with respect to his own ballets, I acknowledge his authority as absolute. I make no attempt to influence his casting choices and even refrain from offering casual suggestions, which he might interpret as a pressure tactic that he must discourage by making a contrary decision. With Jerry Robbins, I can presume to discuss alternative castings, and we usually arrive at a mutually satisfactory solution—which is sometimes disrupted later when an emergency decision has to be made and he is not available.

With Agnes de Mille, I have always felt free to offer suggestions, and we have reached impasses only on the casting of the Cowgirl in *Rodeo*, a role Agnes danced in the original production by the Ballet Russe de Monte Carlo. She maintains that it can be danced only by an accomplished comedienne, and on this point there is no disagreement. However, I am constantly surprised when she is unable to find such a comedienne within the ranks of American Ballet Theatre, a company noted for its actor-dancers. Over the years, at her behest, we have allowed ourselves to be persuaded to engage a series of charming and talented comediennes from the Broadway musical stage, without whom, in Agnes' view, "*Rodeo* could not possibly be performed." There were times when we were able to persuade Agnes to permit a regular member of the company to dance the role, principally on tour in smaller cities. We and the critics, along with the public, found these to be admirable Cowgirls, and in time Agnes was won over to them—so much so that when they left the company, she insisted they be brought back as guest artists, "as there was no one in the company capable of performing the role."

Even when I inform a dancer that I cannot cast her in a role because the choreographer is withholding his permission, she will still insist, "You could do it if you wanted to." Technically, she may be right, particularly in cases where the choreographer was not in a strong bargaining position when negotiating his contract and thus not able to reserve all casting rights to himself. But as a practical matter, I can act in defiance of a choreographer's wishes only if I am prepared to have him decline to choreograph future works for the company or refuse to continue to rehearse those already in the repertory. With the scarcity of choreographers, this is a risk I am seldom willing to take.

Another pressure to which I must respond is exerted by my business associates, whose paramount concern is the sale of tickets and box-office receipts, and it is a fact of theater life that some star performers attract more patrons to the ticket window than do others. Consequently, I am continually being urged to schedule more performances for the more popular principal dancers, and I can do so only by conversely scheduling fewer performances for the less popular dancers. There are a number of systems and procedures for determining who will dance what role in which performance, but none of them can operate with complete fairness to all the dancers, and all of them inevitably give rise to instances of anger and unhappiness. The first of these systems, the so-called "seniority system," functions in most state-supported ballet companies, including those in the Soviet Union. In what is virtually a civil-service organization, the junior members must wait until their seniors relinquish roles or magnanimously permit them an occasional performance. Although this system assures contentment to the senior principals, it leaves the juniors with depressing and discouraging frustrations. A second system is employed in companies where the director operates with the assurance that he (and it is sometimes a "she") knows who should dance which roles and when—with the wishes of the dancer or the public regarded as immaterial. This system can succeed only so long as the dancers and the public concede that the director has earned the right to make such decisions on the basis of his or her experience, accomplishments, and, sometimes, genius. I, for one, would never adopt it.

In Ballet Theatre we have adopted a third system, which though apparently more benevolent in its intentions, in practice, I'm afraid, does not guarantee a greater degree of fairness or any fewer incidents of unhappiness. We try for a more equal distribution of roles, apportioned on the basis of merit, with a concession to the wishes of the public. The inclusion of the factor of public popularity, as indicated by ticket sales, may be said to add a taint of commercialism, yet in the end it may produce what is perhaps the most democratic system. The purchase of tickets can be looked upon as the public's exercise of its franchise. Of course, this policy can be followed only by a company which considers its principal function to be that of entertaining its audiences and providing them with moments of excitement, inspiration, and sheer beauty. And while such a company recognizes the importance of continual exploration and experimentation in order to expand the art of ballet, it must not pay too great attention to those who would nag its conscience by insisting that its primary duty is to educate the public—to give it not necessarily what it likes, but what it *should* like. We seek the happy medium: to maintain our integrity while giving the public what it wants. And my business associates assure me that what the public wants, indeed demands, is performances by star dancers. As it happens, the preponderance of our repertory, particularly the classics, also demands performances by dancers of star quality. To the impresarios who pay us fees and assume the costs of performances, there is no doubt as to which stars are of the greatest magnitude—and they insist that these performers must shine in their theaters. But there is sometimes doubt in the minds of stars of lesser magnitude, those whom connoisseurs appreciate but who shine less brilliantly in the eyes of the general public. Their best friends and ardent fans do not tell them about the empty seats (which cannot be seen from the stage), and they feel that my failure to schedule them for more performances is arbitrary and misguided. However, my associates and I cannot ignore the box-office figures. We do not enjoy the total support of the government, and therefore cannot, even if we wished, operate on the basis of "the public be damned." The sources that contributed funds to make up the deficits that are admitted to be inevitable would be discouraged if we played consistently to only partly filled houses. And so it is that I am frequently frustrated when protests concerning casting and performance scheduling are lodged at my complaint department and I find myself able to do little about them.

I do not, however, mean to overstress the importance of my function as the head of the complaint department. To do so would be to indulge in a negative attitude, which I take such pains to discourage in others. The frustrations I feel when I am forced to refuse dancers' requests are insignificant when compared to the positive joy I derive from delighting and sometimes surprising them with affirmative replies. One of my first satisfying experiences after becoming director occurred in 1945, when I was able to inform the American soloists, whom Hurok had refused to recognize or publicize as stars, that they would henceforth be accorded full status as principal dancers. The ability to bring pleasure to the dancers carries with it greater satisfaction because they are so deserving. They are the hardest workers in the field of entertainment and are the least rewarded. The opportunities for increasing these rewards, with a boost not in salary but rather in morale, usually occur during the rehearsal sessions, the most exciting weeks during the ballet year. It is then that the choreographers are creating and new talents are being discovered in the dancers as they seize the opportunity to learn new roles either at the suggestion of the direction or on their own initiative. We are always encouraging dancers to aim higher, to aspire to new and more difficult roles, and this often results in happy surprises for both the direction and the dancer. It is important that the dancers be made aware of the direction's positive interest in their careers. Otherwise they become discouraged and disgruntled, and individual discontent can spread rapidly and infect the entire company.

Over the years the thrills of discovery and the joys of making deserved awards have been innumerable. To cite a few examples from recent seasons only, there were the times when I could announce to Charles Ward and Clark Tippet that they had been promoted to the rank of principal dancer; when I could tell Marianna Tcherkassky that she would be given performances of the role of Giselle. The excitement of moments like these is exceeded only by the ultimate exhilaration experienced when the curtain falls on the first performance of a new ballet and the roars of applause from the audience bolster my own personal assurance that this time I don't have to wait until I have read the critics' reviews to be convinced that Ballet Theatre has produced another hit. The satisfaction I experienced on the opening nights of, for example, *Pillar of Fire*, *Fancy Free*, and *Theme and Variations*, was doubled recently following the premiere of *Push Comes to Shove*. For on that occasion Ballet Theatre had not only produced another hit but had been instrumental in enabling Mischa Baryshnikov to realize a cherished ambition—that of exploring the new territories being opened up by American choreographers. That evening alone would have convinced me that my thirty years as co-director of Ballet Theatre, with all the headaches, had been well worthwhile, and it encouraged me to continue in the position that I first accepted in 1945 with the understanding that it would be temporary.

PART II

Speculations: Dance Aesthetics, Theory, and Philosophy

"Dance aesthetics, in English especially, is in a pioneering stage; a pioneer may manage to plant a rose bush next to the rhubarb, but he's not going to win any prizes in the flower show back in Boston."

—EDWIN DENBY

Dance and Society

Reviewing two dance books in 1925, T. S. Eliot observed that it wasn't easy to understand ballet. Anyone who would penetrate to the spirit of dancing, Eliot said, should have a deep understanding of dance among primitive peoples; a first-hand knowledge of the technique of the ballet from barre practice to toe work; a familiarity with the society of dancers, musicians, choreographers, and producers; an understanding of the evolution of Christian and other liturgy; and at least some acquaintance with the secrets of rhythm hidden in the science of neurology. "The ideal critic of the dance," Eliot neatly summarized, "should combine the learning of Rome, Cambridge, and Harley Street."

Eliot's remarks remind us that dance, though one of the most basic of arts, is also one of the most complex. Dance may be one of man's earliest and most persistent activities ("The history of dance is the social history of the world," Graham once said), but why and how man dances are complicated issues.

The essays printed here begin to examine the diverse functions of dance in human society. Havelock Ellis' well-known essay provides an overview, describing the general religious, sexual, and social functions of dance. D. H. Lawrence's description of the Hopi snake dance gives us a look at the religious dimensions of a dance in a particular primitive culture. And Ruth Katz' study of the waltz reveals the social and political aspects of a dance in a particular modern society.

It has often been said that every dance, from ballet to disco, reflects the culture that produced it. Ballet, with its expansive use of the body, expresses Western man's urge to conquer space, his confidence in mastering his environment. Oriental dance, by comparison stationary and dependent upon smaller gestures, reveals the East's contemplative, inner life. Dance is such a "sensitive little instrument," said Gordon Craig, the innovative theater director and intimate of Isadora Duncan, "that it can tell you with precision when your nation is just going a little bit too much to the right, or a little bit too much to the left." The essays in this section serve as dance "seismographs," recording the movements and ways of several cultures.

The Dance of Life
by Havelock Ellis

I

Dancing and building are the two primary and essential arts. The art of dancing stands at the source of all the arts that express themselves first in the human person. The art of building, or architecture, is the beginning of all the arts that lie outside the person; and in the end they unite. Music, acting, poetry proceed in the one mighty stream; sculpture, painting, all the arts of design, in the other. There is no primary art outside these two arts, for their origin is far earlier than man himself; and dancing came first.[1]

That is one reason why dancing, however it may at times be scorned by passing fashions, has a profound and eternal attraction even for those one might suppose farthest from its influence. The joyous beat of the feet of children, the cosmic play of philosophers' thoughts rise and fall according to the same laws of rhythm. If we are indifferent to the art of dancing, we have failed to understand, not merely the supreme manifestation of physical life, but also the supreme symbol of spiritual life.

The significance of dancing, in the wide sense, thus lies in the fact that it is simply an intimate concrete appeal of a general rhythm, that general rhythm which marks, not life only, but the universe, if one may still be allowed so to name the sum of the cosmic influences that reach us. We need not, indeed, go so far as the planets or the stars and outline their ethereal dances. We have but to stand on the seashore and watch the waves that beat at our feet, to observe that at nearly regular intervals this seemingly monotonous rhythm is accentuated for several beats, so that the waves are really dancing the measure of a tune. It need surprise us not at all that rhythm, ever tending to be moulded into a tune, should mark all the physical and spiritual manifestations of life. Dancing is the primitive expression alike of religion and of love—

Source: From *The Dance of Life* (Boston, New York: Houghton, Mifflin, 1923).

[1] It is even possible that, in earler than human times, dancing and architecture may have been the result of the same impulse. The nest of birds is the chief early form of building, and Edmund Selous has suggested (*Zoölogist*, December, 1901) that the nest may first have arisen as an accidental result of the ecstatic sexual dance of birds. [All footnotes to the essay are Ellis'.]

of religion from the earliest human times we know of and of love from a period long anterior to the coming of man. The art of dancing, moreover, is intimately entwined with all human tradition of war, of labour, of pleasure, of education, while some of the wisest philosophers and the most ancient civilisations have regarded the dance as the pattern in accordance with which the moral life of men must be woven. To realise, therefore, what dancing means for mankind—the poignancy and the many-sidedness of its appeal—we must survey the whole sweep of human life, both at its highest and at its deepest moments.

II

"What do you dance?" When a man belonging to one branch of the great Bantu division of mankind met a member of another, said Livingstone, that was the question he asked. What a man danced, that was his tribe, his social customs, his religion; for, as an anthropologist has put it, "a savage does not preach his religion, he dances it."

There are peoples in the world who have no secular dances, only religious dances; and some investigators believe with Gerland that every dance was of religious origin. That view may seem too extreme, even if we admit that some even of our modern dances, like the waltz, may have been originally religious. Even still (as Skene has shown among the Arabs and Swahili of Africa) so various are dances and their functions among some peoples that they cover the larger part of life. Yet we have to remember that for primitive man there is no such thing as religion apart from life, for religion covers everything. Dancing is a magical operation for the attainment of real and important ends of every kind. It was clearly of immense benefit to the individual and to society, by imparting strength and adding organised harmony. It seemed reasonable to suppose that it attained other beneficial ends, that were incalculable, for calling down blessings or warding off misfortunes. We may conclude, with Wundt, that the dance was, in the beginning, the expression of the whole man, for the whole man was religious.[2]

Thus, among primitive peoples, religion being so large a part of life, the dance inevitably becomes of supreme religious importance. To

[2] "Not the epic song, but the dance," Wundt says (*Völkerpsychologie*, 3d ed. 1911, Bd. 1, Teil 1, p. 277), "accompanied by a monotonous and often meaningless song, constitutes everywhere the most primitive, and, in spite of that primitiveness, the most highly developed art. Whether as a ritual dance, or as a pure emotional expression of the joy in rhythmic bodily movement, it rules the life of primitive men to such a degree that all other forms of art are subordinate to it."

dance was at once both to worship and to pray. Just as we still find in our Prayer Books that there are divine services for all the great fundamental acts of life,—for birth, for marriage, for death,—as well as for the cosmic procession of the world as marked by ecclesiastical festivals, and for the great catastrophes of nature, such as droughts, so also it has ever been among primitive peoples. For all the solemn occasions of life, for bridals and for funerals, for seed-time and for harvest, for war and for peace, for all these things there were fitting dances. To-day we find religious people who in church pray for rain or for the restoration of their friends to health. Their forefathers also desired these things, but, instead of praying for them, they danced for them the fitting dance which tradition had handed down, and which the chief or the medicine-man solemnly conducted. The gods themselves danced, as the stars dance in the sky—so at least the Mexicans, and we may be sure many other peoples, have held; and to dance is therefore to imitate the gods, to work with them, perhaps to persuade them to work in the direction of our own desires. "Work for us!" is the song-refrain, expressed or implied, of every religious dance. In the worship of solar deities in various countries, it was customary to dance round the altar, as the stars dance round the sun. Even in Europe the popular belief that the sun dances on Easter Sunday has perhaps scarcely yet died out. To dance is to take part in the cosmic control of the world. Every sacred dionysian dance is an imitation of the divine dance.

All religions, and not merely those of primitive character, have been at the outset, and sometimes throughout, in some measure saltatory. That was recognised even in the ancient world by acute observers, like Lucian, who remarks in his essay on dancing that "you cannot find a single ancient mystery in which there is no dancing; in fact most people say of the devotees of the Mysteries that 'they dance them out.' " This is so all over the world. It is not more pronounced in early Christianity, and among the ancient Hebrews who danced before the ark, than among the Australian aborigines whose great corroborees are religious dances conducted by the medicine-men with their sacred staves in their hands. Every American Indian tribe seems to have had its own religious dances, varied and elaborate, often with a richness of meaning which the patient study of modern investigators has but slowly revealed. The Shamans in the remote steppes of Northern Siberia have their ecstatic religious dances, and in modern Europe the Turkish dervishes—perhaps of related stock—still dance in their cloisters similar ecstatic dances, combined with song and prayer, as a regular part of devotional service.

These religious dances, it may be observed, are sometimes ecstatic, sometimes pantomimic. It is natural that this should be so. By each road it is possible to penetrate towards the divine mystery of the world. The auto-intoxication of rapturous movement brings the devotees, for a while at least, into that self-forgetful union with the not-self which the mystic ever seeks. The ecstatic Hindu dance in honour of the pre-Aryan hill god, afterwards Siva, became in time a great symbol, "the clearest image of the *activity* of God," it has been called, "which any art or religion can boast of."[3] Pantomimic dances, on the other hand, with their effort to heighten natural expression and to imitate natural process, bring the dancers into the divine sphere of creation and enable them to assist vicariously in the energy of the gods. The dance thus becomes the presentation of a divine drama, the vital reënactment of a sacred history, in which the worshipper is enabled to play a real part.[4] In this way ritual arises.

It is in this sphere—highly primitive as it is—of pantomimic dancing crystallised in ritual, rather than in the sphere of ecstatic dancing, that we may to-day in civilisation witness the survivals of the dance in religion. The divine services of the American Indian, said Lewis Morgan, took the form of "set dances, each with its own name, songs, steps, and costume." At this point the early Christian, worshipping the Divine Body, was able to join in spiritual communion with the ancient Egyptian or the later Japanese[5] or the modern American Indian. They are all alike privileged to enter, each in his own way, a sacred mystery, and to participate in the sacrifice of a heavenly Mass.

What by some is considered to be the earliest known Christian ritual—the "Hymn of Jesus" assigned to the second century—is nothing but a sacred dance. Eusebius in the third century stated that Philo's description of the worship of the Therapeuts agreed at all points with Christian custom, and that meant the prominence of dancing, to which indeed Eusebius often refers in connection with Christian worship. It has been supposed by some that the Christian Church was originally a theatre, the choir being the raised stage, even the word "choir," it is

[3] See an interesting essay in *The Dance of Siva: Fourteen Indian Essays*, by Ananda Coomaraswamy. New York, 1918.

[4] This view was clearly put forward, long ago, by W. W. Newell at the International Congress of Anthropology at Chicago in 1893. It has become almost a commonplace since.

[5] See a charming paper by Marcella Azra Hincks, "The Art of Dancing in Japan," *Fortnightly Review*, July, 1906. Pantomimic dancing, which has played a highly important part in Japan, was introduced into religion from China, it is said, in the earliest time, and was not adapted to secular purposes until the sixteenth century.

argued, meaning an enclosed space for dancing. It is certain that at the Eucharist the faithful gesticulated with their hands, danced with their feet, flung their bodies about. Chrysostom, who referred to this behaviour round the Holy Table at Antioch, only objected to drunken excesses in connection with it; the custom itself he evidently regarded as traditional and right.

While the central function of Christian worship is a sacred drama, a divine pantomime, the associations of Christianity and dancing are by no means confined to the ritual of the Mass and its later more attenuated transformations. The very idea of dancing had a sacred and mystic meaning to the early Christians, who had meditated profoundly on the text, "We have piped unto you and ye have not danced." Origen prayed that above all things there may be made operative in us the mystery "of the stars dancing in Heaven for the salvation of the Universe." So that the monks of the Cistercian Order, who in a later age worked for the world more especially by praying for it ("orare est laborare"), were engaged in the same task on earth as the stars in Heaven; dancing and praying are the same thing. St. Basil, who was so enamoured of natural things, described the angels dancing in Heaven, and later the author of the "Dieta Salutis" (said to have been St. Bonaventura), which is supposed to have influenced Dante in assigning so large a place to dancing in the "Paradiso," described dancing as the occupation of the inmates of Heaven, and Christ as the leader of the dance. Even in more modern times an ancient Cornish carol sang of the life of Jesus as a dance, and represented him as declaring that he died in order that man "may come unto the general dance."[6]

This attitude could not fail to be reflected in practice. Genuine dancing, not merely formalised and unrecognisable dancing, such as the traditionalised Mass, must have been frequently introduced into Christian worship in early times. Until a few centuries ago it remained not uncommon, and it even still persists in remote corners of the Christian world. In English cathedrals dancing went on until the fourteenth century. At Paris, Limoges, and elsewhere in France, the priests danced in the choir at Easter up to the seventeenth century, in Roussillon up to the eighteenth century. Roussillon is a Catalan province with Spanish traditions, and it is in Spain, where dancing is a deeper and more passionate impulse than elsewhere in Europe, that religious dancing took firmest root and flourished longest. In the cathedrals of Seville, Toledo, Valencia, and Jeres there was formerly dancing,

[6] I owe some of these facts to an interesting article by G. R. Mead, "The Sacred Dance of Jesus," *The Quest*, October, 1910.

though it now only survives at a few special festivals in the first.[7] At Alaro in Mallorca, also at the present day, a dancing company called Els Cosiers, on the festival of St. Roch, the patron saint of the place, dance in the church in fanciful costumes with tambourines, up to the steps of the high altar, immediately after Mass, and then dance out of the church. In another part of the Christian world, in the Abyssinian Church—an offshoot of the Eastern Church—dancing is also said still to form part of the worship.

Dancing, we may see throughout the world, has been so essential, so fundamental, a part of all vital and undegenerate religion, that, whenever a new religion appears, a religion of the spirit and not merely an anæmic religion of the intellect, we should still have to ask of it the question of the Bantu: "What do you dance?"

III

Dancing is not only intimately associated with religion, it has an equally intimate association with love. Here, indeed, the relationship is even more primitive, for it is far older than man. Dancing, said Lucian, is as old as love. Among insects and among birds it may be said that dancing is often an essential part of love. In courtship the male dances, sometimes in rivalry with other males, in order to charm the female; then, after a short or long interval, the female is aroused to share his ardour and join in the dance; the final climax of the dance is the union of the lovers. Among the mammals most nearly related to man, indeed, dancing is but little developed: their energies are more variously diffused, though a close observer of the apes, Dr. Louis Robinson, has pointed out that the "spasmodic jerking of the chimpanzee's feeble legs," pounding the partition of his cage, is the crude motion out of which "the heavenly alchemy of evolution has created the divine movements of Pavlova"; but it must be remembered that the anthropoid apes are offshoots only from the stock that produced Man, his cousins and not his ancestors. It is the more primitive love-dance of insects and birds that seems to reappear among human savages in various parts of the world, notably in Africa, and in a conventionalised and symbolised form it is still danced in civilisation to-day. Indeed, it

[7] The dance of the Seises in Seville Cathedral is evidently of great antiquity, though it was so much a matter of course that we do not hear of it until 1690, when the Archbishop of the day, in opposition to the Chapter, wished to suppress it. A decree of the King was finally obtained permitting it, provided it was performed only by men, so that evidently, before that date, girls as well as boys took part in it. Rev. John Morris, "Dancing in Churches," *The Month*, December, 1892; also a valuable article on the Seises by J. B. Trend, in *Music and Letters*, January, 1921.

is in this aspect that dancing has so often aroused reprobation, from the days of early Christianity until the present, among those for whom the dance has merely been, in the words of a seventeenth-century writer, a series of "immodest and dissolute movements by which the cupidity of the flesh is aroused."

But in nature and among primitive peoples it has its value precisely on this account. It is a process of courtship and, even more than that, it is a novitiate for love, and a novitiate which was found to be an admirable training for love. Among some peoples, indeed, as the Omahas, the same word meant both to dance and to love. By his beauty, his energy, his skill, the male must win the female, so impressing the image of himself on her imagination that finally her desire is aroused to overcome her reticence. That is the task of the male throughout nature, and in innumerable species besides Man it has been found that the school in which the task may best be learnt is the dancing-school. Those who have not the skill and the strength to learn are left behind, and, as they are probably the least capable members of the race, it may be in this way that a kind of sexual selection has been embodied in unconscious eugenics, and aided the higher development of the race. The moths and the butterflies, the African ostrich and the Sumatran argus pheasant, with their fellows innumerable, have been the precursors of man in the strenuous school of erotic dancing, fitting themselves for selection by the females of their choice as the most splendid progenitors of the future race.[8]

From this point of view, it is clear, the dance performed a double function. On the one hand, the tendency to dance, arising under the obscure stress of this impulse, brought out the best possibilities the individual held the promise of; on the other hand, at the moment of courtship, the display of the activities thus acquired developed on the sensory side all the latent possibilities of beauty which at last became conscious in man. That it came about we cannot easily escape concluding. How it came about, how it happens that some of the least intelligent of creatures thus developed a beauty and a grace that are enchanting even to our human eyes, is a miracle, even if not affected by the mystery of sex, which we cannot yet comprehend.

When we survey the human world, the erotic dance of the animal world is seen not to have lost, but rather to have gained, influence. It is no longer the males alone who are thus competing for the love of the

[8] See, for references, Havelock Ellis, *Studies in the Psychology of Sex*, vol. III; *Analysis of the Sexual Impulse*, pp. 29, etc.; and Westermarck, *History of Human Marriage*, vol. I, chap. XIII, p. 470.

females. It comes about by a modification in the earlier method of selection that often not only the men dance for the women, but the women for the men, each striving in a storm of rivalry to arouse and attract the desire of the other. In innumerable parts of the world the season of love is a time which the nubile of each sex devote to dancing in each other's presence, sometimes one sex, sometimes the other, sometimes both, in the frantic effort to display all the force and energy, the skill and endurance, the beauty and grace, which at this moment are yearning within them to be poured into the stream of the race's life.

From this point of view we may better understand the immense ardour with which every part of the wonderful human body has been brought into the play of the dance. The men and women of races spread all over the world have shown a marvellous skill and patience in imparting rhythm and measure to the most unlikely, the most rebellious regions of the body, all wrought by desire into potent and dazzling images. To the vigorous races of Northern Europe in their cold damp climate, dancing comes naturally to be dancing of the legs, so naturally that the English poet, as a matter of course, assumes that the dance of Salome was a "twinkling of the feet."[9] But on the opposite side of the world, in Japan and notably in Java and Madagascar, dancing may be exclusively dancing of the arms and hands, in some of the South Sea Islands of the hands and fingers alone. Dancing may even be carried on in the seated posture, as occurs at Fiji in a dance connected with the preparation of the sacred drink, ava. In some districts of Southern Tunisia dancing, again, is dancing of the hair, and all night long, till they perhaps fall exhausted, the marriageable girls will move their heads to the rhythm of a song, maintaining their hair, in perpetual balance and sway. Elsewhere, notably in Africa, but also sometimes in Polynesia, as well as in the dances that had established themselves in ancient Rome, dancing is dancing of the body, with vibratory or rotatory movements of breasts or flanks. The complete dance along these lines is, however, that in which the play of all the chief muscle-groups of the body is harmoniously interwoven. When both sexes take part in such an exercise, developed into an idealised yet passionate pantomime of love, we have the complete erotic dance. In the beautiful ancient civilisation of the Pacific, it is probable that this ideal was sometimes

[9] At an earlier period, however, the dance of Salome was understood much more freely and often more accurately. As Enlart has pointed out, on a capital in the twelfth-century cloister of Moissac, Salome holds a kind of castanets in her raised hands as she dances; on one of the western portals of Rouen Cathedral, at the beginning of the sixteenth century, she is dancing on her hands; while at Hemelverdeghem she is really executing the *morisco*, the "*danse du ventre.*"

reached, and at Tahiti, in 1772, an old voyager crudely and summarily described the native dance as "an endless variety of posturings and wagglings of the body, hands, feet, eyes, lips, and tongue, in which they keep splendid time to the measure." In Spain the dance of this kind has sometimes attained its noblest and most harmoniously beautiful expression. From the narratives of travellers, it would appear that it was especially in the eighteenth century that among all classes in Spain dancing of this kind was popular. The Church tacitly encouraged it, an Aragonese Canon told Baretti in 1770, in spite of its occasional indecorum, as a useful safety-valve for the emotions. It was not less seductive to the foreign spectator than to the people themselves. The grave traveller Peyron, towards the end of the century, growing eloquent over the languorous and flexible movements of the dance, the bewitching attitude, the voluptuous curves of the arms, declares that, when one sees a beautiful Spanish woman dance, one is inclined to fling all philosophy to the winds. And even that highly respectable Anglican clergyman, the Reverend Joseph Townsend, was constrained to state that he could "almost persuade myself" that if the fandango were suddenly played in church the gravest worshippers would start up to join in that "lascivious pantomime." There we have the rock against which the primitive dance of sexual selection suffers shipwreck as civilisation advances. And that prejudice of civilisation becomes so ingrained that it is brought to bear even on the primitive dance. The pygmies of Africa are described by Sir H. H. Johnston as a very decorous and highly moral people, but their dances, he adds, are not so. Yet these dances, though to the eyes of Johnston, blinded by European civilisation, "grossly indecent," he honestly, and inconsistently, adds, are "danced reverently."

IV

From the vital function of dancing in love, and its sacred function in religion, to dancing as an art, a profession, an amusement, may seem, at the first glance, a sudden leap. In reality the transition is gradual, and it began to be made at a very early period in diverse parts of the globe. All the matters that enter into courtship tend to fall under the sway of art; their aesthetic pleasure is a secondary reflection of their primary joy. Dancing could not fail to be first in manifesting this tendency. But even religious dancing swiftly exhibited the same transformation; dancing, like priesthood, became a profession, and dancers, like priests, formed a caste. This, for instance, took place in old Hawaii. The hula dance was a religious dance; it required a special education and an arduous training; moreover, it involved the observance of important taboos and the exercise of sacred rites; by the very fact of its high specialisation it came to be carried out by paid performers, a professional caste. In India, again, the Devadasis, or sacred dancing girls, are at once both religious and professional dancers. They are married to gods, they are taught dancing by the Brahmins, they figure in religious ceremonies, and their dances represent the life of the god they are married to as well as the emotions of love they experience for him. Yet, at the same time, they also give professional performances in the houses of rich private persons who pay for them. It thus comes about that to the foreigner the Devadasis scarcely seem very unlike the Ramedjenis, the dancers of the street, who are of very different origin, and mimic in their performances the play of merely human passions. The Portuguese conquerors of India called both kinds of dancers indiscriminately Balheideras (or dancers) which we have corrupted in Bayaderes.[10]

In our modern world professional dancing as an art has become altogether divorced from religion, and even, in any biological sense, from love; it is scarcely even possible, so far as Western civilisation is concerned, to trace back the tradition to either source. If we survey the development of dancing as an art in Europe, it seems to me that we have to recognise two streams of tradition which have sometimes merged, but yet remain in their ideals and their tendencies essentially distinct. I would call these traditions the Classical, which is much the more ancient and fundamental, and may be said to be of Egyptian origin, and the Romantic, which is of Italian origin, chiefly known to us as the ballet. The first is, in its pure form, solo dancing—though it may be danced in couples and many together—and is based on the rhythmic beauty and expressiveness of the simple human personality when its energy is concentrated in measured yet passionate movement. The second is concerted dancing, mimetic and picturesque, wherein the individual is subordinated to the wider and variegated rhythm of the group. It may be easy to devise another classification, but this is simple and instructive enough for our purpose.

There can scarcely be a doubt that Egypt has been for many thousands of years, as indeed it still remains, a great dancing centre, the most influential dancing-school the world has ever seen, radiating its influence to south and east and north. We may perhaps even agree with the historian of the dance who terms it "the mother-country of all civilised dancing." We are not entirely dependent on the ancient wall-

[10] For an excellent account of dancing in India, now being degraded by modern civilisation, see Otto Rothfeld, *Women of India*, chap. VII, "The Dancing Girl," 1922.

pictures of Egypt for our knowledge of Egyptian skill in the art. Sacred mysteries, it is known, were danced in the temples, and queens and princesses took part in the orchestra that accompanied them. It is significant that the musical instruments still peculiarly associated with the dance were originated or developed in Egypt; the guitar is an Egyptian instrument and its name was a hieroglyph already used when the Pyramids were being built; the cymbal, the tambourine, triangles, castanets, in one form or another, were all familiar to the ancient Egyptians, and with the Egyptian art of dancing they must have spread all round the shores of the Mediterranean, the great focus of our civilisation, at a very early date.[11] Even beyond the Mediterranean, at Cadiz, dancing that was essentially Egyptian in character was established, and Cadiz became the dancing-school of Spain. The Nile and Cadiz were thus the two great centres of ancient dancing, and Martial mentions them both together, for each supplied its dancers to Rome. This dancing, alike whether Egyptian or Gaditanian, was the expression of the individual dancer's body and art; the garments played but a small part in it, they were frequently transparent, and sometimes discarded altogether. It was, and it remains, simple, personal, passionate dancing, classic, therefore, in the same sense as, on the side of literature, the poetry of Catullus is classic.[12]

Ancient Greek dancing was essentially classic dancing, as here understood. On the Greek vases, as reproduced in Emmanuel's attractive book on Greek dancing and elsewhere, we find the same play of the arms, the same sideward turn, the same extreme backward extension of the body, which had long before been represented in Egyptian

[11] I may hazard the suggestion that the gypsies may possibly have acquired their rather unaccountable name of Egyptians, not so much because they had passed through Egypt, the reason which is generally suggested,—for they must have passed through many countries,—but because of their proficiency in dances of the recognised Egyptian type.

[12] It is interesting to observe that Egypt still retains, almost unchanged through fifty centuries, its traditions, technique, and skill in dancing, while, as in ancient Egyptian dancing, the garment forms an almost or quite negligible element in the art. Loret remarks that a charming Egyptian dancer of the Eighteenth Dynasty, whose picture in her transparent gauze he reproduces, is an exact portrait of a charming Almeh of today whom he has seen dancing in Thebes with the same figure, the same dressing of the hair, the same jewels. I hear from a physician, a gynaecologist now practising in Egypt, that a dancing-girl can lie on her back, and with a full glass of water standing on one side of her abdomen and an empty glass on the other, can by the contraction of the muscles on the side supporting the full glass, project the water from it, so as to fill the empty glass. This, of course, is not strictly dancing, but it is part of the technique which underlies classic dancing and it witnesses to the thoroughness with which the technical side of Egyptian dancing is still cultivated.

monuments. Many supposedly modern movements in dancing were certainly already common both to Egyptian and Greek dancing, as well as the clapping of hands to keep time which is still an accompaniment of Spanish dancing. It seems clear, however, that, on this general classic and Mediterranean basis, Greek dancing had a development so refined and so special—though in technical elaboration of steps, it seems likely, inferior to modern dancing—that it exercised no influence outside Greece. Dancing became, indeed, the most characteristic and the most generally cultivated of Greek arts. Pindar, in a splendid Oxyrhynchine fragment, described Hellas, in what seemed to him supreme praise, as "the land of lovely dancing," and Athenaeus pointed out that he calls Apollo the Dancer. It may well be that the Greek drama arose out of dance and song, and that the dance throughout was an essential and plastic element in it. Even if we reject the statement of Aristotle that tragedy arose out of the Dionysian dithyramb, the alternatives suppositions (such as Ridgeway's theory of dancing round the tombs of the dead) equally involve the same elements. It has often been pointed out that poetry in Greece demanded a practical knowledge of all that could be included under "dancing." Aeschylus is said to have developed the technique of dancing and Sophocles danced in his own dramas. In these developments, no doubt, Greek dancing tended to overpass the fundamental limits of classic dancing and foreshadowed the ballet.[13]

The real germ of the ballet, however, is to be found in Rome, where the pantomime with its concerted and picturesque method of expressive action was developed, and Italy is the home of Romantic dancing. The same impulse which produced the pantomime produced, more than a thousand years later in the same Italian region, the modern ballet. In both cases, one is inclined to think, we may trace the influence of the same Etruscan and Tuscan race which so long has had its seat there, a race with a genius for expressive, dramatic, picturesque art. We see it on the walls of Etruscan tombs and again in pictures of Botticelli and his fellow Tuscans. The modern ballet, it is generally believed, had its origin in the spectacular pageants at the marriage of Galeazzo Visconti, Duke of Milan, in 1489. The fashion for such performances spread to the other Italian courts, including Florence, and Catherine de' Medici, when she became Queen of France, brought the

[13] "We must learn to regard the form of the Greek drama as a dance form," says G. Warre Cornish in an interesting article on "Greek Drama and the Dance" (*Fortnightly Review*, February, 1913), "a musical symphonic dance-vision, through which the history of Greece and the soul of man are portrayed."

Italian ballet to Paris. Here it speedily became fashionable. Kings and queens were its admirers and even took part in it; great statesmen were its patrons. Before long, and especially in the great age of Louis XIV, it became an established institution, still an adjunct of opera but with a vital life and growth of its own, maintained by distinguished musicians, artists, and dancers. Romantic dancing, to a much greater extent than what I have called Classic dancing, which depends so largely on simple personal qualities, tends to be vitalised by transplantation and the absorption of new influences, provided that the essential basis of technique and tradition is preserved in the new development. Lully in the seventeenth century brought women into the ballet; Camargo discarded the complicated costumes and shortened the skirt, so rendering possible not only her own lively and vigorous method, but all the freedom and airy grace of later dancing. It was Noverre who by his ideas worked out at Stuttgart, and soon brought to Paris by Gaetan Vestris, made the ballet a new and complete art form; this Swiss-French genius not only elaborated plot revealed by gesture and dance alone, but, just as another and greater Swiss-French genius about the same time brought sentiment and emotion into the novel, he brought it into the ballet. In the French ballet of the eighteenth century a very high degree of perfection seems thus to have been reached, while in Italy, where the ballet had originated, it decayed, and Milan, which had been its source, became the nursery of a tradition of devitalised technique carried to the finest point of delicate perfection. The influence of the French school was maintained as a living force into the nineteenth century,—when it was renovated afresh by the new spirit of the age and Taglioni became the most ethereal embodiment of the spirit of the Romantic movement in a form that was genuinely classic,—overspreading the world by the genius of a few individual dancers. When they had gone, the ballet slowly and steadily declined. As it declined as an art, so also it declined in credit and in popularity; it became scarcely respectable even to admire dancing. Thirty or forty years ago, those of us who still appreciated dancing as an art—and how few they were!—had to seek for it painfully and sometimes in strange surroundings. A recent historian of dancing, in a book published so lately as 1906, declared that "the ballet is now a thing of the past, and, with the modern change of ideas, a thing that is never likely to be resuscitated." That historian never mentioned Russian ballet, yet his book was scarcely published before the Russian ballet arrived to scatter ridicule over his rash prophecy by raising the ballet to a pitch of perfection it can rarely have surpassed, as an expressive, emotional, even passionate form of living art.

The Russian ballet was an offshoot from the French ballet and illustrates once more the vivifying effect of transplantation on the art of Romantic dancing. The Empress Anna introduced it in 1735 and appointed a French ballet-master and a Neapolitan composer to carry it on; it reached a high degree of technical perfection during the following hundred years, on the traditional lines, and the principal dancers were all imported from Italy. It was not until recent years that this firm discipline and these ancient traditions were vitalised into an art form of exquisite and vivid beauty by the influence of the soil in which they had slowly taken root. This contact, when at last it was effected, mainly by the genius of Fokine and the enterprise of Diaghilev, involved a kind of revolution, for its outcome, while genuine ballet, has yet all the effect of delicious novelty. The tradition by itself was in Russia an exotic without real life, and had nothing to give to the world; on the other hand, a Russian ballet apart from that tradition, if we can conceive such a thing, would have been formless, extravagant, bizarre, not subdued to any fine aesthetic ends. What we see here, in the Russian ballet as we know it today, is a splendid and arduous technical tradition, brought at last—by the combined skill of designers, composers, and dancers—into real fusion with an environment from which during more than a century it had been held apart; Russian genius for music, Russian feeling for rhythm, Russian skill in the use of bright colour, and, not least, the Russian orgiastic temperament, the Russian spirit of tender poetic melancholy, and the general Slav passion for folk-dancing, shown in other branches of the race also, Polish, Bohemian, Bulgarian, and Servian. At almost the same time what I have termed Classic dancing was independently revived in America by Isadora Duncan, bringing back what seemed to be the free naturalism of the Greek dance, and Ruth St. Denis, seeking to discover and revitalise the secrets of the old Indian and Egyptian traditions. Whenever now we find any restored art of theatrical dancing, as in the Swedish ballet, it has been inspired more or less, by an eclectic blending of these two revived forms, the Romantic from Russian, the Classic from America. The result has been that our age sees one of the most splendid movements in the whole history of the ballet.

V

Dancing as an art, we may be sure, cannot die out, but will always be undergoing a rebirth. Not merely as an art, but also as a social custom, it perpetually emerges afresh from the soul of the people. Less than a century ago the polka thus arose, extemporised by the Bohemian servant girl Anna Slezakova out of her own head for the joy of her own heart, and only rendered a permanent form, apt for world-wide popularity, by the accident that it was observed and noted down by an artist. Dancing has for ever been in existence as a spontaneous custom, a social discipline. Thus it is, finally, that dancing meets us, not only as love, as religion, as art, but also as morals.

All human work, under natural conditions, is a kind of dance. In a large and learned book, supported by an immense amount of evidence, Karl Bücher has argued that work differs from the dance, not in kind, but only in degree, since they are both essentially rhythmic. There is a good reason why work should be rhythmic, for all great combined efforts, the efforts by which alone great constructions such as those of megalithic days could be carried out, must be harmonised. It has even been argued that this necessity is the source of human speech, and we have the so-called Yo-heave-ho theory of languages. In the memory of those who have ever lived on a sailing ship—that loveliest of human creations now disappearing from the world—there will always linger the echo of the chanties which sailors sang as they hoisted the topsail yard or wound the capstan or worked the pumps. That is the type of primitive combined work, and it is indeed difficult to see how such work can be effectively accomplished without such a device for regulating the rhythmic energy of the muscles. The dance rhythm of work has thus acted socialisingly in a parallel line with the dance rhythms of the arts, and indeed in part as their inspirer. The Greeks, it has been too fancifully suggested, by insight or by intuition understood this when they fabled that Orpheus, whom they regarded as the earliest poet, was specially concerned with moving stones and trees. Bücher has pointed out that even poetic metre may be conceived as arising out of work; metre is the rhythmic stamping of feet, as in the technique of verse it is still metaphorically called; iambics and trochees, spondees and anapæsts and dactyls, may still be heard among blacksmiths smiting the anvil or navvies wielding their hammers in the streets. In so far as they arose out of work, music and singing and dancing are naturally a single art. A poet must always write to a tune, said Swinburne. Herein the ancient ballad of Europe is a significant type. It is, as the name indicates, a dance as much as a song, performed by a singer who sang the story and a chorus who danced and shouted the apparently meaningless refrain; it is absolutely the chanty of the sailors and is equally apt for the purposes of concerted work.[14] Yet our most com-

[14] It should perhaps be remarked that in recent times it has been denied that the old ballads were built up on dance songs. Miss Pound, for instance, in a book on the subject, argues that they were of aristocratic and not communal origin, which may well be, though the absence of the dance element does not seem to follow.

plicated musical forms are evolved from similar dances. The symphony is but a development of a dance suite, in the first place folk-dances, such as Bach and Handel composed. Indeed a dance still lingers always at the heart of music and even the heart of the composer. Mozart, who was himself an accomplished dancer, used often to say, so his wife stated, that it was dancing, not music, that he really cared for. Wagner believed that Beethoven's Seventh Symphony—to some of us the most fascinating of them and the most purely musical—was an apotheosis of the dance, and, even if that belief throws no light on the intention of Beethoven, it is at least a revelation of Wagner's own feeling for the dance.

It is, however, the dance itself, apart from the work and apart from the other arts, which, in the opinion of many to-day, has had a decisive influence in socialising, that is to say in moralising, the human species. Work showed the necessity of harmonious rhythmic coöperation, but the dance developed that rhythmic coöperation and imparted a beneficent impetus to all human activities. It was Grosse, in his "Beginnings of Art," who first clearly set forth the high social significance of the dance in the creation of human civilisation. The participants in a dance, as all observers of savages have noted, exhibit a wonderful unison; they are, as it were, fused into a single being stirred by a single impulse. Social unification is thus accomplished. Apart from war, this is the chief factor making for social solidarity in primitive life; it was indeed the best training for war. It has been a twofold influence; on the one hand, it aided unity of action and method in evolution: on the other, it had the invaluable function—for man is naturally a timid animal—of imparting courage; the universal drum, as Louis Robinson remarks, has been an immense influence in human affairs. Even among the Romans, with their highly developed military system, dancing and war were definitely allied; the Salii constituted a college of sacred military dancers; the dancing season was March, the war-god's month and the beginning of the war season, and all through that month there were dances in triple measure before the temples and round the altars, with songs so ancient that not even the priests could understand them. We may trace a similar influence of dancing in all the coöperative arts of life. All our most advanced civilisation, Grosse insisted, is based on dancing. It is the dance that socialised man.

Thus, in the large sense, dancing has possessed peculiar value as a method of national education. As civilisation grew self-conscious, this was realised. "One may judge of a king," according to ancient Chinese maxim, "by the state of dancing during his reign." So also among the Greeks; it has been said that dancing and music lay at the foundation of the whole political and military as well as religious organisation of the Dorian states.

In the narrow sense, in individual education, the great importance of dancing came to be realised, even at an early stage of human development, and still more in the ancient civilisations. "A good education," Plato declared in the "Laws," the final work of his old age, "consists in knowing how to sing and dance well." And in our own day one of the keenest and most enlightened of educationists has lamented the decay of dancing; the revival of dancing, Stanley Hall declares, is imperatively needed to give poise to the nerves, schooling to the emotions, strength to the will, and to harmonise the feelings and the intellect with the body which supports them.

It can scarcely be said that these functions of dancing are yet generally realised and embodied afresh in education. For, if it is true that dancing engendered morality, it is also true that in the end, by the irony of fate, morality, grown insolent, sought to crush its own parent, and for a time succeeded only too well. Four centuries ago dancing was attacked by that spirit, in England called Puritanism, which was then spread over the greater part of Europe, just as active in Bohemia as in England, and which has, indeed, been described as a general onset of developing Urbanism against the old Ruralism. It made no distinction between good and bad, nor paused to consider what would come when dancing went. So it was that, as Remy de Gourmont remarks, the drinking-shop conquered the dance, and alcohol replaced the violin.

But when we look at the function of dancing in life from a higher and wider standpoint, this episode in its history ceases to occupy so large a place. The conquest over dancing has never proved in the end a matter for rejoicing, even to morality, while an art which has been so intimately mixed with all the finest and deepest springs of life has always asserted itself afresh. For dancing is the loftiest, the most moving, the most beautiful of the arts, because it is no mere translation or abstraction from life; it is life itself. It is the only art, as Rahel Varnhagen said, of which we ourselves are the stuff. Even if we are not ourselves dancers, but merely the spectators of the dance, we are still —according to that Lippsian doctrine of *Einfühlung* or "empathy" by Groos termed "the play of inner imitation"—which here, at all events, we may accept as true—feeling ourselves in the dancer who is manifesting and expressing the latent impulses of our own being.

It thus comes about that, beyond its manifold practical significance, dancing has always been felt to possess also a symbolic significance. Marcus Aurelius was accustomed to regard the art of life as like the dancer's art, though that Imperial Stoic could not resist adding that in some respects it was more like the wrestler's art. "I doubt not yet to make a figure in the great Dance of Life that shall amuse the spectators in the sky," said, long after, Blake, in the same strenuous spirit. In our own time, Nietzsche, from first to last, showed himself possessed by the conception of the art of life as a dance, in which the dancer achieves the rhythmic freedom and harmony of his soul beneath the shadow of a hundred Damoclean swords. He said the same thing of his style, for to him the style and the man were one: "My style," he wrote to his intimate friend Rohde, "is a dance." "Every day I count wasted," he said again, "in which there has been no dancing." The dance lies at the beginning of art, and we find it also at the end. The first creators of civilisation were making the dance, and the philosopher of a later age, hovering over the dark abyss of insanity, with bleeding feet and muscles strained to the breaking point, still seems to himself to be weaving the maze of the dance.

The Hopi Snake Dance

by D. H. Lawrence

The Hopi country is in Arizona, next to the Navajo country, and some seventy miles north of the Santa Fé railroad. The Hopis are Pueblo Indians, village Indians, so their reservation is not large. It consists of a square track of greyish, unappetising desert, out of which rise three tall arid mesas, broken off in ragged pallid rock. On the top of the mesas perch the ragged, broken, greyish pueblos, identical with the mesas on which they stand.

The nearest village, Walpi, stands in half-ruin, high on a narrow rock-top where no leaf of life ever was tender. It is all grey, utterly grey, utterly pallid stone and dust, and very narrow. Below it all the stark light of the dry Arizona sun.

Walpi is called the 'first mesa'. And it is at the far edge of Walpi you see the withered beaks and claws and bones of sacrificed eagles, in a rock-cleft under the sky. They sacrifice an eagle each year, on the brink, by rolling him out and crushing him so as to shed no blood. Then they drop his remains down the dry cleft in the promontory's farthest grey tip.

Source: From *Mornings in Mexico* (New York: Knopf, 1927).

The trail winds on, utterly bumpy and horrible, for thirty miles, past the second mesa, where Chimopova is, on to the third mesa. And on the Sunday afternoon of August 17th black automobile after automobile lurched and crawled across the grey desert, where low, grey, sage-scrub was coming to pallid yellow. Black hood followed crawling after black hood, like a funeral cortège. The motor-cars, with all the tourists wending their way to the third and farthest mesa, thirty miles across this dismal desert where an odd water-windmill spun, and odd patches of corn blew in the strong desert wind, like dark-green women with fringed shawls blowing and fluttering, not far from the foot of the great, grey, up-piled mesa.

The snake dance (I am told) is held once a year, on each of the three mesas in succession. This year of grace 1924 it was to be held in Hotevilla, the last village on the farthest western tip of the third mesa.

On and on bumped the cars. The lonely second mesa lay in the distance. On and on, to the ragged ghost of the third mesa.

The third mesa has two main villages, Oraibi, which is on the near edge, and Hotevilla, on the far. Up scrambles the car, on all its four legs, like a black-beetle straddling past the school-house and store down below, up the bare rock and over the changeless boulders, with a surge and a sickening lurch to the sky-brim, where stands the rather foolish church. Just beyond, dry, grey, ruined, and apparently abandoned, Oraibi, its few ragged stone huts. All these cars come all this way, and apparently nobody at home.

You climb still, up the shoulder of rock, a few more miles, across the lofty, wind-swept mesa, and so you come to Hotevilla, where the dance is, and where already hundreds of motor-cars are herded in an official camping-ground, among the piñon bushes.

Hotevilla is a tiny little village of grey little houses, raggedly built with undressed stone and mud around a little oblong plaza, and partly in ruins. One of the chief two-storey houses on the small square is a ruin, with big square window-holes.

It is a parched, grey country of snakes and eagles, pitched up against the sky. And a few dark-faced, short, thickly built Indians have their few peach trees among the sand, their beans and squashes on the naked sand under the sky, their springs of brackish water.

Three thousand people came to see the little snake dance this year, over miles of desert and bumps. Three thousand, of all sorts, cultured people from New York, Californians, onward-pressing tourists, cowboys, Navajo Indians, even negroes; fathers, mothers, children, of all ages, colours, sizes of stoutness, dimensions of curiosity.

What had they come for? Mostly to see men hold *live rattlesnakes* in their mouths. "*I never did see a rattlesnake and I'm crazy to see one!*" cried a girl with bobbed hair.

There you have it. People trail hundreds of miles, avidly, to see this circus-performance of men handling live rattlesnakes that may bite them any minute—even do bite them. Some show, that!

There is the other aspect, of the ritual dance. One may look on from the angle of culture, as one looks on while Anna Pavlova dances with the Russian Ballet.

Or there is still another point of view, the religious. Before the snake dance begins, on the Monday, and the spectators are packed thick on the ground round the square, and in the window-holes, and on all the roofs, all sorts of people greedy with curiosity, a little speech is made to them all, asking the audience to be silent and respectful, as this is a sacred religious ceremonial of the Hopi Indians, and not a public entertainment. Therefore, please, no clapping or cheering or applause, but remember you are, as it were, in a church.

The audience accepts the implied rebuke in good faith, and looks round with a grin at the 'church'. But it is a good-humoured, very decent crowd, ready to respect any sort of feelings. And the Indian with his 'religion' is a sort of public pet.

From the cultured point of view, the Hopi snake dance is almost nothing, not much more than a circus turn, or the games that children play in the street. It has none of the impressive beauty of the Corn Dance at Santo Domingo, for example. The big pueblos of Zuni, Santo Domingo, Taos have a cultured instinct which is not revealed in the Hopi snake dance. This last is uncouth rather than beautiful, and rather uncouth in its touch of horror. Hence the thrill, and the crowd.

As a cultured spectacle, it is a circus turn: men actually dancing round with snakes, poisonous snakes, dangling from their mouths.

And as a religious ceremonial: well, you can either be politely tolerant like the crowd to the Hopis; or you must have some spark of understanding of the sort of religion implied.

"Oh, the Indians," I heard a woman say, "they believe we are all brothers, the snakes are the Indians' brothers, and the Indians are the snakes' brothers. The Indians would never hurt the snakes, they won't hurt any animal. So the snakes won't bite the Indians. They are all brothers, and none of them hurt anybody."

This sounds very nice, only more Hindoo than Hopi. The dance itself does not convey much sense of fraternal communion. It is not in the least like St. Francis preaching to the birds.

The animistic religion, as we call it, is not the religion of the Spirit. A religion of spirits, yes. But not of Spirit. There is no One Spirit.

There is no One God. There is no Creator. There is strictly no God at all: because all is alive. In our conception of religion there exists God and His Creation: two things. We are creatures of God, therefore we pray to God as the Father, the Saviour, the Maker.

But strictly, in the religion of aboriginal America, there is no Father, and no Maker. There is the great living source of life: say the Sun of existence: to which you can no more pray than you can pray to Electricity. And emerging from this Sun are the great potencies, the invincible influences which make shine and warmth and rain. From these great interrelated potencies of rain and heat and thunder emerge the seeds of life itself, corn, and creatures like snakes. And beyond these, men, persons. But all emerge separately. There is no oneness, no sympathetic identifying oneself with the rest. The law of isolation is heavy on every creature.

Now the Sun, the rain, the shine, the thunder, they are alive. But they are not persons or people. They are alive. They are manifestations of living activity. But they are not personal Gods.

Everything lives. Thunder lives, and rain lives, and sunshine lives. But not in the personal sense.

How is man to get himself into relation with the vast living convulsions of rain and thunder and sun, which are conscious and alive and potent, but like vastest of beasts, inscrutable and incomprehensible. How is man to get himself into relation with these, the vastest of cosmic beasts?

It is the problem of the ages of man. Our religion says the cosmos is Matter, to be conquered by the Spirit of Man. The yogi, the fakir, the saint try conquest by abnegation and by psychic powers. The real conquest of the cosmos is made by science.

The American-Indian sees no division into Spirit and Matter, God and not-God. Everything is alive, though not personally so. Thunder is neither Thor nor Zeus. Thunder is the vast living thunder asserting itself like some incomprehensible monster, or some huge reptile-bird of the pristine cosmos.

How to conquer the dragon-mouthed thunder! How to capture the feathered rain!

We make reservoirs, and irrigation ditches and artesian wells. We make lightning conductors, and build vast electric plants. We say it is a matter of science, energy, force.

But the Indian says No! It all lives. We must approach it fairly, with profound respect, but also with desperate courage. Because man must conquer the cosmic monsters of living thunder and live rain. The rain that slides down from its source, and ebbs back subtly, with a strange energy generated between its coming and going, an energy which, even to our science, is of life: this, man has to conquer. The serpent-striped, feathery Rain.

We made the conquest by dams and reservoirs and windmills. The Indian, like the old Egyptian, seeks to make the conquest from the mystic will within him, pitted against the Cosmic Dragon.

We must remember, to the animistic vision there is no perfect God behind us, who created us from his knowledge, and foreordained all things. No such God. Behind lies only the terrific, terrible, crude Source, the mystic Sun, the well-head of all things. From this mystic Sun emanate the Dragons, Rain, Wind, Thunder, Shine, Light. The Potencies of Powers. These bring forth Earth, then reptiles, birds, and fishes.

The Potencies are not Gods. They are Dragons. The Sun of Creation itself is a dragon most terrible, vast, and most powerful, yet even so, less in being than we. The only gods on earth are men. For gods, like man, do not exist beforehand. They are created and evolved gradually, with æons of effort, out of the fire and smelting of life. They are the highest thing created, smelted between the furnace of the Life-Sun, and beaten on the anvil of the rain, with hammers or thunder and bellows of rushing wind. The cosmos is a great furnace, a dragon's den, where the heroes and demi-gods, men, forge themselves into being. It is a vast and violent matrix, where souls form like diamonds in earth, under extreme pressure.

So that gods are the outcome, not the origin. And the best gods that have resulted, so far, are men. But gods frail as flowers; which have also the godliness of things that have won perfection out of the terrific dragon-clutch of the cosmos. Men are frail as flowers. Man is as a flower, rain can kill him or succour him, heat can flick him with a bright tail, and destroy him: or, on the other hand, it can softly call him into existence, out of the egg of chaos. Man is delicate as a flower, godly beyond flowers, and his lordship is a ticklish business.

He has to conquer, and hold his own, and again conquer all the time. Conquer the powers of the cosmos. To us, science is our religion of conquest. Hence through science, we are the conquerors and resultant gods of our earth. But to the Indian, the so-called mechanical processes do not exist. All lives. And the conquest is made by the means of the living will.

This is the religion of all aboriginal America, Peruvian, Aztec, Athabascan: perhaps the aboriginal religion of all the word. In Mexico, men fell into horror of the crude, pristine gods, the dragons. But to the pueblo Indian, the most terrible dragon is still somewhat gentle-hearted.

This brings us back to the Hopi. He has the hardest task, the stubbornest destiny. Some inward fate drove him to the top of these parched mesas, all rocks and eagles, sand and snakes, and wind and sun and alkali. These he had to conquer. Not merely, as we should put it, the natural conditions of the place. But the mysterious life-spirit that reigned there. The eagle and the snake.

It is a destiny as well as another. The destiny of the animistic soul of man, instead of our destiny of Mind and Spirit. We have undertaken the scientific conquest of forces, of natural conditions. It has been comparatively easy, and we are victors. Look at our black motor-cars like beetles working up the rock-face at Oraibi. Look at our three thousand tourists gathered to gaze at the twenty lonely men who dance in the tribe's snake dance!

The Hopi sought the conquest by means of the mystic, living will that is in man, pitted against the living will of the dragon-cosmos. The Egyptians long ago made a partial conquest by the same means. We have made a partial conquest by other means. Our corn doesn't fail us: we have no seven years' famine, and apparently need never have. But the other thing fails us, the strange inward sun of life; the pellucid monster of the rain never shows us his stripes. To us, heaven switches on daylight, or turns on the shower-bath. We little gods are gods of the machine only. It is our highest. Our cosmos is a great engine. And we die of ennui. A subtle dragon stings us in the midst of plenty. *Quos vult perdere Deus, dementat prius.*

On the Sunday evening is a first little dance in the plaza at Hotevilla, called the Antelope dance. There is the hot, sandy, oblong little place, with a tuft of green cotton-wood boughs stuck like a plume at the south end, and on the floor at the foot of the green, a little lid of a trap-door. They say the snakes are under there.

They say that the twelve officiating men of the snake clan of the tribe have for nine days been hunting snakes in the rocks. They have been performing the mysteries for nine days, in the kiva, and for two days they have fasted completely. All these days they have tended the snakes, washed them with repeated lustrations, soothed them, and exchanged spirits with them. The spirit of man soothing and seeking and making interchange with the spirits of the snakes. For the snakes are more rudimentary, nearer to the great convulsive powers. Nearer to the nameless Sun, more knowing in the slanting tracks of the rain, the pattering of the invisible feet of the rain-monster from the sky. The snakes are man's next emissaries to the rain-gods. The snakes lie nearer to the source of potency, the dark, lurking, intense sun at the centre of the earth. For to the cultured animist, and the pueblo Indian is such, the earth's dark centre holds its dark sun, our source of isolated being, round which our world coils its folds like a great snake. The snake is nearer the dark sun, and cunning of it.

They say—people say—that rattlesnakes are not travellers. They haunt the same spots on earth, and die there. It is said also that the snake priests (so-called) of the Hopi probably capture the same snakes year after year.

Be that as it may. At sundown before the real dance, there is the little dance called the Antelope Dance. We stand and wait on a house-roof. Behind us is tethered an eagle; rather dishevelled he sits on the coping, and looks at us in unutterable resentment. See him, and see how much 'brotherhood' the Indian feels with animals—at best the silent tolerance that acknowledges dangerous difference. We wait without event. There are no drums, no announcements. Suddenly into the plaza, with rude, intense movements, hurries a little file of men. They are smeared all with grey and black, and are naked save for little kilts embroidered like the sacred dance-kilts in other pueblos, red and green and black on a white fibre-cloth. The fox-skins hang behind. The feet of the dancers are pure ash-grey. Their hair is long.

The first is a heavy old man with heavy, long, wild grey hair and heavy fringe. He plods intensely forward in the silence, followed in a sort of circle by the other grey-smeared, long-haired, naked, concentrated men. The oldest men are first: the last is a short-haired boy of fourteen or fifteen. There are only eight men—the so-called antelope priests. They pace round in a circle, rudely, absorbedly, till the first heavy, intense old man with his massive grey hair flowing, comes to the lid on the ground, near the tuft of kiva-boughs. He rapidly shakes from the hollow of his right hand a little white meal on the lid, stamps heavily, with naked right foot, on the meal, so the wood resounds, and paces heavily forward. Each man, to the boy, shakes meal, stamps, paces absorbedly on in the circle, comes to the lid again, shakes meal, stamps, paces absorbedly on, comes a third time to the lid, or trap-door, and this time spits on the lid, stamps, and goes on. And this time the eight men file away behind the lid, between it and the tuft of green boughs. And there they stand in a line, their backs to the kiva-tuft of green; silent, absorbed, bowing a little to the ground.

Suddenly paces with rude haste another file of men. They are naked, and smeared with red 'medicine', with big black lozenges of smeared paint on their backs. Their wild heavy hair hangs loose, the old, heavy grey-haired men go first, then the middle-aged, then the young men, then last, two short-haired, slim boys, schoolboys. The hair of the young men, growing after school, is bobbed round.

The grown men are all heavily built, rather short, with heavy but shapely flesh, and rather straight sides. They have not the archaic slim waists of the Taos Indians. They have archaic squareness, and a sensuous heaviness. Their very hair is black, massive, heavy. These are the so-called snake-priests, men of the snake clan. And to-night they are eleven in number.

They pace rapidly round, with that heavy wild silence of concentration characteristic of them, and cast meal and stamp upon the lid, cast meal and stamp in the second round, come round and spit and stamp in the third. For to the savage, the animist, to spit may be a kind of blessing, a communion, a sort of embrace.

The eleven snake-priests form silently in a row, facing the eight grey smeared antelope-priests across the little lid, and bowing forward a little, to earth. Then the antelope-priests, bending forward, begin a low, sombre chant, or call, that sounds wordless, only a deep, low-toned, secret Ay-a! Ay-a! Ay-a! And they bend from right to left, giving two shakes to the little, flat, white rattle in their left hand, at each shake, and stamping the right foot in heavy rhythm. In their right hand, that held the meal, is grasped a little skin bag, perhaps also containing meal.

They lean from right to left, two seed-like shakes of the rattle each time and the heavy rhythmic stamp of the foot, and the low, sombre, secretive chant-call each time. It is a strange low sound, such as we never hear, and it reveals how deep, how deep the men are in the mystery they are practising, how sunk deep below our world, to the world of snakes, and dark ways in the earth, where the roots of corn, and where the little rivers of unchannelled, uncreated life-passion run like dark, trickling lightning, to the roots of the corn and to the feet and loins of men, from the earth's innermost dark sun. They are calling in the deep, almost silent snake-language, to the snakes and the rays of dark emission from the earth's inward 'Sun'.

At this moment, a silence falls on the whole crowd of listeners. It is that famous darkness and silence of Egypt, the touch of the other mystery. The deep concentration of the 'priests' conquers for a few seconds our white-faced flippancy, and we hear only the deep Háh-ha! Háh-ha! speaking to snakes and the earth's inner core.

This lasts a minute or two. Then the antelope-priests stand bowed and still, and the snake-priests take up the swaying and the deep chant, that sometimes is so low, it is like a mutter underground, inaudible. The rhythm is crude, the swaying unison is all uneven. Culturally, there is nothing. If it were not for that mystic, dark-sacred concentration.

Several times in turn, the two rows of daubed, long-haired, insunk men facing one another take up the swaying and the chant. Then that too is finished. There is a break in the formation. A young snake-priest takes up something that may be a corn-cob—perhaps an antelope-priest hands it to him—and comes forward, with an old, heavy, but still shapely snake-priest behind him dusting his shoulders with the feathers, eagle-feathers presumably, which are the Indians' hollow prayer-sticks. With the heavy, stamping hop they move round in the previous circle, the young priest holding the cob curiously, and the old priest prancing strangely at the young priest's back, in a sort of incantation, and brushing the heavy young shoulders delicately with the prayer-feathers. It is the God-vibration that enters us from behind, and is transmitted to the hands, from the hands to the corn-cob. Several young priests emerge, with the bowed heads and the cob in their hands and the heavy older priests hanging over them behind. They tread round the rough curve and come back to the kiva, take perhaps another cob, and tread round again.

That is all. In ten or fifteen minutes it is over. The two files file rapidly and silently away. A brief, primitive performance.

The crowd disperses. They were not many people. There were no venomous snakes on exhibition, so the mass had nothing to come for. And therefore the curious immersed intensity of the priests was able to conquer the white crowd.

By afternoon of the next day the three thousand people had massed in the little plaza, secured themselves places on the roofs and in the window-spaces, everywhere, till the small pueblo seemed built of people instead of stones. All sorts of people, hundreds and hundreds of white women, all in breeches like half-men, hundreds and hundreds of men who had been driving motor-cars, then many Navajos, the women in their full, long skirts and tight velvet bodices, the men rather lanky, long-waisted, real nomads. In the hot sun and the wind which blows the sand every day, every day in volumes round the corners, the three thousand tourists sat for hours, waiting for the show. The Indian policeman cleared the central oblong, in front of the kiva. The front rows of onlookers sat thick on the ground. And at last, rather early, because of the masses awaiting them, suddenly, silently, in the same rude haste, the antelope-priests filed absorbedly in, and made the rounds over the lid, as before. To-day, the eight antelope-priests were very grey. Their feet ashed pure grey, like suède soft boots: and their lower jaw was pure suède grey, while the rest of their face was blackish. With that pale-grey jaw, they looked like corpse-faces with swathing-bands. And all their bodies ash-grey smeared, with smears of black, and a black cloth to-day at the loins.

They made their rounds, and took their silent position behind the lid, with backs to the green tuft: an unearthly grey row of men with little skin bags in their hands. They were the lords of shadow, the intermediate twilight, the place of after-life and before-life, where house the winds of change. Lords of the mysterious, fleeting power of change.

Suddenly, with abrupt silence, in paced the snake-priests, headed by the same heavy man with solid grey hair like iron. To-day they were twelve men, from the old one, down to the slight, short-haired, erect boy of fourteen. Twelve men, two for each of the six worlds, or quarters: east, north, south, west, above, and below. And to-day they were in a queer ecstasy. Their faces were black, showing the whites of the eyes. And they wore small black loin-aprons. They were the hot living men of the darkness, lords of the earth's inner rays, the black sun of the earth's vital core, from which dart the speckled snakes, like beams.

Round they went, in rapid, uneven, silent absorption, the three rounds. Then in a row they faced the eight ash-grey men, across the lid. All kept their heads bowed towards earth, except the young boys.

Then, in the intense, secret, muttering chant the grey men began their leaning from right to left, shaking the hand, one-two, one-two, and bowing the body each time from right to left, left to right, above the lid in the ground, under which were the snakes. And their low, deep, mysterious voices spoke to the spirits under the earth, not to men above the earth.

But the crowd was on tenterhooks for the snakes, and could hardly wait for the mummery to cease. There was an atmosphere of inattention and impatience. But the chant and the swaying passed from the grey men to the black-faced men, and back again, several times.

This was finished. The formation of the lines broke up. There was a slight crowding to the centre, round the lid. The old antelope-priest (so-called) was stooping. And before the crowd could realise anything else a young priest emerged, bowing reverently, with the neck of a pale, delicate rattlesnake held between his teeth, the little, naïve, bird-like head of the rattlesnake quite still, near the black cheek, and the long, pale, yellowish, spangled body of the snake dangling like some thick, beautiful cord. On passed the black-faced young priest, with the wondering snake dangling from his mouth, pacing in the original circle, while behind him, leaping almost on his shoulders, was the oldest heavy priest, dusting the young man's shoulders with the feather-prayer-sticks, in an intense, earnest anxiety of concentration such as I have only seen in the old Indian men during a religious dance.

Came another young black-faced man out of the confusion, with another snake dangling and writhing a little from his mouth, and an elder priest dusting him from behind with the feathers: and then another, and another: till it was all confusion, probably, of six, and then four young priests with snakes dangling from their mouths, going round, apparently, three times in the circle. At the end of the third round the young priest stooped and delicately laid his snake on the earth, waving him away, away, as it were, into the world. He must not wriggle back to the kiva bush.

And after wondering a moment, the pale, delicate snake steered away with a rattlesnake's beautiful movement, rippling and looping, with the small, sensitive head lifted like antennæ, across the sand to the massed audience squatting solid on the ground around. Like soft, watery lightning went the wondering snake at the crowd. As he came nearer, the people began to shrink aside, half-mesmerised. But they betrayed no exaggerated fear. And as the little snake drew very near, up rushed one of the two black-faced young priests who held the snake-stick, poised a moment over the snake, in the prayer-concentration of reverence which is at the same time conquest, and snatched the pale, long creature delicately from the ground, waving him in a swoop over the heads of the seated crowd, then delicately smoothing down the length of the snake with his left hand, stroking and smoothing and soothing the long, pale, bird-like thing; and returning with it to the kiva, handed it to one of the grey-jawed antelope-priests.

Meanwhile, all the time, the other young priests were emerging with a snake dangling from their mouths. The boy had finished his rounds. He launched his rattlesnake on the ground, like a ship, and like a ship away it steered. In a moment, after it went one of those two black-faced priests who carried snake-sticks and were the snake-catchers. As it neared the crowd, very close, he caught it up and waved it dramatically, his eyes glaring strangely out of his black face. And in the interim that youngest boy had been given a long, handsome bull-snake, by the priest at the hold under the kiva boughs. The bull-snake is not poisonous. It is a constrictor. This one was six feet long, with a sumptuous pattern. It waved its pale belly, and pulled its neck out of the boy's mouth. With two hands he put it back. It pulled itself once more free. Again he got it back, and managed to hold it. And then as he went round in his looping circle, it coiled its handsome folds twice round his knee. He stooped, quietly, and as quietly as if he were untying his garter, he unloosed the folds. And all the time, an old priest was intently brushing the boy's thin straight shoulders with the feathers. And all the time, the snakes seemed strangely gentle, naïve, wondering and almost willing, almost in harmony with the men. Which of course was the sacred aim. While the boy's expression remained quite still and simple, as it were candid, in a candour where he and the snake should be in unison. The only dancers who showed signs of being wrought-up were the two young snake-catchers, and one of these, particularly, seemed in a state of actor-like uplift, rather ostentatious. But the old priests had that immersed, religious intentness which is like a spell, something from another world.

The young boy launched his bull-snake. It wanted to go back to the kiva. The snake-catcher drove it gently forward. Away it went, towards the crowd, and at the last minute was caught up into the air. Then this snake was handed to an old man sitting on the ground in the audience, in the front row. He was an old Hopi of the Snake clan.

Snake after snake had been carried round in the circles, dangling by the neck from the mouths of one young priest or another, and writhing and swaying slowly, with the small, delicate snake-head held as if wondering and listening. There had been some very large rattlesnakes, unusually large, two or three handsome bull-snakes, and some racers, whipsnakes. All had been launched, after their circuits in the mouth, all had been caught up by the young priests with the snake-sticks, one or two had been handed to old-snake clan men in the audience, who sat holding them in their arms as men hold a kitten. The most of the snakes, however, had been handed to the grey antelope-men who stood in the row with their backs to the kiva bush. Till some of these ash-smeared men held armfuls of snakes, hanging over their arms like wet washing. Some of the snakes twisted and knotted round one another, showing pale bellies.

Yet most of them hung very still and docile. Docile, almost sympathetic, so that one was struck only by their clean, slim length of snake nudity, their beauty, like soft, quiescent lightning. They were so clean, because they had been washed and anointed and lustrated by the priests, in the days they had been in the kiva.

At last all the snakes had been mouth-carried in the circuits, and had made their little outrunning excursion to the crowd, and had been handed back to the priests in the rear. And now the Indian policemen, Hopi and Navajo, began to clear away the crowd that sat on the ground, five or six rows deep, around the small plaza. The snakes were all going to be set free on the ground. We must clear away.

We recoiled to the farther end of the plaza. There, two Hopi women were scattering white corn-meal on the sandy ground. And thither came the two snake-catchers, almost at once, with their arms full of snakes. And before we who stood had realised it, the snakes were all writhing and squirming on the ground, in the white dust of meal, a couple of yards from our feet. Then immediately, before they could writhe clear of each other and steer away, they were gently, swiftly snatched up again, and with their arms full of snakes, the two young priests went running out of the plaza.

We followed slowly, wondering, towards the western, or north-western edge of the mesa. There the mesa dropped steeply, and a broad trail wound down to the vast hollow of desert brimmed up with strong evening light, up out of which jutted a perspective of sharp rock and further mesas and distant sharp mountains: the great, hollow, rock-wilderness space of that part of Arizona, submerged in light.

Away down the trail, small, dark, naked, rapid figures with arms held close, went the two young men, running swiftly down to the hollow level, and diminishing, running across the hollow towards more stark rocks of the other side. Two small, rapid, intent, dwindling little human figures. The tiny, dark sparks of men. Such specks of gods.

They disappeared, no bigger than stones, behind rocks in shadow. They had gone, it was said, to lay down the snakes before a rock called the snake-shrine, and let them all go free. Free to carry the message and thanks to the dragon-gods who can give and withhold. To carry the human spirit, the human breath, the human prayer, the human gratitude, the human command which had been breathed upon them in the mouths of the priests, transferred into them from those feather-prayer-sticks which the old wise men swept upon the shoulders of the young, snake-bearing men, to carry this back, into the vaster, dimmer, inchoate regions where the monsters of rain and wind alternated in beneficence and wrath. Carry the human prayer and will-power into the holes of the winds, down into the octopus heart of the rain-source. Carry the corn-meal which the women had scattered, back to that terrific, dread, and causeful dark sun which is at the earth's core, that which sends us corn out of the earth's nearness, sends us food or death, according to our strength of vital purpose, our power of sensitive will, our courage.

It is a battle, a wrestling all the time. The Sun, the nameless Sun, source of all things, which we call sun because the other name is too fearful, this, this vast dark protoplasmic sun from which issues all that feeds our life, this original One is all the time willing and unwilling. Systole, diastole, it pulses its willingness and its unwillingness that we should live and move on, from being to being, manhood to further manhood, Man, small, vulnerable man, the farthest adventurer from the dark heart of the first of suns, into the cosmos of creation, Man, the last god won into existence. And all the time, he is sustained and threatened, menaced and sustained from the Source, the innermost sun-dragon. And all the time, he must submit and he must conquer. Submit to the strange beneficence from the Source, whose ways are past finding out. And conquer the strange malevolence of the Source, which is past comprehension also.

For the great dragons from which we draw our vitality are all the time willing and unwilling that we should have being. Hence only the heroes snatch manhood, little by little, from the strange den of the Cosmos.

Man, little man, with his consciousness and his will, must both submit to the great origin-powers of his life, and conquer them. Conquered by man who has overcome his fears, the snakes must go back into the earth with his messages of tenderness, of request, and of power. They go back as rays of love to the dark heart of the first of suns. But they go back also as arrows shot clean by man's sapience and courage, into the resistant, malevolent heart of the earth's oldest, stubborn core. In the core of the first of suns, whence man draws his vitality, lies poison as bitter as the rattlesnake's. This poison man must overcome, he must be master of its issue. Because from the first of suns come travelling the rays that make men strong and glad and gods who can range between the known and the unknown. Rays that quiver out of the earth as serpents do, naked with vitality. But each ray charged with poison for the unwary, the irreverent, and the cowardly. Awareness, wariness, is the first virtue in primitive man's morality. And his awareness must travel back and forth, back and forth, from the darkest origins out to the brightest edifices of creation.

And amid all its crudity, and the sensationalism which comes chiefly out of the crowd's desire for thrills, one cannot help pausing in reverence before the delicate, anointed bravery of the snake-priests (so-called), with the snakes.

They say the Hopis have a marvellous secret cure for snake-bites. They say the bitten are given an emetic drink, after the dance, by the old women, and that they must lie on the edge of the cliff and vomit, vomit, vomit. I saw none of this. The two snake-men who ran down into the shadow came soon running up again, running all the while, and steering off at a tangent, ran up the mesa once more, but beyond a deep, impassable cleft. And there, when they had come up to our level, we saw them across the cleft distance washing, brown and naked, in a pool; washing off the paint, the medicine, the ecstasy, to come back into daily life and eat food. Because for two days they had eaten nothing, it was said. And for nine days they had been immersed in the mystery of snakes, and fasting in some measure.

Men who have lived many years among the Indians say they do not believe the Hopi have any secret cure. Sometimes priests do die of bites, it is said. But a rattlesnake secretes his poison slowly. Each time he strikes he loses his venom, until if he strikes several times, he has very little wherewithal to poison a man. Not enough, not half enough to kill. His glands must be very full charged with poison, as they are when he merges from winter-sleep, before he can kill a man outright. And even then, he must strike near some artery.

Therefore, during the nine days of the kiva, when the snakes are bathed and lustrated, perhaps they strike their poison away into some inanimate object. And surely they are soothed and calmed with such things as the priests, after centuries of experience, know how to administer to them.

We dam the Nile and take the railway across America. The Hopi smooths the rattlesnake and carries him in his mouth, to send him back into the dark places of the earth, an emissary to the inner powers.

To each sort of man his own achievement, his own victory, his own conquest. To the Hopi, the origins are dark and dual, cruelty is coiled in the very beginnings of all things, and circle after circle creation emerges towards a flickering, revealed Godhead. With Man as the godhead so far achieved, waveringly and for ever incomplete, in this world.

To us and to the Orientals, the Godhead was perfect to start with, and man makes but a mechanical excursion into a created and ordained universe, an excursion of mechanical achievement, and of yearning for the return to the perfect Godhead of the beginning.

To us, God was in the beginning, Paradise and the Golden Age have been long lost, and all we can do is to win back.

To the Hopi, God is not yet, and the Golden Age lies far ahead. Out of the dragon's den of the cosmos, we have wrested only the beginnings of our being, the rudiments of our Godhead.

Between the two visions lies the gulf of mutual negations. But ours was the quickest way, so we are conquerors for the moment.

The American aborigines are radically, innately religious. The fabric of their life is religion. But their religion is animistic, their sources are dark and impersonal, their conflict with their 'gods' is slow, and unceasing.

This is true of the settled pueblo Indian and the wandering Navajo, the ancient Maya, and the surviving Aztec. They are all involved at every moment, in their old, struggling religion.

Until they break in a kind of hopelessness under our cheerful, triumphant success. Which is what is rapidly happening. The young Indian who have been to school for many years are losing their religion, becoming discontented, bored, and rootless. An Indian with his own religion inside him *cannot* be bored. The flow of the mystery is too intense all the time, too intense, even, for him to adjust himself to circumstances which really are mechanical. Hence his failure. So he, in his great religious struggle for the Godhead of man, falls back beaten. The Personal God who ordained a mechanical cosmos gave the victory to his sons, a mechanical triumph.

Soon after the dance is over, the Navajo begin to ride down the Western trail, into the light. Their women, with velvet bodices and full, full skirts, silver and turquoise tinkling thick on their breasts, sit back on their horses and ride down the steep slope, looking wonderingly around from their pleasant, broad, nomadic, Mongolian faces. And the men, long, loose, thin, long-waisted, with tall hats on their brows and low-slunk silver belts on their hips, come down to water their horses at the spring. We say they look wild. But they have the remoteness of their religion, their animistic vision, in their eyes, they can't see as we see. And they cannot accept us. They stare at us as the coyotes stare at us: the gulf of mutual negation between us.

So in groups, in pairs, singly, they ride silently down into the lower strata of light, the aboriginal Americans riding into their shut-in reservations. While the white Americans hurry back to their motor-cars, and soon the air buzzes with starting engines, like the biggest of rattlesnakes buzzing.

The Egalitarian Waltz

by Ruth Katz

One need not be an anthropologist or a cultural historian to remark that social dancing these days seems to isolate the individual in a trance-like self-absorption which virtually disconnects him from the world and even from his partner. Indeed, the dance of the day—like other art forms—is often a good reflection of the values of a given time and pla[illegible]oday's developments, both in the dance and in society, [illegible] than the usual scholarly justification for looking back to [illegible]liest manifestations of individualism and escape in the [illegible]sociation with the values of liberty, equality and uncer-

[illegible]*ative Studies in Society and History*, June 1973.

tainty which followed upon the French Revolution. The dance was the waltz; the dancers, at first were the middle classes, soon to be joined by both upper and lower classes, the time and place are Central Europe, and soon the whole Western world at the beginning of the nineteenth century.

The history of the dance makes plain that the upper classes of Western society borrowed many of their dance forms from 'the people,' although the dances underwent various transformations in the course of their adaptation. Two forms of the same dance frequently existed side by side, the upper classes preferring the restrained and calmer version, while the country folk preferred the freer and wilder form.[1] Despite the apparent differences between court and folk dance, and the variations in the extent of similarity from dance to dance, and from time to place, the kinship is almost always discernible. Historically, the tie between the two forms was particularly close until the fifteenth century. From that time forward, there is an increasing gap.

We are told that dances tended to be quite simple until the fifteenth century, and their unwritten rules could be learned through observation and participation. The emphasis on both court and folk dance was primarily on their larger basic features, where the relatively few individual components of each dance were fused into an artistic whole. Beginning in the fifteenth century, however, this emphasis on simplicity and on the whole begins to be replaced by a liking for multiple elements, complexity and attention to small details.[2] Without entering into an explanation of the underlying reasons for this new aesthetic outlook—a problem which is not really relevant to the present paper—it will be recalled that this new 'realism of particulars' also found expression in other arts of the period such as the illumination of books, for example, or the importance attached to detail in the weaving of tapestries, etc.

In the dance, the attention to detail gave rise to an elaborate vocabulary of steps. For the first time, intricate features had to be learned with exactitude and memorized carefully. This new development led, eventually, to the establishment of a new profession, the dance teacher, and to the crystallization of a 'theory' of the dance to which the proliferation of dance manuals attests. As a result, courtly dance and folk dance spread further apart. They continued to influence each other, one may say, but their aims and styles were different.[3]

[1] Curt Sachs, *World History of the Dance* (New York, 1937), p. 282.

[2] *Ibid.*, p. 298.

[3] *Ibid.*, pp. 299–302.

The purpose of this paper, however, is not to analyze why the cultural gap between the social classes widened, but rather to point out a moment in history when they converged once again, when 'everybody' danced the waltz. This vantage point, perhaps, may also contribute to the clarification of why and when high culture and popular culture diverge and converge.

The Universality of the Waltz

Popular imagery today has it that in the early decades of the nineteenth century, kings and commoners, nobles and bourgeoisie whiled away their nights waltzing. Hollywood has contributed substantially to this image[4] and perhaps that alone is enough to make it suspect, particularly when one recalls, from cultural history in general, and from the history of the dance alluded to above, that the homogeneity of cultural expression had declined, as the class structure became more heterogeneous. Yet, for all this, a close investigation substantiates the popular image. Indeed, everybody seems to have been dancing the waltz.

No less interesting than the success of the waltz as a dance form is its success from a purely musical point of view. Concert performances of the waltz attracted audiences as significant as those whose legs it propelled. The standing of Johann Strauss Sr. among composers and among concert-goers was very high, and in an era when Beethoven had just died (1827), the waltz was admitted not only to the ballroom and to 'pop' concerts, but to the very halls in which Beethoven had resounded the night before. We know that not only kings and queens lent their ears, but that composers like Schumann, Mendelssohn, Wagner, Rossini, Meyerbeer, Bellini, Auber, Berlioz, Brahms, and even Cherubini, who had lived through the entire high classical era, were among those who praised and applauded Strauss.[5] Farga, with all his exaggerated enthusiasm, seems right when he says, 'Nie vorher und nie nachher erreicht die Unterhaltungsmusik ein derartiges Niveau vie zur Zeit Strauss und Lanners.'[6]

If one holds to the theory that every artistic creation is an expression of the world in which it was created, two questions immediately arise:

[4] One will recall Warner Brothers' 'The Great Waltz' in this connection, as well as more recent offerings, such as a Walt Disney cartoon about Johann Strauss in which both cats and mice join together in the waltz.

[5] H. E. Jacob, *Johann Strauss, Father and Son* (Richmond, Va., 1939), pp. 79–108.

[6] Franz Farga, *Lanner und Strauss* (Vienna, 1948), p. 42.

1. What social conditions account for this radical change? In particular, what changes had taken place in the relationship among the social classes that could be made manifest in this way? 2. Apart from the social basis which may explain the convergence of cultural behavior, one must inquire into the cultural expression itself: What is it about the waltz that made it suitable for this unique role? In what sense does the nature of the dance itself reflect the society which created it? Both of these sets of questions will occupy us in what follows.

The Minuet and the Waltz

To make the argument of this paper more tangible, it is interesting to compare the character of the waltz and its social setting with that of the minuet and its social setting. The major dance which immediately preceded the waltz, the minuet, is a courtly dance whose folk origins had been transferred from their initial unrestrained expressiveness into the classical ideas of clarity, balance and regularity. While outwardly simple, the minuet has to be 'studied,' a fact to which a great number of dance manuals devoted to its rules and regulations attest. Goethe's oft-cited observations, made at one of the carnivals he attended in Rome, substantiates this point even further. He remarks, 'Nobody ventures unconcernedly to dance unless he has been taught the art; the minuet in particular, is regarded as a work of art and is performed, indeed, only by a few couples. The couples are surrounded by the rest of the company, admired and applauded at the end.'[7] Thus, we also learn from Goethe something which is fully corroborated in the dance manuals: the minuet involves not only dancers but onlookers as well, and these latter are an important part of the spectacle.

The delicately planned geometry of the dance steps were the quintessence of dignity and formality. There was no room for individual variation, embellishment or creativity. All is as carefully planned and executed as the architecture of a Le Notre garden. The dancers' dress was costly but moderate, emphasizing an appreciation for the beauty of simplicity. Subdued half-tone colors predominated. The hoop skirt symbolized additional restraint and 'distance.'

But for all the simplicity and uniformity, social status considerations played an important part in the dance. Perhaps it was the presence of an audience which made it so tempting to incorporate into the dance

[7] W. von Goethe, *Italien, Zweiter Aufenthalt in Rom*, 1788. Sachs uses this quotation in a somewhat different connection, primarily to emphasize the aesthetic values of the minuet, *op. cit.*, p. 399.

symbols of the status of the dancers in the social structure; perhaps it was something else. But what we do know is that it took a great deal of research to determine who would open the ball, and in what succession each guest should enter the dance.[8] The minuet, it may be said, reflected and incorporated the wordly ranks which its participants brought with them when they entered the ballroom. Pardoxically, this was made possible by the very uniformity of the minuet.

Not so the waltz. The waltz emphasized not uniformity, but individual expression; there are no rules to be studied, save for a few basic steps; the individual is encouraged to introduce his own variations and interpretations. Here, the dancers surrender their wordly identities upon entering the 'society of the dance' where individuals take on new roles and where recognition is accorded not by virtue of one's status in the larger society, but by virtue of one's performance in the dance. Often, in dances like the waltz where individual expression is encouraged, the best dancers are permitted to bring the dance to a close while the others encircle them to watch and applaud. Except in this latter sense, there are no onlookers or audience in the waltz. The emphasis is on the participation of all, and on the equality of all, while rewarding achievement within the dance itself rather than status one brings to the dance from 'the world outside.'

The Acceptance of the Waltz

If the minuet represented the separateness of the classes and retained social distinctions even within the dance, the waltz represents the breaking down of these distinctions. In trying to explain how this happened, the first thing to note is that the waltz, or something very much like it, had been rejected by the middle and upper classes not very long before.

About the middle of the eighteenth century the word 'walzen' was introduced as the name of a whirling or revolving dance movement. Ultimately, the word is thought to derive from the Latin 'volvere' (to turn around). From both verbal and pictorial documents dating as early as the sixteenth century, it can be deduced that the waltz as a dance

[8] The audience served as an integral part of the dance, the spectators, not only the audience, were saluted with ceremonial bows which preceded the actual dance. Ciambattista Dufort finds it necessary to devote two whole chapters of his manual *Trattato del ballo nobile* (Naples, 1728) to this subject. Gottfried Taubert devotes sixty pages of his *Rechischaffener Tanzmeister* (Leipzig, 1717) to the same, and J. M. de Chavanne devotes almost his entire book *Principes du Minuet* (Luxembourg, 1767) to that crucial opening which so well expresses the atmosphere of the whole dance.

movement is of much older date than that in which it received a definite name. The Weller, the Spinner, and the Volte—noted by sixteenth-century writers such as the Meistersinger, Kunz Has[9] and Thoinot Arbeau in his Orchesographie[10]—show great resemblance to the later waltz in that the dancing couple whirl in close embrace, often revolving about the room, rather than dancing separately side by side in the form that predominated until after the minuet.

These precursors of the waltz were severely criticized by moralists and others. Thoinot Arbeau was concerned with the dizziness caused by the Volte,[11] while a variety of clergymen remarked on the young women who allowed themselves to be grasped anywhere by their partners and lusted to be thrown into the air and twirled about.[12] One such warning is sounded by Cyriacus Spangenberg in his publication of 1578 warning all pious young men against those 'Jungfrauen die da Lust zu den Abendtanzen haben und sich da gerne umbedrehen, unzüchtig küssen und begreifen lassen.'[13]

The upper classes, at least, heeded the warnings, although perhaps for other reasons. Under the influence of the ballet and the increasing distance between folk-dance and court-dance, during the seventeenth and greater part of the eighteenth centuries, courtly dance found little room for the sensual. The minuet, the most dignified representative of those dances the movement of which were conventionalized, was a conscious work of art, lacking that element of spontaneity which characterized the dances it replaced. While some of the whirling dances were 'salonfähig' for a time, the dancing masters easily succeeded in substituting artistic skill and discipline for spontaneity and expressiveness.

The return to naturalness in the dance began in the eighteenth century, together with the renewed interest in folk song, and was part of a movement to recapture the vitality of the folk for the new nationalistic needs of society. Thus, the centuries-old German Dreher was rediscovered, and in a short time became a world-conquering dance which not only dominated dancing itself but succeeded in penetrating into compositions which had little to do with dancing.[14]

Of the many whirling dances, it is particularly the Landler from

[9] See Edward Reeser, *The History of the Waltz* (Stockholm, n.d.), p. 1.

[10] Thoinot Arbeau, *Orchesography*, translated by Mary Stewart Evans (New York, 1967), pp. 119–23.

[11] *Ibid.*, p. 121.

[12] See Paul Nettl, '*Tanz und Tanzmuzik*,' in Adler's *Handbuch der Musikgeschichte* (Berlin, 1930), Vol. II, pp. 979–80.

[13] Cited in Reeser, *op cit.* p. 9.

[14] See Paul Nettl, *The Story of Dance Music* (New York, 1947), pp. 252–86.

which the waltz derived. The couples in close embrace made a turn to each two measures while at the same time following a circular course. The three-four rhythm with the strongly accentuated first beat characteristic of most Landlers was adopted by the waltz.

The waltz attained its true character, however, by being danced like a Schleifer, having given up the skips and the turning under the arm of the Landler in favor of dragging the feet along the floor.[15] The skips unquestioningly represented a certain freedom of expression, but it is these smooth revolutions, the ecstatic gliding motion, which first made it possible to really 'let go.' Of course, this very 'letting go' was the basis on which the ancestors of the waltz had been resisted.

The Waltz in Ideological and Social Perspective

It is well-known that the development of courtly art since the close of the Renaissance came to a standstill toward the middle of the eighteenth century and was superseded by middle-class subjectivism and romanticism. Arnold Hauser, discussing this development, distinguishes, however, between pre-revolutionary romanticism and that of the post-revolutionary period.

The French Revolution, argues Hauser, although it conceived of art as harnessed to the needs of the emerging 'new' society, created an idea of artistic freedom which had no precedent. The revolution itself limited the freedom of the individual artist by focusing on art and not the artist. It declared that art must not be the privilege of the rich and the leisured, or an idle pastime, but that it must 'teach and improve and contribute to the happiness of the general public and be the possession of every man.' By creating a correspondence between the idea of artistic truth and that of social justice, the revolution challenged the dictatorship of the academies and the monopolization of the art market by the court and aristocracy.

The consequent romanticism denied that there existed objective rules of any kind to govern the production or consumption of art. It enshrined the concept of the uniqueness of individual expression and the struggle against the very principle of tradition, authority and rule. Whereas the pre-revolutionary middle class saw art as one means of expressing identification with the aristocracy and aloofness from the lower classes, in the post-revolutionary period it began to think of art as individualistic and idiosyncratic, a 'matter of taste' which might vary

[15] See Sachs, *op. cit.*, p. 433.

among different people, different times and different places.[16] Thus, art which had previously been looked upon as possessing universal validity, in this over-all rebellion against authority of any kind, could no longer be judged by absolute standards. The continuous striving toward the goal of perfection, so characteristic of the eighteenth century, gave way to a kind of relativism in which it became possible to 'like' both a Beethoven and a Strauss, not because they stand comparison, but because they need not be compared.

As the individual was 'freed' from conventional standards and tastes, and the artist was 'freed' from his royal patrons and a market developed in which the artist had to satisfy 'public opinion' and its new leaders, the critics, the demand increased for lighter and less 'complicated' music which led, ultimately, to a division into 'serious' and 'light' music which had not existed previously. The concert societies and later the large concert halls replaced performances at court and drawing rooms, and induced greater concentration on expressiveness and on individual style. 'Individual style' in fact, now characterized the music of the nineteenth century. Emotionalism and sentimentalism now served the middle class as a means of expressing its intellectual independence of the aristocracy, but ultimately led to a cult of sensibility in which the aristocracy itself could join.

Along with nationalism, then, the newly-awakened concern with sensibility, the throwing off of traditional standards and the rise of relativism all cut across barriers to create an ideology of romanticism. This ideology began in the middle classes, but, in time, spread both upwards to the waning aristocracy and downwards to the industrial lower classes. These cohesive forces combined with the economic and political interaction which reduced the barriers between classes.

Yet, for all the equality which the newly-freed individual might experience with those about him, psychologically speaking, there is a loss involved: the sense of having some fixed and proper place in a stable and predictable society. The individual stood alone. This, of course, is the most famous dilemma of modern man, the roots of which are to be found in the post-revolutionary period.[17]

[16] For a suggestive discussion of the above see Arnold Hauser, *The Social History of Art* (London, 1951), Vol. II, pp. 622–710.

[17] For a relevant sociological study of the European drama see Leo Lowenthal, *Literature and the Image of Man* (Boston, 1957), pp. 136–220.

The Appropriateness of the Waltz

The attributes of the waltz are compatible with this social and ideological setting. This was a period of unity, as we tried to point out, in which nationalism, relativism and the over-all ideology of romanticism brought very different kinds of people into contact and sympathy with each other. The university of the waltz gave expression to this unity and mutual accessibility. Furthermore, the period was one of individual assertiveness and achievement, and the waltz allowed for freedom of expression and provided an opportunity for proving oneself. The beautiful commoner, if she waltzed very well, would be invited to dance with the prince.

But with all of this the times were troubled too. Austria, for example, was at war no less than five times between 1792 and 1814, yet she was the leader in the crusade for Gemütlichkeit. The individual who had lost his sense of belonging since the revolution, who no longer had an idea of a proper place in a predictable society, became an object of importance and interest to himself at the expense of his commitment to other social roles. 'Gemütlichkeit' is only one of the symptoms of this new state of being. Self-experiences now replaced the experiences of the world outside and were treated as though they were constantly slipping away and being lost forever. Losing oneself in the waltz is indeed one of the most symbolic cultural expressions of this new frame of mind, and the waltz craze of the first decades of the nineteenth century expresses so well this attitude to experiences and their temporality. It is interesting and amusing to mention in connection with this that the Apollo Palace in Vienna, where the waltz was danced with passion and verve by up to 6,000 persons in five large and thirty-one smaller dancing rooms, is supposed to have contained a hall for pregnant women who were eager not to lose even a moment of the dance, even though they preferred not to mingle with the general crowd.[18]

The waltz not only made it possible for different kinds of individuals to come together on an egalitarian basis, it also made possible a kind of 'escape' from reality through the thrilling dizziness of whirling one's way in a private world of sensuality. The 'letting go' function of the waltz seems relevant to a world without clear standards, in which the individual stood alone having to find his own way. Werther, Goethe's

[18] Jacob, *op. cit.*, p. 24.

romantic hero, confesses to Wilhelm that while waltzing with Lotte, everything around him seemed to disappear. 'Ich war kein Mensch mehr,' he relates, 'das liebenswürdigste Geschöpf in den Armen zu haben und mit ihr herumsufligen wie Wetter, dass alles ringsumher verging.'[19]

Although the waltz seemed like a centrifugal force generated by rotation and threatening to hurl the dancers into space, the support given by each partner to the other was so strong that there was no 'danger' in their abandonment. In other words, the waltz permitted additional 'freedom,' the kind of sexual contact which had heretofore been unthinkable in public. The greater physical contact between the sexes made possible by the waltz is cleverly illustrated in the following sarcastic verses written by Lord Byron on this subject:

> Round all the confines of the yielded waist
> The strongest hand may wander undisplaced;
> The lady's in return may grasp as much
> As princely paunches offer to her touch.
> Pleased round the chalky floor how well they trip;
> One hand reposing on the royal hip;
> The other to the shoulder no less royal
> Ascending with affection truly loyal!
>
> Thus all and each in movement swift or slow,
> The genial contact gently undergo;
> Till some might marvel with the modest Turk
> If "nothing follows all this palming work"?
> Something does follow at a fitter time;
> The breast thus publicly resign'd to man
> In private may resist him—if it can.

The waltz, it seems, not only made it possible to lose consciousness of time and space, but by introducing sensual thrills and encouraging free erotic expressions it also succeeded in providing the 'desert island' to which one might escape. In this sense the waltz may have represented a world in which only the senses were operative, a world which was void of responsibility, an experience of self and self-involvement, an escape from reality and a surrender to the moment which can best

[19] J. W. Goethe, *Die Leiden des Jungen Werther* in *Goethe's Sämtliche Werke* (München, 1910), Vol. II, p. 265.

be understood when contrasted with the element of objectivity and detachment so essential in the execution of the minuet.[20]

Conclusion

Everybody danced the waltz. The waltz, the dance of the middle class, was as expressive for the upper classes who now shared the world view of the middle classes as it was for the lower classes in urban centers who also shared the same world view, not yet having developed one of their own. As was pointed out, the different social strata could share the same cultural expressions because of the greater cultural mobility which resulted from the over-all endorsement of romanticism and its manifold aspects, which directly or indirectly encouraged such a development. The acceptance of some of the basic ideas of the early nineteenth-century philosophy of nationalism directly facilitated cultural mobility.

Louis Philippe with his bourgeois manners and clothes best portrays the changed world view of the upper class. He loved the waltz and paid tribute to one of his major composers. He invited Johan Strauss, Sr., and his orchestra to play some of the waltzes with which he was already familiar at his court.[21]

Louis Philippe is not the only one in whose court the waltz resounded. In 1834 Strauss played for King Friedrich Wilhelm III and the Prussian court. And Czar Nicholas and the Czarina of Russia, upon hearing Strauss in Vienna invited him to introduce his waltzes at St. Petersburg.[22]

The Vienna Congress, held in the years 1814–15, is not only important in modern European history, but also represents an important moment in the history of the waltz. The diplomats and delegates who attended the Congress represented their countries but not a particular social class. The Congress was composed of mixed groups. It consisted of aristocrats of the old regime who applied eighteenth-century diplomatic principles, as well as representatives of other classes who were imbued with post-revolutionary political ideas. The well-known saying

[20] Caillois includes waltzing in the type of game to which he assigns the term *ilinx*—the Greek term for whirlpool—to cover 'the many varieties of such transport . . . which consist of an attempt to momentarily destroy the stability of perception and inflict a kind of voluptuous panic upon an otherwise lucid mind.' See Roger Caillois, *Man, Play and Games* (New York, 1961), pp. 23–6.

[21] Jacob, *op. cit.*, p. 91.

Jacob, *ibid.*, pp. 80–1.

'le Congrès ne marche pas, il danse' is certainly significant of the rage for dancing, but it is doubly significant for us that it was the waltz which propelled the legs of the delegates of all classes.

While the different social classes could share the same cultural expressions, the expressions themselves could now vary, since the new society was no longer guided by absolute values. This was a society for whom art became a matter of changing taste; a society for whom it was 'natural' for varied artistic expressions to co-exist. Moreover, any individual of that society could respond favorably to a diversity of artistic expressions, no longer experiencing the need to rank them in a single continuum of merit.

This is what permitted Berlioz to take Johann Strauss as the starting point and climax of one of his essays for the *Journal des Débats,* to which he was a monthly contributor. With Strauss as his example, Berlioz demonstrated to the Parisians the supremacy of German music and set him on a plane with Gluck, Beethoven and Weber.[23]

Musically speaking, Berlioz is not the only well-known composer of that period to have accepted the waltz and to have praised one of its greatest composers. However, the main supporters of the waltz were the members of the audience who required lighter music and wanted to be entertained. This audience, which was continuously increasing, was catered to because music became a commodity on the free market and made adjustments to the new situation. The idea of making music accessible to the masses can be traced directly to the revolution which made art the possession of every man, and which in the process of democratizing art, lowered its standards. As will be recalled, the social reformers saw a correspondence between the idea of artistic truth and that of social justice. Indeed, the waltz, to this society, represented some kind of artistic truth because it was so socially just. The Congress of 1815, which in a way, tried to eliminate from history both Napoleon and the French Revolution, took over the new dance of the bourgeoisie as its own form of social expression, gazing once more at 'Liberté, égalité, fraternité,' with affection and approval, knowing that the dance, and more specifically the waltz, may have proven to be one of the very few areas where those great ideas could actually be manifested, an area where freedom did not impair equality and vice versa. What a wonderful world in which to get lost!

[23] See Hector Berlioz, *Memoirs* (New York, 1966), pp. 375–7. Also see Jacques Barzun, *Berlioz and the Romantic Century* (Boston, 1950), Vol I, pp. 473–4.

Dance Aesthetics

Balanchine once remarked that any single step in a ballet was like a single frame of a movie and that dance, like film, was a fluid succession of images. Going to the ballet for the first time, many people are both attracted to and bewildered by this fluidity. They can see that ballet has developed specialized codes of movement, but they feel they don't "understand" those codes of movement because it's impossible to stop the flow: the dancer simply will not be caught, we cannot survey him at leisure from head to foot.

The essays in this section explain ballet's codified movements—how ballet uses and displays the body, what classic dancing looks like regardless of the subject matter of a particular ballet. Ballet has its own laws, its own logic, and although it bears many resemblances to poetry, sculpture, music, and drama, ballet cannot be understood by applying literary, musical, and dramatic aesthetics. Ballet generates meaning through its highly specialized and stylized movements; these essays attempt to describe that stylization and its implications.

In his two essays included in this section, Edwin Denby—the most lucid and graceful of all dance writers—tells us how to *look* at the dance, how to see the various qualities (time, space, dynamics) that allow a dancer to turn what otherwise would be a mere collection of unrelated movements into a sequence of steps that has continuity, coherence, and meaning. Denby describes the logic behind the "peculiar" appearance of ballet movement—why ballet distributes the energy through the body the way it does, why it demands verticality, how it uses space. As Denby makes clear in these essays, ballet technique is not merely an outdated, arbitrary, or elitist code of movement; the technique *is* the meaning of dance, the means of generating an extraordinary range of expression.

In "The Spirit of the Classic Dance," André Levinson also explains why the very technique of ballet possesses a beautiful and profound logic. Lamenting that dance has never had a proper aesthetic philosophy of its own, Levinson focuses on those characteristics that belong exclusively to dance. What is the innate quality of a dance step, Levinson asks. What is its intrinsic beauty, its aesthetic reason for being? How does ballet technique intelligently order physical effort? According to Levinson, the essential principle and point of departure of classic choreography—that of turning the body outward from its center—allows the human body an extraordinary, almost a supernatural mobility and flexibility. Because of the turn-out, the dancer can move in more directions, occupy more space, break away from the "exigencies of everyday life," and lose himself in the ideal. Because of the turn-out, the dancer can become a machine for "manufacturing beauty," a machine that in itself is a living, breathing thing, susceptible of the most exquisite and ideal emotions.

John Martin agrees that ballet is an idealistic and not a realistic art. Like Denby and Levinson, Martin maintains that ballet's codified movements are not merely a means for doing something else—for telling a story, let's say—but are an end in and of themselves. According to Martin, the very heart of ballet's aesthetics, the source of its drive, is "a glorification of the person as person, the presentation of its ideal essence freed from the encumbrances of a rationalistic universe of cause and effect . . ." Martin describes how ballet technique uses verticality and balance to create an inexhaustible repertoire of movements that evokes a "transcendent self-containment."

Meaning in Ballet
by Edwin Denby

How to Judge a Dancer

When you watch ballet dancers dancing you are observing a young woman or a young man in fancy dress, and you like it if they look attractive, if they are well built and have what seems to be an open face. You notice the youthful spring in starting, the grace of carriage, the strength in stopping. You like it if they know what to do and where to go, if they can throw in a surprising trick or two, if they seem to be enjoying their part and are pleasantly sociable as performers. All this is

Source: From *Looking at the Dance* (New York: Horizon, 1968), which was originally published in New York, 1949.

proper juvenile charm, and it often gives a very sharp pleasure in watching dancers.

But you are ready too for other qualities besides charm. The audience soon notices if the dancer has unusual control over her movements, if what she is doing is unusually clear to the eye, if there are differences of emphasis and differences of urgency in her motion. Within single slow movements or within a sequence you enjoy seeing the continuity of an impulse and the culmination of a phrase. Now you are not only watching a charming dancer, she is also showing you a dance.

When she shows you a dance, she is showing how the steps are related, that they are coherent and make some sense. You can see that they make some sense in relation to the music or in relation to the story; and now and then the dancer shows you they make sense also as dance phrases purely and simply. You may notice that a dance phrase holds together by its rhythm in time (a rhythm related to that of music), as a sequence of long and short motions set off by a few accents. Again in other passages you may be most interested by the arrangements in space, motions that make up a rhythm of large and small, up and down, right and left, backward and forward. You watch dance figures that combine several directions, done by single dancers or by groups, in place or while covering distance. Such dance phrases are plastically interesting. But at still other moments you notice especially the changes in the dancer's energy, the dynamics of a sequence, which contrasts motion as taut or easy, active or passive, pressing or delaying, beginning or ending. Dynamics, space and time—the dancer may call one or the other to your attention, but actually she keeps these three strands of interest going all the time, for they are all simultaneously present in even the simplest dancing. But a dancer who can make the various factors clear at the proper passage so as to keep you interested in the progress of the dance is especially attractive because she is dancing intelligently. She makes even a complicated choreography distinct to see.

Intelligent dancing—which might as well be called correct dancing—has a certain dryness that appeals more to an experienced dance lover than to an inexperienced one. In any case, everyone in the audience becomes more attentive when he recognizes a personal impetus in an intelligent dancer's movement, when she has a way of looking not merely like a good dancer, but also different from others and like her own self. Her motions look spontaneous, as if they suited her particular body, her personal impulses, as if they were being invented that very moment. This is originality in dancing—and quite different from originality in choreography. The original dancer vivifies the dance—plain or complicated, novel or otherwise—that the choreographer has set. She shows a gift like that of an actor who speaks his lines as if they were being uttered for the first time that very moment, though they have been in print a hundred years or though he has spoken them a hundred nights running.

Such vitality in dancing is not the same thing as that punch in projection sometimes called a "dynamic stage personality." A lively dancer does not push herself on the audience, except, of course, during curtain calls. Projection in serious dancing is a mild and steady force, the dancer who goes out to the audience with a bang cuts herself off from the rest of the stage action. Galvanic projection is a trick appropriate to revue, where there is no drama to interrupt. But in serious dancing the audience must be kept constantly aware of the complete action within the stage area, because the changes—and, therefore, the drama—of dancing are appreciated clearly in relation to that fixed three-dimensional frame. So the best dancers are careful to remain within what one may call the dance illusion, as an actor remains within the illusion of a dramatic action—when you cannot help imagining he is a young man speaking privately to a girl in a garden, though you see perfectly well he is middle aged, that he is talking blank verse for you to hear and standing on a wooden floor.

And just as you become really absorbed at a play when Romeo is not only distinct and spontaneous, but also makes you recognize the emotion of love, which has nothing to do with the actor personally or with acting in itself or with words in themselves, so the dancer becomes absorbing to watch when she makes you aware of emotions that are not make-believe at all. Some of my friends doubt that it is possible to give so much expressive power to dancing, though they grant it is possible to performers of music or of plays. To recognize poetic suggestion through dancing one has to be susceptible to poetic values and susceptible to dance values as well. But I find that a number of people are and that several dancers, for example Miss Danilova and Miss Markova, are quite often able to give them the sense of an amplitude in meaning which is the token of emotion in art. I myself go to dancing looking for this pleasure, which is the pleasure of the grand style, and find a moment or two of satisfaction in the work of a dozen dancers or more. In these remarkable flights the choreographer may be admired even more than the dancer, but here I am describing the merits of dancing only.

What I have said applies to any dance technique, and now that the ballet season is opening, it is a simple matter for anyone to go to the Metropolitan and check for himself the accuracy of it or the mistakes.

—October 10, 1943

Ballet Technique

When they watch a ballet in the theater some people can take ballet technique for granted as easily as school kids take the technique of basketball for granted while they watch a lively game in a gym. These ballet lovers see the dance impulses perfectly clear.

Other people, however, are bothered by the technique. They watch the gestures without feeling the continuity of the dance; the technique seems to keep getting in the way of it. Ballet looks to them chiefly like a mannerism in holding the arms and legs, and in keeping the back stiff as a ramrod. They can see it must be difficult to move about in that way, but why try in the first place? Annoyed at the enthusiasm of their neighbors in the theater, they come to the conclusion that ballet technique is a snobbish fad, the perverse invention of some dead and forgotten foreign esthetic dictator who insisted on making dancing as unnatural as possible.

But ballet technique isn't as unreasonable as that. Just as a dazzling technique in pitching, for instance, is an intelligent refinement of throwing a ball for fun (which everybody does somehow), so ballet technique is a refinement of social dancing and folk dancing, a simple enough thing that everybody has tried doing for fun in his own neighborhood. You know the main technical problem of dancing the first time you try; it's to move boldly without falling flat on the dance floor. You have to get the knack of shifting your weight in a peculiar way. Next you try to keep in rhythm, and then you try to give the conventional steps that extra personal dash which makes the dance come off. It's a question, of course, of doing all this jointly with others, sometimes in groups, sometimes in couples—when a little sex pantomime may be added, by common consent all over the world. And incidental acrobatic feats are welcome if they don't break up the dancers' happy sense of a collective rhythm.

Exhibition dance technique is a way of doing the same things for the pleasure of the neighbors who gather to watch. You see the simple elements of common dance technique refined and specialized, with a particular emphasis placed on one element or another. In recent generations we have seen our own normal folk and social dances evolve into professional tap dancing, into exhibition ballroom, and most recently into exhibition Lindy.

Like these recent dance techniques, ballet, too, is the result of practical experiments by a number of exhibition dancers—a long line of professionals which, in the case of ballet, began in the seventeenth century and has not yet ended. The ballet dancers seem to have taken as their point of emphasis not the small specialty tricks but the first great problem everybody has in dancing—the trouble of keeping in balance. The problem might be described as that of a variable force (the dance impulses) applied to a constant weight (the body). The ballet technicians wanted to find as many ways as possible of changing the impetus of the movement without losing control of the momentum of the body. When a dancer is not sure of his momentum he is like a driver who has no rhythm in driving, who jolts you, who either spurts or dawdles and makes you nervous. Watching a dancer whose momentum is under control, you appreciate the change in impetus as an expression. You follow the dance with pleasure, because the dancer has your confidence.

The foot, leg, arm and trunk positions of ballet, the way it distributes the energy in the body (holding back most of it in the waist and diminishing it from there as from a center)—this is a method of keeping the urgency of the movement in relation to a center of gravity in the body. The peculiar look of ballet movement is not the perverse invention of some dead esthetic dictator. It is a reasonable method which is still being elaborated by experiment. On the basis of a common technical experience—that of equilibrium in motion—this method tries to make the changes of impulse in movement as distinctly intelligible as possible. There have always been great dancers who danced in other techniques than that of ballet. But there have always been great dancers, too, who found in ballet technique an extraordinary range of clear expression. —*July 25, 1943*

About Toe Dancing

To a number of people ballet means toe dancing, that is what they come to see, and they suspect that a dancer only gets down off her "pointes" to give her poor feet a rest. But toesteps are not what ballet is about. They are just one of the devices of choreography, as the sharp hoots of a soprano are one of the devices of opera. Toesteps were invented, the historians say, "toward 1826" or "toward 1830." And the historians also explain that ballet during the century and more before the introduction of toesteps was quite as interesting to its audience as performances at the Metropolitan are nowadays to us. It was fully two hundred years ago that the audience enjoyed the difference between Mlle Camargo, that light, joyous, brilliant creature, and Mlle Sallé, the lovely expressive dramatic dancer. In 1740, too, the public was applauding with enthusiasm the plastic harmony of M. Dupré, "who danced more distinctly (*qui se dessinait mieux*) than anyone in the world." There was evidently plenty to watch before there were any toesteps. Still without toesteps choreography became so expressive that first Garrick and later Stendhal compared dance scenes they saw to scenes of Shakespeare. And long before toesteps Noverre's *Letters on Dancing* discussed the esthetics of ballet so clearly that ever since ballet has been judged by the general standards of art, or has not been judged at all. You can see that toesteps are not the secret of ballet.

I do not mean that the feature of toe dancing is foreign to ballet, quite the contrary. As a matter of fact the principles of ballet technique—its gymnastic as well as its plastic principles—were accurately defined shortly before toesteps were invented, and their addition did not require any revision of the fundamental exercises or postures. Toesteps are an application of an older ballet device, the rigid stretch of knee, ankle and instep to form a single straight line. During the eighteenth century this special expression of the leg was emphasized more and more, though used only when the leg was in the air. Finally a girl discovered she could put her whole weight on two legs and feet so stretched (as in an 1821 ballet print), and even support it on one; that became our modern toestep.

Perhaps toe technique was due to the exceptionally severe exercises to which the dancer Paul Taglioni subjected his brilliant daughter, Marie; certainly it was her expressive genius that made the trick a phenomenal one. But she was a great dancer before she did toesteps, and she had at least six and perhaps ten years of success behind her when the new fashion began. The uncertainty of history over the exact date suggests that these initial toesteps were far less precise than ours. In any case, in the 1830's other dancers beside Marie Taglioni learned them; though done as they then were in a soft slipper darned across the toe every evening, they were often uncertain and dangerous. Now of course any student learns them painlessly and with no heartbreak at all.

But to do them expressively, as Taglioni, Grisi and Elssler did, is still not common. Gautier., the poet-critic of a hundred years ago, described expressive "pointes" as "steel arrows plunging elastically against a marble floor." Unfortunately we have all seen dispirited performances of *Sylphides* where they have been merely a bumpy hobbling. Toesteps inherently have a secret that is not easy for either the dancer or the public: It is the extraordinary tautness of the completely straight leg-and-foot line which seems to alter the usual proportions of the body, not only the proportion of trunk and leg, but also the relation of hard and soft. Dancing on and off the toes may be described in this sense as an expressive play of changing proportions.

But "pointes" have a psychological aspect, too. There is a sense of discomfort, even of cruelty in watching them, a value that often shocks sensitive persons when they fail to find in the emotion of the dance a vividness that would make this savage detail interesting. Well, from a psychological point of view, toesteps have here and there a curious link to the theme of a ballet. In *Giselle* they seem consistent with the shocking fascination of death that is the core of the drama, in *Swan Lake* they are a part of the cruel remoteness of the beloved, in *Noces* they hammer out a savage intoxication. Elsewhere, in scenes of intelligent irony, they can look petulant or particular, absurd or fashionable.

But it would be a complete mistake to tag toesteps in general with a "literary" meaning. Their justification is the shift in the dance, the contrast between taut and pliant motion, between unexpected and expected repose, between a poignantly prolonged line and a normal one. Toesteps also increase the speed and change the rhythm of some figures. On paper these formal aspects sound less dramatic than psychological ones; but they are what one actually sees on the stage, and out of them, seeing them distinctly, the better part of the dance emotion is made.

—October 3, 1943

A Note on Dance Intelligence

Expression in dancing is what really interests everybody and everybody recognizes it as a sign of intelligence in the dancer. But dancing is physical motion, it doesn't involve words at all. And so it is an error to suppose that dance intelligence is the same as other sorts of intelligence which involve, on the contrary, words only and no physical movement whatever. What is expressive in a dance is not the dancer's opinions, psychological, political, or moral. It isn't even what she thinks about episodes in her private life. What is expressive in dancing is the way she moves about the stage, the way she exhibits her body in motion. A dancer's intelligence isn't shown by what intellectual allusions she can make in costume or pantomime, or if she is a choreographer, in her subject matter. It is shown by how interesting to look at she can make her body the whole time she is on the stage.

In the coming ballet season you may be able to compare Alexandra Danilova, Nana Gollner and Alicia Markova, each as the Swan Queen in *Swan Lake* and each one celebrated in that particular part. Each will be interesting to look at the whole time she will be on the stage, but the effect they make will be different. Watching the three in turn you may see what differences in their physical movement parallel their difference of expression and see how the dance intelligence of each leads her to a slightly different visual emphasis in identical steps and gymnastic feats.

For apart from questions of choreography it is variety of visual emphasis that we see when we feel variety of expression. And there are many resources for visual emphasis in dancing. There are the shifts in the pacing of a sequence, the points where the dancer hurries or delays. An identical step or arm gesture can be attacked sharply or mildly, it can subside or be stopped short. These differences draw the eye to one phase of motion rather than another, to one line of the body rather than another, or to the dancer's partner, or else to her momentary position on the stage, or even to a moment in the music which sharpens our sense of her movement.

But the most interesting resource for visual emphasis is the heightened perception of the dancer's body not in a line or silhouette, but in its mass, in its all-aroundness. A dancer can emphasize a passage in the dance by emphasizing the shape her body takes in the air. When she does this she does not call attention merely to the limb that moves, she defines her presence all around in every direction. At such moments she looks large, important, like a figure of imagination, like an ideal human being moving through the air at will. The great dancers seem to do this throughout a dance, but they vary it in intensity.

These are some of the physical characteristics of dance expression, and the brilliant use of them to arouse our interest, to thrill and to satisfy us, is proof of an artist's exceptional dance intelligence. She may have several other sorts of intelligence besides, but it is of no consequence to the public if she has not. It is the boldness and tenderness of her dance intelligence that the public loves her for. *March 26, 1944*

Flight of the Dancer

If you travel all over the world and see every brilliant and flying dance that human beings do, you will maybe be surprised that it is only in our traditional classic ballet dancing that the dancer can leap through the air slowly. In other kinds of dancing there are leaps that thrill you by their impetuousness or accuracy; there are brilliant little ones, savage long ones and powerful bouncing ones. But among all dance techniques only classic ballet has perfected leaps with that special slow-motion grace, that soaring rise and floating descent which looks weightless. It isn't that every ballet leap looks that way. Some are a tough thrust off the ground, some travel like a cat's, some quiver like a fish's, some scintillate like jig steps; but these ways of jumping you can find in other dancing too. The particular expression ballet technique has added to leaping is that of the dancer poised in mid-flight, as easy in the air as if she were suspended on wires. Describing the effect, people say one dancer took flight like a bird, another was not subject to the laws of gravity and a third paused quietly in mid-air. And that is how it does look, when it happens.

To be honest, it doesn't happen very often. It is a way of leaping only a few rare dancers ever quite achieve. But it can be achieved. You can see it in the dancing of Alicia Markova, the English-born star of our present Ballet Theater company; though no one else in this country —perhaps no one else in the world—can "fly" quite as perfectly as she does. No one else is so serenely calm with nothing underneath her. In *Pas de Quatre* she sits collectedly in the air, as if she were at a genteel tea-party, a tea-party where everyone naturally sat down on the air. There is something comic about it. That is because Miss Markova, who in the part of Giselle is a delicate tragic dancer, also has a keen sense of parody. *Pas de Quatre*, a parody ballet, represents the competition in virtuosity of four very great ballerinas at a command performance before Her Majesty Queen Victoria. (It actually happened in 1845.) In the ballet, Miss Markova takes the part of the greatest of the four, Marie Taglioni—Marie *pleine de grâces*, as she was called—who was a sallow little lady full of wrinkles, celebrated not only for her serene flight through the empty air, but also for the "decent voluptuousness" of her expression. Watching Miss Markova's performance one feels that not even the eminently respectable British queen could have found any fault with the female modesty of such a look as hers. And that "refined" look is Miss Markova's joke on Victorian propriety, and a little too on the vanity of exhibiting technique just for its own sake.

Her expression is parody, but the leap itself is no parody of a leap. It is the real, incredibly difficult thing. Taglioni's leap couldn't have been any better. A leap is a whole story with a beginning, a middle and an end. If you want to try it, here are some of the simplest directions for this kind of soaring flight. It begins with a knee bend, knees turned out, feet turned out and heels pressed down, to get a surer grip and a smoother flow in the leg action. The bend goes down softly ("as if the body were being sucked to the floor") with a slight accelerando. The thrust upward, the stretch of the legs, is faster than the bend was.

The speed of the action must accelerate in a continuous gradation from the beginning of the bend into the final spring upward, so there will be no break in motion when the body leaves the ground. The leap may be jumped from two feet, hopped from one, or hopped from one with an extra swing in the other leg. But in any case the propulsive strain of the leap must be taken up by the muscles around the waist, the back must be straight and perpendicular, as if it had no part in the effort. Actually, the back muscles have to be kept under the strictest tension to keep the spine erect—the difficulty is to move the pelvis against the spine, instead of the other way around; and as the spine has no material support in the air, you can see that it's like pulling yourself up by your own bootstraps.

But that isn't all. The shoulders have to be held rigidly down by main force, so they won't bob upward in the jump. The arms and neck, the hands and the head, have to look as comfortable and relaxed as if nothing were happening down below. Really there's as much going on down there as though the arms and head were picnicking on a volcano. Once in the air the legs may do all sorts of things, embellishments sometimes quite unconnected with what they did to spring up, or what they will have to do to land. And if there are such extra embellishments during the leap, there should be a definite pause in the air before they begin and after they are finished. No matter how little time there is for them, the ornaments must never be done precipitately.

But the most obvious test for the dancer comes in the descent from the air, in the recovery from the leap. She has to catch herself in a knee bend that begins with the speed she falls at, and progressively diminishes so evenly that you don't notice the transition from the air to the ground. This knee bend slows down as it deepens to what feels like a final rest, though it is only a fraction of a second long, so short a movie camera will miss it. This is the "divine moment" that makes her look as if she alighted like a feather. It doesn't happen when she lands, you see, it happens later. After that, straightening up from the bend must have the feeling of a new start; it is no part of the jump, it is a new breath, a preparation for the next thing she means to do.

In other words, the action of a leap increases in speed till the dancer leaves the ground. Then it diminishes till it reaches the leap's highest point up in the air. From then on it increases again till the feet hit the ground, when it must be slowed down by the knee bend to a rest; and all these changes must be continuously flowing. But most important of all is the highest point reached in the air. Here, if the dancer is to give the feeling of soaring, she must be completely still. She must express the calm of that still moment. Some dancers hold their breath. Nijinsky used to say he just stopped at that point. But however he does it, the dancer must project that hairs-breadth moment as a climax of repose. The dancer must not be thinking either of how she got up or how she is going to get down. She must find time just then to meditate.

When Nijinsky entered through the window in the *Spectre de la Rose* thirty years ago it was the greatest leap of the century. He seemed to the audience to float slowly down like a happy spirit. He seemed to radiate a power of mysterious assurance as calmly as the bloom of a summer rose does. Such enthusiastic comments sound like complete nonsense nowadays, when you go to the ballet and see a young man thumping about the stage self-consciously. But the comments were made by sensible people, and they are still convinced they were right. You begin to see what they mean when you realize that for Nijinsky in this ballet the leaps and the dance were all one single flowing line of movement, faster or slower, heavier or lighter, a way of moving that could rise up off the ground as easily as not, with no break and no effort. It isn't a question of how high he jumped one jump, but how smoothly he danced the whole ballet. You can see the same quality of technique today in Miss Markova's dancing.

In one respect, though, Nijinsky's way of leaping differed from hers: in his style the knee bend that starts the leap up and the other one that catches it coming down were often almost unnoticeable. This is a difference of appearance, of expression, but not really of technique. Nijinsky could make the transitions in speed I spoke of above with an exceptionally slight bending of the knees—a very unusual accomplishment indeed. When a dancer can do this it gives an expression of greater spontaneity to the leap; but several modern ballet dancers who try to do it aren't able really to land "light as a sylph or a snowflake," as Nijinsky could. The slight jolt when they land breaks the smooth flow and attracts more attention than the stillness of the climax in the air. And so the leap fails to concentrate on a soaring expression. The "correct" soaring leap is a technical trick any ballet dancer can learn in ten or fifteen years if he or she happens to be a genius. The point of learning it is that it enables the dancer to make a particular emotional effect, which enlarges the range of expression in dancing. The effect as we watch Markova's pure flight can only be described as supernatural, as a strangely beneficent magic. It is an approach to those mysterious hints of gentleness that occasionally absorb the human mind. It is a spiritual emotion; so Nijinsky's contemporaries described it, when he danced that way, and so did the Parisian poet Théophile Gautier when he saw first Taglioni and then Grisi take flight a hundred years ago.

It was a hundred years ago, most likely, that the trick was first perfected, together with that other trick so related to it in expression, the moment of airy repose on one toe. (Toe dancing, like leaping, has many kinds of expression, but the suggestion of weightless, poised near-flight is one of its most striking.) Toe dancing, like the technique of aerial flight, took a long series of dance geniuses to develop. The great Mlle Camargo two centuries ago, in Paris and in London, was already "dancing like a bird." But it seems likely that she fluttered enchantingly, rather than soared calm and slow; certainly Camargo's costumes didn't allow some technical resources that are related to our technique of flight; they allowed no horizontal lift of the leg, no deep knee bends, no spring and stretch of foot in a heelless slipper.

In her century, soaring of a different kind was being perfected. They literally hung the dancer on wires, and hoisted him or her through the air. Theaters had machinery called "flight paths," one of them fifty-nine feet long—quite a fine swoop it must have made. Maybe these mechanical effects gradually gave dancers the idea of trying to do the same thing without machinery. In an 1830 ballet, girls dressed as woodland spirits bent down the lower boughs of trees and let themselves be carried upward into the air on the rebound, which sounds like some wire effect. And in 1841 the great dancer Carlotta Grisi—Taglioni's young rival—opened in the ballet *Giselle*, in the second act of which there was one passage at least where her leaps were "amplified" by wiring. (She was supposed to be a ghost in it, and it was meant to look spooky.) In the little engraving of her in this part she certainly floats over her grave in a way no ballet star ever could; but probably the pose is only an imaginary invention by the artist. The same *Giselle* is still being danced today both in America and Europe, and according to report, in Paris, in London and in Leningrad at least, this particular hundred-year-old wire trick is still being pulled. —*October, 1943*

The Spirit of the Classic Dance

by André Levinson

Nothing is more difficult than to reduce the essential esthetic realities of the dance to verbal formulas. Our ordinary methods of analysis are of very little use in dealing with this art, which is primarily a discipline of movement. The dancer in motion is a harmony of living forms,

Source: From *Theatre Arts Monthly* (March 1925).

masses and outlines, whose relations to each other are continually varied by that "motion which causes the lines to flow." We are exceedingly ill equipped for the study of things in flux—even for considering motion itself as such. We cling to things at rest as though they were landmarks in a turbulent chaos. A modern engineer, for example, who wishes to study the mechanism of a revolving screw, would doubtless begin his studies by stopping the motor and taking it apart, in order to understand clearly the technical methods employed by the designer. The dancer has a fairly wide technical vocabulary, but it is one that is useful only to himself. Even the most expert spectator can decipher its hieroglyphics only with great difficulty—not because of ignorance nor unintelligence on his part, but because these technical terms invoke no corresponding muscular association in the layman's consciousness. It is because the art of the dance is so peculiarly inarticulate that it has never possessed a proper esthetic philosophy. Choreographic thought—and here we fall straightway into the use of an improper and misleading term—has always been condemned to expression through paraphrases—high-sounding but inaccurate. It has had to content itself with the shifting, uncertain expedient of the analogy, which is, according to Nietzsche, the surest way of falling into error. We approach the dance by aid of analogous hypotheses and the habits of thought employed in our consideration of other arts with the inevitable result that we substitute the obvious facts of a static art for the elusive dynamics of the dance.

The great Noverre, called the "Shakespeare of the dance" by Garrick and "Prometheus" by Voltaire—who is still the most vital and thorough theoretician who has written on the subject, desired above everything to incorporate the dance into the group of "imitative arts." Carlo Blasis—the same incidentally who established the theory of classic instruction—struggled manfully to evolve some plausible connection between the spectacle of the dance and the poetry of the spoken drama. Others have conceived the dance as strictly limited to the expression of definite ideas—thereby sacrificing it to and confusing it with pantomime. It seems as though everyone had piled upon this art mistaken attributes or supplementary burdens in his efforts to redeem—even if only in a small way—the actual movements of the dance.

I can not think of anyone who has devoted himself to those characteristics which belong exclusively to dancing, or who has endeavored to formulate specifically the laws of this art on its own ground. Those famous dance historians whose names I have mentioned have listed, described and analyzed a certain number of fundamental dance movements and set down the empirical laws which rule the execution of their elements. The grammar of Zorn is complete in its descriptive matter and the recent treatise of Cecchetti is invaluable as a method of instruction. But no one has ever tried to portray the intrinsic beauty of a dance step, its innate quality, its esthetic reason for being. This beauty is referred to the smile of the dancer, to the picturesque quality of his costume, to the general atmosphere surrounding him, to the synchronizing of his bodily rhythm with the beat of the music or again to the emotional appeal of the dramatic libretto of the ballet: but never is it shown to lie in the contours of the movement itself, in the constructive values of an attitude or in the thrilling dynamics of a leap in the air. All the other arts are foisted on the dance as instructors. Blasis even insisted that a dancer should, at any given moment, be a suitable model for the sculptor Canova. But a statue is motion captured and congealed, the eternal prison of one specific form. And while it is true that every movement does break up into moments of action and moments of rest, it is only these moments of rest, of stable equilibrium and not the complete movement of the dance that can be said to find an analogy in sculpture.

I am sure that an artilleryman, thoroughly familiar with the motion of projectiles, able to calculate accurately the trajectory of a shell, the force of the explosion that sets it in motion and the range of the missile released, could much more easily discover the principle of a dancer's leap than some loose-thinking poet, however magnificent his style. For the gunner operates with a knowledge of dynamics. Doubtless his aim is wholly material—destruction, pure and simple—while it is the desire of the dancer to create beauty which causes him to make use of his knowledge of mechanics and that finally dominates this knowledge. He subjects his muscles to a rigid discipline; through arduous practice he bends and adapts his body to the exigencies of an abstract and perfect form. In the end he brings the physiological factors—muscle contraction and relaxation—completely under the domination of the sovereign rhythm of the dance. This is what makes it so difficult to separate the gymnastic elements of the dance from its ideal essence. The technique of a dancer is not like the mechanical workings of a jointed doll; it is physical effort constantly informed by beauty. This technique is no supplementary reënforcement to his art, nor is it a mere device, designed to gain easy applause, like (according to Stendhal) the art of the versifier. It is the very soul of the dance; it *is* the dance itself.

Of all the various techniques it is that of the so-called classic dance —a term designating the style of dancing that is based on the traditional ballet technique—which has prevailed in the Western world. It seems to be in complete accord not only with the anatomical structure of the

European but with his intellectual aspirations as well. We find this technique in all those countries where man is fashioned like us and he thinks in our way. The little definite knowledge we have concerning the system of gymnastics of the ancient Greeks warrants our identifying certain of their "modes" with those of the contemporary dance. Today the universality of the classic style is disputed only by the oriental dance, that finds in the Cambodgian ballet its highest and most complete expression. The superb efflorescence of the dance in Spain is in itself a vestige of an oriental civilization, repelled but not annihilated.

Opponents of the classic dance technique pretend to consider it an academic code, imposed on the dance arbitrarily by pedants and long since obsolete. It is true that it does recapitulate the experience of centuries, for we find that certain of its fundamental ideas were accepted by the dancing masters of the Italian Renaissance. It was they who first broke away from the so-called "horizontal" conception of the dance, based on outlines and figures marked by the feet of the dancer on the floor—what you might call his itinerary. The outlines of the choreographs of the seventeenth century, reproducing on paper the curving path drawn on the ground by the feet of the dancer, are the last vestiges of this "horizontal" idea, which was gradually displaced by the vertical conception of dancing—the configuration of motion in space. This important process, so fruitful in its developments, lasted throughout two centuries and strangely enough has never been even touched upon by any of those many chroniclers of the dance, who, as I have said before, invariably prefer to approach the subject as writers, musicians or historians of folkways and manners. Inasmuch as the verbal formulas that serve to designate dance movements and attitudes have remained practically unchanged all this time, the superficial observer is apt to overlook this development.

As a matter of fact there is no question but that the meaning of these formulas changes with each generation. The five fundamental positions, which are the ABC of the dance, may seem to be the same for Feuillet, the choreographer of the "grand Siècle" and for Mademoiselle Zambelli—to mention one of the fairest flowers of contemporary classic dance. But this is not actually so. In the outlines of Feuillet that have come down to us, the feet in the first position, make an obtuse angle. In the modern they are in the same straight line in the first position, and in the other positions in parallel lines. This may seem to be a trifling detail of growth and change, when one thinks of Isadora Duncan dancing a Beethoven symphony. But this almost imperceptible difference, this slight shift of a geometrical line, these feet pivoting at an angle of so many degrees, represents an enormously important acquisition, capable of infinite combinations and variety. This trifling detail is actually a realization of that essential principle and point of departure of classic choreography which took two centuries to prevail —that of turning the body—and more particularly the legs of the dancer—outward from its centre.

I find myself at times looking at the history of the modern dance as though it were some charming but infinitely obscure romance, that needed a key to unlock its mysteries. This key is an understanding of what a dancer means when he speaks of turning out the body. The movement of the oriental dance is concentric. The knees almost instinctively come together and bend, the curved arms embrace the body. Everything is pulled together. Everything converges. The movement of the classic dance, on the other hand, is ex-centric—the arms and the legs stretch out, freeing themselves from the torso, expanding the chest. The whole region of the dancer's being, body and soul, is dilated. The actual manifestation of this can be readily seen or even better felt in the trained body of a classical ballet dancer. The dancer spreads the hips and rotates both legs, in their entire length from the waist down, away from each other, outward from the body's centre, so that they are both in profile to the audience although turned in opposite directions. The so-called five fundamental positions are merely derivations or variations of this outward turning posture, differentiated by the manner in which the two feet fit in, cross or by the distance that separates them. In the fifth position, where the two feet are completely crossed, toes to heels, you have the very incarnation of this principle of turning outward—that is to say, of the spirit of classic dancing. The fifth position is Taglioni; the third was Carmargo. A whole century of experimentation and of slow, arduous assimilation lies between the two. The orthopedic machines, true instruments of torture, that were used to turn pupils out in the days of Noverre would not be tolerated today. But it does take several years of daily exercise, beginning at the ages of eight or nine years to give a dancer the ability to perform this mechanical feat easily.

At this point, the reader may demand precisely what is gained by this hard won victory over nature. Just this—the body of the dancer is freed from the usual limitations upon human motion. Instead of being restricted to a simple backward and forward motion—the only directions in which the human body, operating normally, can move with ease and grace, this turning outward of the legs permits free motion in any direction without loss of equilibrium; forward, backwards, sideways, obliquely or rotating. The actual extent of motion possible is considerably augmented, and since the feet are thus made to move on lines parallel to each other there is no interference and many motions otherwise impossible are thereby facilitated. As a good example of this, I might cite the *entrechat*—that exhilarating movement where the dancer leaps high in the air and crosses his legs several times while off the ground. This effective "braiding" movement necessitates the turning outward of the body—otherwise the dancer's legs would block each other.

What a tiresome recital, you may be saying and all of this in trying to talk about so elusive and illusive a thing as the dance! But I assure you it is justified, for the very illusion of this enchanting art—which seems to ignore all natural laws—depends on an intelligent ordering of physical effort. The dancer then is a body moving in space according to any desired rhythm. We have seen how the turning outward of the body increases this space to an extraordinary degree, pushing back the invisible walls of that cylinder of air in the centre of which the dancer moves, giving him that extraordinary extension of body which is totally lacking in oriental dancing and multiplying to an infinite degree the direction of the movement as well as its various conformations. It surrounds the vertical of the body's equilibrium by a vortex of curves, segments of circles, arcs; it projects the body of the dancer into magnificent parabolas, curves it into a living spiral; it creates a whole world of animated forms that awake in us a throng of active sensations, that our usual mode of life has atrophied.

I have not tried to explain clearly more than one of the salient and decisive characteristics of the classic technique. The rich development of the dance that increases its sway from generation to generation corresponds to the gradual elaboration of this principle of turning outward.

If at the beginning of the classic period the dance served merely to give law and style to the carriage and deportment of the perfect courtier, or if at the time of the "*fêtes galantes*" it was still skipping and mincing, it has gradually became exalted and transfigured until it is now called upon to express the loftiest emotions of the human soul.

When once the enthusiasm of the romantic period had created the idea of the dance of elevation, it was only one step further to make the dancer rise up on his toes. It would be interesting to know at exactly what moment this second decisive factor entered in. The historians of the dance, unfortunately, are not concerned with telling us. It is however evident that this reform was at least a half century in preparation. The heel of the shoe raised up, the instep arched, the toe reached down —the plant no longer was rooted to the soil. What happened was that the foot simply refused to remain flat any longer. It strove to lengthen out the vertical lines of its structure. It gave up its natural method of functioning to further an esthetic end. And thus it is that when a dancer rises on her points, she breaks away from the exigencies of everyday life, and enters into an enchanted country—that she may thereby lose herself in the ideal.

To discipline the body to this ideal function, to make a dancer of a graceful child, it is necessary to begin by dehumanizing him, or rather by overcoming the habits of ordinary life. His muscles learn to bend, his legs are trained to turn outward from the waist, in order to increase the resources of his equilibrium. His torso becomes a completely plastic body. His limbs stir only as a part of an ensemble movement. His entire outline takes on an abstract and symmetrical quality. The accomplished dancer is an artificial being, an instrument of precision and he is forced to undergo rigorous daily exercise to avoid lapsing into his original purely human state.

His whole being becomes imbued with that same unity, that same conformity with its ultimate aim that constitutes the arresting beauty of a finished airplane, where every detail, as well as the general effect, expresses one supreme object—that of speed. But where the airplane is conceived in a utilitarian sense—the idea of beauty happening to superimpose itself upon it, the constant transfiguration, as you might call it, of the classic dancer from the ordinary to the ideal is the result of a disinterested will for perfection, an unquenchable thirst to surpass himself. Thus it is that an exalted aim transforms his mechanical efforts into an esthetic phenomenon. You may ask whether I am suggesting that the dancer is a machine? But most certainly!—a machine for manufacturing beauty—if it is in any way possible to conceive a machine that in itself is a living, breathing thing, susceptible of the most exquisite emotions.

The Ideal of Ballet Aesthetics

by John Martin

The most advanced word that has yet been spoken with regard to the still unrealized modern ballet is contained perhaps in Lifar's "Choreographer's Manifesto." Though it is incomplete, it at least has had

Source: From *Introduction to the Dance* (New York: Norton, 1939).

the courage to attack the problem boldly. As the modern dance of the non-ballet type has done before it, the ballet must inevitably cast aside, at least for a period of self-discovery, all its accumulation of "aids"—music, décor, drama—and concentrate on its own nature and essential medium. This medium is obviously the academic code of abstract movement, which it has built up over the centuries and from which throughout its history it has never totally separated itself. It is this that needs to be examined from a fresh perspective as something besides traditional mumbo-jumbo, for here, indeed, lies the root of the ballet's aesthetics.

Unless it is willing to discard this code entirely, it must necessarily find its fullest powers in the character of a classic art instead of dallying with romanticism. The classic approach alone allows for an objective vocabulary and an objective mode of procedure, and the academic code itself is incapable of being expressive of human emotion or even imitative of nature. Both ecstasy and mimesis are ruled out of its principle and its historic practice. In its beginnings it was evolved quite coldly, albeit from living sources, by experts who were seeking elegance of carriage, graciousness of gesture, and a general refining of movement away from crude, everyday utilitarianism, for the achievement of an idealized deportment. Ecstasy is patently out of place in such a program, and mimicry focuses on the realistic instead of on the ideal. Such was the basis of the court dance, and even when dramatic action of sorts was introduced into it, impersonation was symbolic rather than realistic, and pantomime was removed as far from nature as possible, taking at most only the outline of nature's gestures and giving them shapely and balanced contours until they became decorative even if unintelligible. Because of the essentially realistic character of pantomime, which makes it resistant to the abstractions of design, it was separated necessarily from the formal element of dancing and confined to sections of its own like recitative between the arias of an opera.

Throughout the development of this system of idealized movement, especially after the ballet was professionalized, its range has been increased by the gymnastic skill of individual executants, by discoveries of new means for enlarging or refining its spectacular appeal, by practical necessities of the stage, but never by the infusion of natural gesture. Its codification has been intellectual and based on geometrical-aesthetic principles, disregarding the nature of the body's movements in life and compelling it to conform to the desired scheme of practice by extending itself or even at times violating itself. It is thus purely an artificial system, in the literal meaning of the word, designed for aesthetic results alone.

Every effort to introduce realistic life impulses (and there have been many) tends to destroy its classic purpose and to nullify its abstract effectiveness. The system itself has always resisted these inroads and at the first opportunity has reasserted itself to the discomfiture of its reformers. The greatest of these, Michel Fokine, understood that to accomplish his richly conceived romantic ends, he must take drastic steps to subdue this traditional force, and we find him urging the dancer to leave the academic vocabulary in the classroom and follow nature. In the creation of his magnificent theatrical synthesis he took the ballet, indeed, as far away from classicism as it can go without ceasing to be ballet altogether. The next step would necessarily have been to leave the academic vocabulary out of the classroom as well and turn directly to subjective movement. (To be sure, in his "Les Sylphides" he also took the ballet nearer to pure classicism than it had been for many years, as if to indicate that his major interest in going the other way was prompted by conviction and not by an inadequate grasp of traditional principles.)

In this direction of synthesis, Fokine has brought the ballet to the ultimate goal that was sought first in the Renaissance, and it would seem that there is nothing more to be added. At the opposite end of its scale, however, it finds itself capable of being not just one element in a synthesis (albeit the dominant one), but self-sufficient dance. In the logic of the aesthetic scheme underlying the academic code it has inherent autonomous potentialities; it is not merely a means for doing something else—for training the body or for interpreting music or for enacting a drama—but an end in itself. As André Levinson, its most able modern aestheticist, said of it, "the technique is no supplementary reinforcement to [the dancer's] art . . . it is the dance itself." Its substance, the basis of its classicism, is its technical material, or more accurately, its technical approach and the theory inherent in its academic code.

It is not thus restricted by any means to "school figures," to jetés and brisés, entrechats and cabrioles. These, indeed, are quite meaningless in themselves; their only function is to illuminate the idealism that underlies them by manifesting its law and logic. The average dancer, unhappily, rattles through them as thoughtlessly as a child through its prayers, perhaps mainly because in our day they and the system they stand for have been nothing but a kind of language in which to express something else. Yet the most elementary steps and the most hackneyed combinations can be touched into life and beauty by the dancer who relates them to their central scheme of aesthetics and makes them simply the means for bringing it into visible action.

With a sense of the unity and the supreme consistency of this central scheme, invention becomes easy and logical but no longer a pressing necessity for its own sake. In the great poetry, the great painting, the great drama of the world, the same simple emotional relationships are invoked time after time, finding fresh validity in every new circumstance; there is no necessity to seek always for psychopathic variations in order to prevent the old sorrows and angers and hatreds and loves from becoming banal. Similarly if the principles of the ballet's aesthetics were better understood and more intuitively sensed by its practitioners, there would be less need for the constant searching out of outré attitudes and contortions for novelty's sake.

The vocabulary, however, is by no means set and closed, for all that its principle is absolute. The sharper dynamisms of today, the increased grasp of beauty in the mechanically functional line and force, the better understanding of the values to be found in dissonance, and the steadily growing gymnastic prowess of the dancer are capable of evolving a wealth of new vocabulary while still not only remaining within the classic principle but even strengthening and revivifying it.

The theory of this geometrical-aesthetic basis involves something quite apart from the arrangement of lines and masses in patterns of purely visual decoration, simply substituting arms and legs and torsos for so many sticks and globes. The body is incapable of translation thus into lifeless mechanics, but even at the height of its abstraction it remains always a living body. Here, indeed, is the very heart of the ballet's aesthetics, the source of its drive. It is a glorification of the person as person, the presentation of its ideal essence freed from the encumbrances of a rationalistic universe of cause and effect, a pragmatical universe of organic drive and utilitarian function. It exemplifies the personal achievement of abstraction, of transcendent self-containment. In its idealization of the body it strips away all necessity for practical accomplishment, turning certain of its conformations to uses more harmonious than the functional processes that have shaped them, and superseding where possible even structural elements which have been bred by utilitarian demands alone. Its idealization, like all other idealizations, struggles constantly to resist being drawn unwittingly into assent with the arguments of that realism which it is its whole purpose to supplant. It does not explore the body's possibilities for life movement, therefore, but concentrates on adapting it to the specialized system of movement that is established for it. In this, to be sure, it is not unique; all the classic dances of the East have long done this, with differences in result comparable to the differences in ideals, but with no difference in process.

This does not argue for either mechanical dehumanizing or stereotyped uniformity for all dancers. Indeed, if the true nature of the theory is understood, these common faults among dancers and misapprehensions among spectators cannot possibly come about. Even so astute and sensitive a critic as Levinson falls into the first trap. In his lively essay on "The Spirit of the Classic Dance," after arguing the necessity for the dancer's being trained along lines contrary to the habits of ordinary life, he writes: "You may ask whether I am suggesting that the dancer is a machine? But most certainly!—a machine for manufacturing beauty." This could be true only if it were possible to conceive of a machine as having a consciousness of its selfhood and a will to archetypal perfection. The precision and the abstraction in a machine's movements, in which there is no choice but to be precise and abstract, deny the essential vitality of the ballet, namely, the personal achievement of these ends. The machine's movement is merely motion; the ballet's movement is motion dictated by taste and selectivity.

As for regimentation, the employment of a common code of movement does not necessarily make all dancers alike any more than the employment of a common language makes all speakers alike. In the latter case there are differences in the quality and pitch of the voice, in the inflection, in the choice of words, which make it impossible for any two speakers to be identical in speech. In the use of the ballet code, the same kind of differences exist, some of them innate in the body and unconscious, and some deliberately and imaginatively assumed. The existence of a specific code actually heightens these differences, serving as a standard of reference against which individual variations are made doubly vivid. The process is automatic and involves a peril as well as an opportunity, for the routine practitioner, who has not the artistry to use the system to his own ends, will inevitably allow it to use him and to expose him in a mental nudity which is all the more revealing because he is unaware of it.

The greatest differentiation is naturally between the dance of men and that of women. Their employment of the same code of movement automatically accentuates their divergences and aids in the idealization of the essentially feminine and the essentially masculine. Again there is a peril involved, and here a more serious one for the health of the art as a whole. With the dancer who is not an artist and the spectator who does not consider that a limitation, it is easy for the glorification of sex to become immediate instead of ideal. At times in its history the ballet has been forced by the insistence on pulchritude and coquetry out of the category of art and into that of polite pandering.

The accent on this element in the last century, with the critical writings of Théophile Gautier as a high example, produced a serious situation for the male dancer, who was jeopardized not only in prestige but also in the maintenance of the virility of his art. The approach to the academic code itself was made predominantly feminine, and even today with men and women taught in the same classes where the women are vastly superior in numbers, there is likely to be a feminine color to the proceedings. This puts upon the classic male dancer the stern necessity of alertness to dominate the system and use it to his own ends instead of unwittingly letting the softness and the curves of his colleagues' technic use him.

The system, indeed, is not inherently feminine in any way, but totally impersonal, an abstraction against which to emphasize the idealized male as well as the idealized female. It reaches its height in this direction in the classical pas de deux, which is in a way the epitome of the ballet. In it we are shown first the static qualities, so to speak, of the medium and of the dancers in relation to each other—balance and line, the strength and stability of the masculine and the lightness and delicacy of the feminine, not in terms of free mobility but sustained and supported. Then follows a section for each dancer in which the idealized masculine and feminine are seen separately in full and free range. The coda, continuing the aspect of free and unsupported movement, climaxes the sequence with a passage of brilliant interplay between the sexes. (How seldom do we see a pas de deux danced with any such realization of its potentialities! It is generally reduced to a kind of contest in which the partners vie with each other for the approval of the spectators.)

Just as the masculine and feminine qualities add their especial flavors to a common code of movement, so individual personal qualities can be made to illuminate it. This potentiality can be extended actually into the territory of impersonation and dramatic action. Such a divagation might be forever unnecessary for dancers whose greatness of spirit, depth of penetration and personal grasp of style were so rich and imaginative that they could give us ever new and engrossing glimpses of themselves in idealization, but such genius is scarcely to be expected in any large numbers, and the perfect classic dancer is perhaps the rarest of all creatures. It becomes essential, therefore, to broaden the scope of the ballet by giving the dancer synthetic increases in personal range. As his natural character affects his manner of exemplifying the standard code, so an assumed character can also be made to do. Thus the ballerina says, in effect: "If I were a gypsy or a peasant maid, a butterfly or an odalisque, this is the particular flavor my arabesques and my pirouettes would take on." She is not pretending to be the peasant maid or the odalisque, nor is she costumed with any realism that might deceive us into thinking she is; she is only showing how such a personality might utilize the established principles of the academic code to project its own idealism and how these principles would react to such use. The personality and individuality of the ballerina herself are thus by no means submerged in such an assumed role, but are actually enhanced by it.

Dramatic situations provide similar occasions, and their selection by scenarist and choreographer, if the true quality of the classic academic ballet is to be maintained, will be dictated not by verisimilitude or psychology or dramaturgy, but by their ability to produce illuminating results upon and by means of the basic code of movement. Emotional situations are not meant to be truly touching or felt sympathetically in any degree, but are designed to be understood and admired in terms of their sensitive and subtle variations on the classic theme of idealized abstraction. Credibility is not an end to be sought, but rather an enemy to be combated, for if it arouses sympathetic response, it only blinds the eye to the dancer's purpose and true art. Logic, the self-contained and impeccable logic of the system, is of supreme importance, but credibility on an emotional or realistic level is a drug to deaden the kind of appreciation that is needed. The ballet, indeed, is neither the actor's medium nor the story-teller's.

Certainly it is not the painter's medium or the musician's, either. It is not a spatial art in the sense of being concerned with the dancer's relation to his environment; it is a timeless and placeless idealization of him and of him alone, against a background of infinity, if you will. Since he must dance upon a stage, there must be décor of some sort, but its proper function is to minimize itself completely and concentrate on maximizing the dancer. As for costume, he is assuredly no couturier's mannequin; his apparel must exhibit him, not he the apparel. There can be no equality of collaboration here; the dancer is king or bondsman.

The situation is much the same where the musician is concerned, for as the décor is the spatial setting of the dance, so the music is the temporal setting, and nothing more. It is as inappropriate to ask a choreographer to create a dance to fit a ready-made score as it would be to ask a dramatist to write a play to fit a series of ready-made settings and costumes. It is not the dancer's business to exhibit the music, but the musician's to exhibit the dancer. Again, there can be no equality; the dancer is either supreme or subordinate.

Theory of Technic

Without some sensing of these matters, the technic of the academic ballet inevitably becomes nothing more than a collection of arbitrary and lifeless acrobatics, and as such it is frequently taught and even more frequently practiced. When its underlying aesthetic intent is apprehended, however, it falls into an easy and vivacious order. If idealistic abstraction is its soul, its body may be said to be dynamic equilibrium. The dancer becomes a sensuous and sentient object maintaining balance against all hazards, inviting and even extending these hazards far beyond the margin of safety and meeting them effortlessly in evidence of a dominion over the inertias and circumscriptions of realism. Heaviness, effort, the overdramatization of difficulties conquered, are essentially vulgar and mark the parvenu in this glorified company.

Verticality is the keynote of the entire procedure, both theoretically and practically. The mechanics of the situation demand a strong vertical axis upon which to erect a postural norm. Both for facility and for effectiveness this axis must be as narrow and as concentrated as possible, in order to bring into immediate range that field of instability which provides the dancer with his challenge and his victory. Thus the position that may be considered as the postural norm is that in which the dancer stands in readiness for the majority of his exercises; his body is erect, turned out at the hips, his feet together so that the heel of each touches the great-toe joint of the other; his legs make one solid column with no space visible between them at any point; his arms curve downwards close in front of him with the fingers all but completing their circle. This is the narrowest stable base that he can maintain, and from it he is able to move in any direction at a moment's notice. Thus we see the turning out of the hip, introduced in the seventeenth century for the attainment of a broader front, serves also to produce a narrowing of base, bringing the vertical axis of the body straight to the floor through the joined arches of the feet instead of allowing it to divide into two lines as it would do if the feet were side by side.

Upon this clearly established verticality, every conceivable variation is played. The arms, besides superimposing arcs of travel, set up a series of concentric planes with the shoulders as a horizontal axis. In conjunction with the legs, they define also those vertical planes which the body sets up about its upright axis; and especially do they effect the torsions in those planes, as when the horizontal of the shoulders is made to cross the horizontal of the hips. The warp that is thus produced replaces the flatness and monotony of the single plane with an accentuation of the body's tridimensionality and the subtleties that inhere in it. It is also a manifestation of that mechanical principle of opposition that underlies not only the ballet's technic but the action of the body in life, and for that matter, of any other object that is subject to gravity. This principle demands that as weight is shifted to one side of a central axis, there must be a compensatory shift to the opposite side if equilibrium is to be maintained. This principle the ballet dramatizes continually, as it maintains its basic verticality against extensions and counterextensions of every variety.

In the pursuit of its fundamental idealism, it habitually transmutes mechanical function thus into aesthetics. The support of the legs is dramatized in countless ways, by freeing one or both of them for the creation of independent designs—crossing and recrossing in the air, describing arcs and circles, approaching the horizontal line of flight in various degrees—and restoring them to their supporting function always at the proper moment, being careful to maintain suspense but never to threaten disaster. Soft knees and ankles remove the harshness of the instant when contact with the earth is restored after a venture into the air, and allow the body to retain its volatility by providing a gently rebounding force from below to meet its gradually settling weight while it is still in descent.

The arms, whose practical necessities are smaller, indulge freely in design, sometimes emphasizing the contours of a large and general movement, sometimes creating a deliberate counterpoint. About the central straightness and vigor of the body, they set in motion circular forces, soft, effortless, elegantly controlled. It is here that the aristocracy of the ballet reveals itself—on those rare occasions when, indeed, it is present.

The parvenu in this ethereal world will expose himself most likely in the use of the torso. Mistaking its upright carriage for rigidity, he will allow it to become a heavy and solid mass carried about with no little effort by the legs. He will forget that the vertical axis of the body is slender and ideally no more a tangible thing than the axis of the earth. Likewise, he will take it for granted that his arms begin at the shoulders, instead of realizing that their point of origin is a common center at the central axis, where they are seen to form one continuous and integrated element, alive from fingertips to fingertips, instead of two rather superfluous appendages whose uselessness is obvious except in a world of eating and drinking and practical accomplishment.

The easy erectness of the trunk and the set of the head above it not only lend a nobility of style, but help to point that play between the shoulder line and the hip line which produces the opposition of planes. The direction of the line of vision is an important element in establishing the scope and the intention of a movement, and this brings the head again into a strategic position. With the sensitive dancer the face will also make a positive contribution, changing subtly and in perfect collaboration with the shifting aspects of the body, though without regard for psychological states of emotion or what is sometimes called expression. Certainly it will not reveal the effort or the physical strain that a mere human undergoes in creating this exalted abstraction of himself, but neither will it wear the hideous mask of a fixed smile.

The actual vocabulary of movement is elaborated from a simple set of five fundamental positions of the feet. These, executed with the hips turned out, place the feet first heel to heel in a straight line, then in the same straight line with a foot's length between them, then with one heel touching the arch of the other foot, and again in the same relationship but with one a foot's length in front of the other, and finally with heel to toe. In practice these are subject to alteration and variation in much the same way that vowel sounds are altered and varied in speech from their cardinal purity. There are five corresponding positions of the arms, others for the head and the hands, and eight directions of the body. Upon these foundations seven types of movement are executed—bending, stretching, rising, jumping, gliding, darting and turning. The five poses called arabesques, in which the line of the horizontal dominates, are largely, though not exclusively, used as climactic attitudes in which to finish sequences of movement. Another pose of similar function answers to the name of attitude, and is an adaptation of Bologna's famous statue of Mercury which Carlo Blasis introduced into the ballet in the early nineteenth century. From these comparatively few elements, an inexhaustible repertoire of combinations is to be achieved, and when the ballerina rises upon the points of her toes, she adds a new dimension which virtually doubles her range.

Such an art obviously makes large demands upon the spectator; it is an art, indeed, for the connoisseur. He must not only be aware of the aesthetic basis of idealized abstraction and be sympathetic to it, but he must also have at least a passing knowledge of the technic and vocabulary if he is really to appreciate its full values. As a result, the strictly classic ballet has had a consistently small audience throughout its life; that is its penalty for being classic. The impulse of contemporary modernism, with its seeking for basic materials and their autonomous formal tendencies, may or may not be capable of winning a wider appeal because of the essentially unifying effect of its processes, but whatever its effect in this direction, it opens a new world to the classic-academic ballet in so far as its individual integrity is concerned. This involves no restoration to some high estate from which it has fallen, but the attainment of a perfection that it has never before enjoyed. Its technic is incomparably more brilliant than it has ever been in the past, and there is now possible for the first time a perspective in which its basic drive stands out clearly and can be seen as permeating all its materials. As it has been progressively humanized, romanticized, democratized, it has won the world's favor, but at the cost of its classicism. Whether this is desirable and in line with social tendencies is beside the question.

Most of the artists who are working in it are conceivably too close to it and to its immediate tradition to realize its possibilities along fresh lines. There is a trend at the moment, it is true, to return to classicism, but this takes the form in the main of a return to the nineteenth century, to the romantic period, in fact—which now passes current for classicism! It is apparently the habit of artists in general, when they sense that the latest great cycle of their art has spent itself, to attempt to go back to the great cycle immediately before that and take up the course from there. Classicism, however, is not to be found there. Blasis, the greatest theorist of the time, argues as a matter of course for synthesis, for music and drama. The course, indeed, must be picked up farther back than that, in no especial period but on the level of fundamental principles.

Perhaps we must look for new values to be discovered not in the line of the established companies at all, with the traditions of La Scala and the Maryinsky, of Fokine and Diaghilev, ingrained in them consciously or unconsciously. It is not unlikely that the last word has been said in that direction, at least for a time, and that in some new field (perhaps America, though there are no signs of it yet) a free choreographer may be able to sense the classic basis of the art in its modern application, skipping over the whole long development toward romanticism.

Certainly, whoever he may be, he will have to be a courageous rebel, for the mere mention of such an idea is likely to produce foamings at the mouth in orthodox circles. He will have to be strong enough to face accusations of destroying progress and of trying to turn back the tide. Just as the modern expressional dance in its return to basic principles of life movement for its procedure has been damned for its alleged effort to revive primitivism, so the modern ballet will meet a bombardment when it returns to the basic principles inherent in the academic code. Actually, however, there is never any retrogression in a return all the way to fundamental principles; only by such action is it possible to learn how to go forward on a solid foundation.

Forms in Motion and in Thought

by Edwin Denby

In dancing one keeps taking a step and recovering one's balance. The risk is a part of the rhythm. One steps out of and into balance; one keeps on doing it, and step by step the mass of the body moves about. But the action is more fun and the risk increases when the dancers step to a rhythmic beat of music. Then the pulse of the downbeat can lift the dancer as he takes a step; it can carry him through the air for a moment, and the next downbeat can do it again. Such a steady beat to dance on is what a dancer dreams of and lives for. The lightness that music gives is an imaginary or an imaginative lightness. You know it is an illusion, but you see it happen; you feel it happen, you enjoy believing it. There is a bit of insanity in dancing that does everybody a great deal of good.

It has been doing people good for a long time. Looking at Paleolithic cave paintings, one can recognize the powerfully developed dance sense our ancestors had fifteen thousand years ago. What are all those bison of theirs floating on, if not on a steady beat? A Brooklyn teen-ager would feel at home among the Magdalenian cave painters once the dancing started and he heard that beat. And a late Paleolithic youth who dropped in on a gym or a ballroom going wild at two in the morning to the blasts of a name band, would see right away that it was a bison ritual. And if he broke into a bison step, the kids near enough to see him would only say, "Wow," or "Dig that rustic shag."

And an educated late Paleolithic magician, if he dropped in on a performance of classic ballet in an air-conditioned theatre would find a good deal he was familiar with—the immense, awesome drafty cavern, the watching tribe huddled in the dark, and in a special enclosure the powerful rhythmic spectacle which it is taboo to join in. As a magic man he would find it proper that the dancers are not allowed to speak, not allowed to make any everyday movements, to show any signs of effort, or even of natural breathing; and equally correct that the musicians are kept hidden in a ritual pit. The orchestra conductor would strike him as a first-class wizard. This singular character stands up in

Source: From *Dancers, Buildings, and People in the Streets* (New York: Horizon, 1965).

the pit waving a wand and is respectfully treated by the audience as invisible. Though it is hard for him, he does his best not to look at the dancers; when his eyes stray to the stage, he pulls them down at once, visibly upset. He keeps in constant agitation, without ever doing a dance step or touching an instrument, and his costume consists of a pair of long black tails. The Magdalenian visitor, familiar with demented clowns who represent pre-male types of fertilization, would recognize the ironic function of this indispensable figure. And as the curtain fell, he would clap with the rest, delighted by a ceremony so clever in its nonsense and so sweeping in its faith.

If a New Yorker were to tell him, "But you're missing the point, ballet is an art, it isn't a ritual," he might answer, "You no like that word 'ritual.' You say it about our ballet, so I think maybe nice word." And his Paleolithic girl friend might add, "Please, are you a critic? We hear critics will roast fat dancer tonight, just like we do at home. Yum, yum."

Students of culture have suggested that an art of dance preceded that of Paleolithic painting. One can see it might well be so. One can see hints of dance at stages of living one thinks of as extremely remote. The stage of culture at which our species showed the first hints of dancing need not have been beyond that of several species of contemporary wild animals. Some of them that can be greedy and fierce have sexual maneuvers that are harmless and take time. On the one hand such a ceremony can be interrupted, it doesn't necessarily lead into the sexual act; on the other hand the act may occur with a minimum of ceremony. The animals seem to be aware of a ritual that is imaginative and that is fairly impractical. Their ceremonies aren't all sexual ones either. Wolves and fishes have special fighting ones. And the birds that swoop low and soar up sharply at dusk over a town square or in a clearing of the woods, are very likely catching an insect in their open bills, but they seem to be ritualizing the action in a way they don't ritualize their feeding during the day. It is a special bedtime one. Standing among the ruins of the Palatine toward sunset late in October, I saw a flock of migrant birds keeping close like a swarm, beating their small wings almost in unison, forming—the swarm of them—a single revolving vibrating shape which kept changing in the air—a shape that distended, that divided like an hour-glass, that streamed out like a spiral nebula, and then condensed again into a close sphere, a series of choreographic figures which rose and fell above the city as the flock drifted upstream and out of sight. A social celebration and a prehistoric pleasure.

Birds seem to have made a number of dance inventions that strikingly resemble our own. They have sociable group numbers, intimate duets and perhaps trios, and private solos. You see the performers assume a submissively graceful or a show-off air. They seem to be enjoying a formal limitation as they move in relation to a center, and even as they move in relation to a lapse of time. Much as we do, they compose their piece out of contrasted energetic and gliding motions, out of reiterated gestures, out of circular paths and straight lines. Bees even use path patterns for a sign language. A returned honeybee performs for her hivemates a varying number of circles which she keeps cutting with a straight line always in one direction, and her audience understands from her choreography in what direction and how far off are the flowers she has newly discovered. After that she passes around samples of the honey, as if she were giving her dance a title. Such an action does not seem like a ritual to us, but the bees find it very practical.

A formal path involves electing a base from which to move, it involves giving a spot an arbitrary imaginative value. It is a feat of imagination essential to dancing. Birds understand the feat. Cats are very good at it when they play games. One can see their cat eyes brightening with an imaginative light as they establish their base. Kittens begin to play with no sense of a base and gradually learn to imagine. It would be fun to see lions playing from a base the same way, pretending to hunt a bright rag on the end of a rope, pouncing, prancing, darting, tumbling head over heels. I imagine they do it in a wild state and would enjoy doing it in the circus if a lion tamer could be found to play with them.

Animals tame or wild do not seem to mimic anybody but themselves. One notices that their dance-like inventions are formal in principle. One may infer from it, how far back in our history or how deep in our nature the formal aspect of dancing is.

But one notices too that the wild animals don't enjoy watching our performances as much as we do theirs. Rattlesnakes are glad to escape from a bunch of fertility-celebrating Indians. Hungry wolves and lions have never been known to venture on a group of enthusiastically stepping Russians or Africans. Our primitive social celebrations intimidate them. It may be they find the energy of them overpowering, or else that they are appalled by the excessive regularity of them, that is foreign to their habits. None of them time their movements to a regular beat of artificial noise as we do. Dancing to a beat is as peculiarly human a habit as is the habit of artificially making a fire.

Stepping to a man-made beat is a dance invention of a formal nature that we alone have made. Presumably we first danced without a beat the way animals and small children do. Even trained animals don't catch the formality of a beat. Seals and monkeys like to clap, they can learn to play tunes, but they can't keep time either way. Riders can direct horses to keep time, and I remember a circus orchestra taking its beat from an old she-elephant who danced the conga, but it was her rhythm, not the orchestra's. How could our species ever have been bright enough to invent the beat; nowadays we aren't even bright enough to explain it.

There used to be an opinion that the beat was invented by externalizing or objectifying our heart beat, that it was first beaten and then stepped to. The prevalent opinion now seems to be that both the regular acoustic beat and the regularly timed step were invented simultaneously, as a single invention. One tries to imagine unknown races of men—tens of thousands of years before the elegant Magdalenians—as they hopped in the glacial snow for fun, laughing and yelling, and first heard a kind of count, an oscillating one two in their ritual action. They may have heard it in the grunt of their own shout, broken as they landed full weight from a leap, over and over. Or else heard it when an older woman out of pleasure at the tumultuous stepping of the young men, clapped sedately, and one of the boys found himself keeping time with her, and both she and he got more and more excited by the mutual communication. Or else they might have heard a beat when a word shouted over and over as they were stepping turned into a unison metric chant that they stepped to. Perhaps as they stepped and exaggerated a hoarse panting noise of breathing, they heard each other's breath and their own coming simultaneously and were thrilled by the simultaneous step action.

However people began to keep time, one imagines the eerie thrill they felt as they found themselves aware of hearing a beat from the outside and of taking a step from the inside, both of them at once. One can still feel a far echo of that thrill as one first finds one's self hitting the beat; or later in life, as one finds one's self stepping securely to a complex rhythm one isn't able to follow consciously. It is a glorious sensation inside and outside of one. For our ancestors the experience, subjective and objective at the same instant, must have been a wonderful intensification of identity. So peculiar a thrill could have been discovered and then forgotten and rediscovered by exceptional geniuses along successive races and successive climatic epochs. The invention ended by becoming an immensely popular one. But we cannot say that it has been entirely successful. Even now after fifty or a hundred thousand years of practice, a number of us still can't keep time, and shuffle about a ballroom floor missing the measure.

Keeping time isn't the same thing as grace of movement. Animals, small children and even adults moving without a beat but with the grace of dancing enjoy what they do and look beautiful to people who like to watch them. But doing it in strict rhythm as much for those who watch as for those who do it has a cumulative excitement and an extra power. The extra power is like a sense of transport. People are so to speak their better selves. They fly by magic.

People who dance till dawn in a ballroom or who are performers on stage can cheerfully pour out as much extra energy as they otherwise would be able to do only grimly in a matter of life and death. The wild animals cannot waste so much energy on fun. To our species the invention of stepping to a regular beat of man-made noise offers an occasion for the extravagant expense of powers which is the special achievement of our human civilization. And when there is grace in the extravagance and beauty in the excess, we are delighted with ourselves.

Looking back then, one can see that animals invented for their ceremonies a formal limitation of movement. They do not move in every possible way, they move in a few particular ways. For us the added formal invention of the beat increased the artificiality much further. What had once been only instinctive animal patterns, became human objective rhythms as well. They gained an objective measure. The subjective-objective or double awareness of stepping which the beat awakened gave an extra exuberance of power to the dancers. It also sharpened a sense of representation, the sense that a step action can also be a magic emblem. So dancing became exhilarating not only to do, but also to watch, to remember and to think about. From being an instinctively formal pleasure, it became the kind of beautiful communication we call an art. In this way our ancestors invented an art—and perhaps all of art—when they regularized their dancing to a timed beat and a timed step.

The rhythmic stress of stepping is a habit of communication or expression which reaches into the present from unrecognizable races, from epochs and festivals when individuals of genius first made fires, first spoke in sentences. They grin and glare at us, and sit down beside us, these astonishing geniuses, and we feel their powerful wonder as they watch our young people dance, as they watch the bright ballet danced on stage at the same time as we do. They wonder at it, but they know how to watch it, they can see that it is some special kind of dancing.

I seem to be prowling about the subject like a nature photographer prowling about the countryside. The subject is expression in ballet. And I think you see what I am concerned with. I am bringing up some very general features of expression, and am trying to catch the expression of ballet from various points of view. Unless you can catch it in motion, you don't catch it at all. What I have caught of it, seems to be as unspecific as a blur on the edge of the camerafield. But you will notice something or other about it, I believe, and recognize something about the expression, and see it independently of what I say, as a fact of nature, I mean as a fact of human nature. That is what I am concerned with.

We were discussing the beat of the step in general terms. As you step to a beat, you feel the rhythmic pressure of your foot against the floor. You have the rhythm in your feet, so people say, and your feet start to dance. The rhythm of steps is beaten by the floor contact. It is stamped, or tapped or heel-struck, or shuffled. The onlookers catch the rhythm and they instinctively participate in the dancing as long as they stay with the step rhythm.

As the dancer steps he can hear the beat elsewhere than in the feet. And he often makes gestures that are visible rhythmic accents. In the Sahara there is a beautiful solo dance in which the girl moves only on her knees and beats the rhythm with sharp elbow, wrist and finger positions. But in any dance the shape of the body is just as evident when it isn't hitting the beat as when it is. Between beats it keeps moving rhythmically, it keeps making contrasting motions. And as it does, it makes visual shapes the rhythm of which is a sculptural one. Watching the dancers, one sees this other rhythm of shape that their bodies make. Sometimes the dancers and onlookers are so obsessed with the acoustic beat of the step rhythm that they take very little interest in the visual shape rhythm; on the other hand, they sometimes take a great deal of interest in the action of the shapes.

Watching the shape of a movement is something we all do a great deal of in everyday life. You may recognize your friends at a distance by the shape of their walk, even unconsciously. One can often recognize foreigners in America or Americans abroad by a characteristic national shape of walking, that one has never particularly thought about. As for average citizens passing down a city street, plenty of them have oddities in the shape of walking one notices right away—a turned-out forearm that dangles across the back, or a head that pecks, a torso that jiggles up and down, a chest that heaves from side to side. Men and women walking on the street keep making personal shapes with their legs—they snap their heels at the sidewalk, they drawl one thigh past the other, they bounce at each step or trip or stalk or lope, or they waddle, they shuffle or bombinate. Sometimes an oddity looks adorable, but one recognizes it perfectly well as an oddity.

Battalions of parading soldiers manage to avoid the oddities of civilian walking. They show very clearly the basic shape of a walking step —the swinging arm following the opposite leg, the twist at the waist, the dip in the figure's height and the roll. Marching West Pointers can give it a massive containment, and marching parachutists can give it an undulant grace. Young women marching don't seem to give it anything pleasantly collective. They don't seem to take an innocent pride in the achievement of a step the way young men do—a pride as innocent as that of a trained dog. A collective step becomes depersonalized or homogenized only after considerable training. And then it is a monotonous shape, of interest only in multiplication.

In a parade the body looks more two-footed than usual. Two feet traveling from place to place haven't mathematically much choice in the order they can go in. Soldiers at Forward March go from two feet to one foot, then they keep going from one foot to the other foot, and they go from one foot to both feet at Halt. That makes three kinds of step and two more exist: a hop on the same foot, a broadjump from both feet to both feet. These five kinds are all there are. Soldiers could be trained to do all five instead of only three, and you can see right away that once they were trained, the five would look hardly less monotonous than the three.

Dancers have no more feet than other people, and so they live with the same limitation. One could try to watch a ballet from the point of view of the five kinds of step, and see how it keeps scurrying about from one kind to another inside the narrow limits of a two-footed fate. One could try, but one doesn't. As you watch a ballet, the dancers do plenty of different steps and often some new ones you hadn't seen before. One doesn't keep watching the feet to see the sequence in which they are contacting the floor. You keep watching the whole shape of the body before and after the floor-contact.

Between a ballet and a parade, take watching a ballroom dance, especially one where the partners break, like a Lindy or a Mambo or a Virginia Reel. You see the steps exhibiting the dancer's figure, the boy's or the girl's, in a series of contrasting shapes. You see it advancing toward a partner, or turning on itself; it lightly bends and stretches; the thighs close and separate, the knees open and shut, the arms swing guardedly in counteraction to the legs, or they lift both at once. The feet, the hands, the head may refuse a direction the body inclines to or they may accept it. When the waist undulates Cuban-style, the extremities delay following it with an air of detachment. As you watch a good dancer, it all looks very cute, the figure and its movable parts, and you get to know them very pleasantly.

The contrasting shapes you see the figure making are as depersonalized as those of a military step—they are sometimes close to a marching step, and the difference is no more than a slight containment, a slight glide of the foot. But the next moment they are quite unmilitary. The dancers move backwards and sideways as much as forward, they kick and spin, they interweave and sway and clap, and the boys and girls keep making mutual shapes. One can see that the dance shapes add particular motions to the basic kind of step they relate to. But one also sees that if you take basic steps to be walking steps then dance steps don't originate in them. Dance steps belong to a different species, so to speak. They don't give the body that useful patient look that walking does. They were invented for mutual fun and for the lively display of sculptural shapes. In Basque folk dancing and in ballet it is normal for a dancer to leap up and make a rapid quivering back-and-forth shape with his feet that is as far from common sense as a bird's brief trill. An entrechat suits the kind of common sense dancing has, but not any other kind.

The action of ballet exhibits the dancer's figure much further and more distinctly than that of a ballroom dance. The shapes are more exact and more extreme. The large reach of all the limbs, the easy erectness of the body regardless, the sharpness of pointed feet, the length of neck, the mildness of wrists, the keen angle of kneebends, the swiftness of sweeping arms, the full visibility of stretched legs turned out from thigh to toe, spreading and shutting; the figure in leaps, spins, stops in balance, slow motion deployments, the feet fluttering and rush and completely still. Passing through such a dazzling series of transformations, you see the powerfully erect figure, effortless and friendly. It appears larger than life, like in an illusion of intimacy. And you are astonished when a performer who on stage looked so big, at a party turns out to be a wisp of a girl or a quite slender-looking boy.

A ballet dancer has been carefully trained to make the shapes of classic dancing, and one can readily see that they have specific limits. Classic steps limit the action of the joints to a few readily visible differences; so the trajectory of the body as it makes the shape is defined. A classic dancer has a habit of many years' standing of rotating, bending and stretching the several joints of legs and arms, of the neck and spine, in movements of which the start, the trajectory and the finish have become second nature. How such a movement draws after it the rest of the body, or how it joins a movement before it or one after it, have become for him instinctive. The whole of the shape is second nature to him, and so are its component parts. He can alter a specific detail without becoming confused in the main shape. He is familiar with the impetus he must give that will mould it very clearly in each of its dimensions. And in all these shapes, whether large or small, the dancer has come to judge his momentum and his balance at varying speeds by instinct. So they appear effortless and unconfused and in harmony.

A classic dancer's legs seem to move not from the hip joint but from further up, from the waist and the small of the back; and the arms not from the shoulder, but from lower down, from the same part of the back as the legs; it lengthens both extremities and harmonizes them. The head moves at the end of a neck like a giraffe's that seems to begin below the shoulderblades. The head can also move without the neck, just from the joint where head and spine meet, tilting against a motionless neck. Then you see its small motion enlarged by the unexpected contrast to so very long and separate a neck. In the same way a flick of ankle or of wrist can be magnified by the long-looking immobile leg or arm it is at the far end of. So aspects of scale appear.

Classic action exhibits the dancer's body very clearly but it steadily exhibits aspects of it that everyday life shows only at rare moments. Classic arms, for instance, keep to a few large trajectories and positions, they keep distinct from the torso, and the quality they exhibit in arms is the long lightness of them. They minimize the activity of elbow and wrists. In everyday life arms and hands do all the chattering, and the legs growl now and then. On the contrary in classic dancing the legs seem to carry the tune, and the arms add to it a milder second voice.

Classic legs turned out from the hip joint down look unusually exposed. One sees the inside surface of them, though the dancer is facing you. One sees the modeling of their parts, the differentiated action of the joints flexing or rotating—the lively bend of the knee especially. One watches the torque and powerful spread of the thighs at their base. The ballerina holds the bone turned in its socket rigid, and the leg extends itself to its complete stretch in the air, sideways, to the back or to the front. The visually exposed action of the legs, fully turned out, fully bending and stretching, can look wonderfully generous.

No matter how large the action of legs and of arms, the classic back does not have to yield, and its stretched erectness is extremely long. It bends in or out when it chooses. The low-held shoulders open the breast or chest. But classicism doesn't feature the chest as a separate attraction the way advertising does; a slight, momentary and beautiful lift of the rib-cage is a movement of the upper back. At the back of the torso or at the front, it is the waist that one keeps looking at. Looking at it you see the figure's changing silhouette at a glance. The waist is the center of the dance shape, or the implied center. You seem to sense in its quickness a lightning anticipation of the next motion. The power of the waist is that of an athlete's, but the quickness of it is a child's.

Among the ways classicism exhibits the body that are different from those of everyday life, the most different is that of toesteps which look like tiny stilts the girl is treading on. She can step onto them, or she can rise into them, rising with a soft flick of both feet. She can step about on them with a fanatic delicacy and a penetrating precision. She can spin on them like a bat out of hell. When she jumps or runs on them one hears a muffled tapping that sometimes sounds fleshy. From the side you see the sole curving like a bending knife-blade with at the back the queer handle of the heel. From the front they over-elongate the leg and alter the body's proportions; and the extreme erectness of the foot seems in keeping with the extremely pulled-up waist and the stretched lightness of the slender ballerina. Sometimes a figure on a single toe-point, as its shape deploys from so narrow a balance, looks intently alone by itself, and even if a partner supports it, intently individual. At other times one feels the contrast between the large pliancy of the knees, the lesser one of the ankles, and the scarcely perceptible give of the bones of the arch.

Toesteps sharpen one's eye to the figure's contact with the floor. The action of rhythm and the action of shape meet and keep meeting at the moment of floor contact. Classic dancing can make that moment keen to the eye so the rhythm it sees has an edge. Take for instance the moment on the ground between two leaps. You see the feet arriving stretched through the air, the ankles flex in a flash, you see the feet on the floor, motionless in their small position, catch the flying body's momentum, and instantly the ankles flash again as the legs stretch off into the air in the new leap. The feet have tossed the dancer's momentum forward, without a wobble or a blur. The eye has caught their moment of stillness the more sharply because the position they held is a familiar one that keeps returning. And that almost imperceptible stillness of theirs cuts the first shape from the second, and makes the rhythm of motion carry.

In these peculiar appearances and the recurrent complete stillness of the classic body, the eye recognizes or the imagination recognizes the sensual meaning of the exhibited parts, and the dramatic implication of their motions. It sees these implications and meanings appear and disappear. They are exhibited without the continuity or the stress that could present them as if in states of greed or of anxiety. Their moment by moment sensual innocence allows the imagination the more unembarrassed play.

The steps keep unfolding the body in large or small ways, and reassembling it in vertical balance like a butterfly. The peculiarity of its grace in motion is consistent and is shared by all the figures on stage. The expressive meaning is divided between recognizable details and the visual grace, the very light alternation of weight of an over-all unrecognizable consistency. The consistency is as if the most usual and easy of ballet steps set a pitch for the eye—a pitch of carriage and balance in action—to which everything that is done on stage keeps a clear relation by its quality of impulse and of carriage. The over-all effect is that of a spontaneous harmony of action. But its common sense remains that of a dance.

The peculiar values of classic style we have been considering are an invention extending from nowadays back into a collective past. They are in that sense traditional values. Ballet began as the kind of dancing current at village festivals around the Mediterranean from the times of King Minos and Daedalus to those of da Vinci. Young Boccaccio and young Dante before him danced these local steps; and Homer had danced them locally as a boy. The village dances changed so slowly that they were always traditional. At the edge of the holiday crowd, when the piper played, the tots tried to do the steps before they could keep time. Everyone had grown up knowing the sequences and the tunes that went with them, and knowing from having watched it the harmony that the dance could show. People always liked to watch the boys and girls do it, and liked giving a prize to the sweetest dancer. The steps were a part of the brightness of the recurrent holiday, and they brought back other bright faces and festivals that the little region had known in the past. The sense of such holidays was strong at the center of civilization for a long time, and one finds echoes of it reaching back from verses of the *Divine Comedy* to a carved Minoan cylinder three thousand years earlier depicting harvesters marching home with a band, singing and joking. In classic Greek representations of a dance step the harmony is sometimes so rich it implies contrary steps and extended phrases. Scholars have traced a number of ballet movements to classic Greek prototypes. No reason to suppose that the ancient dances were simple.

When, around the middle of the millennium before Christ, urban prosperity spread to Europe from the East, the country steps were theatricalized first for Greek theatres, and later for the elaborate and ornate theatres of the Roman Empire. Then prosperity retreated eastward again, and for another thousand years dancing was again that of lively young people doing their local steps at balls or church festivals, with here and there some hired mimes or an anxious acrobat passing the hat. These hard-bitten comics were tramps and outsiders.

When prosperity and a pleasure in grace of behavior spread again—this time from Renaissance Italy—the country dances were theatricalized once more. Like the earlier Greek professionals, the new Italian ones rearranged the steps to new tunes, they turned them out a bit to face the public, and gave them a thread of story. They saw that the pleasure of the dances was their harmony. The pantomime they took over was that of the original holiday occasion, that of pleasant social behavior. Professionals developed indoors a sense of lyric expression in dancing. But the outdoor mimes, thanks to the same prosperity, had developed their capers and their insistent explosive pantomime into a rowdy Italian buffoonery. These two opposite kinds of expression had existed in the ancient theatres as well, and existed time out of mind, sometimes blending, sometimes not. By the seventeenth century, when theatre dancing became organized, the ballet dancers were likely to sustain the sentiment, but the comics were likely to steal the show.

And here we are watching ballet in the prosperous mid-twentieth century. In a number of professional terms and steps dancers can recognize three hundred years of continuity behind them. Ballet-goers can recognize two hundred years in a number of documents that evoke an artistic excitement related to their own. Though the comics still steal the show, the element which holds a ballet together and which creates the big climaxes is the one we call classic dancing. Classicism has stretched the ancient country steps and all the others it has added to them—it has stretched them vertically and horizontally to heighten the drama of dance momentum. But in its extended range of large-scale theatre steps and their spectacular momentum, ballet has kept the gift of harmony it began with. Today's professionals of ballet are artists, they are virtuosos, craftsmen specialized for life. But as one watches them, just when they are at their best, history seems to vanish. The quality of character that makes a dancer seems the same as three or four thousand years ago. The nature of the pleasure they give by their genius as dancers does not seem to have changed much since Minoan times.

One July noon, in an Aegean village on the Greek island of Mykonos, two friends and I, after visiting a monastery, were waiting in the sun for the single daily bus. The torrent of heat and light was so intense that we went into a cafe for shelter. Inside the radio was playing folk tunes and a young farmer was dancing solo to it, while two stood around watching him and waiting for their turn. But when the second young man began, the miracle happened. The traditional steps produced an effect entirely different. The rapidity of decision, the brilliance of impetus, the grace were unforeseeable, as if on another scale. He was a dancer in the class of the classic stars one sees on stage. It was an extraordinary delight to watch him. He finished his turn. But while the next young farmer was dancing, the bus honked outside, and we foreigners ran out to catch it.

An extraordinary delight such as this is the standard of theatre performance. It is the standard that nature sets. A genius for dancing keeps turning up in a particular boy or girl who are doing the regulation steps they grew up with. Outside the theatre or inside it, the gift creates an immediate communication. For some people watching such great moments at a ballet performance, the steps themselves disappear in a blaze of glory. For others the steps remain distinctly visible, but they make as much sense as if one could do them one's self. One understands them. It is like the sensation of understanding a foreign language because a girl has looked so ravishing speaking it.

But for professionals as they watched ballet dancers of genius at such great moments, and knew each step they were doing from long experience, it was the revelation of the large-scale effect possible in the familiar steps that fascinated them. Being professionals they tried to catch the technical method. And what they caught of it during several hundred years has become classic style.

Style in its professional aspect is a question of good habits in the way steps are done. And so ballet has gradually settled on several habits it prefers. It has decided on the turned-out thighs, on the pulled-up waist that joins them to the erect spine, on the low-held shoulder line. It has decided on a few main movements of the head, of the arms, of the torso, of the several leg joints. And on fifty or so main steps. These main steps and the main movements that can modify them are the habitual exercises with which good habits of balance and carriage, with which habits of harmony and rhythm can be trained in apprentices to reach a large-scale theatre effect. They form a common basis of action for professionals. And the history of them is that they have always been specifically dance steps or elements of dance steps, enlarged in scale by constant use in the theatre.

In ancient Italian towns the narrow main street at dusk becomes a kind of theatre. The community strolls affably and looks itself over. The girls and the young men, from fifteen to twenty-two, display their charm to one another with a lively sociability. The more grace they show the better the community likes them. In Florence or in Naples, in the ancient city slums the young people are virtuoso performers, and they do a bit of promenading any time they are not busy. A foreigner in Rome, who loses his way among the fifteenth and sixteenth century alleys and squares, hunting in those neighborhoods for the Sybils of Raphael or the birthplace of Metastasio, discovers how bright about their grace the local young Romans can be. They appreciate it in themselves and in each other equally. Their stroll is as responsive as if it were a physical conversation. Chunkily built though they are, they place their feet, they articulate the arms and legs, the boys stress the opening, and the girls the closing of the limbs. Their necks and waists have an insinuating harmony. They move from the waist turning to look, or stepping back in effacé to let a girl pass, or advancing a sheltering arm (like in croisé). They present their person and they put an arm around each other's waist or shoulder with a graceful intimacy. Their liveliness makes these courteous formalities—that recall ballet—a mutual game of skill. The foreign ballet fan as he goes home through the purple Roman dusk, charmed by the physical caress of it, confuses the shapes of Raphael with those of the performance. But he realizes what it means that ballet was originally an Italian dance, and he becomes aware of the lively sociability of its spirit and of its forms.

The general question I have been considering is harmony in classical dancing. But I hope the reference to Italy has not been misleading. Classic dancing doesn't look Italian when Americans do it, or when English dancers do it, or Russian, or French or Danish dancers; it doesn't, and can't and needn't. But it has harmony when any of them do it. It has a visual harmony of shapes due to the specific action of the body that we were considering earlier. Let us go back to the single step, and make sure where we are, close enough to the Atlantic seaboard.

As one lies with closed eyes in bed or on a beach far from town trying to recall what a single step looks like, one sees several steps and dancers combined in a phrase, and sees the shape of a phrase as if it were an extended step, many-legged and many-armed, with a particular departure, trajectory and arrival. And, as phrases succeed one another, one sees them take direction on stage, and one sees the visual momentum their paths can have with relation to a center of action, or to several centers, coming down stage, retiring back, escaping to the sides, appearing from the wings. The momentum of phrases accentuates the angle at which a figure is presented, or at which it acts, the directions it takes or only aspires to take. The momentum disengages a leading quality of motion, hopping, fluttering, soaring, stopping dead. It carries along a single figure, or several mutually or a group. It draws the figures deeper into dramatic situations, serious or comic ones.

But the action of a step determines the ramifications, the rise and fall of the continuous momentum. You begin to see the active impetus of the dancers creating the impetus moment by moment. They step out of one shape and into another, they change direction or speed, they erect and dissolve a configuration, and their secure and steady impetus keeps coming. The situations that dissolve as one watches are created and swept along by the ease and the fun and the positive lightness of it. They dance and as they do, create in their wake an architectural momentum of imaginary weights and transported presences. Their activity does not leave behind any material object, only an imaginary one.

The stage by its stationary center and its fixed proportions accumulates the imaginative reality. Stage area and stage height appear to be permanent actualities. Within them the brief shape that a dancer's body makes can look small and lost, or it can spread securely and for an instant appear on their scale. One can respond to the visual significance —the visual spaciousness—of such a moment of dance motion without being able to explain it reasonably in other terms.

The shape the dancer makes at such a moment has no specific representational aspect. You have seen the same shape before with different feelings. And yet often the whole house responds to such a moment of classic climax. It seems not to insist on being understood rationally. It presents no problem, it presents a climax of dancing. One can leave the ambiguity of it at that and enjoy at once both the climactic beauty of it and the nonsense.

Or else as one responds in the moment to the effortless sense of completion and of freedom that its spaciousness gives one, one may feel that the expression of the motion one is watching has been seen throughout the piece without being fulfilled until now. It is the expression the piece is about. One feels the cumulative drama it rises on. Then its visual spaciousness offers to one's imagination a large or a tragic image to recognize. It is not frightening, the lucidity of the moment is as sweet as happiness. Like a word you have often heard that spoken without pressure at a certain moment is a final one, as large as your life, so the classic shape is an effortless motion that replies. To the Symbolist poet Mallarmé, it appeared as an emblematic reply—as of blossom or dagger or cup—a climactic perception of mutual identity. Like in a lucidity of perception there is in the motion no sense of intention or pressure. The significance of it appears in the present moment, as the climactic significance of a savage ritual appeared at the moment it occurred in our racial past.

As you lie on the hot deserted beach far from town and with closed eyes recall the visual moment of climax, and scarcely hear the hoarse breathing of the small surf, a memory of the music it rose on returns, and you remember the prolonged melodious momentum of the score as if the musical phrase the step rose on had arrived from so far. So deep in the piece it appears to have been.

The power of projection that music has strikes me as mysterious but it is a fact of nature. I have heard people who considered themselves unmusical modestly make acute remarks on the music of a ballet; and I once sat next to a deaf mute who followed the performance with delight and enrolled in a ballet school afterwards. However one is conscious of it, without music classic dancing is no more real than swimming is real without water around it. The more ballet turns to pantomime, the less intimate its relation to the music becomes; but the more it turns to dancing, the more it enjoys the music's presence, bar by bar. Even when the steps stand aside and let the music alone, they are intimately aware of it.

We spoke of the beat at the beginning and here we are back to it. Take a specific ballet step. An assemblé looks different if it lands on one of the measure or if it lands on four; an entrechat looks different if the push from the floor comes on the downbeat, or if on the downbeat the legs beat in the air. A promenade en arabesque done at the same speed looks different if it is done in three-four time or in four-four. The stress of the measure supports a different phrase of the step; it gives the motion a different lift and visual accent and expression. And as the stress of the beat can give a different look to the step, so can the stresses of the other kinds of musical emphasis—the stresses of dynamics, of melody, of harmony, of timbre, of pathos.

All these stresses offer their various support to the steps. They are like a floor with various degrees of resilience to dance on. The steps step in some places and not in others. They make a choice of stresses.

But as you hear the piece the stresses merge into a musical momentum that varies and into a musical expression that changes; and they build into large coherent sections and finally into a completed structure of musical sound with a coherent identity. We are used to sensing the coherence of music sometimes in one way, sometimes in another. And while we sense a coherence it has, we can believe in the coherence of long sequences of dancing we are watching. We see their coherence from the point of reference of the musical meaning. A long dance gathers power by coherence.

But the relation of eye and ear is a mutual one. The visual action also makes particular stresses in the music more perceptible, and continuities more clearly coherent. Watching the sweep of the dance momentum, you feel more keenly the musical one, and the visual drama can give you an insight to the force of character of the score. A dance happily married to its score likes to make jokes without raising its small voice, and the thundering score likes it too.

But the steps of classic dancing have always enjoyed being timed to the notes of music, and their rhythm has always responded to musical rhythm. Inside the labyrinth of complex musical structures, you see ballet following the clue of the rhythm, you see it hearing the other musical forces as they affect the current of the rhythm, as they leave or don't leave the rhythm a danceable one. You see the dance listening and choosing its own rhythmic response. A dance ballet gets its power of projection by the choice of its response to the larger structures of musical rhythm. So its power of character reveals itself in a more complexly happy marriage. Timed as classic dancing is to strict measures of time, confined to a limited range of motion, lighter in the stress it communicates than everyday motion, the power of character, the power of insight it develops and sustains in reference to its chosen score is a power of its own creation. Mutually to the music, you watch the dance take shape and make sense and show the dazzling grace of an imaginative freedom. It is worth watching for.

What we have been considering is what is usually called the form of classic dancing. I am not suggesting that a ballet has no content, and I am not suggesting either that its form is its content. I have heard these statements but they make no sense to me. I think the meaning of the two words is approximately clear, and that they describe different ways of aproaching an event, or of discussing it. I have been avoiding the distinction because I have been discussing what classic dancing looks like regardless of the subject matter of the ballet, what one is aware of at the moment one sees the dancer move, what one is aware of before one makes the distinction between content and form. It is a fairly confused awareness, but it is real enough. One doesn't, as far as I can see, make any sharp distinction between content and form in the case of pleasant events while one is enjoying them, or of people one is in love with; one instinctively doesn't.

The forms of classic dancing are one may say no less instinctive for being formal. The way a cat comes up to you at night in a deserted city street to be patted, and when you crouch to pat her, the way she will enjoy a stroke or two and then pass out of reach, stop there facing away into the night, and return for another stroke or two, and then pass behind you and return on your other side—all this has a form that you meet again on stage when the ballerina is doing a Petipa adagio. And while cats one meets on different nights all like to follow the same adagio form, one cat will vary it by hunching her back or rolling seductively just out of reach, another another night by standing high on her toes as you pat her, and making little sous-sus on her front paws; a third by grand Petersburg-style tail wavings; a fourth, if you are down close enough, by rising on her hind paws, resting her front ones weightlessly on you, raising her wide ballerina eyes to yours, and then—delicate as a single finger pirouette—giving the tip of your nose a tender nip. When a cat has had enough adagio, she sits down apart; or else, changing to mime, she scampers artificially away, pretending to be scared by the passing of a solitary nocturnal truck. Dogs—dogs you take on daytime country walks are virtuosos of allegro. They invent heroic dashes, sharp zig-zags running low ending in grand jetés that slow down; or else in the midst of a demi-manege at cannonball speed they stop dead. They mean you to get the joke, and they make it dead-pan like troupers. Then they come up to you at an untheatrical dog-trot, smiling, breathing hard, with shining eyes; they enjoy your applause, but they distinguish between the performance when they were pretending and the bow they take after it is finished when they are honest dogs again.

One watches ballet just as one would the animals, but since there is more to be seen, there is more to watch. More to be seen and also more to recognize. Not only the formal shapes but also the pantomime shapes with their specific allusions. And everybody likes to see pantomime in the course of a ballet evening. It gives the feeling of being back in a more familiar rational world, back safe from the flight through the intuitive rhythmic world of irrational symbols and of the charming animals.

We have been considering ballet from its aspect as dancing. Its aspect as pantomime is equally interesting; so is its aspect as an art of the choreographer and as an art of the dancer. They are all part of ballet just as much as what I have been discussing—and I love them just as much, and they don't lose any of their beauty merely by being unmentioned.

Dance Theory

Because the medium of dance is the human body itself, dance has often been dismissed as a physical—and hence frivolous—art. Dance, it has sometimes been said, is only a pretty confection—amusing but not especially serious. When compiling his list of essential arts, Hegel, for example, excluded dance, placing it among the leisure activities of man such as gardening.

The three writers in this section do not agree that the physicality of dance excludes it from serious consideration. Rather they argue that dance succinctly and powerfully expresses both the most basic of human experiences (the rhythm of thought, how feelings come and go) and the most basic of human desires (to reconcile the physical and the metaphysical, to combine somehow the real and the ideal). These essays, in short, pay tribute to the powers of dance, its primal and persistent relevance.

In "Philosophy of the Dance," the French poet and essayist Paul Valéry provides us with one of the most fascinating and original theories of dance ever formulated. According to Valéry, man (and man alone) has too much energy for his own needs: he is capable of performing actions and of thinking ideas that have little "use" in his everyday world of survival. Although dance, according to Valéry, may originate in ordinary useful action, it also breaks away from and even opposes such action. Dance—excessive, self-contained, dream-like—represents man's glorious enchantment with the impractical and the useless. For Valéry, the dance is a kind of visible inner life with its own rhythms.

Susanne Langer—one of America's most prominent philosophers and aestheticians—agrees that dance, although it seems so committed to the physical, nevertheless evokes something beyond physicality. "What is expressed in a dance is an idea," Langer says, "an idea of the way feelings, emotions, and all other subjective experiences come and go—their rise and growth, their intricate synthesis that gives our inner life unity and personal identity." The dancer, living in a world of tensions and resolutions, balance and imbalance, sums up the flux of life.

In "The World as Ballet," English poet and critic Arthur Symons goes one step further: for Symons, dance is life itself—"animal life, having its own way passionately." The dancer—half symbol, half human being—represents the appeal of everything in the world that is passing, colored, to be enjoyed, everything that urges us to give way "luxuriously to the delightful present."

Philosophy of the Dance

by Paul Valéry

Let me begin at once by telling you without preamble that to my mind the dance is not merely an exercise, an entertainment, an ornamental art, or sometimes a social activity; it is a serious matter and in certain of its aspects most venerable. Every epoch that has understood the human body and experienced at least some sense of its mystery, its resources, its limits, its combinations of energy and sensibility, has cultivated and revered the dance.

It is a fundamental art, as is suggested if not demonstrated by its universality, its immemorial antiquity, the solemn uses to which it has been put, the ideas and reflections it has engendered at all times. For the dance is an art derived from life itself, since it is nothing more nor less than the action of the whole human body; but an action transposed into a world, into a kind of *space-time*, which is no longer quite the same as that of everyday life.

Man perceived that he possessed more vigor, more suppleness, more articular and muscular possibilities, than he needed to satisfy the needs of his existence, and he discovered that certain of these movements, by their frequency, succession, or range, gave him a pleasure equivalent to a kind of intoxication and sometimes so intense that only total exhaustion, an ecstasy of exhaustion, as it were, could interrupt his delirium, his frantic motor expenditure.

We have, then, too much energy for our needs. You can easily observe that most, by far the most, of the impressions we receive from our senses are of no use to us, that they cannot be utilized and play no part in the functioning of the mechanisms essential to the con-

Source: From *Aesthetics*, translated by Ralph Manheim, Volume 13 of *The Collected Works* (New York: Pantheon, 1964).

servation of life. We see too many things and hear too many things that we do nothing and *can* do nothing with: the words of a lecturer, for instance.

The same observation applies to our powers of action: we can perform a multitude of acts that have no chance of being utilized in the indispensable, or important, operations of life. We can trace a circle, give play to our facial muscles, walk in cadence; all these actions, which made it possible to create geometry, the drama, and the military art, are in themselves useless, useless to our vital functioning.

Thus life's instruments of relation, our senses, our articulated members, the images and signs which control our actions and the distribution of our energies, co-ordinating the movements of our puppet, might be employed solely for our physiological needs; they might do nothing more than attack the environment in which we live or defend us against it, and then their sole business would be the preservation of our existence.

We might lead a life strictly limited to the maintenance of our living machine, utterly indifferent or insensitive to everything that plays no part in the cycles of transformation which make up our organic functioning; feeling nothing and doing nothing beyond what is necessary, making no move that is not a limited reaction, a finite response, to some external action. For our useful acts are finite. They carry us from one state to another.

Animals do not seem to perceive or do anything that is useless. A dog's eye sees the stars, no doubt, but his being gives no development to the sight. The dog's ear perceives a sound that makes it prick up in alarm; but of this sound the dog assimilates only what he needs in order to respond with an immediate and uniform act. He does not dwell on the perception. The cow in her pasture jumps at the clatter of the passing Mediterranean Express; the train vanishes; she does not pursue the train in her thoughts; she goes back to her tender grass, and her lovely eyes do not follow the departing train. The index of her brain returns at once to zero.

Yet sometimes animals seem to amuse themselves. Cats obviously play with mice. Monkeys perform pantomimes. Dogs chase each other, spring at the heads of horses; and I can think of nothing that suggests free, happy play more fully than the sporting of porpoises we see off shore, leaping free of the water, diving, outracing a ship, swimming under its keel and reappearing in the foam, livelier than the waves amid which they glisten and change color in the sun. Might we not call this a dance?

But all these animal amusements may be interpreted as useful actions, bursts of impulse, springing from the need to consume excess energy, or to maintain the organs designed for vital offense or defense in a state of suppleness or vigor. And I think I am justified in observing that those species, such as the ants and the bees, that seem to be most exactly constructed, endowed with the most specialized instincts, also seem to be those most saving of their time. Ants do not waste a minute. The spider does not play in its web; it lurks in wait. But what about man?

Man is the singular animal who watches himself live, puts a value on himself, and identifies this value with the importance he attaches to useless perceptions and acts without vital physical consequence.

Pascal situated all our dignity in thought; but the thinking that raises us—in our own eyes—above our sensory condition is precisely the kind of thinking that has no useful purpose. Obviously our meditations about the origin of things, or about death, are of no use to the organism; and indeed, exalted thoughts of this kind tend to be harmful if not fatal to our species. Our deepest thoughts are those that are the most insignificant, the most futile as it were, from the standpoint of self-preservation.

But because our curiosity was greater than it had any need to be, and our activity more intense than any vital aim required, both have developed to the point of inventing the arts, the sciences, universal problems, and of producing objects, forms, actions that we could easily have dispensed with.

And moreover, all this free, gratuitous invention and production, all this play of our senses and faculties, gradually provided itself with a kind of *necessity* and *utility*.

Art and science, each in its own way, tend to build up a kind of utility from the useless, a kind of necessity from the arbitrary. Ultimately, artistic creation is not so much a creation of works as the creation of a *need for works;* for works are products, a supply presupposing a demand, a need.

Quite a bit of philosophy, you may think . . . and I admit that I've given you rather too much of it. But when one is not a dancer; when one would be at a loss not only to perform, but even to explain, the slightest step; when, to deal with the miracles wrought by the legs, one has only the resources of a head, there's no help but in a certain amount of philosophy—in other words, one approaches the matter from far off, in the hope that distance will dispel the difficulties. It is much simpler to construct a universe than to explain how a man stands on his feet—as Aristotle, Descartes, Leibnitz, and quite a few others will tell you.

However, it seems perfectly legitimate for a philosopher to watch a dancer in action, and noting that he takes pleasure in it, to try to derive from his pleasure the secondary pleasure of expressing his impressions in his own language.

But first, he may derive some fine images from it. Philosophers have a great taste for images: there is no trade that requires more of them, although philosophers often hide them under dull-gray words. They have created famous ones: the cave; the sinister river you can never cross twice; or Achilles running breathlessly after a tortoise he can never overtake. The parallel mirrors, runners passing on the torch to one another, down to Nietzsche with his eagle, his serpent, his tight-rope dancer. All in all quite a stock of them, quite a pageant of ideas. Think of the metaphysical ballet that might be composed with all these famous symbols.

My philosopher, however, does not content himself with this performance. What, in the presence of the dance and the dancer, can he do to give himself the illusion of knowing a little more than she about something that she knows best, and he not at all? He is compelled to make up for his technical ignorance and hide his perplexity under some ingenious universal interpretation of this art whose wonders he notes and experiences.

He embarks on the task; he goes about it in his own fashion. . . . The fashion of a philosopher. Everyone knows how his dance begins. . . . His first faint step is a *question*. And as befits a man undertaking a useless, arbitrary act, he throws himself into it without foreseeing the end; he embarks on an unlimited interrogation in the interrogative infinitive. That is his trade.

He plays his game, beginning with its usual beginning. And there he is, asking himself:

"What then is the dance?"

What then is the dance? At once he is perplexed, his wits are paralyzed. He is reminded of a famous question, a famous dilemma—that of St. Augustine.

St. Augustine confesses how he asked himself one day what Time is; and he owns that he perfectly well knew as long as he did not think of asking, but that he lost himself at the crossroads of his mind as soon as he applied himself to the term, as soon as he isolated it from any immediate usage or particular expression. A very profound observation. . . .

That is what my philosopher has come to: he stands hesitant on the forbidding threshold that separates a question from an answer, obsessed by the memory of St. Augustine, dreaming in his penumbra of the great saint's perplexity:

"What is Time? But what is the dance?"

But, he tells himself, the dance after all is merely a form of time, the creation of a kind of time, or of a very distinct and singular species of time.

Already he is less worried: he has wedded two difficulties to each other. Each one, taken separately, left him perplexed and without resources; but now they are linked together. Perhaps their union will be fertile. Perhaps some ideas may be born of it, and that is just what he is after—his vice and his plaything.

Now he watches the dancer with the extraordinary, ultralucid eyes that transform everything they see into a prey of the abstract mind. He considers the spectacle and deciphers it in his own way.

It seems to him that this person who is dancing encloses herself as it were in a time that she engenders, a time consisting entirely of immediate energy, of nothing that can last. She is the unstable element, she squanders instability, she goes beyond the impossible and overdoes the improbable; and by denying the ordinary state of things, she creates in men's minds the idea of another, exceptional state—a state that is all action, a permanence built up and consolidated by an incessant effort, comparable to the vibrant pose of a bumblebee or moth exploring the calyx of a flower, charged with motor energy, sustained in virtual immobility by the incredibly swift beat of its wings.

Or our philosopher may just as well compare the dancer to a flame or, for that matter, to any phenomenon that is visibly sustained by the intense consumption of a superior energy.

He also notes that, in the dance, all the sensations of the body, which is both mover and moved, are connected in a certain order—that they call and respond to each other, as though rebounding or being reflected from the invisible wall of a sphere of energy within the living being. Forgive me that outrageously bold expression, I can find no other. But you knew before you came here that I am an obscure and complicated writer. . . .

Confronted by the dance, my philosopher—or a mind afflicted with a mania for interrogation, if you prefer—asks his usual questions. He brings in his *whys* and *hows*, the customary instruments of elucidation, which are the apparatus of his own art; and he tries, as you have just perceived, to replace the immediate and expedient expression of things by rather odd formulas which enable him to relate the graceful phenomenon of the dance to the whole of what he knows, or thinks he knows.

He attempts to fathom the mystery of a body which suddenly, as though by the effect of an internal shock, enters into a kind of life that is at once strangely unstable and strangely regulated, strangely spontaneous, but at the same time strangely contrived and, assuredly, planned.

The body seems to have broken free from its usual states of balance. It seems to be trying to outwit—I should say outrace—its own weight, at every moment evading its pull, not to say its sanction.

In general, it assumes a fairly simple periodicity that seems to maintain itself automatically; it seems endowed with a superior elasticity which retrieves the impulse of every movement and at once renews it. One is reminded of a top, standing on its point and reacting so sensitively to the slightest shock.

But here is an important observation that comes to the mind of our philosopher, who might do better to enjoy himself to the full and abandon himself to what he sees. He observes that the dancing body seems unaware of its surroundings. It seems to be concerned only with itself and one other object, a very important one, from which it breaks free, to which it returns, but only to gather the wherewithal for another flight. . . .

That object is the earth, the ground, the solid place, the plane on which everyday life plods along, the plane of walking, the prose of human movement.

Yes, the dancing body seems unaware of everything else, it seems to know nothing of its surroundings. It seems to hearken to itself and only to itself, to see nothing, as though its eyes were jewels, unknown jewels like those of which Baudelaire speaks, lights that serve no useful purpose.

For the dancer is in another world; no longer the world that takes color from our gaze, but one that she weaves with her steps and builds with her gestures. And in that world acts have no outward aim; there is no object to grasp, to attain, to repulse or run away from, no object which puts a precise end to an action and gives movements first an outward direction and co-ordination, then a clear and definite conclusion.

But that is not all: in this world nothing is unforeseen; though the dancer sometimes seems to be reacting to an unforeseen incident, that too is part of a very evident plan. Everything happens as if. . . . But nothing more.

Thus there is no aim, no real incidents, no outside world. . . .

The philosopher exults. No outside world! For the dancer there is no outside. . . . Nothing exists beyond the system she sets up by her acts—one is reminded of the diametrically contrary and no less closed system constituted by our sleep, whose exactly opposite law is the abolition of all acts, total abstention from action.

He sees the dance as an artificial somnambulism, a group of sensations which make themselves a dwelling place where certain muscular themes follow one another in an order which creates a special kind of time that is absolutely its own. And with an increasingly *intellectual* delight he contemplates this being who, from her very depths, brings forth these beautiful transformations of her form in space; who now moves, but without really going anywhere; now metamorphoses herself on the spot, displaying herself in every aspect; who sometimes skillfully modulates successive appearances as though in controlled phases; sometimes changes herself brusquely into a whirlwind, spinning faster and faster, then suddenly stops, crystallized into a statue, adorned with an alien smile.

But this detachment from the environment, this absence of aim, this negation of explicable movement, these full turns (which no circumstance of ordinary life demands of our body), even this impersonal smile—all these features are radically opposed to those that characterize our action in the practical world and our relations with it.

In the practical world our being is nothing more than an intermediary between the sensation of a need and the impulse to satisfy the need. In this role, it proceeds always by the most economical, if not always the shortest, path: it wants results. Its guiding principles seem to be the straight line, the least action, and the shortest time. A practical man is a man who has an instinct for such economy of time and effort, and has little difficulty in putting it into effect, because his aim is definite and clearly localized: *an external object*.

As we have said, the dance is the exact opposite. It moves in a self-contained realm of its own and implies no reason, no tendency toward completion. A formula for pure dance should include nothing to suggest that it has an end. It is terminated by outside events; its limits in time are not intrinsic to it; the duration of the dance is limited by the conventional length of the program, by fatigue or loss of interest. But the dance itself has nothing to make it end. It ceases as a dream ceases that might go on indefinitely: it stops, not because an undertaking has been completed, for there is no undertaking, but because something else, something outside it has been exhausted.

And so—permit me to put it rather boldly—might one not—and I have already intimated as much—consider the dance as a kind of *inner life*, allowing that psychological term a new meaning in which physiology is dominant?

An inner life, indeed, but one consisting entirely in sensations of time and energy which respond to one another and form a kind of closed circle of resonance. This resonance, like any other, is communicated: a part of our pleasure as spectators consists in feeling ourselves possessed by the rhythms so that we ourselves are virtually dancing.

Carried a little further, this sort of philosophy of the dance can lead to some rather curious consequences or applications. If, in speaking of this art, I have kept to considerations of a very general nature, it has been somewhat with the intention of guiding you to what we are now coming to. I have tried to communicate a rather abstract idea of the dance and to represent it above all as an action that *derives* from ordinary, useful action, but *breaks away* from it, and finally *opposes* it.

But this very general formulation (and this is why I have adopted it today) covers far more than the dance in the strict sense. All action which does not tend toward utility and which on the other hand can be trained, perfected, developed, may be subsumed under this simplified notion of the dance, and consequently, *all the arts can be considered as particular examples of this general idea*, since by definition all the arts imply an element of action, the *action which produces*, or else manifests, the *work*.

A *poem*, for example, is *action*, because a poem exists only at the moment of being spoken, then it is *in actu*. This act, like the dance, has no other purpose than to create a state of mind; it imposes its own laws; it, too, creates a time and a measurement of time which are appropriate and essential to it: we cannot distinguish it from its form of time. To recite poetry is to enter into a verbal dance.

Or consider a virtuoso at work, a violinist, a pianist. Just watch his hands. Stop your ears if you dare. But concentrate on the hands. Watch them act, racing over the narrow stage that is the keyboard. Are they not dancers who have also been subjected for years to a severe discipline, to endless exercises?

Remember that you can hear nothing. You merely see the hands come and go, stop for a moment, cross, play leapfrog; sometimes one waits, while the five fingers of the other seem to be trying out their paces at the other end of the racecourse of ivory and ebony. You begin to surmise that all this follows certain laws, that the whole ballet is regulated, determined. . . .

Let us note in passing that if you hear nothing and are unfamiliar with the music being played, you have no way of knowing what point in his piece the performer has come to. *What you see* gives you *no indication* of the pianist's progress; yet you are quite certain that the action in which he is engaged is at every moment subject to some rather complex system. . . .

With a little more attention you would discover that this system puts certain restrictions on the freedom of movement of these active hands as they fly over the keyboard. Whatever they do, they seem to have undertaken to respect some sort of continuous order. Cadence, measure, rhythm make themselves felt. I do not wish to enter into these questions which, it seems to me, though familiar and without difficulty in practice, have hitherto lacked any satisfactory theory; but then that is true of all questions in which time is directly involved. We are brought back to the remarks of St. Augustine.

But it is easy to note that all automatic movements corresponding to a state of being, and not to a prefigured localized aim, take on a periodic character; this is true of the walker; of the absent-minded fellow who swings his foot or drums on a windowpane; of the thinker who strokes his chin, etc.

If you will bear with me for a few minutes more, we shall carry our thought a little further: a little further beyond the customary, immediate idea of the dance.

I was just saying that all the arts are extremely varied forms of action and may be analyzed in terms of action. Consider an artist at work, eliminate the brief intervals when he sets it aside; watch him act, stop still, and briskly start in again.

Assume that he is so well trained, so sure of his technique that while you are observing him he is a pure executant whose successive operations tend to take place in commensurable lapses of time, that is to say, with a certain *rhythm*. Then you will be able to conceive that the execution of a work of art, of a work of painting or sculpture, is itself a work of art and that its material object, the product of the artist's fingers, is only a pretext, a stage "prop" or, as it were, the subject of the ballet.

Perhaps this view seems bold to you. But remember that for many great artists a work is never finished; perhaps what they regard as a desire for perfection is simply a form of the inner life I have been speaking of, which consists entirely of energy and sensibility in a reciprocal and, one might say, reversible exchange.

Or think, on the other hand, of those edifices that the ancients built, to the rhythm of the flute commanding the movements of the files of laborers and masons.

I might have told you the curious story related in the *Journal* of the Goncourt brothers, about the Japanese painter who, on a visit to Paris, was asked by them to execute a few works in the presence of a little gathering of art lovers.

But it is high time to conclude this dance of ideas round the living dance.

I wanted to show you how this art, far from being futile amusement, far from being a specialty confined to putting on a show now and then for the amusement of the eyes that contemplate it or the bodies that take part in it, is quite simply *a poetry that encompasses the action of living creatures in its entirety:* it isolates and develops, distinguishes and deploys the essential characteristics of this action, and makes the dancer's body into an object whose transformations and successive aspects, whose striving to attain the limits that each instant sets upon the powers of being, inevitably remind us of the task the poet imposes on his mind, the difficulties he sets before it, the metamorphoses he obtains from it, the flights he expects of it—flights which remove him, sometimes too far, from the ground, from reason, from the average notion of logic and common sense.

What is a metaphor if not a kind of pirouette performed by an idea, enabling us to assemble its diverse names or images? And what are all the figures we employ, all those instruments, such as rhyme, inversion, antithesis, if not an exercise of all the possibilities of language, which removes us from the practical world and shapes, for us too, a private universe, a privileged abode of the intellectual dance?

The Dynamic Image: Some Philosophical Reflections on Dance

by Susanne Langer

Once upon a time a student, paging through a college catalogue, asked me in evident bewilderment: "What is 'philosophy of art'? How in the world can art be philosophical?"

Art is not philosophical at all; philosophy and art are two different things. But there is nothing one cannot philosophize about—that is, there is nothing that does not offer some philosophical problems. Art,

Source: From *Problems of Art* (New York: Scribner's, 1957).

in particular, presents hosts of them. Artists do not generally moot such matters explicitly, though they often have fairly good working notions of a philosophical sort—notions that only have to be put into the right words to answer our questions, or at least to move them along toward their answers.

A philosophical question is always a demand for the *meaning* of what we are saying. This makes it different from a scientific question, which is a question of fact; in a question of fact, we take for granted that we know what we mean—that is, what we are talking about. If one asks: "How far from here is the sun?" the answer is a statement of fact, "About ninety million miles." We assume that we know what we mean by "the sun" and by "miles" and "being so-and-so far from here." Even if the answer is wrong—if it fails to state a fact, as it would if you answered "twenty thousand miles"—we still know what we are talking about. We take some measurements and find out which answer is true. But suppose one asks: "What is space?" "What is meant by 'here'?" "What is meant by 'the distance' from here to somewhere else?" The answer is not found by taking measurements or by making experiments or in any way discovering facts. The answer can only be found by thinking—reflecting on what we mean. This is sometimes simple; we analyze our meanings and define each word. But more often we find that we have no clear concepts at all, and the fuzzy ones we have conflict with each other so that as soon as we analyze them, i.e., make them clear, we find them contradictory, senseless, or fantastic. Then logical analysis does not help us; what we need then is the more difficult, but also more interesting part of philosophy, the part that can not be taught by any rule—logical construction. We have to figure out a meaning for our statements, a way to think about the things that interest us. Science is not possible unless we can attach some meaning to "distance" and "point" and "space" and "velocity," and other such familiar but really quite slippery words. To establish those fundamental meanings is philosophical work; and the philosophy of modern science is one of the most brilliant intellectual works of our time.

The philosophy of art is not so well developed, but it is full of life and ferment just now. Both professional philosophers and intellectually gifted artists are asking questions about the meaning of "art," of "expression," of "artistic truth," "form," "reality," and dozens of other words that they hear and use, but find—to their surprise—they cannot define, because when they analyze what they mean it is not anything coherent and tenable.

The construction of a coherent theory—a set of connected ideas about some whole subject—begins with the solution of a central problem; that is, with the establishing of a key concept. There is no way of knowing, by any general rule, what constitutes a central problem; it is not always the most general or the most fundamental one you can raise. But the best sign that you have broached a central philosophical issue is that in solving it you raise new interesting questions. The concept you construct has *implications*, and by implication builds up further ideas, that illuminate other concepts of the whole subject, to answer other questions, sometimes before you even ask them. A key concept solves more problems than it was designed for.

In philosophy of art, one of the most interesting problems—one that proves to be really central—is the meaning of that much-used word, "creation." Why do we say an artist creates a work? He does not create oil pigments or canvas, or the structure of tonal vibrations, or words of a language if he is a poet, or, in the case of a dancer, his body and its mobility. He finds all these things and uses them, as a cook uses eggs and flour and so forth to make a cake, or a manufacturer uses wool to make thread, and thread to make socks. It is only in a mood of humor or extravagance that we speak of the cake Mother "created." But when it comes to works of art, we earnestly call them creations. This raises the philosophical question: What do we mean by that word? What is created?

If you pursue this issue, it grows into a complex of closely related questions: what is created in art, what for, and how? The answers involve just about all the key concepts for a coherent philosophy of art: such concepts as *apparition*, or the image, *expressiveness*, *feeling*, *motif*, *transformation*. There are others, but they are all interrelated.

It is impossible to talk, in one lecture, about all the arts, and not end with a confusion of principles and illustrations. Since we are particularly concerned, just now, with the dance, let us narrow our discussion and center it about this art. Our first question, then, becomes: What do dancers create?

Obviously, a dance. As I pointed out before, they do not create the materials of the dance—neither their own bodies, nor the cloth that drapes them, nor the floor, nor any of the ambient space, light, musical tone, the forces of gravity, nor any other physical provisions; all these things they *use*, to create something over and above what is physically there: the dance.

What, then, is the dance?

The dance is an appearance; if you like, an apparition. It springs from what the dancers do, yet it is something else. In watching a dance, you do not see what is physically before you—people running around or twisting their bodies; what you see is a display of interacting forces, by which the dance seems to be lifted, driven, drawn, closed, or attenuated, whether it be solo or choric, whirling like the end of a dervish dance, or slow, centered, and single in its motion. One human body may put the whole play of mysterious powers before you. But these powers, these forces that seem to operate in the dance, are not the physical forces of the dancer's muscles, which actually cause the movements taking place. The forces we seem to perceive most directly and convincingly are created for our perception; and they exist only for it.

Anything that exists only for perception, and plays no ordinary, passive part in nature as common objects do, is a virtual entity. It is not unreal; where it confronts you, you really perceive it, you don't dream or imagine that you do. The image in a mirror is a virtual image. A rainbow is a virtual object. It seems to stand on the earth or in the clouds, but it really "stands" nowhere; it is only visible, not tangible. Yet it is a real rainbow, produced by moisture and light for any normal eye looking at it from the right place. We don't just dream that we see it. If, however, we believe it to have the ordinary properties of a physical thing, we are mistaken; it is an appearance, a virtual object, a sun-created image.

What dancers create is a dance; and a dance is an apparition of active powers, *a dynamic image*. Everything a dancer actually does serves to create what we really see; but what we really see is a virtual entity. The physical realities are given: place, gravity, body, muscular strength, muscular control, and secondary assets such as light, sound, or things (usable objects, so-called "properties"). All these are actual. But in the dance, they disappear; the more perfect the dance, the less we see its actualities. What we see, hear, and feel are the virtual realities, the moving forces of the dance, and apparent centers of power and their emanations, their conflicts and resolutions, lift and decline, their rhythmic life. These are the elements of the created apparition, and are themselves not physically given, but artistically created.

Here we have, then, the answer to our first question: what do dancers create? The dynamic image, which is the dance.

This answer leads naturally to the second question: for what is this image created?

Again, there is an obvious answer: for our enjoyment. But what makes us enjoy it as intensely as we do? We do not enjoy every virtual image, just because it is one. A mirage in the desert is intriguing chiefly because it is rare. A mirror image, being common, is not an object of wonder, and in itself, just as an image, does not thrill us. But the dynamic image created in dancing has a different character. It is more than a perceivable entity; this apparition, given to the eye, or to the ear and eye, and through them to our whole responsive sensibility, strikes us as something charged with feeling. Yet this feeling is not necessarily what any or all of the dancers feel. It belongs to the dance itself. A dance, like any other work of art, is a perceptible form that expresses the nature of human feeling—the rhythms and connections, crises and breaks, the complexity and richness of what is sometimes called man's "inner life," the stream of direct experience, life as it feels to the living. Dancing is not a symptom of how the dancer happens to feel; for the dancer's own feelings could not be prescribed or predicted and exhibited upon request. Our own feelings simply occur, and most people do not care to have us express them by sighs or squeals or gesticulation. If that were what dancers really did, there would not be many balletomaniacs to watch them.

What is expressed in a dance is an idea; an idea of the way feelings, emotions, and all other subjective experiences come and go—their rise and growth, their intricate synthesis that gives our inner life unity and personal identity. What we call a person's "inner life" is the inside story of his own history; the way living in the world feels to him. This kind of experience is usually but vaguely known, because most of its components are nameless, and no matter how keen our experience may be, it is hard to form an idea of anything that has no name. It has no handle for the mind. This has led many learned people to believe that feeling is a formless affair, that it has causes which may be determined, and effects that have to be dealt with, but that in itself it is irrational—a disturbance in the organism, with no structure of its own.

Yet subjective existence has a structure; it is not only met from moment to moment, but can be conceptually known, reflected on, imagined and symbolically expressed in detail and to a great depth. Only it is not our usual medium, discourse—communication by language—that serves to express what we know of the life of feeling. There are logical reasons why language fails to meet this purpose, reasons I will not try to explain now. The important fact is that what language does not readily do—present the nature and patterns of sensitive and emotional life—is done by works of art. Such works are expressive forms, and what they express is the nature of human feeling.

So we have played our second gambit, answering the second question: What is the work of art for—the dance, the virtual dynamic image? To express its creator's ideas of immediate, felt, emotive life. To set forth directly what feeling is like. A work of art is a composition of tensions and resolutions, balance and unbalance, rhythmic coherence, a precarious yet continuous unity. Life is a natural process of such tensions, balances, rhythms; it is these that we feel, in quietness or emotion, as the pulse of our own living. In the work of art they are expressed, symbolically shown, each aspect of feeling developed as one develops an idea, fitted together for clearest presentation. A dance is not a symptom of a dancer's feeling, but an expression of its composer's knowledge of many feelings.

The third problem on the docket—how is a dance created?—is so great that one has to break it down into several questions. Some of these are practical questions of technique—how to produce this or that effect. They concern many of you but not me, except in so far as solutions of artistic problems always intrigue me. The philosophical question that I would peel out of its many wrappings is: What does it mean to express one's idea of some inward or "subjective" process?

It means to make an outward image of this inward process, for oneself and others to see; that is, to give the subjective events an objective symbol. Every work of art is such an image, whether it be a dance, a statue, a picture, a piece of music, or a work of poetry. It is an outward showing of inward nature, an objective presentation of subjective reality; and the reason that it can symbolize things of the inner life is that it has the same kinds of relations and elements. This is not true of the material structure; the physical materials of a dance do not have any direct similarity to the structure of emotive life; it is the created image that has elements and patterns like the life of feeling. But this image, though it is a created apparition, a pure appearance, is objective; it seems to be charged with feeling because its form expresses the very nature of feeling. Therefore, it is an *objectification* of subjective life, and so is every other work of art.

If works of art are all alike in this fundamental respect, why have we several great domains of art, such as painting and music, poetry and dance? Something makes them so distinct from each other that people with superb talent for one may have none for another. A sensible person would not go to Picasso to learn dancing or to Hindemith to be taught painting. How does dancing, for instance, differ from music or architecture or drama? It has relations with all of them. Yet it is none of them.

What makes the distinction among the several great orders of art is another of those problems that arise in their turn, uninvited, once you start from a central question; and the fact that the question is *what is created* leads from one issue to another in this natural and systematic way makes me think it really is central. The distinction between dancing and all of the other great arts—and of those from each other—lies in the stuff of which the virtual image, the expressive form, is made. We cannot go into any discussion of other kinds, but only reflect a little further on our original query: What do dancers create? What is a dance?

As I said before (so long before that you have probably forgotten), what we see when we watch a dance is a display of interacting forces; not physical forces, like the weight that tips a scale or the push that topples a column of books, but purely apparent forces that seem to move the dance itself. Two people in a *pas de deux* seem to magnetize each other; a group appears to be animated by one single spirit, one Power. The stuff of the dance, the apparition itself, consists of such non-physical forces, drawing and driving, holding and shaping its life. The actual, physical forces that underlie it disappear. As soon as the beholder sees gymnastics and arrangements, the work of art breaks, the creation fails.

As painting is made purely of spatial volumes—not actual space-filling things but virtual volumes, created solely for the eye—and music is made of passage, movements of time, created by tone—so dance creates a world of powers, made visible by the unbroken fabric of gesture. That is what makes dance a different art from all the others. But as Space, Events, Time, and Powers are all interrelated in reality, so all the arts are linked by intricate relations, different among different ones. That is a big subject.

Another problem which naturally presents itself here is the meaning of *dance gesture;* but we shall have to skip it. We have had enough pursuit of meanings, and I know from experience that if you don't make an end of it, there is no end. But in dropping the curtain on this peepshow of philosophy, I would like to call your attention to one of those unexpected explanations of puzzling facts that sometimes arise from philosophical reflection.

Curt Sachs, who is an eminent historian of music and dance, remarks in his *World History of Dance* that, strange as it may seem, the evolution of the dance as a high art belongs to pre-history. At the dawn of civilization, dance had already reached a degree of perfection that no other art of science could match. Societies limited to savage living, primitive sculpture, primitive architecture, and as yet no poetry, quite commonly present the astonished ethnologist with a highly developed tradition of difficult, beautiful dancing. Their music apart from the dance is nothing at all; in the dance it is elaborate. Their worship is dance. They are tribes of dancers.

If you think of the dance as an apparition of interactive Powers, this strange fact loses its strangeness. Every art image is a purified and simplified aspect of the outer world, composed by the laws of the inner world to express its nature. As one objective aspect of the world after another comes to people's notice, the arts arise. Each makes its own image of outward reality to objectify inward reality, subjective life, feeling.

Primitive men live in a world of demonic Powers. Subhuman or superhuman, gods or spooks or impersonal magic forces, good or bad luck that dwells in things like an electric charge, are the most impressive realities of the savage's world. The drive to artistic creation, which seems to be deeply primitive in all human beings, first begets its forms in the image of these all-surrounding Powers. The magic circle around the altar or the totem pole, the holy space inside the Kiwa or the temple, is the natural dance floor. There is nothing unreasonable about that. In a world perceived as a realm of mystic Powers, the first created image is the dynamic image; the first objectification of human nature, the first true art, is Dance.

The World as Ballet

by Arthur Symons

The abstract thinker, to whom the question of practical morality is indifferent, has always loved dancing, as naturally as the moralist has hated it. The Puritan, from his own point of view, is always right, though it suits us, often enough, for wider reasons, to deny his logic. The dance is life, animal life, having its own way passionately. Part of that natural madness which men were once wise enough to include in religion, it began with the worship of the disturbing deities, the gods of ecstasy, for whom wantonness, and wine, and all things in which energy passes into an ideal excess, were sacred. It was cast out of religion when religion cast out nature: for, like nature itself, it is a thing of evil to those who renounce instincts. From the first it has mimed the instincts. It can render birth and death, and it is always going over and over the eternal pantomime of love; it can be all the passions, and all the languors; but it idealises these mere acts, gracious or brutal, into more than a picture; for it is more than a beautiful reflection, it has in it life itself, as it shadows life; and it is farther from life than a picture.

Source: From *Studies in Seven Arts* (New York: Dutton, 1907).

Humanity, youth, beauty, playing the part of itself, and consciously, in a travesty, more natural than nature, more artificial than art: but we lose ourselves in the boundless bewilderments of its contradictions.

The dance, then, is art because it is doubly nature: and if nature, as we are told, is sinful, it is doubly sinful. A waltz, in a drawing-room, takes us suddenly out of all that convention, away from those guardians of our order who sit around the walls, approvingly, unconsciously; in its winding motion it raises an invisible wall about us, shutting us off from the whole world, in with ourselves; in its fatal rhythm, never either beginning or ending, slow, insinuating, gathering impetus which must be held back, which must rise into the blood, it tells us that life flows even as that, so passionately and so easily and so inevitably; and it is possession and abandonment, the very pattern and symbol of earthly love. Here is nature (to be renounced, to be at least restrained) hurried violently, deliberately, to boiling point. And now look at the dance, on the stage, a mere spectator. Here are all these young bodies, made more alluring by an artificial heightening of whites and reds on the face, displaying, employing, all their natural beauty, themselves full of the sense of joy in motion, or affecting that enjoyment, offered to our eyes like a bouquet of flowers, a bouquet of living flowers, which have all the glitter of artificial ones. As they dance, under the changing lights, so human, so remote, so desirable, so evasive, coming and going to the sound of a thin, heady music which marks the rhythm of their movements like a kind of clinging drapery, they seem to sum up in themselves the appeal of everything in the world that is passing, and coloured, and to be enjoyed; everything that bids us take no thought for the morrow, and dissolve the will into slumber, and give way luxuriously to the delightful present.

How fitly then, in its very essence, does the art of dancing symbolise life; with so faithful a rendering of its actual instincts! And to the abstract thinker, as to the artist, all this really primitive feeling, all this acceptance of the instincts which it idealises, and out of which it makes its own beauty, is precisely what gives dancing its preeminence among the more than imitative arts. The artist, it is indeed true, is never quite satisfied with his statue which remains cold, does not come to life. In every art men are pressing forward, more and more eagerly, farther and farther beyond the limits of their art, in the desire to do the impossible: to create life. Realising all humanity to be but a masque of shadows, and this solid world an impromptu stage as temporary as they, it is with a pathetic desire of some last illusion, which shall deceive even ourselves, that we are consumed with this hunger to create, to make something for ourselves, of at least the same shadowy reality as that about us. The art of the ballet awaits us, with its shadowy and real life, its power of letting humanity drift into a rhythm so much of its own, and with ornament so much more generous than its wont.

And something in the particular elegance of the dance, the scenery; the avoidance of emphasis, the evasive, winding turn of things; and, above all, the intellectual as well as sensuous appeal of a living symbol, which can but reach the brain through the eyes, in the visual, concrete, imaginative way; has seemed to make the ballet concentrate in itself a good deal of the modern ideal in matters of artistic expression. Nothing is stated, there is no intrusion of words used for the irrelevant purpose of describing; a world rises before one, the picture lasts only long enough to have been there: and the dancer, with her gesture, all pure symbol, evokes, from her mere beautiful motion, idea, sensation, all that one need ever know of event. There, before you, she exists, in harmonious life; and her rhythm reveals to you the soul of her imagined being.

PART III

In Search of Lost Time: A Short History of Theatrical Dance

"Vainest endeavor, to try to document dance, the most ephemeral of the arts. Suppose that you find the bricks and boards, the levers and pulleys of a theatre intact, and that your lunatic friend who loves the archives helps locate sources from which the scenic decoration, musical orchestration and plot evolution of a famous, forgotten ballet could be reconstructed. Suppose further that you were extremely fortunate in your friend and his treasure hunt uncovered even a precise, pre-Laban notation that enabled one to teach each pas *to contemporary dancers. Still . . . Reason . . . would tell you that the essential movement would be missing. The trappings would be there, but you would not see the "dance urge" Heine saw watching Carlotta Grisi, or recognize with Kleist dance mannerism as a dislocation of the soul from the central still point of movement to the trajectory . . . So you leave the past buried and go back to the new theatre to watch the business at hand, ballet as it is danced today—which is the living tissue, not the death mask of ballet yesterday. You leave reluctantly; besides the ballet's immediate sensual beauty, and its brilliance in time and space as a medium of silent ideas, an urgent part of the reason you had worshipped it before all other arts was the simple wonder of seeing a human body moving in the same step for the same reason as did its predecessors a century or more ago."*

—George Jackson,
"Notes Towards an Anti-History of Ballet in Vienna," *Ballet Review*, 1967.

A Short History of Theatrical Dance

Ballet's relation to history is in a certain sense schizoid. In many ways ballet is the most immediate of the arts, the one that lives most fully in the present—difficult to record, impossible to capture. And yet ballet cannot be separated from its past; it is the art that relies most heavily upon its own tradition. The past is difficult to revive in ballet, but it is impossible to avoid.

The seven essays included in this section outline ballet's past. They provide a convenient survey of the history of theatrical dance, beginning with the Renaissance courts of Europe and ending with the experiments in New York lofts.

From the Courts to the Theaters

by Cyril W. Beaumont

The precise origin of ballet cannot be stated with certainty, but it definitely derives from the several forms of composite entertainment variously styled mummings, masquerades, or interludes, which were of frequent occurrence during the 14th and 15th centuries. The mumming was given by persons disguised and masked who danced without mingling with the spectators; sometimes the dancers appeared suddenly in the midst of an assembly, sometimes they made a more ceremonious entrance on foot or in an allegorical car, preceded by torch-bearers and musicians. The masquerade consisted of a number of gaily-decorated cars filled with actors in costume; the procession filed past the personage it was desired to honour and, as each car stopped before him, the chief actor declaimed a laudatory poem or address. The interlude was a little scene of dancing, singing, and mechanical effects, given between the acts of a play or during a banquet.

Source: From *A Short History of Ballet* (London: Beaumont, 1933).

An excellent example of the interlude, which for all practical purposes may be regarded as the prototype of ballet, was the splendid entertainment given in 1489 by Bergonzio di Botta, of Tortona, on the occasion of the marriage of Galeazzo, Duke of Milan, with Isabella of Aragon. It took the form of a great feast at which each dish was presented with an appropriate dance. This banquet-ballet, most ingeniously contrived and full of graceful allusion, became famous throughout Europe, so that every petty Court aspired to give similar entertainments.

The new fashion found a warm patron in the person of Catherine de Medici (1519–1589), who introduced it to the Court of France, as a diversion for her sons, François II, Charles IX, and Henri III, while she retained a firm grasp of the government. One of the most important spectacles produced at her command was the *Ballet Comique de la Reine* (1581), which celebrated the betrothal of the Duc de Joyeuse and Marguerite de Lorraine. A full account was issued in a costly volume dated 1582, which, incidentally, is regarded as the first printed record of a ballet.

The author was a famous violinist, Baldasarino da Belgiojoso (later frenchified to Balthasar de Beaujoyeulx), who came to France in 1555. He was presented to the Queen who appointed him her *Valet de Chambre*, and later employed him in the capacity of unofficial organiser of Court festivals.

In his preface to the printed version of this ballet, Beaujoyeulx defines ballet as "a geometrical mixture of many persons dancing together to the harmony of several instruments." The designation "*ballet comique*" means "comedy-ballet," and the prime importance of Beaujoyeulx's contribution is that he succeeded in dramatising the ballet, for dancing, music, singing, declamation, and procession are dexterously combined for the expression of the theme, which was the tale of Circe. Some idea of the magnificence of this entertainment may be gained from the fact that it lasted from "ten o'clock in the evening until three and a half hours after midnight, nor did the length of it weary or displease the audience."

In 1588 appeared the first French book devoted to the practice of dancing, the *Orchésographie* of Thoinot Arbeau. This work describes in great detail the courtly dances then in vogue, the Pavane, Gaillarde, Volte, Courante, Allemande, Gavotte, Morisque, and nineteen forms of the Branle.

In England the ballet found expression in masques. Henry VIII (1509–1547) had his disguisings and revels, which became more elaborate during the reign of Elizabeth. But it was not until the accession of James I that the full influence of the *Ballet Comique* was seen, and the masque, with Ben Jonson, Campion, Samuel Daniel, and others as authors, Inigo Jones as designer of scenery and costumes, Alfonso Ferrabosco as composer, and Thomas Giles and Hieronimius Herne as *maîtres de ballet*, achieved full splendour. Among the entertainments given may be mentioned: *The Twelve Goddesses* (Daniel, 1604), *The Masque of Blackness* (Jonson, 1605), and *The Masque of Beauty* (Jonson, 1608). The masque disappeared towards the 17th century.

Thus ballet may be said to have originated in Italy, to have been developed in France to inspire the English masques, which in turn influenced the later French opera-ballets which were the foundation of modern classical ballet.

In France, during the reign of Henri IV (1589–1610), ballet became informal and less a poetic conception. The ballets consisted of *entrées* (entries) at different intervals of groups of masked persons in costume who, having executed their dance, made place for their successors. When all the groups had danced, the whole of the dancers took part in a grand ballet. After this the dancers raised their masks and a ball began.

With the accession of Louis XIII (1610–1643) the ballets consisted likewise of a number of *entrées* having more or less relation to a somewhat vague theme. "Ballets," says a contemporary, "are plays in dumb-show, and should be divided into acts and scenes. Declamations divide the acts, and the dancers' *entrées* correspond to the number of the scenes." The number of acts in a ballet varied from two to five, while the usual number of *entrées* was thirty.

The *entrée* corresponds to what would now be termed a *divertissement*. For instance, the *Ballet de Madame Sœur de Roi* (1613) deals with the three regions of the air. In the first the *entrées* are Snow, Hail, Ice, Fog, and Dew; in the second, Comet, Thunder, and Lightning; in the third, Clouds, Shotting Star, and Rain. Again, in the *Ballet du Monde Renversé* (1625) there are eleven *entrées:* a gentleman walking behind his lackey, a fool teaching philosophy, a sick man prescribing for his doctor, a beggar giving alms to a rich man, and so forth.

But, whatever the nature of the ballet, and whether it was explained by words recited or sung, the sole purpose of the different *entrées* was to provide a suitable excuse for the entry of richly-dressed dancers in similar costumes, and wearing black or gold masks and diadems with plumes or tinselled aigrettes, who danced a number of figures generally containing some complimentary allusion. This particular set of dances was the recognised conclusion to every ballet and was known as the *Grand Ballet*. It was sometimes danced by ladies, sometimes by noblemen, but in the ballets in which the king elected to dance, a proceeding by no means rare, no woman of whatever rank took part.

The majority of the ballets given during the reign of the melancholy Louis XIII were characterised by a departure from good taste, and a marked tendency towards the fantastic and the grotesque, doubtless a natural reaction on the part of his courtiers. Two typical ballets of this period are *Les Fées de la Forêt de Saint-Germain* (1625) and *La Douairière de Billebahaut* (1626).

Under Louis XIV (1643–1715), the ballet became dignified and artistic. In 1651, while still a boy of thirteen, the king appeared in a ballet called *Cassandre*, devised by Benserade. This king made many appearances as a dancer, the last being in the ballet *Flore* (1669). Louis XIV, in accordance with his conception of kingship, represented exalted characters only, such as Apollo, Neptune, and Jupiter. Ballet made great progress during his reign due to his refined taste and the fact that he invited the collaboration of the best talents in his realm. Bocan, Beauchamps, and Pécourt in turn arranged his dances, Lully composed the music, and Molière wrote many of the comedy-ballets. Berain designed many of the costumes and Vigarani was responsible for the stage effects. Louis XIV established the Académie Royale de Danse (1661) and the Académie Royale de Musique (1669). In 1672 a school of dancing was added to the latter, and this was the origin of the state ballet.

The ballet still continued to be a spectacle composed of dancing, music, and singing, but now it passed from restricted performance at Court to the public theatre. The themes were inspired by Greek and Roman mythology. Actually the ballets were operas with opportunities for dancing, the dancing being subservient to the singing. The personnel consisted of men alone, the women's roles being taken by youths of feminine build, whose faces were concealed by masks, at this time a fixed part of the dancer's costume.

In May, 1681, a ballet was given at St. Germain, entitled *Le Triomphe de L'Amour*, in which the composer, Lully, introduced female dancers for the first time. These were drawn from the Court ladies. After Easter the ballet was given publicly at Paris, when the Académie de Musique furnished four *danseuses* of whom Mlle. Lafontaine was the leader, and who consequently became the first *première danseuse*.

In 1708 the Duchesse de Maine devised a novelty for one of the entertainments she was accustomed to give in the private theatre of her residence at Sceaux. She commissioned the composer, Mouret, to write a symphony illustrative of the fourth act of Corneille's *Horace*, where Horace kills Camilla. The music was played and the action mimed by two dancers, Mlle. Prévost and M. Ballon, who, it is said, gave such an excellent performance that the spectators were moved to tears.

The recognised dress for male dancers in the noble or serious style was, broadly considered, the dress of an officer of Ancient Rome seen through 17th century eyes. The ladies wore the tight bodice and long, full skirt. The costumes worn by character dancers displayed a crude symbolism in both cut and decoration.

The tight coats with their padded skirts and close-fitting bodices rendered breathing difficult, and the steps were mainly *terre à terre*. The choreography proceeded on horizontal lines, particular attention being paid to the pattern of the track described by the dancer during his movements. Already the development of ballet had given rise to a definite technique, for R. A. Feuillet, in his *Chorégraphie ou l'Art de De'crire la Danse* (1701), describes a number of steps.

Among the principal dancers of this reign were André Lorin, inventor of a system of dance notation; Pierre Beauchamps, who first laid down the five positions of the feet—he was also an excellent choreographer and dancing-master to the king; Louis Pécourt (1655–1729), the best performer of his day; Ballon (f. a.[1] 1695), noted for his lightness; Blondi, and Lestang. Of *danseuses* there were Marie Subligny (1666–1736?) who succeeded Mlle. Lafontaine (1665?–1738), and Françoise Prévost (1680–1741), who succeeded Mlle. Subligny. The most favoured dances were the Bourée, Courante, Chaconne, Gigue, Menuet, Sarabande, Passepied, and Passacaille. The Menuet, however, did not achieve full favour until the succeeding reign.

Under Louis XV (1715–1774), the epoch of Boucher, Watteau, and Fragonard, the grandiose manner of King Sun was replaced by a refined artificiality. The ballet grew still more elegant and many technical advances were made. In 1726 the *danseuse* Marie Camargo (1710–1770) made her *début*. She introduced the *entrechat quatre*[2] (1730), several types of *jeté*, and the *pas de basque*. To obtain the necessary freedom for the *entrechat* she adopted a heelless shoe and caused her dress to be shortened by several inches, permitting the calf to be seen. This blow to tradition caused an immense scandal, but, since it permitted the execution of many new and pleasing steps, it was accepted. In 1750, another *danseuse*, Louise Lany (1733–1777), achieved the *entrechat six*.

[1] F. a.—first appeared.

[2] It must be stated that some form of *entrechat* was known long before Camargo's time, but there are good grounds for believing that she was the first *danseuse* to execute it.

The same reign saw the execution of the *gargouillade* by Marie Lyonnois (f. a. 1746), a dancer noted for her ability to pirouette.

Early in the 18th century French dancers began to appear on stages abroad. In 1733, Marie Sallé (1707–1756), the rival of Camargo, unable to carry out at the Opera her desired reforms in the dancer's dress, crossed to London[3] and appeared at Covent Garden as Galatea in a ballet of her own composition entitled *Pygmalion*, produced on the 14th February, 1734. On this occasion, according to a contemporary report in the *Mercure de France*, she appeared "without pannier, skirt, or bodice, and with her hair down; she did not wear a single ornament on her head. Apart from her corset and petticoat, she wore only a simple dress of muslin draped about her in the manner of a Greek statue." This novelty added still more to Sallé's graceful and expressive dancing, and created a furore.

In 1760 further pleas for reform were set forth in a remarkable work entitled *Lettres sur la Danse et les Ballets*, by Jean Georges Noverre (1727–1810), a choreographer and pupil of Dupré, who, like Sallé, had to go abroad to secure recognition of his genius and opportunity to put his plans into practice. He produced ballets in most of the principal European capitals with considerable success.

Noverre's *Letters*, considered as an exposition of the theories and laws governing ballet and dance representation, have no equal in the whole of the literature devoted to the art, and no book has exerted so incalculable an influence for good on the manner of production of ballets and dances. Noverre was not only a most talented choreographer, but also a person possessed of an immense knowledge of his subject, and an unusual store of common sense and intelligence which he applied to the reform of every branch of his profession.

What were his ideals? "To break hideous masks, to burn ridiculous perukes, to suppress clumsy panniers, to do away with still more inconvenient hip-pads, to substitute taste for routine, to indicate a dress more noble, more accurate, and more picturesque, to demand action and expression in dancing, to demonstrate the immense distance which lies between mechanical technique and the genius which places dancing beside the imitative arts." Those are his own words.

Noverre reformed stage costume, restored and developed the art of mime, decreed that all ballets must possess a good plot, and insisted that a dance must be designed not as a mere *divertissement*, but as a means of expressing or assisting the development of the theme.

[3] In actual fact, Sallé made her London *début* in 1725, and reappeared in 1730; but in neither case as a reformer of stage costume.

He was the creator of the *ballet d'action* which had been foreshadowed in the experiment of the Duchesse de Maine, a ballet in which the theme was expressed entirely by means of dancing and mime, without the aid of a sung or spoken explanation. It was at Stuttgart, as *maître de ballet* to the Duke of Wurtemburg, that, in conjunction with the dancers Gaetano Vestris and Dauberval, he first worked out his ideas. They were developed by Maximilien and Pierre Gardel, and Dauberval.

In 1766 Anne Heinel, a dancer at the Stuttgart Theatre, invented the *pirouette à la seconde*. The mask was abolished in 1773. This was the result of an incident during the presentation at the Paris Opera of Rameau's opera, *Castor et Pollux*, in 1772. The role of Apollo was taken by Gaetano Vestris, who appeared in the customary wig and mask. One night, however, he was unable to dance and the part was allotted to M. Gardel, who consented to appear provided that he was permitted to discard the wig and mask. The public were pleased and the mask disappeared. It is of interest to note that G. Vestris and M. Gardel are credited with the invention of the *rond de jambe*.

The costumes of the dancers of Louis XV differed to some extent from those of the previous reign. The men who executed the serious dance wore the plumed helmet and cuirass-shaped body as before, but the skirt was shorter, oval, of great width, and so hooped that it projected to a considerable distance beyond the hip. The dress of the *danseuses* consisted of the tight-fitting bodice and a hooped and paniered skirt, adorned with ruchings of various materials, generally lace or feathers. The perukes and costumes were in general more exaggerated than those of the previous reign; on the other hand, the decoration of the costumes, in which allegory and symbolism played their accustomed parts, was more refined and subdued.

The principal dancers during the reign of Louis XV were Louis Dupré (1697–1774), renowned for the nobility and grace of his movements; David Dumoulin; Dupré's pupil, Gaetano Vestris (1729–1808), a fine mime and unsurpassed for the expressiveness and elegance of his dancing; Jean Lany (1718–1786); Charles Le Picq; Dauberval (1742–1806); Maximilien Gardel (1741–1787); and Auguste Vestris (1760–1842), one of the greatest of male dancers, who held the post of *premier danseur* at the Opera for thirty-six years. The last-named was possessed of a sensitive ear for music, an excellent technique, a prodigious elevation, a particular ability to execute *entrechats* and *pirouettes*, and, what is rare indeed, he could adapt his movements and expression to suit any mood or style; lastly, there was never any sense of difficulty or stress in his dancing so that he seemed equally at home on the ground or in the air.

The chief *danseuses* were Marie Sallé (f. a. London, 1725, Paris, 1727); Marie Camargo (f. a. 1726), noted for the brilliancy of her execution; Marie Lyonnois; Marie Allard (1742–1802), celebrated both for her acting and for the charm and gaiety of her dancing; Anne Heinel (1753–1808); Marguerite Peslin (f. a. 1761); and Madeleine Guimard (1743–1816), famous for the precision of her dancing and for her piquant mime.

For the next fifteen years (1774–1789), that is, from the accession of Louis XVI to the outbreak of the French Revolution, there was a remarkable series of interesting ballets produced, for instance: *Médée et Jason* (1775), *Les Caprices de Galathée* (1776), *Les Horaces* (1776)—all by Noverre; *La Chercheuse d'Esprit* (M. Gardel, 1777); *La Fête Chinoise* (1778), *Les Petits Riens* (1778)—both by Noverre; *Ninette à la Cour* (M. Gardel, 1778); *Annette et Lubin* (1778), *La Toilette de Venus* (1779)—both by Noverre; *Mirza* (M. Gardel, 1779); *Medée* (Noverre, 1780); *La Rosière* (1784), *Le Deserteur* (1784), *Le Premier Navigateur* (1785), and *Le Coq du Village* (1787)—all by M. Gardel.

Guimard dominates the scene throughout this epoch, her greatest successes being achieved in *La Chercheuse d'Esprit*, *Ninette à la Cour*, and *Le Premier Navigateur*. Other dancers of the period were Auguste Vestris, Dauberval, and Pierre Gardel (1758–1840), brother of Maximilien. The principal *danseuses* were Mlles. Allard, Peslin, Miller (afterwards Mme. P. Gardel, 1770–1833), and Mlle. Théodore (afterwards Mme. Dauberval).

The advent of the French Revolution exerted a beneficent effect on stage costume. Dress was modelled upon the classic tunics and gowns of the ancient Greek and Roman republics. Fashion ordained that the materials must be light and in some degree transparent in order to reveal the beauty of the human form. With the adoption of the antique tunic it was possible to see the length of the dancer's leg, and now arose a real or fanced dislike to the exhibition of actual nudity on the stage. This led to the introduction of tights, which, while veiling the naked leg, would retain the illusion of flesh. Maillot, the costumier at the Opera at the beginning of the 19th century, is generally credited with the invention of the combined close-fitting knickers and long hose which still bear his name. It must be stated, however, that the use of thighs was certainly known in the time of Guimard, who retired in 1790. The freeing of the legs enabled the dancers to leap upwards, sideways, and forwards, and turn in the air. Soon, the choreographic design included vertical lines.

At the end of the 18th century, France was superior in both dancers and choreographers, and their services were in demand at most of the principal European theatres, from London to Moscow. But the principal attraction of the ballets was still based on technical brilliancy. Noverre laid great stress on the importance of mime and expressiveness of dancing, but he was not so successful in translating his theories into practice. Dauberval, however, one of his best pupils, did much to carry out and develop his master's ideals. His most successful ballet was *La Fille Mal Gardée*. But the person who was to bring Noverre's dreams to full realisation was an Italian, Salvatore Viganò (1769–1821).

His parents were dancers and he was brought up in the same profession, special care being taken to develop his musical gifts. He studied dancing under Dauberval, from whom he imbibed the teaching of Noverre. Viganò married a Spanish dancer, Maria Medina, with whom he gave a series of successful tours from 1793 to 1803, at the same time producing occasional ballets.

In 1812 he established himself at Milan, but, having been left a fortune by an admirer, he gave up dancing and devoted himself to choreography. In some ways he anticipated Fokine. For instance, when the *corps de ballet* took part in mimed scenes, it was the custom for the dancers to take the same pose simultaneously, or for the action to be spread over several groups, each expressing a different contribution to the general effect, with each member of a group taking the same pose. Viganò, however, gave each dancer a distinct individuality by allotting each one a different movement to execute, the actions being continually changed in accordance with the rhythm of the music and the demands of the theme. What Viganò attempted and eventually achieved was to express a theme by means of dancing and mime, both regulated in accordance with the rhythm of the music. The themes for his ballets reveal a remarkable imagination which at times rises to great heights. Indeed, the themes of most ballets seem childish and trivial in comparison with the conceptions of Viganò. He took the same care in the selection of the music for his works and, when he failed to find what he sought, composed the melody himself. His best ballets were *Promethée* (1813), *Psammi* (1817), *Dédale* (1818), *La Vestale* (1818), and *Les Titans* (1819).

An important contribution to the development of technique was the gradual appreciation of the increased facility of execution to be gained from being "well turned out." In all treatises upon dancing up to 1780, the feet are shown turned out at an angle of forty-five degrees. Camargo's brilliancy of execution was due to her being "well turned out," and Noverre in his *Letters* (Letter XIII), declares that "in order to dance well, nothing is so important as the turning out of the thigh. . . . A dancer with his limbs turned inwards is awkward and disagreeable.

The contrary attitude gives ease and brilliancy, it invests steps, position, and attitudes with grace." But C. Blasis, in his *Traité Elémentaire, Théorique et Pratique, de l'Art de la Danse* (Milan, 1820) makes "turning out" imperative to the dancer's success, and, in the drawings accompanying his text, the dancers are shown with their feet turned out at an angle of ninety degrees.

Carlo Blasis (1803–1878) might be termed the first pedagogue of the classical ballet. The son of a musician, he received a very complete education in the arts and studied dancing under Dauberval and P. Gardel.

In 1820 he set forth his theories on the technique of ballet in the *Traité* already mentioned. In that book he lays down a number of principles and establishes a code, the most important of which is the reiterated insistence on the value of line. The pupil is taught to appreciate this important quality by geometric figures which are afterwards expanded into delineations of the human body in dancing positions. In addition to many technical improvements, Blasis devised the position known as *attitude*, based on the statue of Mercury by Jean Bologne (1524–1608), and applied it to the *pirouette*, which he termed *pirouette en attitude*.

In 1837 Blasis became director of the Imperial Academy of Dancing and Pantomime at the Scala Theatre, Milan, and there he put his principles into practice with the most gratifying results. He formed a number of pupils destined to achieve fame, in particular one group whose success earned for them the name of *Les Pléiades*—Pasquale Borri, Marietta Baderna, Augusta Domenichettis, Flora Fabbri, Amalia Ferraris, Sofia Fuoco, and Carolina Granzini. In addition may be mentioned: Aminia Boschetti, Fanny Cerrito, Giovannina King, Carolina Pochini, and Carolina Rosati.

There were no easy paths to success at this academy. Pupils who entered it had to be not under eight or over twelve years of age, physically fit and prepared to remain for eight years, no salary being paid them during the first three years. The daily practice required of each pupil was three hours dancing and one hour mime. As the pupils made progress they were promoted to take part in the various ballets produced in the theatre.

As a choregrapher, Blasis composed upwards of seventy ballets and an immense number of *pas*. He is said to have been the first to make use of biblical themes as a basis for his dance compositions.

To return to France, the French Revolution instituted a much-needed reform in costume, but disestablished the Académie Royale de

Musique, founded by Louis XIV. Several attempts were made to utilise ballet as a medium for political propaganda, for instance P. Gardel's choric ballet to the strains of the Marseillaise (1792), and the later, more ambitious, ambulatory ballet, *La Fête à l'Etre Suprème* (1794). Gardel's most successful production was *Psyche* (1790), which was performed 921 times. The principal dancers during this period were Mmes. Gardel, Clotilde, and Perignon, Mlle. Chevigny, and A. Vestris, Milon, Goyon, Beaupré, Aumer, and Giraud.

Ballet revived a little under Napoleon, but the war between France and England deprived London of the French dancers. An interesting ballet produced during this period was P. Gardel's *La Dansomanie* (1800), in which the waltz was first danced at the Opera. After the Restoration (1815) the State Academy of Dancing was re-formed, and in 1821 English agents made a determined effort to cajole French talent to London. The negotiations were protracted but successful. The dancers, Lise Noblet and Albert, arrived. They were well received and created a renewed interest in ballet. Their appearance marks the beginning of the golden age of ballet in England. Soon, other famous dancers visited London—Mlles. Bigottini, Brocard, Fanny Bias, Mme. Montessu, and M. Paul. The King's Theatre, afterwards Her Majesty's, founded a permanent *corps de ballet*, and crowded houses were the rule at this theatre, the Haymarket, and Covent Garden. Ballet began to outrival opera in popularity.

The Romantic Movement

by Mary Clarke and Clement Crisp

By the end of the eighteenth century the political, social and artistic world of Europe was undergoing extreme stresses and changes that were to alter the whole way of life and way of thinking of men of the next generation. The French revolution and the Napoleonic wars, the spread of the Industrial Revolution, the blossoming of intellectual ideas that had been sown during the later part of the eighteenth century, all brought the most profound changes to life and art. In ballet we have seen how the innovators of the time—Noverre, Viganò, Blasis, Dauberval—were in a sense preparing the ground for a new form of dance.

Source: From *Ballet: An Illustrated History* (New York: Universe, 1973).

In all the arts there was a reaction against the cold, formal classical manner; feeling and sensibility became more important than reason; art, if you like, became subjective rather than objective—what the creator felt, his emotional reaction to the world around him provided the new inspiration. In music, a work like Beethoven's Pastoral Symphony with its portrayal of nature led on to the richer emotional content of Weber, the operas of Meyerbeer, the music of Chopin and Mendelssohn. The publication of Lamartine's *Les Contemplations* in 1820 brought a new voice into poetry; by 1819 Géricault had painted his great canvas of *The Raft of the Medusa*, a thrilling and dramatic portrayal of the survivors of a ship-wreck. In France, always in the forefront of artistic movements, painters, writers and musicians sought fresh inspiration, a freer and more expressive style: they turned to the plays of Shakespeare, the novels of Scott, the poetry of Germany. Painters like Delacroix, Hector Berlioz in his *Fantastic Symphony*, Victor Hugo in his plays and poems, were central influences. Ballet, no less than the other arts, felt this great wind of change, and from 1830 onwards, during the twenty years of the high Romantic movement, ballet became enormously popular and reflected as clearly as any other art the new feeling and the new themes.

In a curious way a picture can evoke a whole age for us. A pose, a grouping of people will reveal a great deal about a society or a way of life, and nothing is more revealing of the Romantic movement in ballet than the lithograph of the *Pas de Quatre*, in which Brandard, a favourite artist of the time, immortalised one of the most extraordinary ballet performances ever given. Compare the view of the ballerinas in this picture—infinitely delicate, lightly poised, sweetly gracious, charmingly clothed in clouds of soft tulle—with the pictures of the dancers of the eighteenth century, and you will see at once the vast change that has taken place. Significantly, there is no male dancer. We are entering a period when men took a very subsidiary place in ballet; this is the era of the ballerina's dominance. The use of point work, the impression of ethereal lightness, are indicative of the change, which altered not only the outward aspect of dancing but also the themes which it treated.

Ballet, like the other arts, had found new inspiration, new stories to tell. In literature, painting and music, artists sought an escape from their world; an interest in the exotic, the supernatural, in distant scenes—distant in place or in time—took them and their audience away from the new industrial world of smoke and grime that was springing up. Ghosts and sprites, far-off lands and far-off times, the local colour of Italy or Spain or Eastern Europe, provided a tremendous new stimulus to choreographers and dancers. And this new view of ballet was reflected in a new view of dancing, epitomised by the first of the ballerinas of this age, the central figure of the *Pas de Quatre*, Marie Taglioni.

Marie Taglioni and La Sylphide

It must have seemed unlikely that the thin, round-shouldered and by no means pretty daughter of Filippo Taglioni, member of a famous Italian dancing family, could become a great ballerina. But her father was determined that she should achieve greatness; her childhood was spent in one European city after another where her father was ballet master, and wherever the family travelled, Marie worked. Her father sometimes drove her almost to exhaustion, training her body mercilessly—so it must seem to us—in order to overcome its physical inelegancies, insisting on leaps and bounding steps to emphasise her natural lightness, on infinitely graceful positions that would disguise the length of her arms, on charm and decorum of manner that would enhance her but modest good looks. By dint of ceaseless and exhausting practice (sometimes six hours a day, during which poor Marie would collapse exhausted, to be bathed, given a change of clothes by her mother and then set to work again) the young girl was ready to make her début in Vienna in 1822, shortly after her eighteenth birthday.

The occasion was a triumph, but it was not until five years later that Marie Taglioni (with Paul, her younger brother, as her partner and her father as choreographer) reached the mecca for all dancers of the time: the Paris Opéra. By this time, Marie's style had been further polished. Its lightness, grace and modesty, the prodigious elevation and feathery delicacy of landing, were totally novel; the Opéra stage had never seen anything like it. Here was an entirely new image of the female dancer. Her success was absolute, despite considerably enmity from the dancers within the Opéra itself, whose jealousy was quickly aroused by this amazingly different artistry. But she had to wait some years yet before a work was created that did justice to her unique qualities.

In 1831 the Opéra staged an opera by Meyerbeer, *Robert the Devil*, a typical Romantic piece telling the story of Duke Robert of Normandy, his love for a princess and his encounter with the devil and with the supernatural; in the third act he enters a cave and ghosts of nuns appear and dance a wild bacchanal. Leading them was Marie Taglioni, a spectral figure in white, and it is generally conceded that the tenor in the opera was so impressed with the scene that he was inspired to devise a libretto for a ballet, using an idea which he drew from a novel dealing with a Scottish elf. In the following year, on 12th March 1832, the ballet *La Sylphide* was staged at the Opéra, with Taglioni in the leading rôle. This is the first true Romantic ballet and in it we see elements that made for the success of *Robert the Devil* (the use of gas-light to simulate moonlight on stage; the extinguishing of the lights in the auditorium; the importance of the supernatural) brought into ballet. The plot introduces ideas dear to the Romantic movement, still in the first flush of enthusiasm: an element of the exotic (Scotland was a distant and curious spot to the good bourgeois of Paris) and the ghostly, the tragic emotions of the theme which portrays the impossible love of a human for a supernatural being—all these are expressed in the role of La Sylphide herself through the novelty and grace of Taglioni's dancing, unbelievably light and delicate, a creature of mist drifting over the stage—and helped by various ingenious pieces of machinery to fly.

The story tells of a young crofter, James, on the eve of his marriage to Effie, a charming girl. But a sylphide has fallen in love with him, and so beguiles him that he deserts his home and fiancée in order to follow her to the forests that are her abode. The romantic artists needed love to be seen as tragic and unattainable; in the second act James unwittingly causes the sylphide's death, and as she drifts away to some sylphide heaven, James is left disconsolate and alone as his erstwhile fiancée, Effie, passes in the distance with a new lover on the way to her wedding. The success of *La Sylphide* and of Taglioni, the visible expression of the Romantic idea, was absolute. The ballet and its star were the heralds of a golden age of ballet, a period of supernatural and exotic creations that starred not only Taglioni but a whole galaxy of great ballerinas during the next twenty years. *La Sylphide* altered the nature of ballet in theme and in decoration (Ciceri's forest set for act II was indicative of a new style of Romantic décor) throughout Europe.

Taglioni's greatness imposed a new image upon dancing. Her successors might differ in style—none could match her lightness and poetic delicacy or the modest grace which she brought to every rôle—but Taglioni remained the first (in every sense) of the Romantic ballerinas, and even today her image is for us the essential picture of the Romantic dancer. For seven years after *La Sylphide* she reigned at the Opéra, but the arrival of brilliant rivals like Fanny Elssler, in every way the opposite of Taglioni, induced her to tour extensively for ten years, triumphing wherever she went: in London in the *Pas de Quatre* among other works, and notably in Russia (where balletomanes acquired a pair of her shoes, had them cooked and served with a sauce, and solemnly proceeded to eat them).

After her retirement in 1847 she settled down to what should have been a happy middle age; she returned to the theatre in 1858 to work at the Paris Opéra, coaching the talented Emma Livry for whom she created her only ballet, *The Butterfly* (Livry was tragically burned to death soon after). Her early marriage to the feckless and ungrateful Count Gilbert de Voisins had been dissolved after three years; her later years were darkened by poverty and she was obliged to giving dancing lessons to well-born young ladies in London. She died in reduced circumstances in Marseilles in 1884. Yet whatever the sadness of her last years, Taglioni is immortal. Her technical authority and the lightness which is particularly associated with her name live on in the ideals of elevation and grace that are still the goal of dancers today, ideals that we can see in Fokine's tribute to the romanticism of Taglioni's manner in *Les Sylphides*.

Fanny Elssler

When the twenty-four-year-old Fanny Elssler arrived in Paris in 1834 she was already celebrated as a dancer in her native Vienna, in Berlin and in London. She was accompanied by her sister Thérèse; taller than Fanny, she served as her partner as well as business manager. It was the astute Dr Véron, director of the Paris Opéra, who sensed that Fanny's style would make a fascinating contrast to Taglioni's. Elssler was already a brilliant dancer, excelling in the most difficult technical feats and in vigorous, fast and dazzling steps; making very skilful use of points. The Romantic age shows the establishment of point work as an essential feature of the ballerina's arts. Its use had been known for twenty years but Taglioni, characteristically, had only used her points to enhance the impression of lightness. When she rose on her toes it seemed as if she was maintaining only the briefest contact with the earth preparatory to flying into the air. With Elssler, point-work was yet another aspect of her virtuosity.

An instant rivalry broke out between the supporters of Taglioni and the adherents of the new star, which reached fresh heights with the triumph of Elssler in 1836 in *Le Diable Boiteux*, a Spanish ballet in which Fanny danced for the first time what was to become her single most celebrated solo, the Cachucha, a display of fiery temperament and voluptuous movement which, although it seems the other side of the artistic coin from Taglioni's style, is yet also true as an image of the Romantic ballet.

Elssler's gifts included one other that was to prove of vital importance to the ballet of this time: she was a superb actress. In ballets both good and (more often) indifferent, she revealed an extraordinary dramatic power that could sustain the feeblest plots. In 1839 *La Gypsy* was staged at the Opéra where she was now reigning ballerina and provided her with a triumph, as did *La Tarentule* later that year. But already rumours were circulating that Fanny was to embark upon an American tour, no mean adventure at this time, and in the spring of 1840 she set out for the New World. Fanny spent two years in the Americas; she visited not only the U.S.A. but also Havana, where she coped with an incredible supporting *corps de ballet* in *La Sylphide;* she wrote of 'plump and swarthy ladies . . . incapable of activity as a superannuated cow' whom the ballet-master daubed with whitewash to make them look more sylph-like. She created a sensation everywhere, dancing amid scenes of unprecedented enthusiasm.

On her return to Europe, in fact to London since as a result of breaking a contract with the Opéra she could not appear in Paris, she reached a new pinnacle of greatness in *Giselle* (staged two years before in Paris), offering a far more dramatic and thrilling rendering of the title rôle than Carlotta Grisi (see below), its creator. She spent much of the next four years working in Italy, and the final glorious period of her active career was spent in Russia, whither she journeyed in 1848. Here she was joined shortly by Perrot and it was in his ballets *La Esmeralda* and *Catarina*, in his own staging of *Giselle* and in several other works that she knew triumphs that rivalled anything she had known previously. Her official farewell performance in 1851 in Moscow occasioned a rain of three hundred bouquets, forty-two curtain calls and gifts of jewels. She returned to her native Vienna to give a brief farewell season, then retired from the stage to devote herself to her family. Her last years were spent quietly and she died in Vienna in 1884, leaving with those fortunate enough to have seen her an indelible memory of a supreme dance actress.

Jules Perrot and Carlotta Grisi

The Romantic age established the dominance of the ballerina. Artists like Taglioni and Elssler, the still thrilling novelty of dancing on point, and the whole attitude of the Romantic artist towards women as either ethereal or thrillingly passionate creatures (typified by the contrasted styles of Taglioni and Elssler) were swiftly relegating male dancers to the position of necessary evils, needed to partner and support the ballerina but not worthy of serious consideration. The great reversal of the state of affairs in the eighteenth century, the age of Vestris, 'Le Dieu de la Danse', was one of the fatal elements in Romantic ballet.

The essential harmonious balance between male and female in dancing was being destroyed, and amid the flood of female stars of the Romantic ballet only a few male names survive: Lucien Petipa (the first Albrecht), Paul Taglioni (Marie's brother), and St Léon and Perrot, both more celebrated now as choreographers than as dancers.

Jules Joseph Perrot was born in 1810 and started his career in his native Lyons as a child acrobat, as well as taking dancing lessons. His earliest successes were as a grotesque mime and dancer, and he copied his light and acrobatic style from the celebrated Mazurier, a famous acrobatic dancer. By the age of thirteen he was in Paris and it was here that he first thought seriously of classic ballet as a career; inevitably this meant lessons with Auguste Vestris, and the great teacher was sufficiently impressed with the young Perrot's talent to promise that with hard work he could overcome his natural disabilities—an ugly face and a thick and rather stocky body, ideal for the rôles of a monkey in which he was first successful as a child performer, but hardly the requisites for a classical *premier danseur*. Perrot worked hard; Vestris advised him to use his natural lightness and *ballon* to keep in constant motion so that the audience would not have time to study his physical defects. Perrot saw the merits of what Vestris said ('Turn, spin, fly, but never give the public time to examine your person closely'), and developed a fast and mercurial style that soon earned him great public success. He was called 'a restless being of indescribable lightness and suppleness, with an almost phosphorescent brightness'.

Perrot thus combined the great style and brilliance of the old *danse noble* technique, which had reached its finest expression in the dancing of Auguste Vestris, with the dramatic traditions of the pantomime clown, and these two disparate elements are to combine later in his own choreographic outlook. By 1830 Perrot's gifts had received the great accolade: he was invited to appear at the Opéra and was soon dancing with Taglioni, herself just at the outset of her career in that theatre. For five years they appeared together, Perrot's boundless lightness and virtuosity providing an admirable foil (and inspiration) to Taglioni's ethereal graces—so much so that he was called Taglioni's dancing brother. But the ballerina was jealous of sharing public acclaim and in 1835 Perrot quit the Opéra after a disagreement about salary and embarked upon a European tour. This eventually brought him to Naples where he discovered a vastly talented sixteen-year-old girl in the ballet company. This was Carlotta Grisi.

Sensing her immense potential, Perrot decided to teach and shape gifts that he saw could rival the greatness of Taglioni and Elssler. For four years he guided Carlotta Grisi, partnered her and staged his first ballets for her, and also gave her his name. After highly successful appearances in Milan, Munich and London, Perrot brought Carlotta to Paris. He hoped, ultimately, that through Carlotta he might make his own return to the Opéra, but this was not to prove possible. In the meantime the couple appeared in a ballet-opera, *Le Zingaro*, at the Théâtre de la Renaissance where Carlotta not only danced but sang—she possessed a fluent soprano voice, and came of a famous family of singers. Carlotta's success in *Le Zingaro* was enough to ensure that early in the following year the Opéra's directorate should approach Perrot with an offer for her. The theatre was without a star dancer, Taglioni being in Russia, Elssler in America and the young Danish ballerina Lucile Grahn injured, and Carlotta's gifts were promising enough to inspire the management of the Opéra. Accordingly in February 1841 she made a successful début, although there was still no invitation for Perrot to appear. But it was Perrot who was to contribute largely to Carlotta's triumph later that summer at the Opéra, when *Giselle* was staged.

This greatest achievement of the Romantic ballet had been inspired by the poet and critic Théophile Gautier's reading in a book by Heine about his native Germany of the Slav legend of Wilis, spectral dancers who lure young men to their death at night. Gautier was already smitten by Carlotta's beauty, and with the assistance of the dramatist Vernoy de St Georges he drew up a scenario that was accepted at the Opéra. Adolphe Adam, the composer, a friend of both Perrot and Grisi, was entrusted with the score, which he drafted in record time, yet the choreography was to be created by Jean Coralli, chief ballet master at the Opéra, and not by Perrot. Nevertheless, although Coralli was credited with the choreography it was common knowledge that it was Perrot who composed all the dances for Carlotta, and in them lies the heart of the ballet. The work's spectacular success needs no further detailing here but it marked the beginning of the most important period of Perrot's career, not as a dancer but as one of the supreme choreographers of the century.

Carlotta's success, and that of *Giselle* to which he had contributed so much, did not open the doors of the Opéra to Perrot, and in the following year he was invited to London to work at Her Majesty's Theatre, then under the direction of an inspired impresario, Benjamin Lumley. After helping to stage *Giselle* for Carlotta, and devising a *pas* for Fanny Cerrito in *Alma*, Perrot was entrusted with most of the ballet at the theatre during the next six years, years in which his genius reached an extraordinary flowering, and he produced some of the finest ballets of the whole Romantic era. *La Esmeralda*, *Eoline*, *Catarina*, *Ondine* and *Lalla Rookh* were big ballets in which the themes and ideas of the Romantic ballet, the exotic, the supernatural, the dramatic, the love of local colour, were given a superb expressiveness. These were true *ballets d'action:* the choreography carried forward the action without relying upon superfluous virtuosity or divertissements, the interpreters were called upon to be expressive at all times, crowd scenes or intimate duets were equally lively in their dramatic interest, and Perrot's daring in achieving his theatrical effects was uniquely successful. His ballets conveyed the fact that the characters were real and sympathetic; mime and dance became fused into a wonderfully convincing style that insisted on naturalism rather than on empty posturing or worn-out balletic traditions. Here, it must seem, were Noverre's theories brought to vivid theatrical life.

In addition to his big ballets Perrot also created a series of divertissements that served as showpieces for the finest dancers of the day. In 1843 Queen Victoria had expressed a wish to see Elssler and Cerrito dancing together, and this undreamed-of confrontation was brought off with consummate skill by Perrot, who balanced with the nicest exactitude the steps and effects that each ballerina would achieve. In 1845 Lumley conceived a plan that must have seemed almost impossible, a *pas de quartre* for the four divinities: Taglioni, Cerrito, Grisi and Grahn. By dint of Lumley's diplomacy and Perrot's choreographic skill the plan was made real, though not without some dramas, particularly in connection with precedence of appearance. Taglioni, of course, would take pride of place, and Lucile Grahn as the most junior of the quartet would come last, but to choose between Grisi and Cerrito, both ladies being inordinately jealous of their position, might have taxed a Solomon. But Lumley was equal even to this, announcing quite simply that the elder of the two goddesses should take precedence, and smiling sweetly both ladies proved amenable to whatever position Perrot chose to give them. The piece was a thunderous success, and in the next three years similar displays were devised to include whatever stars happened to be available: *The Judgement of Paris* in 1846 featured Taglioni, Cerrito and Grahn, with Perrot himself and St Léon (who privately called these affairs 'steeplechases'); in 1847 *The Elements* starred Cerrito, Grisi and Rosati; and in 1848, *The Four Seasons* featured Grisi, Cerrito, Rosati and the younger Marie Taglioni (the great Marie's niece).

By this time the interest in ballet in London was waning, thanks in no small part to the upsurge in public taste for opera occasioned by the arrival of the Swedish Nightingale, Jenny Lind, and in 1848 Perrot made his first visit to Russia, where he was to work with little interruption for the next ten years, restaging his old triumphs, creating some new works and participating in the renaissance of ballet there. His assistant in these productions and interpreter of several rôles was Marius Petipa, who was to maintain the Perrot repertory in Russia for many years. Perrot himself retired in 1859, and returned to Paris where he lived quietly, visiting the ballet and teaching—he can be seen as an old gentleman directing the Opéra ballet class in some Degas paintings. He died in 1892.

Carlotta Grisi's career, launched so magnificently by *Giselle*, continued with undiminished splendour with *La Jolie Fille de Gand* in 1842, *La Péri* in 1843, *Le Diable à Quatre* in 1845 and *Paquita* in 1846. Inevitably, like all her great contemporaries Grisi visited Russia where she had comparable success, in no small part thanks to the presence of Perrot, but in Europe the interest in the ballet was declining and in 1854 she left the stage, still at the height of her powers. She retired, to live quietly and serenely near Geneva for the next forty-five years, dying in 1899.

Fanny Cerrito (1817–1909) and Arthur St Léon (1821–1870)

Of all the divinities of the Romantic era, one in particular became the favourite of London, Fanny Cerrito (who appears in Barham's *Ingoldsby Legends* as Ma'am'selle Cherrytoes). A Neapolitan by birth, Fanny's early successes were at La Scala, Milan, where she enthralled audiences by her brilliant technique, but it was her first London season in 1840 that set the seal on her claim to be considered as one of the brightest stars of this heyday of the Romantic ballet. Bounding, sparkling with life and speed, turning and flying (so it seemed) in the air, Cerrito won London's heart more completely than any dancer had since Taglioni's début ten years previously.

It was in London two years later that she first worked with Perrot, in the *pas* in *Alma* that earned him his engagement at Her Majesty's Theatre with Lumley, and their artistic association over the next years was to bring out much of the best from both. *Ondine* in 1843 remains one of the key works of the period—its *pas de l'ombre* in which Fanny as the water-sprite sported with her own shadow is famous still today and inspired Ashton's own version of it for Fonteyn in his *Ondine*. Between her London triumphs Fanny returned to her native Italy to no less enthusiastic receptions, and although Perrot's next piece for her, *Zélia* in 1844, was a failure, the *Pas de Quatre* and the subsequent divertissements, as rich in ballerinas as a pudding with plums, were occasions that displayed her gifts superbly, as did *Lalla Rookh* in 1846. In 1843 she had met Arthur St Léon, a dancer of impressive gifts and with a virile brilliance that set off her own to perfection in *pas de deux*, and for her St Léon created his first choreography. Two years later the couple were to marry, much to the chagrin of the wealthy English aristocrats who had been laying siege to Fanny's heart for years.

Incredibly, despite her fame in London and Italy and in various other European cities, Fanny had not yet danced at the Paris Opéra, the mecca for any dancer—although London had during the mid-1840s become a vital centre of ballet thanks to the presence of Perrot and the visits of the star ballerinas of whom Fanny was one. In 1847 however, the Opéra made overtures to Fanny and St Léon, and in October of that year St Léon had concocted a version of Fanny's early triumph, *Alma*, cutting out parts of it and renaming it *La Fille de Marbre*. The work proved much to the Parisian taste and during the next three years she starred with St Léon in several of his ballets, outstandingly in *La Vivandière* and in an extraordinary work, *Le Violon du Diable*, for which St Léon was the choreographer, as well as dancing and playing the violin (he was an accomplished performer) as an accompaniment to Fanny's dancing.

In 1851 a visit to dance in Spain brought to light a breach between the pair, which ended in separation. Fanny formed a liaison with a Spanish aristocrat, by whom she had a daughter in 1853, but this did not end her career. Although her technique was suffering with advancing years, she returned for a time to Paris, went to London for some performances and then, although the Crimean War was raging, travelled to St Petersburg in 1855 where she found Perrot as ballet master. Her success here was by no means as complete as were those she had known throughout the rest of Europe, for the Russians were just beginning to realise that their own artists, like the ballerina Muravieva, were as gifted as the foreign stars. By 1857 Fanny was back in Europe, but she could plainly see that her career was near its end; the Paris Opéra seemed closed to her, and her farewell to the stage took place in London, a city which had given her such generous and loving acclaim for so many years. Without any fuss or special announcement, Fanny appeared for the last time in public on 18th June 1857, dancing a Minuet in Mozart's opera *Don Giovanni*.

She lived on in Paris for another fifty-two years, devoting herself first to the education and marriage of her beloved daughter, Mathilde, and to the joys of her grandchildren. Her death in May 1909 coincided almost exactly with the arrival in Paris of the Diaghilev Ballets Russes on their first triumphant season. It is extraordinary to realise that as

Karsavina and Nijinsky rehearsed for *Les Sylphides* a ballerina died who had danced *La Sylphide* sixty-eight years before.

Following the break-up of his marriage to Fanny in 1853 St Léon, who had quit the Paris Opéra the year previously, went to Portugal for some years and after also staging ballets in several other European cities was invited to take over from Jules Perrot as ballet master in St Petersburg. For ten years he travelled between Russia and Paris, spending the winter in St Petersburg and the summer months in Paris. In Russia he was responsible for a considerable number of novelties, works which combined sparkling divertissements with a remarkable interest in national dances, which he seemingly adapted with great skill to the forms of ballet. His *Koniok Gorbonuk*—The Little Hump-backed Horse—was notably successful because of its Russian theme, and it remained for many years in the repertory.

But it was in Paris, after his final departure from St Petersburg, that St Léon created his last and most famous work, *Coppélia* (1870). In it he seems to have poured the best of himself; the charming solos, the clever use of national dance and the divertissements of the final act were all sustained and enhanced by the irresistible charms of the Delibes score. Yet curiously, for this happiest of ballets, it was a work which was attended by great sadness. In the summer following its creation the Franco-Prussian war broke out, sweeping away the elaborate elegance of the Second Empire. St Léon himself died of a heart attack in September of that year, two months later the delightful Giuseppina Bozzacchi who had created the rôle of Swanilda died of small-pox on her seventeenth birthday, and during the fierce winter of the siege of Paris Dauty, the first Coppélius, also died. But the ballet lives on, our only link (in the Paris Opéra's old version) with St Léon, but a priceless and delightful one.

Lucile Grahn and August Bournonville

The junior member of the *Pas de Quatre* was the Danish ballerina, Lucile Grahn, who was born in Copenhagen in 1819. Her career, though less well known than that of her companions in the quartet, followed much the same triumphant pattern of performances throughout Europe, with exultant débuts in Paris and London and St Petersburg, and ended, intriguingly, with her as ballet mistress in Munich helping in the staging of Wagner's *Die Meistersinger* and *Rheingold* (Wagner 'thought highly' of her). It is through her that we make contact with one of the greatest choreographers of the Romantic age, August Bournonville.

Born in Copenhagen in 1805, son of Antoine Bournonville, a French dancer, and his Swedish wife, the young Bournonville made his début as a child in a ballet by Galeotti, who was then ballet master in Copenhagen. Galeotti's ballets reflected the influence of Noverre and Angiolini. For forty years he directed the fortunes of the Royal Danish Ballet, but in his later years (and after his death when Antoine Bournonville directed the troupe) the Royal Danish company fell upon sad times. Antoine, meanwhile, had sent his son to study dancing in Paris, where he worked with Auguste Vestris, absorbing from him all the finesse and nobility as well as the technical virtuosity of the French school of dancing. This style he was to maintain throughout his life, and it formed the basis for the training system which he initiated when, in 1830, he took charge of the Royal Danish Ballet.

He came to power as a brilliant dancer, filled with ambitions to improve the status both of the company and of dancing as a profession. His task was enormously difficult; he had to dance, train his company and provide a repertory, but fortunately his gifts were equal to all this. During the next forty-seven years, with brief interludes when he travelled and worked in the rest of Europe, Bournonville created a fine company and a superb repertory of ballets, some of which have been scrupulously preserved by the Royal Danish Ballet to this day and offer our best idea of what the Romantic ballet was like.

In 1834 Bournonville visited Paris, bringing with him his gifted pupil, the fifteen-year-old Lucile Grahn. They saw Marie Taglioni (Bournonville's 'ideal' as a dancer) in *La Sylphide*, and memories of this must have inspired him two years later to stage his own version of the ballet for the young Lucile. Although the score was different and Bournonville provided new choreography, the ballet was faithful in plot and in style to Filippo Taglioni's original, with the one significant exception characteristic of Bournonville's work: with the male dancer rapidly declining in importance elsewhere in Europe, Bournonville, himself a superior technician, insisted on maintaining the prestige of the man in ballet. His system of training produced, and continues to produce to this day, some of the most elegant, boundingly graceful and virile of male stars.

The fact that Denmark was in an artistic sense something of a backwater meant that the ballet there progressed independently of fashion throughout the rest of Europe. When dancing was losing much public interest in London and Paris (St Petersburg even more distant from the centre of fashion also kept ballet alive at this time), the Royal Danish company benefited from the extraordinary creative genius of Bournonville. More than fifty ballets of all types flowed from him; each was illuminated by Bournonville's poetic imagination and fertile creativity, each maintained the proper balance between male and female dancing, each offered wonderful opportunities for dancing that was firmly based in the great traditions of the Vestris school which Bournonville himself enhanced and developed. Bournonville could compose virtuoso *enchaînements;* he made use of folk-dance that he observed in his travels (he loved Italy and Spain particularly) and in his finest works he produced a picture of the world he knew, showing real people—like the Neapolitan peasants in *Napoli*—and creating a series of superb Romantic *ballets d'action* that are among the best achievements of the ballet of the nineteenth century. He drew on historical subjects (like the trolls of *Et Folkesagn* or *Valdemar* or *Cort Adeler*), topical events (*Zulma or The Crystal Palace in London*), scenes of travel (*Kermesse in Bruges* or *Far from Denmark* or *La Ventana*). Through these and a myriad of other fine works Denmark gained a vital ballet tradition and, through Bournonville's dance teaching, a great academic tradition. These are the basis for the eminence of the company today.

Bournonville's interests also encompassed music: he encouraged native composers to create his scores, he produced plays and operas, particularly his beloved Mozart, and he even introduced Wagner's operas to Denmark by staging *Lohengrin.* He retired in 1877, dying two years later, but on the day before he died he saw the début of a young dancer, Hans Beck, who was to prove the guardian of the illustrious traditions of the Bournonville ballets and the Bournonville school of dancing until his death in 1952.

The Age of Petipa

by Ivor Guest

St Petersburg was the capital city of Imperial Russia. Here, for several months in every year, the Tsars lived in their great Winter Palace, which was only one of the city's many splendid buildings. The setting for the ballet *Petrushka* shows us a view of St Petersburg, with the imposing spire of the Admiralty rising into the sky in the background, but the building with which we are most concerned in this chapter is the Maryinsky Theatre, the great opera house which stands

Source: From *The Dancer's Heritage: A Short History of Ballet* (London: The Dancing Times, 1960).

in the square that used to be called Theatre Square. The Maryinsky replaced the Bolshoi Theatre as the home of the Imperial Russian Ballet in 1885. Both were state theatres in the widest sense. The Director was appointed personally by the Tsar, and staff, singers, dancers and musicians were all in a sense Imperial servants, subject to stern discipline but assured of a pension after long and faithful service. This discipline and the seemingly unlimited funds that were expended on the ballet in nineteenth-century Russia were advantages which no other opera house enjoyed in anything like the same measure. Also, in St Petersburg, ballet was given an equal standing with opera, and important ballet productions filled a whole evening's programme. Elsewhere in Europe, what we now call the full-length ballet did not exist. Even if a ballet were divided into two or three acts, such as *Giselle* or *Coppélia*, it was always given with an opera.

The Maryinsky of the late nineteenth century was probably the most glamorous opera house in the world, and this glamour seemed to shine more and more brightly as the rumblings of discontent throughout the country brought the Revolution closer. Most of the seats were reserved for the Court, the diplomatic corps, and members of exclusive clubs, less than a third—and most of those in the gallery and balcony—being available for the public. A considerable proportion of the audience attended nearly every performance. These were the balletomanes, a closely-knit group which gained immense influence in the management of the theatre, imposing their demands not only in details such as the casting of ballets, but even in weightier matters affecting production and policy. They were very conservative in their outlook, and their influence probably retarded the development of the art they enjoyed so much, for it required a strong Director to ignore their demands. Much more progressive were the enthusiasts in the gallery and balcony, students, clerks and junior officers for the most part who often queued throughout most of a freezing Russian night to be sure of their seats. Unlike the balletomanes downstairs, they confined their admiration solely to the dancers' performances, and if they did not have the ear of the management, they made their opinions no less felt by the vehemence of their cheers or disapproving whistling. Sometimes they became so unruly that the police had to be sent up to restore order.

We shall be mainly concerned in this chapter with St Petersburg, but Russian ballet, even then, had two centres. Moscow, the other centre, was a merchant city, and the Bolshoi Theatre there could not match the Bolshoi and Maryinsky of St Petersburg either in splendour or taste. Ballet in Moscow had started in the eighteenth century when an enterprising dancer began training the inmates of the Orphanage.

Soon a thriving ballet company was in existence which gave performances that were perhaps more vital, if less polished, than those of St Petersburg, because the Moscow audiences were drawn from a much wider cross-section of the public. At least one great dancer, Sankovskaya, had emerged at the Bolshoi Theatre, and Carlo Blasis spent several years there. As the century wore on, the Moscow ballet more and more developed a character of its own. It often presented works that had already been successfully produced in St. Petersburg, but new ballets also figured in its programmes. *Don Quixote* and *Swan Lake* both had their first performance in Moscow. However, Moscow was not to assume international importance as a centre of ballet until the twentieth century, when it became the capital of the Soviet Union.

We must now retrace our steps to St Petersburg, where, in 1847, a young Frenchman called Marius Petipa arrived with a contract as *premier danseur.* Today the name of Petipa is well known to everyone who is interested in ballet, for its appears on the programme whenever *Swan Lake* or *The Sleeping Beauty* is presented, but both these ballets were created many years later, towards the end of his career. Unlike many choreographers, Petipa did not become prominent as a young man. He was fifty before he became principal ballet-master in St Petersburg and well over seventy when he staged *The Sleeping Beauty*.

For the first twenty-two years of his stay in Russia, Marius Petipa learnt the craft of the choreographer in the best possible way. He was able to observe at first hand the methods of Jules Perrot and Arthur Saint-Léon, and also—which was no less useful—to learn, from their experience, how to deal with the authorities whose word was felt in the theatre—with the Director and the many officials, and also with the more influential balletomanes. He would have seen how Perrot, brilliant choreographer though he was, lacked the tact and patience to handle these people and so never received proper support, whereas Saint-Léon, who was a lesser artist, was pliable and always ready to adapt himself to meet their wishes. Perrot, after producing expanded versions of many of his great ballets, such as *La Esmeralda*, became frustrated because he was not given enough opportunity to create new ballets, and left Russia in 1859, after which he was to produce no more ballets, although he was then only forty-nine. While Perrot's ballets were distinguished by their dramatic choreography, Saint-Léon's main quality was his ability to tailor a ballet to suit a ballerina—and that was just what the St Petersburg balletomanes were most interested in at that time. He produced one work which has remained constantly popular in Russia ever since, *The Little Hump-backed Horse*. This ballet was founded on a Russian fairy tale, and although its conventional choreography was by a Frenchman and its music by an Italian, Cesare Pugni, it pointed to the rich material that was to be found in Russian folklore.

During these years, Marius Petipa produced several ballets, one of which, *The Daughter of Pharaoh*, was a resounding success, but his main activity at this time was centred on the ballet school. Here he was in charge of the training, and as a result of his efforts Russian ballerinas began to appear who were capable of standing comparison with the visiting foreign stars. Among these were his wife Marie Petipa, Martha Muravieva and Ekaterina Vazem. Male dancing was not so neglected as it was in the West, but while travesty dancing never obtained a hold as it did in Paris and London, the ballerina was supreme even in Russia. However, St Petersburg possessed several fine male dancers, including Pavel Gerdt, one of the greatest *danseurs nobles* of all time, and the fiery character dancer, Felix Kshesinsky.

When Marius Petipa at last succeeded to the post of principal ballet-master in 1869, ballet in Russia had reached a low ebb, having lost much of the popularity it had enjoyed in Romantic times. Petipa at first showed no unusual originality, and for a dozen years filled his ballets with bravura *variations* and eye-catching scenic effects, and neglected the male dancers, much as Saint-Léon had done before him. When Bournonville visited St Petersburg in the seventies, he was shocked to find that dramatic effect had been sacrificed in the interests of virtuosity and vulgarity. He did not conceal his concern, but Petipa and his colleague Christian Johansson explained that they had no alternative but to give the public what it wanted and comply with the demands of the management. Two of Petipa's ballets from this period have survived: *Don Quixote*, first produced in Moscow in 1869 and still performed in its entirety in Russia, though in a later version by Gorsky, and known in the West chiefly on account of its *grand pas de deux*, which many ballerinas use as a show-piece of technical fireworks; and *The Bayadere*, which dates from 1877.

The rage for ballet which we associate with the Russia of the Tsars did not begin until the eighteen-eighties. It was largely brought about by the intelligent and cultured Director of the Imperial Theatres, Vsevolojsky, who took a very active interest in the ballet. Petipa, who accepted his authority with good grace, then entered upon the most glorious phase of his career. Ballet became fashionable again in St Petersburg quite suddenly with the triumphant appearance in 1885 of Virginia Zucchi, the first of a line of Italian ballerinas to visit Russia, but its popularity was finally sealed with the production of *The Sleeping Beauty* in 1890. This ballet marked the summit of Vsevolojsky's achievement. He had instituted a fundamental reform in suppressing the post of official composer of ballet music, which Pugni and Minkus had held, and instead of facile and tuneful scores of no musical importance the audiences of the Maryinsky now heard the rich melodies of Tchaikovsky.

Tchaikovsky had already composed one ballet, *Swan Lake*, but this had been so wretchedly produced in Moscow in 1877 that he became almost convinced that ballet was not his field. He called his score 'poor stuff' in comparison with Delibes' *Sylvia*, and did not turn his thoughts to ballet again until Vsevolojsky commissioned him to compose *The Sleeping Beauty* twelve years later. Petipa, who had worked out the complete scheme of the ballet in advance, presented him with detailed instructions for the tempo and length of each passage, but this did not appear to hamper him, for he produced a score that sparkled with fresh melodies and rich orchestral effects. The ballet was a triumph for both the composer and the choreographer when given its first performance at the Maryinsky in 1890, even though the Tsar, Nicholas II, could think of nothing better to say than a banal 'Very nice' when Tchaikovsky was presented. The composer was very hurt, and rightly so, for the ballet has remained a classic in Russia and has never left the repertory of the theatre in which it was created. It was also to be revived by Diaghilev in London with great splendour, and later still to become the most popular classic in the repertory of Britain's Royal Ballet.

The leading role of the Princess Aurora was danced, not by a Russian dancer, but by the Milanese ballerina, Carlotta Brianza. This was the result of the influx of Italian stars which had been one of the features of Russian ballet in the eighteen-eighties. It had started in a summer theatre in the Livadia amusement park, where Virginia Zucchi had made her first St Petersburg appearance in a faery extravaganza. In no time everyone was talking of the 'divine Virginia', who opened up new possibilities by her forceful dramatic dancing and her radiant femininity. Her engagement at the Maryinsky, where she enjoyed a fantastic triumph, was largely due to the critic Skalkovsky, who wrote that there was more poetry in her back than in all the modern Italian poets put together. To many, she proved that a dancer could be as great an artist as Sarah Bernhardt or Duse. Alexandre Benois, who was to become one of Diaghilev's principal collaborators, was carried away with enthusiasm, as were so many others that ballet regained its fashionable appeal almost overnight.

Zucchi was a dancer-actress rather than a virtuoso, but the Italian ballerinas who followed her owed their success principally to their technical accomplishments, particularly in turning and *pointe* work. Petipa did not favour the engagement of these Italian ballerinas, because they were not his own pupils. He always preferred working with Russian dancers: with Vazem, a cold but brilliant technician for whom he created *The Bayadere*, with the graceful Evgenia Sokolova, with Varvara Nikitina for whom he staged the first Russian production of *Coppélia* in 1884, or with his daughter who was named Marie after her mother. But none the less he not only accepted the Italian guests but cheerfully created important roles for them.

This Italian invasion was not confined to ballerinas. It also brought to Russia a male dancer, Enrico Cecchetti, whose first experience of a Russian public, like Zucchi's, was in a popular theatre, where he produced and danced in a version of *Excelsior* in 1887. He too was soon engaged by Vsevolojsky, and was given two roles to create in *The Sleeping Beauty:* the wicked fairy Carabosse, which brought our his great talent as a mime, and the Blue Bird, which displayed his equally brilliant gifts as a dancer. To the Russian audiences he was the male counterpart of Zucchi. They were amazed by his virtuosity. His wonderfully intricate *entrechats* and pirouettes surpassed anything which Russian dancers could perform. By his example, Cecchetti did much to restore the popularity and prestige of the male dancer in Russia.

Tchaikovsky followed up *The Sleeping Beauty* with *The Nutcracker*, which was produced in 1892. Petipa had planned this ballet with his usual thoroughness, but he was taken ill during its preparation and the task of arranging the choreography devolved on his assistant, Lev Ivanov. In the brilliant *divertissement* at the end, the part of the Sugar Plum Fairy was danced at the first performance by the Italian ballerina, Antonietta Dell'Era, but at the second performance the role was taken over by a Russian dancer, Varvara Nikitina.

Lev Ivanov was to co-operate in the production of the third Tchaikowsky ballet to be produced at the Maryinsky, *Swan Lake*. As we have already seen, this had been a failure in Moscow, but Marius Petipa was at a loss to understand how this could have happened unless the production and the choreography had been at fault. So he sent to Moscow for the score, and had little difficulty in persuading Vsevolojsky to agree to its being revived, in a revised form, at the Maryinsky. Tchaikowsky had recently died of cholera, and it was Drigo, the conductor, who put the necessary final touches to the score. He orchestrated some of Tchaikovsky's piano pieces to fill out the last act, and composed the music for the Prince's *variation* in the ballroom scene. As usual, Petipa worked out tme scheme for the production, but he only arranged the choreography of the first and third acts. The second and fourth acts—

the lakeside scenes which are filled mainly with the dances for the swans—were left to Ivanov, whose inspired choreography captured the lyrical quality of Tchaikovsky's music to form a wonderful dance poem which has lost none of its emotional impact over the years.

The second act of *Swan Lake* was ready first, and this was first performed on its own at a memorial performance for Tchaikovsky in 1894. The complete ballet was not given until early the following year. Another Italian virtuoso, Pierina Legnani, was given the honour of creating the famous dual role of Odette and Odile—the princess who has been turned into a swan, and the evil magician's daughter who assumes her form—and her great feat of performing thirty-two consecutive *fouettés*, which no one had done in St. Petersburg before her, is still preserved in present-day Russian and British productions of the ballet.

After the death of Tchaikovsky, Petipa had to work with lesser composers. Only one of these could claim distinction as a musician in his own right, and that was Glazounov, a difficult and obstinate man who would not alter his music to suit Petipa's requirements. His most famous ballet score was *Raymonda*, which is still given in Russia, but his music is also heard at Covent Garden when the Royal Ballet dance Ashton's *Birthday Offering*. Another melodious score composed at the turn of the century was Drigo's *Harlequin's Millions*.

It is astonishing to realise that Marius Petipa was a man of seventy-five when *Swan Lake* was first produced in St Petersburg and that even then he had not exhausted his creative activity. Now, in the last years of his long career, he found himself able to work with Russian ballerinas again, for a brilliant new generation was emerging. Much of the credit for this was due to Christian Johansson, a pupil of Bournonville, who, after dancing at the Maryinsky for nearly thirty years, had become the chief teacher in 1869. He, more than anyone else, fashioned what we know today as the Russian school of dancing but which he always insisted was the French school which the French themselves had forgotten.

The Italian brilliance of execution was soon assimilated into the Russian style, and by the turn of the century visiting Italian ballerinas no longer had anything new to offer. Mathilda Kshesinska, for instance, could match all their feats: she was the first Russian ballerina to perform the thirty-two *fouettés*, and she was given the title of *prima ballerina assoluta*, which only Legnani had held before her. Her contemporary, Olga Preobrajenska, did not rise to fame so quickly, but she was no less great in her own way, being a delightful comedienne. A wealth of other dancers followed—Vera Trefilova, Lubov Egorova,

Julia Sedova, Anna Pavlova—all of whom graduated from the Maryinsky ballet school in the nineties, while at the same time, male dancing was coming into its own again with the appearance of Nicolas and Serge Legat, Alexander Gorsky, Georgi Kyaksht and Michel Fokine.

While this brilliant new generation of Russian dancers was emerging, a group of progressive young artists and art-lovers under the growing influence of Serge Diaghilev were airing their views in a magazine called *The World of Art*. Prince Volkonsky was a friend of this group, and when he succeeded Vsevolojsky as Director of the Imperial Theatres, he called in Diaghilev to take complete charge of a new production of *Sylvia*. Unfortunately he regretted this bold act within a few days, but when he asked Diaghilev to relinquish some of his authority so as not to cause too much offence to the officials of the theatre, Diaghilev flatly refused. Volkonsky pleaded with Diaghilev to be reasonable, but events were already beyond his control and soon afterwards the Tsar signed Diaghilev's summary dismissal.

Volkonsky's turn was not long in coming. His reforming zeal was disapproved of in many influential circles, and he was eventually placed in a situation where he had no alternative but to resign. He had given instructions that Kshesinska was to wear panniers in a ballet which was set in the eighteenth century. The ballerina refused, and was duly fined by Volkonsky for disobedience. The Tsar then intervened by having it conveyed to Volkonsky that he wanted the fine publicly cancelled. Volkonsky had no choice in the matter, but after he had complied with the Tsar's wishes he sent in his resignation.

Volkonsky was succeeded by Teliakovsky, a professional soldier who set about the task of introducing reforms with little regard for the feelings of Marius Petipa, who was well over eighty years of age. Petipa's last ballet for the Maryinsky was *The Magic Mirror*, which was produced in 1903. He did not like Koreshchenko's music from the start, but was even unhappier about the sets and costumes, which were designed by Golovine, an artist of the modern school. Teliakovsky refused to withdraw the ballet, and when it proved a failure, Petipa was convinced that he was the victim of a plot. The jeering laughter that greeted the ballet haunted the old man to the end of his days. It was revived just once for the *corps de ballet's* benefit gala, which had been planned to close with a little ceremony when the company were to present Petipa with a silver laurel wreath in the presence of the public. But the management refused to allow the curtain to be raised again at the end, and Vera Trefilova had to make the presentation almost surreptitiously in the wings. Petipa went into retirement, thinking he had been a failure. The management's pettiness was carried to the point of refusing him admittance to the stage of the Maryinsky, a ban that wounded him cruelly.

The turn in Petipa's fortunes was more than a rebellion of the younger generation against the authority he had wielded for so long. New ideas were beginning to emerge that were to influence the future course of ballet. The whole conception of the art, it was felt, needed to be revised. The most important factor in a ballet should be the idea behind it, to which everything else must be subordinated to give it the maximum force and meaning. At the same time, an improvement was called for in the music. Good music was still the exception at the Maryinsky, but the American dancer, Isodora Duncan, was to show how a fine score could add to the emotional impact of the dance when she visited St Petersburg in 1905. Meanwhile, *The World of Art* was campaigning for a more positive approach in the design of scenery and costumes. There was also a choreographer's problem. This was to restore warmth and feeling to the dance, and to assimilate the recent innovations in technique by using them as means of expression rather than as sheer feats of virtuosity. The fulfilment of these ideas was to bring about the great revival of ballet which we associate with the names of Fokine and Diaghilev.

The Diaghilev Era
by Walter Sorell

Three Phases of Diaghilev

> I am, firstly, a charlatan, though rather a brilliant one; secondly, a great charmer; thirdly, frightened of nobody; fourthly, a man with plenty of logic and very few scruples; fifthly, I seem to have no real talent. None the less, I believe that I have found my true vocation—to be a Maecenas, I have everything necessary except money—but that will come!

No one could have described Serge Diaghilev more scathingly than he himself did in a letter written to his stepmother in 1895. An aesthete and an accomplished amateur of the arts, he joined a circle of young

Source: From *The Dance Through the Ages* (New York: Grosset & Dunlap, 1967).

artists in which the painters Léon Bakst and Alexandre Benois were leading figures. In 1899 he founded the magazine *Mir Iskusstva* ("The World of Art") in which he wrote: "Man does not depend on exterior circumstances but on himself alone. One of the greatest merits of our times is to recognize individuality under every guise in every epoch."

He edited the annual of the Imperial Theaters and supervised several productions for a season, but finding that bureaucracy was inimical to art, he resigned. For a while he occupied himself with putting on art exhibitions in St. Petersburg and Paris. In 1908 he decided to become a theatrical impresario, and that year he presented *Boris Godounov* at the Paris Opéra with the famed basso Feodor Chaliapin in the title role. The success of this venture encouraged Diaghilev to bring the Russian ballet to Paris, but an important factor was his break with Teliakovsky, director of the Imperial Theater, which enabled him to take the best dancers with him. What followed was decisive in the history of the dance.

The Concept of Total Theater

Diaghilev saw theater in all of its forms as a challenge. He admired the new, the fresh, the vital and he wanted his ballet theater to reflect a life that was constantly changing. His inner conflict was between his love of the classicism and romanticism of his youth and his desire to be an innovator, always in the vanguard, helping to create the excitement of the new.

When the Ballets Russes opened on May 19, 1909, at the Théâtre du Châtelet, the era of modern ballet began. The dancers—Anna Pavlova, Tamara Karsavina, Vaslav Nijinsky, Ida Rubinstein, Adolf Bolm, Mikhail Mordkin—were the products of the nineteenth century, of the traditional training at the Imperial ballet schools and the Maryinsky Theater. The scenic designers—Benois, Bakst and Nicholas Roerich—came from the circle of the *Mir Iskusstva*. With the exception of Chopin, the composers were Russian. In essence, the first period of the Diaghilev ballet, from 1909 to 1914, was marked by impressionistic, romantic and exotic trends. It was still in transition to twentieth-century ballet. By the end of this period it was undertaking many daring experiments.

What Diaghilev did from the very beginning was synthesize all the theater arts. He knew how to make the most diverse artists work together—even though he lost Pavlova after the first year—and he aimed at one thing only: a dazzling theater. To this end he sought to combine the color provided by great painters; music that was startlingly original; a choreography that did not deny the classical school but could create exciting dancing to match the ideas of great writers. Stravinsky, Ravel, Debussy, Satie, de Falla, Poulenc and Auric worked with him during his reign of twenty years. Some of the best writers—Jean Cocteau, Marcel Proust, Paul Claudel—helped spread his gospel. From Bakst and Benois to Rouault and Picasso, the painters served his cause. In fusing these creative minds, Diaghilev achieved artistic unity and realized the dreams of Lully, Rameau and Noverre: the ballet as a living art.

He was not the first to aim at a total theater. Richard Wagner tried to achieve a similar synthesis in music drama. The French poet Stéphane Mallarmé criticized Wagner for not having gone the whole way and for having minimized the role of poetry and dancing, which he saw as the nucleus of any total theater. The bold scenic designer Gordon Craig deplored the fact that the theater was "split up into departments; it has imprisoned all the arts each in its own cell. . . . I know of but one art." Diaghilev was not alone in believing in the creative power and effectiveness of theatrical synthesis, but he was also able to put it into practice. He wrote:

> The more I thought of that problem of the composition of ballet, the more plainly I understood that perfect ballet can only be created by the very closest fusion of three elements—dancing, painting and music. When I mount a ballet, I always keep these three elements in mind. That is why almost daily I go into the artists' studios, watch their work and the actual execution of the costumes, examine the scores and listen to the orchestra with close attention, and then visit the practice rooms where all the dancers practice and rehearse daily.

The strength of Diaghilev's influence on his collaborators varied, of course, but he had a close relationship with Nijinksy, Cocteau, Massine and Lifar. Lifar admits that "at the beginning" Diaghilev educated and molded him. And he quotes Diaghilev as saying: ". . . in the days of Fokine as producer and Nijinsky as dancer, both decided to carry out my artistic ideas." But Fokine protested emphatically: "No one has ever molded me. I formed myself, realized my own dream of a new ballet, and only then did Diaghilev invite me and take my already completed works." It is fair to say that without Fokine, Diaghilev's dream could easily have turned into a nightmare, or at least would not have achieved immediate acclaim.

Of course, the Ballets Russes had its critics, and André Levinson, the staunch defender of classicism, opposed Diaghilev's basic concept. He condemned him for using a dramatic emotion instead of letting considerations of pure form serve as the *raison d'être* of each step. "Diaghilev consistently seeks his inspiration outside the dance itself," he declared. Another critic, Camille Mauclair, however, appreciated the high standards of Diaghilev's theatrical spectacles. "The Bakst décor," he said, "gives us a feeling of escape into the realms of dream and fantasy. Everything is true, but nothing is real. An aesthetic truth of four arts combined in one." And he saw another truth in these ballets —emotional truth.

With Fokine's help, Diaghilev succeeded in returning to the Aristotelian conception of dancing as the representation of passions, actions and manners. Instead of realism, Diaghilev offered genuine emotions in a setting of unreality, of legend and fantasy, in a flood of color, a symphony of gestures and sound. His sense of theater led him to introduce three or four one-act ballets at each performance instead of one long ballet, as had been customary in Petipa's time. He also rescued the male dancer from his pitiful position as a *porteur* and made the *corps de ballet* significant. The Ballets Russes became a repertory group, but Diaghilev can be criticized for having failed to establish a training school to perpetuate his ideas, to build the dancer of the future.

He failed in it as much as Isadora Duncan did—although she, at least, tried. Perhaps their every day was too dazzling to give them time to think of tomorrow.

Michel Fokine

Fokine did think of the future, although his roots as dancer and teacher were in the past. He had performed important roles under Petipa and was Pavlova's first partner. Pavlova loved to work with him. He had grown up in the great classical tradition and, as Karsavina said in her book, *Theater Street*, "Fokine used classical dance as the basis of his choreography. He embroidered new patterns on it; he invested it with the style of any given epoch into which he made excursions; but his starting point was always the virtuosity of the classical ballet. . . ."

Although he was enormously successful, Fokine's intelligence rebelled against what he saw happening around him. He was twenty-four years old when he began to embarrass his teachers and choreographers with such questions as: "Why is the style of a dance seldom in harmony with its theme, costumes and period? Why does a dancer execute difficult steps if they do not express anything? Why is ballet technique limited to the movements of the lower limbs and a few conventional positions of the arms, when the whole body should be expressive?" The answer was as stereotyped as the dancing: "Because that is the tradition."

Already in 1904 Fokine wrote a letter to the Director of the Imperial Theaters in which he said:

> Dancing should be interpretive. It should not degenerate into mere gymnastics. . . . The ballet must no longer be made up of numbers, entries and so on. It must show artistic unity of conception. The action of the ballet must never be interrupted to allow the danseuse to respond to the applause of the public.
> Ballet must have complete unity of expression, a unity which is made up of a harmonious blending of the three elements—music, painting and plastic art.

His suggestions were rejected, and the letter filed for posterity. These ideas of the young Fokine came close to what Diaghilev was to transform into a reality five years later.

In 1905, Isadora Duncan, the "barefoot" dancer, came to Russia and caused an aesthetic explosion. She wanted to bury all tradition and erase the memory of the immediate past by going back to the simplicity of the ancient Greeks. She startled the dancers at the Ballet School of the Maryinsky Theater. When he saw her, Fokine felt he was not alone in his fight for reform, but having been raised in the spirit of tradition, he wanted only to give the classical school a twentieth-century look.

In April of that same year Fokine made his first attempt at choreography in *Acis and Galatea*, expressing the mythological theme with movements and poses suggested by Greek art. The same year he was asked to compose a *pas seul* of not more than three or four minutes in length for Pavlova. *The Dying Swan*, one of the immortal post-romantic dances, was the result. Fokine said that it "was proof that the dance could not and should not satisfy only the eye, but through the medium of the eye should penetrate into the soul." And like all innovators since the days of Lully, he strove to combine new groups and forms of movement, and to integrate dance, music, decor, lighting, and costuming with theme and action.

He excelled in all styles. After the strongly Duncanesque *Eunice*, created in 1907, in which the ballet dancers appeared barefoot he composed several ballets which were to become the backbone of Diaghilev's repertoire: *Les Sylphides*, *The Firebird*, *Scheherazade*, *Le Spectre de la rose* and *Petrouchka*.

Fokine had a few failures, among them *Le Dieu Bleu* and *Thamar.* He felt Diaghilev's growing indifference and when he found out that Diaghilev had secretly asked Nijinsky to choreograph *The Afternoon of a Faun,* he left the company and only returned in 1914 to stage his successful ballet, *Le Coq d'Or.* In this year he formulated the fundamental ideas of his reform in a letter to the London *Times:*

> 1. To create in each case a new form of movement corresponding to the subject matter, period and character of the music, instead of merely giving combinations of ready-made and established steps.
>
> 2. Dancing and mimetic gesture have no meaning in ballet unless they serve as an expression of dramatic action.
>
> 3. To admit the use of conventional gesture only when it is required by the style of the ballet, and in all other cases to replace the gesture of the hands by movements of the whole body. Man can and should be expressive from head to foot.
>
> 4. The group is not only an ornament. The new ballet advances from the expressiveness of the face and the hands to that of the whole body to groups of bodies and the expressiveness of the combined dancing of a crowd.
>
> 5. The alliance of dancing with other arts. The new ballet, refusing to be slave either of music or of scenic decoration, and recognizing the alliance of arts only on the condition of complete equality, allows perfect freedom both to the scenic artist and to the musician.

Igor Stravinsky

It is usually difficult to assess the importance of a composer's contribution to the growth of a ballet company, but Stravinsky's influence on the theater dance cannot be overstated. If Diaghilev's venture might have failed without the body and form that Fokine provided, it also needed the direction in which Stravinsky's music turned it. He set his own standards and forced them on his collaborators.

Stravinsky's music creates the excitement of nowness, the sound of immediacy, the sound rippling in cascades of surprises but always pure, denuded, unexpectedly earthy. He is never the same, but always recognizable. His innovations derive from an all-embracing awareness and his rhythms are insistent because they reach far back into ritual, into unashamed primitivism.

His compositions are of such theatrical intensity that they become an extension of the imagery of ballet movement giving the dancing bodies a fourth dimension and heightening the visual excitement. His dissonances are a propelling force for the moving body, but at the same time his tempo demands self-discipline, perfect control on the part of the dancer. Stravinsky came to understand the dance better than any other composer, and more often than not he wrote the scenarios for his scores. Of the origin of *Petrouchka* he says:

> I had in mind . . . a puppet, suddenly endowed with life, exasperating the patience of the orchestra with diabolic cascades of arpeggios. The orchestra in turn retaliates with menacing trumpet blasts. The outcome is a terrific noise which reaches its climax and ends in the sorrowful and querulous collapse of the poor puppet. Soon afterwards Diaghilev came to visit me . . . I played him the piece . . . which later became the second scene of *Petrouchka*. He was so much pleased with it that he . . . began persuading me to develop the theme of the puppet's sufferings and make it into a whole ballet. . . .

His eight scores for the Ballets Russes did more to identify the company with a new era than most of the choreography, décors and themes of its early years.

Lully, Rameau and Tchaikovsky all served the dance. Their music was pliant, suggestive, helpful in its rhythmic and melodic richness. But Stravinsky's music is compelling, demanding, leading. If the choreographer is unable to follow the flight of Stravinsky's inventiveness or cannot yield to the complexities of his rhythms, the result is chaos—at least, from Stravinsky's viewpoint. Nijinsky is a case in point. Stravinsky admired him as a dancer and a mime, but was appalled by Nijinsky's utter lack of musical understanding. In 1912 Diaghilev insisted on Nijinsky's staging *The Rite of Spring* ("Le Sacre du Printemps"). Stravinsky felt that it "was a very labored and barren effort rather than a plastic realization flowing simply and naturally from what the music demanded . . . although he had grasped the dramatic significance of the dance, Nijinsky was incapable of giving intelligible form to its essence." Stravinsky was far more satisfied with Leonide Massine's choreography in 1920, which "flowed out of the music and was not, as the first had been, imposed on it."

George Balanchine has fared best with Stravinsky because he recognized the classical austerity of his style and found the most convincing bodily movements for his always surprising and often perplexing atonality. Balanchine claims that working on Stravinsky's *Apollon Musagète*—which took place at the very end of the Diaghilev era—became the turning point of his life. And Stravinsky had great admiration for

Balanchine's inventiveness and craftsmanship, his ability to grasp and express the meaning of the music. Balanchine responded to the vitality in the music; he learned to be guided by Stravinsky's dynamic use of silence; he accepted the constant surprise of his new approaches. Their collaboration is unique in the history of ballet.

If Stravinsky helped the Ballets Russes become what it was, Diaghilev's merit was in having believed in the young composer. By encouraging Stravinsky, he gave the twentieth-century ballet its most important composer.

Vaslav Nijinsky

No artist has ever captured the imagination of the public as Nijinsky did: his one leap in Fokine's *The Spectre of the Rose* became legendary. But it takes more than training and technical ability to achieve perfection. One must have certain other qualities: personality, stage presence, magnetism. Nijinsky had them all.

Diaghilev sensed in this unusual, silent, sad peasant a gift for choreography. And what Nijinsky tried to express in *The Afternoon of a Faun* was close to the hidden primitive in man. His faun had jerky, angular movements that evoked the satyrs on Greek vases, but he also gave his faun a dynamic quality that was a denial of pure classicism. Diaghilev thought that he had found a new choreographer whose work was cerebral; in fact, it was the volcanic expression of a tortured soul haunted by strange images.

At this point Diaghilev needed someone who could prevent a successful formula from becoming rigid and shake his dancers and the public out of their complacency. Nijinsky seemed to be the right man for this task. To give his protégé a sounder foundation for his next choreographic essay, which was to be *The Rite of Spring*, Diaghilev took him to Emile Jaques-Dalcroze in Hellerau, whose influence on many creative dancers had been invaluable. Dalcroze had found that his principles of "eurhythmics"—that is, good rhythm—could help improve the rhythm of dancers. Diaghilev also engaged Miriam Rambach—later known as Marie Rambert—to tutor Nijinsky. Both were Poles, and in her Nijinsky found someone who understood him. If Diaghilev was a kind of father to him, Rambach was the friend who guided him and remedied his lack of a musical education.

Nijinsky's choreography for *The Rite of Spring* may have displeased Stravinsky and shocked the audience—the première caused a furor—but it anticipated a modern mood, a sophisticated approach to archaic movements, a naiveté rooted in primitivism. Nijinsky envisioned a circular dance in unbroken, endless motion, visually exciting, theatrically conceived. Of this choreography his wife says:

> Nijinsky contradicts the classical position by making all steps and gestures turn inward. . . . It is through rhythm, and rhythm only, that the dance identified itself with the music. The rhythmical counterpoint is employed in the choral movements. When the orchestra plays a trill on the flutes, movements thin out, and so do the dancers. Then the tune begins on woodwinds two octaves apart, and on the stage two groups of three dancers each detach themselves from the lines and dance corresponding to the tune. . . . At the end of the first tableau great circles (women dressed in scarlet) run wildly, while shifting masses within are ceaselessly splitting up into tiny groups revolving on eccentric axes.

In 1913, the year in which *The Rite of Spring* had its première, Nijinsky also choreographed a lighter ballet in which he intended to show athletic movements expressed lyrically. *Jeux* was to be a divertissement only but turned out to be revolutionary in the treatment of its subject. The background of the story was a garden party, while the subject was love as revealed through a tennis game. For the first time a choreographer dared introduce the theme of sport and dancers in sport clothes. Moreover, the mood of the dance was conveyed with angular movements and through abstractions rather than conventionally expressed sentiments. A tennis ball bouncing onto the stage started the love game between a boy and two girls, and another ball, which the boy tried to retrieve, ended it. As the boy, Nijinsky, following the balls with two leaps that covered the stage, triumphed with his air-borne movement and grace. But the many innovations in *Jeux* made the first-night audience uneasy. Nijinsky enthralled his public with his leaps. It was "the victory of breath over weight . . . the utilization of the animal by the soul," Paul Claudel said. But the people could not accept his choreography. For he was years ahead of them. His two choreographic failures in 1913 opened the way for more daring experiments to come.

Nijinsky was a genius, but one step removed from the madness that finally overtook him.

Jean Cocteau

Jean Cocteau said: ". . . dancing is the language in which I would prefer to express myself, and my favorite theatrical formula." Like most artists of the day, he was dazzled by the fireworks of the Ballets Russes and drawn to that maker of magic Diaghilev, who wielded his wand like a scepter. Cocteau designed some early posters for the company, wrote about its productions and talked ecstatically of Diaghilev and Nijinsky in Parisian salons. In May 1912, he contributed the scenario for the exotic but unsuccessful Hindu ballet, *Le Dieu Bleu.*

One day Diaghilev startled Cocteau by simply saying, "Surprise me." This was the turning point in Cocteau's life. It was with *Parade*, produced in 1917, that Cocteau eventually surprised Diaghilev and stunned Paris. According to Cocteau, Erik Satie, whose music was sparse, said modestly, "I composed a background for certain noises (dynamos, sirens, trains, planes) which Cocteau considered indispensable in order to establish the mood of his characters." Who were these characters? A Chinese who "pulls out an egg from his pigtail, eats and digests it, finds it again in the toe of his shoe, spits fire, burns himself, stamps to put out the sparks, etc . . ." A little girl who "mounts a race horse, rides a bicycle, quivers like pictures on the screen, imitates Charlie Chaplin, chases a thief with a revolver, dances to ragtime, goes to sleep, is ship-wrecked, rolls on the grass, buys a Kodak, etc . . ." And then: "As for the acrobats—the poor, stupid, agile acrobats—we tried to invest them with the melancholy of a Sunday evening after the circus has ended and the children leave, casting a last glance at the ring."

Parade also introduced Pablo Picasso to the theater as a stage designer. *Parade* had the atmosphere of the street, the music hall, the circus, without their vulgarities. It had an ecstatic quality of the ordered chaos of life, the intense, nostalgic, lyric feeling of childhood memories, with a touch of the disintegration of society after World War I. It was new, different, a scandal.

Cocteau was convinced that "reality alone, even when well concealed, has the power to arouse emotion." He wanted to strip things bare, to see with the imagination of a child. He felt that in an age of subtlety and sophistication it was essential to return to simplicity—but without being banal. He sought to "rehabilitate the commonplace" with the element of surprise. To understand his daring and his zest for anticipating artistic fashion, one must consider some of the influences that shaped him.

Four men were to give Cocteau the confidence he needed. Satie taught him to avoid adornment and to seek a simplicity that attains richness by a refining process. Picasso taught him "to run faster than beauty." ("If you keep step with her, your product will be photographic 'kitsch.' If you run behind her, you accomplish only the mediocre.") Stravinsky taught him to "insult habit," for only in that way can art be kept from becoming sterile. And from his poet friend Raymond Radiguet Cocteau learned to accept no premise and to distrust novelty for its own sake.

Parade was followed by *Le Bœuf sur le Toit ou The Do Nothing Bar*, which Cocteau conceived and staged as a mime show for the famous Fratellini clowns. While the "realistic" *Parade* did not satisfy him completely because, he said, "theater corrupts everything," he derived greater satisfaction from his next ballet. This was *Les Mariés de la Tour Eiffel*, which he did for Rolf de Maré's Ballets Suédois, and which he described as "the first work in which I owe nothing to anyone, which is unlike any other work." He called *Les Mariés* a comedy-ballet and mixed ancient tragedy (the actors wore masks) with music hall numbers.

Bronislava Nijinska's *Les Biches*, on which he collaborated in 1924, was one of the first ballets which, he said, combined classic steps with new gestures. About then Cocteau also devised *Le Train Bleu*, a ballet based on beach games, swimming, tennis and golf movements. The idea emerged from his predilection for clowns and acrobats and seemed very novel at the time.

When, in 1946, he returned to the ballet, he had left behind the idea of any composite spectacle. Experimentation did not stop. *Le Jeune Homme et la Mort* was a great success when the Ballets des Champs-Elysées produced it in Paris with Jean Babilée and Nathalie Philippart in leading roles.

Two years later he designed the sets and costumes for *L'Amour et son Amour* ("Cupid and His Love"), which the Ballet Theater later presented at the Metropolitan Opera House in New York in 1951. It carried the motto by Cocteau: "Love has no explanation—do not seek a meaning in love's gestures." *La Dame à la Licorne*, his last ballet scenario, was choreographed by Heinz Rosen for the Munich Opera Ballet in 1953, later produced by the Paris Opéra and by the Ballet Russe de Monte Carlo in New York in 1955. In that year Jean Cocteau, the "enfant terrible" of art was elected to the Académie Française and became an "immortal."

In Cocteau's sentence: "To be reborn one must burn oneself alive," lies the key to the understanding of his genius. This thought of rising like a phoenix from one's own ashes was echoed in a later statement: "My discipline consists in not letting myself be enslaved by obsolete formulae."

Jean Cocteau was a pioneer in transferring the reflection of everyday life onto the dance stage. Instead of the spectacular sequence of heightened unreality, the fairy-tale atmosphere on which ballet had fed for so long, he offered a heightened reality. What was accepted as avant-garde in dance in the 1950's and 1960's was built in large part on Cocteau's daring and imagination.

The Second and Third Phase

In 1913, after his marriage, Nijinsky left the Ballets Russes. Diaghilev had already commissioned Richard Strauss to write the score for a ballet based on the legend of Joseph; Nijinsky was to have been Joseph. Now the impresario had to find a replacement.

At that time Leonide Massine was a handsome young supernumerary in the ballet *Don Quixote* at the Theater Marny in Moscow. When Diaghilev saw him cross the stage, he felt at once that there was his Joseph. If ever a dancer-choreographer was completely a creation of Diaghilev, it was Massine. Ballet master Enrico Cecchetti had to train the boy for his difficult part; Diaghilev educated him and exposed him to the influence of the avant-garde circle of Cocteau, Picasso and Stravinsky. Diaghilev was certain that Massine would be able to translate the new ideas in the arts into the ballet idiom.

Massine was brilliant in the title role of *The Legend of Joseph* and a year later, in 1915, he choreographed his first ballet, *The Midnight Sun*, a suite of Russian folk dances. As a dancer he possessed more expressive talent than technique and his choreography was strongest in its dramatic and pantomimic aspects. This became obvious in his second ballet, *The Good-Humored Ladies*, which he staged in the style of the *commedia dell'arte* and in which the pantomime was far more brilliant than the dancing. By 1917 he had mastered all styles and non-styles, as he proved when he choreographed Cocteau's *Parade*. In this ballet he made the *non sequitur* effective on stage and transformed the banal into ecstatic reality.

Massine left Diaghilev in 1921, but worked for the Ballets Russes intermittently from 1924 to 1928. Later he was associated with the Ballet Russe de Monte Carlo and other companies on two continents. In 1928 he came to America and accepted the taxing position of ballet master at the Roxy Theater in New York where he staged and appeared in four shows a day. To counteract what must have been an unsympathetic job, he produced in 1930 for the League of Composers *The Rite of Spring*, with Martha Graham in the role of the Chosen Virgin.

When Massine left the Ballets Russes in 1921 Diaghilev had to look for a new choreographer and he chose Bronislava Nijinska, Nijinsky's sister, who had assisted him in mounting *The Sleeping Beauty* in London.

She was more traditional than her brother and gave his harsh, archaic lines a softness. She tried for a "neo-realistic" approach and, probably inspired by her brother's ballet *Jeux*, she included sport, jazz and satire in her works. All this made her appear to vacillate between styles. She fared best when she was under the influence of Stravinsky or Cocteau. Stravinsky characterized her as "an excellent dancer endowed with a profoundly artistic nature, and . . . gifted with a real talent for choreographic creation." However, when she staged Stravinsky's *Les Noces* in 1923, the composer felt that she had listened to Diaghilev but had not followed his intentions. Nevertheless, this ballet of a Russian peasant wedding ceremony was one of her great successes. It was followed by the gently witty sketches of high society, *Les Biches*, some amusing glimpses of the smart set of the 1920's. Next came Cocteau's *Le Train Bleu*, which was full of acrobatics but little dancing.

Diaghilev did not fully appreciate Nijinska's work, for he was seeking the youthful replenishment he more and more required as he grew older. He was impressed by George Balanchine's talent when he saw the work of Balanchine's small Russian company touring Europe in the mid-1920's. Balanchine's approach, though basically classic, was gymnastic, plastic, expressionistically modern. Diaghilev recognized that Balanchine's talent, inventiveness and tongue-in-cheek humor would enrich the Ballets Russes, and in 1925 he asked him to restage Stravinsky's *Le Rossignol*. During the next four years Balanchine created ten more ballets for Diaghilev, of which *Barabau* was the most vital and daring in its theatrical devices, while in *La Chatte*, based on the Aesop fable, he revived the pure classical style. In *Apollon Musagète* he seemed to have found himself.

Balanchine's last work of choreography for Diaghilev was *The Prodigal Son*, in 1929. The title role in this ballet was danced by young Serge Lifar who was another creation and hope of Diaghilev. Balanchine taught Lifar the movements that fitted his gifts and concealed his weaknesses. Lifar was the Nijinsky of the late Diaghilev period: his grace, radiance, and commanding stage presence made him the image of eternal youth of which Diaghilev always dreamed.

For twenty years Diaghilev had sought the new, the contemporaneous expression through the ballet, but he never forgot his first love: the romantic-classical ballet. It may not have been mere coincidence that the last work staged by the Ballets Russes—two weeks before Serge Diaghilev died—was *Swan Lake*.

A Mission for Anna Pavlova

No chapter on the origins of modern ballet would be complete without paying homage to Anna Pavlova who has long signified the ballerina *sublimis.*

The theater dance has never had a more striking representative, a more important pioneer for the idea of ballet itself. And yet so little is left of so much greatness: a few photographs, a short film and the fading memory of those who once saw the "sublime Pavlova."

Diaghilev knew what he wanted from a dancer: a fusion of precision and lightness, of technique and expression. "She is the greatest ballerina in the world," he said, "excelling both in classicism and in character." And he engaged her for the historic Paris opening of the Ballets Russes in 1909. But she left at the end of the first season and went to England to form her own company. What had happened? Nijinsky was, no doubt, favored by Diaghilev—male dancers of such stature are always rarities—and he also received better notices than Pavlova did. Even Ida Rubenstein had a somewhat better press. Moreover, both Diaghilev and Pavlova were despots. They both believed in art *per se*, but Diaghilev thought he summed it up and Pavlova thought that she did.

Some time later, Diaghilev—no doubt, hurt that she had left him—thundered, "Pavlova was never really interested in art as such. The only thing that mattered to her was virtuosity"—but he did add, "and she is a virtuoso without equal." Pavlova realized the gulf between them when she asked the critics, "Are you on my side or Diaghilev's?" and she replied to his charge in an autobiographical sketch saying, "I was essentially a lyric dancer . . . never interested in purposeless virtuosity."

Technical skill alone was not the secret of her greatness, for many a dancer today is better trained than Pavlova ever was. In fact, she rarely turned more than two or three pirouettes, but she executed them with such brio that they had the effect of half a dozen. It was the spirit far more than the body itself which created the illusion of lightness. As a dancer with whom she performed, André Oliveroff, put it: "I knew . . . she would be easy to lift—but I had not divined the uncanny lightness of her. When I caught and supported her in mid-air, I was scarcely conscious of her weight; her elevation seemed to continue—she seemed always to be reaching up, giving you the illusion that she was very much lighter than she really was."

Anna Pavlova was born in St. Petersburg on January 31, 1882, a frail premature baby. At the age of eight she was taken to the Maryinsky Theater, where she saw a performance of *The Sleeping Beauty*. Then and there she decided to become a ballerina. At sixteen she was a *première danseuse*, and her ambition was to be seen as a dancer by the whole world. Taglioni was still the most popular ballerina of the past, and Pavlova conceived the idea of surpassing Taglioni. Theodore Stier, Pavlova's musical director for sixteen years, tells us that he traveled 300,000 miles with her, conducted 3,650 performances and more than 2,000 rehearsals.

She sold ballet to the world and with it her name. She danced before audiences who had never seen dancing "on toe," she appeared in regions where people either disliked or didn't understand ballet. In Java and Mexico, in Japan and India, her name was magic, and ballet schools opened wherever she went. The people needed her. "Everywhere," she said, "our dancing was hailed as the revelation of an undreamed-of art."

Except for a few divertissements and one ballet we have no proof of her choreographic ability, although many critics maintained that she was able to wipe out the difference between "creative" and "interpretative" art by making her interpretation as personal as if it had been her own creation.

The ballet is *Autumn Leaves*, a "choreographic poem" in one act, which she created in 1928 and first produced in Rio de Janeiro. In it she tried to express the inevitability of all that is passing and the tragedy of final rejection. For the poet's tenderness is only caused by a fleeting feeling for the flower's beauty and its fading fragrance, by pity for the doomed. The moment when his betrothed appears, the flower is forgotten.

She was a romantic at heart who saw nature through a poetic prism and translated her dreams into the stage images she loved to dance: *The Snowflake*, *The Dragonfly*, *The Butterfly*, or the *Fleur de Lys*.

The question of what it was that made her such a very great dancer has often been asked, and there are almost as many answers as there are experts. Perhaps it was simply her personality. As Anatole Chujoy has said, "She was great, because she was Pavlova." But if any young dancer should dream of becoming a "second Pavlova" she should remember that she only became what she was because she did not want to be a second Taglioni.

Contemporary Ballet

by Clement Crisp and Edward Thorpe

Within two years of Diaghilev's death in 1929, the other great exponent of the dance, Anna Pavlova had also died. Between them, these two had created a world-wide enthusiasm for ballet. What Diaghilev had offered his public was entertainment employing the finest artistic resources of the time. Pavlova gave her devotees the experience of an incredible star performer, touring world-wide in cities and even townships totally unreachable by the grander Ballet Russe, thrilling audiences by the passionate intensity of her presence. Her influence was incalculable in inspiring a love of dance: in Lima, Peru, a small English boy saw her and determined to make his career as a dancer. He was Frederick Ashton, one of the architects of British ballet as we know it today.

After the dissolution of the Diaghilev and Pavlova companies, there was a vacuum. Just as the itinerant ballet-masters of Italy and France had spread the art of ballet throughout Europe in previous centuries, so now Diaghilev's choreographers and dancers transported their talents and ideas to the central cities of the Western world. During the 1930s the creation of important national ballet companies owed everything to Diaghilev's former artists. In Britain two remarkable women —Marie Rambert and Ninette de Valois—were responsible for the creation of two major companies.

Britain

Both Marie Rambert and Ninette de Valois served an important apprenticeship with Diaghilev. Marie Rambert, born in Warsaw in 1888, was invited to join the Diaghilev enterprise in 1912, to help Nijinsky in his work on the very difficult Stravinsky score for *Rite of Spring*. She came to London during the 1914–1918 war and married the English playwright Ashley Dukes, and thereafter settled in London where she opened a school. From this there developed a classical dance

Source: From *The Colorful World of Ballet* (London: Octopus, 1977).

company, small in numbers but rich in talent. Amongst Rambert's pupils were two men who, in particular, were to become choreographers of international importance: Frederick Ashton (b 1904) and Antony Tudor (b 1909). During the 1930s Rambert's company, ever surviving on a shoe-string, created a repertoire which included several enduring masterpieces by Tudor—notably *Jardin aux Lilas* and *Dark Elegies*—and provided the first opportunities for several subsequently celebrated choreographers and dancers. Marie Rambert's gift for discovering and inspiring creative talent has been vital in the formation of British ballet.

Simultaneously, Ninette de Valois had also set to work. Of Anglo-Irish descent, born in 1898, de Valois had danced with Diaghilev during the 1920s and had then opened a school in London. She had dreams of an English national ballet, and the realization of these dreams owed much to another redoubtable woman, Lilian Baylis. Miss Baylis (1874–1937) was running the Old Vic Theatre at Waterloo, in south London, presenting a repertory of classical plays at popular prices. Ninette de Valois joined forces with her, on the understanding that when Miss Baylis should eventually re-open the derelict Sadler's Wells Theatre in Islington, north London, to house an opera company, Ninette de Valois' ballet school and her dancers should form the nucleus of a permanent ballet company. This plan came to fruition in 1931, and the Vic-Wells ballet company and school, blessed with a permanent home, developed under de Valois' inspiring guidance. During the 1930s the solid foundations of a great national company—the Royal Ballet—were methodically laid. The school—a vital component in any enduring balletic venture—had a home; de Valois herself provided some important choreography, and early on took the vital decision to obtain authentic stagings of the great classics of 19th-century ballet. She invited Nicholas Sergeyev (1876–1951) to revive the repertory which he had supervised at the Maryinsky Theatre in St Petersburg before the Russian revolution and which he had preserved with notation, and by 1934, the infant Vic-Wells ballet was capable of staging *Giselle*, *Swan Lake*, *Coppélia* and *The Nutcracker*.

De Valois was also fortunate in being able to call upon a true classical ballerina to dance several of these great roles. This was Alicia Markova (b 1910) who had been engaged by Diaghilev in 1925 as a phenomenal child dancer, and who had thereafter become an increasingly important member of the Ballet Russe. Now she, and her partner Anton Dolin (b 1904), also British born and an ex-Diaghilev principal, were to lend their support to the fledgling company. (Markova had also appeared with the Rambert ballet in its early days.) In 1935 Markova left the

Wells to form her own company with Anton Dolin; however de Valois had a young dancer on whom she pinned many of her hopes. This was Margot Fonteyn (b 1919) who was to take over Markova's role. At the same time de Valois had an exceptionally gifted dramatic dancer in Robert Helpmann (b 1909) who had already partnered Markova, and who was to become the company's leading male star. Two other great formative talents were also to contribute to the health of this national company. Constant Lambert (1905–1951) was a composer and conductor of magnificent gifts—he had written a score for Diaghilev when only 20—which he dedicated to the service of ballet for most of his life. He arranged scores, composed, conducted, and—very importantly—acted as artistic guide and counsellor to the company.

In 1935 Frederick Ashton, whose talents as a choreographer had been discovered by Marie Rambert, came to join the enterprise at Sadler's Wells Theatre. He had already created ballets for the company, but now his permanent association led to the composition of a series of major works—many starring Margot Fonteyn—which helped to create a style of classical dancing for the company. By 1939, the Sadler's Wells Ballet (as the company was now called) was firmly rooted, and could undertake its most important staging—a revival of *The Sleeping Beauty* with Fonteyn and Helpmann in the leading roles.

With the outbreak of war the company undertook extensive touring, which took it throughout the British Isles. In the process the company acquired a new and faithful audience who were to ensure its popularity in time of peace. During these war years, the contribution of Robert Helpmann as choreographer (with ballets like *Hamlet* and *Miracle in the Gorbals*) and principal dancer was vitally important. With peace came the great opportunity. In 1946 the Royal Opera House, Covent Garden was re-opened as a theatre (after war-time service as a dance-hall) and de Valois was asked to transfer her company there. On 21 February 1946, with an opulent new version of *The Sleeping Beauty*, Fonteyn and Helpmann in the leading roles and Constant Lambert conducting, the Sadler's Wells Ballet entered a new phase in its history. But the Sadler's Wells Theatre was not abandoned. Dame Ninette formed a second company there—the Sadler's Wells Theatre Ballet. Under the guidance of Ursula Moreton and Peggy van Praagh it was to become a cradle for much of the new young talent of the post-war years. This was an exciting time for British ballet: the Sadler's Wells Ballet flourished at Covent Garden, with Frederick Ashton creating a stream of important ballets, many of them designed around the talents of Margot Fonteyn, who was hailed as a great ballerina; the second company at Sadler's Wells Theatre was encouraging new young dancers and most important, a second generation of choreographers (notably John Cranko, and within a few years, Kenneth MacMillan). Within three years the Sadler's Wells Ballet was to be known as a company of international stature following its first appearance in North America: audiences in New York and throughout America and Canada acclaimed not only Margot Fonteyn and Helpmann, but a whole string of outstanding dancers. The world was now to become aware of the English style of dancing and choreography, and of the importance of the classic repertory which was so carefully preserved and presented by what was acknowledged as the British national company.

Ballet was enormously popular. Britain received visits from many important foreign companies, notably New York City Ballet in 1950 and Ballet Theatre from America in 1946; and by the daring young French company—Les Ballets des Champs Elysées (also in 1946)—led by Roland Petit, who continued the Diaghilev tradition of employing outstanding artists to decorate his work. The Ballets Russes, alas, now seemed dead in Europe: de Basil returned in 1947 to give audiences a last glimpse of pre-war magic, but the standard of presentation was disappointing, and the company soon disbanded. Much more exciting was the arrival in London in 1956 of the real Russian ballet, the Bolshoy Ballet from Moscow, with the incomparable Ulanova as its star. The grandeur of the Russians' dancing was to thrill Britain, and thereafter the visits of the Bolshoi Ballet and the aristocratic Kirov from Leningrad (the former Maryinsky Theatre troupe) were to set standards of technical excellence which inspired dancers and public alike. The final establishment of the Sadler's Wells Ballet came in 1956 when Dame Ninette's endeavours were crowned with the granting of a Royal Charter: the Sadler's Wells Ballet and School (which had also flourished wonderfully since the war) were now to become the Royal Ballet. During the next decade, it could be seen how the influence and example of Dame Ninette's work was extending world-wide. Celia Franca (b 1921), a former dancer with both Rambert and the Sadler's Wells Ballets, went to Canada and laboured magnificently to bring about the creation of the National Ballet of Canada. Peggy van Praagh (b 1910), also a former graduate of the Rambert and Sadler's Wells organizations, went to Australia in 1961 to found the Australian Ballet. In 1961 John Cranko (1927–1973) went to Stuttgart from London to revitalize the Stuttgart Ballet and within a dozen years had made it an internationally acclaimed company. Cranko was a member of that generation of commonwealth dancers who hurried to London at the war's end to study at the Sadler's Wells School and then progress into the company (among his contemporaries were Nadia Nerina, Maryon Lane, Alexander

Grant, Elaine Fifield, David Poole and Rowena Jackson, all of whom were to be vitally important as members of the Royal Ballet).

In 1964 Dame Ninette de Valois retired as director of the company she had founded, to be succeeded by Sir Frederick Ashton. Ashton's choreography had become the hallmark of the British national style, and it was particularly important that although he still continued to produce important short ballets, he also embarked upon a series of full-length works which were the logical continuation of the classical traditions he had inherited from Marius Petipa. In 1948 his three-act *Cinderella* was staged at the Royal Opera House. Thereafter, he created *Sylvia* (1952), *Ondine* (1958), *La Fille mal Gardée* (1960) and *The Two Pigeons* (1961) as full-length ballets for the Royal Ballet, and a *Romeo and Juliet* (1955) for the Royal Danish Ballet.

This tradition of full-length works has been continued by the man who succeeded Ashton in 1970 as director of the Royal Ballet, Kenneth MacMillan. MacMillan (b 1929) was another product of the Royal Ballet, moving from school to company, who started to create ballets in 1955. His first full-length work, *Romeo and Juliet*, was staged in 1965, and after three years leave of absence when he went to Berlin to direct the Deutsche Oper Ballet, he returned as Director of the Royal Ballet in 1970. For that company he has created many short works, and has continued the Ashton tradition by producing two further full-length works—*Anastasia* (1971) and *Manon* (1974).

While the Royal Ballet at Covent Garden was established as a national institution, its second company—now known as the Sadler's Wells Royal Ballet following its return to a home base at Sadler's Wells Theatre in 1976—undertook a considerable touring schedule in the regions. As part of the ballet boom during and after the war, several other classical companies were launched. International Ballet led by Mona Inglesby toured classical stagings and a small modern repertory from its inception in 1941 until it was disbanded in 1953. In 1948 Alicia Markova and Anton Dolin returned to London after ten years spent working in America where they had been hailed to be among the greatest ballet stars. So great was their success that in 1949 they embarked upon a regional tour which led to the founding in the following year of London Festival Ballet (named after the Festival of Britain). The company offered classic stagings, revivals of the Diaghilev repertory, and new works, and provided audiences with a wonderful opportunity to see some of the greatest international stars as guest artists. Under the administration of Dr Julian Braunsweg the company flourished despite the absence of any government subsidy—it is worth recording that ballet, like the other performing arts, had now become so prohibitively expensive that official financial support was needed, even with continually full houses. Festival Ballet toured all round Britain and then embarked upon lengthy and very successful world tours; the acquisition of subsidies from the Greater London Council and the Arts Council were well merited. After some managerial changes, a new artistic director was appointed: Beryl Grey, formerly a ballerina with the Royal Ballet, took charge of the company in 1968, and has directed it since then with Paul Findlay as administrator. The company policy of classic staging and Diaghilev repertory as a basis for its work has remained stable, and over the years a varied collection of more contemporary ballets has also been presented.

Ballet Rambert, the oldest of British companies, had long suffered from the fact that the choreographers and dancers who had been discovered and encouraged by Marie Rambert, often left for greater opportunities with larger companies: Frederick Ashton made over a dozen elegant works for Ballet Rambert during the early 1930s—such small gems as *Les Masques* and *Foyer de Danse* featured Alicia Markova; his early comedy *Façade* was preserved by Rambert after it was created for the Camargo Society (which presented brief seasons of ballet in London after Diaghilev's death). Antony Tudor created two of his greatest ballets—*Dark Elegies* and *Jardin aux Lilas*—in the mid 1930s; Andrée Howard (1908–1968) made her amazing *Lady into Fox* in 1939, and two years later created a delicate masterpiece, *La Fête Etrange;* while Walter Gore (b 1910) and Frank Staff (1918–1971) continued the amazing creative record of the Rambert company into the 1940s and 1950s.

But important choreographers such as these had to move on to the challenges of bigger companies. Ashton joined the Sadler's Wells Ballet; Tudor and Andrée Howard both went to America; Walter Gore formed his own company and worked throughout Europe and in Australia; Frank Staff went to South Africa. Dancers, too, naturally wanted more experience, and John Gilpin, a Rambert graduate and one of the brightest young dancers Britain had produced, made a stellar career as the principal male dancer of London Festival Ballet. Despite the loss of fine artists since her earliest seasons Rambert continued to find further talent, and the list of Rambert dancers and choreographers is one of outstanding talent and achievement. After the war a tour of Australia was tremendously successful, although by the end the company had lost much of its personnel. In the following years the need to tour in competition with larger companies was to lead to near disintegration. Nevertheless, excellent stagings (including a fine *Giselle* and *La Sylphide*) were still preserved, and a talented new choreographer, Norman Morrice, was discovered. It was Morrice, who, with Dame Marie, revitalized the company in 1966 with a total change of policy. Inspired by the example of the Nederlands Dans Theater (a ballet company dedicated to adventurous work which combined classic and Modern Dance) Ballet Rambert was re-formed as a small troupe of soloists and its repertory was re-forged: the influence of Glen Tetley (an American choreographer) was important in showing a way in which classic and modern could be combined. Once again—as in the 1930s—Ballet Rambert was doing pioneer work and was in the forefront of the growing interest in Modern Dance. In addition to the ballets of Glen Tetley, new works by Norman Morrice provided the mainstay of the repertory. Within a short while several other choreographers had emerged from within the ranks of the company—a typical facet of the Rambert system. Notable among these is Christopher Bruce, one of the outstanding dancers of our time, and John Chesworth, now director (with Bruce) of the company. The Rambert tradition of encouraging creativity among its dancers is still maintained today in its work-shop seasons co-presented with the Central School of Art and Design.

One of the great champions of Modern Dance in Britain is Robin Howard, a philanthropist who had been inspired by the work of Martha Graham and through his financial generosity, had made possible her visits to Britain. At first British audiences did not appreciate Modern Dance, but persistence paid off: the visits of Graham, of Merce Cunningham, Paul Taylor, Jose Limón and Alvin Ailey with their companies began to attract an appreciative audience. Howard's next move was to plan the establishment of a British dance company and school based upon the Graham technique. To this end he invited Martha Graham's support, and she sent several of her dancers to work with students in London—notably Robert Cohan (b 1925). From this small beginning there developed rapidly the school and company now known as the London Contemporary Dance Theatre. Premises were found in a former army drill hall which was converted into a theatre and teaching studio. This is The Place, the present home of London Contemporary Dance Theatre. Under the guidance of Robert Cohan as artistic director and chief choreographer, the company has established itself in less than a decade as the finest Modern Dance company in Europe. Cohan had 'naturalised' Graham's style to create an authentically British method of Modern Dance: his artists were encouraged to create work, and there now exists a most healthy and exciting nucleus of choreographers who provide the repertory of the London Contemporary Dance Theatre. Among these we must note particularly Siobhan Davies, Robert North, and Micha Bergese. Robert Cohan is an inspiring creator and teacher, and in recent years the company has embarked upon an important programme of working within colleges and schools throughout Britain to encourage a greater interest and participation in dance at every level.

While London has inevitably remained the centre of dance activity, there have been some successful attempts to establish dance in the regions. Most important of these has been the creation of The Scottish Ballet. In 1957 Elizabeth West (1927–1962) and Peter Darrell (b 1929) founded a small company in Bristol. Western Theatre Ballet was dedicated to the presentation of new ballets whose interest was both in their dramatic content and in their use of contemporary themes. Darrell's choreography was well suited to this ideal, and after several years of courageous touring under the most difficult financial circumstances, Western Theatre Ballet was recognized as a vital part of the British dance scene. In 1969, with Arts Council support, the company was transferred to Glasgow to become the Scottish Ballet, where it has now established itself firmly. Both classics and modern repertory are now offered, and its tours in the Northern part of the British Isles, as well as internationally, have made it a cultural force of some renown.

America

Parallel with the expansion of Modern Dance [see following chapter] has been the development of classic ballet in America. The most important figure is, of course, George Balanchine, whose New York City Ballet is one of the great classical ensembles in the world. Balanchine's presence in the USA is due initially to the idealism of Lincoln Kirstein (b 1907), a poet, author and philanthropist of the arts, who was determined that the classical ballet should put down roots in America. He had been a great admirer of Balanchine's work for Diaghilev, and in 1933, he, together with Edward M. M. Warburg, provided the enthusiasm and the funds which would bring Balanchine to America. There Balanchine was to start a school and a company, with Kirstein always at his right hand to administer and support. Initially there were many problems: not least because America was just emerging from the financial crisis of the Depression, and was entering a phase of political isolation in which anything from Europe (even the arts) was viewed with some suspicion. By the late 1930s Balanchine had created a repertory for his American Ballet, but the war and financial problems were to force him to work on Broadway and in Hollywood for some years. It was in 1946 that Balanchine and Kirstein formed the Ballet Society in New York for seasons of dance performances; from this there came the invitation in 1948 to establish the company at the New York City Center, and in October 1948 the New York City Ballet—as such—came into existence. From then on the company's success was rapid: Balanchine had brought his classic style from St Petersburg and had transformed it on the bodies of his athletic young American dancers to create an authentically American classic style; clean, swift and very much of the New World. He has composed a glorious series of ballets, many of them pure dance works, using scores that range from the concert repertory to George Gershwin, John Philip Sousa and electronic music. Balanchine also continued his artistic collaboration with Igor Stravinsky. This had begun with the staging of *Apollo* for the Diaghilev Ballet in 1928, and reached its culmination in the summer of 1972 when in homage to Stravinsky, who had died in the previous year, a festival of 31 ballets to Stravinsky scores was mounted by the City Ballet's choreographers. Chief among these associates of Balanchine is Jerome Robbins (b 1918). Robbins had first come to fame as a dancer with American Ballet Theatre, for whom he made his first, wildly successful ballet, *Fancy Free* in 1944. Robbins moved to New York City Ballet with whom he has been chiefly associated. He has also worked on Broadway—notably in staging *West Side Story* and producing such musicals as *Fiddler on the Roof*, and *The King and I*. For a time he directed his own company, Ballets USA, but the major part of his choreography in recent years has been presented by the New York City Ballet, and his recent *Dances at a Gathering* (1969) and *Goldberg Variations* (1971) have been recognized as masterly creations.

The other major classical company in America, American Ballet Theatre, gave its first performance under the direction of Lucia Chase (b 1907) and Richard Pleasant in January 1940. Over the years the company has presented a wide range of ballets and stars. Its policy has been based on the idea of presenting all kinds of ballet, from the Russian classics and the Diaghilev repertory to contemporary American works. It has engaged some of the greatest choreographers and ballet stars of the past 30 years, and has given its vast public the opportunity to see works and dancers of world-wide importance. Unlike the New York City Ballet which avoids any sort of 'star-system', American Ballet Theatre welcomes stars: such exceptional artists as Erik Bruhn (b 1928), a flawless classical danseur from Copenhagen, Alicia Alonso (b 1917) the Cuban ballerina and today's brightest stars—Natalia Makarova and Mikhail Baryshnikov—have found remarkable opportunities for work with the company. It also contains an impressive number of fine American dancers, notably Nora Kaye (b 1920) who during her career with the company was shown to be a great dramatic ballerina, particularly in the works staged for the company by Antony Tudor who had emigrated to America from London in 1939.

Classical ballet in the United States is not, of course, limited to these two companies. Across the continent there are many companies, indeed, the oldest American ballet company is that in San Francisco which was formed in 1933 by the émigré Russian dancer Adolf Bolm. In 1937 Willam Christensen became its director, and with his brother Lew guided its development, and today it maintains a healthy creativity under Lew Christensen and Michael Smuin. In Chicago the dancer and choreographer Ruth Page (b 1905) has fostered a great deal of ballet activity in collaboration with the Chicago Opera, and other companies in Boston, Cincinnati, Philadelphia, Salt Lake City and other major cities continue valuable work.

In New York the choreographer Robert Joffrey (b 1930) has established a classical company which has been based at the New York City Center (vacant after Balanchine had transferred his company to the impressive theatrical complex at the Lincoln Center). The Joffrey Ballet repertory is a varied one, ranging from traditional works by Massine, Balanchine, Ashton, Bournonville, etc. to 'pop' works by Joffrey himself and his associate choreographer Gerald Arpino (b 1928) which include *Clowns*, *Astarte*, and *The Sacred Grove on Mount Tamalpais*.

One last company must be mentioned: the Dance Theatre of Harlem. In 1971 Arthur Mitchell (b 1934), a leading black dancer who had made a distinguished career with New York City Ballet, was impelled by the ideals of the Negro Civil Rights movement to pioneer a school of classical dance and subsequently a ballet company in Harlem, the predominantly negro quarter of New York. From the hundreds of young people who flocked to his classes, he selected and trained the ensemble known as the Dance Theatre of Harlem, which offers a part classic, part ethnic repertory of ballets and, besides regular New York seasons, has toured throughout America and overseas to great acclaim.

Russia

The Revolution of 1917 affected every aspect of life in Russia, and the ballet, like all the arts, was subjected to revolutionary fervor. Because the ballet was so associated with the Tsar's court and the aristocracy, it may be thought surprising that it survived at all, but the new Commissar for Public Education, Anatoly Lunacharsky, was both a friend of Lenin and a devotee and critic of the ballet. He pointed out that there was no reason why the people should not inherit the glories of the ballet as they were inheriting everything else in Russia. So, after some difficult years, the ballet flourished once more, and the audiences who came to admire the great classics of the 19th century were now drawn from factories rather than palaces. It is significant that the central government moved to Moscow from Petersburg, and the Bolshoi Ballet in Moscow was gradually regarded as the showcase for the new socialist theories of ballet. The style of dancing and production in Moscow had, in any case, always been different, more colourfully dramatic than in aristocratic Petersburg. In Moscow, at the beginning of this century this had been developed by Alexander Gorsky (1871–1924). Gorsky re-staged many of Petipa's ballets at the Bolshoi and made them more obviously dramatic. His own ballets also had considerable theatrical vitality, and even today there is still a distinction to be made between the Moscow and Leningrad (as Petersburg was renamed) styles of dancing. After the Revolution, although many of the old ballets were preserved, new full-length works were gradually produced which expressed the themes of a socialist society: instead of enchanted princesses and fairy tales, ordinary people now became the heroes of ballet. In the first true Soviet ballet, *The Red Poppy*, staged in 1927, the plot showed Russian sailors helping Chinese peasants in an uprising. Later works turned to other revolutionary themes (*The Flames of Paris* which dealt with the French Revolution of 1789), or to Russian and world literature: *Romeo and Juliet*, *Fountain of Bakhchisaray* (from a poem by Pushkin) and most recently Tolstoy's *Anna Karenina*, or to history: *Spartacus*, the story of the Roman slaves' uprising, and *Ivan the Terrible*, about the Tsar who unified Russia in the 16th century.

But while the choreography may be accused of being too restricted in its themes and expression, the long tradition of great teaching in Russia has had a magnificent development thanks to the work of Agrippina Vaganova (1879–1951). Vaganova had been a ballerina at the Maryinsky Theatre in Petersburg, and after the Revolution she opened a school where she was to evolve a wonderful extension of the old classic style of dancing. Invited to become the chief teacher at the Leningrad State School, she trained dancers to use movements which were bigger and more space-consuming, with soaring leaps and more fluid and expressive arms and backs. The Vaganova pupils reflected something of the new exciting spirit of the age, but they retained the perfection of line and aristocracy of style that had always been the best quality of the old Petersburg dancers. So successful was Vaganova that her Leningrad teaching system was adopted throughout Russia, both in Moscow and in the many other theatres and schools which were established during the next decades. Today, thanks to her system, the magnificent qualities of Russian dancers are admired throughout the world. There still remains a certain difference between Leningrad dancers and those in the rest of the Soviet Union: artists like Natalya Makarova and Mikhail Baryshnikov (two Leningrad stars who chose to work in the West) and the occasional visits of the Leningrad company (The Kirov State Theatre Ballet) remind us of the superlative distinction and nobility of the Vaganova style as it is maintained in Leningrad. Moscow dancers seem still more athletic and emotional: such great stars as Maya Plisetskaya, or Vladimir Vasiliev and his wife Ekaterina Maximova exemplify the Moscow style which is exultantly beautiful.

Ballet flourishes today throughout Russia probably more than anywhere else in the world, since it is a vastly popular entertainment for the entire nation, with thriving ballet companies in every major city of the Union of Socialist Republics. Although the Russian dancers excite universal admiration and awe, the same cannot always be said for the ballets that they dance. Because the arts in Russia are subject to some form of government control, the themes of ballets need to reflect the political ideals of the country, and are consequently often narrow in their range of subject. Modern plotless works, of the kind staged by Balanchine, are unknown; the idea that dance can be satisfying as pure dance without any need for a dramatic argument, or even a 'message' is foreign to Soviet ballet's ideals. Experiment of the kind that has brought Modern Dance to the fore in the West, and has so enlivened ballet throughout the rest of the world, is virtually unknown, and it is for this reason that certain dancers—Nureyev, Makarova and Baryshnikov, for example—decided to leave Russia in search of new roles and more challenging choreography. These 'defectors' have had a profound influence on ballet dancers in the West. Even more so have been the visits of Soviet Ballet companies. In 1956 the Bolshoi Ballet from Moscow paid its first visit to Europe, performing at The Royal Opera House, Covent Garden. The effect of the Russians' big, free dance style, and the magic of their prima ballerina, Galina Ulanova, was a great inspiration. Ulanova (b 1910), Leningrad trained, was a supreme lyric artist, and her appearances in *Giselle* and *Romeo and Juliet* have been preserved on film for a grateful posterity.

France and Belgium

During the latter part of the 19th century the performance and appreciation of ballet in France, as elsewhere in Western Europe, had declined enormously. Nevertheless, Paris still remained the artistic centre of Europe, and Paris's acclaim meant success: it was to that city that Diaghilev brought his Ballet Russe. Although the Opéra still maintained a ballet troupe, its work was not of great importance until 1930, when, following the death of Diaghilev, his last male star, Serge Lifar (b 1905), was invited to take over the ballet as director, choreographer and principal dancer. For the next three decades, until his retirement in 1958, Lifar brought the Opéra back into the limelight, creating a large number of ballets, and working with a series of superlative ballerinas. Foremost among these were Olga Spessivtseva (b 1895), arguably the greatest ballerina of our century, who was initially a star in Petersburg and later worked with Diaghilev, Yvette Chauviré (b 1917) a superb French ballerina, and the Franco-Russian star Nina Vyroubova (b 1921). During the Lifar years the Opéra School, the home of great dance tradition, produced a series of exceptional male and female artists, and today it continues to feed the Opéra company with outstanding performers. But with Lifar's departure in 1958 the Opéra fell upon confused times, and since then it has seemed to lack any very positive artistic policy. In spite of this its repertory is continually enlarged with the work of guest choreographers who have ranged from Yuri Grigorovich (b 1927), director of the Bolshoy Ballet in Moscow, to Merce Cunningham, Glen Tetley and Maurice Béjart (b 1927).

While the academic style was being preserved at the Opéra, more adventurous ideas were to be expressed at the war's end in 1944–45 when an extraordinary outburst of dance activity took place in Paris. This centred upon a young dancer trained at the Opéra, Roland Petit (b 1924). With the help of Boris Kochno, formerly secretary and assistant to Serge Diaghilev, and Irène Lidova, a French critic and writer he formed a new ballet company: Les Ballets des Champs Elysées. With the collaboration of many distinguished painters and musicians, with a group of young dancers, and with ballets choreographed by Petit, the Champs Elysées company astonished and delighted audiences by the beauty of its stagings, and the stylishness of its repertory. Its male star, Jean Babilée (b 1923), was one of the most extraordinary dramatic and technical virtuosos of his time, and the company exemplified everything that Paris stood for in the arts: wit, elegance, and true *chic*. However, the Champs Elysées declined, lacking firm foundations. Roland Petit went on to form another company, the Ballets de Paris where he staged several exceptional ballets, particularly *Carmen* which he created for his wife Renée (Zizi) Jeanmaire (b 1924). During this time, several other interesting troupes were formed in France, and then fell on hard times, though not without making their artistic mark. One company in particular, the Grand Ballet du Marquis de Cuevas, did much to revive the glamour of the touring Ballet Russe, and it travelled the world with a fine collection of ballets and some outstandingly good dancers—Nina Vyroubova, Serge Golovine, Rosella Hightower, Georges Skibine, Marjorie Tallchief—until the death of the Marquis de Cuevas who had sustained the enterprise from his private funds. In passing it is worth noting that, to survive, the two prerequisites for a ballet company are a school and a resident choreographer; a permanent theatre can only be placed third on the list of requirements, together with a government subsidy (failing a patron with a bottomless pocket).

There are ballet companies today in France associated with the opera houses or municipal theatres in several important towns, but probably the most interesting development of recent years has been the opening of *Maisons de la Culture* (art complexes) in the French regions. At Amiens, in northern France, the Maison de la Culture was made the home of the *Ballet-Théâtre Contemporain*, founded in 1968. The company was dedicated to the policy of presenting brand new ballets with modern scores and designs by some of the most interesting contemporary artists. Its director, Jean-Albert Cartier, and its choreographic director, Françoise Adret, soon gave the company a vivid modern image. In 1972 the company transferred to Angers, where it now has its base, and continues its distinguished creativity. In the south of France, Roland Petit has recently taken over the direction of the Marseille Ballet, and for this company he has also staged several interesting works, while also continuing to choreograph elsewhere.

It was from Marseille that there came a remarkable choreographer, Maurice Béjart, who trained at the Opéra there, and then toured throughout Europe as a dancer. In 1960, following the success of a work he had staged in Brussels, he was invited to become director of the ballet company at the Théâtre de la Monnaie, Brussels. This company he soon transformed into the Ballet of the Twentieth Century (Le Ballet du XXme Siècle). As its name implies, it is dedicated to the presentation of spectacular modern works. It is also a phenomenon in our time. Using a large company of admirably trained dancers, Béjart stages his works in circus tents and sports stadia as well as theatres, to vast and enthusiastic audiences. In Mexico City he has played to 25,000 people at one time; in West Berlin, he had nightly audiences of 12,000. Wherever the company performs, they are ecstatically received by a predominantly youthful public. While his treatment of his chosen themes may divide critical opinion (he is either adored or loathed by the press in many countries) it must be said that he reaches a vast public who might not otherwise be aware of dance. His ballets can deal with a variety of subjects: *Nijinsky, Clown of God* sought to explain the reasons for Nijinsky's madness; *Golestan* was inspired by Persia; *Bhakti* by Hinduism. His presentations are conceived on a monumental scale: detail is often missing, but there is a broad, simple view which appeals to his audience, and the stagings are often excitingly vital in their massed effects. His school, *Mudra*, in Brussels, attracts students from all over the world.

Germany, Austria, Italy

It is curious that, despite the number of distinguished ballet-masters and dancers who worked in Germany during the 18th and 19th centuries, there has been no continuing tradition of ballet in Germany. During the 1920s and 1930s a form of Modern Dance generally known as the 'Central European' style flourished, especially in the work of Mary Wigman (1886–1973) which reflected the turbulence of the times. There was also Kurt Jooss (b 1901) whose Ballets Jooss based at Essen (and later at Dartington Hall, Devon) toured the world with great success during the 1930s. His best-known work, still in the repertory of several companies, was *The Green Table*, an allegory about war and the cynicism of politicians. The Jooss style, a mixture of comparatively simple, 'free' choreography and forceful, dramatic mime, belonged to the movement that was known as Expressionist theatre—all symbolism and social comment—but it must be looked upon as one of the backwaters of ballet.

After the Second World War, a great change came about. The example of visiting ballet companies inspired a new interest in classical dance. Although there is no national company in West Germany, many cities maintain a ballet company attached to their opera house, and the dancers besides appearing in operas have the opportunity to give occasional evenings of ballet. By far the most celebrated company is that in Stuttgart. It came to prominence following the arrival of John Cranko to revive his full-length *Prince of the Pagodas* there in 1961. Cranko inspired the company, and under his guidance it achieved international renown. This was in part due to Cranko's discovery of Marcia Haydee as his ballerina. Haydee (b 1939) is a Brazilian dancer, trained at the Royal Ballet School, where her contemporaries included Lynn Seymour and Antoinette Sibley. Under Cranko's direction Haydee emerged as a superlative dramatic ballerina, ideal for classic roles as well as those Cranko was to make for her in a number of exciting ballets. In addition Cranko had acquired several other fine principals:

Ray Barra (b 1930), and later Richard Cragun (b 1944) and Egon Madsen (b 1942). The repertory that he created had considerable range, from classic, plotless ballets to high comedy and a series of full-length works: *Onegin*, *Romeo and Juliet*, *The Taming of the Shrew*, *Carmen*, as well as a revival of *Swan Lake:* which arroused enormous public interest in Stuttgart and later round the world. Within a short time Cranko's choreographies and the enthusiastic loyalty he aroused in his dancers had gained the Stuttgart company international success.

Cranko's long training with the Royal Ballet had taught him the importance of a school (the Stuttgart Ballet School is one of the finest in Europe today) and also the importance of the continuity of the classic style. Marcia Haydee and Richard Cragun, Egon Madsen and the first true German ballerina, Birgit Keil (a product of Stuttgart) and the roster of fine soloists who joined the company, brought the Stuttgart Ballet to a pre-eminent position in West Germany. Cranko died in the airplane bringing the Stuttgart Ballet back from a triumphant season in New York in 1973. Despite this tragic loss, it is the measure of the organization he had built and the tremendous company loyalty, to him and what he had created, that the company has continued to flourish. It was directed for a year after Cranko's death by Glen Tetley, who also composed some fine ballets for it, but since 1976 the company has been under the guidance of Marcia Haydee.

There are several other notable companies in West Germany, attached to the Opera Houses—those of Deutsche Oper am Rhein, directed by Erich Walter; the company of the Deutsche Oper in West Berlin; companies in Wuppertal and Munich. Their work is often interesting but they have as yet hardly achieved international status. Rather more significant is the work of the American born choreographer John Neumeier (b 1942) who danced for some years with the Stuttgart Ballet before eventually becoming director of the Hamburg Ballet in 1973. Neumeier is a man of brilliant theatrical ideas, and his stagings in Hamburg, and earlier in Frankfurt, where he was director from 1969 to 1973, have excited a great deal of interest. With such productions as *Romeo and Juliet*, *Meyerbeer-Schumann*, *Don Juan*, *Illusions* and *Swan Lake* he has won a very high reputation in Germany.

Somewhat similar to Germany, in that it was an important centre of ballet during the 18th and 19th centuries, Vienna has also suffered from the lack of a continuous ballet tradition. Today the Vienna State Ballet, while it maintains a large company, makes little creative contribution to the art.

It is interesting to note that in those countries of Europe where, during the 18th century, opera was very popular and continued to be so during the 19th and 20th centuries, ballet has inevitably become the poor and neglected relation. This is true of Germany, Austria and Italy with their unrivalled operatic traditions: in each country ballet has taken second place at best, existing mostly to feed the opera productions with dancers needed in brief ballet scenes. In Italy, as in Germany and Austria, there are ballet companies associated with the opera houses. At La Scala Milan during the 19th century there was still an attempt made to stage important dance works, and the school attached to the theatre has long produced performers of exceptional technical brilliance (witness those virtuoso ballerinas who so amazed the Russian Imperial Ballet at the end of the last century). But in modern times ballet in Italy—in Rome as well as Milan, which are the two chief centres of dance—has declined: there has been too little attempt to give either continuity or real development to the companies associated with the opera-house. A few exceptionally gifted Italian dancers have become known internationally; among them Elisabetta Terabust (b 1946); Carla Fracci (b 1936) and Paolo Bortoluzzi (b 1938) are much admired for their appearances with the major international companies.

Denmark and Sweden

Despite the glorious tradition established by August Bournonville, there was no choreographer to succeed him. Bournonville died in 1879, and two days before his death he saw the debut of a young dancer, Hans Beck (b 1861), who was not to die until 1952. Beck, though not a choreographer of much importance, ensured that the repertory of ballets by Bournonville was properly maintained, as well as the teaching system established by that great master. Although during the 1920s and 1930s certain famous choreographers—Fokine, Balanchine—worked with the company briefly, the Royal Danish Ballet tended almost to be a museum of Bournonville works. During the 1930s it found a distinguished native choreographer in Harald Lander (1905–1971) who created an interesting new repertory, but when the Royal Danish Ballet eventually decided to come out into the world, and undertake a first tour in 1954, it was the beauties of the Bournonville ballets—like *La Sylphide*, *A Folk Tale*, *Napoli*, and the magnificence of the dancers trained in the Bournonville school—which excited immense public admiration. Exposed to the world, the Danes decided that they must try and modernize their ballet. One of the greatest teachers, Vera Volkova (1904–1975), a pupil of A. Y. Vaganova, went to Copenhagen to develop the training system in the Royal Danish

Ballet. A young dancer, Flemming Flindt (b 1936), was appointed director and chief choreographer, and he set about staging a series of daringly innovative ballets such as *The Lesson*, *The Triumph of Death* and *The Young Man Must Marry* which were in violent contrast to the company's Bournonville traditions. Other celebrated choreographers also worked with the company, Ashton, MacMillan and Robbins among them; and today the Royal Danes are held in affectionate esteem throughout the world. It is significant that many companies now try to present Bournonville ballets: they are in the main unsuccessful because of the difficulty of acquiring the genuine Bournonville style which needs training from childhood to assimilate. Great Danish dancers—especially male dancers—have gone out into the world to make magnificent careers: outstandingly is Erik Bruhn (b 1928), hailed as the purest classical stylist of his generation, and Peter Martins (b 1946) who has danced for nearly ten years with the New York City Ballet and is among today's most elegant and powerful *premiers danseurs.* One Danish ballerina, Toni Lander (b 1931), made an exceptional international career, dancing with London Festival Ballet and then with American Ballet Theatre, to great acclaim.

Like the Russian companies of today, the Royal Danish Ballet also excels in producing outstanding character dancers. Its old repertory relies very much upon the service of senior artists who undertake the dramatic supporting roles, and in any production of a Bournonville ballet like *Napoli* or *The Life Guards on Amager*, much of the pleasure in watching the piece lies in the dramatic portrayals by the senior artists of the company.

Sweden

Although the Royal Swedish Ballet was founded as early as 1773, there was no great choreographer or teacher like Bournonville to establish a solid basis of repertory and to ensure a continuity of style. The ballet maintained a rather thin existence for over a century—the most interesting Swedish efforts in ballet being made by the short-lived and independent Ballets Suédois of the early 1920s which was set up to emulate the modernity of Diaghilev. With the ballet boom that followed the end of the Second World War, the English teacher and producer Mary Skeaping (b 1902) became director of the Royal Swedish Ballet for a decade from 1953 to 1962, and produced several fine revivals of the 19th century Russian classics. Various other foreign choreographers, including Tudor and MacMillan have worked in Stockholm, but the company has not known the success of its Danish neighbour. Two other companies in Sweden must be mentioned: the Cullberg Ballet is directed by the choreographer Birgit Cullberg (b 1908) and is dedicated to presenting her ballets; the Gothenberg Ballet was for some years directed by Elsa Marianne von Rosen (b 1927), a Swedish dancer and choreographer who has made some interesting restagings of Bournonville ballets as well as creating her own works.

Holland

With no classical traditions worthy of note before the Second World War, there was a surprising and unexpected interest in ballet in the post-war years. This eventually led, through the work of various dancers, choreographers and teachers, to the establishment of the two main companies in Holland: The National Ballet and the Nederlands Dans Theater. The National Ballet came into being in 1961, as the amalgamation of two existing troupes. The company is large and its repertory wide ranging: classical stagings and modern creativity exist side by side. Nederlands Dans Theater was founded in 1959, and its prolific schedule of new ballets attracted world attention: each year some ten or more creations are staged, many of them highly experimental. Chief among its choreographers at one time was Hans van Manen (b 1932), the foremost Dutch ballet-maker, and he composed a series of very effective works for the company, some of which were later to enter the repertory of major European companies—the Royal Ballet has no less than 6 of his works.

Hans van Manen then went on to work with the Dutch National Ballet, where he joined two other choreographers—Rudi van Dantzig (b 1933) and Toer van Schayk (b 1936). All three have maintained a constant stream of new works for the company, many of them somewhat controversial. Nederlands Dans Theater has—like Ballet Rambert—owed much to the influence of the work of Glen Tetley, who for a time was director of the company. Latterly it suffered from the injection of too many pretentious American dance ideas, which sapped it of its real identity, but now under the directorship of Jiří Kylián it is rediscovering its original character.

A third Dutch company, which has contributed considerably to the national interest in the art, is the Scapino Ballet, which tours throughout the country giving performances for school audiences.

It is interesting to note that, in contrast to all the other major national companies in Europe, the Dutch are alone in not having a school directly linked to their companies.

Eastern Europe

At the end of the war in 1945, when much of Eastern Europe fell under the dominance of the Soviet Union, countries such as Latvia, Poland, Hungary, Rumania, Bulgaria, Czechoslovakia, and the rather more independent Yugoslavia, all set about developing their ballet companies. In Poland, there was a long balletic heritage; and in many of the others there is a strong and vital interest in folk-dance as a means of expression. The ballet troupes and schools established in these countries after the war have received considerable encouragement and practical help from the Soviet Union, but much of their work remains unknown in the West.

Canada, Australia, South Africa

The flourishing national ballets in Canada and Australia are direct descendants of the Royal Ballet. The Canadian National Ballet was founded by Celia Franca who went to Canada at the suggestion of Dame Ninette de Valois after the Royal Ballet's first triumphant tour of North America in 1949. For 20 years Celia Franca had to work tremendously hard to sustain the growth of her company, and in this she was aided by the presence of the outstanding National Ballet School in Toronto, under the direction of Betty Oliphant. The National School is one of the finest we know, and its graduates now form the major part of the National Ballet's ensemble: outstanding are Karen Kain, Frank Augustyn, Nadia Potts, Veronica Tennant and Mary Jago. The style and repertory of the company are recognizably linked with that of the Royal Ballet, but the Canadians' freshness of manner and their youthful charm are especially their own. Canada has not yet found a major choreographer, but the National Ballet, like the Royal Ballet, maintains a strong classical repertory; its dancers are extremely impressive, and in recent years it has toured abroad with great success. The special relationship with the Royal Ballet has been continued with the appointment of Alexander Grant (b 1925) as Director in 1976. Grant, a character dancer of genius, joined the Sadler's Wells School as a scholar from New Zealand in 1946, and thereafter rose to become a principal of the company and created many important roles—unforgettably, Alain in Ashton's *La Fille mal Gardée*.

For an enormous country, which still remains relatively under-populated, Canada maintains several other companies: The Grands Ballets Canadiens, The Royal Winnipeg Ballet, and several experimental modern groups.

In Australia a somewhat similar situation exists. The Ballets Russes of the 1930s toured Australia, as did Pavlova, but it was the work of Edouard Borovansky (1902–1959) (a Ballet Russe dancer who settled in Australia) who did much to encourage a public interest in ballet during the 1940s and '50s. His company disbanded in 1960 and its members were the nucleus of the Australian Ballet which was founded two years later. Under the direction of Dame Peggy van Praagh (who had directed the Sadler's Wells Theatre Ballet for many years) the new young company quickly established itself. In 1965 the Australian-born dancer and choreographer Sir Robert Helpmann joined Dame Peggy in directing the company, and for them he produced a number of ballets. Like their Canadian contemporaries, the Australian dancers were given the benefit of a fine school and the existence of sound classical stagings in the company repertory. Rudolf Nureyev staged *Don Quixote* and *Raymonda* for them (just as he had mounted *The Sleeping Beauty* for the Canadian company).

The Australian Ballet has toured internationally with great success: visiting Poland and Russia in 1973, as well as Britain on three occasions. Its principals include Lucette Aldous (who danced with the Royal Ballet, Ballet Rambert and Festival Ballet as ballerina before going to Australia), Kelvin Coe, Marilyn Jones, John Meehan, and a strong group of soloists. In 1976, Anne Woolliams (b 1926) was appointed director of the company. She had previously been ballet-mistress in Stuttgart during John Cranko's directorate of the ballet there. Australia also numbers several small ensembles which produce new work and tour throughout the vastness of the continent.

In South Africa the Royal Ballet's influence is less direct. The country has produced many fine dancers—notably Nadia Nerina (b 1927), who became a leading ballerina of the Royal Ballet and was the original Lise in *La Fille mal Gardée*, Maryon Lane and John Cranko. The work of an outstanding teacher, Dulcie Howes, in Cape Town, did much to stimulate public interest in ballet, and the establishment of a ballet company on the Cape developed from her school. This is the CAPAB Ballet, which is now directed by yet another one-time Royal Ballet principal, David Poole (b 1925). The PACT Ballet, like CAPAB, is based in Johannesburg in the Transvaal, and is also a classical company. The permanent troupe has been host to a series of very celebrated guests, from Dame Margot Fonteyn, Natalia Makarova and

Anthony Dowell to Sir Frederick Ashton and Sir Robert Helpmann (who appeared as the Ugly Sisters in Ashton's *Cinderella*).

Elsewhere throughout the world, ballet and dance flourish as never before. From Japan to Norway, from South Africa to South America, in China and Cuba, there is a continuing and developing interest in dance. This world-wide interest in the art has meant that performers and dance students travel long distances in search of fine teaching or of engagements: there is a true internationalism now apparent in dance, and during any year in the major centres of ballet—New York, London, Paris, Moscow—dancers from all parts of the globe will be found at work.

The Modern Dance

by Jack Anderson

After Martha Graham's debut concert in 1926 a bewildered acquaintance exclaimed, "It's dreadful! Martha, how long do you expect to keep this up?" Graham replied, "As long as I have an audience." Many other theatergoers experienced similar bewilderment in the early days of modern dance, but their confusion did not deter the dancers, whose persistence eventually gained them a wide and highly enthusiastic audience.

The term "modern dance" has never pleased anyone—critics, choreographers, or dance historians. It has stuck, however, and a better name has yet to be found. Nor has anyone managed to invent a concise definition of just what modern dance is, although the historian, pressed for a description, might say that modern dance is a form of Western theatrical dancing that has developed almost entirely outside the ballet tradition. Its spiritual ancestors are Isadora Duncan, Ruth St. Denis, and Ted Shawn, but its pioneers include dancers who rebelled against Denishawn's artistic limitations, just as St. Denis and Shawn had rebelled against the limitations of an earlier era of dance.

Modern dance is not simply a matter of chronology, however, nor is it a rigid technical system. In essence, it is a point of view that stresses artistic individualism and encourages dancers to develop personal cho-

Source: From *Dance* (New York: *Newsweek*, 1974).

reographic styles. According to this philosophy, there are as many valid ways of dancing as there are skillful choreographers—an outlook that was cogently expressed in 1927 in program notes for a concert by Helen Tamiris: "There are no general rules. Each work of art creates its own code."

The early days of modern dance—the 1920's and 1930's—were days of adventure. Despite the Great Depression and the bewilderment of audiences, choreographers proceeded undaunted. They virtually reinvented dance as they went along, a process that began with the rejection of ballet, which they considered hidebound and trivial. It is perhaps significant that the two nations in which modern dance took strongest hold, America and Germany, were nations that had no celebrated ballet companies, a situation that led ambitious dancers to experiment with new forms. Their iconoclasm occasionally went to grim extremes, however. Because ballet movements were by and large rounded and symmetrical, for example, modern dancers emphasized angular asymmetries. The result was that early modern dance tended to be fierce; it hugged the ground and was resolutely unglamorous. Its exponents disdained frills, preferring to look sturdy and earthy rather than conform to stereotyped ideals of grace.

Save for Harald Kreutzberg in Germany and Ted Shawn and Charles Weidman in America, most modern dance pioneers were women. A public that branded male dancers effeminate—and thereby discouraged many potentially great dancers from entering the field—tolerated female dancers, even while suspecting their virtue. Modern dance gave women an opportunity to proclaim their independence from conventionality, both as artists and as women, and many seized the opportunity.

In general, the moderns focused upon the expressive powers of movement. So, of course, did Isadora Duncan and the Diaghilev choreographers. But whereas Isadora and Diaghilev combined movement with fine music—and, in Diaghilev's case, with fine art—in order to prove that movement could hold its own with the other two, the early moderns minimized the other arts. Music was frequently composed after a dance had been choreographed and it sometimes consisted only of percussion rhythms. Costumes were spartan, and as a result wags have called this the "long woolens" period of modern dance.

Modern dance developed independently in America and Germany, thriving in the former locale but fading in the latter in the wake of the Nazi holocaust. Before World War II, the greatest exponent of German modern dance was Mary Wigman, who had been a student of Emile Jacques-Dalcroze, inventor of a system designed to foster a sense of musical rhythm, and of Rudolf von Laban, who tried to apply scientific principles to movement analysis. Despite her teachers' intellectuality, Wigman's art appealed to the instincts. A stocky, muscular woman who fitted no one's idea of prettiness, Wigman created sombre, macabre, almost demonic dances that hinted at the primitive drives still lurking beneath the veneer of civilization. Wigman felt she was in contact with primordial forces that took possession of her as she performed, and she often wore masks in order to escape her ordinary personality and yield herself to these powers. So awesome were these forces on occasion that Wigman, convinced that the mask represented a spirit attempting to consume her utterly, became terrified by her own choreography.

Wigman toured America in the 1930's, and shortly thereafter she sent one of her assistants, Hanya Holm, to open a New York branch of the Wigman school. After a few years Holm realized that American bodies and temperaments were so markedly different from those she had encountered in Germany that she could not replicate Wigman's style. She therefore asked for and received permission to rename the school the Hanya Holm Studio and to run it as an independent institution. Over the ensuing years Holm has choreographed for her own company and has set the dances for such well-known musicals as *Kiss Me, Kate* and *My Fair Lady*.

Of American modern dancers, the most famous is surely Martha Graham. Indeed, to many people her name is virtually synonymous with modern dance. She once said that she views each of her works as "a graph of the heart," a statement that reveals much about her art. Equally significant is the fact that when she was a little girl her father, a physician specializing in nervous disorders, warned her never to lie because he would always know when she was lying by the tensions in her body. She remembered that warning, and in her dances she has tried to tell the truth, however unpleasant it may be. Graham can be equally strong-willed offstage; as a young woman, she disconcerted friends by her tendency, when aroused, to bare her teeth like a shark.

Like that other artistic experimentalist, Gertrude Stein, Graham was born in Allegheny, Pennsylvania. Able to trace her ancestry back to Miles Standish, Graham grew up in an atmosphere of Presbyterian rectitude. When her family moved to Santa Barbara because of her sister's asthma, Graham found herself in a less stern environment—and it was in California that she first saw Ruth St. Denis perform. She knew then that she wanted to dance, but she did not dare enroll in the Denishawn school until after her father's death. The force of family tradition had battled against her personal desires, a conflict that would be reflected in her choreography.

After some years with Denishawn, Graham was encouraged to go her own choreographic way by Louis Horst, who was Denishawn's conductor at the time. (Later Horst was to serve as accompanist and father confessor to the whole early generation of American modern dancers.) Graham started choreographing programs in which Denishawn exoticism gave way to a strident angularity that caused some observers to compare her to a cube. She also started teaching, taking in a young actress named Bette Davis as one of her early pupils. Among other things, Graham taught Davis to fall down a flight of stairs without injury—it was such a spectacular stunt that Davis got one role on the basis of that trick alone.

Like many modern dancers, past and present, Graham invented her technique as she went along. The kinds of movements she and her company practiced were based upon whatever creative problems were troubling her. Early Graham technique was notorious for its nervous jerks and tremblings. Yet it was by no means irrational, for she based it upon a fundamental fact of life: breathing. Graham studied the bodily changes that occur during inhalation and exhalation, and from her observations developed the principles known as contraction and release. She then experimented with the dynamics of the process, allowing contractions to possess whiplash intensity. Unlike classical ballet, which typically tried to conceal effort, Graham sought to reveal it because she believed that life itself was effort. Eventually her technique incorporated softer, more lyrical, elements, but it never ceased to be a vehicle for passion. Her productions also grew richer in terms of music and scenery, many being collaborations with sculptor Isamu Noguchi.

Graham's percussive style enabled her to express emotional extremes. Some of her dances, to the dismay of rationalists, resembled visions of medieval mystics, who could combine flagellation with exaltation. Graham's finest early achievement in this vein is *Primitive Mysteries*, a 1931 work based upon the rites of Christianized Indians in the American Southwest that features a cult of female worshipers trying to emulate the Virgin Mary, sinking into dolor at the Crucifixion and rejoicing at the Resurrection.

After the Depression, many choreographers turned to themes of social protest. Graham, who seldom chose overtly topical themes, did choose during the course of the next decade to examine the forces that helped shape American society. *Frontier* (1935) offered a portrait of a pioneer woman facing the vastness of the American continent, at first with trepidation but ultimately with confidence. *Act of Judgment* attacked the crippling influence of Puritanism, a theme to which Graham returned with *Letter to the World*, in which the New England poet Emily Dickinson is thwarted by Puritan repression as personified by a terrifying dowager called the Ancestress. In *Appalachian Spring* (1944), a fire-and-brimstone revivalist preacher thunders at a housewarming for a newly married couple. But the newlyweds' love for each other and the common sense of a pioneer woman triumph over Calvinism. With this resolution Graham apparently made peace with her heritage, for she has never taken up the theme again. Over the years, Graham has repeatedly commissioned works by contemporary composers, the music Aaron Copland provided for *Appalachian Spring* being possibly the best single score of her career.

Since the 1940's, Graham has largely concerned herself with dance dramas depicting figures from history, literature, and mythology. She uses these characters as embodiments of psychological traits that are universal to mankind. *Errand into the Maze*, for instance, derives from the myth of Theseus and the Minotaur but does not literally tell that story. Rather, it shows a woman shuddering her way through a labyrinth, where she confronts a creature—half man, half beast—who personifies her own fears. *Deaths and Entrances*, suggested by the life of the Brontë sisters, mingles fancy and fact as three sisters handle objects in their house (a vase, a shell, a chesspiece) that trigger memories.

Graham's dances often begin at a climactic moment in the protagonist's life, with the heroine—for they are usually about women—recalling past events as she moves toward her destiny. This retrospective approach is most elaborately developed in the evening-long *Clytemnestra*, in which the ancient Greek queen, condemned to Hades, reflects upon her murderous past and slowly comes to terms with herself. Another favorite Graham device is to divide a character into different facets and have each personified by a separate dancer, as in *Seraphic Dialogue*, in which the spirit of Joan of Arc contemplates herself as maiden, warrior, and martyr.

Throughout her career, Graham has prompted adulation and controversy. Some have faulted her for obscurity, others for obviousness; occasionally her work has been called obscene. Yet she continues to choreograph, and no matter how much her style changes, her works share one common quality—total commitment.

Graham was not the only influential early modern dancer. The list also includes Helen Tamiris, for instance. She was born Helen Becker, but changed her name when she found a poem about a Persian queen that contained the line "Thou art Tamiris, the ruthless queen who banishes all obstacles." At a time when many modern dancers favored a gaunt look, Tamiris was flamboyant and something of a hellion. Fascinated by the American past, she choreographed dances to Whitman poems, Revolutionary War songs, and Louisiana bayou ballads.

Her *Negro Spirituals* was one of the first works choreographed by a white to take black culture seriously. As adept on Broadway as she was on the concert stage, Tamiris also choreographed several musicals, including *Up in Central Park* and *Annie Get Your Gun*.

If Graham had a real rival for choreographic eminence, however, it was Doris Humphrey, who grew up in the Chicago area where her parents managed a hotel that had a theatrical clientele. She took ballet lessons as a girl and, as often happened in a period when standards of dance training varied considerably, studied with both eminent masters and unbalanced eccentrics. The latter ranged from a Viennese lady who claimed that a diet of gooseberries promoted bodily agility to a gentleman who pinched little Doris as she went through her exercises. Humphrey joined Denishawn in 1917, only to rebel against that method eleven years later. She and her partner, Charles Weidman, thereupon established their own group. Weidman became famous for his deft pantomime, his compositions spoofing silent films, and his mimetic studies inspired by James Thurber. Humphrey, for her part, had more cosmic ambitions. Like Graham, she forged a technique from elementary principles of movement. But whereas Graham had emphasized breathing, Humphrey concentrated upon balance, her key words being "fall" and "recovery."

Humphrey's choreography was based upon the muscular drama of balance and imbalance, the contrasts between giving way to gravity altogether and resisting gravity to regain equilibrium. Conflict is inherent in such movement, and many Humphrey works were monumental explorations of human conflict. *The Shakers* (1931) examined the customs of a nineteenth-century celibate sect that believed one could rid oneself of sin by literally shaking it out of the body. Humphrey's dance, in depicting this process of shaking, hinted that sexual repression was an unacknowledged source of the devotees' frenzy. During 1935 and 1936 Humphrey choreographed the *New Dance* trilogy, her most ambitious treatment of conflict and resolution. The first section, *Theatre Piece*, satirized the rat race of competitive society. *With My Red Fires*, the second piece, castigated possessive love as personified by a matriarchal figure who thwarts her daughter's romantic desires. Having chastised communal and personal failings, Humphrey finally attempted to visualize an ideal social order in which the individual and the group could exist in accord. This finale, called simply *New Dance*, was entirely abstract in form.

Modern dance's stress upon creativity encouraged dancers to go out and organize new companies. Just as Graham and Humphrey left Denishawn, so fledglings started leaving Graham and Humphrey-Weidman. Anna Sokolow, for example, left Graham in 1938 and later created works, set to jazz scores, about the loneliness and alienation of life in big cities. A Humphrey-Weidman dancer who headed an unusually successful troupe was José Limón. His declaration of independence from Humphrey-Weidman was accomplished without rancor, and until her death Humphrey served as Limón's artistic advisor. The Mexican-born Limón, with his deep-set eyes and hollow cheeks, possessed a brooding presence that suggested an Indian heritage. His dances tended to be strongly dramatic, and his heroes were saints, sinners on a grand scale, and holy fools. Limón's most durable composition has been *The Moor's Pavane* (1949), an adaptation of *Othello* that sustains tension by placing the machinations of Iago and the jealousy of Othello within the strict decorum of old court dances. Maintaining surface politeness, the characters dance out a pavane that finally explodes into catastrophe.

By the 1950's, modern dance was recognized as an authentic American art. Lamentably, some of its original energy had been drained away over the years, a factor that led disenchanted younger choreographers to declare that modern dance was so oriented toward drama and narrative that it had become a form of pantomime and had lost sight of movement as something beautiful and fascinating for its own sake. The new choreographers advocated a dance that was abstract, nonliteral, and evocative rather than explicit.

Erick Hawkins, Graham's former husband, proclaimed what he called "movement quality" to be the essence of all dancing. The qualities he seemed most fond of were softness, gentleness, and ceremoniousness—attributes that give his work an almost Oriental serenity. Paul Taylor, on the other hand, is a dancer with a strong, heavy body who can nonetheless move with wit and grace—and those qualities abound in his choreography. His compositions include *Aureole*, a lyric dance that has a balletic feeling although its actual steps would astonish Petipa; *Orbs*, a meditation upon the seasons of the year, set to Beethoven quartets; and *American Genesis*, which gives familiar Bible stories American settings, turning Cain and Abel into feuding cowboys, Noah's ark into a Mississippi riverboat, and the Creation itself into the landing of the Pilgrims. Taylor is aware of human frailty but, unlike some of the dramatic choreographers of the 1940's who wrapped themselves in the gloom of Freudian dogma, he makes his social comments with an unmistakable twinkle in his eye.

Alwin Nikolais boasts that he is an artistic polygamist. What he seeks, he says, is "a polygamy of motion, shape, color, and sound." A complete man of the theater, Nikolais choreographs the dances, composes the electronic music, and designs the scenery, costumes, and lighting for all his productions, which are abstract mixed-media pieces of dazzling complexity. These pieces, surprising as conjuring tricks, could be regarded as contemporary equivalents of the masques and spectacles that delighted monarchs back in the seventeenth century. But if the old masques glorified monarchy, Nikolais's spectacles extol the wonders of the electronic age. He likes to transform dancers by encasing them in fantastic costumes or by attaching sculptural constructions to them to alter the body's natural shape. He then further transforms his dancers by flooding them with patterns of light and shadow so that audiences cannot tell what is dancer and what is scenery, what is illusion and what is reality. Through these devices, Nikolais hopes to transcend the limitations of ordinary theater and to extend the possibilities of the human anatomy.

One of the most controversial and influential choreographic experimentalists is Merce Cunningham. His performance style is almost balletically elegant, although unlike ballet dancers Cunningham's dancers seldom try to appear ethereal. Despite their latent classicism, Cunningham productions—many of them collaborations with composer John Cage—have prompted extremes of rage and enthusiasm. Three aspects of Cunningham's approach have been especially provocative: his use of chance and indeterminacy; his treatment of stage space as an open field; and his treatment of the elements that comprise a dance production as independent entities. Most notably, Cunningham uses chance elements in compositions so that his dances will possess some of the unpredictability of life itself. But he uses them with discretion; his dances are not free-for-alls. For instance, he may prepare in advance a multitude of movement possibilities—more than he needs for a work —and then decide by flipping coins which sequences will actually occur in that work. Or he may create works in which a set number of episodes may be performed in any order.

It may be asked why, if Cunningham prepares so much, he bothers with chance at all. Advocates of his method will reply that chance can reveal to the choreographer ways of combining movements which his conscious mind might not otherwise have thought of; our conscious minds are, to an extent, prisoners of habit, prisoners of thought patterns that we have been building up all our lives. By utilizing chance in choreography, it is possible to discover attractive combinations of movements that our conscious minds might not otherwise have thought of on their own.

Concern with indeterminacy is only to be expected in an age where live performances are, in a sense, in subtle competition with such mechanical forms as films and television. One characteristic of the mechanical is its fixity: once something has been captured on film, it will stay that way forever, or at least until the film wears out. But every live performance is different, even if only slightly, from every other live performance. Cunningham merely exploits the element of indeterminacy inherent in all theater.

A second important aspect of Cunningham's approach is his treatment of stage space. Unlike classical ballet, which is often structured around a central focus—usually the ballerina, performing front-and-center, framed by the ensemble—Cunningham gives equal importance to each area of the stage. The corners and sides can be as important as the center, and many things can happen simultaneously in different parts of the stage. The spectator's eye, instead of being riveted to one point, is free to wander as it wishes across a field of activity. There is no necessary reason why this should create difficulties for the spectator, since our eyes are regularly used to assimilate situations of greater visual complexity than can be found in most dances—for example, we readily adjust to the sight of pedestrians in the street or crowds at beaches or in bus stations.

Lastly, Cunningham tends to regard the elements of a work—movement, sound, decor—as independent entities which coexist together. The dance does not attempt to duplicate the musical phrase. Nor does the scenery illustrate the choreography. Choreography, music, and scenery simply occupy time and space together. Yet, oddly enough, these elements, though separate, manage to give each Cunningham work its own special climate. *Rainforest*, for instance, contains lush, sensuous movement; David Tudor's electronic score chugs gently along like a motorboat going up a river; Andy Warhol's decor consists of floating silver pillows. There is nothing specifically tropical about this piece, yet it is thoroughly luxuriant in tone.

The best advice one can give to anyone unfamiliar with Cunningham is simply to forget the theories and watch the dances with a keen eye and open mind. Gradually, each dance will reveal its personality. Thus *Summerspace* shimmers like August heat; *Winterbranch* is filled with so many suggestions of oppression that it frequently reminds audiences of the horrors of war; *Landrover* eats up space with enthusiastic abandon; and *Suite for Five* is as cool as spring water. Cunningham dances are like landscapes; the separate elements in them cohere to produce an unmistakable atmosphere, just as certain aggregations of people, traffic, and buildings are, in appearance, unmistakably those of a city's main street or financial district, its parks or its suburbs.

Since the 1960's there has been an extraordinary resurgence of modern dance experimentation. During the early years of the decade, many dancers performed at New York City's Judson Memorial Church, a Baptist church that has long been concerned with liberal social action and support of the arts (even though the grandmother of one of its ministers once announced that "A praying knee and a dancing foot never grew on the same leg"). Most of the important choreographers associated with Judson have established independent careers, while still other choreographers have conducted their experiments totally apart from the Judson milieu.

Recent experimentation has concentrated upon two broad areas: the kinds of movements that may be used in a dance, and the space in which a dance may be performed. It now appears that virtually any movement from the simplest to the most complex may be legitimately employed by choreographers. Twyla Tharp has on occasion covered space with intricate webs of nimble, twisting movements. In contrast, Yvonne Rainer has emphasized an athletic roughhouse kind of movement derived from gymnastics and work activities. Several lesser-known choreographers—in a development parallel to minimal painting and sculpture—have choreographed pieces with people assembling and dispersing in geometrical formations and have deliberately cast them with nondancers so that they will have a realistic appearance.

Going to another extreme, James Waring has been wildly eclectic. He has combined Bach and 1920's pop songs within a single piece, while other works include florid pantomimes, austere abstractions, tributes to Jeanette MacDonald movies, and romantic ballets *en pointe*. He roams from period to period with a genuine affection that makes him want to revivify the past. He demonstrates that any style can be theatrically valid, provided a choreographer treats it with respect. Other choreographers juxtapose many kinds of movement in dances: Rudy Perez uses movement which seems rich in emotional implications but which he measures out with tight, stoic control; Murray Louis is the master of a peppery comic style; while Dan Wagoner often plays perception games with audiences. In Wagoner's *Brambles*, for example, a live dancer performs while another person describes him in relation to totally imaginary scenery.

Just as any kind of movement may be used in a dance, so dances may be given in all kinds of spaces. The spaces in which dances are being presented today include churches, gymnasiums, armories, museums, parks, and city streets. And these areas are being used for their own sake, not as second-best substitutes for conventional theaters. Twyla Tharp once produced an event called *Medley* at twilight in New York City's Central Park. Its most striking episode was its conclusion, in which forty-odd dancers were spread across the grass, some near the audience, others almost as far away as the eye could see. All performed identical steps, but each was told to dance them as slowly as he personally could. Some moved so slowly that it was not always possible to discern if they were moving at all. In the fading light the almost imperceptible movement suggested a sculpture garden come magically to life.

Among young choreographers, Meredith Monk has been particularly interested in environmental theater productions staged on lawns, in empty lots, and in the interiors of museums and churches. She utilized New York's Solomon R. Guggenheim Museum for *Juice*, in which dancers moved along the great spiral interior ramp designed by Frank Lloyd Wright. Set in the vast nave of the Cathedral of St. John the Divine, *Education of the Girl Child* showed the course of life from birth to old age, then reversed the process and unwound life from old age back to birth. In *Needle Brain Lloyd and the Systems Kid*, Monk filled the Connecticut College lawn with a zany assortment of characters that included croquet players, mobsters, pioneers, and a motorcycle gang.

A form of dance that has been attracting ever wider attention is black dance, a choreographic amalgam of elements derived from jazz and tap, from conventional modern dance, and from the history and traditions of Africa, the Caribbean, the American South, and the big-city ghetto. The result is a dance form of tremendous energy, fervor, and rage. Pioneers of black dance include Asadata Dafora Horton, who in the 1930's created dance dramas about tribal life, and Katherine Dunham and Pearl Primus, who achieved prominence in the 1940's. Dunham treated Caribbean and American black themes in a series of revues that were exuberant combinations of scholarly research and showbiz flair. Primus's repertoire ranged from recreations of African ceremonies to *Strange Fruit*, which concerned lynching in the South. Both Dunham and Primus are university-trained anthropologists as well as choreographers.

Notable compositions on black themes created since the 1950's include Talley Beatty's *Road of the Phoebe Snow*, based upon childhood memories of games, fights, and dances along the railroad tracks; and Donald McKayle's *Rainbow Round My Shoulder*, depicting convicts on the chain gang, and *District Storyville*, a look at New Orleans in the early days of jazz when musicians earned their living by playing in brothels. One of the most popular American dance companies is that of Alvin Ailey. Like the New York City Ballet and the Joffrey Ballet, it is affiliated with the New York City Center. Its repertoire contains Ailey's own rousing *Revelations*, set to spirituals, and an assortment of works by many choreographers, black and white.

Modern dance remains volatile. No one can ever predict what the next trend will be, but one can assume there will be constant stylistic changes. Increasingly, modern dance and ballet, once bitter rivals, are regarding each other with cordial respect. Many dancers are now versed in both idioms, and several modern dance works have been taken into ballet repertoires. But even as the innovations of one era of modern dance are being assimilated by the dance world as a whole, new choreographers are breaking fresh ground. Modern dance would not be modern if it were not in a state of constant ferment.

Appendix I: A Chronology of Dance

1558 Beginning of the court ballet when on April 24 Francis, the eldest son of Catherine De Médici, marries Mary Queen of Scots and an extravagant courtly spectacle is presented to celebrate the occasion: a combination of music, dialogue, pantomime, and dancing.

1581 Beaujoyeulx presents *Ballet comique de la Reine*—generally considered the first ballet in history—on October 15 as part of the wedding celebration of Duc de Joyeuse to Marguerite of Lorraine, Catherine de Médici's sister. The ballet, which lasts five-and-a-half hours, depicts scenes from the Circe legend.

1588 Publication of *Orchésographie*, Thoinot Arbeau's illustrated dance manual, one of the first in history.

1607 Monteverdi's opera *Orfeo* premieres in Mantua: development of *ballet comique*.

1653 Louis XIV portrays the Sun King in *Ballet de la Nuit* on February 23. The ballet lasts thirteen hours and gives prominence to Jean Baptiste Lully, who is now appointed court composer of the king's ballets.

1661 Académie de Danse is founded by Louis XIV.

1669 Louis XIV establishes L'Académie de Musique et de Danse to present opera, drama, and music. The institution survives today as the Paris Opéra.

1670 Molière's *Le Bourgeois Gentilhomme* premieres—a comedy with music by Lully and choreography by Pierre Beauchamp. The play contains a one-act ballet: *Ballet des nations*.

1671 Paris Académie opens on March 19 with its presentation of *Pomone*, a pastoral ballet choreographed by Beauchamp.

1671 Beauchamp is appointed first ballet master of the Académie.

1681 Women perform for the first time as professional dancers in Lully's *The Triumph of Love*. Mademoiselle Lafontaine becomes ballet's first *première danseuse*.

1682 Père Claude François Ménestrier's *Ballets Ancient and Modern* appears: the first published history of dancing.

1687 Louis Pécourt succeeds Beauchamp as ballet master of the Académie.

c. 1700 Beauchamp names the five basic foot positions of classic dance.

1701 *Choreography: of the Art of Writing Dance*—one of the earliest works on dance notation—is published in Paris. Edited by Raoul Ager Feuillet; often attributed to Louis Pécourt.

1717 John Weaver stages *The Loves of Mars and Venus* in London: first *ballet d'action* (ballet without spoken narration) on record.

1721 Weaver's *Anatomical and Mechanical Lectures Upon Dancing* is published in England.

1726 Marie Camargo makes debut at Paris Opéra.

1734 Marie Sallé, Camargo's principal rival, stages ballet version of *Pygmalion*, one of the earliest works choreographed by a woman. Sallé wears only a simple muslin dress, thus freeing women to dance with greater ease and hence greater virtuosity.

1735 Jean-Philippe Rameau's spectacular opera-ballet *Les Indes Galantes* is performed at the Opéra with Dupré, Camargo, and Sallé.

1738 Imperial St. Petersburg Theatrical Academy is founded in Russia. Headed by Jean Baptiste Landé, the institution is the forerunner of the Maryinsky Ballet Company, now the Kirov.

1743 Jean-Georges Noverre makes his debut at the Paris Opéra Comique.

1748 The Royal Theatre opens in Copenhagen, home of the Royal Danish Ballet.

1754 Noverre stages his successful production of *Les Fêtes Chinoises* at the Paris Opéra Comique.

1760 Noverre publishes *Letters on Dancing and Ballets*, one of the most influential books in the history of dance, in Lyon and Stuttgart.

1761 Dauberval, student of Noverre, makes debut at the Opéra.

1761 Premiere of Gasparo Angiolini's *Don Juan*, an early *ballet d'action*.

1775 Vincenzo Galeotti is appointed ballet master, choreographer, and *premier danseur* at the Royal Theatre, Copenhagen, and over the next fifty years creates a repertory of more than fifty ballets.

1776 Gaetan Vestris becomes ballet master of Paris Opéra.

1776 Noverre succeeds Vestris as ballet master of Paris Opéra.

1780 Noverre becomes ballet master at King's Theatre, London.

1783 Noverre's *Letters* translated into English.

1783 The Bolshoi Theatre opens in St. Petersburg.

1786 *La Fille Mal Gardée*, choreographed by Jean Dauberval and said to be the first comic ballet, is presented in France.

1786 Vincenzo Galeotti presents *The Whims of Cupid and the Ballet*

Master for the Royal Theatre, Copenhagen. The ballet is still performed today and is thus the oldest extant ballet with its original choreography intact.

1796 Charles Didelot's *Flore and Zéphire* opens in London: dancers are suspended from wires to produce the illusion of flight.

1796 M. L. E. Moreau de Saint-Méry's *Danse* is published in Philadelphia: often thought to be the first dance book published in the United States.

1801 Charles Didelot is appointed director of the Imperial Russian Ballet School. Didelot has been called the "father of Russian ballet."

1816 Antoine Bournonville, a pupil of Noverre, becomes ballet master of the Royal Theatre, Copenhagen.

1820 Carlo Blasis' *Elementary Treatise on the Theory and Practice of the Art of Dancing* is published in Milan: the book codifies dance technique and becomes one of the most important texts of classic dance.

1821 First known print of a dancer *en pointe:* toe dancing becomes one of the most important aspects of the Romantic Ballet.

1822 Gas lighting first used at Paris Opéra: the soft lighting enhances the supernatural stories of the Romantic Ballet.

1822 Marie Taglioni, one of the great Romantic ballerinas, makes her debut in Vienna.

1825 First performance at the Bolshoi Theatre in Moscow.

1829 August Bournonville, son of Antoine, succeeds his fathers as ballet master of Royal Theater, Copenhagen. Bournonville becomes the greatest choreographer the company has known; many of his ballets are still performed today.

1829 Blasis publishes his *Code of Terpischore.*

1830 Jules Perrot, one of the few men who survived the otherwise female-dominated Romantic ballet, makes his debut at the Paris Opéra.

1832 Premiere of *La Sylphide* with Marie Taglioni: the first great Romantic ballet.

1834 Fanny Elssler—Taglioni's rival—makes her debut at the Paris Opéra.

1835 Fanny Cerrito makes her debut in Naples.

1836 August Bournonville stages his version of *La Sylphide* for Lucile Grahn at the Royal Theatre, Copenhagen. The version is still in the company's repertory.

1837 Carlo Blasis is appointed director of the Royal Academy of Dance at La Scala, Milan.

1838 Lucile Grahn makes her Paris debut.

1839 American ballerina August Maywood makes her Paris Opéra debut.

1840 Carlotta Grisi makes her Paris debut.

1841 Premiere of *Giselle* with music of Adolph Adam and choreography of Perrot and Coralli. Carlotta Grisi performs the title role. This becomes the great ballet from the Romantic era.

1845 The four famous Romantic ballerinas—Taglioni, Elssler, Grisi, and Cerrito—perform in Jules Perrot's *Pas de quatre* in London.

1847 Taglioni retires.

1847 Mazilier is appointed ballet master at the Paris Opéra, succeeding Coralli.

1847 Marius Petipa arrives in St. Petersburg and performs at the Imperial Theatre.

1851 Elssler retires.

1860 The Maryinsky Theatre opens in St. Petersburg: still the home of what is now the Kirov.

1860 Christian Johansson starts teaching at the Russian Imperial School and becomes one of the great teachers in ballet history.

1862 *The Daughter of Pharaoh*—Petipa's first great choreographic success in Russia—premieres. Petipa is to become the greatest force in nineteenth-century Russian ballet.

1865 Lucien Petipa becomes ballet master at Paris Opéra.

1867 Arthur Saint-Léon is appointed ballet master at Paris Opéra.

1870 *Coppélia*—choreography by Saint-Léon, music by Delibes—premieres in Paris: the comic masterpiece of nineteenth-century ballet.

1870 Enrico Cecchetti makes his debut at La Scala, Milan.

1877 First production of *Swan Lake*—choreography by Reisinger, music by Tchaikovsky—presented at Bolshoi Theatre, Moscow.

1885 Virginia Zucchi, a student of Blasis, makes her Russian debut and dazzles audiences with her technical virtuosity.

1885 Lev Ivanov becomes second ballet master of the Imperial Russian Ballet.

1887 Cecchetti performs with the Imperial Theatre in St. Petersburg. From 1892 to 1902 he is the company's greatest teacher. His pupils include Pavlova, Nijinsky, and Karsavina.

1890 Premiere of *The Sleeping Beauty*—music by Tchaikovsky, choreography by Petipa—in St. Petersburg. Many consider this Petipa's crowning achievement.

1892 *The Nutcracker* premieres in St. Petersburg—music by Tchaikovsky, choreography by Ivanov following Petipa's instructions.

1895 Premiere of the full-length *Swan Lake*—Tchaikovsky's music, choreography by Petipa and Ivanov. Pierina Legnani stars.
1898 Michel Fokine makes debut at Imperial Theatre.
1899 Anna Pavlova makes her debut at the Maryinsky.
1899 Isadora Duncan dances in Chicago.
1899 First issue of the magazine, *The World of Art*. The magazine is founded by Serge Diaghilev, Léon Bakst, and Alexandre Benois—the great forces behind the Ballets Russes.
1900 Vaslav Nijinsky enters the Imperial Academy in St. Petersburg.
1902 Tamara Karsavina makes her debut at the Imperial Theatre.
1904 Michel Fokine, weary of dance gymnastics, submits reforms to enhance ballet's expressiveness to director of Imperial Theatre. Reforms are rejected.
1905 Fokine choreographs *The Dying Swan* for Pavlova: the ballet is to become Pavlova's signature piece.
1905 Duncan appears in Russia.
1906 Premiere of Ruth St. Denis' *Radha*.
1908 Fokine presents *Chopiniana*, the first version of *Les Sylphides*.
1909 First appearance of Diaghilev's Ballets Russes in Paris on May 18: one of the most important premieres in ballet history.
1909 Cecchetti becomes the instructor for the Ballets Russes.
1910 Pavlova appears in the United States.
1910 Premiere of *Firebird*—choreography by Fokine and music by Stravinsky.
1911 Premiere of *Petroushka*—choreography by Fokine, music by Stravinsky. Nijinsky and Karsavina star.
1911 Diaghilev's Ballets Russes perform in London.
1912 Nijinsky choreographs his first ballet, *Afternoon of a Faun*, to Debussy's music.
1913 Nijinsky's third ballet—*Le Sacre du printemps* (*Rite of Spring*)—premieres. The production results in riots. Soon after this premiere, Nijinsky marries and Diaghilev dismisses the famous dancer from the Ballets Russes. Leonide Massine will begin choreographing for the company in 1915.
1914 Fokine writes letter to the London *Times* on July 6 stating his now famous five principles of the New Ballet.
1914 Ted Shawn joins the Ruth St. Denis Company and marries St. Denis. The couple found Denishawn, the first famous modern dance company.
1916 Diaghilev's Ballets Russes appears in United States. Nijinsky dances with them.

1916 Martha Graham starts dance training at Denishawn school in Los Angeles.
1917 Premiere of *Parade*, a "cubist" ballet with story by Cocteau, sets by Picasso, music by Satie, and choreography by Massine. A production of the Ballets Russes in Paris.
1917 Margaret H'doubler starts teaching dance at University of Wisconsin; dance enters the universities.
1917 Doris Humphrey joins Denishawn.
1918 Cecchetti opens Academy of Dancing in London.
1919 Nijinsky retires and tragically ends his brief career: he suffers from mental illnesses the rest of his life.
1920 Royal Academy of Dancing is founded in London.
1921 Diaghilev revives *The Sleeping Beauty* in London. The elaborate production is not popular; the audience, accustomed to Diaghilev's experiments, finds the ballet too old-fashioned.
1921 Charles Weidman joins Denishawn.
1923 Martha Graham leaves Denishawn and embarks on her own career.
1924 George Balanchine starts to choreograph for Diaghilev.
1926 Graham gives her first recital on April 18 in New York.
1926 University of Wisconsin becomes the first college to grant bachelor and master degrees in dance.
1926 Ninette de Valois opens ballet school in London.
1926 Ballet Club (now Ballet Rambert) gives first performance with a ballet by Frederick Ashton—*A Tragedy of Fashion*. Beginning of British ballet.
1927 Duncan gives her last performance on July 8 and dies two months later.
1927 John Martin is appointed first dance critic of the New York *Times;* Mary Watkins becomes first dance critic of the New York *Herald Tribune*.
1928 Doris Humphrey and Charles Weidman, leaving Denishawn, form their own company.
1928 Premiere of Balanchine's *Apollo* to music by Stravinsky: beginning of their great collaboration and of a neo-classicism in dance.
1929 Last performance of Diaghilev's Ballets Russes in London on July 26. Diaghilev dies August 19 in Venice.
1930 Pavlova makes her last public appearance on December 13, dies one month later.
1930 José Limón joins the Humphrey-Weidman Company.
1930 Anna Sokolow joins the Martha Graham Company.
1931 Premiere of Doris Humphrey's *The Shakers*.

1931 Premiere of Martha Graham's *Primitive Mysteries.*

1931 Ninette de Valois' Vic-Wells Ballet gives its first performance at the Old Vic Theatre, London. Later performances presented at Sadler's Wells Theatre: beginning of the Sadler's Wells Ballet, now the Royal Ballet.

1931 Final performances of Denishawn in New York.

1932 Ballet Russe de Monte Carlo is founded by René Blum and Colonel W. de Basil.

1932 Premiere of Kurt Jooss' now famous anti-war ballet, *The Green Table.*

1933 Premiere of *Les Présages* in Monte Carlo—music by Tchaikovsky, choreography by Massine. This is the first ballet set to a full symphony (Tchaikovsky's Fifth).

1933 Ted Shawn establishes his all-male modern dance company.

1934 First all-English production of *Giselle* by the Vic-Wells Ballet. Alicia Markova stars.

1934 The School of American Ballet, the official training grounds for what is now the New York City Ballet, opens in New York on January 2: Lincoln Kirstein has brought George Balanchine to America to start a company and school.

1934 Bennington College Summer School of the Dance offers its first courses in Bennington, Vermont. Faculty includes Martha Graham, Doris Humphrey, Charles Weidman, and Hanya Holm.

1934 The 92nd St. "Y" in New York presents modern dance concerts.

1934 School of American Ballet presents Balanchine's ballets—among them *Serenade*—on December 6 in Hartford, Connecticut.

1935 Littlefield Ballet is founded by Catherine Littlefield in Philadelphia: first American ballet company with American director and American dancers.

1935 The American Ballet, directed by Balanchine, is named resident ballet company at the Metropolitan Opera in New York.

1936 Premiere of Antony Tudor's *Jardin aux Lilas* on January 26 in London: ballet is given a contemporary psychological complexity.

1936 Doris Humphrey completes her trilogy: *New Dance*, *Theater Piece*, and *With My Red Fires.*

1936 Lincoln Kirstein organizes Ballet Caravan to stimulate American dancers, choreographers, composers, and designers. The company tours the United States and produces ballets by Eugene Loring, Lew Christensen, and Erick Hawkins to the music of such composers as Aaron Copland and Elliott Carter, Jr.

1937 American Ballet presents a Stravinsky Festival on April 27 at the Metropolitan Opera House: an all-Stravinsky, all-Balanchine program.

1937 Martha Graham performs at the White House.

1937 San Francisco Ballet organized.

1938 Eugene Loring's *Billy the Kid* premieres in Chicago: one of the first American-theme ballets using American movements.

1939 Sadler's Wells Ballet presents its *Sleeping Beauty* on February 2, staged by Nicholas Serguyev and starring Margot Fonteyn. The ballet is to become the company's signature piece.

1939 Royal Winnipeg Ballet of Canada founded.

1939 Merce Cunningham joins the Martha Graham Company.

1940 Ballet Theatre (now American Ballet Theatre) gives its first performance on January 11 in New York. Founded by Lucia Chase and Richard Pleasant, the company will become one of the world's major dance companies.

1940 Dance Notation Bureau is founded in New York.

1941 Ted Shawn establishes the Jacob's Pillow Dance Festival: one of the major American summer dance attractions.

1942 Tudor's *Pillar of Fire* premieres at Ballet Theatre in New York. Nora Kaye stars.

1942 Premiere of Agnes De Mille's *Rodeo*.

1942 Edwin Denby becomes dance critic of the New York *Herald Tribune*.

1944 Cunningham choreographs his first works.

1944 Premiere of Martha Graham's *Appalachian Spring*.

1944 Premiere of Jerome Robbins' *Fancy Free* by Ballet Theatre in New York.

1944 Doris Humphrey retires from dancing; Charles Weidman forms his own company.

1946 Sadler's Wells Ballet becomes resident company of Covent Garden in London.

1946 Ballet Society is founded in July in New York by Lincoln Kirstein and George Balanchine; the company gives its first performances in November.

1947 Cunningham choreographs *The Seasons* for Ballet Society.

1948 The Dance Collection of the New York City Public Library is established.

1948 The American Dance Festival at Connecticut College is founded.

1948 Ballet Society becomes the New York City Ballet and is appointed the resident company of City Center.

1949 Sadler's Wells Ballet presents its first American tour: a triumph.

1949 Jerome Robbins is appointed associate artistic director of the New York City Ballet.
1950 New York City Ballet performs in London for the first time.
1950 Ballet Theatre begins its first European tour.
1952 The Dance Department of the Juilliard School of Music in New York is established.
1952 National Ballet of Canada is founded.
1954 Paul Taylor organizes his own company.
1954 José Limón tours South America: the first time the State Department sponsors a modern dance troupe.
1956 Robert Joffrey founds the Joffrey Ballet.
1956 Sadler's Wells receives royal charter and becomes the Royal Ballet.
1956 The Bolshoi appears in London: the first performance of the Russian company in the West.
1957 Premiere of Balanchine's *Agon*, to Stravinsky's music.
1957 Bolshoi tours the United States and Canada.
1957 Alvin Ailey forms his own company.
1958 Les Grands Ballets Canadien founded in Montreal.
1958 Graham's *Clytemnestra* premieres, a full-length modern dance ballet.
1959 Graham and Balanchine collaborate in *Episodes* for the New York City Ballet.
1960 Ballet Theatre tours U.S.S.R. for the first time.
1961 The Kirov tours the United States and Canada.
1961 Rudolf Nureyev defects from the Kirov and begins dancing in the West: he stimulates male dancing throughout the Western world.
1962 The Judson Dance Theater is established at the Judson Memorial Church in New York: a home for experimental modern dance.
1962 New York City Ballet tours U.S.S.R.
1963 The Joffrey Ballet tours U.S.S.R.
1963 Martha Graham performs in Europe.
1963 The Ford Foundation begins its ten-year program to develop dance in the United States.
1964 New York City Ballet moves into its new home, the State Theater.
1964 The Paul Taylor and Merce Cunningham companies tour Europe.
1965 Twyla Tharp forms her own troupe.
1965 The National Foundation of the Arts and Humanities is established in Washington, D.C.

1967 The Association of American Dance Companies is founded.
1967 Robert Joffrey's *Astarte* is presented: a multi-media ballet.
1969 The Stuttgart Ballet appears in the United States.
1970 Eliot Feld forms his own ballet company.
1971 Maurice Béjart's *Ballet of the Twentieth Century* tours the United States.
1972 Alvin Ailey becomes resident company of New York City Center.
1972 New York City Ballet presents its week-long Stravinsky Festival.
1973 Martha Graham re-organizes her company and begins reviving her classics.
1973 Experimental choreographer Twyla Tharp choreographs *Deuce Coupe* for the Joffrey. The following year she creates *As Time Goes By*, also for the Joffrey. In 1976 she choreographs *Push Comes to Shove* for American Ballet Theatre.
1974 Mikhail Baryshnikov defects. Joins American Ballet Theatre.
1975 Martha Graham choreographs *Lucifer* for ballet stars Margot Fonteyn and Rudolf Nureyev: the "war" between ballet and modern is declared over.
1978 Baryshnikov moves to New York City Ballet.

Appendix II: The Family Trees of Dance

Family Trees of Ballet Masters

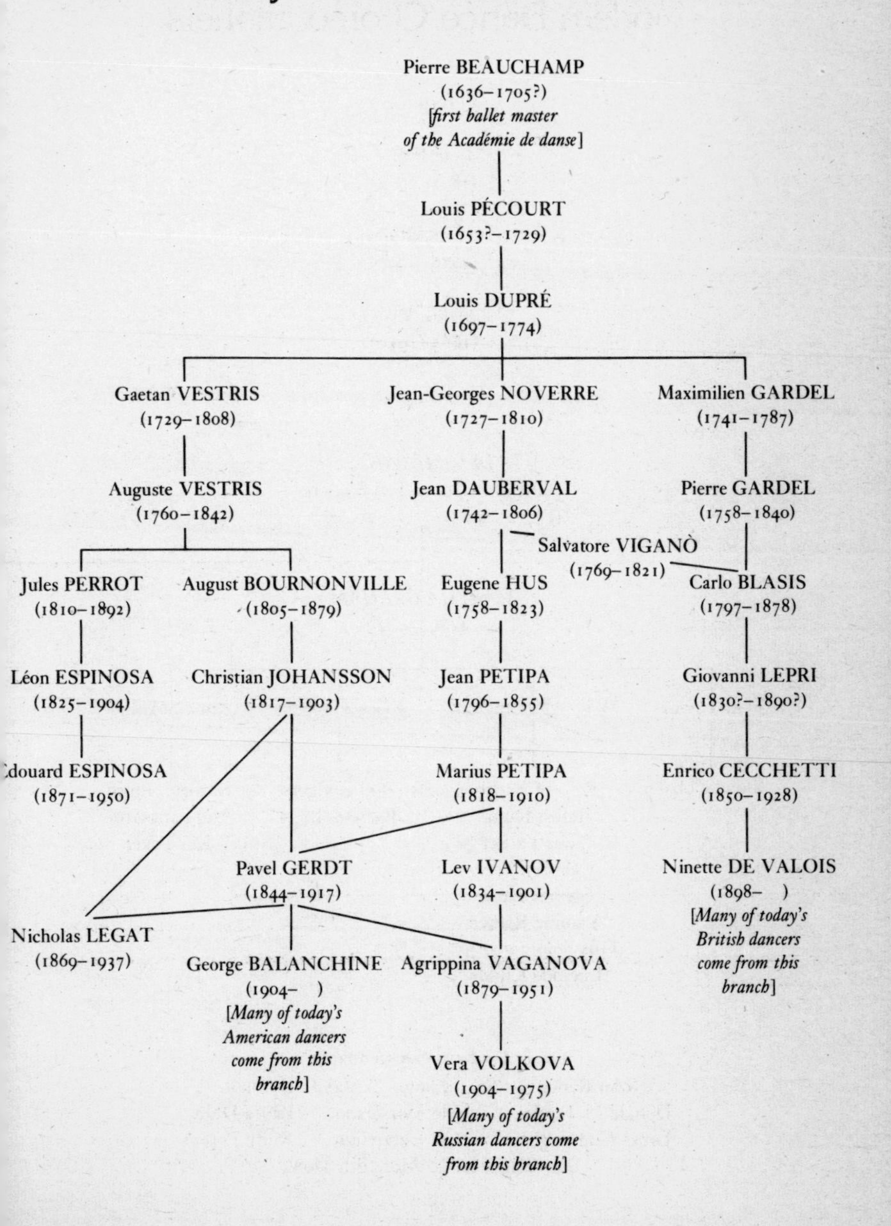

Family Trees of Modern Dance Choreographers

Forerunners

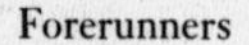

Loie Fuller
(1862–1928)

Isadora Duncan
(1878–1927)

Maud Allan
(1883–1956)

DENISHAWN
Ruth St. Denis-Ted Shawn
(1877?–1968) (1891–1972)

MARTHA GRAHAM
(1894–)

Paul Taylor	Merce Cunningham	Erick Hawkins	Anna Sokolow
Twyla Tharp	Remy Charlip	Rod Rodgers	Kathryn Posin
	Judith Dunn	Barbara Roan	Paul Sanasardo
	Viola Farber		Kei Takei
	Deborah Hay		
	Steve Paxton		
	Yvonne Rainer		
	Gus Solomons, Jr.		
	Lucinda Childs		

Other Graham "Descendants":
John Butler Pearl Lang May O'Donnell
Donald McKayle Merle Marsicano Laura Dean
James Cunningham Lar Lubovitch Rudy Perez
Dan Wagoner Meredith Monk

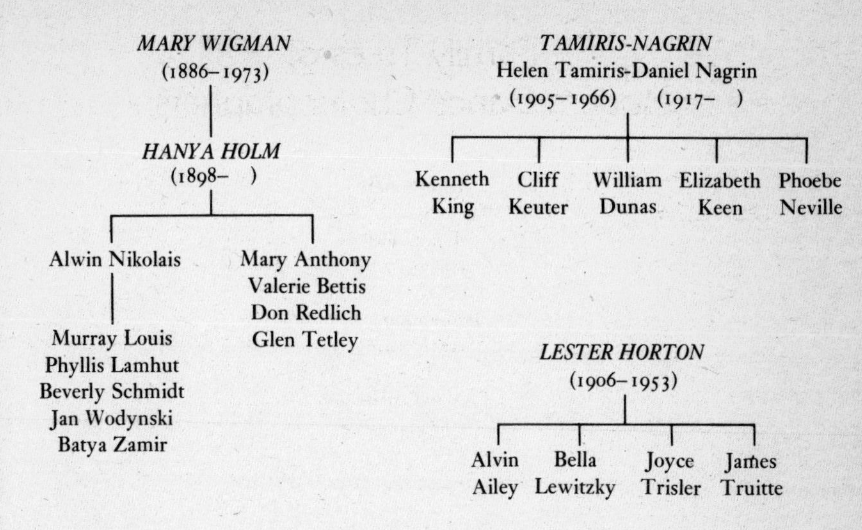

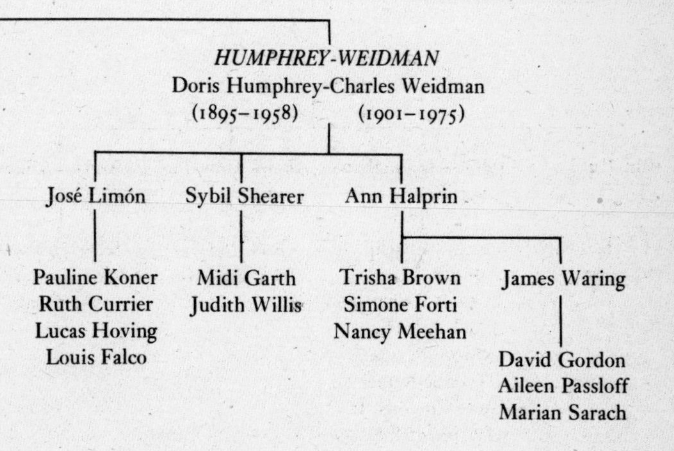

Other Humphrey-Weidman "Descendants":
Katherine Litz William Bales Eleanor King
Marion Scott

Appendix III: A Guide to Dance Literature, Libraries, and Booksellers

Dictionaries and Encyclopedias

("*" denotes especially useful publication.)

d'Albert, Charles. *Encyclopedia of Dancing*. London, T. M. Middleton and Company, n.d.

Beaumont, C. W. *A French-English Dictionary of Technical Terms Used in Classical Ballet*. London, Beaumont, 1970.

Chujoy, Anatole and Manchester, P. W. *The Dance Encyclopedia*. New York, Simon and Schuster, 1977 (revised edition).

Clarke, Mary and Vaughan, David. *The Encyclopedia of Dance and Ballet*. New York, G. P. Putnam's Sons, 1977.

Crosland, Margaret. *Ballet Lovers' Dictionary*. New York, Archer House, 1962.

Espinosa, Eduard. *Technical Dictionary of Dancing*. London, 1935.

Gadan, Francis and Maillard, Robert. *Dictionary of Modern Ballet*. New York, Tudor, 1959. Translated by John Montague and Peggie Cochrane; American editor Selma Jeanne Cohen.

Grant, Gail. *Technical Manual and Dictionary of Classical Ballet*. New York, Dover, 1967.

Kersley, Leo and Sinclair, Janet. *A Dictionary of Ballet Terms*. London, Adam and Charles Black, 1969.

*Koegler, Horst. *The Concise Oxford Dictionary of Ballet*. London, New York, Toronto, Oxford University Press, 1977.

Mara, Thara. *The Language of Ballet: An Informal Dictionary*. New York, World Publishing Company, 1966.

Raffé, W. G. *Dictionary of the Dance*. New York, A. S. Barnes, 1964.

Reyna, Ferdinand. *Concise Encyclopedia of Ballet*. Glasgow, William Collins' Sons and Company, 1974. Translated by André Gâteau.

Wilson, G. B. L. *A Dictionary of Dancing*. London, 1957.

Bibliographies

Beaumont, C. W. (ed). *A Bibliography of the Dance Collection of Doris Niles and Serge Leslie. Part I: A–K.* Annotated by Serge Leslie. London, Beaumont, 1968.

———. *A Bibliography of the Dance Collection of Doris Niles and Serge Leslie. Part II: L–Z.* Annotated by Serge Leslie. London, Beaumont, 1968.

———. *A Bibliography of the Dance Collection of Doris Niles and Serge Leslie. Part III: A–Z. Mainly 20th Century Publications.* London, Beaumont, 1974.

Beaumont, C. W. *A Bibliography of Dancing.* New York, B. Blom, 1963. A reprint of the 1929 original.

*Belknap, Sara (ed). *A Guide to Dance Periodicals.* Gainesville, Florida, University of Florida Press. In 10 volumes, first volume covers 1931–35; thereafter issued bi-annually through 1960.

Dance Perspectives. "Current Bibliography for Dance." Compiled annually, 1959, 1960, 1961, and 1962.

Fentress, Roy. "A Bibliography of Dance Books," *Dance Magazine,* March 1969, pp. 51–59.

Fletcher, Ifan Kyrle. *A Bibliographical Description of Forty Rare Books Relating to the Art of Dancing.* London, 1954.

Forrester, F. S. *Ballet in England: A Bibliography and Survey c. 1700–June 1966.* London, Library Association, 1968.

Kaprelian, Mary H. *Aesthetics for Dancers: A Selected Annotated Bibliography.* Washington, D.C., American Alliance for Health, Physical Education and Recreation, 1976.

*Magriel, Paul David. *A Bibliography of Dancing; A List of Books and Articles on the Dance and Related Subjects.* New York, H. W. Wilson, 1936. Reprinted in 1974.

*New York (City). Public Library. Performing Arts Research Center. *Dictionary Catalog of the Dance Collection: A List of Authors, Titles, and Subjects of Multi-Media Materials in the Dance Collection of the Performing Arts Research Center of the New York Public Library.* Boston, G. K. Hall, 1974. In 10 volumes. Annual Supplements.

Guides to Ballet Plots and Characters

*Balanchine, George and Mason, Francis. *Complete Stories From the Great Ballets.* Garden City, New York, Doubleday, 1977 (revised edition).

*Beaumont, C. W. *Complete Book of Ballets: A Guide to the Principal Ballets of the 19th and 20th Centuries.* New York, G. P. Putnam's Sons, 1938.
———. *Supplement to the Complete Book of Ballets.* London, Beaumont, 1942.
———. *Ballets of Today: Being a Supplement to the Complete Book of Ballets.* London, Beaumont, 1954.
———. *Ballets Past and Present: Being a Third Supplement to the Complete Book of Ballets.* London, Beaumont, 1955.
Brinson, Peter and Crisp, Clement. *The International Book of Ballet.* New York, Stein and Day, 1971.
Crosland, Margaret. *Ballet Carnival: A Companion to Ballet.* London, Arco, 1957.
Crowle, Pigeon. *Come to the Ballet.* New York, G. P. Putnam's Sons, 1957.
———. *Tales From the Ballet.* London, Faber and Faber, 1955.
Davidson, Gladys. *Stories of the Ballets.* London, Werner Laurie, 1958.
Drew, David (ed). *The Decca Book of Ballets.* London, Muller, Ltd., n.d.
Goode, Gerald. *The Book of Ballets Classic and Modern.* New York, Crown, 1939.
*Kirstein, Lincoln. *Movement and Metaphor: Four Centuries of Ballet.* New York, Praeger, 1970.
Krokover, Rosalyn. *New Borzoi Book of Ballets.* New York, Knopf, 1956.
Lawrence, Robert. *The Victor Book of Ballets and Ballet Music.* New York, Simon and Schuster, 1950.
Robert, Grace. *The Borzoi Book of Ballets.* New York, Knopf, 1947.
Sharp, Harold S. and Marjorie Z. *Index to Characters in the Performing Arts. Part III: Ballet A–Z and Symbols.* New York, 1972.
Untermeyer, Louis. *Tales From the Ballet.* London, Paul Hamlyn, 1969.
Verwer, Hans. *Guide to the Ballet.* New York, Barnes and Noble, 1963.
Viveash, Cherry. *Tales From the Ballet.* London, George Ronald, 1958.

Collections of Reviews and Interviews

Coton, A. V. *Writings on Dance, 1938–68.* London, Dance Books, 1975.
Craig, Gordon, *Gordon Craig on Movement and Dance.* New York, Dance Horizons, 1977.
*Croce, Arlene. *Afterimages.* New York, Knopf, 1977.
*Denby, Edwin. *Dancers, Buildings, and People in the Streets.* New York, Horizon, 1965.

*———. *Looking at the Dance*. New York, Horizon, 1968 (reprint of 1949 edition).

*Gautier, Théophile. *The Romantic Ballet; As Seen By Théophile Gautier. Being His Notices Of All the Principal Performances of Ballet Given at Paris During the Years 1837–1848*. New York, Dance Horizons, 1972. Translated by C. W. Beaumont.

Gruen, John. *The Private World of Ballet*. New York, Viking, 1975.

Haggin, B. H. *Ballet Chronicle*. New York, Horizon, 1970.

Haskell, Arnold. *Balletomania; Then and Now*. New York, Knopf, 1977.

Jackson, Graham. *Dance as Dance: Selected Reviews and Essays*. Ontario, Catalyst Press, 1978.

Johnston, Jill. *Marmelade Me*. New York, Dutton, 1971.

Jowitt, Deborah. *Dance Beat: Selected Views and Reviews, 1967–76*. New York, Marcel Dekker, 1977.

Lyle, Cynthia. *Dancers on Dancing*. New York, Drake, 1977.

Siegel, Marcia B. *At the Vanishing Point: A Critic Looks at Dance*. New York, Saturday Review Press, 1972.

———. *Watching the Dance Go By*. Boston, Houghton Mifflin, 1977.

Terry, Walter. *I Was There: Selected Dance Reviews and Articles, 1936–1976*. New York, Marcel Dekker, 1978.

Van Vechten, Carl. *The Dance Writings of Carl Van Vechten*. New York, Dance Horizons, 1974.

Influential Reviewers

Jack Anderson, *The New York Times;* Clive Barnes, *Ballet News;* Arlene Croce, *The New Yorker;* Jennifer Dunning, *The New York Times;* Nancy Goldner, *The Nation;* Deborah Jowitt, *The Village Voice;* Anna Kisselgoff, *The New York Times;* Alan M. Kriegsman, *The Washington Post;* Marcia B. Siegel, *Soho Weekly News;* Walter Terry, *Saturday Review*.

Magazines and Periodicals

Ballet. London, irregularly. Volume 1, #1 (July–August 1939) through Volume 12, #10 (October 1952). Edited by Richard Buckle.

The Ballet Annual: A Record and Year Book of the Ballet. London, annually. 1946–1963. Edited by Arnold Haskell.

**Ballet Review*. New York, now quarterly. Founded in 1965 by Arlene Croce; as of Volume 7, #1, edited by Robert Cornfield.

Ballet Today. London, monthly then bi-monthly, 1946–1970.
CCT Review (Composers and Choreographers Theatre). New York, quarterly.
Dance and Dancers. London, monthly, 1950 to the present.
Dance Chronicle: Studies in Dance and the Related Arts. New York, quarterly, 1977 to the present. Edited by George Dorris and Jack Anderson.
Dance Dimensions. Milwaukee (Department of Philosophy, Marquette University), quarterly.
Dance Gazette. London, three times a year. Published by the Royal Academy of Dancing.
Dance in Canada. Toronto, quarterly.
**Dance Index*. New York, irregularly, 1942–1948. Largely edited by Lincoln Kirstein. Reprinted in 7 volumes in 1971 by Arno Press.
Dance Life. New York, three times a year.
**Dance Magazine*. New York, monthly, 1936 to the present. The largest dance magazine in the world. Trendy but still indispensable.
**Dance Magazine Annual: A Catalogue of Dance Artists and Attractions, Programs, and Services*. New York, annually.
Dance News. New York, monthly except for July and August, 1942 to the present.
Dance Observor. New York, monthly, 1934–1964. Run predominantly by Louis Horst.
**Dance Perspectives*. New York, quarerly, 1958–1976. Founded by Al Pischl, later edited by Selma Jeanne Cohen.
Dance Research Journal. New York, twice a year. Published by the Committee on Research in Dance, New York University.
Dance Scope. New York, twice a year from 1964 through 1978, now quarterly. Published by the American Dance Guild.
**The Dancing Times*. London, monthly. Founded in 1910.
**Dance World*. New York, annually. Edited by John Willis. Annual compilation of dance seasons in the United States.
Eddy. New York, irregularly.
Impulse: An Annual of Contemporary Dance. San Francisco, annually. 1951–61.

Anthologies of Essays

Brahms, Caryl (ed). *Footnotes to the Ballet*. London, Peter Davies, 1936.
Brown, Jean Morrison (ed). *The Vision of Modern Dance*. Princeton, Princeton Book Company, 1979.

Cohen, Selma Jeanne (ed). *Dance as a Theatre Art: Source Readings in Dance History From 1581 to the Present*. New York, Harper & Row, 1974.

Livet, Anne (ed). *Contemporary Dance: An Anthology of Lectures, Interviews, and Essays with Many of the Most Important Contemporary American Choreographers, Scholars and Critics*. New York, Abbeville Press, 1978.

Nadel, Myron Howard and Miller, Constance Nadel (eds). *The Dance Experience: Readings in Dance Appreciation*. New York, Universe Books, 1978.

Pops, Martin Leonard (ed). *Dance*. *Salmagundi*, #33–34, Spring–Summer, 1976.

Sorell, Walter (ed). *The Dance Has Many Faces*. New York, World, 1951. Second Edition: New York, Columbia University Press, 1966.

Twenty Five Years of American Dance. New York, 1951. An Anthology of *Dance Magazine* articles.

Van Tuyl, Marian (ed). *Anthology of Impulse*. New York, Dance Horizons, 1969.

Historical Overviews

World Overviews

*Anderson, Jack. *Dance*. New York, Newsweek Books, 1974.

Beaumont, C. W. *A Short History of Ballet*. London, Beaumont, 1944.

Bland, Alexander. *A History of Ballet and Dance in the Western World*. New York, Praeger, 1976.

Clarke, Mary and Crisp, Clement. *Ballet: An Illustrated History*. New York, Universe Books, 1978.

Crisp, Clement and Thorpe, Edward. *The Colorful World of Ballet*. London, Octopus Books, 1977.

*De Mille, Agnes. *The Book of the Dance*. New York, Golden Press, 1963.

*Guest, Ivor. *The Dancer's Heritage: A Short History of Ballet*. London, The Dancing Times, 1960.

*Kirstein, Lincoln. *Dance: A Short History of Classic Theatrical Dancing*. New York, Dance Horizons, 1974 (reprint of the 1935 edition).

Haskell, Arnold. *Ballet Retrospect*. New York, Viking, 1965.

Kraus, Richard. *History of the Dance in Art and Education*. Englewood Cliffs, New Jersey, Prentice-Hall, 1969.

Lawson, Joan. *A History of Ballet and Its Makers*. London, Pitman, 1964.

Martin, John. *The Dance*. New York, Tudor, 1946.

Reyna, Ferdinando. *A Concise History of Ballet*. New York, Grosset & Dunlop, 1965.

Sorell, Walter. *The Dance Through the Ages.* New York, Grosset & Dunlop, 1967.
Swinson, Cyril. *Guidebook to the Ballet.* New York, Macmillan, 1961.
Woodward, Ian. *Ballet.* London, Hodder and Stoughton, 1977.

American Overviews

Amberg, George. *Ballet in America.* New York, Duell, Sloan, and Pearce, 1949.
Martin, John. *America Dancing.* New York, Dodge, 1936.
Mazo, Joseph H. *Prime Movers: The Makers of Modern Dance in America.* New York, Morrow, 1977.
Maynard, Olga. *The American Ballet.* Philadelphia, Macrae Smith, 1959.
———. *American Modern Dancers: The Pioneers.* Boston and Toronto, Little Brown, 1965.
*McDonagh, Don. *The Complete Guide to Modern Dance.* Garden City, New York, Doubleday, 1976.
———. *The Rise and Fall and Rise of Modern Dance.* New York, Outerbridge & Dienstfrey, 1970. New American Library, paperback.
Palmer, Winthrop. *Theatrical Dancing in America.* New York, Bernard Ackerman, 1945. (Revised edition, New York, Barnes, 1978.)
*Siegel, Marcia B. *The Shapes of Change: Images of American Dance.* Boston, Houghton Mifflin, 1979.
Terry, Walter. *The Dance in America.* New York, Harper & Row, 1956. Revised edition, 1973.

Technical Manuals

Agnew, Eric M. *Anatomical Studies for Dancers and Teachers of the Classical Ballet.* London, Imperial Society of Teachers of Dancing, 1964.
Ambrose, Kay. *The Ballet-Lover's Pocketbook: Technique Without Tears for the Ballet-Lover.* New York, Knopf, 1954.
*Beaumont, C. W. and Idzikowski, Stanislas. *A Manual of the Theory and Practice of Classical Theatrical Dancing (Méthode Cecchetti).* New York, Dover, 1975 (reprint of 1922 original).
Blasis, Carlo. *An Elementary Treatise Upon the Theory and Practice of the Art of Dancing.* New York, Dover, 1968 (originally published in 1820).
*Bruhn, Erik and Moore, Lillian. *Bournonville and Ballet Technique.* London, A. & C. Black, 1961.
Craske, Margaret and De Moroda, Derra. *The Theory and Practice of Advanced Allegro. (Cecchetti Method).* London, 1971.

Dolin, Anton. *Pas de Deux: The Art of Partnering*. London, A. & C. Black, 1950.

Featherstone, Donald F. and Allen, Rona. *Dancing Without Danger: The Prevention and Treatment of Ballet Dancing Injuries*. London, Kaye and Ward, 1970.

French, Ruth and Demery, Felix. *First Steps in Ballet*, London, 1966.

Guillot, Genevieve and Prodhommeau, Germaine. *The Book of Ballet*. New York, 1975.

Hammer, Sylvia. *Technique for the Dancer*. New York, 1974.

*Karsavina, Tamara. *Classical Ballet: The Flow of Movement*. London, A. & C. Black, 1962.

*———. *Ballet Technique. A Series of Practical Essays*. London, A. & C. Black, 1957.

*Kirstein, Lincoln; Stuart, Muriel; Dyer, Carlus; and Balanchine, George. *The Classic Ballet: Basic Technique and Terminology*. New York, 1953. Revised edition, 1979.

Lawson, Joan. *Classical Ballet: Its Style and Technique*. London, A. & C. Black, 1960.

Lifar, Serge. *Lifar on Classical Ballet*. London, Wingate, 1951.

*Messerer, Asaf. *Classes in Classical Ballet*. New York, 1975.

Ralov, Kirsten. *The Bournonville School* (4 volumes). New York, Marcel Dekker, 1978.

Sparger, Celia, *Anatomy and Ballet*. London, A. & C. Black, 1970.

Spessivtzeva, Olga. *Technique for the Ballet Artiste*. London, Frederick Muller, 1967.

*Vaganova, Agrippina. *Basic Principles of Classical Ballet*. New York, Dover, 1969.

Notation Guides

Arbeau, Thoinot. *Orchesography, 15th and 16th Century Dances*. New York, Dover, 1966. Originally published in 1588, translated by Mary Stewart Evans.

Benesh, Rudolf. *Choreology; Benesh Movement Notation*. London, 1955.

*Benesh, Rudolf and Benesh, Joan. *An Introduction to Benesh Dance Notation*. London, A. & C. Black, 1956.

Causley, Marguerite. *An Introduction to Benesh Movement Notation*. London, 1967.

Cook, Ray. *The Dance Director*. New York, Dance Notation Bureau, 1977.

Eshkol, Noa and Wachmann, Abraham. *Movement Notation*. London, Weidenfeld and Nicholson, 1958.

*Hutchinson, Ann. *Labanotation*. New York, Theatre Arts Books, 1977 (revised edition).

Laban, Rudolf von. *Principles of Dance and Movement Notation*. London, 1956.

Pemberton, E. *An Essay for the Improvement of Dancing*. London, 1970 (facsimile of 1711 text).

Stepanow, V. I. *Alphabet of Movements of the Human Body*. New York, Dance Horizons, 1969. Translated by Raymond Lister from the French edition of 1892.

Zorn, Friedrich Albert. *Grammar of the Art of Dancing*. New York, Dance Horizons, 1975. Reprint of the 1905 edition.

Notation Bureaus:

Dance Notation Bureau
505 Eighth Avenue
New York, New York 10018
(212) 736-4350

Institute of Choreology
Highdown Tower
Littlehampton Road
Worthing, Sussex NB126PF
England

Dance Notation Bureau Extension
Ohio State University
1813 North High Street
Columbus, Ohio 43210
(614) 422-6446

Studies in Dance Design

*Amberg, George. *Art in Modern Ballet*. New York, Pantheon, 1946.

Arsène, Alexandre and Cocteau, Jean. *The Decorative Art of Leon Bakst*. New York, Dover, 1972 (reprint of the 1913 edition).

Beaton, Cecil. "Designing for Ballet," *Dance Index*, Volume 5, #8, August 1946, pp. 184–198.

Beaumont, C. W. *Five Centuries of Ballet Design*. London, Studio Ltd., n.d.

———. *Design for the Ballet*. London, 1938.

*———. *Ballet Design, Past and Present*. New York, Studio Publications, 1946.

Buckle, Richard. *Modern Ballet Design*. London. A. & C. Black, 1955.
*Clarke, Mary and Crisp, Clement. *Design for Ballet*. London, Macmillan, 1978.
Cooper, Douglas, *Picasso: Theatre*. London, Weidenfeld and Nicolson, 1968.
Delarue, Allison, "The Stage and Ballet Designs of Eugene Berman," *Dance Index*, Volume 5, #2, February 1946, pp. 4–24.
Lassaigne, Jacques. *Marc Chagall: Drawings and Water Colors for the Ballet*. New York, Tudor, 1969.
Levinson, André. *Bakst, The Story of the Artist's Life*. London, Bayard Press, 1923.
———. *The Designs of Leon Bakst for "The Sleeping Beauty."* London, Benn Brothers, 1923.
Lieberman, William S. "Picasso and the Ballet," *Dance Index*, Volume 5, #11–12, November–December 1946, pp. 266–308.
Rischbieter, Henning and Storch, Wolfgang (eds). *Art and the Stage in the Twentieth Century: Painters and Sculptors Work for the Theater*. Greenwich, Connecticut, New York Graphic Society, Ltd. 1968.
Rosenthal, Jean and Wertenbaker, Loel. *The Magic of Light*. Boston, Little Brown, 1972.
Windham, Donald. "The Stage and Ballet Designs of Pavel Tchelitchew," *Dance Index*, Volume VIII, #1–2, January–February 1944, pp. 4–32.

Studies in Dance Music

*Arvey, Verna. *Choreographic Music; Music for the Dance*. New York, 1941.
Austin, Richard. "The Dance and Music," *Images of the Dance*. London, Vision Press, 1975.
Berger, Arthur. "Music for the Ballet," *Dance Index*, Volume 6, pp. 258–277.
Calvocoressi, Michel D. *Music and Ballet*. London, 1934.
Dorris, George. "Music for Spectacle," *Ballet Review*, Volume 6, #1, 1977/78, pp. 45–55.
Evans, Edwin. *Music and the Dance, for Lovers of the Ballet*. London, Jenkins, 1948.
Fiske, Roger. *Ballet Music*. London, Harrap, 1958.
Gould, Morton, "Music and the Dance," *The Dance Has Many Faces* (ed) Walter Sorell. New York, Columbia University Press, 1966.
Knight, Judith. *Ballet and Its Music*. London, 1973.

*Lederman, Minna (ed). *Stravinsky in the Theatre.* New York, Da Capo, 1975 (reprint of *Dance Index* tribute to Stravinsky).

Levinson, André. "Stravinsky and the Dance," *Theatre Arts*, November 1924, pp. 741–754.

Limón, José. "Music Is the Strongest Ally to a Dancer's Way of Life," *The Dance Experience* (ed) Myron Howard Nadel. New York, Universe Books, 1978.

Nettl, Paul. *The Dance in Classical Music.* New York, Philosophical Library, 1963.

———. *The Story of Dance Music.* New York, 1947.

Porter, Evelyn. *Music Through the Dance.* London, 1937.

*Searle, Humphrey. *Ballet Music: An Introduction.* New York, Dover, 1973 (second edition).

Studwell, William E. "The Choreographic Chain: Seventy Years of Ballet Music," *Dance Scope*, Volume 10, #2, Spring–Summer 1976, pp. 51–55.

Willinger, Edward. "Music at the Ballet," *Ballet Review*, Volume 6, #2, 1977/78, pp. 86–95.

Dance Film Catalogues

Catalog of Dance Films. New York, Dance Film Associates, 1974.

*Mueller, John. *Dance Film Directory: An Annotated and Evaluative Guide to Films on Ballet and Modern Dance.* Princeton, Princeton Book Company, 1979.

Parker, David L. and Siegel, Esther. *Guide to Dance in Films*, Detroit, Gale Research Company, 1977.

Dance Libraries and Archives

American

Allen A. Brown Collection
Boston Public Library
Boston, Massachusetts 02116

Anatole Chujoy Memorial Dance Collection
Gorno Memorial Music Library
College Conservatory of Music
University of Cincinnati
101 Emery Hall
Cincinnati, Ohio 45221

Cleveland Public Library
325 Superior Avenue, N.E.
Cleveland, Ohio 44114

Collins Collection of the Dance
Birmingham Public and Jefferson County Free Library
2020 Seventh Avenue N.
Birmingham, Alabama 35203

*Dance Collection
New York Public Library
Library and Museum of the Performing Arts
111 Amsterdam Avenue
New York, New York 10023
(perhaps the finest dance library in the world)

Dance Collection
Walter Clinton Jackson Library
University of North Carolina
Greensboro, North Carolina 27412

George Chaffee Ballet Collection
Harvard Theatre Collection
Houghton Library
Cambridge, Massachusetts 02138

Hoblitzelle Theatre Arts Library
University of Texas
Austin, Texas 78712

Jan Veen-Katrine Amory Hooper Memorial Dance and Art Collection
Albert Alphin Music Library
Boston Conservatory of Music
8 The Fenway
Boston, Massachusetts 02215

Wadsworth Atheneum
600 Main Street
Hartford, Connecticut 06103
(houses the Serge Lifar Collection of set and costume designs)

European

The Arsenal Library
Theater Section
1 Rue Sully
75004 Paris

Covent Garden Archives
Royal Opera House
Covent Garden
London WC2E 7QA

London School of Contemporary Dance Library
The Place
17 Dukes Road
London WC1H 9AB

Paris Opera Library
Place de l'Opéra
75009 Paris
(more than 80,000 volumes—houses important collection on Diaghilev's Balles Russes)

Pavlova Memorial Library
Westminster Reference Library
St. Martin's Street
London WC2

Royal Academy of Dancing Library
48 Vickerage Crescent
London SW11 3LT

Theatre Museum at the Victoria and Albert Museum
Exhibition Road
South Kensington
London SW7 2RL

Vic-Wells Association Library
Sadler's Wells Theatre
Roseberry Avenue
London EC1

Dance Booksellers

AMERICAN

The Ballet Shop
1887 Broadway
New York, New York 10023

Dance Etc.
5897 College Avenue
Oakland, California 94618

The Dance Mart
Box 48
Homecrest Station
Brooklyn, New York 11229

Drama Book Shop
150 West 52nd Street
New York, New York 10019

Footnotes
F. Randolph Associates
1300 Arch Street
Philadelphia, Pennsylvania 19107

Library and Museum of the Performing Arts Sales Shop
111 Amsterdam Avenue
New York, New York 10023

EUROPEAN

Le Coupe Papier
19 Rue de l'Odéon
75006 Paris

Dance Books, Ltd. (Ballet Bookshop)
9 Cecil Court
London WC2N 4EZ

Dancing Times
18 Hand Court
High Holborn
London WC1

Danse
14 Rue de Beaune
75007 Paris

Notes on Contributors

JACK ANDERSON reviews dance for *The New York Times* and is a regular contributor to *Dance Magazine*, *Ballet Review*, and the *Dancing Times* of London. He has taught dance criticism at Connecticut College and at the New School for Social Research in New York City. He is the author of *Dance* in the Newsweek World of Culture series.

GEORGE BALANCHINE was born in St. Petersburg and received his training at the Imperial Ballet Academy. He left Russia and began choreographing for Diaghilev's Ballets Russes in 1924. After Diaghilev's death, Balanchine was brought to America by Lincoln Kirstein in 1933, where he founded the School of American Ballet and the company now known as the New York City Ballet. By even the most conservative estimates, Mr. Balanchine is one of the most prolific and most influential choreographers in ballet history.

C. W. BEAUMONT (1891–1976) was one of England's best-known dance scholars and its favorite bookseller. The tireless Mr. Beaumont was, moreover, on the boards of several dance academies and institutes, and it was he who preserved the Cecchetti teaching method. Mr. Beaumont's books include *A Bibliography of Dancing*, *Michel Fokine and His Ballets*, *The Complete Book of Ballets*, *The Diaghilev Ballet in London*, *Ballet Design: Past and Present*, and translations of Noverre, Gautier, and Rameau.

ALEXANDRE BENOIS (1870–1960) was one of the founding members of the Ballets Russes and functioned as the company's artistic director in its early years. He designed the sets and costumes for *Le Pavillon d'Armide*, *Les Sylphides*, and *Petrouchka*, among many other ballets. His books include *Reminiscences of the Russian Ballet* and *Memoirs.*

LUCIA CHASE is the director and co-founder of the American Ballet Theatre, one of the world's major companies and one into which Miss Chase has invested a large portion of her personal fortune. She studied dance under Fokine, Mordkin, Vilzak, and Tudor, and created the role of Eldest Sister in Tudor's *Pillar of Fire*.

MARY CLARKE is an editor of the London dance magazine, *Dancing Times.* Her books include *The Sadler's Wells Ballet*, *Dancers of the Mercury: The Story of Ballet Rambert*, and (with Clement Crisp) *Ballet: An Illustrated History*, *Making a Ballet*, and *Design for Ballet.*

CLEMENT CRISP is the dance critic for the British *Financial Times* as well as the Librarian for the Royal Academy of Dancing. His books include (with Peter Brinson) *The International Book of Ballet* and (with Mary Clarke) *Ballet: An Illustrated History*, *Making a Ballet*, and *Design for Ballet*.

ARLENE CROCE founded the distinguished dance journal *Ballet Review* in 1965. Often praised as the finest dance critic currently working in America, she reviews dance for *The New Yorker*.

NORMAN DELLO JOIO studied music at Juilliard and Yale and has himself taught at Sarah Lawrence and Mannes College of Music. His score for José Limón's *Meditations on Ecclesiastes* won the Pulitzer Prize in 1957. Mr. Dello Joio has also composed the scores for Martha Graham's *Diversion of Angels* and *Seraphic Dialogue*.

AGNES DE MILLE—born in New York and raised in California—studied dance with Kosloff and Rambert. After dancing in the early Tudor ballets in England, she returned to America and began creating some of the best-known and most popular American-theme ballets, among which *Rodeo* is the most famous. Her choreography for *Oklahoma!*, *Carousel*, and *Paint Your Wagon* revolutionized Broadway dancing. Her fine books include *Dance to the Piper*, *And Promenade Home*, *Speak to Me*, *Dance with Me*, and *The Book of the Dance*.

EDWIN DENBY—often considered the finest dance critic America has ever produced—reviewed dance for *Modern Music* and *The New York Herald Tribune*. His books include *Looking at Dance*, and *Dancers, Buildings, and People in the Streets*.

ISADORA DUNCAN (1878–1927) was born and raised in San Francisco but lived most of her adult life—and enjoyed most of her immense success—in Europe. Wishing to free dance from the restraints of classical ballet and to return dance to a more "natural" state, she performed barefoot, wearing loose tunics, to great classical music. She was a phenomenon of her times, and if she founded no lasting academy or no permanent technique, her influence has nonetheless been profound.

HAVELOCK ELLIS (1859–1939), English psychologist and author, is perhaps best-known for his pioneering work in the field of human sexuality, *Studies in the Psychology of Sex*.

MICHEL FOKINE (1880–1942)—like Balanchine, Nijinsky, Nureyev, and Baryshnikov—was trained at the Imperial Ballet Academy in St. Petersburg. Annoyed by the storytelling conventions of the ballets of his time, he tried to give ballet a greater dramatic unity—to achieve a consistency of plot, music, decor, and choreography. His reforms are now famous. His best-known works, choreographed for the Ballets Russes, include *Les Sylphides*, *Firebird*, and *Petrushka*.

THÉOPHILE GAUTIER (1811–1872)—poet, novelist, critic—was one of the great figures of French Romanticism. As a theater critic, Gautier saw the best dancers of the Romantic Era, and his reviews remain some of the finest examples of dance criticism we have.

NANCY GOLDNER, the dance critic for *The Nation*, is the author of *The Stravinsky Festival of the New York City Ballet*.

MARTHA GRAHAM, perhaps the most celebrated of all American modern dancers/choreographers, began studying dance under Denishawn in California. In 1927 she founded the Martha Graham School of Contemporary Dance and has ever since devoted herself to developing her own special breed of dance, which is at once personal and mythic and undeniably American in perspective. One of the great figures in dance history, she is arguably the most imitated choreographer in the field of modern dance.

IVOR GUEST is one of England's most-respected dance historians. His books include *The Ballet of the Second Empire, 1858–1870*, *The Romantic Ballet in England*, *Fanny Cerrito*, *The Dancer's Heritage*, *The Romantic Ballet in Paris*, and *Fanny Elssler*.

LOUIS HORST (1884–1964) was the musical mentor for many of America's best modern dance choreographers. A close collaborator of Martha Graham, Horst created the scores for her *Primitive Mysteries*, *Frontier*, and *El Penitente*. In 1934, Horst founded *Dance Observor*, a magazine devoted to modern dance. Mr. Horst is also the author of *Modern Dance Forms*.

RUTH KATZ is a professor at Hebrew University.

CONSTANT LAMBERT (1905–1951), one of the principal figures in British dance music, was the musical director of Vic-Wells and Sadler's Wells Ballet (now Royal Ballet). Mr. Lambert composed the scores for several of Ashton's early works (*Rio Grande*, *Pomona*, *Horoscope*) as well as arranged the score for Ashton's *Les Patineurs*.

SUSANNE LANGER, one of American's best-known philosophers and aestheticians, is the author of *An Introduction to Symbolic Logic*, *Philosophy in a New Key*, *Feeling and Form*, *Problems of Art*, *Reflections on Art*, and *Mind*.

D. H. LAWRENCE (1885–1930) is one this century's most controversial and celebrated novelists, author of *Sons and Lovers*, *Women in Love*, *The Rainbow*, and *Lady Chatterly's Lover*. His travel books include *Mornings in Mexico* and *Etruscan Places*.

ANDRÉ LEVINSON (1887–1933), the Russian dance critic, taught languages at St. Petersburg University before becoming a journalist in Paris in 1918. A defender of the pure classical style in dance, he opposed the new dance of Fokine and Diaghilev. His works include *Ballet Romantique*, *La Vie de Noverre*, *Anna Pavlova*, *Marie Taglioni*, and *Serge Lifar*. Unfortunately, all too little of his fine criticism has been translated into English.

PRINCE PETER LIEVEN (1887–1943), born and educated in Russia, lived in Europe after World War I. His intense interest in music and theater brought him to the Ballets Russes and he become a first-hand observer of that company's success. His recollections of those days were published in *The Birth of the Ballets Russes.*

NORMAN LLOYD has taught music at New York University, Sarah Lawrence, Juilliard, and Oberlin. His scores for dance include Graham's *Panorama* and *Opening Dance*, Charles Weidman's *Quest* and *This Passion*, and Doris Humphrey's *Inquest* and *Lament for Ignacio Sanchez Mejias.*

JOHN MARTIN, one of America's first professional dance critics, reviewed dance for *The New York Times* from 1927 to 1962. His books include *The Modern Dance*, *Introduction to the Dance*, *The Dance*, and *World Book of Modern Ballet*.

ISAMU NOGUGHI designed the sets for Balanchine's *Orpheus* as well as those for many of Graham's best-known works—*Frontier*, *Appalachian Spring*, *Dark Meadow*, *Cave of the Heart*, *Errand in the Maze*, *Seraphic Dialogue*, and *Clytemnestra*.

JEAN-GEORGES NOVERRE (1727–1810) is one of the great choreographers, ballet masters, and dance theoreticians in the history of ballet. Today, he is best known as the author of *Letters on Dancing and Ballets.*

GUNTER SCHULLER has played French horn for both the American Ballet Theatre and the Metropolitan Opera. He composed the scores for Balanchine's *Modern Jazz: Variants* and José Limón's *The Traitor* and *Barren Sceptre*.

WALTER SORELL's books on dance include *The Dance Through the Ages*, *Hanya Holm*, *The Dancer's Image*, *The Mary Wigman Book*, and *The Dance Has Many Faces.*

ARTHUR SYMONS (1865–1945), English poet and critic, was one of the leading figures in England's Symbolist movement. His books include *The Symbolist Movement in Literature*, *The Romantic Movement in English Poetry*, and *Studies in Seven Arts*.

ROUBEN TER-ARUTUNIAN designed the sets for Balanchine's *The Seven Deadly Sins* (1958 version), *The Flood*, *Ballet Imperial*, *The Nutcracker*, *Harlequinade*, *Coppelia*, *Union Jack* and *Vienna Waltzes*, as well as those for Glen Tetley's *Pierrot Lunaire*, *Sargasso*, *Field Mass*, and *Voluntaries*.

EDWARD THORPE is the author (with Clement Crisp) of *The Colorful World of Ballet*.

PAUL VALÉRY (1871–1945), French poet, dramatist, critic, essayist, and philosopher, is one of the most brilliant men of letters in the twentieth century. His *Collected Works* are now available in English.